Annotations to the Front Cover

1. This is a watercolor sketch of Jane Austen by her sister, Cassandra. Sketching and drawing were among the most popular of the various accomplishments ladies of the time were taught and encouraged to pursue; others are discussed in this novel.

2. The picture was made while the Austen family was visiting Lyme Regis, on the southern coast of England. An excursion to Lyme, a popular vacation spot, plays a central role in *Persuasion*.

3. Jane Austen's face is unfortunately obscured by her bonnet. It was standard then for people to wear hats or bonnets when outdoors; women also usually wore caps indoors.

4. Cassandra made this picture during one of her outings with Jane to the picturesque countryside near Lyme, which is described as "very fine" in *Persuasion*. Jane Austen's love of natural beauty appears in her letters, and she gives that same love to the heroine of this novel, Anne Elliot.

The Annotated

PERSUASION

Annotated and Edited by

DAVID M. SHAPARD

David M. Shapard is the author of *The Annotated Pride and Prejudice*. He graduated with a Ph.D. in European History from the University of California at Berkeley; his specialty was the eighteenth century. Since then he has taught at several colleges. He lives in upstate New York.

ALSO BY DAVID M. SHAPARD

The Annotated Pride and Prejudice

The Annotated

PERSUASION

———

Woman in contemporary dress at the seaside, with bathing machines in the background.

[From William Alexander, *Picturesque Representations of the Dress & Manners of the English* (1813)]

The Annotated

PERSUASION

———

JANE AUSTEN

Annotated and Edited, with an Introduction, by
DAVID M. SHAPARD

ANCHOR BOOKS
A Division of Random House, Inc.
New York

AN ANCHOR BOOKS ORIGINAL, OCTOBER 2010

Library of Congress Cataloging-in-Publication Data
Austen, Jane, 1775–1817.
[Persuasion]
The annotated Persuasion / by Jane Austen ; annotated and
edited, with an introduction by David M. Shapard.
p. cm.
Includes bibliographical references.
ISBN 978-0-307-39078-3 (pbk.)
1. Austen, Jane, 1775–1817. Persuasion. 2. Young women—
England—Fiction. 3. Gentry—England—Fiction. 4. Mate
selection—Fiction. 5. Ship captains—Fiction. 6. England—
Social life and customs—19th century—Fiction.
I. Shapard, David M. II. Title.
PR4034.P4 2010
823'.7—dc22
2010021617

Book design by Rebecca Aidlin
Maps by R. Bull

www.anchorbooks.com

Printed in the United States of America

Contents

PERSUASION

VOLUME I
(Note: The following chapter headings are not found in the novel.
They are added here by the editor to assist the reader.)

VOLUME II

Notes to the Reader

The *Annotated Persuasion* contains several features
that the reader should be aware of:

Literary interpretations: the comments on the techniques and
themes of the novel, more than other types of entries, represent
the personal views and interpretations of the editor. Such views
have been carefully considered, but inevitably they will still provoke disagreement among some readers. I can only hope that
even in those cases the opinions expressed provide useful food for
thought.

Differences of meaning: many words then, like many words now,
had multiple meanings. The meaning of a word that is given at
any particular place is intended to apply only to the way the word
is used there; it does not represent a complete definition of the
word in the language of the time. Thus some words are defined
differently at different points, while many words are defined only
in certain places, since in other places they are used in ways that
remain familiar today.

Repetitions: this book has been designed so it can be used as a
reference. For this reason many entries refer the reader to other
pages where more complete information about a topic exists. This,
however, is not practical for definitions of words, so definitions of
the same word are repeated at each appropriate point, except in
cases when such definitions are extremely close together.

Acknowledgments

My first, and greatest, expression of gratitude must go to my editor, Diana Secker Tesdell. She has patiently responded to a continued series of questions and concerns throughout the gestation of this book, and she has played a vital role in the preparation of the manuscript, sharpening up the prose, forcing me to clarify my ideas, and identifying several important points in the novel that I had missed. Further thanks are owed to Nicole Pedersen and to others at Anchor Books for their work in preparing the final manuscript.

I am also grateful to Professor Phyllis Roth of Skidmore College, and her seminar class on Jane Austen, who allowed me to participate in two lively discussions that were enjoyable and useful in stimulating my thinking about Austen and *Persuasion*.

Additional thanks go to the staff of the Bethlehem Public Library, the New York State Library, and the New York Public Library for helping me procure the materials essential for my research, with particular appreciation for the efforts of Gordon Noble at the first institution and Elizabeth C. Denlinger at the last one.

Finally, I must thank my mother and other members of my family for their continued encouragement and support.

Introduction

Persuasion was the last complete novel by Jane Austen, the capstone to a literary career that started when she was young. Born on December 16, 1775, in the southern English county of Hampshire, she grew up in a large family of six boys and two girls that valued books and education. Her father, George Austen, was a clergyman and her mother, Cassandra Austen Leigh, whose father was a clergyman, came from a family mostly of landed gentry; thus Jane Austen grew up among the social class she consistently depicts in her novels. Her father supplemented his income by running a school for boys, and several of her brothers tried their hand at literary composition. The family also encouraged Jane's literary efforts, the first surviving examples of which date to when she was thirteen. Her earliest writings were highly comical and show the influence of other literary works of the time, many of which she satirized. As she matured, she wrote longer and more serious works, which reveal an increasing interest in the delineation of character. In 1795 she wrote her first full novel, *Elinor and Marianne*, and followed this in the next few years with *First Impressions* and *Susan*. She tried to publish the latter two books, but without success.

During this time Jane Austen lived with her parents and her sister, Cassandra, in Steventon. Her surviving letters indicate regular attendance at balls and other social events, and an interest in men, but no sustained romance or offer of marriage. The first known major event of her life occurred in 1801, when her father retired and moved the family to the popular spa and resort town of

Bath, which was to serve as the setting for a substantial portion of *Northanger Abbey* and *Persuasion*. The family lived there, at various addresses, for the next four years. In 1805 Mr. Austen died, after which Mrs. Austen and her two daughters left Bath, settling eventually in Southampton, a port city in Hampshire. During this whole period Jane Austen did not complete any other novels; she also rejected, after briefly accepting, her one known offer of marriage. Finally, in 1809, she and her mother and sister were able to move into a cottage owned by her brother Edward in the quiet village of Chawton in Hampshire.

In these new circumstances Jane Austen resumed her writing with vigor. In 1810 she finished *Sense and Sensibility*, a revised version of *Elinor and Marianne*. In 1811 it became her first published book—though not one that revealed her name, for its title page simply read, "By a Lady." Its modest success encouraged a similar revision of *First Impressions*, resulting in the appearance of *Pride and Prejudice* in early 1813, and even greater success. Her next two books, *Mansfield Park* and *Emma*, appeared in 1814 and 1815, and in the latter year she began work on *Persuasion*. Unfortunately, she grew increasingly ill during the following year. Her ailment is not certain, though many have suggested it was what is now known as Addison's disease, an endocrine disorder caused by a malfunction of the adrenal glands. She managed to finish *Persuasion* in 1816, though it is possible she was unable to revise and polish it as fully as she wished—the principal evidence for this is its short length, especially compared to the long novels that immediately preceded it, and its sketchily developed subplot involving Mr. Elliot and Mrs. Clay. She also managed to begin another novel, *Sanditon*. Eventually, however, she grew too weak to write, and on July 18, 1817, she died in the town of Winchester.

Shortly afterward, in December 1817, her brother Henry arranged for the joint publication of *Persuasion* and *Northanger Abbey* (the new title of *Susan*). He added a brief biographical notice in which he informed the world of his sister's death and revealed her identity for the first time.

Persuasion stands out in several ways from other Jane Austen novels. It is by far the shortest, the only one to comprise two volumes rather than three, with the exception of *Northanger Abbey*, which was completed many years before the final versions of any of the others and bears the mark of a much less mature author. *Persuasion*'s brevity is linked to other features that distinguish it from the other novels. While it contains a comparable number of characters, most of these characters are developed in much less detail. It contains fewer passages of dialogue, relying far more on authorial description to summarize what the other novels show through the characters' speech and action. This has furnished another argument for the influence of the author's declining health on its composition: "One may suspect, however, that Jane Austen might well have revised the novel had she lived, and expanded many of these résumés into the dialogues she so obviously enjoyed."[1] Finally, this novel stands out for being the least humorous of all the novels, the only one without two or three supporting characters who provide substantial comic relief.

All this might lead logically to *Persuasion*'s being by far the least popular of Jane Austen's novels, for comedy, a rich array of supporting characters, and brilliant dialogue are central to her appeal. But this has not been the fate of *Persuasion*. Sales figures show it roughly tied with *Sense and Sensibility* and *Emma* for second place in popularity, behind *Pride and Prejudice* and ahead of both *Mansfield Park* and *Northanger Abbey*. Indeed, many readers have declared a particular fondness for it.

An important reason for this fondness lies in *Persuasion*'s most distinctive feature: its plot. Like all Jane Austen novels it is primarily a romance, in which the principal characters form a happy marital union at the end. But in *Persuasion* this union occurs against the background of an unhappy rupture in the past, one

---

[1] W. A. Craik, *Jane Austen: The Six Novels* (London, 1965), p. 172.

that has led to years of misery for both characters, especially the heroine, the person around whom the novel revolves. This gives the novel a bittersweet flavor and is one reason for its less comical spirit. It also gives the novel's resolution a unique poignancy. Rather than having to overcome misunderstandings or difficulties that last merely for months and that still allowed them frequently to enjoy each other's company and friendship, these lovers have overcome years of total estrangement, an estrangement both have long assumed to be final. Added to this is the heroine's attainment of an age that, in this society, usually consigned a woman to permanent spinsterhood, and the dependence and low status that accompanied it.

Such misery makes the final joy of reconciliation stand out all the more sharply. The letter from Captain Wentworth bringing about this joy is probably the single most moving event in Jane Austen. His "You pierce my soul. I am half agony, half hope," and "I have loved none but you," represent far more intense language than that used by any Austen hero, the words of a man who has suffered for years from the thwarting, and the attempted self-suppression, of his love. And these words have an impact on the heroine and the reader that probably exceeds that in any other Austen novel, the product of the heroine's long period of even greater suffering and the reader's immersion in her pain for most of the novel.

There are other advantages to the novel that flow from its protagonists' lengthy separation. One is a far more mature heroine. Anne is twenty-seven; the next-oldest Austen heroine is Emma Woodhouse, who is twenty-one. Moreover, partly because of her bitter experiences and her years spent struggling against unhappiness, Anne has attained a degree of wisdom and self-control rare even for her age. This makes a significant difference in the presentation of the story. Jane Austen always tells her tales from the perspective of her heroine, with only occasional interruptions. Yet, even as she does this, there is generally an important divergence between the author's consciousness and that of the heroine, due to the flaws or follies or misunderstandings of the latter. This means that the narration must switch between expressing the point of view of the heroine, with all its limitations and possible errors, and expressing the all-knowing perspective of the author. The gap between these two can be a fruitful source of ironic commentary, but it also can create abrupt transitions, as well as possible uncertainty or confusion regarding which perspective is being conveyed in particular passages.

In *Persuasion*, however, there is little gap between heroine and author. During the first three chapters, and in occasional passages thereafter, the author alone speaks in order to provide essential background information. Otherwise, she speaks almost completely through Anne, who is so reflective that she is constantly analyzing the characters and actions around her, and so perceptive that her analyses are almost invariably correct. This means that these passages can furnish the reader with essential information both about what is happening generally and about the state of Anne's mind. The case in Jane Austen closest to this is that of Elinor Dashwood in *Sense and Sensibility*, yet she, while very intelligent and sensible, does not possess as comprehensive a vision as Anne. Moreover, a character with Elinor's high level of wisdom and self-control who is only nineteen creates serious problems of plausibility.

Anne's past experience also gives her a dimension of personal development lacking in Elinor or in Fanny Price, the other heroine who proves to be consistently right. One important opportunity afforded the Jane Austen heroines who prove to be wrong is that they can experience a great degree of moral growth. As they realize their errors and suffer the adverse consequences, they are forced to learn essential lessons about their own flaws and about what conduct or attitudes to avoid. Anne has experienced similar moral growth insofar as her adult life has been dominated by the tragic results of an earlier decision, albeit one in which her friend Lady Russell bears a heavier blame than herself. Anne has been forced to reflect on mistaken decisions and to learn to cope with their consequences. Yet because this process is mainly in the past, she is still able to be consistently wise over the course of the novel, and thus a completely reliable vehicle for the author's narration.

Persuasion's distinctive plot also allows for an especially insightful presentation of the hero, Captain Wentworth. All Jane Austen's novels are written from the perspective of the heroine, with only occasional brief glimpses of the hero's thoughts. There are good reasons for this. One is that it gives each novel a consistent tone and outlook. Another is brevity: a crucial strength of Jane Austen is the minute analysis she continually provides of the heroine's thoughts and feelings, but providing the same analysis for another character could stretch the novels out to an inordinate length, relative to the material of the plot. The only way to avoid this would be to reduce significantly the wide array of supporting characters and numerous lengthy dialogues—yet these are crucial parts of her work, of great value for their comedy and social and psychological portraiture and for their contribution to the development of the principal characters and the themes of the novel. A final reason for this exclusive focus on the heroine's perspective, perhaps the most important, is Jane Austen's ardent commitment to the strictest possible accuracy. This can be seen in her comments on others' writing, in which even the smallest implausibilities are criticized, and in the extraordinary precision with which she presents even minute matters—something that can be attested to by anyone who has done detailed research on the novels. This leads her to avoid any scenes in which only men are present. For while she had plenty of exposure to men, having grown up in a family of numerous brothers, and portrays, with great astuteness, almost as wide a variety of male characters as female ones, she evidently believed that her own inexperience with exclusively male conversation meant she should not hazard depictions of such conversation. The same logic would apply to a detailed presentation of a man's thoughts and feelings.

Yet, as understandable as this scruple is, it creates difficulties in novels that center around the union of a man and a woman. Each must naturally come to love the other and to regard marriage to the other as feasible and desirable. This usually means, for both, a process of growth and enlightenment. Yet inevitably Jane Austen presents only one-half of the story in detail. The reader follows every twist and turn of the woman's thoughts and feelings concerning the man but remains mostly ignorant of his thoughts and feelings, except for what can be discerned through his outward behavior. It is only at the end of each novel, after the lovers' union has been assured, that a retrospective history of the man's emotional evolution is provided. Since this evolution is generally as eventful and interesting as the woman's, its abbreviated presentation represents a definite loss. This loss is particularly acute in *Sense and Sensibility* and *Pride and Prejudice*, for their plots require the hero to spend much of the novel away from the heroine, and thus away from the reader's awareness as well. In *Northanger Abbey* the hero is more continually present, but the heroine's lack of familiarity with him means that his inner thoughts remain murky. Finally, *Mansfield Park* and *Emma* both involve heroes who are close friends with the heroine throughout the story, thus allowing their characters to be fully presented, but because each story hinges upon either the hero or the heroine regarding the other solely as a friend and close relation, and focusing on other objects of interest, the issue of a romantic union of the two is barely raised.

Persuasion is the one Austen novel to avoid these limitations. The past affair between Anne and Captain Wentworth ensures attention throughout to the issue of their feelings toward each other—he is always a figure of potential romance. In addition, this past affair, in which they briefly achieved a full and intimate union of souls, ensures that Anne is highly interested in him and able to draw upon a deep knowledge of his character. Throughout the novel, even when Captain Wentworth is holding himself aloof from Anne, her mind offers a continual stream of observations on him, observations that consistently prove correct. She can guess his reactions and motivations on particular occasions and reflect on his general state. The end of the novel contains, like the others, a summary of his prior evolution, but in this case the summary, at least on the central question of his feelings toward Anne, only confirms what has already been suggested rather than reveals new information. All this means that Captain Wentworth, despite the novel's brevity and his aloofness or absence for much of it, is one of the most, if not the most, fully realized of all Jane Austen's heroes.

These advantages of *Persuasion*'s distinctive romantic plot are accompanied, however, by important disadvantages. One of these is the limited nature of the plot. A principal reason for the novel's brevity is that it has by far the thinnest story of any Austen novel, with the possible exception of *Northanger Abbey*, whose satirical and comical nature makes story matter less. In all the others the plot has many twists and turns, since its central romance effectively starts from scratch. The two lovers either do not know each other at the outset, or they have come to know each other so well in a nonromantic context that it requires a major adjustment by at least one of the two to think of the other in a different sense. This creates many possibilities for one or both of the potential lovers to be diverted by an involvement with a third person, a misunderstanding of the other's character or intentions, or a failure to imagine even the possibility of this romance. The development of these distractions or barriers, and the eventual triumph over them, provide ample material for incident and story.

In contrast, by having a pair of lovers who came close to marriage earlier and who still harbor powerful affection for each other, even if this affection has been suppressed by resentment in one case, *Persuasion* has limited means of delaying or complicating their eventual union. Once events have brought Anne and Captain Wentworth in close proximity again, the course is basically set. All that is really needed is sufficient time to soften old bitterness and to remind the person harboring this bitterness of the worth of the other. Rivals—Louisa Musgrove and William Elliot—do appear. But since both Anne and Captain Wentworth have already been reexposed to each other, neither can really become attracted to the rival. That could happen only if one of them lacked the true love for the other that they both ultimately manifest and acknowledge. The only way to lengthen the plot, while preserving the characters of the two principals, would be to introduce improbable contrivances that impede their union or to expand the treatment of supporting characters and subplots to the point that the story of the principals becomes obscured. Wisely avoiding such expedients, Jane Austen is left with a beautiful but slim tale.

Another handicap of the tale is the passive role it necessarily imposes on its main character. Though Anne Elliot forms the complete focus of the novel, she does very little. This contrasts to other Jane Austen heroines. Those who are flawed have much to do, first in committing their serious errors and then in suffering the consequences, realizing their mistakes, and making amends. Even the two other relatively faultless heroines, Elinor Dashwood and Fanny Price, are given a far more active role in the plot. Elinor has to fall in love, learn that her lover is engaged elsewhere, fend off the sneers and barbs of her rival, and cope with her apparent definitive loss before being finally united with him. She also has to devote considerable effort to coping with her sister's woes, which constitute half the plot. As for Fanny Price, she is forced to resist, in the face of considerable temptation and pressure from those she loves, the prolonged and persistent courtship of a man she disapproves of. She also is given the tasks of observing and detecting an all-important illicit entanglement that nobody else discerns, and of revising significantly her long-held nostalgia for her original home.

Anne Elliot has almost nothing like this to do. The mistake she suffers from occurred in the past, and she has fully absorbed its lesson when the action begins. Her feelings for Captain Wentworth are already set, and she has no important discoveries to make about herself. She does not observe anything of great significance not witnessed by others; her superior insights into Captain Wentworth's mind result primarily from her state of prior knowledge, not from anything that she does over the course of the novel. Nor does she need to cope with or overcome any major external difficulties. The sole exceptions are the falls of her nephew and of Louisa, both brief episodes and only the second of which is important to the plot. She also has to deliberate over the desirability of William Elliot's attentions and to alert Captain Wentworth to her continued interest in him, but the first takes little time or mental effort, and the second involves only two relatively brief conversations in the final chapters. Otherwise she watches, waits, reflects on her situation and on Captain Wentworth, controls her feelings as best she can, and engages in the usual trivialities of everyday life.

This poses a challenge to maintenance of continued interest in the heroine. It also limits how much attention can be paid to other characters, for doing so could make them overshadow a main character with little active function. Thus, while *Persuasion* contains almost as rich an array of supporting characters as the other novels, these characters are developed less. Sir Walter, Mary Musgrove, Admiral Croft, and the obsequious father and daughter team of Mr. Shepherd and Mrs. Clay are all distinctive individual studies with rich comic potential, such as those that provide much of the glory of other Austen novels. Here, however, this potential is never exploited to the full. This underdevelopment also occurs with the more significant character of Lady Russell, the closest friend of the heroine and the one whose decision caused the rupture that is the basis of the plot. Like all the supporting characters, she appears only occasionally, and the exact mixture of parts that make her both inclined to judge wrongly and worthy of being still loved and esteemed by Anne is only sketched generally. In the last part of the book, precisely when her errors are becoming apparent, she disappears, and one reason is that her presence would distract from Anne during the only section of the book in which the latter enjoys some opportunity for action.

Yet even as it suffers from these particular limitations, *Persuasion* compensates with two other important features that distinguish it somewhat from other Austen novels and that help to maintain interest in a story with so few dramatic developments and so little for its heroine to do: its use of external atmosphere and its focus on the subtle fluctuations and evolution of emotion.

Persuasion is far from unique in moving its characters from one place to another. All Austen novels except *Emma* do that. But generally these moves serve only to bring certain characters together or to spur a new plot development (the sole exception is the Portsmouth episode in *Mansfield Park*, where the far poorer circumstances of the heroine's home shock her by the contrast to her usual elegant surroundings). In contrast, *Persuasion*, which transfers its heroine a number of times in its short span, imparts a distinct atmosphere to each place, partly by placing in each one a set of characters with common traits. The first chapters establish the cold, heartless elegance of Kellynch Hall, which then gives way to the informal, warm, and unsophisticated world of the Musgroves' Uppercross. The latter characteristics appear even more strongly in the small naval society of Lyme. Furthermore, in Lyme, as well as in the country walk that precedes the venture there, nature itself is used to establish a mood that in some respects corresponds to the situation of the heroine. The walk is autumnal and melancholy in imagery, and forlorn for Anne in much of what it reveals, while Lyme, the site of inspiring and energizing scenic beauty, is where Anne's looks and Captain Wentworth's admiration for her are revived. Finally, after a brief interval at Lady Russell's, the scene shifts to Bath, which combines further cold elegance, a reminder of Anne's unfortunate family situation, with the busier social swirl of a popular resort town, a sign of increased opportunities for Anne that will eventually bear fruit. These alterations of atmosphere form a miniature drama in themselves, one that gives a sense of overall development even when the events being chronicled, especially those relating to the heroine, are slight.

Another miniature drama is formed by the minute depiction of the heroine's evolving emotions. All Austen novels focus greatly on such emotions, but in *Persuasion* there is a particular emphasis on their continual and subtle change. Within various scenes Anne is shown undergoing a succession of different feelings, sometimes in reaction to other people or events and sometimes in response to her own reflections. In many of these scenes this inner evolution is almost more eventful than what is happening around Anne.

Virginia Woolf wrote that in *Persuasion* Jane Austen sees life "through the eyes of a woman who, unhappy herself, has a special sympathy for the happiness and unhappiness of others, which, until the very end, she is forced to comment upon in silence. Therefore the observation is less of facts and more of feelings than is usual."[2] Woolf goes on to speculate that, had she lived, Jane Austen would have moved further in this direction and composed novels focusing even more on the subtleties and complexities of human nature (in other words, novels more like those of Virginia Woolf herself). This of course is only speculation, and in fact Austen's last work, *Sanditon*, shows her, in the few unpolished chapters she managed to write, returning to the more comical and satirical strain of her earlier writings. But *Persuasion* does have a heightened emotional sensitivity, corresponding to the character of its heroine. Since at least some of that sensitivity, as Woolf suggests, stems from the heroine's unhappy history, this is one more way in which the distinctive nature of the novel's plot, even as it limits the external drama, compensates with subtler, yet still powerful, forms of drama. The continued focus on Anne's emotions throughout the book means that when those emotions are raised to their highest peak by the one highly important external action of the novel, Captain Wentworth's letter, the impact on the reader is all the greater, and all the more likely to ensure the enduring affection so many feel for it.

---

[2] Virginia Woolf, "Jane Austen," in Ian Watt, ed., *Jane Austen: A Collection of Critical Essays* (Englewood Cliffs, NJ, 1963), p. 23.

The Annotated

PERSUASION

Chapter One

Sir Walter Elliot, of Kellynch-hall, in Somersetshire,[1] was a man who, for his own amusement, never took up any book but the Baronetage;[2] there he found occupation for an idle hour, and consolation in a distressed one; there his faculties were roused into admiration and respect, by contemplating the limited remnant of the earliest patents; there any unwelcome sensations, arising from domestic affairs, changed naturally into pity and contempt, as he turned over the almost endless creations of the last century[3]—and there, if every other leaf were powerless, he could read his own history with an interest which never failed—this was the page at which the favourite volume always opened:

"ELLIOT OF KELLYNCH-HALL.

"Walter Elliot, born March 1, 1760, married, July 15, 1784, Elizabeth, daughter of James Stevenson, Esq.[4] of South Park, in the county of Gloucester;[5] by which lady (who died 1800) he has issue Elizabeth, born June 1, 1785; Anne, born August 9, 1787; a still-born son,[6] Nov. 5, 1789; Mary, born Nov. 20, 1791."[7]

Precisely such had the paragraph originally stood from the printer's hands; but Sir Walter had improved it by adding, for the information of himself and his family, these words, after the date of Mary's birth—"married, Dec. 16, 1810, Charles, son and heir of Charles Musgrove, Esq. of Uppercross, in the county of Somerset,"—and by inserting most accurately the day of the month on which he had lost his wife.

Then followed the history and rise of the ancient and

1. *Somersetshire:* A county in southwestern England (see map, p. 512).

2. The baronetage is a book listing baronets. Baronets are hereditary knights: both baronets and knights are called "Sir," but baronets pass down their title to a descendant; for this reason they are more prestigious. Various baronetages were published, including ones in 1804 and 1808 with entries similar to that here and in a duodecimo format (see note 14 below).

3. The book listed families in order of receipt of the title. Thus Sir Walter would first see the earliest patents (i.e., grants conferring the baronetcy); there would be only a "limited remnant" of them because most early baronetcies had expired by this point due to the death of all possible heirs. Sir Walter could only know this by consulting another book such as Dugdale (see note 9 below) and comparing its list of all baronetcies with the entries in his baronetage, for the latter would show only existing titles—that he has done this indicates how obsessed he is with the matter. This carefully acquired knowledge arouses Sir Walter to admiration for himself as the holder of a surviving baronetcy. He would later come to the many pages showing the creations, or new titles, of the last (i.e., eighteenth) century and feel contempt for their relative newness (his came from 1660; see note 12 below).

4. *Esq.:* Esquire. This was an informal title, often given to gentlemen, especially prominent landowners, who had no other title. It derives from the medieval term "squire," one who served a knight (knight being the lowest of the formal titles).

5. *Gloucester:* a county to the immediate northeast of Somerset (see map, p. 512).

6. Stillborn children were not unusual then. Jane Austen mentions one in a letter, and not as a remarkable event (Oct. 27, 1798).

7. This entry is very similar to ones in actual baronetages of the time, albeit with slight differences in the wording and the exact information included (Jane Austen may have been recalling a book she had seen years earlier). A history of the current baronet begins each family entry; similar histories of all preceding baronets, starting from the oldest, comprise the rest of the entry.

respectable family, in the usual terms: how it had been first settled in Cheshire;[8] how mentioned in Dugdale[9]—serving the office of High Sheriff,[10] representing a borough in three successive parliaments,[11] exertions of loyalty, and dignity of baronet, in the first year of Charles II.,[12] with all the Marys and Elizabeths they had married;[13] forming altogether two handsome duodecimo[14] pages, and concluding with the arms and motto:[15] "Principal seat, Kellynch-hall, in the county of Somerset," and Sir Walter's handwriting again in this finale:

"Heir presumptive, William Walter Elliot, Esq., great grandson of the second Sir Walter."[16]

Vanity was the beginning and the end of Sir Walter Elliot's character; vanity of person[17] and of situation. He had been remarkably handsome in his youth; and, at fifty-four, was still a very fine man. Few women could think more of their personal appearance than he did; nor could the valet of any new made lord be more delighted with the place he held in society.[18] He considered the blessing of beauty as inferior only to the blessing of a

Gaunt House: a prominent country house, such as Kellynch Hall is.

[From John Preston Neale, *Views of the Seats of Noblemen and Gentlemen, Vol. V* (1822)]

8. *Cheshire:* a county farther north from Somerset (see map, p. 512).

9. Sir William Dugdale had in 1682 published *The Antient Usage in Bearing of such Ensigns of Honour as are commonly call'd Arms.* It included lists of those holding various titles and honors, including baronets.

10. The High Sheriff (often simply called sheriff) was, after the Lord Lieutenant, the leading official in a county, responsible for the execution of the laws. He served for one year. The position, usually held by a member of the gentry, carried great prestige and would be a source of family pride.

11. Representing a borough, the main unit sending representatives to Parliament, would be an even greater source of pride. Successive parliaments meant consecutive sessions; members often changed from one session to another, so serving for three in a row would be a further distinction.

12. This means the Elliot family sided with the monarchy during the English Civil War and was later rewarded with a baronetcy. The civil war was a struggle between the king and parliament in the 1640s that ended with the execution of Charles I; in 1660 his son Charles II returned and restored the monarchy. More baronetcies were created in the first year of his reign than in any other year, as the monarchy had many loyal supporters to reward.

13. Mary and Elizabeth were traditionally two of the most popular female names in England. The strong family traditions that kept them popular is shown in their being used again in this generation, with the eldest daughter given the mother's name of Elizabeth, a common procedure.

14. *duodecimo:* book in a small format; see p. 157, note 7, for more on book sizes.

15. At the end of each entry the family arms and crest would be listed, along with (in most cases) the family motto, and (in some cases) the family seal.

16. The exact relationship of William Elliot and Sir Walter is never specified. If William's father was of the same generation as Sir Walter, he would be a first cousin, and William a second cousin. William Elliot's name probably came from his father, with his middle name being in honor of the baronetcy (in most cases each successive baronet had the same first name). He is the heir presumptive because the baronetcy cannot be inherited by a woman; in the absence of a son, it goes to the male relative next in line. This was also usually the case with landed estates, and later it is revealed that William Elliot is indeed the expected heir of Sir Walter's estate.

17. *person:* personal appearance.

18. A new made lord was someone who had just been raised by the king to

baronetcy; and the Sir Walter Elliot, who united these gifts, was the constant object of his warmest respect and devotion.

His good looks and his rank had one fair claim on his attachment; since to them he must have owed a wife of very superior character to any thing deserved by his own. Lady Elliot[19] had been an excellent woman, sensible and amiable;[20] whose judgment and conduct, if they might be pardoned the youthful infatuation which made her Lady Elliot, had never required indulgence afterwards. — She had humoured, or softened, or concealed his failings, and promoted his real respectability for seventeen years; and though not the very happiest being in the world herself, had found enough in her duties,[21] her friends, and her children, to attach her to life, and make it no matter of indifference to her when she was called on to quit them. — Three girls, the two eldest sixteen and fourteen, was an awful[22] legacy for a mother to bequeath; an awful charge rather, to confide to the authority and guidance of a conceited, silly father. She had, however, one very intimate friend, a sensible, deserving woman, who had been brought, by strong attachment to herself, to settle close by her, in the village of Kellynch; and on her kindness and advice, Lady Elliot mainly relied for the best help and maintenance of the good principles and instruction which she had been anxiously giving her daughters.[23]

This friend, and Sir Walter, did *not* marry, whatever might have been anticipated on that head by their acquaintance. — Thirteen years had passed away since Lady Elliot's death, and they were still near neighbours and intimate friends; and one remained a widower, the other a widow.

That Lady Russell,[24] of steady age and character, and extremely well provided for, should have no thought of a second marriage, needs no apology to the public, which is rather apt to be unreasonably discontented when a woman *does* marry again, than when she does *not*;[25] but Sir Walter's continuing in singleness requires explanation. — Be it known then, that Sir Walter, like a good father, (having met with one or two private disappointments in very unreasonable applications) prided himself on remaining

the nobility, or peerage; this position, higher than a baronet, gave the possessor the right to sit in the House of Lords. It was an exclusive honor, enjoyed by fewer than three hundred men at this time. A valet was a male servant who took care of his master's clothing and grooming, and often accompanied him wherever he went. Servants frequently identified with their employers, and the nature of a valet's position, along with the high rank among servants he enjoyed, made him especially prone to this. Since servants' social status rose with that of their employers, a valet whose master was recently ennobled would have even more reason to be delighted with his position.

19. The wife of a baronet was called "Lady + last name." Only women from the upper ranks of the nobility used both first and last name after "Lady."

20. *amiable:* kind, friendly, good-natured. The word then suggested general goodness, not just outward agreeableness.

21. Her duties, as the wife of a baronet, would have centered around managing the household, which included purchasing what was needed, keeping the household budget, planning meals, and, most of all, supervising the servants and their various labors. It was generally expected that men would allow their wives to take charge of these matters, without substantial interference—on p. 10 the mistress of the house is referred to as "laying down the domestic law at home." Other duties of such a mistress would have been entertaining guests, attending church regularly, and performing charitable acts in the neighborhood.

22. *awful:* impressive, solemn; worthy of awe and respect.

23. This may refer to formal instruction as well as to general maternal guidance; young children, and girls in later years, were frequently educated at home, either by a governess or their mother. It is soon revealed that Anne went away to school, probably for the first time, after her mother's death (see p. 26).

24. Lady Russell is the widow of a knight (see p. 20), a rank just below baronet. As with Lady Elliot, this means she uses just her last name with "Lady."

25. Widows who remarried were often subject to disapproval. One reason was that a woman, on marrying, was considered a permanent part of her husband's family. Remarriage would mean abandoning that family for another, which could be regarded as a betrayal, especially if the woman was able to take property with her into the new marriage. Remarriage was also condemned as an indulgence in lust improper in women, who were expected to

single for his dear daughter's[26] sake. For one daughter, his eldest, he would really have given up any thing, which he had not been very much tempted to do. Elizabeth had succeeded, at sixteen, to all that was possible, of her mother's rights and consequence; and being very handsome, and very like himself, her influence had always been great, and they had gone on together most happily. His two other children were of very inferior value. Mary had acquired a little artificial importance, by becoming Mrs. Charles Musgrove; but Anne, with an elegance of mind and sweetness of character, which must have placed her high with any people of real understanding, was nobody with either father or sister: her word had no weight; her convenience was always to give way;— she was only Anne.

To Lady Russell, indeed, she was a most dear and highly valued god-daughter, favourite, and friend. Lady Russell loved them all; but it was only in Anne that she could fancy the mother to revive again.

A few years before, Anne Elliot had been a very pretty girl, but her bloom[27] had vanished early; and as even in its height, her father had found little to admire in her, (so totally different were her delicate features and mild dark eyes from his own); there could be nothing in them now that she was faded and thin, to excite his esteem. He had never indulged much hope, he had now none, of ever reading her name in any other page of his favourite work. All equality of alliance[28] must rest with Elizabeth; for Mary had merely connected herself with an old country family of respectability and large fortune,[29] and had therefore given all the honour, and received none: Elizabeth would, one day or other, marry suitably.

It sometimes happens, that a woman is handsomer[30] at twenty-nine than she was ten years before; and, generally speaking, if there has been neither ill health nor anxiety, it is a time of life at which scarcely any charm is lost. It was so with Elizabeth; still the same handsome Miss Elliot that she had begun to be thirteen years ago; and Sir Walter might be excused, therefore, in forgetting her age, or, at least, be deemed only half a fool, for thinking

be chaste, or as a violation of the undivided and permanent love a woman was supposed to feel for her husband. In a letter Jane Austen seems to give voice to this last sentiment when, commenting on a woman who remarried, she writes, "had her first marriage been of affection . . . I should not have forgiven her" (Dec. 27, 1808). At the same time, she explains that, in this case, she believes the woman justified in remarrying, and the wording here suggests she regards this condemnation of widows as unfair.

26, *daughter's:* It may be that the apostrophe was wrongly placed in the original printing, as happened with punctuation marks in the initial editions of Jane Austen's works, and that this is supposed to be *daughters.'* Later Elizabeth, speaking to Anne, says that their father has "kept himself single so long for *our* sakes" (see p. 66; emphasis added). While Sir Walter does care truly only for Elizabeth, he would probably not *pride himself* on such flagrant partiality, just as Elizabeth would not claim to be its beneficiary.

27. *bloom:* prime of beauty, state of greatest loveliness. The word is frequently used in Jane Austen in this sense, applied particularly to young women in their freshest looks. A contemporary book on beauty (*The Mirror of Graces,* 1811) gives a sense of the origins of the term by comparing, in a chapter discussing how best to preserve "the bloom of beauty," the progression of a woman's appearance both to the progression of the seasons, with spring first and winter last, and to the blossoming and ultimate fading and death of a flower. One reason for particular concern about bloom in this period was that facial cosmetics, which might help disguise the effects of age, had become generally frowned upon—see p. 409, note 34.

28. *alliance:* marriage. The term connoted especially the union of different families through marriage, which was often a central purpose of marriage.

29. An old country family is one that had long been prominent in this country, i.e., county. Such antiquity would be a mark of additional distinction, though it still would not make a family rank as high as one with a baronetcy.

30. "Handsome" was often used to describe women at this time. It had no suggestion of masculine appearance.

himself and Elizabeth as blooming as ever, amidst the wreck of the good looks of every body else; for he could plainly see how old all the rest of his family and acquaintance were growing. Anne haggard, Mary coarse, every face in the neighbourhood worsting;[31] and the rapid increase of the crow's foot about Lady Russell's temples had long been a distress to him.

Elizabeth did not quite equal her father in personal contentment. Thirteen years had seen her mistress of Kellynch Hall,[32] presiding and directing with a self-possession and decision[33] which could never have given the idea of her being younger than she was. For thirteen years had she been doing the honours, and laying down the domestic law at home, and leading the way to the chaise and four,[34] and walking immediately after Lady Russell out of all the drawing-rooms and dining-rooms in the country.[35] Thirteen winters' revolving frosts had seen her opening every ball of credit which a scanty neighbourhood afforded;[36] and thirteen springs shewn their blossoms, as she travelled up to London with her father,[37] for a few weeks annual enjoyment of the great world.[38] She had the remembrance of all this; she had the consciousness of being nine-and-twenty, to give her some regrets and some apprehensions. She was fully satisfied of being still quite as handsome as ever; but she felt her approach to the years of danger,[39] and would have rejoiced to be certain of being properly solicited by baronet-blood within the next twelvemonth or two. Then might she again take up the book of books with as much enjoyment as in her early youth; but now she liked it not. Always to be presented with the date of her own birth, and see no marriage follow but that of a youngest sister,[40] made the book an evil; and more than once, when her father had left it open on the table near her, had she closed it, with averted eyes, and pushed it away.

She had had a disappointment, moreover, which that book, and especially the history of her own family, must ever present the remembrance of. The heir presumptive, the very William Walter Elliot, Esq. whose rights had been so generously supported by her father, had disappointed her.

She had, while a very young girl, as soon as she had known him

31. *worsting*: growing worse, deteriorating.

32. After her mother died Elizabeth, as the eldest daughter, and already sixteen at that point, would have assumed her place as mistress of the house; see p. 7, note 21, for a description of a mistress's duties.

33. *decision*: determination, firmness.

34. *chaise and four*: a chaise was a type of carriage; "four" refers to the number of horses driving it. The chaise, from the French word for "chair," was one of the most popular carriages of the time, used especially for long-distance transportation. It was a small enclosed carriage with one seat, which could accommodate three people facing forward (in contrast to the coach, which had two seats facing each other); see pictures, pp. 59, 221, 223. The Elliots need only a chaise since there are only three family members living there; it would also be useful for Sir Walter and Elizabeth's journeys to London. Chaises could use only two horses, but four would make for a faster journey and be a sign of distinction, while also costing more. The conflict of distinction and expense on this very point will shortly arise (see p. 23, note 12).

35. They would proceed according to rules of precedence, which were especially in force at formal dinner parties: usually everyone would gather in the drawing room, and then go into the dining room in order of rank; afterward the ladies, also in order, would return to the drawing room. Lady Russell precedes Elizabeth because, even though her husband ranked below Sir Walter, she was his wife and Elizabeth is only the daughter of Sir Walter. Elizabeth precedes Anne because she is the eldest sister (for more, see p. 89, note 31).

36. To open a ball is to be part of the lead couple in the first dance. It would be an honor normally enjoyed by the unmarried gentleman and lady of highest rank, which would always be Elizabeth in this neighborhood. A ball of credit would be a formal ball attended by people of good families. Such balls would be especially likely to occur in the winter in the country, when outdoor amusements were less available. *Pride and Prejudice* and *Mansfield Park* depict elaborate country balls in, respectively, November and December.

37. Spring was the time of the London season, to which the aristocracy and many country gentry would flock for a variety of social events and amusements.

38. *great world*: the world of the highest-ranking people in society.

39. These are the years when a woman lost her marital eligibility. This happened early in this society (see p. 53, note 27). For many women twenty-nine would already be in those years; Elizabeth's beauty and birth have extended her eligibility a little.

40. Because of the importance of marriage for women in this society — it was

to be, in the event of her having no brother, the future baronet, meant to marry him; and her father had always meant that she should. He had not been known to them as a boy, but soon after Lady Elliot's death Sir Walter had sought the acquaintance, and though his overtures had not been met with any warmth, he had persevered in seeking it, making allowance for the modest drawing back of youth; and in one of their spring excursions to London, when Elizabeth was in her first bloom, Mr. Elliot had been forced into the introduction.

He was at that time a very young man, just engaged in the study of the law;[41] and Elizabeth found him extremely agreeable, and every plan in his favour was confirmed. He was invited to Kellynch-Hall; he was talked of and expected all the rest of the year; but he never came. The following spring he was seen again in town,[42] found equally agreeable, again encouraged, invited and expected, and again he did not come; and the next tidings were that he was married. Instead of pushing his fortune in the line marked out for the heir of the house of Elliot, he had purchased independence[43] by uniting himself to a rich woman of inferior birth.[44]

Sir Walter had resented it. As the head of the house,[45] he felt that he ought to have been consulted, especially after taking the young man so publicly by the hand: "For they must have been seen together," he observed, "once at Tattersal's,[46] and twice in the lobby of the House of Commons."[47] His disapprobation was expressed, but apparently very little regarded. Mr. Elliot had attempted no apology, and shewn himself as unsolicitous of being longer noticed by the family, as Sir Walter considered him unworthy of it: all acquaintance between them had ceased.

This very awkward history of Mr. Elliot, was still, after an interval of several years, felt with anger by Elizabeth, who had liked the man for himself, and still more for being her father's heir, and whose strong family pride could see only in *him*, a proper match for Sir Walter Elliot's eldest daughter. There was not a baronet from A to Z, whom her feelings could have so willingly acknowledged as an equal. Yet so miserably had he conducted himself,

considered a woman's natural destiny and duty, and it was usually the only way she could achieve wealth, influence, and high status—there was a strong belief that sisters should ideally marry in order of birth. Some families, if an older daughter had not married, would even delay letting their younger daughters "come out," or socialize freely with eligible young men; the delay would keep the younger girls from competing with the eldest. This could lead to rivalry between sisters as well: in a youthful satire, "Three Sisters," Jane Austen depicts a woman who marries a man she does not like out of fear that, if she does not, one of her younger sisters will marry him. Hence, for Elizabeth it is a further pain and humiliation that she, the eldest, is preceded in marriage by her youngest sister.

41. Mr. Elliot would have been studying to become a barrister, the branch of the law considered genteel. For what this study involved, see p. 379, note 32.

42. *town:* London.

43. *independence:* financial independence.

44. For this woman's history, and its significance as an example of social climbing in this society, see p. 383, note 45.

45. He sees himself as head of the house, or family, because he is the one Elliot who has a title.

46. Tattersal's, or Tattersalls in more recent spelling, was the main place in London for buying and selling horses. Horses were a particular concern of gentlemen, who would use them for their carriages, for riding, and for hunting, and who in consequence often owned several. All this made Tattersalls a popular venue for upper-class men. For a picture of Tattersalls, giving a sense of its clientele, see the following page.

47. The House of Commons is the lower, though also the more powerful, of the two houses of Parliament. It was dominated then by country gentry like Sir Walter. While he himself does not appear to have a seat, he probably has friends who do, and he would see it as a natural place to meet other men of his class and to introduce his heir to them.

that though she was at this present time, (the summer of 1814,) wearing black ribbons for his wife,[48] she could not admit him to be worth thinking of again.[49] The disgrace of his first marriage might, perhaps, as there was no reason to suppose it perpetuated by offspring, have been got over, had he not done worse; but he had, as by the accustomary intervention of kind friends they had been informed, spoken most disrespectfully of them all,[50] most slightingly and contemptuously of the very blood he belonged to, and the honours which were hereafter to be his own. This could not be pardoned.

Such were Elizabeth Elliot's sentiments and sensations; such the cares to alloy, the agitations to vary, the sameness and the elegance, the prosperity and the nothingness, of her scene of life — such the feelings to give interest to a long, uneventful residence in one country circle, to fill the vacancies which there were no habits of utility abroad, no talents or accomplishments for home, to occupy.[51]

Tattersal's: the main venue for buying and selling horses in London.

[From Fiona St. Aubyn, *Ackermann's Illustrated London*, illustrations by Augustus Pugin and Thomas Rowlandson (Ware, 1985), p. 82]

48. Mourning attire was a universal practice among the more affluent classes at this time, with an elaborate etiquette indicating what was worn and for how long. The ribbons worn by Elizabeth represent a bare minimum: full mourning for women included black gowns as well as other articles, and such mourning was often adopted for people no closer than cousins. Since Mrs. Elliot has just died—in a conversation in the following February Anne says she has "not been dead much above half a year" (see chronology, p. 487; and p. 370)—the limited mourning adopted here suggests the estrangement of Sir Walter and his children from Mr. Elliot.

49. There was no prohibition against marriage between cousins; see p. 143, note 9.

50. Their hearing this gossip from friends, whether truly kind or not, suggests the relatively small upper-class society of this time, something indicated at other places in Jane Austen. There were only around six hundred baronetcies in all of England at this time, along with almost three hundred noble families of higher rank.

51. Upper-class women had a great deal of leisure time, even if, like Elizabeth, they had the duties of a mistress of the house. This would be especially true if they had no children. The "habits of utility abroad" (i.e., outside the house) probably refers to charitable activities: assisting and visiting the local poor was considered an important activity for elite ladies, though, as Elizabeth shows, not all did it. Talents and accomplishments included music, drawing, and various decorative activities such as embroidery: these were taught to girls, and young women were encouraged to continue cultivating them. One argument made in favor of such continued cultivation was that these activities—along with reading, another pastime later shown (p. 408) to be of no interest to Elizabeth—helped fill ladies' leisure hours in productive ways.

But now, another occupation and solicitude of mind was beginning to be added to these. Her father was growing distressed for money. She knew, that when he now took up the Baronetage, it was to drive the heavy bills of his tradespeople,[52] and the unwelcome hints of Mr. Shepherd, his agent,[53] from his thoughts. The Kellynch property was good, but not equal to Sir Walter's apprehension of the state[54] required in its possessor.[55] While Lady Elliot lived, there had been method, moderation, and economy, which had just kept him within his income; but with her had died all such right-mindedness, and from that period he had been constantly exceeding it. It had not been possible for him to spend less; he had done nothing but what Sir Walter Elliot was imperiously called on to do; but blameless as he was, he was not only growing dreadfully in debt,[56] but was hearing of it so often, that it became vain to attempt concealing it longer, even partially, from his daughter.[57] He had given her some hints of it the last spring in town; he had gone so far even as to say, "Can we retrench? does it occur to you that there is any one article in which we can retrench?"—and Elizabeth, to do her justice, had, in the first ardour of female alarm, set seriously to think what could be done, and had finally proposed these two branches of economy: to cut off some unnecessary charities,[58] and to refrain from new-furnishing the drawing-room; to which expedients she afterwards added the happy thought of their taking no present down to Anne, as had been the usual yearly custom.[59] But these measures, however good in themselves, were insufficient for the real extent of the evil, the whole of which Sir Walter found himself obliged to confess to her soon afterwards. Elizabeth had nothing to propose of deeper efficacy. She felt herself ill-used and unfortunate, as did her father; and they were neither of them able to devise any means of lessening their expenses without compromising their dignity, or relinquishing their comforts in a way not to be borne.

There was only a small part of his estate that Sir Walter could dispose of; but had every acre been alienable,[60] it would have made no difference. He had condescended to mortgage as far as

52. His tradespeople would be the merchants he bought from. It was standard commercial practice then to sell items by credit, especially when dealing with wealthy customers, and then send them periodic bills.

53. Mr. Shepherd is a lawyer who manages Sir Walter's affairs; see p. 21, note 1.

54. *state*: dignity, pomp, grandeur.

55. It was commonly believed that those of high status should demonstrate and support that status by external display. This would mean both expensive and impressive possessions—houses, furnishings, clothes, carriages, horses—and a general willingness to spend money freely. Those who did not could lose prestige, while also seeing themselves outdone by others of their rank. Thus Sir Walter has a powerful social reinforcement for his natural extravagance.

56. Many wealthy landowners fell into debt. This had long been the case, and it may have become more common during the half century preceding this novel, despite rising incomes from agriculture. The principal cause was excessive expenditure. Maintaining a large country house, with its attendant army of servants, was itself an enormous expense, and in the eighteenth century many owners—spurred by changes in tastes, desire for greater comfort, or simple competitive emulation—undertook the additional expense, potentially enormous, of improving or even completely rebuilding the house and installing new elaborate landscaping as well. Increasing numbers of wealthy people also added to their expenses by living for substantial parts of the year in London, which had been growing tremendously in size and in the opportunities for enjoyment it offered, and which was increasingly accessible thanks to improvements in the speed and ease of travel. To all these pressures and temptations were added a relaxed attitude to debt among much of the elite and a willingness among many people to lend to those of high status.

57. It is notable that Sir Walter thinks only of informing and consulting Elizabeth.

58. Charity then was a basic function of the upper classes, especially if they were prominent landowners. In a letter Jane Austen writes of the standard Christmas duty of "laying out Edward's money for the poor"—Edward was a brother of hers who had inherited a wealthy estate. Hence even someone as selfish as Sir Walter has regular charities he contributes to, and even when Elizabeth selects their charities as prime candidates for elimination, a sign of her similar selfishness, she does not propose eliminating them all.

59. London offered a great variety of shops, so it would be natural for those visiting it to buy gifts for those who remained in the country.

60. *alienable*: capable of being transferred to another's ownership.

he had the power,[61] but he would never condescend[62] to sell.[63] No; he would never disgrace his name so far. The Kellynch estate should be transmitted whole and entire, as he had received it.[64]

Their two confidential friends, Mr. Shepherd, who lived in the neighbouring market town,[65] and Lady Russell, were called on to advise them; and both father and daughter seemed to expect that something should be struck out by one or the other to remove their embarrassments and reduce their expenditure, without involving the loss of any indulgence of taste or pride.

61. Sir Walter's estate, like most estates of the time, was governed by a system of strict settlement, under which the current owner was only a life tenant, who received the current income from the property but was bound to hand it intact to the next holder, his heir. The central purpose of the system was to preserve family property through the generations, which meant, among other things, keeping profligate or foolish owners like Sir Walter from selling to pay off debts. In many cases, as is true here, a small portion of the estate was granted outright to the current owner to give him some flexibility to deal with unexpected problems; this is what Sir Walter could dispose of or sell if he wished.

62. *condescend:* lower himself.

63. Mortgaging was a standard way for landowners to raise money, whether for paying debts or for other purposes. Sir Walter has been able to mortgage only the small part of the estate under his control; the strict settlement would block him from mortgaging the rest.

64. Sir Walter's strong scruples, and fear of disgracing his name, stem from the powerful emphasis in upper-class society on preserving family tradition and family social position through the generations. Sir Walter's own obsession with his ancestry shows how much he shares this ethos. Someone who failed to pass on his inheritance intact would be regarded as having violated one of the most basic of his duties, to his family and to society as a whole (since an elite landowning class with strong traditions and strong ties to its land was considered an essential source of political and social leadership and stability).

65. *market town:* town in a rural area that is a center for local trade and shopping. It would be a natural residence for a local lawyer like Mr. Shepherd.

Chapter Two

Mr. Shepherd, a civil, cautious lawyer, who, whatever might be his hold or his views on Sir Walter,[1] would rather have the *disagreeable* prompted by any body else, excused himself from offering the slightest hint, and only begged leave to recommend an implicit deference to the excellent judgment of Lady Russell,—from whose known good sense he fully expected to have just such resolute measures advised, as he meant to see finally adopted.

Lady Russell was most anxiously zealous on the subject, and gave it much serious consideration. She was a woman rather of sound than of quick abilities,[2] whose difficulties in coming to any decision in this instance were great, from the opposition of two leading principles. She was of strict integrity herself, with a delicate sense of honour; but she was as desirous of saving Sir Walter's feelings, as solicitous for the credit of the family, as aristocratic in her ideas of what was due to them, as any body of sense and honesty could well be.[3] She was a benevolent, charitable, good woman, and capable of strong attachments; most correct in her conduct, strict in her notions of decorum, and with manners that were held a standard of good-breeding.[4] She had a cultivated[5] mind, and was, generally speaking, rational and consistent—but she had prejudices on the side of ancestry; she had a value for rank and consequence,[6] which blinded her a little to the faults of those who possessed them.[7] Herself, the widow of only a knight,[8] she gave the dignity of a baronet all its due; and Sir Walter, independent of his claims as an old acquaintance, an attentive neighbour, an obliging landlord,[9] the husband of her very dear friend, the father of Anne and her sisters, was, as being Sir Walter, in her apprehension entitled to a great deal of compassion and consideration under his present difficulties.

1. Mr. Shepherd has already been identified as Sir Walter's agent (p. 16). He is an attorney: attorneys constituted the majority of lawyers at the time; unlike the more prestigious barristers, they could not try cases in court. Attorneys' business consisted principally of property and financial transactions, and they were usually selected by wealthy landowners to manage their estates and finances (see p. 25, note 19). Some attorneys gave up their normal practice to full-time agents, though a later reference by Mr. Shepherd to consultation on another matter suggests this is not the case with him.

The description of Mr. Shepherd's possible "hold or his views on Sir Walter" refers to the dependence someone as incapable as Sir Walter of managing his finances might have on the person who does it for him, and the low opinion that close dealings have probably given the attorney of his client. But, as explained, and shown over the next couple of chapters, none of this causes Mr. Shepherd to be other than deferential in speaking to Sir Walter.

2. *abilities:* mental powers.

3. Respect for those of high rank was a basic tenet of this society. In principle it went along with respect for the high moral standards that those of high rank were supposed to embody. In practice, the latter, as the case of Sir Walter shows, did not always fulfill those standards, and this created a tension, seen in Lady Russell's attitudes, between moral respect and social respect.

4. *good-breeding:* politeness, courtesy.

5. *cultivated:* well-educated, cultured. Lady Russell's strong interest in books, and regard for those who read, will be mentioned at several points.

6. *consequence:* social status or distinction.

7. This indicates Jane Austen's own moral standards. While not condemning all concern for social distinction or deference, she always upholds the primacy of moral considerations. She also takes care to delineate the precise moral virtues and failings of each character, whether explicitly, as in this passage, or implicitly, through showing the character in speech and action.

8. A knight was someone distinguished by the king for meritorious action or service of some kind. The knighthood gave him the right to be called "Sir," and his wife the right to be called "Lady," for their lifetimes.

9. This means Lady Russell rents her house from Sir Walter. She had earlier been described as having moved to the village of Kellynch to be near Lady Elliot. Landowners often owned much of the property in the local village; Sir Walter may have already owned a house there, or he may have built one to accommodate his wife's friend. The house in which Jane Austen lived in the last decade of her life, and wrote most of her novels, was one owned by her brother, whose estate near the village included the house, and who offered it, rent-free, to his mother and sisters.

They must retrench;[10] that did not admit of a doubt. But she was very anxious to have it done with the least possible pain to him and Elizabeth. She drew up plans of economy, she made exact calculations, and she did, what nobody else thought of doing, she consulted Anne, who never seemed considered by the others as having any interest in the question. She consulted, and in a degree was influenced by her, in marking out the scheme of retrenchment, which was at last submitted to Sir Walter. Every emendation of Anne's had been on the side of honesty against importance.[11] She wanted more vigorous measures, a more complete reformation, a quicker release from debt, a much higher tone of indifference for every thing but justice and equity.

"If we can persuade your father to all this," said Lady Russell, looking over her paper, "much may be done. If he will adopt these regulations, in seven years he will be clear; and I hope we may be able to convince him and Elizabeth, that Kellynch-hall has a respectability in itself, which cannot be affected by these reductions;[12] and that the true dignity of Sir Walter Elliot will be very far from lessened, in the eyes of sensible people, by his acting like a man of principle. What will he be doing, in fact, but what very many of our first families have done, — or ought to do?[13] — There will be nothing singular in his case; and it is singularity which often makes the worst part of our suffering, as it always does of our conduct.[14] I have great hope of our prevailing. We must be serious and decided — for, after all, the person who has contracted debts must pay them; and though a great deal is due to the feelings of the gentleman, and the head of a house, like your father, there is still more due to the character of an honest man."

This was the principle on which Anne wanted her father to be proceeding, his friends to be urging him. She considered it as an act of indispensable duty to clear away the claims of creditors, with all the expedition which the most comprehensive retrenchments could secure, and saw no dignity in any thing short of it. She wanted it to be prescribed, and felt as a duty.[15] She rated Lady Russell's influence highly, and as to the severe degree of self-

It is notable that Sir Walter is described as an obliging landlord. This may stem from his regard for Lady Russell as a family friend and a person with a title, or it may reflect his general tendency in such matters. With all his faults, he is never shown as rapacious or dishonest in his dealings with others. Jane Austen consistently gives even her worst characters some redeeming features, and even her best some flaws: her firm moral judgments are complemented by an equally firm realism in depicting the complexities of human nature. In her satirical sketch "Plan for a Novel," she imagines a novel that is the antithesis of what she values; among its features are that "All the Good will be unexceptionable in every respect—and there will be no foibles or weaknesses but with the Wicked, who will be completely depraved & infamous, hardly a resemblance of Humanity left in them."

10. Retrenchment, particularly by cutting down on one's expenses, was the frequent response of landowners who fell into debt. Some tried instead to augment their income, whether through marriage to an heiress or lucrative political office or agricultural improvements. Sir Walter, however, is rather old for marriage and has clearly not pursued politics until now. As for improving the productivity and income from his land, that might be insufficient for his needs; moreover, he hardly seems like someone to undertake such a task. Some indebted landowners tried defaulting, or even defrauded their creditors in some manner, but Sir Walter is sufficiently honorable, or desirous of preserving a good name, that this course is never considered.

11. *importance*: social position, dignity.

12. Grand country houses like Kellynch Hall were built in part to support the status of the owner by displaying his wealth and grandeur; for example, they frequently had more rooms than were really needed by the family to live, even to live luxuriously. Lady Russell's fear, which turns out to be justified, is that Sir Walter will not accept a reduced style of living because he believes a grand style is too important to the dignity of the house.

13. As discussed earlier (see p. 17, note 56), many aristocrats fell into debt, including the leading aristocrats, i.e., the "first families." Lady Russell's final words, "ought to do," represents her reluctant admission that not all behaved sensibly and responsibly in response to their misfortunes.

14. Lady Russell's disapproval of singular conduct, i.e., deviation from established social norms, was standard in this society, though not everyone would have disapproved as strongly as she. For more on this issue, and Jane Austen's probable attitude, see p. 277, note 13.

15. This is the first time we see Anne, the main character of the novel, actually doing or deciding on something. It is notable that what she does is to recommend self-denial and the strongest adherence to duty and conscience.

denial, which her own conscience prompted, she believed there might be little more difficulty in persuading them to a complete, than to half a reformation. Her knowledge of her father and Elizabeth, inclined her to think that the sacrifice of one pair of horses would be hardly less painful than of both,[16] and so on, through the whole list of Lady Russell's too gentle reductions.

How Anne's more rigid requisitions might have been taken, is of little consequence. Lady Russell's had no success at all—could not be put up with—were not to be borne. "What! Every comfort of life knocked off! Journeys, London, servants, horses, table,[17]— contractions and restrictions every where. To live no longer with the decencies even of a private gentleman![18] No, he would sooner quit Kellynch-hall at once, than remain in it on such disgraceful terms."

"Quit Kellynch-hall." The hint was immediately taken up by Mr. Shepherd, whose interest was involved in the reality of Sir Walter's retrenching,[19] and who was perfectly persuaded that nothing would be done without a change of abode.[20]—"Since the idea had been started in the very quarter which ought to dictate, he had no scruple,"[21] he said, "in confessing his judgment to be entirely on that side. It did not appear to him that Sir Walter could materially alter his style of living in a house which had such a character of hospitality and ancient dignity to support.[22]—In any other place, Sir Walter might judge for himself; and would be looked up to, as regulating the modes of life, in whatever way he might choose to model his household."[23]

Sir Walter would quit Kellynch-hall;—and after a very few days more of doubt and indecision, the great question of whither he should go, was settled, and the first outline of this important change made out.

There had been three alternatives, London, Bath, or another house in the country. All Anne's wishes had been for the latter. A small house in their own neighbourhood, where they might still have Lady Russell's society, still be near Mary, and still have the pleasure of sometimes seeing the lawns and groves[24] of Kellynch, was the object of her ambition. But the usual fate of Anne

16. The horses are used for the family chaise: see p. 11, note 34. Horses represented a considerable expense, including the initial cost of purchase (and of subsequent purchases, for they would need to be replaced periodically, especially if subjected to frequent use), numerous pieces of necessary equipment, food, servants to attend to them, and a stable to keep them.

17. Travel was expensive then, especially if done by private carriage, as anyone of their standing would do. The Elliots do not need to rent a carriage, but theirs would suffer costly wear on any lengthy voyage along the often rough roads of the time, and they would still need to hire new horses every ten miles (for how this worked, see p. 221, note 90), pay frequent tolls on the main roads (which were built by turnpike trusts that financed them through tolls), and stay at inns for many trips, including any to London, which was around twenty hours from Somerset at the time. Staying in London, as well as servants, horses, and table (i.e., food), were further heavy expenses.

18. A private gentleman was someone of high rank who did not play a prominent role in society, as Sir Walter does, at least in his own mind, and to a certain degree in reality by virtue of his title.

19. Mr. Shepherd probably gains much of his income from the fees he charges for serving as Sir Walter's agent. Agents often undertook the daily managing of estates, which could include collecting rents, paying wages, ordering repairs, and selling products from the estate; it is highly unlikely Sir Walter bothers with such matters. Mr. Shepherd would also take care of legal transactions, such as the mortgages mentioned above, and probably advises Sir Walter on his investments. Moreover, Mr. Shepherd would gain social prestige from being the agent of a high-ranking client. Thus he would have good reason to work assiduously to save this client from bankruptcy, while making sure, during the difficult process, to avoid causing any offense.

20. The house and its grounds, both requiring many servants to maintain and operate, usually constituted much of a typical landowner's expenses.

21. *scruple*: hesitation, uncertainty.

22. Hospitality was frequently fundamental to the life of a wealthy landowner. This could mean large parties of houseguests, or annual celebrations in which the entire neighborhood, rich and poor, was invited to the grounds and offered food and entertainment. Such hospitality was considered a basic social duty, while offering the opportunity to display one's wealth and importance. Of course, all this represented a considerable expense.

23. When no longer occupying a prominent house, with its rich history, Sir Walter would be freed from external pressure to maintain a certain level of expense. Whether he would still be looked up to in his new situation is debatable: this is probably just flattery to help secure his agreement.

24. Country houses were usually surrounded by elaborate landscapes offer-

attended[25] her, in having something very opposite from her inclination fixed on. She disliked Bath, and did not think it agreed
with her—and Bath was to be her home.[26]

Sir Walter had at first thought more of London, but Mr. Shepherd felt that he could not be trusted in London, and had been
skilful enough to dissuade him from it, and make Bath preferred.
It was a much safer place for a gentleman in his predicament:—
he might there be important at comparatively little expense.[27]—
Two material advantages of Bath over London had of course been
given all their weight, its more convenient distance from Kellynch, only fifty miles,[28] and Lady Russell's spending some part of
every winter there; and to the very great satisfaction of Lady Russell, whose first views on the projected change had been for Bath,
Sir Walter and Elizabeth were induced to believe that they should
lose neither consequence nor enjoyment by settling there.

Lady Russell felt obliged to oppose her dear Anne's known
wishes. It would be too much to expect Sir Walter to descend into
a small house in his own neighbourhood. Anne herself would
have found the mortifications of it more than she foresaw, and to
Sir Walter's feelings they must have been dreadful. And with
regard to Anne's dislike of Bath, she considered it as a prejudice
and mistake, arising first from the circumstance of her having
been three years at school there, after her mother's death,[29] and,
secondly, from her happening to be not in perfectly good spirits
the only winter which she had afterwards spent there with herself.[30]

Lady Russell was fond of Bath in short, and disposed to think it
must suit them all; and as to her young friend's health, by passing
all the warm months with her at Kellynch-lodge, every danger
would be avoided; and it was, in fact, a change which must do
both health and spirits good. Anne had been too little from home,
too little seen. Her spirits were not high. A larger society would
improve them. She wanted her to be more known.[31]

The undesirableness of any other house in the same neighbourhood for Sir Walter, was certainly much strengthened by one
part, and a very material part of the scheme, which had been hap-

ing beautiful views and attractive walks. They would include lawns and groves of trees, the latter often planted as part of the landscaping design.

25. *attended*: awaited.

26. Bath, thanks to several warm springs beneath its surface, had developed into the most popular spa town in England. Visitors hoped that bathing in or drinking its warm waters could heal their ailments, and their presence also made it a center for social life and entertainment, with many coming purely for enjoyment. Throughout the eighteenth century it was England's leading resort, attracting the elite of society and providing the setting for a number of novels and plays. Jane Austen sets substantial portions of two of her novels there, this one and *Northanger Abbey,* and she refers to it in all her novels.

Around 1800 its character began to change. It lost popularity as a vacation destination, as the seaside became increasingly the venue of choice for those seeking pleasure or health, while becoming more popular as a permanent residence, especially for retirees. After Jane Austen's father retired from his clerical position in 1801, he and his wife and daughters moved to Bath, staying until his death five years later. For them and others Bath offered a combination of beautiful architecture, the result of its eighteenth-century boom, a wide variety of entertainments, excellent shopping, and the presence of many other genteel people. Hence Sir Walter's consideration of Bath, and decision to settle there, reflects a growing trend—though the visits of others to Bath later in the novel show that its old functions had not disappeared.

27. The cost of living was higher in London, which by this time had more than a million people (as opposed to Bath's fewer than 40,000). London also offered many further temptations to spend, including an array of expensive shops, numerous entertainments, and the presence of the wealthiest people in England, whose extravagance would be emulated by those eager to win acceptance in the best social circles. This may be why Mr. Shepherd believes Sir Walter cannot be trusted there.

28. Proximity to Bath is one of the reasons Somerset has been chosen as the home of the main characters; the other is proximity to Lyme (see map, p. 513). Jane Austen, who had no connection to Somerset, always chooses her settings according to what will work best for the plot. Her characters never display distinctive regional traits; such traits had in actuality ceased to be very prominent among upper-class English people by this time.

29. Girls then usually received most of their education at home, but wealthy girls would sometimes attend boarding schools for part of their adolescence.

30. Winter was the most popular time to visit Bath (see p. 63, note 11).

31. Lady Russell is probably thinking, at least in part, of the much greater opportunities in Bath for Anne to find a mate. As a popular national venue

pily engrafted on the beginning. He was not only to quit his home, but to see it in the hands of others; a trial of fortitude, which stronger heads than Sir Walter's have found too much.— Kellynch-hall was to be let. This, however, was a profound secret; not to be breathed beyond their own circle.[32]

Sir Walter could not have borne the degradation of being known to design letting his house.[33]—Mr. Shepherd had once mentioned the word, "advertise";[34]—but never dared approach it again; Sir Walter spurned the idea of its being offered in any manner; forbad the slightest hint being dropped of his having such an intention; and it was only on the supposition of his being spontaneously solicited by some most unexceptionable applicant, on his own terms, and as a great favour, that he would let it at all.

How quick come the reasons for approving what we like!— Lady Russell had another excellent one at hand, for being extremely glad that Sir Walter and his family were to remove from the country. Elizabeth had been lately forming an intimacy, which she wished to see interrupted. It was with a daughter of Mr. Shepherd, who had returned, after an unprosperous[35] marriage, to her father's house, with the additional burthen of two children. She was a clever young woman, who understood the art of pleasing; the art of pleasing, at least, at Kellynch-hall; and who had made herself so acceptable to Miss Elliot,[36] as to have been already staying there more than once, in spite of all that Lady Russell, who thought it a friendship quite out of place, could hint of caution and reserve.

Lady Russell, indeed, had scarcely any influence with Elizabeth, and seemed to love her, rather because she would love her, than because Elizabeth deserved it. She had never received from her more than outward attention, nothing beyond the observances of complaisance;[37] had never succeeded in any point which she wanted to carry, against previous inclination. She had been repeatedly very earnest in trying to get Anne included in the visit to London, sensibly open to all the injustice and all the discredit of the selfish arrangements which shut her out, and on many lesser occasions had endeavoured to give Elizabeth the

for wealthy people, it would far surpass their limited country neighborhood in this regard.

32. Letting, or renting, his house would be typical for a landowner not living in it, especially if he had left due to indebtedness. It would be an additional trial not only because he would witness another resident in his home, but also because the latter's presence would ensure that his financial troubles would become public knowledge—were the house left empty, others might assume he had simply gone on an extended vacation, something many wealthy people did. Fear of imparting this knowledge is what makes Sir Walter wish to maintain secrecy, though of course such secrecy will delay the inevitable only slightly.

33. One reason he sees this as a further degradation is that aristocratic pride included standing above commerce, which was regarded as vulgar, and having sufficient social and financial independence that one never needed to hawk one's wares to anyone else.

34. Newspapers had become a prominent feature of English life, with a variety of dailies and weeklies in circulation, and advertisements formed a considerable portion of newspapers, with numerous notices, often on the front page, offering or promoting a wide variety of goods and services.

35. *unprosperous:* unsuccessful, unfortunate. This does not mean she came home after a divorce, something almost impossible at this time, but that the marriage was unhappy. Later she is identified as a widow.

36. "Miss Elliot" means Elizabeth. The eldest unmarried daughter in a family was always described or addressed as "Miss + last name." Younger unmarried daughters had their first name put after "Miss"; thus Anne will shortly be called "Miss Anne." For an exception to this rule, see p. 137, note 58.

37. *complaisance:* civility, obligingness.

advantage of her own better judgment and experience—but always in vain; Elizabeth would go her own way—and never had she pursued it in more decided opposition to Lady Russell, than in this selection of Mrs. Clay; turning from the society of so deserving a sister to bestow her affection and confidence on one who ought to have been nothing to her but the object of distant civility.[38]

From situation,[39] Mrs. Clay was, in Lady Russell's estimate, a very unequal, and in her character she believed a very dangerous companion—and a removal that would leave Mrs. Clay behind, and bring a choice of more suitable intimates within Miss Elliot's reach, was therefore an object of first-rate importance.

38. Those of different social ranks were not supposed to mix intimately. All characters in Jane Austen show some support or acceptance of this principle, and a character with Lady Russell's value for rank would support it strongly. Mrs. Clay, as the daughter of an attorney, is considerably lower on the social scale than the Elliots (nor is there any indication that her marriage has raised her position). The critical dividing line in English society at the time was between the genteel, meaning gentlemen and their families, and the non-genteel. Gentlemen were those who possessed enough property, preferably landed property, to avoid having to work, except to supervise that property, or those who earned a living from one of the genteel professions, the principal ones being army and naval officer, clergyman, and barrister (the type of lawyer able to try cases in court). The Elliots, as substantial landowners with a title, are in the upper ranks of this class, the vast majority of whose members were either untitled landowners or members of the above professions.

Attorneys, in contrast, were not considered gentlemen at all. Their prestige was rising slightly during this time, but they, like merchants, were still regarded as being on a distinctly lower level. Though attorneys were a basic part of the rural society depicted in each of Jane Austen's novels, these novels almost never show attorneys socializing with the genteel characters who dominate them. The one exception is in *Pride and Prejudice*, in which one of the heroine's uncles is an attorney, but he and his wife are consistently depicted as vulgar, and they never associate with the highest-ranking figures in the novel. Moreover, having an uncle who is an attorney, as well as a maternal grandfather who was one, is a social mark against the heroine, one provoking sharp strictures from others.

39. *situation:* social position.

Chapter Three

"*I* must take leave to observe, Sir Walter," said Mr. Shepherd one morning at Kellynch Hall, as he laid down the newspaper, "that the present juncture is much in our favour. This peace will be turning all our rich Navy Officers ashore.[1] They will be all wanting a home. Could not be a better time, Sir Walter, for having a choice of tenants, very responsible tenants. Many a noble[2] fortune has been made during the war. If a rich Admiral were to come in our way, Sir Walter—"

"He would be a very lucky man, Shepherd,"[3] replied Sir Walter, "that's all I have to remark. A prize indeed would Kellynch Hall be to him; rather the greatest prize of all, let him have taken ever so many before—hey, Shepherd?"[4]

Mr. Shepherd laughed, as he knew he must, at this wit, and then added,

"I presume to observe, Sir Walter, that, in the way of[5] business, gentlemen of the navy are well to deal with. I have had a little knowledge of their methods of doing business, and I am free to confess that they have very liberal[6] notions, and are as likely to make desirable tenants as any set of people one should meet with.[7] Therefore, Sir Walter, what I would take leave to suggest is, that if in consequence of any rumours getting abroad[8] of your intention—which must be contemplated as a possible thing, because we know how difficult it is to keep the actions and designs of one part of the world from the notice and curiosity of the other,—consequence has its tax[9]—I, John Shepherd, might conceal any family-matters that I chose, for nobody would think it worth their while to observe me,[10] but Sir Walter Elliot has eyes upon him which it may be very difficult to elude—and therefore, thus much I venture upon, that it will not greatly surprise me if, with all our caution, some rumour of the truth should get

1. It is the summer of 1814. In March of 1814 Napoleon, the Emperor of France, abdicated, ending the French Revolutionary and Napoleonic Wars (though there would be a brief, limited revival of the war in early 1815, after which the fighting completely ceased). These wars had been going on since 1792, with only a short interlude of peace in 1802–1803. They had pitted France against various coalitions of European powers, in which Britain consistently played a leading role. Britain's main weapon against France was its large navy, which expanded enormously during these years. The end of the war meant that large numbers of those serving would now return home.

2. *noble:* magnificent, splendid.

3. Sir Walter's use of only his last name indicates his relatively low status. Were he of higher rank Sir Walter would call him "Mr." Were he of even lower rank Sir Walter would use only his first name, as with most servants.

4. Sir Walter's feeble witticism refers to the prize money naval officers received when they captured an enemy ship, i.e., a prize. This ship could be a rival warship or an enemy commercial vessel—intercepting such vessels to choke off the other side's commerce was a standard part of warfare then. The navy would assess the value of the ship and its cargo, and distribute the sum, according to a set formula, among the members of the capturing ship. The captain received the greatest share (three-eighths until 1808, one-sixth thereafter), while the rest was apportioned among others on the ship, with the highest-ranking officers receiving the most per person, and ordinary crewmen the least. If the ship was sailing, as it often was, under the command of a higher-ranking officer such as an admiral, the captain had to give this superior officer one-third of his share. Because naval salaries, at all levels, were low, and the value of captured ships usually high, prize money was often the main source of remuneration for those in the navy, and it provided a strong incentive for ships to act aggressively against the enemy. Many captains and admirals made substantial fortunes through this means.

5. *in the way of:* as regards, with a view to.

6. *liberal:* generous (in a financial sense).

7. In addition to any possible liberality, naval officers would be less experienced in these matters, having spent much of their adult lives in the confined world of their ships, and thus probably less able to drive hard bargains.

8. *abroad:* outside the family, in general circulation.

9. *consequence has its tax:* social importance has its burden.

10. Mr. Shepherd refers to his low social status as an attorney; see p. 31, note 38.

abroad—in the supposition of which, as I was going to observe, since applications will unquestionably follow, I should think any from our wealthy naval commanders particularly worth attending to—and beg leave to add, that two hours will bring me over at any time, to save you the trouble of replying."

Sir Walter only nodded. But soon afterwards, rising and pacing the room, he observed sarcastically,

"There are few among the gentlemen of the navy, I imagine, who would not be surprised to find themselves in a house of this description."

"They would look around them, no doubt, and bless their good fortune," said Mrs. Clay, for Mrs. Clay was present; her father had driven her over, nothing being of so much use to Mrs. Clay's health as a drive to Kellynch: "but I quite agree with my father in thinking a sailor might be a very desirable tenant.[11] I have known a good deal of the profession; and besides their liberality, they are so neat and careful in all their ways![12] These valuable pictures of yours, Sir Walter, if you chose to leave them, would be perfectly safe.[13] Every thing in and about the house would be taken such excellent care of! The gardens and shrubberies would be kept in almost as high order as they are now.[14] You need not be afraid, Miss Elliot, of your own sweet flower-garden's being neglected."[15]

"As to all that," rejoined Sir Walter coolly, "supposing I were induced to let my house, I have by no means made up my mind as to the privileges to be annexed to it. I am not particularly disposed to favour a tenant. The park would be open to him of course, and few navy officers, or men of any other description, can have had such a range; but what restrictions I might impose on the use of the pleasure-grounds is another thing.[16] I am not fond of the idea of my shrubberies being always approachable; and I should recommend Miss Elliot to be on her guard with respect to her flower-garden. I am very little disposed to grant a tenant of Kellynch Hall any extraordinary favour, I assure you, be he sailor or soldier."

After a short pause, Mr. Shepherd presumed to say,[17]

"In all these cases, there are established usages which make

11. Mrs. Clay wishes to assist her father in persuading Sir Walter to accept a sailor as a tenant; she also has her own reasons for trying to please Sir Walter. Her speech shows a consistent resemblance to her father's in its careful tact, frequent professions of humility, and assiduous flattery.

12. The confined quarters of a ship forced those living on it to be neat and well organized. The constant threat of illness, due to intense crowding and the frequent absence of fresh food, also made the navy put a premium on cleanliness. Thus ships were normally given a thorough washing every day.

13. Most wealthy families had pictures in their homes. They would normally have portraits of family members of each generation, and they would frequently possess other paintings as well, bought from genuine appreciation of art or from a desire to display their taste and affluence.

14. Gardens of various types and shrubberies were standard features of country houses at this time; Jane Austen's family had both, though they had a less grand home than Kellynch Hall. Shrubberies were usually planted in elaborate patterns that would be both interesting visually and suitable for taking strolls; they could also contain places to sit down and relax.

15. Flower gardens were one of the most popular types of gardens. They often included exotic flowers and shrubs. Such plants could require special care, whether from adjoining greenhouses, special beds, sheltering walls, or artificial sources of heat, and this is why Mrs. Clay makes a point of assuring Elizabeth that the flower garden will not be neglected.

16. "Park" and "pleasure-grounds" were the standard terms then for the two principal parts of a landscape garden. The pleasure grounds, which were usually near the house, consisted of those areas with ornamental plantings. Thus it generally included the shrubbery and the flower garden, which is why Sir Walter, in the next sentence, includes them in his discussion of possible restrictions. The park referred to the lawns and woodlands that were farther afield. While in general carefully landscaped, with planted trees and often bodies of water that were created or enlarged, these parks had been made to appear as natural as possible. They could be very extensive, which is why Sir Walter boasts of the range of his.

17. The pause suggests Sir Walter's unreasonableness—though of course Mr. Shepherd offers no direct contradiction. The pleasure garden's proximity to the house would make keeping it off-limits particularly ridiculous.

every thing plain and easy between landlord and tenant. Your interest, Sir Walter, is in pretty safe hands. Depend upon me for taking care that no tenant has more than his just rights.[18] I venture to hint, that Sir Walter Elliot cannot be half so jealous for his own, as John Shepherd will be for him."

Here Anne spoke,—

"The navy, I think, who have done so much for us, have at least an equal claim with any other set of men, for all the comforts and all the privileges which any home can give. Sailors work hard enough for their comforts, we must all allow."[19]

"Very true, very true. What Miss Anne[20] says is very true," was Mr. Shepherd's rejoinder, and "Oh! certainly," was his daughter's; but Sir Walter's remark was, soon afterwards—

"The profession has its utility, but I should be sorry to see any friend of mine belonging to it."

"Indeed!" was the reply, and with a look of surprise.

"Yes; it is in two points offensive to me; I have two strong grounds of objection to it. First, as being the means of bringing persons of obscure birth into undue distinction, and raising men to honours which their fathers and grandfathers never dreamt of;[21] and secondly, as it cuts up a man's youth and vigour most horribly; a sailor grows old sooner than any other man; I have observed it all my life. A man is in greater danger in the navy of being insulted by the rise of one whose father, his father might have disdained to speak to, and of becoming prematurely an object of disgust himself, than in any other line. One day last spring, in town, I was in company with two men, striking instances of what I am talking of, Lord St. Ives, whose father we all know to have been a country curate,[22] without bread to eat; I was to give place[23] to Lord St. Ives, and a certain Admiral Baldwin, the most deplorable looking personage you can imagine, his face the colour of mahogany, rough and rugged to the last degree, all lines and wrinkles,[24] nine grey hairs of a side, and nothing but a dab of powder at top.[25]—'In the name of heaven, who is that old fellow?' said I, to a friend of mine who was standing near, (Sir Basil Morley). 'Old fellow!' cried Sir Basil, 'it is Admiral Baldwin.

18. There were a number of books then that set down the laws governing the relationship between a landlord and tenant, in various circumstances, and that sometimes gave advice on the best type of arrangement.

19. The navy played an absolutely critical role in Britain's war with Napoleon. It shielded Britain from invasion at a time when he dominated all of Europe, ensuring that Britain was the one major European country never attacked by his armies. It also protected Britain's commerce with the rest of the world, despite Napoleon's attempts to cut off Britain's European trade, foiled French attempts to extend the war outside Europe, and allowed Britain to land armies in various places in Europe to exploit French weaknesses. Thus Anne's gratitude, at a juncture when Britain had just emerged victorious, represents a standard attitude, though, as will be seen, she has particular reasons of her own for holding the navy in high esteem.

20. *Miss Anne:* this is what Anne, as a younger sister, is called.

21. The navy offered greater possibilities of social mobility than most institutions in this society. Generally only the sons of gentlemen (see p. 31, note 38), or perhaps of wealthy middle-class parents, could begin the path that led to becoming an officer. But once there a man could rise through his own merit to a high position, even above those who had more distinguished origins. The importance of the navy to Britain's defense led to an unwillingness to promote less qualified people just because of their social background, though a good background and social or political connections could still help. Moreover, while the hierarchical nature of this society created opposition in general to social climbing, the high prestige of the navy meant that most people, unlike Sir Walter, would not object to someone whose distinguished service there had raised him higher than his origins.

22. A curate was a low-ranking and poorly paid clergyman; see p. 45, note 48. Since his father, however poor, was still classed as a gentleman, Lord St. Ives would have had the opportunity to begin as a midshipman.

23. *give place.* yield precedence; for more on precedence, see p. 11, note 35. Lord St. Ives is a nobleman; thus he outranks Sir Walter and would precede him in formal settings. Naval officers could be ennobled for meritorious action, an example of the social climbing Sir Walter deplores.

24. Naval officers would frequently have tanned and rough skin, for their jobs involved being on top of an exposed ship deck. Britain's worldwide naval interests also required many of its ships to go to climates in which the sun would beat down far more fiercely than in Britain itself. At this time, tanned skin, even on a smooth face, was regarded as unattractive.

25. Hair powder had been a standard feature of male grooming during the

What do you take his age to be?' 'Sixty,' said I, 'or perhaps sixty-two.' 'Forty,' replied Sir Basil, 'forty, and no more.' Picture to your-selves my amazement; I shall not easily forget Admiral Baldwin. I never saw quite so wretched an example of what a sea-faring life can do: but to a degree, I know it is the same with them all; they are all knocked about, and exposed to every climate, and every weather, till they are not fit to be seen. It is a pity they are not knocked on the head at once, before they reach Admiral Bald-win's age."

"Nay, Sir Walter," cried Mrs. Clay, "this is being severe indeed. Have a little mercy on the poor men. We are not all born to be handsome. The sea is no beautifier, certainly; sailors do grow old betimes; I have often observed it; they soon lose the look of youth. But then, is not it the same with many other professions, perhaps most other?[26] Soldiers, in active service, are not at all better off: and even in the quieter professions, there is a toil and a labour of the mind, if not of the body, which seldom leaves a man's looks to the natural effect of time. The lawyer plods, quite care-worn; the physician is up at all hours,[27] and travelling in all weather; and even the clergyman —" she stopt a moment to consider what might do for the clergyman; — "and even the clergyman, you know, is obliged to go into infected rooms,[28] and expose his health and looks to all the injury of a poisonous atmosphere.[29] In fact, as I have long been convinced, though every profession is necessary and honourable in its turn, it is only the lot of those who are not obliged to follow any, who can live in a regular way, in the coun-try, choosing their own hours, following their own pursuits, and living on their own property, without the torment of trying for more; it is only *their* lot, I say, to hold the blessings of health and a good appearance to the utmost: I know no other set of men but what lose something of their personableness when they cease to be quite young."[30]

It seemed as if Mr. Shepherd, in this anxiety to bespeak Sir Walter's goodwill towards a naval officer as tenant, had been gifted with foresight; for the very first application for the house was from an Admiral Croft, with whom he shortly afterwards fell

eighteenth century, but it had declined starting in the 1790s, spurred by a general change toward a more natural look for both men and women as well as by a tax on hair powder. By this point it was mostly used by older men who continued the fashions of their youth. Thus Admiral Baldwin's use of powder marks him out both as behind the current fashions and as desperate to hide his baldness.

26. The professions in Mrs. Clay's list are the ones whose practitioners could be considered gentlemen, and thus the only ones worthy of notice and comparison for Sir Walter: naval and army officer, clergyman, lawyer (and among lawyers, only barristers were considered gentlemen), and physician.

27. The physician was one of the three main types of medical practitioners, the other two being surgeon and apothecary. Physicians were the only ones who received formal education at a university (the others simply underwent an apprenticeship with an existing practitioner), and the only ones considered genteel. They were relatively few in number, were concentrated especially in cities and large towns, and were often consulted in serious cases that seemed beyond the ability of other practitioners.

Consulting and treating patients at home was standard medical practice; one reason was that most medical tools or equipment were simple and easily transportable. For doctors attending patients in rural areas this could mean long and difficult journeys. Even physicians might have to do this, for some were based in the provinces, and they frequently attended affluent patients in a position to insist that their doctor come to them.

28. Visiting the sick was a basic part of the duty of the clergy.

29. Contemporary medical thinking attributed the onset of many diseases to the effects of unhealthy atmospheres. People understood that certain illnesses were infectious—hence Mrs. Clay's comment about "infected rooms"—but, knowing nothing of microorganisms, did not understand why and looked frequently to environmental factors such as stale air, dampness, or dirt.

30. Mrs. Clay's argument is a parody of a basic justification for the prestige and power of the landowning elite, which was that their freedom from normal monetary striving allowed them to cultivate a concern for the public good as well as various moral virtues. Few making that argument would have regarded the cultivation of one's appearance as a sufficient justification for privilege.

into company in attending the quarter sessions at Taunton;[31] and indeed, he had received a hint of the admiral from a London correspondent.[32] By the report which he hastened over to Kellynch to make, Admiral Croft was a native of Somersetshire, who having acquired a very handsome fortune, was wishing to settle in his own country,[33] and had come down to Taunton in order to look at some advertised places in that immediate neighbourhood, which, however, had not suited him; that accidentally hearing—(it was just as he had foretold, Mr. Shepherd observed, Sir Walter's concerns could not be kept a secret,)—accidentally hearing of the possibility of Kellynch Hall being to let, and understanding his (Mr. Shepherd's) connection with the owner, he had introduced himself to him in order to make particular inquiries, and had, in the course of a pretty long conference, expressed as strong an inclination for the place as a man who knew it only by description could feel; and given Mr. Shepherd, in his explicit account of himself, every proof of his being a most responsible, eligible[34] tenant.

"And who is Admiral Croft?" was Sir Walter's cold suspicious inquiry.

Mr. Shepherd answered for his being of a gentleman's family, and mentioned a place; and Anne, after the little pause which followed, added—

"He is rear admiral of the white.[35] He was in the Trafalgar action,[36] and has been in the East Indies[37] since; he has been stationed there, I believe, several years."[38]

"Then I take it for granted," observed Sir Walter, "that his face is about as orange as the cuffs and capes of my livery."[39]

Mr. Shepherd hastened to assure him, that Admiral Croft was a very hale, hearty, well-looking man, a little weather-beaten, to be sure, but not much; and quite the gentleman in all his notions and behaviour;—not likely to make the smallest difficulty about terms;—only wanted a comfortable home, and to get into it as soon as possible;—knew he must pay for his convenience;—knew what rent a ready-furnished house of that consequence might fetch;—should not have been surprised if Sir Walter had asked

31. The quarter sessions were meetings of local magistrates, usually covering an entire county, that occurred every three months; Taunton is the county town (or seat) of Somerset (see map, p. 513). The quarter sessions settled many legal cases, while also deciding on the principal matters of government for the county. They were major events, which attracted many people, and which lawyers like Mr. Shepherd would be especially likely to attend.

32. It was standard for a provincial attorney to have a contact in London, for much of the legal business in England then took place in the capital. Most likely Mr. Shepherd sent word to this London correspondent, and perhaps to others, to be discreetly on the watch for a potential renter of Kellynch Hall. Thus when Admiral Croft made his inquiries, either by going to London himself or by approaching someone with his own London contacts, the information eventually made its way to Mr. Shepherd's correspondent, and some kind of meeting at Taunton was arranged.

33. *country*: county.

34. *eligible*: suitable.

35. Rear admiral is the lowest of the three admiral ranks. The highest is full admiral, then vice admiral. Each rank had three levels, the red, the white, and the blue (in descending order), creating nine total levels. Admirals, who were promoted on the basis of seniority, started at the lowest level, rear admiral of the blue, and gradually worked their way up. Hence Admiral Croft has reached the second level of ascent.

36. Trafalgar, fought in 1805 off the coast of Spain, was Britain's most important naval victory of the war. In it the British fleet, commanded by Lord Nelson, destroyed much of the French and Spanish fleets, ensuring that Napoleon would be unable to invade Britain. Trafalgar Square, dominated by a column with a statue of Nelson, is one of the leading landmarks in London.

37. *East Indies*: India and the islands of Southeast Asia. India was Britain's most important colony, and the British navy was needed to protect trade with it. Britain also had important commercial interests in Southeast Asia.

38. This is the second time in the novel that Anne has spoken. In both cases she speaks about the navy, and in this case with a great deal of knowledge. The reason for her strong interest will soon appear.

39. A livery was a special uniform worn by male servants. Each family had its own distinctive livery, and most of its male servants would wear it. Designed

more;—had inquired about the manor;—would be glad of the deputation, certainly, but made no great point of it;—said he sometimes took out a gun, but never killed;—quite the gentleman.[40]

Mr. Shepherd was eloquent on the subject; pointing out all the circumstances of the admiral's family, which made him peculiarly desirable as a tenant. He was a married man, and without children; the very state to be wished for. A house was never taken good care of, Mr. Shepherd observed, without a lady: he did not know, whether furniture might not be in danger of suffering as much where there was no lady, as where there were many children. A lady, without a family, was the very best preserver of furniture in the world. He had seen Mrs. Croft, too; she was at Taunton with the admiral, and had been present almost all the time they were talking the matter over.

"And a very well-spoken, genteel, shrewd lady, she seemed to be," continued he; "asked more questions about the house, and terms, and taxes,[41] than the admiral himself, and seemed more conversant with business. And moreover, Sir Walter, I found she was not quite unconnected in this country, any more than her husband; that is to say, she is sister to a gentleman who did live amongst us once; she told me so herself: sister to the gentleman who lived a few years back, at Monkford. Bless me! what was his name? At this moment I cannot recollect his name, though I have heard it so lately. Penelope, my dear, can you help me to the name of the gentleman who lived at Monkford—Mrs. Croft's brother?"

But Mrs. Clay was talking so eagerly with Miss Elliot, that she did not hear the appeal.

"I have no conception whom you can mean, Shepherd; I remember no gentleman resident at Monkford since the time of old Governor Trent."[42]

"Bless me! how very odd! I shall forget my own name soon, I suppose. A name that I am so very well acquainted with; knew the gentleman so well by sight; seen him a hundred times; came to consult me once, I remember, about a trespass of one of his neigh-

to display the family's importance, the liveries were often very gaudy and elaborate. This is indicated in this case by the use of a bright color like orange (at a time when men normally wore dark, sober colors), and what would seem to be the contrast in color between the cuffs and capes and the rest of the coat—capes in this context refer not to a separate garment, but to one or more smaller pieces that were attached to the coat at the neck and covered the tops of the shoulders.

40. Mr. Shepherd is speaking about hunting, or shooting, rights, which is why he refers to taking out a gun. By law this right was essentially restricted to landed gentlemen (the principal qualification was owning an estate worth at least a hundred pounds a year). At the same time, any lord of a manor—a category embracing most substantial landowners of the time, a manor being land with tenants on it—had the right to authorize another person to kill game on his land by conferring on him the deputation of gamekeeper. Many landowners granted this right to those renting their house; a character in *Pride and Prejudice*, Mr. Bingley, enjoys it as a renter. Shooting game was extremely popular among upper-class men.

41. Mrs. Croft could be asking about several taxes. There were two national taxes that varied according to the house: the window tax, assessed on the number of windows, and the tax on inhabited houses, assessed on the estimated fair rental value of the house; both these taxes were imposed on the occupier, not the owner. There were also various local taxes, including the poor rate, for relief of the local poor, and the county rate, for a variety of government expenses. These could differ greatly from place to place, as could the methods of determining them, and whether they were imposed on the owner or the occupier of a property.

42. Governor could be used for someone holding high authority in a variety of institutions, public or private. But it was always a designation of distinction, and not one enjoyed by many people.

bours; farmer's man[43] breaking into his orchard—wall torn down—apples stolen[44]—caught in the fact; and afterwards, contrary to my judgment, submitted to an amicable compromise.[45] Very odd indeed!"

After waiting another moment—

"You mean Mr. Wentworth, I suppose," said Anne.[46]

Mr. Shepherd was all gratitude.

"Wentworth was the very name! Mr. Wentworth was the very man. He had the curacy of Monkford, you know, Sir Walter, some time back, for two or three years. Came there about the year —5,[47] I take it. You remember him, I am sure."

"Wentworth? Oh! ay,—Mr. Wentworth, the curate of Monkford. You misled me by the term *gentleman*. I thought you were speaking of some man of property:[48] Mr. Wentworth was nobody, I remember; quite unconnected; nothing to do with the Strafford family. One wonders how the names of many of our nobility become so common."[49]

As Mr. Shepherd perceived that this connexion of the Crofts did them no service with Sir Walter, he mentioned it no more; returning, with all his zeal, to dwell on the circumstances more indisputably in their favour; their age, and number, and fortune; the high idea they had formed of Kellynch Hall, and extreme solicitude for the advantage of renting it; making it appear as if they ranked nothing beyond the happiness of being the tenants of Sir Walter Elliot: an extraordinary taste, certainly, could they have been supposed in the secret of Sir Walter's estimate of the dues of a tenant.

It succeeded, however; and though Sir Walter must ever look with an evil eye on any one intending to inhabit that house, and think them infinitely too well off in being permitted to rent it on the highest terms, he was talked into allowing Mr. Shepherd to proceed in the treaty, and authorising him to wait on Admiral Croft, who still remained at Taunton, and fix a day for the house being seen.

Sir Walter was not very wise; but still he had experience enough of the world to feel, that a more unobjectionable tenant,

43. *farmer's man:* man working for a farmer. Farmers formed the middle rank of rural society. At the top were wealthy landowners like Sir Walter. They normally rented sections of their land to farmers, who would undertake the actual business of farming it and selling the produce, and then keep the earnings (minus what they paid the landowner in rent). Farmers, who usually rented substantial allotments and could be very prosperous, would hire laborers, such as the man here, to work under them.

44. Mrs. Croft's brother is shortly revealed to be a curate, a low-ranking clergyman. A clerical position often included agricultural land, which formed one of the principal sources of the position's income. Jane Austen's father, a clergyman, raised vegetables and fruit along with various livestock. Apples had long been one of the most popular English fruits.

45. Such an amicable compromise, done out of court, would be normal. The eighteenth century had witnessed a considerable decline in litigation, especially in rural areas; people there regarded the law as too full of complexities, delays, and costs to be worth resorting to and preferred informal means of settling disputes. Mr. Shepherd, in recommending action, is conforming to a common stereotype of lawyers, as men out to multiply litigation in order to garner fees, that accompanied this general disgust with the court system (though attorneys like Mr. Shepherd could not try cases, they still would earn fees from other work connected with a trial).

46. This is the third time Anne has spoken, and, as will soon appear, this statement, though ostensibly about a clergyman, also has an important naval dimension.

47. 1805. His presence led to important events in 1806 (see next chapter).

48. A curate was a clergyman in the Church of England, the church attended by the majority of the population and supported in its supreme position by the law. He was hired by the person actually holding a clerical position and receiving the income to reside in the parish and perform the duties in his place. A curate could be hired because a clergyman held more than one position, or living, and was unable to perform the duties of each one, or because the holder simply preferred paying the curate's stipend, which was usually much less than the income from the position, to performing the duties himself. The excess of qualified clergymen, compared to positions available, meant that curates could generally be hired for low salaries. As members of the Anglican clergy, curates were, strictly speaking, gentlemen. This is why Mr. Shepherd calls Mr. Wentworth one. But the subordinate nature of their position and, even more, their low incomes could cause men like Sir Walter to hold them in disdain.

49. Sir Walter is thinking of the Earls of Strafford, who were prominent in

in all essentials, than Admiral Croft bid fair to be, could hardly offer. So far went his understanding; and his vanity supplied a little additional soothing, in the admiral's situation in life, which was just high enough, and not too high. "I have let my house to Admiral Croft," would sound extremely well; very much better than to any mere Mr. ——; a Mr. (save, perhaps, some half dozen in the nation,) always needs a note of explanation. An admiral speaks his own consequence,[50] and, at the same time, can never make a baronet look small. In all their dealings and intercourse, Sir Walter Elliot must ever have the precedence.[51]

Nothing could be done without a reference to Elizabeth; but her inclination was growing so strong for a removal, that she was happy to have it fixed and expedited by a tenant at hand; and not a word to suspend decision was uttered by her.

Mr. Shepherd was completely empowered to act; and no sooner had such an end been reached, than Anne, who had been a most attentive listener to the whole, left the room, to seek the comfort of cool air for her flushed cheeks;[52] and as she walked along a favourite grove, said, with a gentle sigh, "A few months more, and *he*, perhaps, may be walking here."[53]

the seventeenth and eighteenth centuries and whose family name was Wentworth. The most famous earl was Thomas Wentworth, First Earl of Strafford, who rose to high political office under Charles I, was made an earl, and shortly afterward was convicted of high treason by Parliament and executed in 1641. His execution was one of the principal early events in the English Civil War, or English Revolution, which eventually led to Charles I's own execution in 1649. Jane Austen ends her juvenile *History of England* with a brief discussion of Charles I, including a mention of Strafford. This history, and the names of Wentworth and Strafford, would resonate with Sir Walter because, as he would know well from his favorite book, the baronetage, his own family had been granted its title as a reward for its support of the monarchy during the civil war (see p. 5, note 12).

At the same time, the Wentworth name had existed for centuries as a nonnoble one prior to Thomas Wentworth's becoming an earl, and there continued to be many other Wentworths who were not members of the nobility. Thus it makes little sense for Sir Walter to lament the name's having become common.

50. *speaks his own consequence*: announces or indicates his own importance.

51. Rules of precedence dictated that a baronet would precede an admiral, unless the latter had been raised to the rank of a lord like Lord St. Ives.

Sir Walter's reasoning contrasts with Mr. Shepherd's, who had focused on practical questions of the case of the terms and the likelihood that these tenants would maintain the house well, obviously thinking that this would convince Sir Walter of their desirability.

52. Anne's pursuit of cool air outdoors suggests that they have a fire in the house, even though it is now summer (see chronology, p. 487). This would not be that unusual, especially for someone like Sir Walter, who is more concerned with comfort than with cost. Summers in England can sometimes be cool: in a letter written at the end of June, while she was staying at the home of her wealthy brother, Jane Austen writes of her enjoyment at finding a fire in the house (June 30, 1808).

53. For the first time, the novel moves to a focus on Anne. The focus will remain there until the end.

One writer, Josephine Ross, has suggested that the name Anne Elliot is a subtle compliment to Austen's publisher, John Murray. The maiden name of his wife was Anne Elliot, including the unusual spelling of "Elliot" (usually it is spelled with one "l" and one "t," or two of both letters). Ross speculates that Jane Austen may have been trying to please Murray because he had expressed reservations about her last book, *Emma* (Josephine Ross, "Diary," *The Times*, June 11, 2003).

Chapter Four

*H*e was not Mr. Wentworth,[1] the former curate of Monkford, however suspicious appearances may be, but a captain Frederick Wentworth, his brother, who being made commander in consequence of the action off St. Domingo,[2] and not immediately employed,[3] had come into Somersetshire, in the summer of 1806; and having no parent living, found a home for half a year, at Monkford. He was, at that time, a remarkably fine[4] young man, with a great deal of intelligence, spirit and brilliancy; and Anne an extremely pretty girl, with gentleness, modesty, taste, and feeling.[5] — Half the sum of attraction, on either side, might have been enough, for he had nothing to do, and she had hardly any body to love; but the encounter of such lavish recommendations could not fail. They were gradually acquainted, and when acquainted, rapidly and deeply in love. It would be difficult to say which had seen highest perfection in the other, or which had been the happiest; she, in receiving his declarations and proposals, or he in having them accepted.

A short period of exquisite felicity followed, and but a short one. — Troubles soon arose. Sir Walter, on being applied to, without actually withholding his consent,[6] or saying it should never be, gave it all the negative of great astonishment, great coldness, great silence, and a professed resolution of doing nothing for his daughter.[7] He thought it a very degrading alliance;[8] and Lady Russell, though with more tempered and pardonable pride, received it as a most unfortunate one.

Anne Elliot, with all her claims of birth, beauty, and mind, to throw herself away at nineteen; involve herself at nineteen in an engagement with a young man, who had nothing but himself to recommend him, and no hopes of attaining affluence, but in the

1. *Mr. Wentworth:* This indicates that he is the elder brother. Younger brothers would be called "Mr + first name." The respective forms would be used even if one brother, as in this case, is called Captain. The usage is analogous to that of "Miss" with the names of unmarried sisters.

2. Santo (or San) Domingo was a Spanish colony in the Caribbean; it is now the Dominican Republic. A major battle between British and French fleets occurred offshore in 1806, resulting in the destruction of most of the latter. Jane Austen's brother commanded a ship there. After major battles, especially victorious ones, each participating ship's first lieutenant, the officer just below the captain and Wentworth's probable position, was usually promoted to commander. This enabled a man to command a small ship.

3. He had not yet been assigned a ship; there were more officers with the rank of commander and captain than ships that they could command.

4. *fine:* handsome.

5. These two lists of qualities contrast the main characters and reveal their suitability. In his case, spirit means ardor, vigor, or assertiveness; brilliancy means sparkling cleverness, with a similar connotation of energy and vivacity. In her case, modesty means especially sexual modesty and restraint, a prime female virtue in this society. Taste, an important quality in Jane Austen, refers to a general sense of what is proper as well as to aesthetic discernment, while feeling means sensitivity, tenderness, and a susceptibility to the finest emotions.

It will be noted that his qualities are more intellectual, hers more emotional. This corresponds to ideas at the time regarding what is characteristic, and most worthy, in men and women. For example, the heroine of *Evelina,* by one of Austen's favorite novelists, Frances (or Fanny) Burney, says of a clever, sharp-tongued woman, "her understanding, indeed, may be called *masculine:* but, unfortunately, her manners deserve the same epithet; for, in studying to acquire the knowledge of the other sex, she has lost all the softness of her own." She adds that gentleness is "a virtue which . . . seems so essential a part of the female character." Thus Anne Elliot, in combining her intelligence, a quality that is certainly respected in women, with softness and gentleness, fulfills far better the prevailing feminine ideal.

6. In this society people were free to select their marriage partners on their own, but parents retained, by general consent, a right of veto. Thus characters in Austen, after making their choice, usually ask for parental permission.

7. This refers particularly to any financial assistance he might offer. Anne is entitled to a dowry of ten thousand pounds (see p. 474, and p. 475, note 7), but parents would sometimes give more, in money or other benefits, to encourage the marriage and assist the young couple afterward.

8. *alliance:* marriage. The term reflects the tendency then to view marriage

chances of a most uncertain profession,[9] and no connexions[10] to secure even his farther rise in that profession; would be, indeed, a throwing away, which she grieved to think of! Anne Elliot, so young; known to so few, to be snatched off by a stranger without alliance or fortune; or rather sunk by him into a state of most wearing, anxious, youth-killing dependance![11] It must not be, if by any fair interference of friendship, any representations[12] from one who had almost a mother's love, and mother's rights, it would be prevented.

Captain Wentworth had no fortune. He had been lucky in his profession, but spending freely, what had come freely, had realized nothing. But, he was confident that he should soon be rich;[13]—full of life and ardour, he knew that he should soon have a ship, and soon be on a station that would lead to every thing he wanted.[14] He had always been lucky; he knew he should be so still.—Such confidence, powerful in its own warmth, and bewitching in the wit which often expressed it, must have been enough for Anne; but Lady Russell saw it very differently.—His sanguine temper, and fearlessness of mind,[15] operated very differently on her. She saw in it but an aggravation of the evil. It only added a dangerous character to himself. He was brilliant,[16] he was headstrong.—Lady Russell had little taste for wit; and of any thing approaching to imprudence a horror. She deprecated the connexion[17] in every light.

Such opposition, as these feelings produced, was more than Anne could combat. Young and gentle as she was, it might yet have been possible to withstand her father's ill-will, though unsoftened by one kind word or look on the part of her sister;— but Lady Russell, whom she had always loved and relied on, could not, with such steadiness of opinion, and such tenderness of manner, be continually advising her in vain.[18] She was persuaded to believe the engagement a wrong thing—indiscreet, improper, hardly capable of success, and not deserving it.[19] But it was not a merely selfish caution, under which she acted, in putting an end to it. Had she not imagined herself consulting his good, even more than her own, she could hardly have given him up.—The

as a link between families, one joining their interests and affecting their social positions. In this case Sir Walter feared the harm from a link with Captain Wentworth. His contempt is particularly ironic since now, eight years later, his debts are forcing him to rent his house to a wealthy naval officer.

9. Naval success was uncertain. Many officers were killed; many never got promoted to a high level; others spent much of their careers on ship assignments that offered little possibility of prize money or other rewards.

10. *connexions:* connections—particularly family connections or relations. That could be valuable, though it was not necessary for success: the navy was more meritocratic than most institutions in this society. Lady Russell, who seems to be unaffiliated with the navy, may be shaped more by knowledge of how society in general worked, than of the navy in particular, and thus more fearful of the effects of not having connections than is warranted.

11. *dependance:* condition of resting in expectation or waiting for something. In this case Anne could have to spend years waiting to see if Captain Wentworth enjoyed the success needed for them to establish a home.

12. *representations:* arguments, remonstrances; statements made with a view to influencing or changing someone's opinion.

13. His casual attitude reflects his own personality, but it is also characteristic of his profession, which was dominated by uncertainty and chance, and required confidence and boldness in facing its risks.

14. A station would be the assignment of his ship.

15. Mind then referred to emotional as well as intellectual attributes.

16. Brilliant, or brilliancy (just used to describe Captain Wentworth), could mean a sparkling or playful wit, which the next sentence explains is not appealing to Lady Russell. The word could also have a slight connotation of insufficient seriousness, and of more show than substance.

17. *connexion:* marriage, i.e., the establishment of a family connection.

18. Strong respect for family was a fundamental principle of this society, and while Lady Russell is not related to Anne, she has stood in place of Anne's mother since the latter died. The need for such respect, and obedience, was stressed particularly for girls, who in actual fact were in a condition of great dependence on their families.

19. This sentence announces the central theme of the novel. In this case, as is soon shown, Anne's susceptibility to persuasion and lack of confidence in her own judgment have created misery for her.

belief of being prudent, and self-denying principally for *his* advantage, was her chief consolation, under the misery of a parting[20] — a final parting; and every consolation was required, for she had to encounter all the additional pain of opinions, on his side, totally unconvinced and unbending, and of his feeling himself ill-used by so forced a relinquishment. — He had left the country[21] in consequence.

A few months had seen the beginning and the end of their acquaintance; but, not with a few months ended Anne's share of suffering from it. Her attachment and regrets had, for a long time, clouded every enjoyment of youth; and an early loss of bloom[22] and spirits had been their lasting effect.

More than seven years were gone since this little history of sorrowful interest had reached its close; and time had softened down much, perhaps nearly all of peculiar[23] attachment to him, — but she had been too dependant on time alone; no aid had been given in change of place, (except in one visit to Bath soon after the rupture,) or in any novelty or enlargement of society. — No one had ever come within the Kellynch circle, who could bear a comparison with Frederick Wentworth, as he stood in her memory. No second attachment, the only thoroughly natural, happy, and sufficient cure, at her time of life, had been possible to the nice[24] tone of her mind, the fastidiousness of her taste, in the small limits of the society around them.[25] She had been solicited, when about two-and-twenty, to change her name, by the young man, who not long afterwards found a more willing mind in her younger sister; and Lady Russell had lamented her refusal; for Charles Musgrove was the eldest son of a man, whose landed property and general importance, were second, in that country, only to Sir Walter's,[26] and of good character and appearance; and however Lady Russell might have asked yet for something more, while Anne was nineteen, she would have rejoiced to see her at twenty-two, so respectably removed from the partialities and injustice of her father's house, and settled so permanently near herself.[27] But in this case, Anne had left nothing for advice to do;[28] and though Lady Russell, as satisfied as ever with her own discretion, never

20. The reasons why this would be to his advantage are not spelled out. The most obvious one would be the financial burden on him of supporting a wife. Her dowry would provide some support, but not a great amount, especially if she had many children (birth control was not generally practiced then). At this stage he had only his naval salary, which was too low to make much difference, and there was no certainty of his gaining prize money.

21. *country:* county. Country then also had the current meaning of nation, but the context suggests Captain Wentworth left only the area in which Anne resided.

22. For the idea, and importance, of a woman's bloom, see p. 9, note 27.

23. *peculiar:* particular.

24. *nice:* delicate, refined.

25. Members of the landed gentry would mostly socialize only with others of their class in the neighborhood. This would generally mean other landed families and the family of the local clergyman. In this case, the Elliots and the Musgroves seem to be the only wealthy landowners in the vicinity, and the clergyman in the Musgroves' village, Dr. Shirley, is an old man (see p. 148) who is never mentioned as having children. The only other local clergyman cited is Captain Wentworth's brother, later described as married, and his presence provided the basis for Anne's meeting Captain Wentworth. This restricted range of options is why in every Jane Austen novel—except *Northanger Abbey*, set in Bath—the arrival of unmarried young persons from elsewhere sets in motion much of the plot. Here Captain Wentworth's reappearance is the crucial generator of events.

26. As the eldest son Charles will eventually inherit that substantial property.

27. Lady Russell's change of attitude reflects her knowledge of how much a woman's youthfulness determined her marital eligibility. One reason was the premium placed on women's beauty and the focus on youthful bloom as the basis of beauty. Another reason was that bearing children was the main function of a wife, which meant men preferred a bride in a state of maximum fertility (there were no medical treatments then for infertility). Thus even a woman in her early twenties could be less desirable than one in her late teens, while a woman in her late twenties was rapidly losing her eligibility, and one thirty or older had generally lost her chance.

28. Thus in this case Anne proves resistant to persuasion. Her refusal also shows her high standards.

wished the past undone, she began now to have the anxiety which borders on hopelessness for Anne's being tempted, by some man of talents and independence,[29] to enter a state for which she held her to be peculiarly fitted by her warm affections and domestic habits.[30]

They knew not each other's opinion, either its constancy or its change, on the one leading point of Anne's conduct, for the subject was never alluded to,[31]—but Anne, at seven-and-twenty, thought very differently from what she had been made to think at nineteen.—She did not blame Lady Russell, she did not blame herself for having been guided by her; but she felt that were any young person, in similar circumstances, to apply to her for counsel, they would never receive any of such certain immediate wretchedness, such uncertain future good.—She was persuaded that under every disadvantage of disapprobation at home, and every anxiety attending his profession, all their probable fears, delays and disappointments, she should yet have been a happier woman in maintaining the engagement, than she had been in the sacrifice of it; and this, she fully believed, had the usual share, had even more than a usual share of all such solicitudes and suspense[32] been theirs, without reference to the actual results of their case, which, as it happened, would have bestowed earlier prosperity than could be reasonably calculated on. All his sanguine expectations, all his confidence had been justified. His genius[33] and ardour had seemed to foresee and to command his prosperous path. He had, very soon after their engagement ceased, got employ; and all that he had told her would follow had taken place. He had distinguished himself, and early gained the other step in rank[34]—and must now, by successive captures, have made a handsome fortune.[35] She had only navy lists and newspapers for her authority, but she could not doubt his being rich;[36]—and, in favour of his constancy, she had no reason to believe him married.

How eloquent could Anne Elliot have been,—how eloquent, at least, were her wishes on the side of early warm attachment, and a cheerful confidence in futurity, against that over-anxious cau-

29. *independence:* financial independence.

30. In addition to the attractions of marriage for one of Anne's character, and its general attractions in any time and place, women in this society had a number of strong reasons to wish to be married. As marriage was held to be the natural and best state for a woman, one who married automatically gained social prestige, and the prospect of even further improvement in status in the event of having children or a husband who gained prominence. Marriage also usually improved a woman's financial position and offered her some financial security, even if her husband died, while providing her the best opportunity to exercise, as mistress of a household, genuine power and influence. In contrast, single women were frequent objects of scorn, especially as they aged (when they would gain the derogatory label of old maid). They also had limited ability to support themselves, for few jobs were open to them, and among genteel women almost no paid work was considered acceptable. Anne inherits enough to provide for herself reasonably, but it still is less than she would enjoy if married to a man of her class. Finally, prevailing mores forbade single women from living alone, except perhaps if they were older, so such a woman would have to spend her life in another's household, subject to others' rules and the continual knowledge of being a dependent, possibly an unwanted one—as is true of Anne at present.

31. Lady Russell may consider the matter closed, while, knowing Anne's distress at the time and fretting over her not marrying since, she may consider that raising the subject would only distress Anne further. Anne may be inhibited by a similar desire to avoid a painful subject, and by a disinclination to articulate opinions that would call into question Lady Russell's judgment.

32. *suspense:* delay, uncertainty.

33. *genius:* natural talent.

34. The other step in rank is captain, which allowed him to command a larger ship than he could as commander, and which guaranteed that he would eventually become an admiral, and at a relatively early age since he became a captain when young (promotion to admiral was automatic, and happened according to the chronological order of when those eligible had risen to captain).

35. For captures and prize money, see p. 33, note 4.

36. Navy lists would give information about ships and officers; newspapers would report recent actions (see p. 123, note 9, and p. 127, note 25). These would also have given her knowledge of Admiral Croft's rank and history, he being of natural interest to her as the brother-in-law of Captain Wentworth.

tion which seems to insult exertion and distrust Providence!— She had been forced into prudence in her youth, she learned romance as she grew older—the natural sequel of an unnatural beginning.[37]

With all these circumstances, recollections and feelings, she could not hear that Captain Wentworth's sister was likely to live at Kellynch, without a revival of former pain; and many a stroll and many a sigh were necessary to dispel the agitation of the idea. She often told herself it was folly, before she could harden her nerves sufficiently to feel the continual discussion of the Crofts and their business no evil. She was assisted, however, by that perfect indifference and apparent unconsciousness, among the only three of her own friends[38] in the secret of the past, which seemed almost to deny any recollection of it. She could do justice to the superiority of Lady Russell's motives in this, over those of her father and Elizabeth; she could honour all the better feelings of her calmness[39]—but the general air of oblivion among them was highly important, from whatever it sprung;[40] and in the event of Admiral Croft's really taking Kellynch-hall, she rejoiced anew over the conviction which had always been most grateful to her, of the past being known to those three only among her connexions, by whom no syllable, she believed, would ever be whispered, and in the trust that among his, the brother only with whom he had been residing, had received any information of their short-lived engagement.—That brother had been long removed from the country— and being a sensible man, and, moreover, a single man at the time, she had a fond dependance on no human creature's having heard of it from him.

The sister, Mrs. Croft, had then been out of England, accompanying her husband on a foreign station,[41] and her own sister, Mary, had been at school while it all occurred[42]—and never admitted by the pride of some, and the delicacy of others, to the smallest knowledge of it afterwards.

With these supports, she hoped that the acquaintance between herself and the Crofts, which, with Lady Russell, still resident in

37. The normal sequence would be to start romantically, perhaps by trying to marry purely for love, and to become more attuned to the importance of prudence as one aged. A copy of the novel once owned by Jane Austen's sister, Cassandra, contains a marginal note, presumably by Cassandra, next to this paragraph that reads, "Dear dear Jane! This deserves to be written in letters of gold." An obvious inspiration for the note would be the tragic story of Cassandra's own engagement. She and her fiancé, a clergyman, decided to wait to marry: his current income was too small, but he expected to attain a better position soon from his patron. Unfortunately, his patron, not knowing of the engagement, asked him to accompany him as his chaplain on a military expedition to the Caribbean; while there, off St. Domingo, in fact (see p. 49, note 2), the young man died of yellow fever. The patron is supposed to have said he would not have asked him along on such a dangerous mission if he had known of the engagement. Cassandra may have felt that she and her fiancé had shown the same overanxious caution mentioned in this passage.

38. *friends*: friends, or family members. It obviously includes Sir Walter and Elizabeth in this case.

39. The following paragraph speaks of "the pride of some, and the delicacy of others" as the reasons the matter was not mentioned to Mary, Anne's sister. The clear implication is that Sir Walter and Elizabeth were motivated by pride, in particular the wish to conceal that a member of their family had initially accepted the hand of a man of inferior birth, while Lady Russell was motivated by delicacy about mentioning a matter so painful to Anne.

40. Thus her father's pride, and his indifference toward her, prove beneficial to Anne in this particular case.

41. British naval officers were frequently stationed overseas, for Britain had naval ports in various parts of the world.

42. Anne went to a boarding school after the death of her mother. It is likely Mary did the same and, being younger, remained in school longer.

Kellynch, and Mary fixed[43] only three miles off, must be anticipated, need not involve any particular awkwardness.

Woman's walking dress.

[From Elisabeth McClellan, *Historic Dress in America, 1800–1870*
(Philadelphia, 1910), p. 87]

43. *fixed*: settled.

A curricle (Ashstead Park, a country house, is in the background).

[From John Preston Neale, *Views of the Seats of Noblemen and Gentlemen, Vol. V* (1822)]

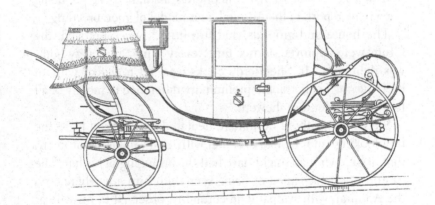

A coach. Most would not have such fancy trimmings.

[From T. Fuller, *Essay on Wheel Carriages* (London, 1828), Plate no. 11]

Chapter Five

O n the morning appointed for Admiral and Mrs. Croft's seeing
Kellynch-hall, Anne found it most natural to take her almost
daily walk to Lady Russell's,[1] and keep out of the way till all was
over; when she found it most natural to be sorry that she had
missed the opportunity of seeing them.

This meeting of the two parties proved highly satisfactory, and
decided the whole business at once. Each lady was previously
well disposed for an agreement, and saw nothing, therefore, but
good manners in the other; and, with regard to the gentlemen,
there was such an hearty good humour, such an open, trusting
liberality on the Admiral's side, as could not but influence Sir
Walter, who had besides been flattered into his very best and most
polished behaviour by Mr. Shepherd's assurances of his being
known, by report, to the Admiral, as a model of good breeding.[2]

The house and grounds, and furniture,[3] were approved, the
Crofts were approved, terms, time, every thing, and every body,
was right; and Mr. Shepherd's clerks were set to work,[4] without
there having been a single preliminary difference to modify of all
that "This indenture sheweth."[5]

Sir Walter, without hesitation, declared the Admiral to be the
best-looking sailor he had ever met with, and went so far as to say,
that, if his own man might have had the arranging of his hair,[6] he
should not be ashamed of being seen with him any where; and
the Admiral, with sympathetic cordiality, observed to his wife as
they drove back through the Park,[7] "I thought we should soon
come to a deal, my dear, in spite of what they told us at Taunton.[8]
The baronet will never set the Thames on fire, but there seems no
harm in him:"—reciprocal compliments, which would have been
esteemed about equal.

The Crofts were to have possession at Michaelmas,[9] and as Sir

1. Regular outdoor exercise was recommended by writers as healthful, both for the exertion and the fresh air. For adult women, who rarely engaged in any outdoor sports, this usually meant daily walks. Many women in Jane Austen, especially younger ones, are described as regularly taking walks. Anne is also depicted as having a strong love of nature. For an example of a walking dress of the time, see p. 58.

2. *good breeding:* politeness.

3. *furniture:* furnishings; the term was often broader then, referring to all the items inside a house.

4. Clerks would assist attorneys with matters like drawing up documents; usually they had been apprenticed to attorneys in order to learn the trade themselves. Many attorneys of the time had only one clerk, so Mr. Shepherd's having more than one indicates his relative prosperity.

5. An indenture is a contract or agreement. Samples of rental agreements from the time show them consistently beginning with "This indenture," as well as frequently employing archaic grammar, as "sheweth" (or "showeth") would have been at this time.

6. Sir Walter's own man would be his valet, the most personal servant for any man (see p. 5, note 18). The valet was responsible for his master's appearance, and arranging his hair was a critical part of this; some valets, or aspiring valets, would work under a professional hairdresser in order to master the art. Sir Walter would likely be particularly keen to have such a well-qualified man.

7. The park is the name for the grounds surrounding the house (see p. 35, note 16). A park would normally be large enough—Sir Walter had boasted of the range of his—that one would need to drive through it, using roads built for carriages.

8. Presumably the experience of others in the county with Sir Walter has led to a general opinion of his being difficult to deal with, whether because of folly, irrationality, or excessive pride.

9. *Michaelmas:* September 29. Michaelmas was one of the four days used to divide the year into quarters. The others were Christmas, Lady Day (March 25), and Midsummer Day (June 24). Rent payments were frequently due on those days, and it would be standard to have somebody begin leasing a house on one of them.

Walter proposed removing to Bath in the course of the preceding month,[10] there was no time to be lost in making every dependant arrangement.

Lady Russell, convinced that Anne would not be allowed to be of any use, or any importance, in the choice of the house which they were going to secure, was very unwilling to have her hurried away so soon, and wanted to make it possible for her to stay behind, till she might convey her to Bath herself after Christmas;[11] but having engagements of her own, which must take her from Kellynch for several weeks, she was unable to give the full invitation she wished; and Anne, though dreading the possible heats of September in all the white glare of Bath,[12] and grieving to forego all the influence so sweet and so sad of the autumnal months in the country,[13] did not think that, every thing considered, she wished to remain. It would be most right, and most wise, and, therefore, must involve least suffering, to go with the others.

Something occurred, however, to give her a different duty. Mary, often a little unwell, and always thinking a great deal of her own complaints, and always in the habit of claiming Anne when any thing was the matter, was indisposed; and foreseeing that she should not have a day's health all the autumn, entreated, or rather required her, for it was hardly entreaty, to come to Uppercross Cottage, and bear her company as long as she should want her, instead of going to Bath.

"I cannot possibly do without Anne," was Mary's reasoning; and Elizabeth's reply was,[14] "Then I am sure Anne had better stay, for nobody will want her in Bath."

To be claimed as a good, though in an improper style, is at least better than being rejected as no good at all; and Anne, glad to be thought of some use, glad to have any thing marked out as a duty,[15] and certainly not sorry to have the scene of it in the country, and her own dear country, readily agreed to stay.

This invitation of Mary's removed all Lady Russell's difficulties, and it was consequently soon settled that Anne should not go to Bath till Lady Russell took her, and that all the intervening time should be divided between Uppercross Cottage and Kellynch-lodge.

10. Later information indicates that they left four weeks before Michaelmas, or right around the beginning of September (see chronology, p. 487).

11. Lady Russell's choice of when to go to Bath was standard. At this time its season extended from September to June, with the winter being especially popular; in both this novel and *Northanger Abbey* the characters' visits to Bath occur during the winter. One reason was that Bath offered mainly indoor amusements, in contrast to destinations such as the increasingly popular seaside resorts that were best enjoyed in warmer weather. Another reason was that Bath tended to be warm, due to its location in the southwest of England and its being in a bowl surrounded by hills.

Anne must choose between going with her father or with Lady Russell because she cannot travel to Bath on her own. At this time it was considered inappropriate for genteel women, especially young and unmarried ones, to travel alone. An escort, preferably a male relative, was considered essential to guard against danger or any possible sexual impropriety. Jane Austen and her sister had to adjust their plans at various times to ensure that a man, usually one of their brothers, could accompany them. This would be less of an issue for Lady Russell, who is older and widowed, and who can use her own carriage (Anne would have to use a hired one).

12. *white glare of Bath:* Bath is distinguished by almost every building being of the same light yellow stone, a natural reflector of sunlight. Much of it also has little shade from trees.

13. Anne's interest in experiencing both what is sweet and what is sad reflects a bent toward serious, and sometimes melancholy, reflection. A later passage will describe how the scenes of autumn evoke in her mind poetic descriptions of the season (p. 160).

14. Mary has written or spoken to Elizabeth because the latter, as mistress of the house, should be consulted, or at least informed, when requesting the presence of someone who is part of that household. It is not clear whether Mary thought to ask Anne herself, though, as Anne's above deliberations show, she is not under Elizabeth's authority and can decide for herself, within certain limitations, where she will go.

15. This emphasis on duty will characterize Anne throughout the novel. It was seen just above in her rueful decision to go to Bath because that would be right.

So far all was perfectly right; but Lady Russell was almost star-tled by the wrong of one part of the Kellynch-hall plan, when it burst on her, which was, Mrs. Clay's being engaged to go to Bath with Sir Walter and Elizabeth, as a most important and valuable assistant to the latter in all the business before her.[16] Lady Russell was extremely sorry that such a measure should have been resorted to at all—wondered, grieved, and feared—and the affront it contained to Anne, in Mrs. Clay's being of so much use, while Anne could be of none, was a very sore aggravation.

Anne herself was become[17] hardened to such affronts; but she felt the imprudence of the arrangement quite as keenly as Lady Russell. With a great deal of quiet observation, and a knowledge, which she often wished less, of her father's character, she was sen-sible[18] that results the most serious to his family from the inti-macy, were more than possible.[19] She did not imagine that her father had at present an idea of the kind. Mrs. Clay had freckles,[20] and a projecting tooth,[21] and a clumsy wrist, which he was con-tinually making severe remarks upon, in her absence; but she was young, and certainly altogether well-looking, and possessed, in an acute mind and assiduous pleasing manners,[22] infinitely more dangerous attractions than any merely personal might have been. Anne was so impressed by the degree of their danger, that she could not excuse herself from trying to make it perceptible to her sister. She had little hope of success; but Elizabeth, who in the event of such a reverse would be so much more to be pitied than herself, should never, she thought, have reason to reproach her for giving no warning.[23]

She spoke, and seemed only to offend. Elizabeth could not conceive how such an absurd suspicion should occur to her; and indignantly answered for each party's perfectly knowing their situ-ation.

"Mrs. Clay," said she warmly, "never forgets who she is; and as I am rather better acquainted with her sentiments than you can be, I can assure you, that upon the subject of marriage they are particularly nice;[24] and that she reprobates all inequality of condi-tion[25] and rank more strongly than most people.[26] And as to my

16. This means Mrs. Clay is leaving her children behind, presumably with her father (and mother, if she is living). Other cases of parents leaving children will occur in the novel, though never for the many months Mrs. Clay remains in Bath. Her decision indicates how determined she is to win the favor of Sir Walter.

17. *was become*: had become. This use of "to be" for the past tense, where "to have" is currently employed, can be found elsewhere in this novel and in the language of the time generally.

18. *sensible*: aware, conscious.

19. Meaning a marriage between Sir Walter and Mrs. Clay.

20. In *Pride and Prejudice* a young woman is denigrated for having freckles.

21. The limited dentistry and orthodontia available during this period meant that many people had problems with their teeth.

22. Mind and manners, both of which had broader meanings than they do at present, were frequently paired in phrases, with the first referring to someone's inner character and the second to outer character or behavior.

23. Elizabeth would be more deserving of pity in such a case because any wife of Sir Walter's would displace Elizabeth as mistress of the house, thereby undermining both her power and her status. She also would be displaced, at least partly, in her father's affections, which are directed far more toward her than toward his other daughters.

24. *nice*: scrupulous, delicate.

25. *condition*: social position.

26. Elizabeth means Mrs. Clay reprobates a marriage based on inequality of rank, not that she reprobates inequality of rank. Acceptance of such inequality was standard at the time, as was disapproval of unequal marriages — though one can assume that Mrs. Clay's strong expression of reprobation stemmed primarily from her wish to flatter Sir Walter and Elizabeth and to avoid any suspicion that she might be seeking such a marriage.

father,[27] I really should not have thought that he, who has kept himself single so long for our sakes, need be suspected now.[28] If Mrs. Clay were a very beautiful woman, I grant you, it might be wrong to have her so much with me; not that any thing in the world, I am sure, would induce my father to make a degrading match; but he might be rendered unhappy. But poor Mrs. Clay, who, with all her merits, can never have been reckoned tolerably pretty! I really think poor Mrs. Clay may be staying here in perfect safety. One would imagine you had never heard my father speak of her personal misfortunes, though I know you must fifty times. That tooth of her's! and those freckles! Freckles do not disgust me so very much as they do him: I have known a face not materially disfigured by a few, but he abominates them. You must have heard him notice Mrs. Clay's freckles."

"There is hardly any personal defect," replied Anne, "which an agreeable manner might not gradually reconcile one to."

"I think very differently," answered Elizabeth, shortly; "an agreeable manner may set off handsome features, but can never alter plain ones. However, at any rate, as I have a great deal more at stake on this point than any body else can have, I think it rather unnecessary in you to be advising me."

Anne had done—glad that it was over, and not absolutely hopeless of doing good. Elizabeth, though resenting the suspicion, might yet be made observant by it.

The last office[29] of the four carriage-horses[30] was to draw Sir Walter, Miss Elliot, and Mrs. Clay to Bath. The party drove off in very good spirits; Sir Walter prepared with condescending[31] bows for all the afflicted tenantry and cottagers who might have had a hint to shew themselves:[32] and Anne walked up at the same time, in a sort of desolate tranquillity, to the Lodge, where she was to spend the first week.

Her friend was not in better spirits than herself. Lady Russell felt this break-up of the family exceedingly. Their respectability was as dear to her as her own; and a daily intercourse had become precious by habit. It was painful to look upon their deserted grounds, and still worse to anticipate the new hands they were to

27. *my father:* saying "my" rather than "our" when speaking of one's parent to a sibling is standard in Jane Austen. In her own letters to her sister she consistently refers to "my mother" or "my father." She was sensitive to such matters of usage: in one letter she notes, as an apparent curiosity, a servant's speaking of "Mother" rather than "my mother" (Jan. 24, 1809).

28. His keeping himself single could serve his children's interests by guaranteeing that they would remain foremost in his affection, that they would never be placed under the authority of a stepmother, and that his available income would not be diverted into expenditure on his wife. In fact, it was earlier stated that Sir Walter made some efforts at marriage after his wife died, and decided to remain single for his progeny's sake only after he failed (pp. 6–8).

29. *office:* service, task.

30. Because of the easy availability of hired means of transport in Bath, the Elliots will not need to own horses or carriages there—that is one way they will save money. The horses will presumably be sold now. Sir Walter may employ them this last time to keep his neighbors from suspecting this sale.

31. *condescending:* gracious—or condescending in the current sense. The term then could be one of praise as well as of criticism.

32. The tenantry and cottagers would be those who lived, and probably worked, on the Elliot estate (cottages were the standard dwellings of poorer people in the country). Ideally, according to norms of the time, there should be a paternalistic relationship between them and the landowner, with the latter extending charity and benevolent supervision and the former offering deference and gratitude, as well as good service, in return. This is why the tenantry and cottagers would normally gather to pay their respects to a departing landowner, why he would offer condescending bows in return, and why they are supposed to be afflicted by his leaving. But in this case they had to be encouraged to come, perhaps by the manager of the estate, who would know that Sir Walter, probably believing himself to be loved and expecting signs of deference, would be humiliated and angered if nobody appeared. It is easy to imagine that Sir Walter was far from an ideal landlord.

fall into; and to escape the solitariness and the melancholy of so altered a village, and be out of the way when Admiral and Mrs. Croft first arrived, she had determined to make her own absence from home begin when she must give up Anne. Accordingly their removal was made together, and Anne was set down at Uppercross Cottage, in the first stage of Lady Russell's journey.[33]

Uppercross was a moderate-sized village, which a few years back had been completely in the old English style; containing only two houses superior in appearance to those of the yeomen and labourers,[34]—the mansion of the 'squire, with its high walls, great gates, and old trees, substantial and unmodernized[35]—and the compact, tight parsonage,[36] enclosed in its own neat garden, with a vine and a pear-tree trained round its casements;[37] but upon the marriage of the young 'squire, it had received the improvement of a farm-house elevated into a cottage for his residence; and Uppercross Cottage, with its viranda, French windows, and other prettinesses, was quite as likely to catch the traveller's eye, as the more consistent and considerable aspect[38] and premises of the Great House, about a quarter of a mile farther on.[39]

Here Anne had often been staying. She knew the ways of Uppercross as well as those of Kellynch. The two families were so continually meeting, so much in the habit of running in and out of each other's house at all hours, that it was rather a surprise to her to find Mary alone; but being alone, her being unwell and out of spirits, was almost a matter of course. Though better endowed than the elder sister, Mary had not Anne's understanding or temper. While well, and happy, and properly attended to, she had great good humour and excellent spirits; but any indisposition sunk her completely; she had no resources for solitude; and inheriting a considerable share of the Elliot self-importance, was very prone to add to every other distress that of fancying herself neglected and ill-used. In person, she was inferior to both sisters, and had, even in her bloom, only reached the dignity of being "a fine girl." She was now lying on the faded sofa of the pretty little drawing-room, the once elegant furniture of which had been

33. Journeys were made in stages, for horses needed to be changed approximately every ten miles (for this system of traveling, see p. 221, note 90).

34. Yeomen were men who owned small pieces of land and farmed them. They would thus rank above laborers, who worked others' land, but they would still be below large landowners like the Musgroves and would not have substantial houses.

35. "Squire" is a term frequently used for an important landowner; in this case it means Mr. Musgrove. The high walls and large gates were standard features of older houses. Many such houses had been rebuilt in more recent style, for the sake of convenience and appearance, but this one has not.

36. A parsonage is the home of the resident clergyman. Though generally not as wealthy as the leading landowners, the clergy belonged to the same genteel class, and their homes would reflect that.

37. Casement windows, which open out or in through hinges, mark this house as old-fashioned. They had been the main type of window in earlier times, but in the eighteenth century they had been largely superseded by sash windows, which go up and down.

38. *aspect:* appearance.

39. It is this cottage that marks the village as departing from the old English style, especially because, unlike the parsonage or the squire's mansion, or Great House, it was built in the latest architectural style.

Traditionally a cottage was a small, humble dwelling for poorer people (like those described above as cottagers). Thus it would have represented no improvement or enlargement over a farmhouse, a term used for ordinary rural houses. But this period saw a brief vogue for cottages as habitations of the wealthy. One character in *Sense and Sensibility*, Robert Ferrars, proclaims his great love of cottages, even drawing up plans for one, while in Austen's unfinished novel, *Sanditon*, one person is constructing a Cottage Ornée, the term (from the French for "adorned" or "decorated") used for these cottages. This vogue was linked to the Romantic movement of the time, with its celebration of nature and the picturesque. This made cottages appealing due to their simple, bucolic associations, though cottages built for the wealthy were significantly larger and more comfortable than traditional ones. Their frequently elaborate design usually incorporated quaint, rustic elements, which gave them the "prettinesses" mentioned here—a contrast to the classical grandeur typical of the period's country houses. Verandas and French windows were popular features of these cottages. Verandas, typically made of black-painted cast iron (the veranda here is described as black on p. 230) shaped into elaborate decorative patterns, had recently become a feature of many houses, and for cottages they offered access to the open air that

gradually growing shabby, under the influence of four summers and two children;[40] and, on Anne's appearing, greeted her with,

"So, you are come at last! I began to think I should never see you. I am so ill I can hardly speak. I have not seen a creature the whole morning!"[41]

"I am sorry to find you unwell," replied Anne. "You sent me such a good account of yourself on Thursday!"

"Yes, I made the best of it; I always do; but I was very far from well at the time; and I do not think I ever was so ill in my life as I have been all this morning—very unfit to be left alone, I am sure.[42] Suppose I were to be seized[43] of a sudden in some dreadful way, and not able to ring the bell![44] So, Lady Russell would not get out. I do not think she has been in this house three times this summer."

Anne said what was proper, and enquired after her husband. "Oh! Charles is out shooting. I have not seen him since seven o'clock.[45] He would go, though I told him how ill I was. He said he should not stay out long; but he has never come back, and now it is almost one. I assure you, I have not seen a soul this whole long morning."

"You have had your little boys with you?"

"Yes, as long as I could bear their noise; but they are so unmanageable that they do me more harm than good. Little Charles does not mind a word I say, and Walter is growing quite as bad."[46]

"Well, you will soon be better now," replied Anne, cheerfully. "You know I always cure you when I come. How are your neighbours at the Great House?"[47]

"I can give you no account of them. I have not seen one of them to-day, except Mr. Musgrove,[48] who just stopped and spoke through the window, but without getting off his horse; and though I told him how ill I was, not one of them have been near me. It did not happen to suit the Miss Musgroves, I suppose, and they never put themselves out of their way."

"You will see them yet, perhaps, before the morning is gone. It is early."

"I never want them, I assure you. They talk and laugh a great

fit with the rustic appeal of such dwellings. French windows, meaning floor-length ones, had also became popular, and they were a good complement to verandas, offering a full view of the outside world beyond the veranda, and frequently offering access as well, since many French windows opened and functioned as doors.

40. "Once elegant" probably means the furniture was new. Jane Austen often describes the current style of furniture as elegant (see p. 231, note 27).

41. Mary is exaggerating. Morning at the time meant most of the day, and Anne says below, without being contradicted, that it is still early. It is appropriate that Mary's first words should involve exaggeration, complaints of others' mistreatment of her, and moans about the extremity of her illness (which does not stop her from talking at length). In these respects, and in her general selfishness and pride, Mary forms an excellent foil for Anne.

42. Jane Austen often ridicules hypochondria: Mrs. Bennet in *Pride and Prejudice* is another example. In a letter Austen describes someone as "the sort of woman who gives the idea of being determined never to be well—& who likes her spasms & nervousness & the consequence they give her, better than anything else" (Sept. 25, 1813).

43. Seized was often used to mean being afflicted with an ailment, especially one that drastically impacted someone.

44. She would ring the bell for a servant to attend her. By this time most houses of the wealthy were equipped with bells attached to wires running through the house: people in one room could pull a cord, and a bell would ring in the servants' quarters, indicating where attendance was required.

45. Shooting game birds, usually partridges and pheasants, was a popular gentlemen's pursuit. It often kept them out much of the day. One reason for Charles's zeal may be that it is early September (see chronology, p. 487), and the shooting season just started on September 1.

46. The family follows standard naming practice. The eldest boy is named after his father, the next oldest after his maternal grandfather—the paternal grandfather is probably also Charles.

47. This is the first extended conversation involving Anne. She exhibits here, in her attempts to cheer up Mary, two of her leading traits: a strong inclination to help others and a habit of trying to make the best of things.

48. Mr. Musgrove is Charles Musgrove's father. He is consistently called only "Mr. Musgrove," a sign of superior status. Charles is always called "Charles Musgrove"; once his father dies, he will be "Mr. Musgrove."

deal too much for me. Oh! Anne, I am so very unwell! It was quite unkind of you not to come on Thursday."

"My dear Mary, recollect what a comfortable account you sent me of yourself! You wrote in the cheerfullest manner, and said you were perfectly well, and in no hurry for me; and that being the case, you must be aware that my wish would be to remain with Lady Russell to the last: and besides what I felt on her account, I have really been so busy, have had so much to do, that I could not very conveniently have left Kellynch sooner."

"Dear me! what can *you* possibly have to do?"

"A great many things, I assure you. More than I can recollect in a moment: but I can tell you some. I have been making a duplicate of the catalogue of my father's books and pictures.[49] I have been several times in the garden with Mackenzie, trying to understand, and make him understand, which of Elizabeth's plants are for Lady Russell.[50] I have had all my own little concerns to arrange—books and music to divide,[51] and all my trunks to repack, from not having understood in time what was intended as to the waggons.[52] And one thing I have had to do, Mary, of a more trying nature; going to almost every house in the parish, as a sort of take-leave. I was told that they wished it.[53] But all these things took up a great deal of time."

"Oh! well";—and after a moment's pause, "But you have never asked me one word about our dinner at the Pooles yesterday."

"Did you go then? I have made no enquiries, because I concluded you must have been obliged to give up the party."

"Oh! yes, I went. I was very well yesterday; nothing at all the matter with me till this morning. It would have been strange if I had not gone."

"I am very glad you were well enough, and I hope you had a pleasant party."

"Nothing remarkable. One always knows beforehand what the dinner will be, and who will be there. And it is so very uncomfortable, not having a carriage of one's own.[54] Mr. and Mrs. Musgrove took me, and we were so crowded! They are both so very large, and take up so much room! And Mr. Musgrove always sits

49. A large library was a standard feature of country houses, even for someone like Sir Walter, whose reading seems to consist of only one book. Much of the library would have been handed down from earlier generations. Most houses also had numerous pictures (see p. 35, note 13).

50. Mackenzie would be the gardener. Gardeners, whose work required great skill and knowledge, especially on properties with extensive landscaping, were upper servants; this is why Anne refers to him by his last name, a mark of respect. First names were used for lower servants.

51. This would be printed music. Large amounts of music were printed at this time, either in single sheets or in volumes with various pieces. Jane Austen, who played the piano daily for much of her life, owned numerous pieces, including many she had copied herself. Anne, who is soon revealed to be an accomplished pianist, would naturally have a substantial collection, and the task of division may not have been easy for her—presumably some music is to stay with her now, and some is to be sent to Bath for future use.

52. Wagons were the principal vehicles for transporting goods over land; in this case they would be conveying the Elliots' possessions to Bath. By this time regular wagon service between important towns had become common in England; the wagons themselves could be very large, requiring as many as eight horses to pull them (see picture, p. 79).

53. The Elliots would be the leading family in their parish, the basic unit of local government and rural society. Their departure would be an important event for others living there. Anne's willingness to undertake the task of seeing all the residents shows her exercising the social duties of her class that Sir Walter and Elizabeth neglect. One of the most important of these duties, especially for women, was charity; this often involved visiting the houses of the local poor, so it is likely that Anne saw many people she had seen before and who genuinely wished to say good-bye. That may be why Anne describes it as trying. Later, when Anne is staying with Lady Russell, and thus back in the same parish, she engages in visits of charity in the village (p. 250).

54. It is later revealed that Charles has a curricle, a small open carriage (for a picture, see p. 59). He may have driven in it on this occasion (see note 55 below), but an open carriage would not be good for conveying ladies in evening clothes, which were typically made of lightweight, delicate material and were often white. A larger, enclosed carriage was very expensive to buy and maintain, and it would require hiring a coachman to drive it; moreover, carriages were taxed, and the rates were greater for larger ones and second family vehicles. Thus Charles and Mary, or at least Charles, presumably decided that a second carriage was not worth it, especially since Charles's parents have a coach and live within easy walking distance.

forward. So, there was I, crowded into the back seat with Henrietta and Louisa. And I think it very likely that my illness to-day may be owing to it."[55]

A little farther perseverance in patience, and forced cheerfulness on Anne's side, produced nearly a cure on Mary's. She could soon sit upright on the sofa, and began to hope she might be able to leave it by dinner-time. Then, forgetting to think of it, she was at the other end of the room, beautifying a nosegay; then, she ate her cold meat;[56] and then she was well enough to propose a little walk.

"Where shall we go?" said she, when they were ready. "I suppose you will not like to call at the Great House before they have been to see you?"

"I have not the smallest objection on that account," replied Anne. "I should never think of standing on such ceremony with people I know so well as Mrs. and the Miss Musgroves."[57]

"Oh! but they ought to call upon you as soon as possible. They ought to feel what is due to you as *my* sister. However, we may as well go and sit with them a little while, and when we have got that over, we can enjoy our walk."

Anne had always thought such a style of intercourse highly imprudent; but she had ceased to endeavour to check it, from believing that, though there were on each side continual subjects of offence, neither family could now do without it.[58] To the Great House accordingly they went, to sit the full half hour in the old-fashioned square parlour, with a small carpet and shining floor,[59] to which the present daughters of the house were gradually giving the proper air of confusion by a grand piano forte[60] and a harp,[61] flower-stands and little tables placed in every direction.[62] Oh! could the originals of the portraits against the wainscot,[63] could the gentlemen in brown velvet and the ladies in blue satin have seen what was going on,[64] have been conscious of such an overthrow of all order and neatness! The portraits themselves seemed to be staring in astonishment.

The Musgroves, like their houses, were in a state of alteration, perhaps of improvement. The father and mother were in the old

55. As shown later, Mr. and Mrs. Musgrove have a coach, an enclosed carriage with two seats facing each other (see p. 95, note 58; and picture, p. 59). That is why Mrs. and Mr. Musgrove's size could have inconvenienced Mary. At the same time, since coach seats were designed to seat three, Mary was not really crowded. Charles would have either gone separately, perhaps in his curricle, or would have sat on one of the outside seats on the coach.

56. Because there was no meal between breakfast and dinner, usually at four or five o'clock, substantial snacks such as cold meat were often eaten during the day. For nosegays, see note 62 below.

57. Standard etiquette dictated that when someone new arrived, existing residents should make the first visit. Anne, while not disavowing this etiquette in general, sees no reason to follow it here, since she is not really a stranger.

58. This shows the difference in manners between the more aristocratic and formal Elliots and the Musgroves. The difference will surface frequently.

59. Carpets had been smaller in earlier periods. This would naturally put a premium on shiny floors.

60. *grand piano forte*: grand piano. Pianoforte was the initial name for the piano, and around 1790, a little more than fifty years after the appearance of pianofortes, an English manufacturer, John Broadwood, created a large, wing-shaped version. Broadwood's manufacturing improvements also made the instrument very affordable: in 1815, the year this novel was begun, he was selling a simple pianoforte for less than 20 pounds, and a grand one for 46. The latter would be a modest sum for the Musgroves (see p. 145, note 14, for the value of money), so their possession of a grand pianoforte does not necessarily indicate any great dedication to music.

61. *harp*: see p. 89, note 34.

62. In earlier times all furniture was usually arranged against the wall, and taken out when needed. Scattering it permanently around the room was a recent development, a product of a greater casualness in decoration. This encouraged the placement of a variety of little tables next to the scattered chairs and sofas (for an example, see p. 78), and the resulting additional surfaces allowed for the increasing display of flowers, whose indoor use had been growing in popularity since the mid eighteenth century (as just seen in Mary's "beautifying a nosegay"). Plant and flower stands became a standard feature of interiors, with many of these stands being made with multiple tiers and in highly elaborate designs; for an example, see p. 78.

63. *wainscot*: the wooden paneling or covering on the wall.

64. Brown velvet and blue satin were fashionable materials in earlier times.

English style, and the young people in the new. Mr. and Mrs. Musgrove were a very good sort of people; friendly and hospitable, not much educated, and not at all elegant. Their children had more modern minds and manners.[65] There was a numerous family; but the only two grown up, excepting Charles, were Henrietta and Louisa, young ladies of nineteen and twenty, who had brought from a school at Exeter all the usual stock of accomplishments,[66] and were now, like thousands of other young ladies, living to be fashionable,[67] happy, and merry. Their dress had every advantage, their faces were rather pretty, their spirits extremely good, their manners unembarrassed and pleasant; they were of consequence at home, and favourites abroad.[68] Anne always contemplated them as some of the happiest creatures of her acquaintance; but still, saved as we all are by some comfortable feeling of superiority from wishing for the possibility of exchange, she would not have given up her own more elegant and cultivated mind for all their enjoyments;[69] and envied them nothing but that seemingly perfect good understanding and agreement together, that good-humoured mutual affection, of which she had known so little herself with either of her sisters.

They were received with great cordiality. Nothing seemed amiss on the side of the Great House family, which was generally, as Anne very well knew, the least to blame. The half hour was chatted away pleasantly enough; and she was not at all surprised, at the end of it, to have their walking party joined by both the Miss Musgroves, at Mary's particular invitation.[70]

Jane Austen could have seen many examples of such attire from the generations of family portraits usually hanging in country houses (see also p. 35, note 13).

65. In a letter Jane alludes to such changes when she writes, "Like other young Ladies she is considerably genteeler than her Parents" (Sept. 14, 1804).

66. Young ladies at the time were praised for their accomplishments, and teaching these was the primary business of girls' boarding schools; Exeter, a large town near Somerset, would be a natural place for Henrietta and Louisa to attend one of these schools. These accomplishments could include music, dancing (which was taught as a skill), drawing, various decorative crafts including embroidery, and a polished and elegant manner of speaking and comporting oneself. Foreign languages, especially French and Italian, were also frequently taught. This teaching, and the influence of other girls at the school, some of them perhaps from wealthier and more distinguished families, is probably the main reason for their more up-to-date and elegant manners.

67. *fashionable*: in accord with the behavior and style of upper-class society. It also had a connotation of "fashionable" in the current sense.

68. *abroad*: outside the family.

69. "Elegant and cultivated mind" would refer to her more refined taste, and to her greater knowledge and education, especially from her reading. Anne will later be given particular reason to treasure this superiority, over the lively and fun spirits of the Miss Musgroves, from the effect it has on someone (see p. 346).

70. Mary's invitation directly contradicts her statement on p. 74 that she and Anne should, after seeing the Musgroves, set out on their own walk.

Contemporary design for a flower stand.

[From Andrew Tuer, *The Follies and Fashions of Our Grandfathers* (1807)
(London, 1886), p. 120]

A small table, representing the style of the time.

[From Thomas Arthur Strange, *English Furniture in the 18th Century:
A Guide to Collectors*, p. 350]

A wagon, the main vehicle for transporting goods on land. Many would be this large and have this many horses pulling them.

[From John Ashton, *The Dawn of the XIXth Century in England* (London, 1906), p. 184]

Queen Square, Bath (contemporary drawing).

[From Mowbray Aston Green, *The Eighteenth Century Architecture of Bath* (Bath, 1904), p. 65]

Chapter Six

Anne had not wanted[1] this visit to Uppercross, to learn that a removal from one set of people to another, though at a distance of only three miles, will often include a total change of conversation, opinion, and idea. She had never been staying there before, without being struck by it, or without wishing that other Elliots could have her advantage in seeing how unknown, or unconsidered there, were the affairs which at Kellynch-hall were treated as of such general publicity[2] and pervading interest; yet, with all this experience, she believed she must now submit to feel that another lesson, in the art of knowing our own nothingness beyond our own circle, was become necessary for her;[3]—for certainly, coming as she did, with a heart full of the subject which had been completely occupying both houses in Kellynch for many weeks, she had expected rather more curiosity and sympathy than she found in the separate, but very similar remark of Mr. and Mrs. Musgrove—"So, Miss Anne, Sir Walter and your sister are gone; and what part of Bath do you think they will settle in?" and this, without much waiting for an answer;—or in the young ladies' addition of, "I hope *we* shall be in Bath in the winter; but remember, papa, if we do go, we must be in a good situation—none of your Queen-squares for us!"[4] or in the anxious supplement from Mary, of "Upon my word, I shall be pretty well off, when you are all gone away to be happy at Bath!"

She could only resolve to avoid such self-delusion in future, and think with heightened gratitude of the extraordinary blessing of having one such truly sympathising friend as Lady Russell.

The Mr. Musgroves had their own game to guard, and to destroy;[5] their own horses, dogs, and newspapers to engage them;[6] and the females were fully occupied in all the other common sub-

1. *wanted*: needed.

2. *publicity*: notoriety, part of general knowledge.

3. It is significant that Anne takes note of this lesson and resolves to put it to good use. The principal characters in Jane Austen are distinguished by their ability and willingness to learn from their experience, including their own mistakes, and to improve their characters. In contrast, the other characters, whether good or bad, generally make no effort to learn or improve.

4. *Queen-squares*: Queen Square was one of the most prominent venues in Bath (see map, p. 516, and picture on p. 79). It was built in the 1730s, and its grand houses were initially inhabited by wealthy and prominent people. But as Bath expanded northward and eastward, these newer areas, farther from the poorer old sections of the city and, in some cases, with even grander architecture, became the most fashionable and sought-after places to live. The Miss Musgroves are attuned to this new reality, while they may fear, or know from past discussions, that their parents, judging by an earlier time, overrate the current desirability of the square.

When Jane Austen visited Bath with her family for six weeks in 1799, they resided in Queen Square. The possible conflict of Louisa and Henrietta with their parents has an echo in Jane Austen's own experience, for later, when the family was living in Bath and needed to change residences, she worries that they will not choose the location she favors, one next to excellent gardens for walking, because her mother "hankers after the Square dreadfully, & it is but natural to suppose that my Uncle will take *her* part" (Jan. 22, 1801).

5. Guarding game was critical for allowing its destruction. England's density of population and agricultural cultivation meant there was far too little wild area to support, unaided, a sufficient population of game. Landed gentlemen undertook great efforts to encourage the reproduction of game and to guard the resulting concentrations from animal predators, poachers, and other country gentlemen. For more, see p. 413, note 48.

6. Other typical masculine concerns. Riding horses was very popular, either as part of the hunt or as a recreation in its own right, and many gentlemen owned more than one; women rode also, but much less. Dogs, which could be kept as pets by either men or women, were a particular preoccupation of men because they played a central role in pursuing game; many gentlemen devoted great attention to the breeding and raising of dogs for this purpose. Finally, newspapers were a particular interest of men (and Jane Austen consistently depicts them as such). One reason was that only men could participate in politics, which formed a primary subject of newspapers; even provincial papers, such as the Musgroves would be likely to read, often devoted much of their space to reprints of national news from London papers.

jects of house-keeping, neighbours, dress, dancing, and music.[7] She acknowledged it to be very fitting, that every little social commonwealth[8] should dictate its own matters of discourse; and hoped, ere long, to become a not unworthy member of the one she was now transplanted into. —With the prospect of spending at least two months at Uppercross, it was highly incumbent on her to clothe her imagination, her memory, and all her ideas[9] in as much of Uppercross as possible.

She had no dread of these two months. Mary was not so repulsive[10] and unsisterly as Elizabeth, nor so inaccessible to all influence of hers; neither was there any thing among the other component parts of the cottage inimical to comfort. —She was always on friendly terms with her brother-in-law; and in the children, who loved her nearly as well, and respected her a great deal more than their mother, she had an object of interest, amusement,[11] and wholesome exertion.

Charles Musgrove was civil and agreeable; in sense and temper[12] he was undoubtedly superior to his wife; but not of powers,[13] or conversation, or grace, to make the past, as they were connected together, at all a dangerous contemplation;[14] though, at the same time, Anne could believe, with Lady Russell, that a more equal match might have greatly improved him; and that a woman of real understanding[15] might have given more consequence[16] to his character, and more usefulness, rationality, and elegance[17] to his habits and pursuits. As it was, he did nothing with much zeal, but sport,[18] and his time was otherwise trifled away, without benefit from books, or any thing else. He had very good spirits, which never seemed much affected by his wife's occasional lowness; bore with her unreasonableness sometimes to Anne's admiration; and, upon the whole, though there was very often a little disagreement, (in which she had sometimes more share than she wished, being appealed to by both parties) they might pass for a happy couple. They were always perfectly agreed in the want of more money, and a strong inclination for a handsome present from his father; but here, as on most topics, he had the superiority, for while Mary thought it a great shame that such

7. A similar list of feminine interests and occupations. Housekeeping, which at this level of society meant mostly supervising servants' work, was the main task of mistresses of households such as Mrs. Musgrove and Mary, and it would also interest those like the Miss Musgroves, who could expect to become mistresses. Jane Austen also shows women exhibiting a particular interest in their neighbors' affairs—and the charitable activities they often performed involved helping poorer neighbors—and in dress; she herself often refers to both subjects in her letters. As for dancing, it was an activity enjoyed by both men and women, but it was taught to girls in school, and Jane Austen frequently depicts them as being particularly fond of it. Finally, while music could be appreciated by either sex, it was mostly performed by women: young ladies often learned to play an instrument or to sing, while men rarely received musical education.

8. *commonwealth*: community, body politic. The term was regularly used in political writing and discussion at this time.

9. *ideas*: thoughts.

10. *repulsive*: cold, repellent—i.e., tending to repulse someone.

11. *amusement*: occupation, diversion. The term did not necessarily suggest a comical or humorous state.

12. *temper*: emotional qualities. The term had a broader meaning then.

13. *powers*: abilities.

14. There is no danger of her suffering from regrets for not marrying him.

15. *understanding*: intelligence. This term is frequently used to refer to the mind or general intellectual attributes of a person.

16. *consequence*: dignity, weight.

17. *elegance*: refinement, taste.

18. *sport*: the pursuit of game. The principal types of sport were shooting (see p. 113, note 29) and hunting hares or foxes with horses and dogs (only the latter was usually called hunting in the parlance of the time). Fishing, or angling, along with coursing, the pursuit of hares by greyhounds alone, were also popular activities falling under the rubric of sport. Sport was one of the leading pursuits of English gentlemen at the time and a subject of great passion and interest—one sign of this was the constant appearance of books offering detailed advice on sport. Jane Austen's letters contain numerous references to the sporting activities of her male relatives.

a present was not made, he always contended for his father's having many other uses for his money, and a right to spend it as he liked.[19]

As to the management of their children, his theory was much better than his wife's, and his practice not so bad. — "I could manage them very well, if it were not for Mary's interference," — was what Anne often heard him say, and had a good deal of faith in; but when listening in turn to Mary's reproach of "Charles spoils the children so that I cannot get them into any order," — she never had the smallest temptation to say, "Very true."

One of the least agreeable circumstances of her residence there, was her being treated with too much confidence by all parties, and being too much in the secret of the complaints of each house.[20] Known to have some influence with her sister, she was continually requested, or at least receiving hints to exert it, beyond what was practicable. "I wish you could persuade Mary not to be always fancying herself ill," was Charles's language; and, in an unhappy mood, thus spoke Mary; — "I do believe if Charles were to see me dying, he would not think there was any thing the matter with me. I am sure, Anne, if you would, you might persuade him that I really am very ill—a great deal worse than I ever own."[21]

Mary's declaration was, "I hate sending the children to the Great House, though their grandmamma is always wanting to see them, for she humours and indulges them to such a degree, and gives them so much trash and sweet things, that they are sure to come back sick and cross for the rest of the day." — And Mrs. Musgrove took the first opportunity of being alone with Anne, to say, "Oh! Miss Anne,[22] I cannot help wishing Mrs. Charles[23] had a little of your method with those children. They are quite different creatures with you! But to be sure, in general they are so spoilt![24] It is a pity you cannot put your sister in the way of managing[25] them. They are as fine healthy children as ever were seen, poor little dears, without partiality; but Mrs. Charles knows no more how they should be treated! — Bless me, how troublesome they are sometimes! — I assure you, Miss Anne, it prevents my wishing

19. One reason they would have a particular interest in Mr. Musgrove's financial generosity is that they primarily depend on that for their income. The standard settlement governing landed estates gave the estate to the eldest son, but no separate sum of money, as was given to daughters and younger sons. Thus Charles, while set to inherit considerable property once his father dies, depends until then on the latter's largesse. Mary brought a dowry of ten thousand pounds (this is the sum later specified for Anne—p. 474—and daughters almost always had the same dowries). But the income from that would not suffice to meet their needs, especially with children. Mr. Musgrove seems to be generous, as in his financing of their fashionable cottage, and he would wish his son and heir to live like a gentleman of means— he may have even settled informally a regular stipend on them. But, as Charles says, he has other expenses, since they are a numerous family, and Charles and Mary's situation inevitably encourages them to wonder what else Mr. Musgrove might give them.

20. Anne's move to Uppercross has plunged her into a very different world and altered the atmosphere of the novel. She is treated with more kindness by the Musgroves than by her father and sister, and the Musgroves' more casual manners, compared to the Elliots and to Lady Russell, encourage greater friendliness and warmth. But these manners, a reflection in part of their less aristocratic background and position, also have their drawbacks, such as this forcing of Anne to listen to confidences she would rather not hear and to take sides, in effect, in the various family quarrels the different Musgroves proceed to rehearse before her. This is something that Anne herself, or Lady Russell, would never impose upon someone else.

21. *own:* acknowledge.

22. With no elder sister present, Anne should now be called "Miss Elliot," as other characters will. Mrs. Musgrove's use of "Miss Anne," seen elsewhere, may reflect a long-standing habit of using this when Elizabeth was present.

23. *Mrs. Charles:* Mary. The name distinguishes her from Mrs. Musgrove herself.

24. These two descriptions of the treatment of children suggest a certain degree of indulgence toward children. There had been a trend in the eighteenth century toward less strict child rearing, and some of this is reflected in Jane Austen. In fact, the few small children who appear in her novels tend to be depicted as rather spoiled. The principle of respect and obedience toward parents was basic in this culture, and her novels almost never show open defiance, including by adult children, but she also does not show parents enforcing this obedience with harsh discipline, much less with physical punishment, which never appears.

25. *put your sister in the way of managing:* get your sister to be able to manage.

to see them at our house so often as I otherwise should. I believe Mrs. Charles is not quite pleased with my not inviting them oftener; but you know it is very bad to have children with one, that one is obliged to be checking every moment; 'don't do this, and don't do that';—or that one can only keep in tolerable order by more cake than is good for them."

She had this communication, moreover, from Mary. "Mrs. Musgrove thinks all her servants so steady, that it would be high treason to call it in question; but I am sure, without exaggeration, that her upper house-maid and laundry-maid,[26] instead of being in their business, are gadding about[27] the village, all day long. I meet them wherever I go; and I declare, I never go twice into my nursery without seeing something of them. If Jemima were not the trustiest, steadiest creature in the world, it would be enough to spoil her; for she tells me, they are always tempting her to take a walk with them.[28] And on Mrs. Musgrove's side, it was,—"I make a rule of never interfering in any of my daughter-in-law's concerns, for I know it would not do; but I shall tell *you*, Miss Anne, because you may be able to set things to rights, that I have no very good opinion of Mrs. Charles's nursery-maid: I hear strange stories of her; she is always upon the gad: and from my own knowledge, I can declare, she is such a fine-dressing lady, that she is enough to ruin any servants she comes near.[29] Mrs. Charles quite swears by her, I know; but I just give you this hint, that you may be upon the watch; because, if you see any thing amiss, you need not be afraid of mentioning it."

Again; it was Mary's complaint, that Mrs. Musgrove was very apt not to give her the precedence that was her due, when they dined at the Great House with other families; and she did not see any reason why she was to be considered so much at home as to lose her place. And one day, when Anne was walking with only the Miss Musgroves, one of them, after talking of rank, people of rank, and jealousy of rank, said, "I have no scruple[30] of observing to *you*, how nonsensical some persons are about their place, because, all the world knows how easy and indifferent you are

26. The upper housemaid would be the highest-ranking of the housemaids, who were responsible for cleaning the house; the laundry maid washed and ironed clothes, which was a substantial chore at this time. The existence of at least two housemaids and a laundry maid (in many households housemaids also did the washing) indicates a large domestic establishment. A book of 1825, *The Complete Servant*, identifies incomes of 2,000 to 3,000 pounds per year as the lowest that would normally lead to employing a laundry maid (for the value of money, see p. 145, note 14).

27. *gadding about:* wandering about idly. "Upon the gad," used below, has the same meaning.

28. Jemima's being in the nursery, the room for young children, indicates she is the nursery maid. Very wealthy families might have a head nurse, later called a nanny, to take charge of the children's upbringing, but in ordinary gentry families like this the mother would undertake the main responsibility. In either case the nursery maid would assist, particularly with the more menial tasks of child rearing. Nursery maids were lower servants, which is why Mary refers to her by her first name (last names were used for upper servants).

29. Complaints about the overly fine dressing of servants, especially female servants, were common at this time. Rising prosperity, and falling prices for clothes, allowed more servants to buy the latest fashions, and many did, seeking to emulate their masters or other servants who dressed nicely—this last process is what worries Mrs. Musgrove. Those employing servants objected to this for undermining the distinctions of rank, which were partly expressed through clothing, and for leading servants into excessive spending, which in turn could lead to vice, including theft from their employers. In *Mansfield Park*, the heroine's mother, Mrs. Price, became "discomposed if she saw . . . Rebecca [her servant] pass by with a flower in her hat."

30. *scruple:* hesitation.

about it: but I wish any body could give Mary a hint that it would be a great deal better if she were not so very tenacious; especially, if she would not be always putting herself forward to take place of mamma. Nobody doubts her right to have precedence of mamma, but it would be more becoming in her not to be always insisting on it. It is not that mamma cares about it the least in the world, but I know it is taken notice of by many persons."[31]

How was Anne to set all these matters to rights? She could do little more than listen patiently, soften every grievance, and excuse each to the other; give them all hints of the forbearance necessary between such near neighbours, and make those hints broadest which were meant for her sister's benefit.

In all other respects, her visit began and proceeded very well. Her own spirits improved by change of place and subject, by being removed three miles from Kellynch: Mary's ailments lessened by having a constant companion; and their daily intercourse with the other family, since there was neither superior affection, confidence, nor employment in the cottage, to be interrupted by it, was rather an advantage.[32] It was certainly carried nearly as far as possible, for they met every morning, and hardly ever spent an evening asunder; but she believed they should not have done so well without the sight of Mr. and Mrs. Musgrove's respectable forms in the usual places, or without the talking, laughing, and singing of their daughters.[33]

She played a great deal better than either of the Miss Musgroves; but having no voice, no knowledge of the harp,[34] and no fond parents to sit by and fancy themselves delighted,[35] her performance was little thought of, only out of civility, or to refresh the others, as she was well aware. She knew that when she played she was giving pleasure only to herself; but this was no new sensation: excepting one short period of her life, she had never, since the age of fourteen, never since the loss of her dear mother, known the happiness of being listened to, or encouraged by any just appreciation or real taste.[36] In music she had been always used to feel alone in the world; and Mr. and Mrs. Musgrove's fond partiality for their own daughters' performance, and total indifference to

31. Rules of precedence dictated the order in which people would proceed when dining and at social events. This order was based on social rank and followed an elaborate set of rules. Mary, though Mrs. Musgrove's daughter-in-law, takes precedence because she is the daughter of a baronet, whereas Mrs. Musgrove is only the wife of an untitled country gentleman. Because wife is a more important connection than daughter, a wife whose husband ranks slightly below another woman's father can still take precedence. This is what happens with Lady Russell and Elizabeth (see p. 11, note 35). But the difference between a baronet and an untitled gentleman is large enough that it overrides the difference between a wife and a daughter. These precise rankings, which were laid out in books, would be well known by everyone.

These rules were adhered to particularly on formal occasions. This passage suggests that the Musgroves do not worry about precedence when only the family, including Mary and Charles, dine together, and that Mary does not protest (whatever her possible private misgivings). Her complaint is that they continue to disregard precedence when other families are present. The words of the Miss Musgroves indicate they accept that Mary is right on the merits, but wish she cared less about these matters.

32. Since there is no strong affection or intimacy between Anne and Mary, nor activities to occupy their time, the constant intercourse with the Musgroves is a benefit, not an interference. The female activities they might pursue include household and maternal duties, as well as reading, music, drawing, or decorative activities like embroidery—Mary seems negligent of the former and is not shown engaged in the latter except for occasional references to embroidery.

33. Singing was often taught to genteel young ladies at schools.

34. Harps were, after pianos, the most popular instruments for young ladies. The harp had the advantage of making its user look elegant while playing: a number of portraits from the time show aristocratic young ladies playing a harp. In *Mansfield Park* the fashionable Mary Crawford plays one well, and the sounds and image formed as she plays help fix the love of the main male character for her. All this makes it ideal for the Miss Musgroves, with their fashionable tastes and the seductiveness they soon reveal. For a contemporary picture of a young woman playing a harp, see p. 416.

35. The suggestion is that the Musgroves have no real appreciation for what their daughters are playing and admire it purely from parental fondness. Other commentators of the time take satirical note of such parental fondness, for musical prowess was encouraged in young ladies, and those who displayed it could be sources of family pride. The Musgroves' lack of musical taste is further shown in their reaction on p. 90 to Anne's playing.

36. The short period would be the courtship between her and Captain Wentworth, for he is revealed to have a great love and appreciation for music.

any other person's, gave her much more pleasure for their sakes, than mortification for her own.

The party at the Great House was sometimes increased by other company. The neighbourhood was not large, but the Musgroves were visited by every body, and had more dinner parties, and more callers, more visitors by invitation and by chance,[37] than any other family. They were more completely popular.

The girls were wild for dancing; and the evenings ended, occasionally, in an unpremeditated little ball.[38] There was a family of cousins within a walk of Uppercross, in less affluent circumstances, who depended on the Musgroves for all their pleasures: they would come at any time, and help play at any thing, or dance any where; and Anne, very much preferring the office[39] of musician to a more active post, played country dances to them by the hour together;[40] a kindness which always recommended her musical powers to the notice of Mr. and Mrs. Musgrove more than any thing else, and often drew this compliment;—"Well done, Miss Anne! very well done indeed! Lord bless me! how those little fingers of yours fly about!"[41]

So passed the first three weeks. Michaelmas came; and now Anne's heart must be in Kellynch again. A beloved home made over to others; all the precious rooms and furniture, groves, and prospects,[42] beginning to own other eyes and other limbs! She could not think of much else on the 29th of September; and she had this sympathetic touch in the evening, from Mary, who, on having occasion to note down the day of the month, exclaimed, "Dear me! is not this the day the Crofts were to come to Kellynch? I am glad I did not think of it before. How low it makes me!"

The Crofts took possession with true naval alertness,[43] and were to be visited.[44] Mary deplored the necessity for herself. "Nobody knew how much she should suffer. She should put it off as long as she could." But was not easy till she had talked Charles into driving her over on an early day; and was in a very animated, comfortable state of imaginary agitation, when she came back. Anne had very sincerely rejoiced in there being no means of her going.[45] She wished, however, to see the Crofts, and was glad to

37. They invited visitors, but also happily welcomed unexpected ones.

38. This contrasts with the more formal balls discussed in relation to Elizabeth Elliot (see p. 11, note 36), just as the above encouragement of frequent visitors differs from the more formal Elliot procedures, seen later when they are in Bath.

39. *office:* duty, function, position.

40. Country dances were the most popular type of dance in England at the time. They were usually longways dances, in which the couples lined up one after the other, with men and women forming two opposing rows. Two reasons for their popularity were their flexibility, since any number of couples could participate, and their sociable nature, since the dances required every couple to meet and dance with every other couple.

   Jane Austen may have played a role similar to Anne's. In a letter to her sister she anticipates their purchase of a pianoforte and declares, "I will practise country dances, that we may have some amusement for our nephews & neices [*sic*], when we have the pleasure of their company" (Dec. 28, 1808).

41. Country dances were lively, so someone playing them would move her fingers rapidly across the piano. That such a visible sign of Anne's proficiency is what mainly draws the notice and praise of Mr. and Mrs. Musgrove is a further sign of their lack of musical sophistication.

42. *prospects:* views (from the house, or other vantage points on the property). These views could include the groves, already mentioned as part of the landscaped park surrounding Kellynch.

43. *alertness:* briskness, rapidity. Sailing a ship would often demand quick action, whether in dealing with the sea, engaging in battle, or following orders.

44. It was considered an obligatory courtesy to visit new neighbors of one's own social level. This meant going to them first, thereby offering one's greetings.

45. Charles's carriage, a curricle, carries only two people (see p. 201, note 26). Thus Anne cannot accompany them. Her relief contrasts with her earlier wish of still residing in this area in order to "have the pleasure of sometimes seeing the lawns and groves of Kellynch" (p. 24). Presumably the sobering reality of their possession by others has altered her perspective.

be within when the visit was returned.[46] They came; the master of
the house was not at home, but the two sisters were together; and
as it chanced that Mrs. Croft fell to the share of Anne, while the
admiral sat by Mary, and made himself very agreeable by his
good-humoured notice of her little boys, she was well able to
watch for a likeness, and if it failed her in the features, to catch it
in the voice, or the turn of sentiment and expression.

Mrs. Croft, though neither tall nor fat, had a squareness,
uprightness, and vigour of form, which gave importance to her
person. She had bright dark eyes, good teeth,[47] and altogether an
agreeable face; though her reddened and weather-beaten complexion, the consequence of her having been almost as much at
sea as her husband, made her seem to have lived some years
longer in the world than her real eight-and-thirty. Her manners[48]
were open, easy,[49] and decided, like one who had no distrust of
herself, and no doubts of what to do;[50] without any approach to
coarseness, however, or any want[51] of good humour. Anne gave
her credit, indeed, for feelings of great consideration towards herself, in all that related to Kellynch; and it pleased her: especially,
as she had satisfied herself in the very first half minute, in the
instant even of introduction, that there was not the smallest symp-
tom of any knowledge or suspicion on Mrs. Croft's side, to give a
bias of any sort. She was quite easy on that head, and consequently full of strength and courage, till for a moment electrified[52] by Mrs. Croft's suddenly saying, —

"It was you, and not your sister, I find, that my brother had the
pleasure of being acquainted with, when he was in this country."

Anne hoped she had outlived the age of blushing; but the age
of emotion[53] she certainly had not.

"Perhaps you may not have heard that he is married," added
Mrs. Croft.

She could now answer as she ought; and was happy to feel,
when Mrs. Croft's next words explained it to be Mr. Wentworth of
whom she spoke,[54] that she had said nothing which might not do
for either brother. She immediately felt how reasonable it was,
that Mrs. Croft should be thinking and speaking of Edward,[55] and

46. Once Charles and Mary made the initial gesture, it was standard courtesy for the Crofts to return it.

47. The quality of people's teeth is often described in Jane Austen's novels. Oral hygiene was limited, though some people would brush their teeth; dental care mainly consisted of either pulling teeth or offering dentures or other cosmetic improvements. Sugar was also becoming an increasingly large part of people's diets, causing even more decay to teeth.

48. *manners*: outward bearing or characteristics; general mode of behavior.

49. *easy*: unembarrassed; free from awkwardness or stiffness.

50. In these respects she shows a strong resemblance to her brother Captain Wentworth.

51. *want*: lack.

52. The term "electrified"—though it may seem incongruous in Austen's world, in which no electrical devices for ordinary use existed—had been in circulation for more than fifty years, used both in reference to specific electrical phenomena and in the more metaphorical sense employed here. Electricity had been first identified in the early 1700s, and by the middle of the century it had become an object of great interest on the part of both scientists and the general public. Electrical demonstrations were popular public entertainments. In a letter Jane Austen speaks of her brother trying electricity as a health treatment (June 2, 1799).

53. *emotion*: agitation.

54. Mr. Wentworth, without a first name, is the elder brother (see also p. 49, note 1)

55. It is reasonable because Edward Wentworth resided in this area when he was a curate at Monkford. This would make someone naturally assume that Anne knew him better.

not of Frederick; and with shame at her own forgetfulness, applied herself to the knowledge of their former neighbour's present state, with proper interest.[56]

The rest was all tranquillity; till just as they were moving, she heard the admiral say to Mary,

"We are expecting a brother of Mrs. Croft's here soon; I dare say you know him by name."

He was cut short by the eager attacks of the little boys, clinging to him like an old friend, and declaring he should not go; and being too much engrossed by proposals of carrying them away in his coat pocket, &c. to have another moment for finishing or recollecting what he had begun, Anne was left to persuade herself, as well as she could, that the same brother must still be in question. She could not, however, reach such a degree of certainty, as not to be anxious to hear whether any thing had been said on the subject at the other house, where the Crofts had previously been calling.

The folks of Great House were to spend the evening of this day at the Cottage; and it being now too late in the year for such visits to be made on foot,[57] the coach was beginning to be listened for,[58] when the youngest Miss Musgrove walked in. That she was coming to apologize, and that they should[59] have to spend the evening by themselves, was the first black idea; and Mary was quite ready to be affronted, when Louisa made all right by saying, that she only came on foot, to leave more room for the harp,[60] which was bringing in[61] the carriage.

"And I will tell you our reason," she added, "and all about it. I am come on to give you notice, that papa and mamma are out of spirits this evening, especially mamma; she is thinking so much of poor Richard! And we agreed it would be best to have the harp, for it seems to amuse[62] her more than the piano-forte.[63] I will tell you why she is out of spirits. When the Crofts called this morning, (they called here afterwards, did not they?) they happened to say, that her brother, Captain Wentworth, is just returned to England, or paid off, or something,[64] and is coming to see them almost directly; and most unluckily it came into mamma's head, when

56. Here, as elsewhere, Anne's feelings regarding Captain Wentworth make her depart from her usual high standards of reasonableness, and comprehension of others, though she quickly realizes this and strives to resume her normal attentiveness.

57. This is probably because evenings are now dark (it being October), though it could also refer to the coldness of nights at this time of year. No street lighting would exist in rural villages.

58. The coach is the Musgroves' vehicle (see p. 75, note 55).

59. *should:* would. Thus there is no suggestion of moral obligation or urging in the sentence. This use of "should" is found elsewhere in the novel.

60. A harp being, then as now, as tall as a person, it could have required enough room in the coach to leave space for only a few people. Louisa, as the youngest of the family, would be the one selected to give way (for her being younger than Henrietta, see p. 147, note 22). She or Henrietta would also be better suited to venture on foot, whether it was darkness or cold that was making the others go by coach—though if darkness was the reason, she might be accompanied by a servant now.

61. *bringing:* being brought. This use of an active verb in a passive sense was a traditional construction that can be found elsewhere in Jane Austen. The construction "be + past participle" (as in "being brought") was also used, but it was subject to disapproval by grammarians.

62. *amuse:* entertain.

63. This suggests that Charles and Mary also own a pianoforte, for otherwise it would not be mentioned as an option (Mr. and Mrs. Musgrove's grand pianoforte would be too cumbersome to be conveyed elsewhere for an evening). It is possible Mary learned when she was a girl; even without that, because the instrument was very popular, relatively inexpensive, and a standard sign of taste and gentility, it was found in homes throughout England, regardless of musical taste or ability (see p. 75, note 60).

64. Louisa's uncertainty about exactly what happened indicates her ignorance of the navy, even though, as shortly revealed, she had a brother in the service.

they were gone, that Wentworth, or something very like it, was the name of poor Richard's captain, at one time, I do not know when or where, but a great while before he died, poor fellow![65] And upon looking over his letters and things, she found it was so; and is perfectly sure that this must be the very man, and her head is quite full of it, and of poor Richard! So we must all be as merry as we can, that she may not be dwelling upon such gloomy things."

The real circumstances of this pathetic piece of family history were, that the Musgroves had had the ill fortune of a very troublesome, hopeless son; and the good fortune to lose him before he reached his twentieth year; that he had been sent to sea, because he was stupid and unmanageable on shore; that he had been very little cared for at any time by his family, though quite as much as he deserved; seldom heard of, and scarcely at all regretted, when the intelligence[66] of his death abroad had worked its way to Uppercross, two years before.[67]

He had, in fact, though his sisters were now doing all they could for him, by calling him "poor Richard," been nothing better than a thick-headed, unfeeling, unprofitable Dick Musgrove,[68] who had never done any thing to entitle himself to more than the abbreviation of his name, living or dead.

He had been several years at sea, and had, in the course of those removals to which all midshipmen are liable, and especially such midshipmen as every captain wishes to get rid of,[69] been six months on board Captain Frederick Wentworth's frigate,[70] the Laconia; and from the Laconia he had, under the influence of his captain, written the only two letters which his father and mother had ever received from him during the whole of his absence; that is to say, the only two disinterested letters; all the rest had been mere applications for money.[71]

In each letter he had spoken well of his captain; but yet, so little were they in the habit of attending to such matters, so unobservant and incurious were they as to the names of men or ships, that it had made scarcely any impression at the time; and that Mrs. Musgrove should have been suddenly struck, this very day, with a recollection of the name of Wentworth, as connected with

65. The language of Louisa's speech reveals her character. It is not foolish or ungrammatical, but it does show her—through its exclamation points, its mostly brief clauses, its jumping from one point to another, and its occasional repetition of the same points—to be excitable and not prone to careful reflection.

66. *intelligence*: news.

67. This passage, especially the statement that the Musgroves were fortunate that their son died, has shocked some readers. Its cynicism does reflect a tough-minded attitude found frequently in eighteenth-century literature, and in Jane Austen, though usually in more modulated form. This attitude included an at times brutal honesty about the unpleasant facts of existence, such as the possible benefit to people of losing a child who had caused them trouble, and a willingness to draw sharp moral distinctions between people, which included identifying some people as completely bad and therefore better off gone. One could argue that Jane Austen's strong realism about life, and her strict moral standards, lead logically to both these perspectives. Some commentators suggest that she might have softened this passage if she had enjoyed more time to revise the novel. Similar statements in earlier novels never attain the brutal frankness of this one.

The issue of Dick Musgrove and his parents' grief for him, when continued a little later (p. 126, and p. 128), does serve to reveal important facets of Captain Wentworth's character and his relationship to Anne—though the author could have accomplished this without such pointed language.

68. The man's name, and its derogatory abbreviation here, may be an inside joke. In a letter to her sister Jane Austen jokes about someone named Richard putting off his marriage "till he has got a Better Christian name" (Sept. 15, 1796). There may have been a personal reason why she and her sister disliked the name; she never uses it for a speaking character in her novels.

69. Midshipmen were, in effect, officer apprentices. All who wished to become commissioned officers (lieutenant and higher) had to serve first as midshipmen. Midshipmen generally started when they were adolescents, as was the case with the Musgroves' son.

70. Frigates were one of the three main types of ships in the navy. The other two were sloops, the smallest kind, and ships of the line (or men-of-war), the largest kind. Captain Wentworth's command of this frigate will figure prominently when he gives a brief history of his naval career in Chapter VIII.

71. Those in the navy could engage in regular correspondence, though their receipt of letters could be very uncertain due to the vagaries of where ships sailed. The main character in *Mansfield Park*, Fanny, receives frequent letters from her brother, who is at sea, and Jane Austen corresponded with her naval brothers.

her son, seemed one of those extraordinary bursts of mind which do sometimes occur.

She had gone to her letters, and found it all as she supposed; and the reperusal of these letters, after so long an interval, her poor son gone for ever, and all the strength of his faults forgotten, had affected her spirits exceedingly, and thrown her into greater grief for him than she had known on first hearing of his death. Mr. Musgrove was, in a lesser degree, affected likewise; and when they reached the cottage, they were evidently in want, first, of being listened to anew on this subject, and afterwards, of all the relief which cheerful companions could give.

To hear them talking so much of Captain Wentworth, repeating his name so often, puzzling over past years, and at last ascertaining that it *might*, that it probably *would*, turn out to be the very same Captain Wentworth whom they recollected meeting, once or twice, after their coming back from Clifton;[72]—a very fine young man; but they could not say whether it was seven or eight years ago,—was a new sort of trial to Anne's nerves.[73] She found, however, that it was one to which she must enure[74] herself. Since he actually was expected in the country, she must teach herself to be insensible[75] on such points. And not only did it appear that he was expected, and speedily, but the Musgroves, in their warm gratitude for the kindness he had shewn poor Dick, and very high respect for his character, stamped as it was by poor Dick's having been six months under his care, and mentioning him in strong, though not perfectly well spelt praise, as "a fine dashing felow, only two perticular about the school-master,"[76] were bent on introducing themselves, and seeking his acquaintance, as soon as they could hear of his arrival.

The resolution of doing so helped to form the comfort of their evening.[77]

72. Clifton is a small town next to Bristol (by now it has been largely absorbed into Bristol; see map, p. 513). It developed into a popular spa and resort during the eighteenth century, thanks to the hot springs discovered there, the spectacular beauty of the adjacent river gorge, and its proximity to Bath. In *Northanger Abbey* some of the characters, who are staying in Bath, take a day-trip to Clifton. Jane Austen lived there for a brief period. Being close to Somerset, it would be a natural place for the Musgroves to vacation.

73. It is a trial because they met Captain Wentworth during the same period when he was staying nearby at Monkford with his brother and romancing Anne. This has earlier been described as "more than seven years" ago (p. 52). The Musgroves, however, would have no knowledge of what happened between Anne and Captain Wentworth, since at that time, before the marriage of Charles and Mary, they had no particular connection with the Elliot family.

74. *enure*: inure, i.e., accustom.

75. *insensible*: indifferent, unmoved.

76. The navy wished its midshipmen to be educated, since they were designed to become its commanding officers. It stipulated that they should receive instruction from a schoolmaster. But many ships did not have schoolmasters, and how much schooling was offered, or enforced, was in practice left up to the captain. Sometimes the ship's chaplain would undertake the responsibility, sometimes the captain himself. The letter quoted here suggests that Captain Wentworth was more conscientious than most captains, through his apparent insistence that Dick Musgrove do his lessons.

77. Such resolutions of calm and forbearance have formed a good part of the comfort of Anne's life until now. Her statement above about teaching herself to be insensible harkens back to her determination at the outset of the chapter to draw an important lesson from her experience on joining the Musgroves.

Chapter Seven

A very few days more, and Captain Wentworth was known to be at Kellynch, and Mr. Musgrove had called on him, and come back warm in his praise, and he was engaged with the Crofts to dine at Uppercross, by the end of another week. It had been a great disappointment to Mr. Musgrove, to find that no earlier day could be fixed, so impatient was he to shew his gratitude, by seeing Captain Wentworth under his own roof, and welcoming him to all that was strongest and best in his cellars.[1] But a week must pass; only a week, in Anne's reckoning, and then, she supposed, they must meet; and soon she began to wish that she could feel secure even for a week.

Captain Wentworth made a very early return to Mr. Musgrove's civility, and she was all but calling there in the same half hour! — She and Mary were actually setting forward for the great house, where, as she afterwards learnt, they must inevitably have found him, when they were stopped by the eldest boy's being at that moment brought home in consequence of a bad fall. The child's situation put the visit entirely aside, but she could not hear of her escape with indifference, even in the midst of the serious anxiety which they afterwards felt on his account.

His collar-bone was found to be dislocated, and such injury received in the back, as roused the most alarming ideas. It was an afternoon of distress, and Anne had every thing to do at once — the apothecary to send for[2] — the father to have pursued and informed — the mother to support and keep from hysterics — the servants to control[3] — the youngest child to banish, and the poor suffering one to attend and soothe;[4] — besides sending, as soon as she recollected it, proper notice to the other house, which brought her an accession rather of frightened, enquiring companions, than of very useful assistants.

1. His wine cellars.

2. Apothecaries were one of the main types of medical practitioner. Originally they only dispensed drugs, but over time they expanded their role to include prescribing drugs and offering general medical advice. In strict terms, injuries like a dislocated collarbone fell under the purview of the surgeon, who was traditionally distinct from the apothecary. But in practice by this time the two roles were frequently melded, especially in rural areas like this, where the small population of patients made it impractical for a medical man to restrict himself to one type of case. Lists of the time show surgeon-apothecaries, sometimes just called apothecaries, making up the majority of practitioners.

3. Managing and supervising servants was one of the basic duties of the mistress of a household. Anne's apparent facility with that indicates her suitability for being such a mistress, if she should ever have the opportunity.

4. Anne's calm, sensible actions in the face of an emergency foreshadow her behavior during a far greater emergency (pp. 210–212).

Her brother's[5] return was the first comfort; he could take best care of his wife, and the second blessing was the arrival of the apothecary. Till he came and had examined the child, their apprehensions were the worse for being vague;—they suspected great injury, but knew not where; but now the collar-bone was soon replaced,[6] and though Mr. Robinson felt and felt, and rubbed, and looked grave, and spoke low words both to the father and the aunt, still they were all to hope the best, and to be able to part and eat their dinner in tolerable ease of mind; and then it was just before they parted, that the two young aunts were able so far to digress from their nephew's state, as to give the information of Captain Wentworth's visit;[7]—staying five minutes behind their father and mother, to endeavour to express how perfectly delighted they were with him, how much handsomer, how infinitely more agreeable they thought him than any individual among their male acquaintance, who had been at all a favourite before—how glad they had been to hear papa invite him to stay dinner—how sorry when he said it was quite out of his power—and how glad again, when he had promised in reply to papa and mamma's farther pressing invitations, to come and dine with them on the morrow, actually on the morrow!—And he had promised it in so pleasant a manner, as if he felt all the motive of their attention just as he ought!—And, in short, he had looked and said every thing with such exquisite grace, that they could assure them all, their heads were both turned by him![8]—And off they ran, quite as full of glee as of love, and apparently more full of Captain Wentworth than of little Charles.[9]

The same story and the same raptures were repeated, when the two girls came with their father, through the gloom of the evening, to make enquiries; and Mr. Musgrove, no longer under the first uneasiness about his heir,[10] could add his confirmation and praise, and hope there would be now no occasion for putting Captain Wentworth off, and only be sorry to think that the cottage party, probably, would not like to leave the little boy, to give him the meeting.—"Oh, no! as to leaving the little boy!"—both father and mother were in much too strong and recent alarm to bear the

5. *brother's:* brother-in-law's.

6. *replaced:* put back in its original position. This was the original definition of "replace," and still the most common one at this time, though the
present-day meaning, "take the place of," had also become current by the
eighteenth century.

Medical science of the time possessed a good knowledge of human
anatomy and was able to deal well with many bone fractures and dislocations. A book of surgical advice described the treatment of a dislocated collarbone, or clavicle, as fairly simple and straightforward; it also pointed out
that the lack of muscles around the bone made abnormalities in it easy to
detect, which is seen here in the detection of the injury before the arrival of
the doctor. To treat the usual dislocations the writer advised "taking off the
weight of the arm, by placing the elbow and fore arm in a sling," pushing the
bone back in position, and "applying compresses and a spica [reverse spiral]
bandage, for the purpose of keeping the end of the clavicle from ascending
again" (Samuel Cooper, *First Lines of the Practice of Surgery,* p. 433).

7. The two young aunts are Henrietta and Louisa Musgrove.

8. The second half of this paragraph is an example of what is known as free
indirect speech. This technique, in which Jane Austen was a pioneer, consists of rendering the characters' words or thoughts in the third person, without quotation marks, but in a way that replicates the manner and language of
those words. In this case, the exclamation points, the frequent dashes, the
switch from glad to sorry to glad, and the fulsome language with which Captain Wentworth is praised and their feelings are described, all serve to convey
the breathless excitement of the characters who are speaking.

9. One reason for their delight in him is that there are few unmarried
young men within their social circle, limited as it is by neighborhood and
class (see p. 53, note 25). Henrietta has already been wooed by one of the
only eligible men in their area, and he is neither that close geographically
nor their complete equal socially (pp. 140–142). The arrival of a man as attractive and charming, and socially and financially suitable, as Captain Wentworth represents an important event for them.

At the same time, their willingness to switch their concerns so quickly to
him, and away from their just injured nephew, contrasts them with Anne,
who bears the same relationship to little Charles but shows far more solicitude.

10. As the eldest son of Charles Musgrove, Mr. Musgrove's eldest son, little
Charles is in line ultimately to inherit the Musgrove estate. Preserving one's
property and position across the generations was a central concern of the
landed elite.

thought; and Anne, in the joy of the escape, could not help adding her warm protestations to theirs.

Charles Musgrove, indeed, afterwards shewed more of inclination; "the child was going on so well—and he wished so much to be introduced to Captain Wentworth, that, perhaps, he might join them in the evening; he would not dine from home, but he might walk in for half an hour." But in this he was eagerly opposed by his wife, with "Oh, no! indeed, Charles, I cannot bear to have you go away. Only think, if any thing should happen!"

The child had a good night, and was going on well the next day. It must be a work of time to ascertain that no injury had been done to the spine,[11] but Mr. Robinson found nothing to increase alarm, and Charles Musgrove began consequently to feel no necessity for longer confinement. The child was to be kept in bed, and amused[12] as quietly as possible; but what was there for a father to do? This was quite a female case,[13] and it would be highly absurd in him, who could be of no use at home, to shut himself up. His father very much wished him to meet Captain Wentworth, and there being no sufficient reason against it, he ought to go; and it ended in his making a bold public declaration, when he came in from shooting, of his meaning to dress directly,[14] and dine at the other house.

"Nothing can be going on better than the child," said he, "so I told my father just now that I would come, and he thought me quite right. Your sister being with you, my love, I have no scruple[15] at all. You would not like to leave him yourself, but you see I can be of no use. Anne will send for me if any thing is the matter."

Husbands and wives generally understand when opposition will be vain. Mary knew, from Charles's manner of speaking, that he was quite determined on going, and that it would be of no use to teaze him. She said nothing, therefore, till he was out of the room, but as soon as there was only Anne to hear,

"So! You and I are to be left to shift by ourselves, with this poor sick child—and not a creature coming near us all the evening! I knew how it would be. This is always my luck! If there is any thing

11. They are worried about the spine because they had already noted that the boy's injury was in the back as well as the collarbone.

12. *amused*: entertained, occupied.

13. See below, note 16, for the issue of this as a female case.

14. It was standard practice to change into one's nicer clothes for a dinner that included more than one's immediate family.

15. *scruple*: hesitation.

disagreeable going on, men are always sure to get out of it, and Charles is as bad as any of them. Very unfeeling! I must say it is very unfeeling of him, to be running away from his poor little boy; talks of his being going on so well! How does he know that he is going on well, or that there may not be a sudden change half an hour hence? I did not think Charles would have been so unfeeling. So, here he is to go away and enjoy himself, and because I am the poor mother, I am not to be allowed to stir;—and yet, I am sure, I am more unfit than any body else to be about the child. My being the mother is the very reason why my feelings should not be tried. I am not at all equal to it. You saw how hysterical I was yesterday."

"But that was only the effect of the suddenness of your alarm— of the shock. You will not be hysterical again. I dare say we shall have nothing to distress us. I perfectly understand Mr. Robinson's directions, and have no fears; and indeed, Mary, I cannot wonder at your husband. Nursing does not belong to a man, it is not his province.[16] A sick child is always the mother's property, her own feelings generally make it so."

"I hope I am as fond of my child as any mother—but I do not know that I am of any more use in the sickroom than Charles, for I cannot be always scolding and teazing[17] a poor child when it is ill; and you saw, this morning, that if I told him to keep quiet, he was sure to begin kicking about. I have not nerves[18] for the sort of thing."

"But, could you be comfortable yourself, to be spending the whole evening away from the poor boy?"

"Yes; you see his papa can, and why should not I?—Jemima is so careful! And she could send us word every hour how he was. I really think Charles might as well have told his father we would all come. I am not more alarmed about little Charles now than he is. I was dreadfully alarmed yesterday, but the case is very different to-day."

"Well—if you do not think it too late to give notice for yourself, suppose you were to go, as well as your husband. Leave little Charles to my care. Mr. and Mrs. Musgrove cannot think it

16. *province:* duty; sphere of action. Anne reflects current opinion and practice as to women's natural suitability for nursing. The sick were generally cared for at home by the women of the house, who were already at home, or by female servants — the hospitals existing then were charitable institutions treating the poor, and full-time outside nurses were not frequently hired (for one example of the latter, see p. 292). Anne's readiness to nurse, and apparent aptitude, indicates the domestic habits that, in the opinion of Lady Russell, make her especially fit to become a wife and mother. It thereby underlines the poignancy of her current single state.

17. *teazing:* bothering, disturbing (in a petty way). It is significant that it is this and scolding that Mary sees as her primary parental tasks.

18. *nerves:* this could refer simply to what are now called nerves, or it could have a wider connotation. Medical thinking at the time attributed a large number of ailments to nerves or nervous disorders. Hence Mary could also be warning of the possibility of damaging her own health, which would be in keeping with her hypochondriacal nature. A similar character in *Pride and Prejudice*, Mrs. Bennet, complains frequently about her nerves.

wrong, while I remain with him."

"Are you serious?" cried Mary, her eyes brightening. "Dear me! that's a very good thought, very good indeed. To be sure I may just as well go as not, for I am of no use at home—am I? and it only harasses me. You, who have not a mother's feelings, are a great deal the properest person. You can make little Charles do any thing; he always minds you at a word. It will be a great deal better than leaving him with only Jemima. Oh! I will certainly go; I am sure I ought if I can, quite as much as Charles, for they want me excessively to be acquainted with Captain Wentworth, and I know you do not mind being left alone. An excellent thought of yours, indeed, Anne! I will go and tell Charles, and get ready directly. You can send for us, you know, at a moment's notice, if any thing is the matter; but I dare say there will be nothing to alarm you. I should not go, you may be sure, if I did not feel quite at ease about my dear child."

The next moment she was tapping at her husband's dressing-room door,[19] and as Anne followed her up stairs, she was in time for the whole conversation, which began with Mary's saying, in a tone of great exultation,

"I mean to go with you, Charles, for I am of no more use at home than you are. If I were to shut myself up for ever with the child, I should not be able to persuade him to do any thing he did not like. Anne will stay; Anne undertakes to stay at home and take care of him. It is Anne's own proposal, and so I shall go with you, which will be a great deal better, for I have not dined at the other house since Tuesday."

"This is very kind of Anne," was her husband's answer, "and I should be very glad to have you go; but it seems rather hard that she should be left at home by herself, to nurse our sick child."[20]

Anne was now at hand to take up her own cause, and the sincerity of her manner being soon sufficient to convince him, where conviction was at least very agreeable, he had no farther scruples as to her being left to dine alone, though he still wanted her to join them in the evening, when the child might be at rest for the night, and kindly urged her to let him come and fetch her;

19. A dressing room attached to the bedroom had become a standard feature of affluent houses. Both the man and woman of the house would usually each have their own dressing rooms; they also could have their own bedrooms.

20. Charles's noticing this elementary point shows his greater fair-mindedness than Mary, as does his offering, after Anne insists on her wish to stay, to come fetch her so she can join them later.

but she was quite unpersuadable;[21] and this being the case, she had ere long the pleasure of seeing them set off together in high spirits. They were gone, she hoped, to be happy, however oddly constructed such happiness might seem; as for herself, she was left with as many sensations of comfort, as were, perhaps, ever likely to be hers. She knew herself to be of the first utility to the child; and what was it to her, if Frederick Wentworth were only half a mile distant, making himself agreeable to others![22]

She would have liked to know how he felt as to a meeting. Perhaps indifferent, if indifference could exist under such circumstances. He must be either indifferent or unwilling. Had he wished ever to see her again, he need not have waited till this time; he would have done what she could not but believe that in his place she should have[23] done long ago,[24] when events had been early giving him the independence[25] which alone had been wanting.[26]

Her brother and sister came back delighted with their new acquaintance, and their visit in general. There had been music, singing, talking, laughing, all that was most agreeable; charming manners in Captain Wentworth, no shyness or reserve; they seemed all to know each other perfectly, and he was coming the very next morning to shoot with Charles. He was to come to breakfast, but not at the Cottage, though that had been proposed at first; but then he had been pressed to come to the Great House instead, and he seemed afraid of being in Mrs. Charles Musgrove's way, on account of the child; and therefore, somehow, they hardly knew how, it ended in Charles's being to meet him to breakfast at his father's.

Anne understood it. He wished to avoid seeing her. He had enquired after her, she found, slightly, as might suit a former slight acquaintance, seeming to acknowledge such as she had acknowledged, actuated, perhaps, by the same view of escaping introduction when they were to meet.[27]

The morning hours of the Cottage were always later than those of the other house; and on the morrow the difference was so great, that Mary and Anne were not more than beginning breakfast

21. Another sign that Anne can easily resist persuasion when she has a strong reason for her actions.

22. The last sentence—another example of free indirect speech—reveals the contradictory nature of Anne's thoughts. She asks what Captain Wentworth is to her, in a manner meant to suggest he means nothing, even as the very need to ask that, as if in reassurance, shows that he means a lot, and that his presence nearby occupies her mind.

23. *should have:* would have.

24. Anne contrasts her place to his because, as a woman, she cannot go to him. Women were never supposed to take the initiative in romantic matters; a woman who did so would be scorned as wanton and immodest. Moreover, a young, unmarried woman like Anne could neither travel on her own, nor live on her own.

25. *independence:* financial independence.

26. *wanting:* lacking. Since his lack of fortune and uncertain prospects were the principal reasons Anne was persuaded to refuse him, Captain Wentworth has long been in an excellent position to renew his addresses to Anne—if he wished to do so.

27. Anne's immediate instinct is to interpret his action as one motivated by aversion to her. This shows both her confidence in knowing his character, a confidence that will be justified on a number of occasions, and her tendency to see things through the prism of her earlier experience with him. This tendency will often prove justified, but not in every case.

when Charles came in to say that they were just setting off,[28] that he was come for his dogs,[29] that his sisters were following with Captain Wentworth, his sisters meaning to visit Mary and the child, and Captain Wentworth proposing also to wait on[30] her for a few minutes, if not inconvenient; and though Charles had answered for the child's being in no such state as could make it inconvenient, Captain Wentworth would not be satisfied without his running on to give notice.[31]

Mary, very much gratified by this attention, was delighted to receive him; while a thousand feelings rushed on Anne, of which this was the most consoling, that it would soon be over. And it was soon over. In two minutes after Charles's preparation, the others appeared; they were in the drawing-room. Her eye half met Captain Wentworth's; a bow, a curtsey passed;[32] she heard his voice — he talked to Mary, said all that was right; said something to the Miss Musgroves, enough to mark an easy footing: the room seemed full — full of persons and voices — but a few minutes ended it. Charles shewed himself at the window, all was ready, their visitor had bowed and was gone; the Miss Musgroves were gone too,[33] suddenly resolving to walk to the end of the village with the sportsmen: the room was cleared, and Anne might finish her breakfast as she could.

"It is over! it is over!" she repeated to herself again, and again, in nervous gratitude. "The worst is over!"

Mary talked, but she could not attend. She had seen him. They had met. They had been once more in the same room!

Soon, however, she began to reason with herself, and try to be feeling less. Eight years, almost eight years had passed, since all had been given up. How absurd to be resuming the agitation which such an interval had banished into distance and indistinctness! What might not eight years do? Events of every description, changes, alienations, removals, — all, all must be comprised in it; and oblivion of the past — how natural, how certain too! It included nearly a third part of her own life.

Alas! with all her reasonings, she found, that to retentive feelings eight years may be little more than nothing.[34]

28. Mary's different breakfast hours could result from her family background. Generally, the more affluent people were the later they ate breakfast: one reason was that wealthier and more fashionable people ate dinner and went to bed later. Mary probably picked up her daily habits when growing up and has maintained them, at least for breakfast, especially since they are a source of social distinction. Charles's having obviously eaten earlier may reflect, in addition to his eagerness to begin his sport, the Musgroves' lesser rank and elegance.

29. The dogs are to assist Charles and Captain Wentworth in their shooting. Dogs played two essential roles, locating the live birds by their scent and retrieving them after they had been shot. Once birds were located the standard method at the time was "shooting flying," which meant hitting the birds as they flew up in the air; the method's widespread use resulted from improvements in guns in the immediately preceding decades, which had caused it to supersede older methods of shooting birds on the ground or catching them with nets and snares. Another innovation of the period was the battue, in which birds were flushed out by beating the trees, but it was not widely practiced at this juncture.

30. *wait on:* call on.

31. Captain Wentworth's evident wish to call on Mary, when he must know Anne will be in, might suggest that he is not as averse to her as Anne suspects. But it also could be his way to pay his courtesy to Mary, and perhaps satisfy his curiosity about how Anne looks, without having to spend much time in her presence, as he would have to if he ate breakfast there.

32. Bowing and curtseying are standard greetings. In this case they allow the two people to acknowledge each other without having to speak directly to each other.

33. The rapid sequence of thoughts represents Anne's state of mind, nervous and barely able to register what is happening.

34. Anne frequently struggles to subdue her feelings and remain rational. Her inability to do so here shows both the limits of reason and the strength of these particular feelings.

Now, how were his sentiments to be read? Was this like wishing to avoid her? And the next moment she was hating herself for the folly which asked the question.[35]

On one other question, which perhaps her utmost wisdom might not have prevented, she was soon spared all suspense; for after the Miss Musgroves had returned and finished their visit at the Cottage, she had this spontaneous information from Mary:

"Captain Wentworth is not very gallant by[36] you, Anne, though he was so attentive to me. Henrietta asked him what he thought of you, when they went away; and he said, 'You were so altered he should not have known you again.' "

Mary had no feelings to make her respect her sister's in a common way; but she was perfectly unsuspicious of being inflicting[37] any peculiar[38] wound.

"Altered beyond his knowledge!" Anne fully submitted, in silent, deep mortification. Doubtless it was so; and she could take no revenge, for he was not altered, or not for the worse. She had already acknowledged it to herself, and she could not think differently, let him think of her as he would. No; the years which had destroyed her youth and bloom had only given him a more glowing, manly, open look, in no respect lessening his personal advantages. She had seen the same Frederick Wentworth.

"So altered that he should not have known her again!" These were words which could not but dwell with her. Yet she soon began to rejoice that she had heard them. They were of sobering tendency; they allayed agitation; they composed, and consequently must make her happier.[39]

Frederick Wentworth had used such words, or something like them, but without an idea that they would be carried round to her. He had thought her wretchedly altered, and, in the first moment of appeal, had spoken as he felt.[40] He had not forgiven Anne Elliot. She had used him ill; deserted and disappointed him; and worse, she had shewn a feebleness of character in doing so, which his own decided, confident temper could not endure. She had given him up to oblige others. It had been the effect of over-persuasion. It had been weakness and timidity.[41]

35. The folly is her obsessive inclination to study him constantly and try to analyze everything he does, along with, perhaps, her inclination to interpret everything he does as motivated by his feelings toward her.

36. *gallant by*: gallant to. There are other instances in Jane Austen like this; "by" was sometimes used then where "to" is used now.

37. *being inflicting*: inflicting.

38. *peculiar*: particular.

39. Anne is trying to convince and reassure herself that his words must make her happier: by convincing her that he no longer cares for her and that there is no possibility of renewing their intimacy, his words will make her cease wondering about how he feels and help her look upon him with calm indifference.

40. It is appropriate that the first action by Captain Wentworth depicted in the novel involves speaking as he feels. He will exhibit this spontaneity on a number of occasions, and it will turn out to be one of the critical differences between him and another man who will interest Anne. It will also be a notable characteristic of other naval officers.

41. These last lines, a series of short emphatic sentences, convey the decisive character of Wentworth's thoughts. They are particularly appropriate when those thoughts are expressions of contempt for timidity.

He had been most warmly attached to her, and had never seen a woman since whom he thought her equal; but, except from some natural sensation of curiosity, he had no desire of meeting her again. Her power with him was gone for ever.[42]

It was now his object to marry. He was rich, and being turned on shore,[43] fully intended to settle[44] as soon as he could be properly tempted; actually looking round, ready to fall in love with all the speed which a clear head and quick taste could allow. He had a heart for either of the Miss Musgroves, if they could catch it; a heart, in short, for any pleasing young woman who came in his way, excepting Anne Elliot. This was his only secret exception, when he said to his sister, in answer to her suppositions,[45]

"Yes, here I am, Sophia, quite ready to make a foolish match.[46] Any body between fifteen and thirty may have me for asking. A little beauty, and a few smiles, and a few compliments to the navy, and I am a lost man. Should not this be enough for a sailor, who has had no society among women to make him nice?"[47]

He said it, she knew, to be contradicted. His bright, proud eye spoke the happy conviction that he was nice; and Anne Elliot was not out of his thoughts, when he more seriously described the woman he should wish to meet with. "A strong mind, with sweetness of manner,"[48] made the first and the last of the description.

"This is the woman I want," said he. "Something a little inferior I shall of course put up with, but it must not be much. If I am a fool, I shall be a fool indeed, for I have thought on the subject more than most men."

42. As with Anne's thoughts about him, Captain Wentworth's thoughts are contradictory, and revelatory. Logically it would be odd to be so determined on never again meeting the woman one considered superior to all others. Moreover, his having such strong feelings about Anne—for the thoughts described here seem his current ones, made as he thinks back on their affair—suggests that she still has the power to occupy his mind, however much he consciously believes otherwise.

43. This means his ship is no longer sailing. The navy would quickly reduce the number of ships sailing as soon as a war ended, in part to save the considerable expense that active ships involved.

44. *settle:* marry.

45. The following dialogue is the only one in the novel that Anne is not present to witness. It thus departs from the consistent presentation of the action through her eyes. Doing this allows the author to present Captain Wentworth's ideas and motivations regarding love, for he would not reveal them in front of Anne, especially now that he is so aloof from her. It also suggests Anne is broadly correct in her analysis of him and thereby validates the observations she will continue to make about him, which will be the principal means of conveying his inner thoughts during the rest of the novel.

46. It could be asked why he is here, considering that he claims no desire to meet Anne again. He, given his fortune and personal attractions, could certainly go elsewhere and have a good chance of finding a mate. One interpretation would be that he unconsciously does wish to see her again, but there are other explanations. He may not expect to see her: knowing the Crofts are renting Kellynch Hall, he could logically expect, before he decided to come, that Anne would be gone with her family; he never met Mary and would have no reason to expect her to be offering a home for Anne in the same area. He also would wish to visit his sister, as he talks of later visiting his brother, and while there he would be happy to see what young ladies were available. If the Miss Musgroves were not here, he might soon decide to end this visit.

47. *nice:* fastidious, choosy, careful.

48. Anne inspires his ideal in both a positive and a negative way. Her sweetness of manner, or outer character, provides the standard he seeks to find elsewhere, while the weakness he believes she showed earlier has made him identify strength as the most valuable quality of mind, or inner character. His standards are high, showing that he is indeed choosy and fastidious. He has yet to meet the woman who equals Anne, yet now he seeks a woman who is even better. It is possible that his experience with her, by inspiring such high standards, is one reason he has never married.

British ships of the line, or men-of-war. Ships of this class would have two or three decks of guns.

[From A. T. Mahan, *The Life of Nelson* (Boston, 1897), p. 180]

A naval battle between a British frigate and a French frigate.

[From Constance Hill, *Jane Austen: Her Homes and Her Friends* (London, 1904), p. 42]

Naval officers dining on board ship.

[From Alfred Burton, *The Adventures of Johnny Newcome in the Navy* (London, 1818; 1904 reprint), p. 34]

The main room of the Admiralty, the central headquarters of the navy.

[From Fiona St. Aubyn, *Ackermann's Illustrated London*, illustrations by Augustus Pugin and Thomas Rowlandson (Ware, 1985), p. 54]

Chapter Eight

*F*rom this time Captain Wentworth and Anne Elliot were repeatedly in the same circle. They were soon dining in company together at Mr. Musgrove's, for the little boy's state could no longer supply his aunt with a pretence for absenting herself; and this was but the beginning of other dinings and other meetings.

Whether former feelings were to be renewed, must be brought to the proof; former times must undoubtedly be brought to the recollection of each; *they* could not but be reverted to; the year of their engagement could not but be named by him, in the little narratives or descriptions which conversation called forth. His profession qualified him, his disposition led him, to talk; and *"That* was in the year six";[1] *"That* happened before I went to sea in the year six," occurred in the course of the first evening they spent together: and though his voice did not falter, and though she had no reason to suppose his eye wandering towards her while he spoke, Anne felt the utter impossibility, from her knowledge of his mind, that he could be unvisited by remembrance any more than herself.[2] There must be the same immediate association of thought, though she was very far from conceiving it to be of equal pain.

They had no conversation together, no intercourse but what the commonest civility required. Once so much to each other! Now nothing! There *had* been a time, when of all the large party now filling the drawing-room at Uppercross, they would have found it most difficult to cease to speak to one another. With the exception, perhaps, of Admiral and Mrs. Croft, who seemed particularly attached and happy, (Anne could allow no other exception even among the married couples) there could have been no two hearts so open, no tastes so similar, no feelings so in unison, no countenances so beloved.[3] Now they were as strangers; nay,

1. The year six, i.e., 1806, was the year of Captain Wentworth's abortive wooing of Anne (it happened eight years ago, and it is now 1814).

2. Later statements by Captain Wentworth in this chapter will validate her surmise.

3. Her recollections give a powerful sense of how ideally suited the two were for each other, and thus how much has been lost by both.

Pelisse — back view. It would close completely in front.

[From Elisabeth McClellan, *Historic Dress in America, 1800–1870* (Philadelphia, 1910), p. 139]

worse than strangers, for they could never become acquainted. It was a perpetual estrangement.

When he talked, she heard the same voice, and discerned the same mind. There was a very general ignorance of all naval matters throughout the party;[4] and he was very much questioned, and especially by the two Miss Musgroves, who seemed hardly to have any eyes but for him, as to the manner of living on board, daily regulations, food, hours, &c.; and their surprise at his accounts, at learning the degree of accommodation and arrangement which was practicable, drew from him some pleasant ridicule, which reminded Anne of the early days when she too had been ignorant,[5] and she too had been accused of supposing sailors to be living on board without any thing to eat, or any cook to dress[6] it if there were, or any servant to wait, or any knife and fork to use.[7]

From thus listening and thinking, she was roused by a whisper of Mrs. Musgrove's, who, overcome by fond regrets, could not help saying,

"Ah! Miss Anne, if it had pleased Heaven to spare my poor son, I dare say he would have been just such another by this time."

Anne suppressed a smile, and listened kindly,[8] while Mrs. Musgrove relieved her heart a little more; and for a few minutes, therefore, could not keep pace with the conversation of the others. — When she could let her attention take its natural course again, she found the Miss Musgroves just fetching the navy-list,[9] — (their own navy list, the first that had ever been at Uppercross); and sitting down together to pore over it, with the professed view of finding out the ships which Captain Wentworth had commanded.

"Your first was the Asp, I remember; we will look for the Asp."

"You will not find her there. — Quite worn out and broken up. I was the last man who commanded her. — Hardly fit for service then. — Reported fit for home service for a year or two,[10] — and so I was sent off to the West Indies."[11]

The girls looked all amazement.

"The admiralty,"[12] he continued, "entertain themselves now and then, with sending a few hundred men to sea, in a ship not fit

4. It is ironic that Anne, the person Captain Wentworth avoids speaking to, is the one person, aside from the Crofts, with any knowledge of the navy.

5. Thus his growing friendship with the Miss Musgroves, which will develop into a courtship of one of them, replicates in many ways his courtship of Anne. She herself notes the parallels.

6. *dress*: prepare.

7. Naval officers attempted to live on board in the same manner that gentlemen lived onshore, so their accommodations differed significantly from the rest of the ship's company. They would have a special cook for themselves, nice eating materials including glassware, and servants (servants being seen, by those of this class, as one of the necessities of life). Those outside the navy, knowing of the size of ships and the numbers of men aboard but not of the many contrivances the navy had developed to cope with their small spaces, could easily imagine that conditions were harder than they were. For a picture of officers dining, see p. 119.

8. Anne's reaction is similar to Captain Wentworth's later. She thinks of Mrs. Musgrove's absurdity but shows outward kindness. The absurdity stems from Mrs. Musgrove's lamenting her son so extravagantly, even though when alive he "had been very little cared for at any time by his family," as well as from her projection of a completely implausible future for him.

9. They could be referring to *Steel's Original and Correct List of the Royal Navy*, a private publication that had been coming out regularly for several decades, or an official *Navy List* that the navy, inspired by Steel's example, began publishing in 1814. Both publications contained, among other things, a list of all officers in the navy, grouped according to rank and showing the date they attained that rank, and a list of active ships, including their number of guns, current station, and, in most cases, commanding officer.

10. Home service involved guarding Britain's own coasts. This, because it meant the ship could easily return to port for repairs, was more suitable for ships that were old and in poor condition.

11. The West Indies are the islands of the Caribbean. Since both Britain and its rivals France and Spain had colonies there, it was a leading center of naval action, as each country attempted to protect its own colonies and the trade with them, and to attack its enemy's. The irony in his statement is that, because the West Indies could be a dangerous place to sail (for one thing, it experiences frequent hurricanes), it would not be an ideal place to be sent in a ship only "fit for home service for a year or two."

12. The Admiralty was the official government department in charge of the navy (for a picture, see p. 119).

to be employed.[13] But they have a great many to provide for; and among the thousands that may just as well go to the bottom as not, it is impossible for them to distinguish the very set who may be least missed."[14]

"Phoo! phoo!" cried the admiral, "what stuff these young fellows talk! Never was a better sloop[15] than the Asp in her day.—For an old built sloop, you would not see her equal. Lucky fellow to get her!—He knows there must have been twenty better men than himself applying for her at the same time. Lucky fellow to get any thing so soon, with no more interest than his."[16]

"I felt my luck, admiral, I assure you"; replied Captain Wentworth, seriously.—"I was as well satisfied with my appointment as you can desire. It was a great object with me, at that time, to be at sea,—a very great object. I wanted to be doing something."[17]

"To be sure you did.—What should a young fellow, like you, do ashore, for half a year together?—If a man has not a wife, he soon wants to be afloat again."

"But, Captain Wentworth," cried Louisa, "how vexed you must have been when you came to the Asp, to see what an old thing they had given you."

"I knew pretty well what she was, before that day," said he, smiling. "I had no more discoveries to make, than you would have as to the fashion[18] and strength of any old pelisse,[19] which you had seen lent about among half your acquaintance, ever since you could remember, and which at last, on some very wet day, is lent to yourself.—Ah! she was a dear old Asp to me. She did all that I wanted. I knew she would.—I knew that we should either go to the bottom together, or that she would be the making of me; and I never had two days of foul weather all the time I was at sea in her; and after taking privateers[20] enough to be very entertaining, I had the good luck, in my passage home the next autumn, to fall in with the very French frigate I wanted.[21]—I brought her into Plymouth; and here was another instance of luck. We had not been six hours in the Sound,[22] when a gale came on, which lasted four days and nights, and which would have done for poor old

13. Constructing ships was expensive and required enormous amounts of the right type of wood (the most commonly used was oak due to its hardness). Hence the navy tried as much as possible to repair existing ships.

14. Wentworth's casual attitude toward risk reflects his own character, as well as what naval officers generally had to develop, given the hazards of their job.

15. A sloop is the smallest of the main naval vessels. It would be all he could command at this stage of his career, as only a commander.

16. Interest, or personal influence and connections, was valuable for securing ships, though, as Captain Wentworth's example shows, it was not essential. It could come from influential friends outside the navy, but came most often from senior officers one had served under and who were in a position to help those they liked and considered worthy. Many officers did not get ships at this time. War led to frequent promotions, since it was the principal way to reward brave conduct, and this created a surplus of officers at ranks fit for command.

17. This is just after Anne rejected him, something he is obviously thinking of. His statement indicates the difference in men's and women's situations. He can plunge into his work and focus his mind on that; she has no such outlet. This difference will later be an object of important discussion (p. 444).

18. *fashion:* make, form.

19. *pelisse:* a popular female overcoat, whose use was encouraged by the thin, lightweight fashions of the period. Jane Austen refers to pelisses frequently in her letters. Originally a half-length cloak, it had by this time become a close-fitting overcoat extending to the ankles (for a picture, see p. 121).

20. *privateers:* ships authorized by a government to prey on the commercial ships of an enemy; in effect, licensed pirates. France, due to the defeat of much of its navy by Britain, relied heavily on privateers for its naval efforts.

21. A frigate is larger than a sloop, so he was attacking a stronger ship. This was a common practice of the British navy. Its superior ship construction (in many cases), battle tactics, and practice in sailing and firing guns—the last a product of its ships being constantly at sea, where they would gain sailing experience and could practice firing, while French ships were mostly bottled up in port by the British—gave it advantages in any battle. Moreover, this very success gave it a confidence in its prowess that proved a further advantage. For a picture of a battle between British and French frigates, see p. 118.

22. This is Plymouth Sound, the bay leading into Plymouth, a city in southwest England and one of the main British naval bases.

Asp, in half the time; our touch with the Great Nation[23] not having much improved our condition.[24] Four-and-twenty hours later,
and I should only have been a gallant Captain Wentworth, in a
small paragraph at one corner of the newspapers,[25] and being lost
in only a sloop, nobody would have thought about me."

Anne's shudderings were to herself, alone:[26] but the Miss Musgroves could be as open as they were sincere, in their exclamations of pity and horror.

"And so then, I suppose," said Mrs. Musgrove, in a low voice, as
if thinking aloud, "so then he went away to the Laconia, and there
he met with our poor boy.—Charles, my dear, (beckoning him to
her), "do ask Captain Wentworth where it was he first met with
your poor brother. I always forget."

"It was at Gibraltar, mother, I know. Dick had been left ill at
Gibraltar, with a recommendation from his former captain to
Captain Wentworth."[27]

"Oh!—but, Charles, tell Captain Wentworth, he need not be
afraid of mentioning poor Dick before me, for it would be rather
a pleasure to hear him talked of, by such a good friend."

Charles, being somewhat more mindful of the probabilities of
the case, only nodded in reply, and walked away.

The girls were now hunting for the Laconia; and Captain
Wentworth could not deny himself the pleasure of taking the precious volume into his own hands to save them the trouble, and
once more read aloud the little statement of her name and rate,
and present non-commissioned class,[28] observing over it, that she
too had been one of the best friends man ever had.

"Ah! those were pleasant days when I had the Laconia! How
fast I made money in her.—A friend of mine, and I, had such a
lovely cruise together off the Western Islands.[29]—Poor Harville,
sister! You know how much he wanted money—worse than
myself. He had a wife.—Excellent fellow! I shall never forget his
happiness. He felt it all, so much for her sake.—I wished for him
again the next summer, when I had still the same luck in the
Mediterranean."[30]

"And I am sure, Sir," said Mrs. Musgrove, "it was a lucky day for

23. *Great Nation:* a translation of *La Grande Nation*, the name the French used for themselves in this period, thanks to their conquest of much of Europe. Wentworth's use of it has a sarcastic ring, for he, like his listeners, knows that Britain and its allies have just decisively defeated France.

24. Damage from battle would make ships less seaworthy.

25. Newspapers often printed accounts of naval matters, including stories of battles of sea. Most papers also had a special section called "Ship News," in which they listed ship arrivals and departures, as well as ships lost at sea; this helped merchants and shipowners keep track of merchant vessels, and the families of those on any kind of vessel learn the fate of loved ones.

Captain Wentworth's account of his near disaster shows the importance of chance in the navy. It also provides some validity to Lady Russell's fears about the risk Anne would have run if she had accepted his proposal.

26. Her reaction indicates he would have been missed by someone at least, though right now he may not be aware, or even wish to be aware, of that.

27. Gibraltar, which is at the bottom tip of Spain, was an important British base, because it controlled the narrow passageway between the Atlantic and the Mediterranean. As a base it could provide medical care to ill soldiers. It is possible that Dick's illness was not that serious, but his captain, wishing to get rid of him, had decided to leave him there for treatment anyway, with a recommendation sufficient to ensure that another captain took him.

28. Noncommissioned class means she is no longer in use. All ships in the British navy were rated, according to the number of guns.

29. The Western Islands is another name for the Azores, a chain of Atlantic islands west of Portugal. They would be an excellent place to make prize money, for they lie next to the route between France and its Caribbean colonies, a prime source of its overseas trade. Frigates, the type of ship he was commanding then, were especially good ships for making money, for they tended to sail on their own, attacking enemy ships. Larger ships often spent their time engaging enemy fleets, or, especially in the later part of the war, blockading those fleets; such activities provided little opportunity for captures.

30. The Mediterranean was another prime area of naval activity, for it allowed Britain to attack the coastal trade of France (and of Spain earlier, though by this point, after 1808—see chronology, p. 486—Spain was occupied by Napoleon and no longer really his ally). We will later meet Captain Harville and his wife; his children are also mentioned, and they would be a further reason for him to desire money. His not sailing again with Captain

us, when you were put captain into that ship. We shall never forget what you did."

Her feelings made her speak low; and Captain Wentworth, hearing only in part, and probably not having Dick Musgrove at all near his thoughts, looked rather in suspense, and as if waiting for more.

"My brother," whispered one of the girls; "mamma is thinking of poor Richard."

"Poor dear fellow!" continued Mrs. Musgrove; "he was grown so steady, and such an excellent correspondent, while he was under your care! Ah! it would have been a happy thing, if he had never left you. I assure you, Captain Wentworth, we are very sorry he ever left you."

There was a momentary expression in Captain Wentworth's face at this speech, a certain glance of his bright eye, and curl of his handsome mouth, which convinced Anne, that instead of sharing in Mrs. Musgrove's kind wishes, as to her son, he had probably been at some pains to get rid of him; but it was too transient an indulgence of self-amusement to be detected by any who understood him less than herself; in another moment he was perfectly collected and serious; and almost instantly afterwards coming up to the sofa, on which she and Mrs. Musgrove were sitting, took a place by the latter, and entered into conversation with her, in a low voice, about her son, doing it with so much sympathy and natural grace, as shewed the kindest consideration for all that was real and unabsurd in the parent's feelings.[31]

They were actually on the same sofa,[32] for Mrs. Musgrove had most readily made room for him;—they were divided only by Mrs. Musgrove. It was no insignificant barrier indeed. Mrs. Musgrove was of a comfortable substantial size, infinitely more fitted by nature to express good cheer and good humour, than tenderness and sentiment; and while the agitations of Anne's slender form, and pensive face, may be considered as very completely screened, Captain Wentworth should be allowed some credit for the self-command with which he attended to her large fat sighings over the destiny of a son, whom alive nobody had cared for.[33]

Wentworth may have resulted from the serious injury he is described as having suffered two years prior to the events of the novel.

31. Wentworth's willingness to do this, despite his lack of affection for Dick Musgrove, exhibits the goodness of his character. Such exhibitions are of particular value at this stage, when his resentment and aloof behavior toward Anne make it more difficult to perceive his character in a good light.

32. The sofa developed as a piece of furniture only around 1800. It quickly attained wide popularity. For a picture of a contemporary sofa, see below.

33. This continuation of the theme of Dick Musgrove, and the author's astringent comments on him and his parents' grief, shows its role in the development of the novel. The scene displays further positive qualities of Captain Wentworth, his self-command and good manners, even more in evidence through his ability to maintain them despite the absurdity, in the author's view, of the lamentations that he is called upon to console. It also links him to Anne; she had earlier, while amused inwardly by Mrs. Musgrove's laments, exercised similar self-control and manifested similar sympathy. Finally, in suggesting that grief can be excessive or absurd, even that of a parent for a dead child, it prepares for the treatment later of a character's loudly proclaimed sorrow regarding his dead fiancée, which does not prove to be very lasting.

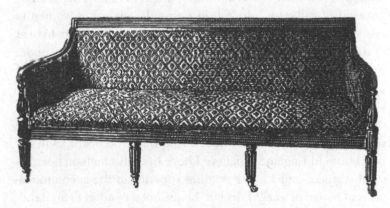

Contemporary sofa.

[From Esther Singleton, *The Furniture of Our Forefathers*, p. 643]

Personal size and mental sorrow have certainly no necessary proportions. A large bulky figure has as good a right to be in deep affliction, as the most graceful set of limbs in the world. But, fair or not fair, there are unbecoming conjunctions, which reason will patronize in vain,—which taste cannot tolerate,—which ridicule will seize.[34]

The admiral, after taking two or three refreshing turns about the room with his hands behind him,[35] being called to order by his wife,[36] now came up to Captain Wentworth, and without any observation of what he might be interrupting, thinking only of his own thoughts,[37] began with,

"If you had been a week later at Lisbon, last spring, Frederick, you would have been asked to give a passage to Lady Mary Grierson and her daughters."[38]

"Should I? I am glad I was not a week later then."

The admiral abused him for his want[39] of gallantry. He defended himself; though professing that he would never willingly admit any ladies on board a ship of his, excepting for a ball,[40] or a visit, which a few hours might comprehend.

"But, if I know myself," said he, "this is from no want of gallantry towards them. It is rather from feeling how impossible it is, with all one's efforts, and all one's sacrifices, to make the accommodations on board, such as women ought to have. There can be no want of gallantry, admiral, in rating the claims of women to every personal comfort *high*—and this is what I do. I hate to hear of women on board, or to see them on board; and no ship, under my command, shall ever convey a family of ladies any where, if I can help it."

This brought his sister upon him.

"Oh Frederick!—But I cannot believe it of you.—All idle refinement!—Women may be as comfortable on board, as in the best house in England. I believe I have lived as much on board as most women, and I know nothing superior to the accommodations of a man of war.[41] I declare I have not a comfort or an indulgence about me, even at Kellynch-hall," (with a kind bow to

34. This last statement gives a further sense of the author's perspective. She makes a distinction she frequently makes, between principles of morality and principles of taste. The former are more important, but the latter still have their value and influence. One can sympathize morally with Mrs. Musgrove's grief and believe in her right to it, while still finding its appearance ridiculous, and therefore likely to provoke amusement, even in the best persons—though such persons will, like Anne and Captain Wentworth, conceal their amusement from its target.

35. The admiral's behavior would come from long habit. Captains often walked around the area of the deck from which they commanded the ship with their hands clasped behind their back.

36. Mrs. Croft is consistently depicted as having more polished manners than her husband; she probably has past experience calling him to order when he is doing things, like walking around instead of sitting when at a social gathering, that would not be considered polite.

37. The admiral's peremptory air would be a natural product of his years spent commanding ships.

38. Lisbon, a port, is the capital of Portugal, a strong British ally against Napoleon. It provided the base for Wellington's army, which fought the French in Spain during the period being discussed; this made it an important location for the British navy, which supplied the army.

39. *want:* lack.

40. Balls on ships could be organized by the captain. They would occur while the ship was in port, which meant the women who came would not be sailing with it. Entertainments were often organized for the ship while it was docked.

41. A man-of-war, or ship of the line, was the largest type of ship in the navy. An enormous craft, it contained anywhere from 64 to 120 cannons, placed on two or three decks, and was staffed by as many as 800 men. It was used to fight enemy warships and thus took the lead at all major battles. Its size, and the high rank and importance of those commanding it, meant that a man-of-war had the most spacious and luxurious accommodations of any naval ship. For a picture, see p. 118.

Anne) "beyond what I always had in most of the ships I have lived in; and they have been five altogether."

"Nothing to the purpose," replied her brother. "You were living with your husband; and were the only woman on board."

"But you, yourself, brought Mrs. Harville, her sister, her cousin, and the three children, round from Portsmouth to Plymouth.[42] Where was this superfine, extraordinary sort of gallantry of yours, then?"

"All merged in my friendship, Sophia. I would assist any brother officer's wife that I could, and I would bring any thing of Harville's from the world's end, if he wanted it. But do not imagine that I did not feel it an evil[43] in itself."

"Depend upon it they were all perfectly comfortable."

"I might not like them the better for that, perhaps. Such a number of women and children have no *right* to be comfortable on board."[44]

"My dear Frederick, you are talking quite idly. Pray, what would become of us poor sailors' wives, who often want to be conveyed to one port or another, after our husbands, if every body had your feelings?"

"My feelings, you see, did not prevent my taking Mrs. Harville, and all her family, to Plymouth."

"But I hate to hear you talking so, like a fine gentleman, and as if women were all fine ladies,[45] instead of rational creatures. We none of us expect to be in smooth water all our days."[46]

"Ah! my dear," said the admiral, "when he has got a wife, he will sing a different tune. When he is married, if we have the good luck to live to another war,[47] we shall see him do as you and I, and a great many others, have done. We shall have him very thankful to any body that will bring him his wife."

"Ay, that we shall."

"Now I have done," cried Captain Wentworth—"When once married people begin to attack me with, 'Oh! you will think very differently, when you are married,' I can only say, 'No, I shall not'; and then they say again, 'Yes, you will,' and there is an end of it."

He got up and moved away.

42. Portsmouth, the most important British naval base, was approximately 150 miles from Plymouth (see map, p. 512), so he did not take these passengers a long distance.

43. *evil*: bad thing; the word then had a weaker connotation than now.

44. Naval ships were staffed only by men. Women could be transported in them and sometimes captains' wives would accompany them. Jane Austen's brother Charles, as captain, had his wife and children on board for a while.

There are several additional reasons for Captain Wentworth to object to women on board that he could not mention before mixed company. One is that sailors were notorious for profane language. Another is that naval discipline could involve harsh physical punishments, including repeated floggings of bare-backed men before the entire ship's company. A third is that while ships were in port it was normal for large numbers of prostitutes to come on board ship, often smuggling liquor with them. The reason was that because most crewmen had been pressed into service against their will, they were kept on board while the ship was docked to keep them from deserting, but experience had shown that, if never allowed to carouse and get sexual satisfaction during their years in service, they could become extremely discontented. One officer commented, not untypically, about these episodes: "The whole of the shocking, disgraceful transactions of the lower deck it is impossible to describe" (Brian Lavery, *Nelson's Navy*, p. 210).

His attitude, which clearly contrasts with Admiral Croft's, may also be spurred by his rejection by Anne. It had meant he could never take his own beloved on board, and it may have made him, while at sea, dislike seeing women because they reminded him of what he had lost.

45. *fine*: refined, dainty, fastidious. Mrs. Croft is using the term in an at least partly pejorative sense, and applying it to both gentlemen and ladies.

46. This is a natural metaphor for a naval wife to use, especially one frequently at sea. It also harkens to a passage in a poem, "Henry and Emma," alluded to later (see p. 223, note 94). There Emma, vowing her eternal love for Henry, responds to his warning that she will face rough times with him:

> Thy Rise of Fortune did I only wed,
> From it's Decline determined to recede?
> Did I but purpose to embark with Thee,
> On the smooth Surface of a Summer's Sea . . .
> But would forsake the Ship, and make the Shoar,
> When the Winds whistle, and the Tempests roar?

47. His good luck would result from the superior chance to make money in war from capturing enemy ships. The admiral's statement also reflects a general acceptance of war at this time. While not regarded as good, it was seen as a natural fact of life, and few people protested against war or imagined a future state in which it would not be a regular occurrence.

"What a great traveller you must have been, ma'am!" said Mrs. Musgrove to Mrs. Croft.

"Pretty well, ma'am, in the fifteen years of my marriage; though many women have done more. I have crossed the Atlantic four times, and have been once to the East Indies, and back again; and only once,[48] besides being in different places about home—Cork, and Lisbon, and Gibraltar.[49] But I never went beyond the Streights[50]—and never was in the West Indies. We do not call Bermuda or Bahama, you know, the West Indies."[51]

Mrs. Musgrove had not a word to say in dissent; she could not accuse herself of having ever called them any thing in the whole course of her life.

"And I do assure you, ma'am," pursued Mrs. Croft, "that nothing can exceed the accommodations of a man of war; I speak, you know, of the higher rates.[52] When you come to a frigate, of course, you are more confined—though any reasonable woman may be perfectly happy in one of them; and I can safely say, that the happiest part of my life has been spent on board a ship. While we were together, you know, there was nothing to be feared. Thank God! I have always been blessed with excellent health, and no climate disagrees with me. A little disordered always the first twenty-four hours of going to sea, but never knew what sickness was afterwards. The only time that I ever really suffered in body or mind, the only time that I ever fancied myself unwell, or had any ideas of danger, was the winter that I passed by myself at Deal, when the Admiral (*Captain* Croft then) was in the North Seas.[53] I lived in perpetual fright at that time, and had all manner of imaginary complaints from not knowing what to do with myself, or when I should hear from him next; but as long as we could be together, nothing ever ailed me, and I never met with the smallest inconvenience."

"Ay, to be sure.—Yes, indeed, oh yes, I am quite of your opinion, Mrs. Croft," was Mrs. Musgrove's hearty answer. "There is nothing so bad as a separation. I am quite of your opinion. *I* know what it is, for Mr. Musgrove always attends the assizes,[54] and I am so glad when they are over, and he is safe back again."

48. The East Indies are India and the islands of Southeast Asia; Admiral Croft served there (see p. 41, note 37). They required a long time to reach from Britain in a sailing ship, which is why Mrs. Croft mentions the voyage there and back.

49. Cork is in southern Ireland, which was ruled by Britain then. That it, and Lisbon and Gibraltar—already mentioned, and around a thousand miles from Britain—are called "places about home" demonstrates the sense of perspective and scale generated by the navy's wide-ranging activities.

50. The Streights are the Straits of Gibraltar, the entrance to the Mediterranean, where many British ships went.

51. Bermuda and the Bahamas are near the islands of the Caribbean and so could be included in the West Indies, and probably are by some, to judge from Mrs. Croft's explaining the distinction to her listener. Her scrupulous precision in detailing where she went indicates the sharp mind, and honesty, that will continue to characterize her.

52. See p. 127, note 28, for ship ratings; and p. 131, note 41, for man-of-war. The navy had six rates, or levels; the top three comprised the men-of-war.

53. Deal is a city in southeast England that was a naval base. It would be a good base for a ship patrolling the North Sea, the sea between Britain and Scandinavia. It is not certain, however, if that is what is meant by North Seas, plural. *The Oxford English Dictionary* defines that as "seas of the northern hemisphere," though its last example of this usage is from 1706.

54. The assizes were courts held in each county. A small number of judges were at the pinnacle of the English legal system, and they all resided in London. To enable the most serious cases in the provinces to be tried—magistrates, or justices of the peace, handled less serious cases there—pairs of judges would go on circuit to each region of England and hear cases in every county. In most counties, including Somerset, this occurred twice a year and was the most important event in the county calendar, conducted with elaborate public ceremony and attended by leading local figures. As a prominent landowner, Mr. Musgrove would be a natural attendee.

At the same time, he would be running no risk in attending, except that of a carriage accident while traveling back and forth. Such accidents did occur, perhaps even more than automobile ones now, and could be fatal, but they paled in comparison to the dangers run by naval officers, whether from the sea, accidents on board, disease, or enemy ships. Moreover, assizes generally lasted a short time, so Mr. Musgrove's absence would be nothing like the months, or even years, of those in the navy. Hence Mrs. Musgrove, in comparing her experience with Mrs. Croft's, is only being ridiculous and giving further indication of her complete ignorance of naval matters.

The evening ended with dancing. On its being proposed, Anne offered her services, as usual, and though her eyes would sometimes fill with tears as she sat at the instrument, she was extremely glad to be employed, and desired nothing in return but to be unobserved.[55]

It was a merry, joyous party, and no one seemed in higher spirits than Captain Wentworth. She felt that he had every thing to elevate him, which general attention and deference, and especially the attention of all the young women could do. The Miss Hayters, the females of the family of cousins already mentioned, were apparently admitted to the honour of being in love with him; and as for Henrietta and Louisa, they both seemed so entirely occupied by him, that nothing but the continued appearance of the most perfect good-will between themselves, could have made it credible that they were not decided rivals.[56] If he were a little spoilt by such universal, such eager admiration, who could wonder?

These were some of the thoughts which occupied Anne, while her fingers were mechanically at work, proceeding for half an hour together, equally without error, and without consciousness. Once she felt that he was looking at herself—observing her altered features, perhaps, trying to trace in them the ruins of the face which had once charmed him; and once she knew that he must have spoken of her;[57]—she was hardly aware of it, till she heard the answer; but then she was sure of his having asked his partner whether Miss Elliot[58] never danced? The answer was, "Oh! no, never; she has quite given up dancing. She had rather play. She is never tired of playing."[59] Once, too, he spoke to her. She had left the instrument on the dancing being over, and he had sat down to try to make out an air which he wished to give the Miss Musgroves an idea of.[60] Unintentionally she returned to that part of the room; he saw her, and, instantly rising, said, with studied politeness,

"I beg your pardon, madam,[61] this is your seat"; and though she immediately drew back with a decided negative, he was not to be induced to sit down again.

55. Anne's tears, and actions, serve as a reminder of her in a chapter that necessarily keeps her in the background. Her actions also show her continued usefulness despite her distress, as well as how her habits of employment, and of fortitude, make things easier for her by keeping her from wallowing in her emotion, and thereby possibly behaving in a way, such as by crying openly, that would attract the attention from others that she dreads.

56. Their lack of rivalry indicates the good characters of the two sisters. Two sisters in *Mansfield Park*, previously on good terms, develop strong feelings of rivalry and jealousy toward each other due to interest in the same man.

57. Thus even amidst her mechanical playing her senses are still attuned to what he might be doing.

58. "Miss Elliot" is the correct way for someone not related to her to speak of her now, when her elder sister is gone, and therefore no need exists to say "Miss Anne Elliot" to distinguish the two.

59. Most of the characters who dance in Jane Austen's novels are young people, who would naturally be more drawn to what she calls in *Emma* "the felicities of rapid motion," and who would have more strength for it (each pair of dances, which is what people would be expected to stand up for at a minimum, would last half an hour, and whole balls could last many hours). Yet Anne, at twenty-seven and in apparent good health, would still be perfectly fit for participating—this fitness is what helps inspire the question. The answer suggests that she has even ceased dancing at the local balls given by her elder sister, but it is doubtful this answer resulted from careful reflection. It may be Captain Wentworth's presence that helps keep Anne off the floor. The answer also keeps him from conceiving that at least part of the reason for her playing the instrument rather than dancing is her wish and willingness to be helpful to others.

60. To make out an air, or melody, on the pianoforte would presumably require some knowledge of the instrument. This would be unusual for a man at this time: music, while strongly promoted as an accomplishment for ladies, was generally scorned as a subject of study for gentlemen. It thus indicates the strength of his love of music, referred to elsewhere (p. 342). That love had earlier made him so ideally suited to Anne: now, in a truly painful irony for her, the same love leads to an encounter that mortifies her by revealing the extent of his coldness to her—a coldness that contrasts notably with his behavior in the rest of the scene, in which "no one seemed in higher spirits than Captain Wentworth."

61. His use of "madam" is very formal and indicates his aloofness. It was mostly employed in letters, with the less formal "ma'am" preferred in speech, and even the latter was mostly used for addressing older women.

Anne did not wish for more of such looks and speeches. His cold politeness, his ceremonious grace,[62] were worse than any thing.

62. *grace:* kindness, favor.

British admiral of the time.

[From William Alexander, *Picturesque Representations
of the Dress & Manners of the English* (1813)]

Chapter Nine

Captain Wentworth was come to Kellynch as to a home, to stay as long as he liked, being as thoroughly the object of the Admiral's fraternal kindness as of his wife's. He had intended, on first arriving, to proceed very soon into Shropshire,[1] and visit the brother settled in that county, but the attractions of Uppercross induced him to put this off. There was so much of friendliness, and of flattery, and of every thing most bewitching in his reception there; the old were so hospitable, the young so agreeable, that he could not but resolve to remain where he was, and take all the charms and perfections of Edward's wife upon credit a little longer.

It was soon Uppercross with him almost every day. The Musgroves could hardly be more ready to invite than he to come, particularly in the morning, when he had no companion at home, for the Admiral and Mrs. Croft were generally out of doors together, interesting themselves in their new possessions, their grass, and their sheep,[2] and dawdling about in a way not endurable to a third person, or driving out in a gig,[3] lately added to their establishment.[4]

Hitherto there had been but one opinion of Captain Wentworth, among the Musgroves and their dependencies. It was unvarying, warm admiration every where. But this intimate footing was not more than established, when a certain Charles Hayter returned among them, to be a good deal disturbed by it, and to think Captain Wentworth very much in the way.

Charles Hayter was the eldest of all the cousins, and a very amiable, pleasing young man, between whom and Henrietta there had been a considerable appearance of attachment previous to Captain Wentworth's introduction. He was in orders,[5] and having a curacy in the neighbourhood where residence was not required,[6]

1. Shropshire is a county north of Somerset (see map, p. 512).

2. The grass would be part of the park around Kellynch (see p. 35, note 16). The grass is being grazed by sheep to keep it low, which would be necessary to preserve its appearance and to make it suitable for walking (grass not serving those purposes could be allowed to grow and then harvested for hay). This would also provide nourishment for the sheep, one of the most popular types of livestock in Britain, cultivated for wool and for food.

3. *gig*: an open two-wheeled carriage. It was the most popular of open carriages and would be a good choice for riding about the countryside when the weather was not inclement. For more on their specific choice of a gig, see p. 177, note 79.

4. *establishment*: household.

5. *in orders*: qualified as a clergyman in the Church of England.

6. A curacy is a position as a curate, someone hired to fulfill the duties of the person holding a clerical position (for more, see p. 45, note 48). Residence would frequently be required for curacies so that the curate could perform the duties well, but in this case Charles Hayter's residence in the neighborhood means he would be able to go to the parish often. The most essential duties were performing the Sunday service and presiding at baptisms, weddings, and funerals, and these would not require a constant presence.

lived at his father's house, only two miles from Uppercross. A short absence from home had left his fair one[7] unguarded by his attentions at this critical period, and when he came back he had the pain of finding very altered manners,[8] and of seeing Captain Wentworth.

Mrs. Musgrove and Mrs. Hayter were sisters.[9] They had each had money, but their marriages had made a material difference in their degree of consequence.[10] Mr. Hayter had some property of his own, but it was insignificant compared with Mr. Musgrove's; and while the Musgroves were in the first class of society in the country, the young Hayters would, from their parents' inferior, retired, and unpolished way of living, and their own defective education, have been hardly in any class at all, but for their connexion with Uppercross; this eldest son of course excepted, who had chosen to be a scholar and a gentleman,[11] and who was very superior in cultivation and manners to all the rest.

The two families had always been on excellent terms, there being no pride on one side, and no envy on the other, and only such a consciousness of superiority in the Miss Musgroves, as made them pleased to improve their cousins.—Charles's attentions to Henrietta had been observed by her father and mother without any disapprobation. "It would not be a great match for her; but if Henrietta liked him,—and Henrietta *did* seem to like him."

Henrietta fully thought so herself, before Captain Wentworth came; but from that time Cousin Charles had been very much forgotten.

Which of the two sisters was preferred by Captain Wentworth was as yet quite doubtful, as far as Anne's observation reached. Henrietta was perhaps the prettiest, Louisa had the higher spirits; and she knew not *now*, whether the more gentle or the more lively character were most likely to attract him.

Mr. and Mrs. Musgrove, either from seeing little, or from an entire confidence in the discretion of both their daughters, and of all the young men who came near them, seemed to leave every thing to take its chance.[12] There was not the smallest appearance

7. *fair one:* lady, i.e., member of the fairer sex.

8. *manners:* outward behavior—specifically Henrietta's toward him.

9. Among the landed classes at this time, marriage between cousins, even first cousins, was completely acceptable (those lower in the social scale were more likely to regard it as incestuous). *Mansfield Park* concludes with the marriage of the hero and heroine, who are first cousins. One reason for this elite attitude was that marriage between cousins could consolidate family wealth, sometimes even by uniting two different estates—in this case that is not a factor.

Another reason, which does apply here, was the limited population of the landed classes, which restricted the number of suitable marriage partners, and thus made people prefer not to exclude relatives from consideration. Among the high aristocracy, which set standards that others followed, the number of possible partners was especially limited. The lower-ranking gentry, portrayed here, was much larger in number, but their resources usually restricted their socializing to their immediate rural neighborhood, and any particular neighborhood rarely contained more than a handful of elite families. The main characters in this novel come from a few families and spend all their time with one another; a similar pattern prevails in other Jane Austen novels. As for marriage choices, Elizabeth Elliot has found no suitable man pursuing her since her disappointment with William Elliot, Anne has seen no one suitable since Captain Wentworth, and Charles Musgrove directed his proposals, in succession, to two daughters of the only other prominent family in the vicinity.

10. *consequence:* social position.

11. Among the meanings of "scholar" was someone attending a university, and someone who was well-educated. Both could be applicable here. Study at Oxford or Cambridge, the only two English universities then, was the principal way for someone to become qualified for the clergy, which in turn would automatically confer gentleman status on him. Becoming well-educated would also be a way for Charles Hayter to distinguish himself, and thereby help people forget about his less genteel origins. At this time, people who were from modest social levels rarely received much education.

12. The Musgroves' behavior suggests some of the problems that could result from their easygoing manners. Confusion about marital intentions later develops regarding Captain Wentworth and one of their daughters, and had events transpired differently, and had he been less than highly honorable, that daughter could have been left with a broken heart and possibly some degree of social humiliation (see p. 463, note 88).

of solicitude or remark[13] about them, in the Mansion-house; but it was different at the Cottage: the young couple there were more disposed to speculate and wonder; and Captain Wentworth had not been above four or five times in the Miss Musgroves' company, and Charles Hayter had but just reappeared, when Anne had to listen to the opinions of her brother and sister, as to *which* was the one liked best. Charles gave it for Louisa, Mary for Henrietta, but quite agreeing that to have him marry either would be extremely delightful.

Charles "had never seen a pleasanter man in his life; and from what he had once heard Captain Wentworth himself say, was very sure that he had not made less than twenty thousand pounds by the war.[14] Here was a fortune at once; besides which, there would be the chance of what might be done in any future war; and he was sure Captain Wentworth was as likely a man to distinguish himself as any officer in the navy. Oh! it would be a capital match for either of his sisters."

"Upon my word it would," replied Mary. "Dear me! If he should rise to any very great honours! If he should ever be made a Baronet![15] 'Lady Wentworth' sounds very well. That would be a noble thing, indeed, for Henrietta! She would take place of me then,[16] and Henrietta would not dislike that. Sir Frederick and Lady Wentworth! It would be but a new creation, however, and I never think much of your new creations."[17]

It suited Mary best to think Henrietta the one preferred, on the very account of Charles Hayter, whose pretensions she wished to see put an end to. She looked down very decidedly upon the Hayters, and thought it would be quite a misfortune to have the existing connexion between the families renewed—very sad for herself and her children.

"You know," said she, "I cannot think him at all a fit match for Henrietta; and considering the alliances[18] which the Musgroves have made, she has no right to throw herself away. I do not think any young woman has a right to make a choice that may be disagreeable and inconvenient to the *principal* part of her family,[19] and be giving bad connexions[20] to those who have not been used

13. *remark*: observation or comment, often of a critical nature.

14. His fortune is elsewhere specified as 25,000 pounds. At the standard investment return, from government bonds, of 5%, this would give him 1,250 pounds a year, a sum that would make him, and any wife of his, very comfortable, though not as rich as many landowners. As regards present monetary values, a pound then was approximately the equivalent, measured in purchasing power, of 55 pounds today (2010), or 80 to 85 dollars at current exchange rates. Thus Wentworth's annual income would be $100,000 or a little more.

These comparisons are tricky, for relative economic costs have changed greatly. Goods have become much cheaper since then, and labor much more expensive. Thus at that time, purchases of books or clothing or household furnishings could absorb a large portion of people's income, and even the wealthy had to be careful about them, but many people could afford live-in servants, with wealthy families having many, sometimes dozens, and even middle-class families having one or two. But, however his wealth is calculated in today's terms, at the time Captain Wentworth's fortune would have put him in the richest one percent of the population.

15. Naval officers could be given honors like baronetcies for distinguished service. Earlier Sir Walter discussed an officer who had been made a lord, which was even higher.

16. This would be by rules of precedence (see p. 89, note 31). The wife of a baronet would supersede the daughter of a baronet like Mary.

17. The newer a title was the less prestigious. Mary's father was shown looking down on those baronetcies that were granted later than his (p. 2).

18. *alliances*: marriages, or unions (with other families) through marriage.

19. By principal part of the family Mary means herself, husband, and children, for Charles, as the eldest son, will eventually inherit the Musgrove property, and thus be the leading member of the family. The idea of obligations to one's family, including in marital decisions, was standard in this society, though that mostly meant one's parents. Few would have argued for a binding duty to avoid marrying someone who was looked down upon by one's brother and his wife.

20. *connexions*: connections, that is, family ties or relationships (including those formed by marriage).

to them. And, pray, who is Charles Hayter? Nothing but a country curate.[21] A most improper match for Miss Musgrove,[22] of
Uppercross."

Her husband, however, would not agree with her here; for
besides having a regard for his cousin, Charles Hayter was an
eldest son, and he saw things as an eldest son himself.[23]

"Now you are talking nonsense, Mary," was therefore his
answer. "It would not be a *great* match for Henrietta, but Charles
has a very fair chance, through the Spicers, of getting something
from the Bishop in the course of a year or two;[24] and you will
please to remember, that he is the eldest son; whenever my uncle
dies, he steps into very pretty property. The estate at Winthrop is
not less than two hundred and fifty acres, besides the farm near
Taunton,[25] which is some of the best land in the country.[26] I grant
you, that any of them but Charles would be a very shocking match
for Henrietta, and indeed it could not be;[27] he is the only one that
could be possible; but he is a very good-natured, good sort of a fellow; and whenever Winthrop comes into his hands, he will make
a different sort of place of it, and live in a very different sort of way;
and with that property, he will never be a contemptible man.
Good, freehold property.[28] No, no; Henrietta might do worse than
marry Charles Hayter; and if she has him, and Louisa can get Captain Wentworth, I shall be very well satisfied."

"Charles may say what he pleases," cried Mary to Anne, as soon
as he was out of the room, "but it would be shocking to have Henrietta marry Charles Hayter; a very bad thing for *her,* and still
worse for *me;* and therefore it is very much to be wished that Captain Wentworth may soon put him quite out of her head, and I
have very little doubt that he has. She took hardly any notice of
Charles Hayter yesterday. I wish you had been there to see her
behaviour. And as to Captain Wentworth's liking Louisa as well as
Henrietta, it is nonsense to say so; for he certainly *does* like Henrietta a great deal the best. But Charles is so positive! I wish you
had been with us yesterday, for then you might have decided
between us; and I am sure you would have thought as I did, unless
you had been determined to give it against me."

21. Curates had a low status, relative to other gentlemen, and low incomes (see p. 45, note 48).

22. She uses a more formal title here, rather than "Henrietta" as she has been saying, to emphasize Henrietta's social status, and thus her social superiority to Charles Hayter. Her use of "Miss Musgrove," rather than "Miss Henrietta Musgrove," indicates that Henrietta is the eldest sister. At a few points later Louisa is called "Miss Louisa" or "Miss Louisa Musgrove," titles appropriate for a younger sister.

23. Eldest sons were the ones who inherited the family property.

24. Charles could mean that the Spicers control a church living, or position, and will present Charles Hayter to the bishop of the diocese, who would then, as required, officially grant the appointment. Approximately half the livings in England were controlled by individual families such as the Spicers. Charles could also mean that the bishop himself controls the living—as was true of around ten percent of livings—and will appoint Charles Hayter on the basis of a personal recommendation from the Spicers. Such exercise of personal connections and influence was standard in both the church and society at this time.

25. An estate normally meant a substantial piece of property, though this one is not that large by the standards of estates. A farm meant a piece of land that one rented from the owner and could cultivate in order to get the profits above the rental payments (for more, see p. 45, note 43). A farm would therefore be less valuable, though in this case, since Charles goes on to praise the quality of the land, it could bring in substantial profits. All this would be on top of Charles Hayter's income as a clergyman (to avoid interference with his clerical duties, he could hire people to take care of cultivating the land he owns or rents).

26. *country*: county.

27. Charles's comment indicates how important social status is, even for those like the Musgroves, who are more relaxed about it than the Elliots.

28. Freehold property is owned outright. This is what principally distinguishes the estate at Winthrop from the farm Charles also mentioned, and naturally freehold property is considered better than rented property.

A dinner at Mr. Musgrove's had been the occasion, when all these things should[29] have been seen by Anne; but she had staid at home, under the mixed plea of a headache of her own, and some return of indisposition in little Charles. She had thought only of avoiding Captain Wentworth; but an escape from being appealed to as umpire was now added to the advantages of a quiet evening.

As to Captain Wentworth's views, she deemed it of more consequence that he should know his own mind, early enough not to be endangering the happiness of either sister, or impeaching his own honour,[30] than that he should prefer Henrietta to Louisa, or Louisa to Henrietta. Either of them would, in all probability, make him an affectionate, good-humoured wife. With regard to Charles Hayter, she had delicacy[31] which must be pained by any lightness[32] of conduct in a well-meaning young woman, and a heart to sympathize in any of the sufferings it occasioned;[33] but if Henrietta found herself mistaken in the nature of her feelings, the alteration could not be understood too soon.

Charles Hayter had met with much to disquiet and mortify him in his cousin's behaviour. She had too old a regard for him to be so wholly estranged, as might in two meetings extinguish every past hope, and leave him nothing to do but to keep away from Uppercross; but there was such a change as became very alarming, when such a man as Captain Wentworth was to be regarded as the probable cause. He had been absent only two Sundays; and when they parted, had left her interested even to the height of his wishes, in his prospect of soon quitting his present curacy, and obtaining that of Uppercross instead. It had then seemed the object nearest her heart, that Dr. Shirley, the rector,[34] who for more than forty years had been zealously discharging all the duties of his office,[35] but was now growing too infirm for many of them, should be quite fixed on engaging a curate; should make his curacy quite as good as he could afford,[36] and should give Charles Hayter the promise of it. The advantage of his having to come only to Uppercross, instead of going six miles another way; of his having, in every respect, a better curacy; of his belonging to

29. *should:* would.

30. He would impeach, or discredit, his honor because in that day a man was never supposed to woo a woman he was not seriously interested in, and since he could not marry two women, making advances toward two would mean inevitably abandoning one. It is notable that Anne, despite the pain she feels from seeing his flirtation with other women, concentrates her reflections on the dangers posed to others' happiness or honor.

31. *delicacy:* sensitivity for the feelings of others.

32. *lightness:* fickleness, thoughtlessness, frivolity.

33. In addition to her general concerns, she would feel a natural identification with someone spurned by the person he or she loves and forced to watch that person flirting with another.

34. A rector was a clergyman entitled to all the tithes from his parish. A vicar, the other principal type, was entitled to only some of the tithes. Since tithes constituted much of a clergyman's income, a rector was generally in a superior position (though, since the incomes from clerical positions varied widely, due to the great differences in the size and wealth of parishes, there were vicars who were wealthier than rectors).

35. His zeal is shown by his not engaging a curate to take over his work, even though he is apparently getting old. Since curates could often be hired cheaply, and since, as a rector, it is likely the income from his position is good, he would probably still be able to live well after the expense of a curate. Many clergy at the time did not show such zeal, though there was a movement to encourage greater devotion and stricter performance of duties.

36. Henrietta would naturally wish this, and was probably, in articulating this wish, aware that many curates were hired at salaries far below what the person hiring them could afford.

their dear Dr. Shirley, and of dear, good Dr. Shirley's being relieved from the duty which he could no longer get through without most injurious fatigue, had been a great deal, even to Louisa, but had been almost every thing to Henrietta. When he came back, alas! the zeal of the business was gone by. Louisa could not listen at all to his account of a conversation which he had just held with Dr. Shirley: she was at window, looking out for Captain Wentworth; and even Henrietta had at best only a divided attention to give, and seemed to have forgotten all the former doubt and solicitude of the negociation.[37]

"Well, I am very glad indeed, but I always thought you would have it; I always thought you sure. It did not appear to me that— In short, you know, Dr. Shirley *must* have a curate, and you had secured his promise.[38] Is he coming, Louisa?"

One morning, very soon after the dinner at the Musgroves, at which Anne had not been present, Captain Wentworth walked into the drawing-room at the Cottage, where were only herself and the little invalid Charles, who was lying on the sofa.

The surprise of finding himself almost alone with Anne Elliot, deprived his manners of their usual composure: he started, and could only say, "I thought the Miss Musgroves had been here— Mrs. Musgrove told me I should find them here," before he walked to the window to recollect himself, and feel how he ought to behave.

"They are up stairs with my sister—they will be down in a few moments, I dare say,"—had been Anne's reply,[39] in all the confusion that was natural; and if the child had not called her to come and do something for him, she would have been out of the room the next moment, and released Captain Wentworth as well as herself.

He continued at the window; and after calmly and politely saying, "I hope the little boy is better," was silent.[40]

She was obliged to kneel down by the sofa, and remain there to satisfy her patient; and thus they continued a few minutes, when, to her very great satisfaction, she heard some other person crossing the little vestibule. She hoped, on turning her head, to see the

37. Henrietta's fickleness suggests the limitations of her character. It also foreshadows similar behavior on the part of her highly similar sister later in the novel.

38. Eventual clerical retirement was standard, though there was nothing to force it. Jane Austen's father eventually retired from his duties as a clergyman and moved with his family to Bath. He hired a curate to replace him while continuing, like any such clergyman, to receive the income from the position.

39. He, as a nonrelated man, would never go upstairs to where the bedrooms were.

40. In seeing her nurse the boy Wentworth has an opportunity to witness Anne's willingness to help others, and the skill and gentleness with which she provides that help. In *Pride and Prejudice* the hero, Darcy, is first alerted to the good moral qualities of the heroine, Elizabeth, by seeing her devotedly nurse her ill sister.

master of the house; but it proved to be one much less calculated for making matters easy—Charles Hayter, probably not at all better pleased by the sight of Captain Wentworth, than Captain Wentworth had been by the sight of Anne.

She only attempted to say, "How do you do? Will not you sit down? The others will be here presently."

Captain Wentworth, however, came from his window, apparently not ill-disposed for conversation; but Charles Hayter soon put an end to his attempts, by seating himself near the table, and taking up the newspaper; and Captain Wentworth returned to his window.

Another minute brought another addition. The younger boy, a remarkable stout,[41] forward[42] child, of two years old, having got the door opened for him by some one without, made his determined appearance among them, and went straight to the sofa to see what was going on, and put in his claim to any thing good that might be giving away.[43]

There being nothing to be eat, he could only have some play; and as his aunt would not let him teaze[44] his sick brother, he began to fasten himself upon her, as she knelt, in such a way that, busy as she was about Charles, she could not shake him off. She spoke to him—ordered, intreated, and insisted in vain. Once she did contrive to push him away, but the boy had the greater pleasure in getting upon her back again directly.

"Walter," said she, "get down this moment. You are extremely troublesome. I am very angry with you."

"Walter," cried Charles Hayter, "why do you not do as you are bid? Do not you hear your aunt speak? Come to me, Walter, come to cousin Charles."

But not a bit did Walter stir.

In another moment, however, she found herself in the state of being released from him; some one was taking him from her, though he had bent down her head so much, that his little sturdy hands were unfastened from around her neck, and he was resolutely borne away, before she knew that Captain Wentworth had done it.[45]

41. *stout:* vigorous, strong. The meaning of "bulky" or "overweight" was just coming into usage at this time and was still not the standard one.

42. *forward:* precocious, bold.

43. *giving away:* being given away; see also p. 95, note 61, on this construction.

44. *teaze:* tease, meaning, in this case, bother or disturb.

45. The nineteenth-century American novelist William Dean Howells commented, regarding this scene of rescue by Captain Wentworth, "As any practiced reader of fiction could easily demonstrate, this is not the sort of rescue to bring about a reconciliation between lovers in a *true* novel. There it must be something more formidable than a naughty little boy that the heroine is saved from: it must be a deadly miscreant, or a mad bull, or a frightened horse, or an express train, or a sinking ship. Still it cannot be denied that this simple, this homely scene, is very pretty, and is very like things that happen in life, where there is reason to think that love is oftener shown in quality than quantity, and does its effect as perfectly in the little as in the great events" (from *Heroines of Fiction*).

Her sensations on the discovery made her perfectly speechless. She could not even thank him. She could only hang over little Charles, with most disordered feelings. His kindness in stepping forward to her relief—the manner—the silence in which it had passed—the little particulars of the circumstance—with the conviction soon forced on her by the noise he was studiously making with the child, that he meant to avoid hearing her thanks, and rather sought to testify that her conversation was the last of his wants,[46] produced such a confusion of varying, but very painful agitation, as she could not recover from, till enabled by the entrance of Mary and the Miss Musgroves to make over her little patient to their cares, and leave the room. She could not stay. It might have been an opportunity of watching the loves and jealousies of the four; they were now all together, but she could stay for none of it. It was evident that Charles Hayter was not well inclined towards Captain Wentworth. She had a strong impression of his having said, in a vext[47] tone of voice, after Captain Wentworth's interference, "You ought to have minded *me*, Walter; I told you not to teaze your aunt"; and could comprehend his regretting that Captain Wentworth should do what he ought to have done himself. But neither Charles Hayter's feelings, nor any body's feelings, could interest her, till she had a little better arranged her own. She was ashamed of herself, quite ashamed of being so nervous, so overcome by such a trifle; but so it was; and it required a long application of solitude and reflection to recover her.[48]

46. In the next chapter, when performing another service for Anne, he will show a similar disinclination to converse with her about it. She assumes, along the lines she has been consistently thinking, that his aversion to conversation results from continued aloofness toward her, and that is certainly plausible. But it may also result from simple dislike of thanks. Mr. Knightley, the hero of Jane Austen's previous novel, *Emma*, and a man with some similar qualities to Captain Wentworth, is described as having a particular aversion to being thanked for the many services he renders others.

47. *vext*: vexed, annoyed.

48. Her inability to feel interest in anyone else's feelings because of her own, while normal for most people, represents a departure from Anne's usual altruistic spirit. It indicates how much the incident, despite its trivial nature, has affected her.

Chapter Ten

Other opportunities of making her observations could not fail to occur. Anne had soon been in company with all the four together often enough to have an opinion, though too wise to acknowledge as much at home, where she knew it would have satisfied neither husband nor wife; for while she considered Louisa to be rather the favourite, she could not but think, as far as she might dare to judge from memory and experience, that Captain Wentworth was not in love with either.[1] They were more in love with him; yet there it was not love. It was a little fever of admiration; but it might, probably must, end in love with some.[2] Charles Hayter seemed aware of being slighted, and yet Henrietta had sometimes the air of being divided between them. Anne longed for the power of representing to them all what they were about, and of pointing out some of the evils they were exposing themselves to. She did not attribute guile to any. It was the highest satisfaction to her, to believe Captain Wentworth not in the least aware of the pain he was occasioning.[3] There was no triumph, no pitiful[4] triumph[5] in his manner. He had, probably, never heard, and never thought of any claims of Charles Hayter. He was only wrong in accepting the attentions—(for accepting must be the word) of two young women at once.[6]

After a short struggle, however, Charles Hayter seemed to quit the field. Three days had passed without his coming once to Uppercross; a most decided change. He had even refused one regular invitation to dinner; and having been found on the occasion by Mr. Musgrove with some large books before him, Mr. and Mrs. Musgrove were sure all could not be right, and talked, with grave faces, of his studying himself to death.[7] It was Mary's hope and belief, that he had received a positive dismissal from Henrietta, and her husband lived under the constant dependance of seeing

1. Her discernment of this shows the usefulness, to the story, of her previous knowledge of him.

2. That two women are in this fever of admiration, and that he is, at this stage, apparently interested in them equally, is important for suggesting that Anne's surmise about his lack of real love may be correct. He would know that he cannot have both, and if really in love with one would avoid flirting with the other. When, later in this chapter, he does veer toward one, it is more her doing than his—a sharp contrast to the active initiative he usually shows.

3. A sign of how much she still identifies with him, despite all she is witnessing.

4. *pitiful*: petty, small-minded.

5. *triumph*: exultation.

6. One reason for his negligence may be his lack of strong feelings for either, which makes him not bother choosing and may make him underestimate the seriousness of what is happening. Another reason may be his having spent most of his adult life at sea, removed from women. That would make him inexperienced in the ways of courtship and less likely to perceive the dangers of irregular behavior there. Toward the end of the book he provides further insight into his state of mind at this point (p. 462).

7. "Large" could refer to thickness but is more likely to refer to length and width. At this time books came in widely varying sizes. The principal ones were folios, in which a standard sheet of paper was folded in two to make the pages, quartos, in which the paper was folded into quarters, octavos, in which the paper was folded into eight pieces, and duodecimos, in which the paper was folded into twelve pieces. Thus the length and width of a duodecimo would be one-sixth those of a folio. The type of book would influence its size. Popular books, especially novels, tended to come in smaller sizes, while serious, scholarly ones were usually larger. Thus the size of Charles Hayter's books helps spur the Musgroves' worries about excessive studying. They might be naturally inclined to such worries, not seeming bookish at all themselves.

him to-morrow. Anne could only feel that Charles Hayter was wise.[8]

One morning, about this time, Charles Musgrove and Captain Wentworth being gone a shooting together, as the sisters in the cottage were sitting quietly at work,[9] they were visited at the window by the sisters from the mansion-house.

It was a very fine November day, and the Miss Musgroves came through the little grounds,[10] and stopped for no other purpose than to say, that they were going to take a *long* walk, and, therefore, concluded Mary could not like to go with them; and when Mary immediately replied, with some jealousy, at not being supposed a good walker, "Oh, yes, I should like to join you very much, I am very fond of a long walk," Anne felt persuaded, by the looks of the two girls, that it was precisely what they did not wish, and admired[11] again the sort of necessity which the family-habits seemed to produce, of every thing being to be communicated, and every thing being to be done together, however undesired and inconvenient. She tried to dissuade Mary from going, but in vain; and that being the case, thought it best to accept the Miss Musgroves' much more cordial invitation to herself to go likewise, as she might be useful in turning back with her sister, and lessening the interference in any plan of their own.[12]

"I cannot imagine why they should suppose I should not like a long walk!" said Mary, as she went up stairs. "Every body is always supposing that I am not a good walker! And yet they would not have been pleased, if we had refused to join them. When people come in this manner on purpose to ask us, how can one say no?"

Just as they were setting off, the gentlemen returned. They had taken out a young dog, who had spoilt their sport,[13] and sent them back early. Their time and strength, and spirits, were, therefore, exactly ready for this walk, and they entered into it with pleasure. Could Anne have foreseen such a junction, she would have staid at home; but, from some feelings of interest and curiosity, she fancied now that it was too late to retract, and the whole six set forward together in the direction chosen by the Miss Musgroves, who evidently considered the walk as under their guidance.[14]

8. Anne is the only one to perceive what is really happening, even though she knows Charles Hayter far less well than Mr. or Mrs. Musgrove.

9. *work:* needlework. The usage, found often in Jane Austen, illustrates how basic an activity needlework was for genteel women.

10. The little grounds would be those around the cottage of Charles and Mary. The cottage's location in the village means its grounds could not be extensive, but having some kind of landscaped grounds was considered essential to a country house, and this cottage was already described in terms of its "prettinesses" and its fashionable features (see p. 69, note 39). This would naturally call for grounds as picturesque as available space would permit.

11. *admired:* marveled at.

12. Anne again shows her dutifulness. In this case it will receive a reward of sorts.

13. The various books of the time on hunting and shooting devote considerable attention to the issue of young dogs. They discuss the various risks posed by the dogs' excitability and lack of experience and propose elaborate training regimens, often lasting more than a year—though the authors warn that mishaps may still occur when the dogs are first used. The most frequently cited problem, and the one that has probably spoiled the gentlemen's sport here, is the tendency of young dogs to chase game as soon as they find it, rather than stopping and simply indicating its location. The former causes the birds to fly away before the shooters are in a suitable position.

14. The same group of six will undertake an even grander, and more consequential, excursion to Lyme in the next chapter. They are a natural grouping, being the young adults currently part of or connected with the Musgrove family. This grouping means Anne is regularly being placed in company with Captain Wentworth.

Anne's object was, not to be in the way of any body, and where the narrow paths across the fields made many separations necessary,[15] to keep with her brother and sister. Her *pleasure* in the walk must arise from the exercise and the day, from the view of the last smiles of the year upon the tawny leaves and withered hedges, and from repeating to herself some few of the thousand poetical descriptions extant of autumn,[16] that season of peculiar[17] and inexhaustible influence on the mind of taste and tenderness, that season which has drawn from every poet, worthy of being read, some attempt at description, or some lines of feeling.[18] She occupied her mind as much as possible in such like musings and quotations; but it was not possible, that when within reach of Captain Wentworth's conversation with either of the Miss Musgroves, she should not try to hear it; yet she caught little very remarkable. It was mere lively chat, — such as any young persons, on an intimate footing, might fall into. He was more engaged with Louisa than with Henrietta. Louisa certainly put more forward for his notice than her sister. This distinction appeared to increase, and there was one speech of Louisa's which struck her. After one of the many praises of the day, which were continually bursting forth, Captain Wentworth added,

"What glorious weather for the Admiral and my sister! They meant to take a long drive this morning; perhaps we may hail them from some of these hills. They talked of coming into this side of the country. I wonder whereabouts they will upset to-day. Oh! it does happen very often, I assure you[19] — but my sister makes nothing of it — she would as lieve[20] be tossed out as not."

"Ah! You make the most of it, I know," cried Louisa, "but if it were really so, I should do just the same in her place. If I loved a man, as she loves the Admiral, I would be always with him, nothing should ever separate us, and I would rather be overturned by him, than driven safely by anybody else."[21]

It was spoken with enthusiasm.

"Had you?" cried he, catching the same tone; "I honour you!" And there was silence between them for a little while.

15. This discourages conversation during the walk. This has important consequences, for when two of the characters do engage in a long and serious talk, it is after they have stopped, and Anne ends up being in a position to overhear them.

16. Anne's love of poetry is fully demonstrated here by how readily poetic quotations spring to her mind. It will lead to a significant plot development in the next chapter. The sentence evoking her love itself has a poetic cast, using language, such as "smiles of the year" and "tawny leaves," that is often found in poetry.

17. *peculiar*: particular.

18. Anne's wish to spend autumn in the country was mentioned earlier (p. 62). The poignant and almost rueful atmosphere often associated with autumn would also suit her state of mind at this point.

19. Carriage accidents were a regular hazard of using them. Jane Austen's next, unfinished novel, *Sanditon*, begins with a carriage accident. Toward the end of this chapter it is revealed that they are a particular hazard for the Crofts.

20. *lieve*: lief, i.e., gladly, willingly.

21. The emphatic enthusiasm of this speech gives an indication of Louisa's character, while its fervent expression of willingness to undergo an accident will soon prove eerily prescient.

Anne could not immediately fall into a quotation again. The sweet scenes of autumn were for a while put by—unless some tender sonnet, fraught with the apt analogy of the declining year, with declining happiness, and the images of youth and hope, and spring, all gone together, blessed her memory.[22] She roused herself to say, as they struck by order into another path, "Is not this one of the ways to Winthrop?" But nobody heard, or, at least, nobody answered her.

Winthrop, however, or its environs—for young men are, sometimes, to be met with, strolling about near home, was their destination;[23] and after another half mile of gradual ascent through large enclosures,[24] where the ploughs at work, and the fresh-made path spoke[25] the farmer, counteracting the sweets of poetical despondence, and meaning to have spring again,[26] they gained the summit of the most considerable hill, which parted Uppercross and Winthrop, and soon commanded a full view of the latter, at the foot of the hill on the other side.

Winthrop, without beauty and without dignity, was stretched before them; an indifferent house, standing low, and hemmed in by the barns and buildings of a farm-yard.[27]

Mary exclaimed, "Bless me! here is Winthrop—I declare I had no idea!—Well, now I think we had better turn back; I am excessively tired."

Henrietta, conscious[28] and ashamed, and seeing no cousin Charles walking along any path, or leaning against any gate, was ready to do as Mary wished;[29] but "No," said Charles Musgrove, and "no, no," cried Louisa more eagerly, and taking her sister aside, seemed to be arguing the matter warmly.

Charles, in the meanwhile, was very decidedly declaring his resolution of calling on his aunt, now that he was so near; and very evidently, though more fearfully, trying to induce his wife to go too. But this was one of the points on which the lady shewed her strength, and when he recommended the advantage of resting herself a quarter of an hour at Winthrop, as she felt so tired, she resolutely answered, "Oh! no, indeed!—walking up that hill again would do her more harm than any sitting down could do

22. What she has heard has darkened her poetic memory, though the scenes around her have not changed. Personal concerns have overridden the influence of the external atmosphere.

23. That this was intended as their destination is probably why nobody answered Anne just now (the wording of that passage suggests that at least some heard her statement about heading toward Winthrop). The description of Henrietta below indicates that she has selected the destination—Louisa will soon afterward confirm that and signal her collaboration in the scheme, which did start, after all, with their meaning to take a long walk by themselves. Henrietta may be a little reluctant to avow her design from fear of arousing Mary's disapproval, given the latter's disdain for the Hayters, or from not wishing to look as if she is pursuing Charles Hayter, which would be considered immodest. The last concern is probably why the "environs" of Winthrop are identified as their target, rather than the house itself. Her hope presumably was to meet Charles Hayter while he was walking in the vicinity: then she could claim to have simply happened upon him while visiting the area, and not be accused of improperly going after him. Similar considerations lead a woman in *Pride and Prejudice*, Charlotte Lucas, to leave her house when she sees a man coming that she hopes will propose to her, in order to meet him "accidentally" in the lane outside.

24. Enclosures were fields for farming. During the half century or so preceding the novel, large sections of England had undergone enclosure, in which, frequently with the support of acts of Parliament, substantial tracts of land were consolidated into the hands of a single owner by buying out the long-held rights of various other people. The purpose was to allow these lands to be farmed more efficiently.

25. *spoke:* testified to, indicated.

26. This brings the story back to a more practical, prosaic reality after the poetic strains of the last few pages. It also suggests a possible end to the gloom currently dominating Anne's mind. For a contemporary picture of a field being plowed, see next page.

27. Its low position and placement amid other buildings would add to its lack of dignity and beauty, in contemporary eyes. The ideal house at the time stood on top of a hill, where it could be seen to best advantage and would have the finest view of the surrounding landscape. Thus the house's placement marks the poorer character of the Hayter family, for those with less money often needed to worry more about practical considerations, such as shelter from wind and rain or proximity to barns, when deciding on sites.

28. *conscious:* guilty, i.e., conscious of doing wrong.

29. Henrietta's hesitation reveals her indecisive character. That will soon form a critical point of discussion.

her good;"—and, in short, her look and manner declared, that go she would not.

After a little succession of these sort of debates and consultations, it was settled between Charles and his two sisters, that he, and Henrietta, should just run down for a few minutes, to see their aunt and cousins, while the rest of the party waited for them at the top of the hill. Louisa seemed the principal arranger of the plan; and, as she went a little way with them, down the hill, still talking to Henrietta, Mary took the opportunity of looking scornfully around her, and saying to Captain Wentworth,

"It is very unpleasant, having such connexions! But I assure you, I have never been in the house above twice in my life."

She received no other answer, than an artificial, assenting smile, followed by a contemptuous glance, as he turned away, which Anne perfectly knew the meaning of.

The brow of the hill, where they remained, was a cheerful spot; Louisa returned, and Mary finding a comfortable seat for herself, on the step of a stile, was very well satisfied so long as the others all stood about her; but when Louisa drew Captain Wentworth away, to try for a gleaning of nuts in an adjoining hedge-row,[30] and they were gone by degrees quite out of sight and sound, Mary was happy no longer; she quarrelled with her own seat,—was sure Louisa had got a much better somewhere,—and nothing could prevent her from going to look for a better also. She turned through the same gate,—but could not see them.—Anne found a nice seat for her, on a dry sunny bank, under the hedge-row, in which she had no doubt of their still being—in some spot or other. Mary sat down for a moment, but it would not do; she was sure Louisa had found a better seat somewhere else, and she would go on, till she overtook her.

Anne, really tired herself, was glad to sit down; and she very soon heard Captain Wentworth and Louisa in the hedge-row, behind her, as if making their way back, along the rough, wild sort of channel, down the centre.[31] They were speaking as they drew near. Louisa's voice was the first distinguished. She seemed to be in the middle of some eager speech. What Anne first heard was,[32]

30. Hedgerows were a common feature of the English countryside. Jane Austen's nephew James Edward Austen-Leigh, who in 1870 published the first important biography of Jane Austen, based on family reminiscences, declared that, "the chief beauty of Steventon [the village where Jane Austen grew up] consisted in its hedgerows."

31. In the above memoir, Jane Austen's nephew writes that the hedgerows around her childhood home were "an irregular border of copse-wood and timber, often wide enough to contain within it a winding footpath, or a rough lane." He adds that "two such hedgerows radiated, as it were, from the parsonage garden," the parsonage being the clerical home in which she and her family lived. This sort of hedgerow provides an ideal setting for this scene in the novel, for its large channel allows Captain Wentworth and Louisa to walk side by side and talk, while its thick, tall woods mean that they cannot see outside it to realize that somebody else is just on the other side and able to hear them.

32. Anne's overhearing of Captain Wentworth and Louisa is a significant moment in the novel. It also foreshadows an even more significant scene in which he overhears Anne talking to someone else.

Field being plowed, with a country house (Cusworth) in the background.
[From John Preston Neale, *Views of the Seats of Noblemen and Gentlemen, Vol. V* (1822)]

"And so, I made her go. I could not bear that she should be frightened from the visit by such nonsense. What!—would I be turned back from doing a thing that I had determined to do, and that I knew to be right, by the airs and interference of such a person?[33]—or, of any person I may say. No,—I have no idea of being so easily persuaded. When I have made up my mind, I have made it. And Henrietta seemed entirely to have made up hers to call at Winthrop to-day—and yet, she was as near giving it up, out of nonsensical complaisance!"[34]

"She would have turned back then, but for you?"

"She would indeed. I am almost ashamed to say it."

"Happy for her, to have such a mind[35] as yours at hand!—After the hints you gave just now, which did but confirm my own observations, the last time I was in company with him, I need not affect to have no comprehension of what is going on. I see that more than a mere dutiful morning-visit to your aunt was in question;[36]— and woe betide him, and her too, when it comes to things of consequence, when they are placed in circumstances, requiring fortitude and strength of mind, if she have not resolution enough to resist idle interference in such a trifle as this. Your sister is an amiable creature; but *yours* is the character of decision and firmness, I see. If you value her conduct or happiness, infuse as much of your own spirit[37] into her, as you can. But this, no doubt, you have been always doing. It is the worst evil of too yielding and indecisive a character, that no influence over it can be depended on.—You are never sure of a good impression being durable.[38] Every body may sway it; let those who would be happy be firm.— Here is a nut," said he, catching one down from an upper bough. "To exemplify,—a beautiful glossy nut, which, blessed with original strength, has outlived all the storms of autumn. Not a puncture, not a weak spot any where.—This nut," he continued, with playful solemnity,—"while so many of its brethren have fallen and been trodden under foot, is still in possession of all the happiness that a hazel-nut can be supposed capable of."[39] Then, returning to his former earnest tone: "My first wish for all, whom I am interested in, is that they should be firm. If Louisa Musgrove

33. There is an irony in Louisa's moralistic tone, for while she may have been right about Henrietta's going, and may have been motivated in part by this sense of its being right, the action also served her own interest very well by rejoining her sister to Charles Hayter and thereby leaving Captain Wentworth completely to herself.

34. Thus Louisa announces explicitly her own stance on the issue of persuasion, one that seems to be the exact opposite of the susceptibility that Captain Wentworth perceived in Anne earlier. Louisa, of course, does not know this, but his lengthy speech in reply bears clear marks of his earlier experience with Anne, and the lessons he has drawn from it.

35. *mind*: character, disposition.

36. Captain Wentworth is perceptive enough to grasp Henrietta's relationship with Charles Hayter, but he fails to perceive, in his fulsome praise of Louisa, her less than pure reasons for urging her sister so forcefully. He also is failing to perceive, as he admits later (p. 462), the exact effects his words and behavior are having on Louisa, and on the perceptions of those around them.

37. *spirit*: ardor, vigor, assertiveness.

38. The exact durability of the impression made by Captain Wentworth on Louisa will later be revealed. It does make a powerful impression now, however, and will soon lead to highly important developments. Since these words are being influenced in turn by his own earlier experience with Anne, and his recoil from what he believed to be her weakness of character, that episode is continuing to play a vital role in the plot.

39. A rare instance of symbolism in Jane Austen, though here it is the character, not the author, who is employing it.

would be beautiful and happy in her November of life,[40] she will cherish all her present powers of mind."

He had done,—and was unanswered. It would have surprised Anne, if Louisa could have readily answered such a speech— words of such interest, spoken with such serious warmth![41]—she could imagine what Louisa was feeling. For herself—she feared to move, lest she should be seen. While she remained, a bush of low rambling holly protected her,[42] and they were moving on. Before they were beyond her hearing, however, Louisa spoke again.

"Mary is good-natured enough in many respects," said she; "but she does sometimes provoke me excessively, by her nonsense and her pride; the Elliot pride. She has a great deal too much of the Elliot pride.—We do so wish that Charles had married Anne instead.—I suppose you know he wanted to marry Anne?"

After a moment's pause, Captain Wentworth said,[43]

"Do you mean that she refused him?"

"Oh! yes, certainly."

"When did that happen?"

"I do not exactly know, for Henrietta and I were at school at the time; but I believe about a year before he married Mary. I wish she had accepted him. We should all have liked her a great deal better; and papa and mamma always think it was her great friend Lady Russell's doing, that she did not.—They think Charles might not be[44] learned and bookish enough to please Lady Russell, and that therefore, she persuaded Anne to refuse him."

The sounds were retreating, and Anne distinguished no more.[45] Her own emotions[46] still kept her fixed. She had much to recover from, before she could move.[47] The listener's proverbial fate was not absolutely hers; she had heard no evil of herself,—but she had heard a great deal of very painful import.[48] She saw how her own character was considered by Captain Wentworth; and there had been just that degree of feeling and curiosity about her in his manner, which must give her extreme agitation.[49]

As soon as she could, she went after Mary, and having found, and walked back with her to their former station, by the stile, felt some comfort in their whole party being immediately afterwards

40. Its being November endows the metaphor with extra resonance. His use of two metaphors in a row also provides another link with Anne. They are the sort of metaphors often found in poetry, and Anne's own taste for poetry, especially that evoking the seasons and natural phenomena like hazelnuts, has just been shown.

41. These words are particularly significant in the context of this society, for unmarried men were never supposed to express such heartfelt praise and affection to an unmarried woman unless they had serious intentions of being more than friends.

42. Holly trees have long been a common feature of English hedgerows.

43. The pause suggests Captain Wentworth has been affected by her words about Anne and Charles. He will later explain that the information had a significant effect on his thinking (p. 464).

44. *might not be:* may not have been. She is using "might" as the past tense of "may," a traditional usage found elsewhere in Jane Austen.

45. Their movement away means that we (and Anne) do not learn Captain Wentworth's reaction to this last suggestion. The idea that Anne was persuaded by Lady Russell would be one he could easily believe, based on his own experience, and that would confirm his negative verdict on Anne's character. Anne has good reason to expect him to draw a negative conclusion— though she knows that her refusal of Charles was her decision alone, one that Lady Russell in fact lamented (p. 52). This would add to Anne's distress, for whether or not she still harbors any hope of renewed love between herself and Captain Wentworth, her high regard for him makes her still wish for his good opinion.

46. *emotions:* agitations.

47. Their being on a country walk thus assists Anne by allowing her to remain alone while she recovers. Were she in a more social setting, others might notice her agitation, and this might lead to suspicion of her true feelings, including by Captain Wentworth himself.

48. The wrongness of eavesdropping is a principle developed clearly at various points in Jane Austen. Anne has not been doing that intentionally, for she did not pursue the two she overheard, but she also made no attempt to move away, and it could be argued that the painful impact of what she has heard forms a fitting punishment, in the author's moral calculus.

49. She has perceived a genuine interest in her on his part, but she has also heard him say things that indicate his continued disapproval of her, and received information from Louisa that might lower his opinion of Anne further.

collected, and once more in motion together. Her spirits wanted the solitude and silence which only numbers could give.

Charles and Henrietta returned, bringing, as may be conjectured, Charles Hayter with them. The minutiæ of the business Anne could not attempt to understand; even Captain Wentworth did not seem admitted to perfect confidence here; but that there had been a withdrawing on the gentleman's side, and a relenting on the lady's, and that they were now very glad to be together again, did not admit a doubt. Henrietta looked a little ashamed, but very well pleased;—Charles Hayter exceedingly happy, and they were devoted to each other almost from the first instant of their all setting forward for Uppercross.

Every thing now marked out Louisa for Captain Wentworth; nothing could be plainer; and where many divisions were necessary, or even where they were not, they walked side by side, nearly as much as the other two. In a long strip of meadow-land, where there was ample space for all, they were thus divided—forming three distinct parties; and to that party of the three which boasted least animation, and least complaisance,[50] Anne necessarily belonged. She joined Charles and Mary, and was tired enough to be very glad of Charles's other arm;—but Charles, though in very good humour with her, was out of temper[51] with his wife. Mary had shewn herself disobliging to him, and was now to reap the consequence, which consequence was his dropping her arm almost every moment, to cut off the heads of some nettles in the hedge with his switch;[52] and when Mary began to complain of it, and lament her being ill-used, according to custom, in being on the hedge side, while Anne was never incommoded on the other, he dropped the arms of both to hunt after a weasel which he had a momentary glance of;[53] and they could hardly get him along at all.

This long meadow bordered a lane, which their foot-path, at the end of it, was to cross;[54] and when the party had all reached the gate of exit,[55] the carriage advancing in the same direction, which had been some time heard, was just coming up, and proved to be Admiral Croft's gig.[56]—He and his wife had taken their intended drive, and were returning home. Upon hearing

50. *complaisance*: civility, agreeableness, willingness to please others.

51. *out of temper*: angry.

52. It would be normal for a man to take a woman's arm as they walked together, or two women's arms in this case, in order to offer support.

53. Charles's hunting after a weasel would be natural for a sportsman like him. The delays it causes, and his dropping of Anne's arm, could also add to her weariness, which soon has important consequences.

54. The mention of a footpath is a little curious since the earlier description of the meadow, "where there was ample space for all," seemed to imply they were simply walking in the meadow itself.

55. The gate was probably to keep livestock inside. Meadowland, which would mean land that was not plowed, was generally used for grazing.

56. The gig has been advancing somewhat parallel to the walkers, which is why they have long heard it. It would not have been going much faster than they. Even the fastest carriages, on the best roads, could reach ten miles per hour at most, and a gig, a carriage with one horse pulling two people, that was traveling over a rough country lane would achieve far less speed.

how long a walk the young people had engaged in, they kindly offered a seat to any lady who might be particularly tired; it would save her full a mile, and they were going through Uppercross. The invitation was general, and generally declined. The Miss Musgroves were not at all tired, and Mary was either offended, by not being asked before any of the others, or what Louisa called the Elliot pride could not endure to make a third in a one-horse chaise.[57]

The walking-party had crossed the lane, and were surmounting an opposite stile;[58] and the admiral was putting his horse into motion again, when Captain Wentworth cleared the hedge in a moment to say something to his sister.[59]—The something might be guessed by its effects.

"Miss Elliot, I am sure *you* are tired," cried Mrs. Croft. "Do let us have the pleasure of taking you home. Here is excellent room for three, I assure you. If we were all like you, I believe we might sit four.—You must, indeed, you must."

Anne was still in the lane; and though instinctively beginning to decline, she was not allowed to proceed. The admiral's kind urgency came in support of his wife's; they would not be refused; they compressed themselves into the smallest possible space to leave her a corner,[60] and Captain Wentworth, without saying a word, turned to her, and quietly obliged her to be assisted into the carriage.

Yes,—he had done it. She was in the carriage, and felt that he had placed her there, that his will and his hands had done it, that she owed it to his perception of her fatigue, and his resolution to give her rest.[61] She was very much affected by the view of his disposition towards her which all these things made apparent. This little circumstance seemed the completion of all that had gone before. She understood him. He could not forgive her,—but he could not be unfeeling. Though condemning her for the past, and considering it with high and unjust resentment, though perfectly careless[62] of her, and though becoming attached to another, still he could not see her suffer, without the desire of giving her relief. It was a remainder of former sentiment; it was an

57. *one-horse chaise:* a term often applied to gigs, as well as other vehicles at times—"chaise," which usually meant a small, enclosed vehicle, could be used for light carriages in general. The term "one-horse" has a negative connotation, which would resonate particularly with the status-conscious Mary: later she is said to exult at traveling in a carriage pulled by four horses (p. 416).

58. *stile:* barriers that separated fields, and that humans could cross, but that were impassable by animals. Turnstiles were one form. Stiles were a common feature of the English countryside, due to the heavy emphasis on livestock in English agriculture.

59. Captain Wentworth's clearing the hedge in a moment to help a lady in distress signals a heroic, and highly active, aspect of his character.

60. A gig generally had seats for two, which is why the Crofts must compress themselves. Their eagerness to do so to accommodate Anne contrasts with Mary's earlier complaints about being crowded on a coach seat with Louisa and Henrietta, even though coach seats were wider and it is probable that the Musgrove girls took up less room than the Crofts. For a contemporary picture of a couple in a gig, see below.

61. The mention of his hands implies he was the one helping her into the carriage. The sum of his action shows him both heroic and gentle, and perhaps with a special sensitivity to Anne, one that made him notice her fatigue sooner than he might have noticed another woman's.

62. *careless:* unsolicitous, regardless.

Elderly couple arriving in a gig.

[From William Combe, *The Tour of Doctor Syntax in Search of the Picturesque* (London, 1817; 1903 reprint), p. 265]

impulse of pure, though unacknowledged friendship; it was a proof of his own warm and amiable[63] heart, which she could not contemplate without emotions so compounded of pleasure and pain, that she knew not which prevailed.[64]

Her answers to the kindness and the remarks of her companions were at first unconsciously given. They had travelled half their way along the rough lane,[65] before she was quite awake to what they said. She then found them talking of "Frederick."

"He certainly means to have one or other of those two girls, Sophy," said the admiral;—"but there is no saying which.[66] He has been running after them, too, long enough, one would think, to make up his mind. Ay, this comes of the peace. If it were war, now, he would have settled it long ago.—We sailors, Miss Elliot, cannot afford to make long courtships in time of war. How many days was it, my dear, between the first time of my seeing you, and our sitting down together in our lodgings at North Yarmouth?"[67]

"We had better not talk about it, my dear," replied Mrs. Croft, pleasantly; "for if Miss Elliot were to hear how soon we came to an understanding, she would never be persuaded that we could be happy together. I had known you by character,[68] however, long before."

"Well, and I had heard of you as a very pretty girl; and what were we to wait for besides?[69]—I do not like having such things so long in hand.[70] I wish Frederick would spread a little more canvas,[71] and bring us home one of these young ladies to Kellynch. Then, there would always be company for them.[72]—And very nice young ladies they both are; I hardly know one from the other."[73]

"Very good-humoured, unaffected girls, indeed," said Mrs. Croft, in a tone of calmer praise, such as made Anne suspect that her keener powers[74] might not consider either of them as quite worthy of her brother; "and a very respectable family. One could not be connected with better people.[75]—My dear admiral,[76] that post!—we shall certainly take that post."[77]

But by coolly giving the reins a better direction herself, they happily passed the danger; and by once afterwards judiciously

63. *amiable*: kind, benevolent.

64. The pleasure would be the proof of his good character and concern for her, but that would lead to the pain of an increased awareness of how much she has lost.

65. Country roads of the time, being unpaved, were generally rough lanes.

66. His words show how others are interpreting Wentworth's actions. Wentworth will later mention this as a general phenomenon, one that surprised him (p. 462).

67. Yarmouth, on England's east coast, was a small naval base (see map, p. 512).

68. *character*: reputation.

69. Their two descriptions stand in contrast. She had thought of his reputation, which would involve his overall qualities; he thought only of her being pretty. At the same time, their willingness to marry quickly, despite any risk, unites them and forms a sharp contrast with Anne's earlier actions.

70. *in hand*: in expectation or suspense; in process.

71. Spreading canvas, meaning sails, which were made of canvas, is what a ship would do when it needed to increase speed.

72. One editor, R. W. Chapman, thinks this is probably a misprint, and should read "us," which would seem more logical.

73. Admiral Croft's words say something of his own lack of perceptiveness, a natural adjunct to his rough and ready ways, and also something of the Miss Musgroves themselves, who do seem almost interchangeable at times.

74. *powers*: abilities.

75. A statement that indicates how much marriage is regarded as a connection between families, with a preference for prominent families, even by people as little concerned with social distinctions as Mrs. Croft.

76. Her calling him "Admiral," albeit with "dear," is a good exhibit of standard formality, even in such an affectionate and down-to-earth couple.

77. The post is next to the road. Main roads would have mileposts, marking distance traversed, but the post here could simply be a marker of property.

putting out her hand, they neither fell into a rut, nor ran foul of a dung-cart;[78] and Anne, with some amusement at their style of driving, which she imagined no bad representation of the general guidance of their affairs,[79] found herself safely deposited by them at the cottage.

78. The dung cart would be for spreading dung on fields as fertilizer. An innovation of the time, which improved the productivity of the land, was collecting dung and distributing it systematically, rather than letting animals drop it wherever they grazed.

79. Admiral Croft's near mishaps confirm Captain Wentworth's earlier observation of the frequency with which he and his wife are upset while driving. They also may be one reason why they drive a gig, rather than a curricle like Charles Musgrove. The gig used one horse, the curricle two. This made the latter more expensive, but also more fashionable and more suitable for long distances. The Crofts could afford a curricle, but it is possible Mrs. Croft, with the same judicious care of her husband shown here, decided that the gig was safer. One of its advantages was that, with only one horse, it took up less room and could more easily travel along the narrow roads common in the country without running into objects along the side.

Their near mishap here, and the ones they do suffer at other times, serve to show that their bold indifference to risk can have its disadvantages.

Chapter Eleven

*T*he time now approached for Lady Russell's return; the day was even fixed, and Anne, being engaged to join her as soon as she was resettled, was looking forward to an early removal to Kellynch, and beginning to think how her own comfort was likely to be affected by it.

It would place her in the same village with Captain Wentworth, within half a mile of him; they would have to frequent the same church,[1] and there must be intercourse between the two families. This was against her; but, on the other hand, he spent so much of his time at Uppercross, that in removing thence she might be considered rather as leaving him behind, than as going towards him; and, upon the whole, she believed she must, on this interesting[2] question, be the gainer, almost as certainly as in her change of domestic society, in leaving poor Mary for Lady Russell.[3]

She wished it might be possible for her to avoid ever seeing Captain Wentworth at the hall;—those rooms had witnessed former meetings which would be brought too painfully before her; but she was yet more anxious for the possibility of Lady Russell and Captain Wentworth never meeting any where. They did not like each other, and no renewal of acquaintance now could do any good; and were Lady Russell to see them together, she might think that he had too much self-possession, and she too little.[4]

These points formed her chief solicitude in anticipating her removal from Uppercross, where she felt she had been stationed quite long enough. Her usefulness to little Charles would always give some sweetness to the memory of her two months' visit there,[5] but he was gaining strength apace, and she had nothing else to stay for.

1. Regular church attendance was a standard practice and social obligation at the time. Jane Austen's letters contain frequent mentions of attending church on Sunday, sometimes both in the morning and the evening.

2. *interesting:* important.

3. "Poor Mary" probably represents the thoughts of Anne, who is able to sympathize with her sister for the way she suffers from her own querulousness and pride, even as Anne is glad to be able now to escape the sufferings those qualities inflict on her.

4. Lady Russell had earlier considered Captain Wentworth's bold confidence one of his dangerous qualities and might consider a high degree of self-possession on his part a continuation of that quality. Lady Russell would also be distressed to see how much Captain Wentworth continues to affect Anne.

5. She arrived in Uppercross approximately a week into September, so it would be early November if "two months" is a precise designation. It may not be so precise, for other information suggests the trip to Lyme, which is about to occur now, takes place a little later in November (see chronology, p. 487, for September; and p. 488, for the sequence after Lyme).

Picture of Lyme Regis and the Cobb from the early eighteenth century. The Cobb had been connected to the mainland by the time of the novel.

[From Emma Austen-Leigh, *Jane Austen and Lyme Regis* (London, 1941), p. 4]

The conclusion of her visit, however, was diversified in a way which she had not at all imagined. Captain Wentworth, after being unseen and unheard of at Uppercross for two whole days, appeared again among them to justify himself by a relation[6] of what had kept him away.

A letter from his friend, Captain Harville, having found him out at last,[7] had brought intelligence of Captain Harville's being settled with his family at Lyme for the winter;[8] of their being, therefore, quite unknowingly, within twenty miles of each other. Captain Harville had never been in good health since a severe wound which he received two years before, and Captain Wentworth's anxiety to see him had determined him to go immediately to Lyme. He had been there for four-and-twenty hours. His acquittal was complete,[9] his friendship warmly honoured, a lively interest excited for his friend, and his description of the fine country about Lyme so feelingly attended to by the party, that an earnest desire to see Lyme themselves, and a project for going thither was the consequence.[10]

The young people were all wild to see Lyme. Captain Wentworth talked of going there again himself; it was only seventeen miles from Uppercross; though November, the weather was by no means bad;[11] and, in short, Louisa, who was the most eager of the eager, having formed the resolution to go, and besides the pleasure of doing as she liked, being now armed with the idea of merit in maintaining her own way, bore down all the wishes of her father and mother for putting it off till summer;[12] and to Lyme they were to go—Charles, Mary, Anne, Henrietta, Louisa, and Captain Wentworth.

The first heedless scheme had been to go in the morning and return at night, but to this Mr. Musgrove, for the sake of his horses, would not consent;[13] and when it came to be rationally considered, a day in the middle of November would not leave much time for seeing a new place, after deducting seven hours, as the nature of the country required, for going and returning.[14] They were consequently to stay the night there, and not to be

6. *relation:* account, narration.

7. Captain Wentworth would have been difficult to find, since he has no apparent home of his own. The letter might have been sent to his brother, or a fellow officer, and then sent on, or, if sent to Mrs. Croft at another address, could have been forwarded by the post office, which had recently established a special office and procedures for forwarding missent letters. The warm friendship between him and Captain Harville was mentioned on p. 126.

8. *Lyme:* Lyme, or Lyme Regis, is a town on the southern coast, near Somerset (see map, p. 513). In the eighteenth century it became a popular vacation spot.

9. The others, learning his reason, acquit him of having deserted them.

10. The seaside, after a long period of being shunned, had from the 1600s gradually become a popular destination, sought for the supposed health benefits of sea-bathing and drinking seawater, and for simple pleasure. By this time numerous towns along the coasts of England had developed into resorts, catering to the enthusiasm displayed by the young people here.

11. Jane Austen's family visited Lyme in November 1803, when the town suffered a major fire. Thus she knew the state of the weather in Lyme then.

12. The expedition to Lyme is the first important result of this new conviction of Louisa. It will lead to another display of unpersuadable determination on her part, one with momentous consequences. The terms "wild" and "heedless" in the opening sentence of this and the next paragraph signal the reckless attitude of those pushing the trip. Mr. and Mrs. Musgrove wish to wait until summer because that is the normal time for visiting the sea.

13. He wishes to save his horses from the overwork resulting from such a lengthy journey in one day. Horses were expensive, and overworking them was the main reason for needing to replace them; those that worked the busier transportation routes could need replacing as often as every three years. They would become particularly exhausted when pulling a heavy vehicle like the Musgroves' coach, and when traveling at the speeds expected by those going beyond their immediate locale. Horses pulling public coaches, which went at top speeds, were usually rested after ten miles.
    The party could advance their speed by hiring horses, but they may have decided it was not worth the trouble and expense (see also p. 221, note 90).

14. The "nature of the country" around Lyme is hilly, which is why, instead of the 7–8 miles per hour carriages would usually attain then over smooth roads, they would make only around 5 miles per hour (seven hours for a round-trip of 34 miles, Lyme being 17 miles from Uppercross—see p. 180).
    England's northerly latitude makes days in late fall and winter very short.

expected back till the next day's dinner. This was felt to be a considerable amendment; and though they all met at the Great House at rather an early breakfast hour,[15] and set off very punctually, it was so much past noon before the two carriages, Mr. Musgrove's coach containing the four ladies, and Charles's curricle, in which he drove Captain Wentworth,[16] were descending the long hill into Lyme, and entering upon the still steeper street of the town itself,[17] that it was very evident they would not have more than time for looking about them, before the light and warmth of the day were gone.

After securing accommodations, and ordering a dinner at one of the inns,[18] the next thing to be done was unquestionably to walk directly down to the sea. They were come too late in the year for any amusement or variety which Lyme, as a public place, might offer; the rooms were shut up,[19] the lodgers almost all gone, scarcely any family but of the residents left—and, as there is nothing to admire in the buildings themselves, the remarkable situation of the town, the principal street almost hurrying into the water, the walk to the Cobb, skirting round the pleasant little bay, which in the season is animated with bathing machines and company,[20] the Cobb itself, its old wonders and new improvements,[21] with the very beautiful line of cliffs stretching out to the east of the town, are what the stranger's eye will seek; and a very strange stranger it must be, who does not see charms in the immediate environs of Lyme, to make him wish to know it better. The scenes in its neighbourhood, Charmouth, with its high grounds and extensive sweeps of country, and still more its sweet retired bay, backed by dark cliffs, where fragments of low rock among the sands make it the happiest spot for watching the flow of the tide, for sitting in unwearied contemplation;—the woody varieties of the cheerful village of Up Lyme, and, above all, Pinny, with its green chasms between romantic rocks,[22] where the scattered forest trees and orchards of luxuriant growth declare that many a generation must have passed away since the first partial falling of the cliff prepared the ground for such a state, where a scene so

15. The most common breakfast time then for those of their class was ten o'clock.

16. A coach seats six, so they all could have traveled in it, but they may have thought this arrangement more comfortable. If servants were accompanying them, as would often be the case, they may have wished to have room inside for them, though servants could sit on outside perches on the coach (even if there were servants with them it would be normal for the author not to bother mentioning them). Charles also may have wished to demonstrate his curricle to Captain Wentworth; he is later shown to be interested in comparing his vehicle to another's (see p. 202, and for a curricle, see p. 201, note 26).

17. Lyme sits below a sharp ascent of land, while its main street, Broad Street, is very steep and terminates at the beach (see map, p. 514).

18. One book of 1804 catering to the interest in seaside resorts, Feltham's *A Guide to All the Watering and Sea-Bathing Places*, identified two inns in Lyme, "The Golden Lion" and "Three Cups," where "lodging may be procured on easy terms."

19. "Rooms" mean assembly rooms, where dances were held and which also had a card room and a billiard table. In a letter from Lyme, written in September, Jane Austen describes attending a ball (Sept. 14, 1804). By November Lyme, like most seaside venues, would have been well past its main visiting season.

20. Bathing machines were small cabins with a door on each end and wheels attached to the bottom. They were parked on the beach, where the user would enter the door facing the shore and change into swimming clothes. The machine would be rolled into the water, whereupon the swimmer could open the door facing seaward and plunge into the water; once done the process would be reversed. They had developed in the eighteenth century and soon became ubiquitous features of seaside resorts (for a picture, see frontispiece).

21. The Cobb, which was first built in the thirteenth century and then repaired and improved at different times, has long been Lyme's most distinctive feature. It is a curved structure, slightly west of the town, that extends into the sea and, by blocking the prevailing west winds and currents, provides an artificial harbor. This harbor was long the basis for Lyme's economy, though during the eighteenth century it declined because of its inability to accommodate the larger ships of the time. (For its location and general shape, see map, p. 514).

22. Charmouth is another coastal town (see p. 245, note 8, for a description). Up Lyme sits atop the ascent next to Lyme, and offers views of the town and sea. Pinny is a spot a little west of Lyme. (For locations, see map, p. 514.)

wonderful and so lovely is exhibited, as may more than equal any of the resembling scenes of the far-famed Isle of Wight:[23] these places must be visited, and visited again, to make the worth of Lyme understood.[24]

The party from Uppercross passing down by the now deserted and melancholy looking rooms, and still descending, soon found themselves on the sea shore, and lingering only, as all must linger and gaze on a first return to the sea, who ever deserve to look on it at all, proceeded towards the Cobb, equally their object in itself[25] and on Captain Wentworth's account; for in a small house, near the foot of an old pier of unknown date,[26] were the Harvilles settled. Captain Wentworth turned in to call on his friend; the others walked on, and he was to join them on the Cobb.

They were by no means tired of wondering and admiring; and not even Louisa seemed to feel that they had parted with Captain Wentworth long, when they saw him coming after them, with three companions, all well known already by description to be Captain and Mrs. Harville, and a Captain Benwick, who was staying with them.

Captain Benwick had some time ago been first lieutenant of the Laconia; and the account which Captain Wentworth had given of him, on his return from Lyme before; his warm praise of him as an excellent young man and an officer, whom he had always valued highly, which must have stamped him well in the esteem of every listener, had been followed by a little history of his private life, which rendered him perfectly interesting in the eyes of all the ladies. He had been engaged to Captain Harville's sister, and was now mourning her loss. They had been a year or two waiting for fortune and promotion. Fortune came, his prize-money as lieutenant being great,[27]—promotion, too, came at last;[28] but Fanny Harville did not live to know it. She had died the preceding summer, while he was at sea. Captain Wentworth believed it impossible for man to be more attached to woman than poor Benwick had been to Fanny Harville, or to be more deeply afflicted under the dreadful change. He considered his dis-

23. The Isle of Wight is a large island just off the southern coast, which was recommended by guidebooks then for its natural beauty. Jane Austen lived for two years in the nearby city of Southampton, and thus would have been in a good position to compare its beauties with those of Pinny.

24. This lengthy and enthusiastic description of Lyme and its environs is unusual for Jane Austen. Unlike many novelists of her time and later, she rarely gives more than the briefest description of physical settings, and when referring to specific places, she generally says little about them. The description also seems to represent a deviation from her usual artistic discipline, for it does not advance the story in any clear way. For this reason, some speculate that she would have eliminated it if she had enjoyed greater opportunity to revise and polish the novel. One possible justification for it is the way its enthusiastic evocation of beauty seems to foreshadow the improvement in appearance and spirits that Anne experiences at Lyme.

Whatever the artistic justifications, Jane Austen's willingness to include this description does indicate her own love of Lyme. Jane Austen went there with her family in both 1803 and 1804; in a letter from the second visit she writes favorably of her experience there. It is an understandable affection, for Lyme and its environs do present a truly beautiful site.

25. The Cobb can be strolled upon. It provides striking views of the sea, Lyme itself, and the cliffs and hills all around Lyme.

26. While the principal part of the town has always been a little removed from the Cobb, there have long been a few houses very close to it. Since this is the location of the harbor, there would also have been piers in the vicinity. It is not certain if Jane Austen had a specific pier or house in mind.

27. For prize money generally, see p. 33, note 4. Lieutenants, while not receiving as much as those who captained the ship, still received a decent share, which could represent a lot of money if the ship had been very successful. Yet, because he was only a lieutenant, his fortune is probably much less than that of Captain Wentworth.

28. He would have been promoted while at sea, probably because of some action of his there. Waiting to marry until fortune and promotion came would be standard practice for those in various walks of life. The ensuing tragedy could be seen as another lesson in the perils of waiting and being overly cautious, though in this case, if they had married, the principal difference would have been that Captain Benwick lost a wife rather than a fiancée.

position as of the sort which must suffer heavily, uniting very
strong feelings with quiet, serious, and retiring manners,[29] and a
decided taste for reading, and sedentary pursuits. To finish the
interest of the story, the friendship between him and the Harvilles
seemed, if possible, augmented by the event which closed all
their views of alliance,[30] and Captain Benwick was now living
with them entirely. Captain Harville had taken his present house
for half a year, his taste, and his health, and his fortune all directing him to a residence unexpensive, and by the sea;[31] and the
grandeur of the country, and the retirement[32] of Lyme in the winter, appeared exactly adapted to Captain Benwick's state of
mind.[33] The sympathy and good-will excited towards Captain
Benwick was very great.[34]

"And yet," said Anne to herself, as they now moved forward to
meet the party, "he has not, perhaps, a more sorrowing heart than
I have. I cannot believe his prospects so blighted for ever. He is
younger than I am; younger in feeling, if not in fact; younger as a
man. He will rally again, and be happy with another."[35]

They all met, and were introduced. Captain Harville was a tall,
dark man, with a sensible, benevolent countenance; a little lame;
and from strong features, and want[36] of health, looking much
older than Captain Wentworth. Captain Benwick looked and was
the youngest of the three, and, compared with either of them, a
little man. He had a pleasing face and a melancholy air, just as he
ought to have, and drew back from conversation.

Captain Harville, though not equalling Captain Wentworth in
manners, was a perfect gentleman, unaffected, warm, and obliging. Mrs. Harville, a degree less polished than her husband,
seemed however to have the same good feelings; and nothing
could be more pleasant than their desire of considering the whole
party as friends of their own, because the friends of Captain Wentworth, or more kindly hospitable than their entreaties for their all
promising to dine with them. The dinner, already ordered at the
inn,[37] was at last, though unwillingly, accepted as an excuse; but
they seemed almost hurt that Captain Wentworth should have

29. *manners:* outward bearing or behavior.

30. *alliance:* union through marriage.

31. Feltham's A *Guide to All the Watering and Sea-Bathing Places,* which calls Lyme one of the better sea-bathing places in England, adds that it has the further advantage of being less expensive than most such places.

32. *retirement:* seclusion, privacy.

33. Captain Benwick is soon shown to have a strong interest in the Romantic poetry of the age. Appreciation of natural beauty was a central theme in that poetry, so a place like Lyme would suit that aspect of his nature.

34. Captain Benwick's situation of loss and regret has parallels to Anne's, as she notes in the next line. But this description of others' sympathy indicates a crucial difference. She, in contrast, must keep her sufferings completely to herself. An early work of Jane Austen's, "Catharine," speaks of "that assertion which says that sorrows are lightened by communication."

35. Men maintained marital eligibility longer than women (for the latter, see p. 53, note 27). Thus in Jane Austen, while the female characters who marry are all below thirty, and are usually in their early twenties or younger, a number of comparable male characters are in their thirties, sometimes even late thirties. Later events will demonstrate the comparative validity of Anne's prediction about Captain Benwick's future, as opposed to the belief of Captains Wentworth and Harville that their friend is inconsolable.

36. *want:* lack.

37. Inns, which catered to the most affluent classes, offered meals, often lavish, as well as accommodations. The party was already said to have ordered dinner at the inn as soon as they arrived. Busy inns would normally have dinners readily available; this was especially important for those that served travelers, who frequently needed to eat immediately before their carriage left again. That is not true here, for Lyme is away from main traveling routes, and during the off-season the inn would have relatively few visitors (though inns could also be places for locals to meet). The inn probably needs time not only to cook but also to procure food from local shops, for lack of refrigeration meant that many items would need to be bought fresh.

brought any such party to Lyme, without considering it as a thing of course that they should dine with them.

There was so much attachment to Captain Wentworth in all this, and such a bewitching charm in a degree of hospitality so uncommon, so unlike the usual style of give-and-take invitations, and dinners of formality and display,[38] that Anne felt her spirits not likely to be benefited by an increasing acquaintance among his brother-officers. "These would have been all my friends," was her thought; and she had to struggle against a great tendency to lowness.[39]

On quitting the Cobb, they all went indoors with their new friends, and found rooms so small as none but those who invite from the heart could think capable of accommodating so many. Anne had a moment's astonishment on the subject herself;[40] but it was soon lost in the pleasanter feelings which sprang from the sight of all the ingenious contrivances and nice arrangements of Captain Harville, to turn the actual space to the best possible account, to supply the deficiencies of lodging-house furniture, and defend the windows and doors against the winter storms to be expected.[41] The varieties in the fitting-up[42] of the rooms, where the common necessaries provided by the owner, in the common indifferent plight,[43] were contrasted with some few articles of a rare species of wood, excellently worked up,[44] and with something curious and valuable from all the distant countries Captain Harville had visited,[45] were more than amusing[46] to Anne: connected as it all was with his profession, the fruit of its labours, the effect of its influence on his habits, the picture of repose and domestic happiness it presented, made it to her a something more, or less, than gratification.[47]

Captain Harville was no reader; but he had contrived excellent accommodations,[48] and fashioned very pretty shelves, for a tolerable collection of well-bound volumes,[49] the property of Captain Benwick. His lameness prevented him from taking much exercise; but a mind of usefulness and ingenuity seemed to furnish him with constant employment within. He drew, he varnished,

38. Standard etiquette dictated that people should issue invitations to dine with them and should carefully alternate which family invited the other. Dinners could also be opportunities, ones Sir Walter and Elizabeth would certainly seize, to display the elegance of one's possessions, manners, and serving procedures. The Harvilles' hospitality contrasts with the relative lack of hospitality toward her own relatives that Elizabeth displays later (p. 418).

39. This demonstration of the goodness of those in the navy, which will continue throughout the novel, highlights for Anne what she has lost. It also helps reveal Captain Wentworth's goodness, through the quality of his friends.

40. Her astonishment would be increased by having lived almost all her life in spacious and luxurious Kellynch Hall.

41. Lyme, being along the coast, is windy, and can suffer strong winter storms.

42. *fitting-up*: furnishing.

43. *common indifferent plight*: standard mediocre condition (of lodging houses).

44. *worked up*: improved, brought to a superior state.

45. Naval officers would stop at various ports around the world, and thus have opportunities to buy a variety of souvenirs. Such souvenirs would have particular value then, because the slowness and costs of overseas trade meant that numerous products were available only in their country of origin. He also may have procured his "rare species of wood" on these overseas voyages.

46. *amusing*: interesting, diverting.

47. The "more than gratification" would be the feelings, even stronger than simple satisfaction (the rough meaning of "gratification" then), that this inspiring picture stirs in her; the "less than gratification" would be the reminder the scene brings of what she has lost by not connecting herself with the navy.

48. *accommodations*: arrangements.

49. At this time the binding of books would indicate something of the owner. A book was generally sold with little or no binding; most purchasers would then have it rebound themselves, with the quality and elegance of the binding varying according to the means and wishes of the owner. Thus Captain Benwick's well-bound books suggest the value he places on them.

he carpentered, he glued; he made toys for the children, he fashioned new netting-needles and pins with improvements;[50] and if
every thing else was done, sat down to his large fishing-net at one
corner of the room.[51]

Anne thought she left great happiness behind her when they
quitted the house; and Louisa, by whom she found herself walking, burst forth into raptures of admiration and delight on the
character of the navy—their friendliness, their brotherliness, their
openness, their uprightness; protesting that she was convinced of
sailors having more worth and warmth than any other set of men
in England; that they only knew how to live, and they only
deserved to be respected and loved.

They went back to dress and dine;[52] and so well had the
scheme answered already, that nothing was found amiss; though
its being "so entirely out of the season," and the "no-thorough-fare
of Lyme,"[53] and the "no expectation of company," had brought
many apologies from the heads of the inn.

Anne found herself by this time growing so much more hardened to being in Captain Wentworth's company than she had at
first imagined could ever be, that the sitting down to the same
table with him now, and the interchange of the common civilities
attending on it—(they never got beyond) was become a mere
nothing.[54]

The nights were too dark for the ladies to meet again till the
morrow,[55] but Captain Harville had promised them a visit in the
evening; and he came, bringing his friend also, which was more
than had been expected, it having been agreed that Captain Benwick had all the appearance of being oppressed by the presence of
so many strangers.[56] He ventured among them again, however,
though his spirits certainly did not seem fit for the mirth of the
party in general.

While Captains Wentworth and Harville led the talk on one
side of the room, and, by recurring to former days, supplied anec-
dotes in abundance to occupy and entertain the others, it fell to
Anne's lot to be placed rather apart with Captain Benwick; and a

50. The needles and pins could help him make his own fishing net, mentioned just below, or they could be intended for other forms of netting. Netting purses or other small items was a popular activity for women: the heroine of *Mansfield Park*, Fanny Price, owns a netting box for keeping her netting supplies. The handicrafts described here, and the woodworking mentioned above, were popular pastimes for sailors on ships, who often needed ways to fill the long hours of waiting and inaction that were a frequent part of life at sea. The many contrivances on ships, to minimize the handicaps of a small space and difficult conditions, could also foster the spirit of practical ingenuity that Captain Harville displays.

51. Making nets for fishing or hunting was a popular male activity. In a letter Jane Austen writes of two of her nephews, "They amuse themselves very comfortably in the Even^g — by netting; they are each about a rabbit net," and then compares them in this to her brother Frank, who was a naval officer noted for his handiness and fondness for various crafts (Oct. 11, 1813). He may have inspired this depiction of Captain Harville.

52. Dressing for dinner would be standard practice, especially when visiting a public place.

53. Lyme was away from the main roads, being perched at the edge of the sea and separated from inland areas by steep hills. If it were a thoroughfare it could experience people passing through, even during the off-season.

54. This suggests an evolution in their relationship, but a limited one.

55. The darkness of the nights probably refers to the absence of moonlight. By this time larger towns had street lighting, but many smaller ones like Lyme (it had fewer than two thousand inhabitants at this time) still had little or no public lighting. In such towns, and in rural areas, people had to rely on the moon at night, and of course it fluctuated, whatever light it did offer would be further diluted by the overcast conditions prevailing over England throughout the colder months. Moreover, the artificial light generated by houses, shops, public buildings, and carriages, which played an important role in helping illuminate towns, would all be less in Lyme during the winter off-season.

56. This suggests that Captain Benwick may not be as completely oppressed by sorrow as others suspect. He will show other signs of wishing for company.

very good impulse of her nature obliged her to begin an acquaintance with him. He was shy, and disposed to abstraction; but the engaging mildness of her countenance, and gentleness of her manners, soon had their effect; and Anne was well repaid the first trouble of exertion. He was evidently a young man of considerable taste in reading, though principally in poetry; and besides the persuasion of having given him at least an evening's indulgence in the discussion of subjects, which his usual companions had probably no concern in, she had the hope of being of real use to him in some suggestions as to the duty and benefit of struggling against affliction,[57] which had naturally grown out of their conversation. For, though shy, he did not seem reserved; it had rather the appearance of feelings glad to burst their usual restraints; and having talked of poetry, the richness of the present age, and gone through a brief comparison of opinion as to the first-rate poets,[58] trying to ascertain whether *Marmion* or *The Lady of the Lake* were to be preferred,[59] and how ranked the *Giaour* and *The Bride of Abydos*;[60] and moreover, how the *Giaour* was to be pronounced,[61] he shewed himself so intimately acquainted with all the tenderest songs of the one poet, and all the impassioned descriptions of hopeless agony of the other; he repeated, with such tremulous feeling, the various lines which imaged a broken heart, or a mind destroyed by wretchedness,[62] and looked so entirely as if he meant to be understood, that she ventured to hope he did not always read only poetry; and to say, that she thought it was the misfortune of poetry, to be seldom safely enjoyed by those who enjoyed it completely; and that the strong feelings which alone could estimate it truly, were the very feelings which ought to taste it but sparingly.[63]

His looks shewing him not pained, but pleased with this allusion to his situation, she was emboldened to go on; and feeling in herself the right of seniority of mind, she ventured to recommend a larger allowance of prose in his daily study; and on being requested to particularize mentioned such works of our best moralists, such collections of the finest letters, such memoirs of characters of worth and suffering, as occurred to her at the

57. This idea that struggling against affliction was not only a benefit to one-self, but also a duty to one's fellow creatures and to God, was widespread at the time. Anne's own struggles along these lines would certainly make her likely to preach such a message, just as her own afflictions would tend to make her sympathize with, and attend to, someone who has suffered and whose sufferings have affinities to hers.

58. This period, that of the Romantic poets, was indeed one of the richest in the history of English poetry, though many of the poets currently regarded as first-rate were far less heeded in their own time. Wordsworth and Coleridge, who helped launch the Romantic movement in poetry, were slow to gain popularity and respect; their seminal inaugural work, *Lyrical Ballads*, was read by few people when it appeared in 1798. Jane Austen has only a brief mention of Wordsworth in her last work, *Sanditon*. Two other famous poets, Shelley and Keats, who were just beginning to publish during the second decade of the nineteenth century, also did not attain quick recognition.

59. These are two long narrative poems by Walter Scott. In contrast to the above poets, Scott immediately achieved great popularity. The two poems cited here, his most widely read, were among the best sellers of the age—and in this age, poetry generally outsold novels, at least until Scott's own novels appeared. Both poems are stories of love and war, set in sixteenth-century Scotland; a critical element of Romanticism was fascination with the past, especially the medieval past, and Scott was central to fostering this senti-ment. Jane Austen mentions each of these poems in her letters.

60. These are two narrative poems by Lord Byron, the other highly popular poet of the time. Both are tragic love stories set in the Middle East; fascina-tion with foreign lands, especially ones regarded as highly exotic, was another feature of Romanticism.

61. The title of the *Giaour*, based on the main character, comes from a Mus-lim term of reproach for infidels. Byron himself admitted the difficulty of pro-nouncing it (one literary dictionary writes the pronunciation as "dja-oor").

62. The tenderest songs would refer to Scott, and the descriptions of hope-less agony to Byron. Scott's poems include a variety of songs, often full of ten-der sentiment and telling of lovers who come to grief; such lovers also figure prominently in the narratives of his poems. Byron presents a more despairing picture, with more extreme emotions: The *Bride of Adybos* ends with the deaths of the bride and her beloved, while in the *Giaour* the title character's beloved is cruelly slain and he, retreating to a monastery, concludes the poem with an extended lament of the bitterest anguish.

63. Anne's advice of a moderate course corresponds to her own behavior.

moment as calculated to rouse and fortify the mind by the highest precepts, and the strongest examples of moral and religious endurances.[64]

Captain Benwick listened attentively, and seemed grateful for the interest implied; and though with a shake of the head, and sighs which declared his little faith in the efficacy of any books on grief like his, noted down the names of those she recommended, and promised to procure and read them.

When the evening was over, Anne could not but be amused at the idea of her coming to Lyme, to preach patience and resignation to a young man whom she had never seen before; nor could she help fearing, on more serious reflection, that, like many other great moralists and preachers, she had been eloquent on a point in which her own conduct would ill bear examination.[65]

While a person of acute feelings, and a lover of poetry, she has always tried, even when it required great struggle, to temper her feelings with reason. This picture of Captain Benwick, and suggestion of the possible excess in his romantic emotionalism, also corresponds to Jane Austen's own treatment of such emotionalism in other works. *Sense and Sensibility* criticizes the cult of sensibility that was linked to Romanticism, and *Northanger Abbey* directly satirizes the highly charged, and popular, Gothic novels that appealed to similar sentiments. Her last work, *Sanditon*, written just after this, portrays one character whose infatuation with Romantic poetry, especially that of Robert Burns, and overflowing enthusiasm for natural beauty, especially that of the sea, leads him to ludicrous extremes in both his thoughts and his language, and even helps inspire a planned course of immoral seduction.

64. These could refer to a wide array of works, especially from earlier years. The eighteenth century, whose spirit Jane Austen exudes in many respects, was characterized by a general preference for prose and an emphasis on greater rationalism than the Romantic period. Moral essays, frequently supported by observations on life and contemporary mores, were popular throughout the century. Collections of letters, often highly polished, also appeared. Finally, biography developed as a significant genre, and it, like much of the prose of the time, often had a moralizing tone, pointing out lessons and presenting examples of virtuous behavior.

65. The difficulty in following precepts of patience and resignation had been a popular theme of many writers, especially when discussing the influential philosophy of Stoicism, which counseled rational indifference to the ills of life. Similarly, as in all ages, many who preached virtue did not always live up to their preaching. One of the most influential prose moralists of the eighteenth century, and a favorite author of Jane Austen's, Samuel Johnson, addresses this point in one of his essays (*The Rambler*, #14). He writes that "for many reasons a man writes much better than he lives." But he argues, "Nothing is more unjust, however common, than to charge with hypocrisy him that expresses zeal for those virtues, which he neglects to practice; since he may be sincerely convinced of the advantages of conquering his passions, without having yet obtained the victory." Rather, he claims that such a man should be commended for attempting to impart to others some of his own, possibly hard-earned, wisdom. From this perspective, Anne's counsel to Captain Benwick, which does certainly come from her own extensive experience, would represent a valuable and benevolent service to him, whatever her own failings in achieving patience or self-control.

Chapter Twelve

Anne and Henrietta, finding themselves the earliest of the party the next morning, agreed to stroll down to the sea before breakfast.—They went to the sands, to watch the flowing of the tide, which a fine south-easterly breeze was bringing in with all the grandeur which so flat a shore admitted.[1] They praised the morning; gloried in the sea; sympathized[2] in the delight of the fresh-feeling breeze—and were silent; till Henrietta suddenly began again, with,

"Oh! yes,—I am quite convinced that, with very few exceptions, the sea-air always does good. There can be no doubt of its having been of the greatest service to Dr. Shirley, after his illness, last spring twelvemonth.[3] He declares himself, that coming to Lyme for a month, did him more good than all the medicine he took;[4] and, that being by the sea, always makes him feel young again. Now, I cannot help thinking it a pity that he does not live entirely by the sea. I do think he had better leave Uppercross entirely, and fix at[5] Lyme.—Do not you, Anne?—Do not you agree with me, that it is the best thing he could do, both for himself and Mrs. Shirley?—She has cousins here, you know, and many acquaintance, which would make it cheerful for her,—and I am sure she would be glad to get to a place where she could have medical attendance at hand, in case of his having another seizure.[6] Indeed I think it quite melancholy to have such excellent people as Dr. and Mrs. Shirley, who have been doing good all their lives, wearing out their last days in a place like Uppercross, where, excepting our family, they seem shut out from all the world.[7] I wish his friends would propose it to him. I really think they ought. And, as to procuring a dispensation, there could be no difficulty at his time of life, and with his character.[8] My only doubt is, whether any thing could persuade him to leave his parish. He is so very

1.   On a flat shore a rise in water would cause a large stretch of beach to be speedily inundated. Because Lyme faces to the south, a southeasterly breeze would add to the rapid advance of the water.

2.   *sympathized:* were affected similarly.

3.   *spring twelvemonth:* a year prior to last spring.

4.   Sea air, like bathing in and drinking seawater, was recommended by many doctors of the time as healthy. Medical thinking placed a great emphasis on environmental factors in causing disease, with the quality of the air considered to be one of the principal determinants. Jane Austen visited the seaside at one point for purposes at least partly of health.

5   *fix at:* settle or establish his residence in.

6.   *seizure:* sudden attack, especially an attack of apoplexy, i.e., a stroke. Seaside resorts were noted for their large numbers of medical practitioners, who were attracted to them by the many visitors, usually wealthy, who came there in search of health.

7.   As already shown, the number of genteel families was very limited in rural areas. A place like Lyme, with many affluent visitors from elsewhere, would offer the possibility of far greater companionship for someone like Dr. Shirley.

8.   A dispensation would be from the church, granting him permission to retire from his post. Henrietta is probably right that someone of his age, and with his character, or reputation, would have no difficulty procuring one. Jane Austen's father had no trouble retiring from his post, and many clergymen who did not have the excuse of old age were able to hire curates to perform their duties.

strict and scrupulous in his notions; over-scrupulous, I must say.[9]
Do not you think, Anne, it is being over-scrupulous? Do not you
think it is quite a mistaken point of conscience, when a clergyman
sacrifices his health for the sake of duties, which may be just as
well performed by another person? — And at Lyme too, — only seventeen miles off, — he would be near enough to hear, if people
thought there was any thing to complain of."[10]

Anne smiled more than once to herself during this speech, and
entered into the subject, as ready to do good by entering into the
feelings of a young lady as of a young man, — though here it was
good of a lower standard, for what could be offered but general
acquiescence?[11] — She said all that was reasonable and proper on
the business; felt the claims of Dr. Shirley to repose, as she ought;
saw how very desirable it was that he should have some active,
respectable young man, as a resident curate,[12] and was even courteous enough to hint at the advantage of such resident curate's
being married.

"I wish," said Henrietta, very well pleased with her companion,
"I wish Lady Russell lived at Uppercross, and were intimate with
Dr. Shirley. I have always heard of Lady Russell, as a woman of
the greatest influence with every body! I always look upon her as
able to persuade a person to any thing! I am afraid of her, as I have
told you before, quite afraid of her, because she is so very clever;
but I respect her amazingly, and wish we had such a neighbour at
Uppercross."

Anne was amused by Henrietta's manner of being grateful, and
amused also, that the course of events and the new interests of
Henrietta's views[13] should have placed her friend at all in favour
with any of the Musgrove family;[14] she had only time, however,
for a general answer, and a wish that such another woman were at
Uppercross, before all subjects suddenly ceased, on seeing Louisa
and Captain Wentworth coming towards them. They came also
for a stroll till breakfast was likely to be ready;[15] but Louisa recollecting, immediately afterwards, that she had something to procure at a shop, invited them all to go back with her into the town.
They were all at her disposal.

9. Dr. Shirley's scrupulousness, shown by his not retiring yet, was already indicated (see p. 149, note 35).

10. Meaning if people complained about the curate he hired.

11. The young man was Captain Benwick. In his case she was able to offer useful advice he had not heard before, which means she was offering good of greater value, or higher standard, than her simple acquiescence to Henrietta.

12. A curate who needs to reside in the parish. Currently Charles Hayter has a curacy that does not require residency.

13. *views:* prospects, expectations (that is, of marriage).

14. The sentence implies that Lady Russell is not in favor with the Musgrove family. No aversion between her and them is otherwise shown, though she is consistently portrayed as more formal than they in her conduct and manners, and more bookish and serious in her tastes and interests. Louisa said earlier that her parents believed that Lady Russell persuaded Anne to refuse to marry Charles Musgrove. It is possible this belief has spurred resentment of Lady Russell on their part, whether because of wounded pride that she thought their eldest son, and heir, not good enough for Anne, or because of a wish that they had Anne rather than Mary as a daughter-in-law.

15. As indicated elsewhere, breakfast was not eaten early by wealthier people at this time. They would usually have a couple of hours beforehand for other things. One standard practice making this possible was a light supper late in the evening.

When they came to the steps, leading upwards from the beach,[16] a gentleman at the same moment preparing to come down, politely drew back, and stopped to give them way.[17] They ascended and passed him; and as they passed, Anne's face caught his eye, and he looked at her with a degree of earnest admiration, which she could not be insensible[18] of. She was looking remarkably well; her very regular, very pretty features, having the bloom and freshness of youth restored by the fine wind which had been blowing on her complexion, and by the animation of eye which it had also produced. It was evident that the gentleman, (completely a gentleman in manner) admired her exceedingly. Captain Wentworth looked round at her instantly in a way which shewed his noticing of it. He gave her a momentary glance,—a glance of brightness, which seemed to say, "That man is struck with you,—and even I, at this moment, see something like Anne Elliot again."[19]

After attending Louisa through her business, and loitering about a little longer, they returned to the inn; and Anne in passing afterwards quickly from her own chamber to their dining-room, had nearly run against the very same gentleman, as he came out of an adjoining apartment.[20] She had before conjectured him to be a stranger like themselves, and determined that a well-looking[21] groom,[22] who was strolling about near the two inns as they came back, should be his servant. Both master and man being in mourning, assisted the idea.[23] It was now proved that he belonged to the same inn as themselves; and this second meeting, short as it was, also proved again by the gentleman's looks, that he thought hers very lovely, and by the readiness and propriety of his apologies, that he was a man of exceedingly good manners. He seemed about thirty, and, though not handsome, had an agreeable person.[24] Anne felt that she should like to know who he was.

They had nearly done breakfast, when the sound of a carriage, (almost the first they had heard since entering Lyme)[25] drew half the party to the window. "It was a gentleman's carriage—a curricle[26]—but only coming round from the stable-yard to the front

16. The beach at Lyme is at a lower elevation from the town, so steps to get from one to the other are necessary.

17. This gentleman, who will soon be identified, will consistently display very polite manners.

18. *insensible:* unaware, unconscious.

19. This is a significant moment in the novel. It shows Anne regaining some of her good looks. It is also the first time Captain Wentworth has indicated actual admiration for her, as opposed to sympathy for her distress. And it introduces the possibility of rivalry between the two men struck or inspired by Anne. Later Captain Wentworth will mention the effect of the other's look upon him (p. 462). One possible inspiration for the episode is an incident Jane Austen recounted in a letter from her own visit to Lyme, when she was almost the same age as Anne Elliot. She mentions "a new odd-looking Man who had been eyeing me for some time, & at last without any introduction asked me if I meant to dance again" (Sept. 14, 1804).

20. *apartment:* room, or suite of rooms. The term was used in both senses then, and it is not clear from the context which is meant here.

21. *well-looking:* good-looking.

22. A groom is a male servant who takes care of horses. Grooms could also double as valets (see p. 5, note 18), and it is likely this groom does so, since he seems to be the only servant attending his master (see note 28 below).

23. It was standard for servants to adopt the mourning of their masters.

24. *person:* personal appearance.

25. A sign of how quiet Lyme was in the off-season. Local people, who would mostly be working people without much money, would walk, for the town was small enough to go everywhere on foot. Visitors would be more likely to use carriages: some, like the party here, would come in their own carriages; others would be able to hire a vehicle.

26. *curricle:* an open carriage pulled by two horses; other open carriages used one. This meant two horses were pulling a lightweight vehicle, allowing them to go longer distances without becoming tired. This made it suitable to convey Charles and Captain Wentworth all the way to Lyme. Charles's interest in comparing this other curricle to his suggests he may have enjoyed showing it off: a contemporary writer states that no vehicles "are so much regarded for fashion as these [curricles] are by those who are partial to drive their own horses" (William Felton, *A Treatise on Carriages*).

door[27]—Somebody must be going away.—It was driven by a servant in mourning."[28]

The word curricle made Charles Musgrove jump up, that he might compare it with his own, the servant in mourning roused Anne's curiosity, and the whole six were collected to look, by the time the owner of the curricle was to be seen issuing from the door amidst the bows and civilities of the household,[29] and taking his seat, to drive off.

"Ah!" cried Captain Wentworth, instantly, and with half a glance at Anne; "it is the very man we passed."

The Miss Musgroves agreed to it; and having all kindly watched him as far up the hill as they could, they returned to the breakfast-table. The waiter came into the room soon afterwards.

"Pray," said Captain Wentworth, immediately, "can you tell us the name of the gentleman who is just gone away?"

"Yes, Sir, a Mr. Elliot; a gentleman of large fortune,—came in last night from Sidmouth,[30]—dare say you heard the carriage, Sir, while you were at dinner; and going on now for Crewkherne, in his way to Bath and London."[31]

"Elliot!"—Many had looked on each other, and many had repeated the name, before all this had been got through, even by the smart[32] rapidity of a waiter.

"Bless me!" cried Mary; "it must be our cousin;—it must be our Mr. Elliot, it must, indeed!—Charles, Anne, must not it? In mourning, you see, just as our Mr. Elliot must be. How very extraordinary! In the very same inn with us! Anne, must not it be our Mr. Elliot; my father's next heir? Pray Sir,"[33] (turning to the waiter), "did not you hear,—did not his servant say whether he belonged to the Kellynch family?"[34]

"No, ma'am,—he did not mention no particular family; but he said his master was a very rich gentleman, and would be a baronight[35] some day."

"There! you see!" cried Mary, in an ecstasy, "Just as I said! Heir to Sir Walter Elliot!—I was sure that would come out, if it was so. Depend upon it, that is a circumstance which his servants take

27. The stable yard is probably attached to the inn. Inns normally kept horses and carriages to rent (this one is described as doing so on p. 220), and thus would have facilities for lodgers' horses and vehicles.

28. The wording of the passage leaves some ambiguity as to whether this is the same servant as the groom just mentioned. That would be logical, for the man and a servant in mourning are shortly described as driving away in the curricle, and it could seat only two comfortably. A second servant would have to travel separately in a public coach, which would involve additional complications and expense.

29. This refers to the household of the inn. Inns would often be run by a family; even if not, "household" could mean any group of people living under the same roof. Innkeepers were of a lower social level than their usual guests, so they would behave very solicitously and courteously to them.

30. *Sidmouth:* another fashionable seaside resort, about ten miles west of Lyme (see map, p. 513). The man's visiting both Sidmouth and Lyme, and then Bath, suggests he is a gentleman of leisure, as turns out to be the case.

31. Crewkherne is a town north of Lyme, and the first significant stop on the way to Bath (see map, p. 513); they will probably change horses there.

32. *smart:* brisk, prompt.

33. Mary calls him "sir" even though he is from a lower social class. Jane Austen's novels, and other works of the time, even as they show people socializing only with those of their own class, depict them mostly treating everyone, even those lower than they are, with respectful formality.

34. While Mr. Elliot was staying at the inn, his servant would have associated with employees of the inn like the waiter, who were of similar social rank. Thus it would be logical to ask the latter about conversations with the servant.

35. *baronight:* an incorrect amalgamation of "baronet" and "knight." The waiter, and perhaps Mr. Elliot's servant as well, does not understand the distinction between the ranks (which were close). This mistake, and some of the poor grammar of this speech and his preceding one, indicates his lower class. Jane Austen rarely reproduces lower-class speech, but when she does it always has a marked plainness and awkwardness, an accurate reflection of the tremendous gap in education and culture between classes at this time.

care to publish[36] wherever he goes.[37] But, Anne, only conceive how extraordinary! I wish I had looked at him more. I wish we had been aware in time, who it was, that he might have been introduced to us. What a pity that we should not have been introduced to each other!—Do you think he had the Elliot countenance? I hardly looked at him, I was looking at the horses; but I think he had something of the Elliot countenance. I wonder the arms did not strike me! Oh!—the great-coat[38] was hanging over the pannel,[39] and hid the arms;[40] so it did, otherwise, I am sure, I should have observed them, and the livery too; if the servant had not been in mourning, one should have known him by the livery."[41]

"Putting all these very extraordinary circumstances together," said Captain Wentworth, "we must consider it to be the arrangement of Providence, that you should not be introduced to your cousin."

When she could command Mary's attention, Anne quietly tried to convince her that their father and Mr. Elliot had not, for many years, been on such terms as to make the power of attempting an introduction at all desirable.[42]

At the same time, however, it was a secret gratification to herself to have seen her cousin, and to know that the future owner of Kellynch was undoubtedly a gentleman, and had an air of good sense. She would not, upon any account, mention her having met with him the second time; luckily Mary did not much attend to their having passed close by him in their early walk, but she would have felt quite ill-used by Anne's having actually run against him in the passage, and received his very polite excuses, while she had never been near him at all; no, that cousinly little interview must remain a perfect secret.

"Of course," said Mary, "you will mention our seeing Mr. Elliot, the next time you write to Bath. I think my father certainly ought to hear of it; do mention all about him."

Anne avoided a direct reply, but it was just the circumstance which she considered as not merely unnecessary to be communicated, but as what ought to be suppressed. The offence which had

36. *publish*: announce, make generally known.

37. Mary's suspicion is characteristic, for she instinctively attributes to others her own obsession with social status. But it also may be correct, for since servants' status derived largely from their master's, they had a natural incentive to boast of the latter.

38. *great-coat*: a large, loose coat for outerwear, reaching below the knees, that was worn by men. It was warm, but also heavy and awkward—a man in *Northanger Abbey* is described as hating to wear one. In this case its owner wishes to have it for traveling, for he is using an open carriage in November, but he leaves it on the carriage while walking around.

39. The pannel, or panel, was a piece of wood set within the door; it would be where various insignia could be placed. Private carriages would often have family arms displayed there. In an open vehicle like a curricle the door would be low, so it would be natural to hang a coat over it, thereby covering the panel.

40. For family arms, see p. 299, note 44.

41. A livery was specific to each family (see p. 41, note 39). Since liveries tended to be gaudy and brightly colored, they would be particularly inappropriate to wear during mourning. For more on mourning attire, see p. 279, note 20.

42. Anne's waiting until she could catch Mary's attention, and the quietness of her words, indicate both her discretion, for she would not wish to announce her family's quarrel with Mr. Elliot, and her politeness. In this section of the book, even as she enjoys and extols the more open and informal manners of the Harvilles, she maintains her own careful and discreet manners.

been given her father, many years back, she knew; Elizabeth's particular share in it she suspected;[43] and that Mr. Elliot's idea[44] always produced irritation in both, was beyond a doubt. Mary never wrote to Bath herself; all the toil of keeping up a slow and unsatisfactory correspondence with Elizabeth fell on Anne.[45]

Breakfast had not been long over, when they were joined by Captain and Mrs. Harville, and Captain Benwick, with whom they had appointed to take their last walk about Lyme. They ought to be setting off for Uppercross by one, and in the meanwhile were to be all together, and out of doors as long as they could.

Anne found Captain Benwick getting near her, as soon as they were all fairly in the street. Their conversation, the preceding evening, did not disincline him to seek her again; and they walked together some time, talking as before of Mr. Scott[46] and Lord Byron, and still as unable, as before, and as unable as any other two readers, to think exactly alike of the merits of either, till something occasioned an almost general change amongst their party, and instead of Captain Benwick, she had Captain Harville by her side.

"Miss Elliot," said he, speaking rather low, "you have done a good deed in making that poor fellow talk so much.[47] I wish he could have such company oftener. It is bad for him, I know, to be shut up as he is; but what can we do? we cannot part."

"No," said Anne, "that I can easily believe to be impossible; but in time, perhaps — we know what time does in every case of affliction, and you must remember, Captain Harville, that your friend may yet be called a young mourner — only last summer, I understand."

"Ay, true enough," (with a deep sigh) "only June."

"And not known to him, perhaps, so soon."

"Not till the first week in August, when he came home from the Cape,[48] — just made into the Grappler.[49] I was at Plymouth, dreading to hear of him; he sent in letters, but the Grappler was under orders for Portsmouth.[50] There the news must follow him,

43. She means Elizabeth's disappointment and anger at Mr. Elliot's marrying someone else. The narrator explicitly stated Elizabeth to have felt this (p. 12). Anne would not have witnessed the incident, for it took place just after her mother's death, and she was away at school then. Hence she can only surmise, but, as with most of her surmises, she is correct.

44. *Mr. Elliot's idea:* the idea or conception of Mr. Elliot.

45. Thus Anne maintains contact with her family in Bath by corresponding with Elizabeth rather than her father. It is probable that Anne feels closer to her sister, even with the latter's coldness, and even though the unsatisfactory nature of the correspondence probably results from Elizabeth's neglect rather than Anne's. In addition, letter writing was an activity especially likely to be undertaken by women. Jane Austen, who wrote numerous letters herself, describes it as something women are often highly devoted to, and other evidence indicates that genteel women, even more than men, would engage in continual and lengthy correspondence with friends and relations. One reason was that women had less freedom to go outside the home and travel; letters could be their principal, or only, means of staying in touch with others.

46. Mr. Scott is Walter Scott, the poet already discussed by these two. This was what he would be called then, for it was not until several years later, in 1820, that he was made a baronet and became Sir Walter Scott.

47. His praise, along with Captain Benwick's interest, show Anne's stature increasing. Their high opinion might influence Captain Wentworth; it at least signals that he could potentially be influenced by the same considerations that made them regard her favorably.

48. The Cape of Good Hope, where Britain had a naval base (see p. 445, note 21).

49. This means he was just promoted to a position, probably captain, of the *Grappler.* It is an appropriate name for a ship, for naval vessels sometimes grappled enemy ships in order to board them during a battle.

50. He would have sent in letters for his fiancée, who was probably staying with Captain Harville, her brother, in Plymouth.

but who was to tell it? not I. I would as soon have been run up to the yard-arm.[51] Nobody could do it, but that good fellow, (pointing to Captain Wentworth). The Laconia had come into Plymouth the week before; no danger of her being sent to sea again.[52] He stood his chance for the rest—wrote up for leave of absence,[53] but without waiting the return,[54] travelled night and day till he got to Portsmouth,[55] rowed off to the Grappler that instant,[56] and never left the poor fellow for a week; that's what he did, and nobody else could have saved poor James.[57] You may think, Miss Elliot, whether he is dear to us!"[58]

Anne did think on the question with perfect decision,[59] and said as much in reply as her own feelings could accomplish, or as his seemed able to bear, for he was too much affected to renew the subject—and when he spoke again, it was of something totally different.

Mrs. Harville's giving it as her opinion that her husband would have quite walking enough by the time he reached home, determined the direction of all the party in what was to be their last walk; they would accompany them to their door, and then return and set off themselves. By all their calculations there was just time for this; but as they drew near the Cobb, there was such a general wish to walk along it once more, all were so inclined, and Louisa soon grew so determined,[60] that the difference of a quarter of an hour, it was found, would be no difference at all, so with all the kind leave-taking, and all the kind interchange of invitations and promises which may be imagined, they parted from Captain and Mrs. Harville at their own door, and still accompanied by Captain Benwick, who seemed to cling to them to the last, proceeded to make the proper adieus to the Cobb.[61]

Anne found Captain Benwick again drawing near her. Lord Byron's "dark blue seas" could not fail of being brought forward by their present view,[62] and she gladly gave him all her attention as long as attention was possible. It was soon drawn per force another way.

There was too much wind to make the high part of the new

51. *run up to the yard-arm:* hanged. The yardarm is the outer part of a wooden beam extending horizontally across the ship, on which sails can be hung. Sailors sentenced to death would be hanged from the yardarm.

52. Ships normally stayed in harbor for a period of time because, having inevitably sustained wear and tear, if not damage, during their voyage, they would need repairs to be seaworthy again. Both Portsmouth and Plymouth contained substantial dockyards for performing these repairs.

53. He would have written to the Admiralty for leave of absence. He would have known that the ship would not return to sea: being away when it was due to leave would be a serious breach of duty. But he could not be certain the request for leave would be granted, so he stood, or took, his chance on that less grave eventuality by departing before hearing from the Admiralty.

54. *return:* reply.

55. He would have traveled by land, most likely via post chaises (see p. 221, note 90). Plymouth is approximately 150 miles from Portsmouth in a straight line and it would have been longer by the main roads, which veered substantially inland. The trip would have taken more than twenty-four hours, perhaps much more, which was why he needed to travel night and day.

56. He would have rowed in a boat to the ship, sitting in harbor.

57. The words seem to imply Captain Benwick would have killed himself otherwise. If so, this would suggest a clear flaw in his character, perhaps a product of the highly emotional nature he has shown.

58. This is the most powerful example of Captain Wentworth's goodness that is presented in the story. It is valuable because his role in the novel gives him limited opportunity to display that goodness, even as it is necessary to have Anne regret him acutely. The incident also establishes a link between him and Anne, through their mutual service to Captain Benwick in his grief.

59. *decision:* determination.

60. Another instance of the determination Louisa has been consistently displaying since Captain Wentworth's praise of that quality on their walk.

61. Captain Benwick's remaining with the party, a product particularly of the rapport Anne has established with him, will soon lead to his being available for a mission that will have momentous consequences.

62. Byron's *The Corsair*, a work Jane Austen mentions reading in a letter (March 5, 1814), begins with the lines, "O'er the glad waters of the dark blue sea, / Our thoughts as boundless, and our souls as free."

Cobb[63] pleasant for the ladies, and they agreed to get down the steps to the lower,[64] and all were contented to pass quietly and carefully down the steep flight, excepting Louisa; she must be jumped down them by Captain Wentworth. In all their walks, he had had to jump her from the stiles;[65] the sensation was delightful to her. The hardness of the pavement for her feet, made him less willing upon the present occasion; he did it, however; she was safely down, and instantly, to shew her enjoyment, ran up the steps to be jumped down again. He advised her against it, thought the jar too great; but no, he reasoned and talked in vain; she smiled and said, "I am determined I will": he put out his hands; she was too precipitate by half a second, she fell on the pavement on the Lower Cobb, and was taken up lifeless!

There was no wound, no blood, no visible bruise; but her eyes were closed, she breathed not, her face was like death. — The horror of that moment to all who stood around!

Captain Wentworth, who had caught her up, knelt with her in his arms, looking on her with a face as pallid as her own, in an agony of silence. "She is dead! she is dead!" screamed Mary, catching hold of her husband, and contributing with his own horror to make him immoveable; and in another moment, Henrietta, sinking under the conviction, lost her senses too, and would have fallen on the steps, but for Captain Benwick and Anne, who caught and supported her between them.

"Is there no one to help me?" were the first words which burst from Captain Wentworth, in a tone of despair, and as if all his own strength were gone.

"Go to him, go to him," cried Anne, "for heaven's sake go to him. I can support her myself. Leave me, and go to him. Rub her hands, rub her temples; here are salts,[66] — take them, take them."

Captain Benwick obeyed, and Charles at the same moment, disengaging himself from his wife, they were both with him; and Louisa was raised up and supported more firmly between them, and every thing was done that Anne had prompted, but in vain; while Captain Wentworth, staggering against the wall for his support, exclaimed in the bitterest agony,

63. *new Cobb:* this probably refers to the outer section of the Cobb (see p. 182, and p. 183, note 21). It had been swept away by a storm in 1792 and rebuilt using larger, more solid blocks of stone, fastened together by pieces of iron. This would have clearly distinguished it from the older sections, which consisted of uncut stones that were not secured by any external fastening.

64. The Cobb contains an upper and lower level, with steps at various points leading between them. The upper is fully exposed to the wind, which can be very strong at Lyme. It would be especially difficult to walk along for ladies wearing the long, loose dresses of the time. In contrast, the lower Cobb is sheltered from the prevailing western winds by the upper Cobb, which can be as much as ten feet higher. This difference in height, in addition to making walking much easier, makes the steps more formidable, and, combined with the hardness of the pavement, makes Louisa's game a dangerous one.

There have been attempts to identify which set of steps might have been used by Louisa (for one set, see below). But one cannot be certain if Jane Austen had a specific set in mind: she had last visited Lyme ten years before she wrote the novel. Even if there were a specific one, it might not exist today, at least not in the same state, for in 1824 the Cobb was heavily damaged in the worst storm in Lyme's history and had to be rebuilt in many places.

65. *stiles:* barriers that animals cannot pass at the entrances to fields. That this had become her practice suggests her boldness, if not recklessness, and the acquiescence, if not encouragement, Wentworth gave this behavior.

66. *salts:* smelling salts. These, usually consisting of ammonium carbonate,

One of the sets of steps from the lower to the upper Cobb. The wall behind the steps is what Captain Wentworth would have staggered against for his support.

[From Constance Hill, *Jane Austen: Her Homes and Her Friends* (London, 1904), p. 147]

"Oh God! her father and mother!"

"A surgeon!"[67] said Anne.

He caught the word; it seemed to rouse him at once, and saying only "True, true, a surgeon this instant," was darting away, when Anne eagerly suggested,

"Captain Benwick, would not it be better for Captain Benwick? He knows where a surgeon is to be found."

Every one capable of thinking felt the advantage of the idea, and in a moment (it was all done in rapid moments) Captain Benwick had resigned the poor corpse-like figure entirely to the brother's care, and was off for the town with the utmost rapidity.

As to the wretched party left behind, it could scarcely be said which of the three, who were completely rational, was suffering most, Captain Wentworth, Anne, or Charles, who, really a very affectionate brother, hung over Louisa with sobs of grief, and could only turn his eyes from one sister, to see the other in a state as insensible, or to witness the hysterical agitations of his wife, calling on him for help which he could not give.

Anne, attending with all the strength and zeal, and thought, which instinct supplied, to Henrietta, still tried, at intervals, to suggest comfort to the others, tried to quiet Mary, to animate Charles, to assuage the feelings of Captain Wentworth. Both seemed to look to her for directions.

"Anne, Anne," cried Charles, "what is to be done next? What, in heaven's name, is to be done next?"

Captain Wentworth's eyes were also turned towards her.[68]

"Had not she better be carried to the inn? Yes, I am sure, carry her gently to the inn."

"Yes, yes, to the inn," repeated Captain Wentworth, comparatively collected, and eager to be doing something. "I will carry her myself. Musgrove, take care of the others."

By this time the report of the accident had spread among the workmen and boatmen about the Cobb,[69] and many were collected near them, to be useful if wanted, at any rate, to enjoy the sight of a dead young lady, nay, two dead young ladies, for it

were the normal means used to rouse those who fainted or lost consciousness. Women often carried them, something indicated here by Anne's having
some with her (even though she does not seem one to faint).

67. She calls for a surgeon, rather than an apothecary, and that is what is
found. This is in contrast to the apothecary mentioned as coming to examine
little Charles's dislocated collarbone (see p. 101, note 2). The reason is that in
Lyme, with its larger number of patients and medical practitioners, it would
be feasible for the latter to specialize in one branch of practice. In the case of
the surgeon, this would mean treatment of wounds—internal surgery such as
exists today was almost unknown then.

68. Everyone, most notably Captain Wentworth, is looking toward Anne for
leadership. This makes it a critical moment in the novel, during which Anne
can display qualities she has never needed to show previously. At the same
time, it also represents continuity, for her ability to maintain her composure
in a tense and difficult situation results, at least in part, from her frequent, and
mostly successful, struggles to steady and control her emotions in other trying
circumstances. Her doing so also provides a lesson for Captain Wentworth, if
he wishes to draw it. His evaluation of her has been that she possessed the
sweetness of manner he considered essential, but lacked the equally necessary strength of mind. Now he is exposed to a display of her strength, and in
the sort of emergency that he, as a naval officer, has experienced before.

His prior experience in the navy has led to questions about the plausibility
of his relative paralysis in the face of Louisa's accident. On a ship in battle he
would have seen people wounded and killed in front of him, often in grue-
some ways. He also, in order to succeed as he has, would have needed to show
great coolness of mind in the face of such deaths and other dangers and fast-
moving developments. It is possible that his different reaction here results
from his not expecting to meet with such an accident while strolling with a
young lady, whereas he expects danger on board ship. That she is a young lady
may also exacerbate his distress—he earlier spoke of his hatred of anything
that physically inconvenienced women. Added to this would be his consciousness of being partly responsible for a possibly fatal injury to someone
who, unlike a sailor, is not expected to risk her life. Whatever the reason, and
the plausibility, he will soon return to his usual active and decisive character.

69. The harbor adjacent to the Cobb continued to be used by many vessels;
there was also an active shipbuilding industry nearby. Hence there would be
many workers in the area during a normal workday.

proved twice as fine as the first report.[70] To some of the best-
looking[71] of these good people Henrietta was consigned, for,
though partially revived, she was quite helpless; and in this manner, Anne walking by her side, and Charles attending to his wife,
they set forward, treading back with feelings unutterable, the
ground which so lately, so very lately, and so light of heart, they
had passed along.

They were not off the Cobb, before the Harvilles met them.
Captain Benwick had been seen flying by their house, with a
countenance which shewed something to be wrong; and they had
set off immediately, informed and directed, as they passed,[72]
towards the spot. Shocked as Captain Harville was, he brought
senses and nerves that could be instantly useful; and a look
between him and his wife decided what was to be done. She must
be taken to their house — all must go to their house — and wait the
surgeon's arrival there.[73] They would not listen to scruples: he was
obeyed; they were all beneath his roof; and while Louisa, under
Mrs. Harville's direction, was conveyed up stairs, and given possession of her own bed, assistance, cordials, restoratives were supplied by her husband to all who needed them.[74]

Louisa had once opened her eyes, but soon closed them again,
without apparent consciousness. This had been a proof of life,
however, of service to her sister; and Henrietta, though perfectly
incapable of being in the same room with Louisa, was kept, by the
agitation of hope and fear, from a return of her own insensibility.
Mary, too, was growing calmer.

The surgeon was with them almost before it had seemed possible. They were sick with horror while he examined; but he was
not hopeless. The head had received a severe contusion, but he
had seen greater injuries recovered from: he was by no means
hopeless; he spoke cheerfully.

That he did not regard it as a desperate case — that he did not
say a few hours must end it — was at first felt, beyond the hope of
most; and the ecstasy of such a reprieve, the rejoicing, deep and
silent, after a few fervent ejaculations of gratitude to Heaven had
been offered, may be conceived.

70. A young lady, even a fully conscious one, would be a distinctive sight to ordinary workmen. Their voyeuristic curiosity, and the sardonic description of it, shift the tone of the narrative from intense and emotional to ironic and comic. This shift may be a way of reassuring the reader that, despite the horror of the event and the horror felt by the characters, no great tragedy will result.

71. *best-looking:* looking most willing or able to help. The previous sentence stated that some of the onlookers were interested in being useful, and the succeeding description suggests that those they selected carried Henrietta back toward the town, with Anne walking next to them as they did so.

72. Meaning as they passed other people. The description implies that they continually did this, which would indicate the busyness of the Cobb.

73. The Harvilles show the same hospitality seen the previous night. It will prove important for what happens later.

74. Cordials and restoratives could refer to a variety of substances—foods, drinks, or medicines—that were supposed to revive people and restore vigor and strength. Cordials frequently contained alcohol, which was considered to have a variety of medicinal properties.

The tone, the look, with which "Thank God!" was uttered by Captain Wentworth, Anne was sure could never be forgotten by her; nor the sight of him afterwards, as he sat near a table, leaning over it with folded arms, and face concealed, as if overpowered by the various feelings of his soul, and trying by prayer and reflection to calm them.[75]

Louisa's limbs had escaped. There was no injury but to the head.

It now became necessary for the party to consider what was best to be done, as to their general situation. They were now able to speak to each other, and consult. That Louisa must remain where she was, however distressing to her friends to be involving the Harvilles in such trouble, did not admit a doubt. Her removal was impossible. The Harvilles silenced all scruples; and, as much as they could, all gratitude. They had looked forward and arranged every thing, before the others began to reflect. Captain Benwick must give up his room to them, and get a bed elsewhere—and the whole was settled. They were only concerned that the house could accommodate no more; and yet perhaps by "putting the children away in the maids' room,[76] or swinging a cot somewhere,"[77] they could hardly bear to think of not finding room for two or three besides, supposing they might wish to stay;[78] though, with regard to any attendance on Miss Musgrove, there need not be the least uneasiness in leaving her to Mrs. Harville's care entirely. Mrs. Harville was a very experienced nurse;[79] and her nursery-maid, who had lived with her long and gone about with her every where,[80] was just such another. Between those two, she could want[81] no possible attendance by day or night. And all this was said with a truth and sincerity of feeling irresistible.

Charles, Henrietta, and Captain Wentworth were the three in consultation, and for a little while it was only an interchange of perplexity and terror. "Uppercross,—the necessity of some one's going to Uppercross,—the news to be conveyed—how it could be broken to Mr. and Mrs. Musgrove—the lateness of the morning,—an hour already gone since they ought to have been off,—the impossibility of being in tolerable time. At first, they were

75. Just as Anne has just displayed an outward strength and decisiveness she has not exhibited previously, Captain Wentworth, in praying, reveals a gentler and more reflective side than he has shown. Both are establishing greater affinities with the other.

76. The maids' room would be where the maids slept. Lower servants, such as maids were likely to be, usually shared rooms; conditions tended to be especially cramped in townhomes like this one.

77. This suggestion would be inspired by the Harvilles' naval background, for on ships cots that were suspended from the ceiling were the standard beds for officers. Their crucial advantage was that they could be taken up during the day, thereby freeing up space in the cramped living quarters. For the same reason lower-ranking sailors all slept on easily removable hammocks; for a picture of midshipmen on hammocks, see next page.

78. Their assumption that those who stayed in Lyme with Louisa would wish to sleep at the Harvilles' may partly reflect the latter's lesser affluence. They might find it hard to imagine incurring the expense of an inn for an extended stay.

79. For nursing as a basic task of women, see p. 107, note 16.

80. The nursery maid would help the mistress take care of the children (see p. 87, note 28). This could involve nursing, especially given the frequency, and dangers, of childhood illnesses at this time; the maid may also have done other nursing. Her long service with the Harvilles, something also true of the Musgroves' nursery maid (see p. 228), fulfills the contemporary ideal of the strong and lasting bond between mistress and servant. It was an ideal, however, that was frequently not fulfilled, as numerous servants would leave their places, sometimes after very short stays, for employment elsewhere. Mrs. Harville's ability to retain her servant, even with her limited means, suggests her good character.

81. *want*: lack.

capable of nothing more to the purpose than such exclamations; but, after a while, Captain Wentworth, exerting himself, said,

"We must be decided, and without the loss of another minute.[82] Every minute is valuable. Some must resolve on being off for Uppercross instantly. Musgrove, either you or I must go."

Charles agreed; but declared his resolution of not going away. He would be as little incumbrance as possible to Captain and Mrs. Harville; but as to leaving his sister in such a state, he neither ought, nor would. So far it was decided; and Henrietta at first declared the same. She, however, was soon persuaded to think differently.[83] The usefulness of her staying!—She, who had not been able to remain in Louisa's room, or to look at her, without sufferings which made her worse than helpless! She was forced to acknowledge that she could do no good; yet was still unwilling to be away, till touched by the thought of her father and mother, she gave it up; she consented, she was anxious to be at home.

The plan had reached this point, when Anne, coming quietly down from Louisa's room, could not but hear what followed, for the parlour door was open.

"Then it is settled, Musgrove," cried Captain Wentworth, "that you stay, and that I take care of your sister home.[84] But as to the rest;—as to the others;—If one stays to assist Mrs. Harville, I think it need be only one.—Mrs. Charles Musgrove will, of course, wish to get back to her children; but, if Anne will stay, no one so proper, so capable as Anne!"[85]

She paused a moment to recover from the emotion of hearing herself so spoken of. The other two warmly agreed to what he said, and she then appeared.

"You will stay, I am sure; you will stay and nurse her"; cried he, turning to her and speaking with a glow, and yet a gentleness, which seemed almost restoring the past.—She coloured[86] deeply; and he recollected himself, and moved away.—She expressed herself most willing, ready, happy to remain. "It was what she had been thinking of, and wishing to be allowed to do.—A bed on the floor in Louisa's room would be sufficient for her, if Mrs. Harville would but think so."[87]

82. Captain Wentworth is now again making clear decisions, like the captain he is.

83. Henrietta has earlier been shown as susceptible to persuasion. That quality has helped spare her the fate of her sister, and in this instance it leads her to agree to wise advice.

84. Meaning he will conduct Henrietta home.

85. A sign that Captain Wentworth has appreciated Anne's recent actions, and raised his opinion of her. His use of her first name, something normally used only for relatives or close friends, is further testimony to his changed feelings. Anne's hearing his words makes them of even greater significance.

86. *coloured:* blushed.

87. This would represent an especially big change for Anne, accustomed as she has always been to comfortable physical accommodations.

Midshipmen sleeping in hammocks on board a ship.

[From Alfred Burton, *The Adventures of Johnny Newcome in the Navy* (London, 1818; 1904 reprint), p. 40]

One thing more, and all seemed arranged. Though it was rather desirable that Mr. and Mrs. Musgrove should be previously alarmed by some share of delay;[88] yet the time required by the Uppercross horses to take them back, would be a dreadful extension of suspense;[89] and Captain Wentworth proposed, and Charles Musgrove agreed, that it would be much better for him to take a chaise from the inn,[90] and leave Mr. Musgrove's carriage and horses to be sent home the next morning early, when there would be the farther advantage of sending an account of Louisa's night.

Captain Wentworth now hurried off to get every thing ready on his part, and to be soon followed by the two ladies. When the plan was made known to Mary, however, there was an end of all peace in it. She was so wretched, and so vehement, complained so much of injustice in being expected to go away, instead of Anne;—Anne, who was nothing to Louisa, while she was her sister, and had the best right to stay in Henrietta's stead! Why was not she to be as useful as Anne? And to go home without Charles, too—without her husband! No, it was too unkind! And, in short, she said more than her husband could long withstand; and as none of the others could oppose when he gave way, there was no help for it: the change of Mary for Anne was inevitable.

Anne had never submitted more reluctantly to the jealous and ill-judging claims of Mary; but so it must be, and they set off for the town, Charles taking care of his sister, and Captain Benwick attending to her. She gave a moment's recollection, as they hurried along, to the little circumstances which the same spots had witnessed earlier in the morning. There she had listened to Henrietta's schemes for Dr. Shirley's leaving Uppercross; farther on, she had first seen Mr. Elliot; a moment seemed all that could now be given to any one but Louisa, or those who were wrapt up in her welfare.

Captain Benwick was most considerately attentive to her; and, united as they all seemed by the distress of the day, she felt an increasing degree of good-will towards him, and a pleasure even

88. It is good that the delay in their return from Lyme will already alarm Mr. and Mrs. Musgrove. They will thus be less shocked when they hear the actual news.

89. At the same time, they do not wish to prolong Mr. and Mrs. Musgrove's state of alarm and anxiety.

90. They would hire a chaise and horses, along with a postilion to drive. After approximately ten miles they would change horses, which in this case would be only once. This would allow the horses at each stage to gallop at maximum speed. In contrast, the Musgrove horses would need to conserve their strength for the entire journey, especially since the road from Lyme involves a considerable uphill climb; their speed would be further slowed by having to pull a coach, a heavier vehicle than a chaise (for further explanation, see p. 11, note 34; for pictures, see p. 59 and below).

A system in which inns in towns, and along main roads, had carriages and horses available and could make the change of horses very quickly had become a prominent feature of English life. Thanks to it travel was much faster than in earlier ages, a fact commented upon by many living then. The system also supported an elaborate network of public coaches, though the characters in Jane Austen, like wealthy people in general then, are consistently shown traveling post, which meant hiring private carriages and horses or using their own carriages with hired horses; this was more expensive, and not necessarily faster, than public coaches, but it offered greater privacy and seclusion from social inferiors. Chaises, enclosed but also small and fast, were the standard vehicles for traveling post.

A chaise of the period. The postilion is sitting on the horse (see above note); those driving post, or hired, horses always sat there, instead of on the carriage. The illustration on the following page shows the same practice.

[From John Ashton, *Social England Under the Regency* (London, 1899), p. 350]

in thinking that it might, perhaps, be the occasion of continuing their acquaintance.

Captain Wentworth was on the watch for them, and a chaise and four[91] in waiting, stationed for their convenience in the lowest part of the street;[92] but his evident surprise and vexation, at the substitution of one sister for the other—the change of his countenance—the astonishment—the expressions begun and suppressed, with which Charles was listened to, made but a mortifying reception of Anne;[93] or must at least convince her that she was valued only as she could be useful to Louisa.

She endeavoured to be composed, and to be just. Without emulating the feelings of an Emma towards her Henry,[94] she would have attended on Louisa with a zeal above the common claims of regard, for his sake; and she hoped he would not long be so unjust as to suppose she would shrink unnecessarily from the office[95] of a friend.

In the meanwhile she was in the carriage. He had handed them both in, and placed himself between them; and in this manner, under these circumstances full of astonishment and emotion to Anne, she quitted Lyme. How the long stage would pass;[96] how it was to affect their manners;[97] what was to be their sort of intercourse, she could not foresee. It was all quite natural, however. He was devoted to Henrietta; always turning towards her; and when he spoke at all, always with the view of supporting her hopes and raising her spirits. In general, his voice and manner were studiously calm. To spare Henrietta from agitation seemed the governing principle. Once only, when she had been grieving over the last ill-judged, ill-fated walk to the Cobb, bitterly lamenting that it ever had been thought of, he burst forth, as if wholly overcome—

"Don't talk of it, don't talk of it," he cried. "Oh God! that I had not given way to her at the fatal moment! Had I done as I ought! But so eager and so resolute! Dear, sweet Louisa!"

Anne wondered whether it ever occurred to him now, to question the justness of his own previous opinion as to the universal felicity and advantage of firmness of character; and whether it

91. *chaise and four*: chaise with four horses (see p. 11, note 34). Four horses, instead of two, would ensure a faster journey.

92. The two principal inns in Lyme were on the main street, which is very steep. But they were near the bottom of the street, where it meets a flatter road. Hence a carriage waiting at the lowest part would be on flatter ground, where it would be easier to ascend the steps into it.

93. Her inference, as indicated by her reflections in the next paragraph, is that he suspects Anne was the author of the change regarding who will remain in Lyme, due to her unwillingness to stay.

94. "Henry and Emma" is a poem from 1709 by Matthew Prior. In it Henry, to test Emma's love for him, tells her that he must flee to remote and wild woods and that she, if she wishes to remain with him, will have to follow and endure terrible hardships. She consistently avers she will endure anything, whereupon he switches to declaring that he is really in love with another woman. She, though shocked, responds that she will follow and attend this other woman as a mere servant because of the love she bears him. This finally convinces him of her love, and he declares that in fact he loves only her and can offer her a happy home. Thus, in attending Louisa, Anne would show a similar, though less extreme, willingness to put aside her own self-interest for the sake of the man she cares for.

95. *office*: duty, function.

96. Meaning the stage of their journey until they have to change horses.

97. *manners*: external conduct or demeanor.

A chaise arriving at a house.

[From William Combe, *The Dance of Life* (London, 1817; 1903 reprint), p. 166]

might not strike him, that, like all other qualities of the mind, it should have its proportions and limits. She thought it could scarcely escape him to feel, that a persuadable temper might sometimes be as much in favour of happiness, as a very resolute character.[98]

They got on fast. Anne was astonished to recognise the same hills and the same objects so soon. Their actual speed,[99] heightened by some dread of the conclusion, made the road appear but half as long as on the day before. It was growing quite dusk, however, before they were in the neighbourhood of Uppercross, and there had been total silence among them for some time, Henrietta leaning back in the corner, with a shawl over her face,[100] giving the hope of her having cried herself to sleep; when, as they were going up their last hill, Anne found herself all at once addressed by Captain Wentworth. In a low, cautious voice, he said,

"I have been considering what we had best do. She must not appear at first. She could not stand it. I have been thinking whether you had not better remain in the carriage with her, while I go in and break it to Mr. and Mrs. Musgrove. Do you think this a good plan?"[101]

She did: he was satisfied, and said no more. But the remembrance of the appeal remained a pleasure to her—as a proof of friendship, and of deference for her judgment, a great pleasure; and when it became a sort of parting proof, its value did not lessen.[102]

When the distressing communication at Uppercross was over, and he had seen the father and mother quite as composed as could be hoped, and the daughter all the better for being with them, he announced his intention of returning in the same carriage to Lyme; and when the horses were baited, he was off.[103]

98. This offers a crucial lesson of the book. Its recommendation of a mean of behavior, in this case between being resolute and being persuadable, is typical of Jane Austen.

99. Their actual speed is faster because, unlike in their journey to Lyme, they have been able to change horses (see note 90 above).

100. Shawls were widely used by women in this period, for the thin and loose fashions, and predominance of lightweight material like muslin, created a need for additional layers for warmth. The most popular were cashmere shawls, which were first imported from India in the late 1700s, a product of British colonization and increased trade with India, but which by this time were also being made in Britain.

101. She appreciates his appeal to her judgment. The style of his communication—its simple brevity and lack of formality—might also be indications of a friendlier, more relaxed attitude toward her.

102. They will not see each other again until a number of chapters later.

103. *baited:* given food and drink. Normally new horses would be hired, allowing the first set of horses to rest as well as to eat and drink. But here, at a private rural residence rather than an inn, such horses are not readily available, so Captain Wentworth, in a hurry to return, must continue with the same horses.

This departure ends Volume I. It could be asked why the author broke the book at this point. Anne's departure for Bath, which will happen shortly, changes the setting of the book more sharply and occurs at a point closer to the exact middle, measured by the number of pages. The most logical reason for the current division is that it marks a critical turning point in the relationship of Captain Wentworth and Anne. The events later in the book will demonstrate the effects of the change seen here.

VOLUME TWO

Chapter One

*T*he remainder of Anne's time at Uppercross, comprehending only two days, was spent entirely at the mansion-house, and she had the satisfaction of knowing herself extremely useful there, both as an immediate companion, and as assisting in all those arrangements for the future, which, in Mr. and Mrs. Musgrove's distressed state of spirits, would have been difficulties.[1]

They had an early account from Lyme the next morning.[2] Louisa was much the same. No symptoms worse than before had appeared. Charles came a few hours afterwards, to bring a later and more particular account.[3] He was tolerably cheerful. A speedy cure must not be hoped, but every thing was going on as well as the nature of the case admitted. In speaking of the Harvilles, he seemed unable to satisfy his own sense of their kindness, especially of Mrs. Harville's exertions as a nurse.[4] "She really left nothing for Mary to do. He and Mary had been persuaded to go early to their inn last night. Mary had been hysterical again this morning. When he came away, she was going to walk out with Captain Benwick, which, he hoped, would do her good. He almost wished she had been prevailed on to come home the day before; but the truth was, that Mrs. Harville left nothing for any body to do."

Charles was to return to Lyme the same afternoon, and his father had at first half a mind to go with him, but the ladies could not consent. It would be going only to multiply trouble to the others, and increase his own distress; and a much better scheme followed and was acted upon. A chaise[5] was sent for from Crewkherne,[6] and Charles conveyed back a far more useful per-

1.   Anne's natural inclination toward usefulness and helping others could be strengthened here by her regret at having been forced to leave Lyme while Mary stayed. She may see assisting the Musgroves as one way to make up for her inability to help with Louisa.

2.   It was decided the previous day (see p. 220) that the Musgroves' coach would return early the next morning with the latest news. It does not seem that any of the family come with the coach, so the news was likely conveyed by a letter. The coachman and any family servant who traveled with him could supplement this account.

The Musgroves' reliance on personal messengers for news probably results, at least in part, from the limitations of rural mail. While the post office at the time offered good service within and between towns, many rural areas were barely covered, or covered through uncertain or inconsistent methods of delivery.

3.   Charles would be driving his curricle, which he had used to drive himself and Captain Wentworth to Lyme.

4.   Mrs. Harville's nursing experience was mentioned when the decision was made to leave Louisa in her care; the earnest efforts described here provide more proof of the generosity and hospitality attributed to the Harvilles, and to naval society generally.

5.   *chaise*: for chaises, and the system of hiring them, see p. 11, note 34, and p. 221, note 90).

6.   Crewkherne, a town in southern Somerset, was mentioned earlier as the first important stop on the road north from Lyme (see map, p. 513). It would not be far from Uppercross and would be a logical place for hiring a chaise.

son in the old nursery-maid of the family,[7] one who having brought up all the children, and seen the very last, the lingering and long-petted master Harry,[8] sent to school after his brothers,[9] was now living in her deserted nursery to mend stockings, and dress all the blains[10] and bruises she could get near her,[11] and who, consequently, was only too happy in being allowed to go and help nurse dear Miss Louisa.[12] Vague wishes of getting Sarah thither, had occurred before to Mrs. Musgrove and Henrietta; but without Anne, it would hardly have been resolved on, and found practicable so soon.

They were indebted, the next day, to Charles Hayter for all the minute knowledge of Louisa, which it was so essential to obtain every twenty-four hours. He made it his business to go to Lyme,[13] and his account was still encouraging. The intervals of sense and consciousness were believed to be stronger. Every report agreed in Captain Wentworth's appearing fixed in Lyme.

Anne was to leave them on the morrow, an event which they all dreaded. "What should they do without her? They were wretched comforters for one another!" And so much was said in this way, that Anne thought she could not do better than impart among them the general inclination to which she was privy, and persuade them all to go to Lyme at once. She had little difficulty; it was soon determined that they would go, go to-morrow, fix themselves at the inn, or get into lodgings,[14] as it suited, and there remain till dear Louisa[15] could be moved. They must be taking off some trouble from the good people she was with; they might at least relieve Mrs. Harville from the care of her own children; and in short they were so happy in the decision, that Anne was delighted with what she had done, and felt that she could not spend her last morning at Uppercross better than in assisting their preparations, and sending them off at an early hour, though her being left to the solitary range of the house was the consequence.

She was the last, excepting the little boys at the cottage,[16] she was the very last, the only remaining one of all that had filled and animated both houses, of all that had given Uppercross its cheerful character. A few days had made a change indeed!

7. The nursery maid would help raise the young children of the family.

8. Master Harry would be what she, as a servant, would call him.

9. Upper-class boys were usually sent to boarding school at an early age. This passage suggests Harry was sent later than usual, and being petted was probably a reason. Boys' schools were often brutal environments, in which boys were subject both to frequent beatings by the schoolmasters and to the unrestrained tyranny of older boys. Such an environment was justified as essential for inculcating the toughness and assertiveness that men needed to perform their social roles, and for this reason fathers insisted on sending their sons to school. Mothers often disliked subjecting their sons to such an ordeal, and in this case Mr. Musgrove, perhaps softening as he grew older, may have been persuaded to keep the boy at home longer.

10. *blains:* inflammatory swellings or sores on the skin; blisters.

11. The Musgroves therefore are keeping her with them, even though she now has little employment left. Many employers provided some kind of assistance to old servants, including pensions and legacies in wills. This reflected a strong ethos of upper-class paternalism in this society.

12. *Miss Louisa:* the name the maid would use for Louisa. She is "Miss Louisa" rather than "Miss Musgrove" because Henrietta is older (see p. 147, note 22). Her use of this respectful name, despite being much older, along with her simply being called "Sarah" by the family in the next sentence, indicates how entrenched hierarchical distinctions were in this society, even in an easygoing and unpretentious family like the Musgroves. Her eagerness to be employed, which obviously results from her lack of other occupation, also reflects many servants' strong, often lifelong identification with their masters.

13. Charles Hayter would be happy to perform any service that would gratify the Musgroves, for he would be aware that a marriage between him and Henrietta is not regarded by them as a great match, socially or financially.

14. *lodgings:* regular rooms or houses for rent, as opposed to rooms at an inn.

15. *dear Louisa:* what the Musgroves would call her.

16. These would be the two boys of Charles and Mary, who would now be left completely in the hands of their nursery maid and other servants (during the initial visit to Lyme, Mr. and Mrs. Musgrove would have been there to help with them). It is later revealed that Mary and Charles stayed two weeks in Lyme (p. 244). There are other cases in Jane Austen of children being left with only servants to attend them, though none for so long or with children this young. Thus this does indicate a rather casual attitude on the part of the parents, especially since, as already indicated, they are hardly necessary to help out with Louisa.

If Louisa recovered, it would all be well again. More than former happiness would be restored.[17] There could not be a doubt, to her mind there was none, of what would follow her recovery. A few months hence, and the room now so deserted, occupied but by her silent, pensive self, might be filled again with all that was happy and gay, all that was glowing and bright in prosperous love, all that was most unlike Anne Elliot![18]

An hour's complete leisure for such reflections as these, on a dark November day,[19] a small[20] thick rain almost blotting out the very few objects ever to be discerned from the windows,[21] was enough to make the sound of Lady Russell's carriage exceedingly welcome;[22] and yet, though desirous to be gone, she could not quit the mansion-house, or look an adieu to the cottage, with its black, dripping, and comfortless veranda,[23] or even notice through the misty glasses[24] the last humble tenements of the village,[25] without a saddened heart. — Scenes had passed in Uppercross, which made it precious. It stood the record of many sensations of pain, once severe, but now softened; and of some instances of relenting feeling, some breathings of friendship and reconciliation, which could never be looked for again, and which could never cease to be dear. She left it all behind her; all but the recollection that such things had been.[26]

Anne had never entered Kellynch since her quitting Lady Russell's house, in September. It had not been necessary, and the few occasions of its being possible for her to go to the hall she had contrived to evade and escape from. Her first return, was to resume her place in the modern and elegant apartments of the lodge,[27] and to gladden the eyes of its mistress.

There was some anxiety mixed with Lady Russell's joy in meeting her. She knew who had been frequenting Uppercross. But happily, either Anne was improved in plumpness and looks,[28] or Lady Russell fancied her so; and Anne, in receiving her compliments on the occasion, had the amusement of connecting them with the silent admiration of her cousin, and of hoping that she was to be blessed with a second spring of youth and beauty.

When they came to converse, she was soon sensible of some

17. Meaning that Louisa would be able to marry Captain Wentworth.

18. These are clearly Anne's thoughts, at least in part, and form a melancholy coda to her time spent with the Musgroves. They also show that the greater than usual attention she received at Lyme has not brought about a fundamental change in her situation, or her perception of it.

19. Late fall and winter days in England can be quite dark, for its very northerly latitudes mean short days and an extremely low and dim sun.

20. *small:* composed of minute drops. The term was often used for rain then.

21. The earlier description of the elder Musgroves' house (p. 68) spoke of its old trees, which would presumably be large enough to block views from the windows, especially since a house in a village, even a mansion, would not have ample space around it, causing the trees to be close to the windows.

22. Anne's welcoming the carriage, rather than preferring further indulgence in melancholy reflections, signals the difference between her and Captain Benwick, one that informed their discussion at Lyme (see p. 192).

23. *veranda:* see p. 69, note 39. The veranda's exposure to the outside and its dark iron material would make it a particularly forlorn object in the rain.

24. These would be the window glasses of the carriage.

25. These would be the dwellings of the poorer people who constitute the majority of the village. It is notable that while Anne notices their homes, during her entire time at Uppercross only the inhabitants, guests, and occasionally servants of the two Musgrove houses are ever mentioned. All important social life was conducted exclusively among people of one's own class; others were dealt with only as practical necessity demanded.

26. Anne's parting thoughts concern Wentworth. Her feelings for him are such that she treasures the brief instances of his softening toward her, even as she believes, as shown by the words "never be looked for again," that he is soon to be permanently separated from her by marriage.

27. The modernity and elegance of the apartments, or rooms, of the lodge, Lady Russell's residence, stem from the furniture and possibly the architecture being in the latest style. In a letter Jane Austen describes a drawing room as "full of all the modern Elegancies"(May 24, 1813), and in *Pride and Prejudice* she gives a sense of what she means by describing a room as "lately fitted up with greater elegance and lightness"—the furniture of the time being lighter in character than older furniture. As mentioned earlier (p. 21, note 9), Sir Walter may have built this house for Lady Russell, which would mean it was constructed and furnished in the latest style; even if not, she, a wealthy woman with no one else to support, could have easily furnished it anew.

28. When Anne next sees her father he will perceive her to be "less thin in

mental change. The subjects of which her heart had been full on leaving Kellynch, and which she had felt slighted, and been compelled to smother among the Musgroves, were now become but of secondary interest. She had lately lost sight even of her father and sister and Bath. Their concerns had been sunk under those of Uppercross, and when Lady Russell reverted to their former hopes and fears, and spoke her satisfaction in the house in Camden-place, which had been taken, and her regret that Mrs. Clay should still be with them, Anne would have been ashamed to have it known, how much more she was thinking of Lyme, and Louisa Musgrove, and all her acquaintance there; how much more interesting to her was the home and the friendship of the Harvilles and Captain Benwick, than her own father's house in Camden-place,[29] or her own sister's intimacy with Mrs. Clay. She was actually forced to exert herself, to meet Lady Russell with any thing like the appearance of equal solicitude, on topics which had by nature the first claim on her.[30]

There was a little awkwardness at first in their discourse on another subject. They must speak of the accident at Lyme. Lady Russell had not been arrived five minutes the day before, when a full account of the whole had burst on her;[31] but still it must be talked of, she must make enquiries, she must regret the imprudence, lament the result, and Captain Wentworth's name must be mentioned by both. Anne was conscious of not doing it so well as Lady Russell. She could not speak the name, and look straight forward to Lady Russell's eye, till she had adopted the expedient of telling her briefly what she thought of the attachment between him and Louisa. When this was told, his name distressed her no longer.

Lady Russell had only to listen composedly, and wish them happy; but internally her heart revelled in angry pleasure, in pleased contempt,[32] that the man who at twenty-three had seemed to understand somewhat of the value of an Anne Elliot, should, eight years afterwards, be charmed by a Louisa Musgrove.

The first three or four days passed most quietly, with no circumstance to mark them excepting the receipt of a note or two

her person" (p. 274) and will also regard this as a positive development. Various passages in Jane Austen, and in other writings of the time, indicate that thinness was not equated with attractiveness; in an unfinished novel of hers, *The Watsons*, the heroine, who is generally lauded for her beauty, is described as "well made & plump, with an air of healthy vigour." This does not mean that actual obesity was considered desirable. Instead a more moderate figure was regarded as ideal, both on the grounds of health and appearance. One character in *Emma*, Jane Fairfax, is praised for being "a most becoming medium, between fat and thin." One possible reason for not idealizing thinness then is that, with food less abundant, fewer people were overweight, while excessive thinness could be a sign of poverty.

29. *Camden-Place:* (see p. 259, note 1; and map, p. 516).

30. This forced transition of her thoughts is similar to that experienced by Anne when she first came to Uppercross and found little concern there with Elliot affairs (see p. 80). In this case Lady Russell does show some interest in what Anne has left behind, and a willingness to speak of it, thereby indicating her superiority in courtesy to the Musgroves.

31. Jane Austen consistently depicts the ubiquity and speed of village or country gossip in her novels. It was one area of life where different classes would interact, for gossip about the elite classes was often spread by servants or other lower-class people. It is possible that Lady Russell heard the news from a servant, for it was before she saw Anne.

32. Her reveling in such emotions indicates her moral inferiority to Anne, who never derives pleasure from anger or contempt.

from Lyme, which found their way to Anne, she could not tell how, and brought a rather improving account of Louisa. At the end of that period, Lady Russell's politeness could repose no longer,[33] and the fainter self-threatenings of the past,[34] became in a decided tone, "I must call on Mrs. Croft; I really must call upon her soon. Anne, have you courage to go with me, and pay a visit in that house? It will be some trial to us both."

Anne did not shrink from it; on the contrary, she truly felt as she said, in observing,

"I think you are very likely to suffer the most of the two; your feelings are less reconciled to the change than mine. By remaining in the neighbourhood, I am become inured to it."

She could have said more on the subject; for she had in fact so high an opinion of the Crofts, and considered her father so very fortunate in his tenants, felt the parish[35] to be so sure of a good example,[36] and the poor of the best attention and relief,[37] that however sorry and ashamed for the necessity of the removal, she could not but in conscience feel that they were gone who deserved not to stay, and that Kellynch-hall had passed into better hands than its owners. These convictions must unquestionably have their own pain, and severe was its kind;[38] but they precluded that pain which Lady Russell would suffer in entering the house again, and returning through the well-known apartments.

In such moments Anne had no power of saying to herself, "These rooms ought to belong only to us. Oh, how fallen in their destination! How unworthily occupied! An ancient family to be so driven away![39] Strangers filling their place!" No, except when she thought of her mother, and remembered where she had been used to sit and preside, she had no sigh of that description to heave.

Mrs. Croft always met her with a kindness which gave her the pleasure of fancying herself a favourite; and on the present occasion, receiving her in that house, there was particular attention.

The sad accident at Lyme was soon the prevailing topic; and on comparing their latest accounts of the invalid, it appeared that each lady dated her intelligence[40] from the same hour of yester

33. Lady Russell has put off what she is about to propose for a little, but her strong politeness now compels her to undertake the duty.

34. She had earlier threatened herself with the need for the unpleasant task, but too faintly, at that time, to force her into action.

35. *parish:* the local Kellynch area (for more on this and the accompanying issue of help for the poor, shortly to be mentioned, see p. 73, note 53).

36. Setting an example of correct and responsible behavior was considered an important function of the highest-ranking members of society.

37. As residents of the leading house in the neighborhood the Crofts would be in a position to assume the standard upper-class duty of local charity.

38. The pain of being forced to feel shame regarding one's family. The importance of family in this society could make such a pain acute; one sees throughout the novel that as much as Anne is aware of the failings of her father, she still identifies with him in many respects.

39. Strong respect for tradition would make the departure of a family long resident in an abode especially unfortunate in people's eyes.

40. *intelligence:* news, information.

morn, that Captain Wentworth had been in Kellynch yesterday—
(the first time since the accident) had brought Anne the last note,
which she had not been able to trace the exact steps of,[41] had staid
a few hours and then returned again to Lyme—and without any
present intention of quitting it any more.—He had enquired after
her, she found, particularly;—had expressed his hope of Miss
Elliot's not being the worse for her exertions, and had spoken of
those exertions as great.—This was handsome,—and gave her
more pleasure than almost any thing else could have done.

As to the sad catastrophe itself, it could be canvassed[42] only in
one style by a couple of steady, sensible women, whose judgments
had to work on ascertained events; and it was perfectly decided
that it had been the consequence of much thoughtlessness and
much imprudence; that its effects were most alarming, and that it
was frightful to think, how long Miss Musgrove's recovery might
yet be doubtful, and how liable she would still remain to suffer
from the concussion hereafter!—The Admiral wound it all up
summarily by exclaiming,

"Ay, a very bad business indeed.—A new sort of way this, for a
young fellow to be making love,[43] by breaking his mistress's
head!—is not it, Miss Elliot?—This is breaking a head and giving
a plaister[44] truly!"

Admiral Croft's manners were not quite of the tone to suit Lady
Russell, but they delighted Anne. His goodness of heart and sim-
plicity of character were irresistible.[45]

"Now, this must be very bad for you," said he, suddenly rousing
from a little reverie, "to be coming and finding us here.—I had
not recollected it before, I declare,—but it must be very bad.—
But now, do not stand upon ceremony.—Get up and go over all
the rooms in the house if you like it."

"Another time, Sir, I thank you, not now."

"Well, whenever it suits you.—You can slip in from the shrubbery at any time.[46] And there you will find we keep our umbrellas,
hanging up by that door.[47] A good place, is not it? But" (checking
himself) "you will not think it a good place, for yours were always
kept in the butler's room.[48] Ay, so it always is, I believe. One man's

41. Captain Wentworth's taking the trouble to deliver a note to Anne indicates that the warmer feelings he recently showed for her have persisted.

42. *canvassed:* discussed, examined.

43. *making love:* courting, expressing one's love for someone. It had no stronger connotation than this at the time.

44. *plaister:* plaster. Adhesive plasters of various kinds were commonly applied to wounds, to help close them or to fix a soothing medication. "To break my head and give me a plaster" is a traditional expression, meaning to injure and then make amends. In this case, Admiral Croft expects that Captain Wentworth's ultimate marriage to Louisa, the natural conclusion of his lovemaking, will be the amends.

45. Lady Russell probably finds Admiral Croft's comment about "breaking a head," a humorous remark about a serious injury, to be inappropriate. He is consistently shown to be casual and bluff in his speech and behavior, something that has led his wife, who is shortly described as pleasing Lady Russell very well, to call him to order (see p. 130). Anne's delight in the admiral, a result in part of her recent experience with naval manners, marks a crucial difference between her and Lady Russell, one that will soon play an important role in the plot, through their different reactions to Mr. Elliot (see pp. 300–306).

That the manners of Admiral Croft, notwithstanding his general likability, have their flaws is indicated in a brief episode in a chapter of the first version of the novel, which was replaced by Chapters X and XI of Volume II. In it, a mishap placed the Crofts' servant in a foolish position: "The Adm. enjoyed the joke exceedingly. Anne thought his triumph over Stephen too long."

46. The shrubbery would normally be near the house (see p. 35, note 16).

47. Originally umbrellas had completely straight handles, and some still did at this time, but others had handles curved or bent at the end, which allowed for easy hanging (for more on umbrellas, see p. 337, note 17).

48. The butler, the principal male servant in a house, would have at least one room—in some houses butlers had a whole suite of rooms—for performing such tasks as preparing wine, cleaning cutlery, silver, and glassware, and caring for lamps. The butler was frequently the servant who would attend to the inhabitants of the house when they called, so his room would be a logical place to store umbrellas, if one wished to have a servant fetch one rather than getting it oneself. That Sir Walter preferred the former course, and Admiral Croft seems to favor the latter, suggests the difference in their characters.

ways may be as good as another's, but we all like our own best.
And so you must judge for yourself, whether it would be better for
you to go about the house or not."

Anne, finding she might decline it, did so, very gratefully.

"We have made very few changes either!" continued the Admiral, after thinking a moment. "Very few.—We told you about the
laundry-door,[49] at Uppercross. That has been a very great
improvement. The wonder was, how any family upon earth could
bear with the inconvenience of its opening as it did, so long![50]—
You will tell Sir Walter what we have done, and that Mr. Shepherd thinks it the greatest improvement the house ever had.[51]
Indeed, I must do ourselves the justice to say, that the few alterations we have made have been all very much for the better. My
wife should have the credit of them, however. I have done very little besides sending away some of the large looking-glasses from
my dressing-room, which was your father's. A very good man, and
very much the gentleman I am sure—but I should think, Miss
Elliot" (looking with serious reflection) "I should think he must
be rather a dressy man for his time of life.—Such a number of
looking-glasses![52] oh Lord! there was no getting away from oneself. So I got Sophy to lend me a hand, and we soon shifted their
quarters; and now I am quite snug, with my little shaving glass[53] in
one corner, and another great thing that I never go near."

Anne, amused in spite of herself, was rather distressed for an
answer, and the Admiral, fearing he might not have been civil
enough, took up the subject again, to say, "The next time you
write to your good father, Miss Elliot, pray give my compliments
and Mrs. Croft's, and say that we are settled here quite to our liking, and have no fault at all to find with the place. The breakfast-
room chimney smokes a little,[54] I grant you, but it is only when
the wind is due north and blows hard, which may not happen
three times a winter. And take it altogether, now that we have
been into most of the houses hereabouts and can judge, there is
not one that we like better than this. Pray say so, with my compliments. He will be glad to hear it."

Lady Russell and Mrs. Croft were very well pleased with each

49. This probably means the door to the room in which laundry was done, which was one meaning of the term "laundry." Washing clothes was an elaborate task under the technology of the time, and country houses would often have more than one room devoted to the various parts of the operation.

50. The admiral's action and comment suggest his less exalted attitudes: Sir Walter would probably never deign to bother with something so common as laundry, which may be why the inconvenience noted by the admiral was tolerated so long. The latter's inclination to fix things may also reflect his naval background, for the difficult conditions and confined quarters of a ship put a premium on practical efficiency.

51. Mr. Shepherd shows with the Crofts the same tendency toward courteous flattery that he showed earlier with Sir Walter.

52. It is possible Sir Walter left all of his dressing room mirrors behind, though given his character he could have taken some to Bath and still left enough behind to astonish Admiral Croft. All the Elliots' furnishings may have remained at Kellynch as part of the rental arrangement: later they boast of the elegant style with which they have furnished their Bath house (p. 258), and they have Charles and Mary admire their china and mirrors during their visit (p. 416), both of which suggest the purchase of new items in Bath.

53. A shaving glass or mirror could be tall and freestanding, with the mirror atop a large frame, or could be designed to rest on top of a cabinet or dresser; it often had hinges on the side allowing it to be adjusted to the height of the user. Admiral Croft's description of his as little suggests it is one that rested on something else (for a picture of this type, see next page). Shaving was a universal practice among men then; almost nobody sported facial hair.

54. A breakfast room was a standard part of a country house; it would be a place for informal casual dining, and sometimes other activities during the day. The Crofts' casual style may cause them to use it frequently instead of the more formal dining room. Smoking chimneys were a common problem, since fireplaces were the universal source of heat, though recent innovations had improved the efficiency of chimneys and reduced their tendency to smoke.

other; but the acquaintance which this visit began, was fated not to proceed far at present; for when it was returned,[55] the Crofts announced themselves to be going away for a few weeks, to visit their connexions[56] in the north of the county,[57] and probably might not be at home again before Lady Russell would be removing to Bath.

So ended all danger to Anne of meeting Captain Wentworth at Kellynch-hall, or of seeing him in company with her friend. Every thing was safe enough, and she smiled over the many anxious feelings she had wasted on the subject.[58]

55. Returning a visit soon, especially one of introduction, was standard etiquette.

56. *connexions*: connections, i.e., relations. These relations are not identified, but earlier Admiral Croft was said to be a native of Somersetshire, so he could easily have family members residing elsewhere in the county.

57. The description of Kellynch as fifty miles from Bath (p. 26), and of the nearby Uppercross as seventeen miles from Lyme (p. 180), indicates that both are in southern Somersetshire (see map, p. 513).

58. Thus even Anne is subject to the usual human frailties, though her ability to smile at them signals her continued superiority to most people.

Contemporary shaving glasses or mirrors.

[From Thomas Arthur Strange, *English Furniture in the 18th Century: A Guide to Collectors*, p. 273]

Chapter Two

*T*hough Charles and Mary had remained at Lyme much longer after Mr. and Mrs. Musgrove's going, than Anne conceived they could have been at all wanted,[1] they were yet the first of the family to be at home again, and as soon as possible after their return to Uppercross, they drove over to the lodge.—They had left Louisa beginning to sit up; but her head, though clear, was exceedingly weak, and her nerves susceptible to the highest extreme of tenderness; and though she might be pronounced to be altogether doing very well, it was still impossible to say when she might be able to bear the removal home; and her father and mother, who must return in time to receive their younger children for the Christmas holidays,[2] had hardly a hope of being allowed to bring her with them.

They had been all in lodgings together. Mrs. Musgrove had got Mrs. Harville's children away as much as she could, every possible supply from Uppercross had been furnished, to lighten the inconvenience to the Harvilles, while the Harvilles had been wanting them to come to dinner every day; and in short, it seemed to have been only a struggle on each side as to which should be most disinterested and hospitable.

Mary had had her evils;[3] but upon the whole, as was evident by her staying so long,[4] she had found more to enjoy than to suffer.— Charles Hayter had been at Lyme oftener than suited her, and when they dined with the Harvilles there had been only a maid-servant to wait,[5] and at first, Mrs. Harville had always given Mrs. Musgrove precedence;[6] but then, she had received so very handsome an apology from her on finding out whose daughter she was, and there had been so much going on every day, there had been so many walks between their lodgings and the Harvilles, and she had got books from the library and changed them so often,[7] that

1. *wanted:* needed.

2. The children would be home from school during the holidays. The calendar of social life in upper-class families often revolved around school holidays.

3. *evils:* troubles, pains.

4. See p. 229, note 16, on Mary and Charles leaving children behind.

5. Waiting at table, unlike most household tasks, could be performed by either male or female servants. Male servants were more expensive, for they commanded much higher wages, usually needed to be furnished with a livery (see p. 41, note 39), and were subject to a special tax. Partly because of their cost, male servants were more prestigious and highly sought by families that could afford them (this was why the government opted to tax them specially). Thus status-conscious Mary is grieved at their absence from meals, an absence due to the Harvilles' limited means and possibly their lesser concern for display.

6. Mrs. Musgrove, as the mother of Mary's husband, would take precedence were Mary not the daughter of a baronet (see p. 89, note 31). Thus Mrs. Harville, until she learned of Mary's birth, had assumed she came after her mother-in-law.

7. Circulating libraries had become a basic feature of English life during the second half of the eighteenth century; in 1801 a magazine estimated them to number around one thousand. The libraries were all private enterprises, in which users paid a subscription fee for periods ranging between a week and a year. Resort towns like Lyme, with their large number of affluent people with time on their hands, particularly abounded in libraries; Lyme itself, though small, was described in 1823, a few years after this novel, as having three circulating libraries.

   Mary's having changed her books at the library several times does not necessarily indicate a great appetite for reading on her part, for libraries often allowed patrons to borrow only one book at a time. Mary also may have been attracted by the sheer novelty of frequent borrowing: while some rural villages had libraries by this point, many did not, and rural libraries that did exist offered a smaller selection than those in towns.

the balance had certainly been much in favour of Lyme. She had been taken to Charmouth too,[8] and she had bathed,[9] and she had gone to church, and there were a great many more people to look at in the church at Lyme than at Uppercross,[10]—and all this, joined to the sense of being so very useful, had made really an agreeable fortnight.[11]

Anne enquired after Captain Benwick. Mary's face was clouded directly.[12] Charles laughed.

"Oh! Captain Benwick is very well, I believe, but he is a very odd young man. I do not know what he would be at. We asked him to come home with us for a day or two; Charles undertook to give him some shooting,[13] and he seemed quite delighted, and for my part, I thought it was all settled; when behold! on Tuesday night, he made a very awkward sort of excuse; "he never shot" and he had "been quite misunderstood,"—and he had promised this and he had promised that, and the end of it was, I found, that he did not mean to come. I suppose he was afraid of finding it dull; but upon my word I should have thought we were lively enough at the Cottage for such a heart-broken man as Captain Benwick."

Charles laughed again and said, "Now Mary, you know very well how it really was.—It was all your doing," (turning to Anne.) "He fancied that if he went with us, he should find you close by; he fancied every body to be living in Uppercross; and when he discovered that Lady Russell lived three miles off, his heart failed him, and he had not courage to come. That is the fact, upon my honour. Mary knows it is."

But Mary did not give into it very graciously; whether from not considering Captain Benwick entitled by birth and situation[14] to be in love with an Elliot, or from not wanting to believe Anne a greater attraction to Uppercross than herself, must be left to be guessed. Anne's good-will, however, was not to be lessened by what she heard. She boldly acknowledged herself flattered, and continued her enquiries.

"Oh! he talks of you," cried Charles, "in such terms,"—Mary interrupted him. "I declare, Charles, I never heard him mention

8. *Charmouth*: a coastal town approximately two and a half miles east of Lyme (see map, p. 514). It, along with the impressive cliffs on either side, can be seen easily from Lyme. It also was a seaside resort; John Feltham's *A Guide to all the Watering and Sea-Bathing Places* (1804) says that, while Charmouth contains no fashionable amusements, it "commands many vast and beautiful prospects both of the sea and the land."

9. Meaning she went into the sea. For sea-bathing, see p. 181, note 10.

10. This suggests where Mary's thoughts were during church.

11. Their being in Lyme for two weeks, and the previous suggestion that Mr. and Mrs. Musgrove will probably return soon for their children's Christmas holidays (which suggests it is already December), indicates that the initial visit to Lyme was in late November (see chronology, p. 488).

12. *directly*: immediately.

13. Charles earlier took Captain Wentworth to shoot with him and would regard it as a natural attraction for a man. He also may be eager to shoot more himself, for the legal shooting season will be over at the end of the following month (see p. 411, note 39).

14. *situation*: social position.

Anne twice all the time I was there. I declare, Anne, he never talks of you at all."

"No," admitted Charles, "I do not know that he ever does, in a general way—but however, it is a very clear thing that he admires you exceedingly.—His head is full of some books that he is reading upon your recommendation, and he wants to talk to you about them; he has found out something or other in one of them which he thinks—Oh! I cannot pretend to remember it, but it was something very fine—I overheard him telling Henrietta all about it—and then 'Miss Elliot' was spoken of in the highest terms!—Now Mary, I declare it was so, I heard it myself, and you were in the other room.—'Elegance, sweetness, beauty,' Oh! there was no end of Miss Elliot's charms."[15]

"And I am sure," cried Mary warmly, "it was very little to his credit, if he did. Miss Harville only died last June. Such a heart is very little worth having; is it, Lady Russell? I am sure you will agree with me."

"I must see Captain Benwick before I decide," said Lady Russell, smiling.

"And that you are very likely to do very soon, I can tell you, ma'am," said Charles. "Though he had not nerves for coming away with us and setting off again afterwards to pay a formal visit here, he will make his way over to Kellynch one day by himself, you may depend on it. I told him the distance and the road,[16] and I told him of the church's being so very well worth seeing, for as he has a taste for those sort of things,[17] I thought that would be a good excuse, and he listened with all his understanding and soul; and I am sure from his manner that you will have him calling here soon. So, I give you notice, Lady Russell."

"Any acquaintance of Anne's will always be welcome to me," was Lady Russell's kind answer.

"Oh! as to being Anne's acquaintance," said Mary, "I think he is rather my acquaintance, for I have been seeing him every day this last fortnight."

"Well, as your joint acquaintance, then, I shall be very happy to see Captain Benwick."[18]

"You will not find any thing very agreeable in him, I assure you,

15. This praise of Anne from an eligible young man, even one she has no interest in, suggests the gradual change in her fortunes that is occurring.

16. He probably means the quality and condition of the road. This was a common topic of conversation then and would be a natural point to discuss with a traveler, for road conditions varied greatly at the time. Rural roads were maintained by the local authorities, and though there were some national regulations about how this should be done, many localities did a poor job. Main roads were generally better, but because each was built and administered by separate turnpike trusts, they also varied in quality.

17. Captain Benwick's interest in church architecture corresponds to a popular trend of the time. Starting around 1800 a number of books about architecture, especially church architecture, appeared and enjoyed wide circulation. One publisher experienced particular success with two series, *Architectural Antiquities of Great Britain* and *Cathedral Antiquities*, featuring superb engravings of buildings. A central force behind these books, which focused particularly on Britain's many Gothic churches and cathedrals, was the movement known as the Gothic Revival. This movement, which began in the late eighteenth century and continued through much of the nineteenth century, spurred a renewed interest in the Gothic styles of the Middle Ages and led to extensive building in that style, especially for religious buildings.

It is appropriate that Captain Benwick should be the one to manifest this interest. The Gothic Revival was closely linked to the Romanticism of the time, which fostered a tremendous vogue for the Middle Ages, and Captain Benwick had earlier expressed his love for two of the leading Romantic poets, Byron and Scott. The latter was perhaps the single leading force in promoting greater interest in the Middle Ages. *Northanger Abbey* also presents a similar link, through a heroine whose passionate love of Romantic literature leads to a fascination for Gothic architecture, albeit not church architecture particularly.

18. Here, and elsewhere in the conversation, Lady Russell demonstrates, by carefully deflecting Mary's intrusive comments without causing offense, the cultivated manners she is consistently described as having. This conversation represents the most sustained presentation of Lady Russell in speech or action. Many commentators have complained that, given her importance to the story, she is presented sketchily, and mostly through authorial description. A related problem is that, while she is generally praised for her good sense and virtue and shown as possessing Anne's regard and affection, her two actions of significance—her earlier persuasion of Anne regarding Captain Wentworth and her later advice regarding Mr. Elliot—are both revealed to be actually or potentially harmful. Thus any scene that displays her in a more positive light serves a valuable function.

ma'am. He is one of the dullest young men that ever lived. He has walked with me, sometimes, from one end of the sands to the other, without saying a word.[19] He is not at all a well-bred[20] young man. I am sure you will not like him."

"There we differ, Mary," said Anne. "I think Lady Russell would like him. I think she would be so much pleased with his mind, that she would very soon see no deficiency in his manner."

"So do I, Anne," said Charles. "I am sure Lady Russell would like him. He is just Lady Russell's sort. Give him a book, and he will read all day long."

"Yes, that he will!" exclaimed Mary, tauntingly. "He will sit poring over his book, and not know when a person speaks to him, or when one drops one's scissors,[21] or any thing that happens. Do you think Lady Russell would like that?"

Lady Russell could not help laughing. "Upon my word," said she, "I should not have supposed that my opinion of any one could have admitted of such difference of conjecture, steady and matter of fact as I may call myself. I have really a curiosity to see the person who can give occasion to such directly opposite notions. I wish he may be induced to call here. And when he does, Mary, you may depend upon hearing my opinion; but I am determined not to judge him beforehand."

"You will not like him, I will answer for it."

Lady Russell began talking of something else. Mary spoke with animation of their meeting with, or rather missing, Mr. Elliot so extraordinarily.

"He is a man," said Lady Russell, "whom I have no wish to see. His declining to be on cordial terms with the head of his family, has left a very strong impression in his disfavour with me."[22]

This decision[23] checked Mary's eagerness, and stopped her short in the midst of the Elliot countenance.

With regard to Captain Wentworth, though Anne hazarded no enquiries, there was voluntary communication sufficient. His spirits had been greatly recovering lately, as might be expected. As Louisa improved, he had improved; and he was now quite a different creature from what he had been the first week. He had not

19. The beach at Lyme is less than half a mile long, so Captain Benwick's silence would not have lasted over an enormous distance.

20. *well-bred:* polite.

21. Mary's scissors—one can assume with Mary that she is speaking of herself—were probably being used as part of her needlework, the standard daily activity of genteel ladies.

22. Sir Walter had earlier identified himself as the head of the house or family (p. 12), because he is the member with the baronet title. Respect for rank would make most in this society agree, and Lady Russell's particularly strong respect for rank may make her agreement especially emphatic.

23. *decision:* firmness, decidedness.

Happy domestic scene, such as could occur at the Musgroves'. Note the portraits on the wall, a common feature of houses then.

[From William Combe, *The Dance of Life* (London, 1817; 1903 reprint), p. 244]

seen Louisa; and was so extremely fearful of any ill consequence to her from an interview, that he did not press for it at all; and, on the contrary, seemed to have a plan of going away for a week or ten days, till her head were stronger. He had talked of going down to Plymouth[24] for a week, and wanted to persuade Captain Benwick to go with him;[25] but, as Charles maintained to the last, Captain Benwick seemed much more disposed to ride over to Kellynch.

There can be no doubt that Lady Russell and Anne were both occasionally thinking of Captain Benwick, from this time. Lady Russell could not hear the door-bell[26] without feeling that it might be his herald;[27] nor could Anne return from any stroll of solitary indulgence in her father's grounds,[28] or any visit of charity in the village,[29] without wondering whether she might see him or hear of him. Captain Benwick came not, however. He was either less disposed for it than Charles had imagined, or he was too shy;[30] and after giving him a week's indulgence, Lady Russell determined him to be unworthy of the interest which he had been beginning to excite.

The Musgroves came back to receive their happy boys and girls from school, bringing with them Mrs. Harville's little children, to improve the noise of Uppercross, and lessen that of Lyme. Henrietta remained with Louisa; but all the rest of the family were again in their usual quarters.

Lady Russell and Anne paid their compliments to them once, when Anne could not but feel that Uppercross was already quite alive again. Though neither Henrietta, nor Louisa, nor Charles Hayter, nor Captain Wentworth were there, the room presented as strong a contrast as could be wished, to the last state she had seen it in.[31]

Immediately surrounding Mrs. Musgrove were the little Harvilles, whom she was sedulously guarding from the tyranny of the two children from the Cottage, expressly arrived to amuse them. On one side was a table, occupied by some chattering girls, cutting up silk and gold paper;[32] and on the other were tressels

24. Plymouth, as one of the principal bases of the navy, would be a natural destination for Captain Wentworth, who probably has acquaintances stationed there. It is also not far from Lyme (see map, p. 512).

25. The real reasons for these plans of Captain Wentworth, and for his behavior toward Louisa, are revealed at the end (p. 464).

26. Doorbells were a recent phenomenon; doors at this time typically had large metal knockers. This passage is the first example of the term's use cited by *The Oxford English Dictionary*. Thus Lady Russell's having one indicates the modernity of her residence, something already mentioned on p. 230.

27. *herald:* something announcing someone's arrival. Traditionally the herald was an actual person employed to announce an arrival, but by this time the term was used mostly in the metaphorical sense it has here.

28. Anne was earlier described as regretting her loss of the familiar lawns and groves of Kellynch (p. 24). Such a stroll would satisfy both her nostalgia for her old home and her love of nature, for there is every indication that the Kellynch grounds, like those of most country houses at the time, were elaborately landscaped to create pleasing views and walks.

29. Thus, even while indulging her own pleasure, Anne still finds time to serve others; before she left Kellynch in the fall she had also visited poor families. Such visits were a frequent activity of genteel women, who were usually the ones playing the most active role in fulfilling the upper-class duty of charity. A scene in *Emma* shows the heroine on an actual visit to a local family.

30. The real reason why Captain Benwick remained in Lyme will be revealed in later chapters.

31. When last there, Anne was alone and engaged in melancholy reflections (p. 230).

32. They may be making Christmas decorations. Skill in decorative projects was an accomplishment often taught to girls, and one they were encouraged to pursue. A number of books for young women explained the technique of various decorative crafts. *Mansfield Park* describes two girls turning to "whatever might be the favourite holiday sport of the moment, making artificial flowers or wasting gold paper"—the wording suggests the frivolity of some of these efforts.

and trays,[33] bending under the weight of brawn and cold pies,[34] where riotous boys were holding high revel; the whole completed by a roaring Christmas fire,[35] which seemed determined to be heard, in spite of all the noise of the others. Charles and Mary also came in, of course, during their visit; and Mr. Musgrove made a point of paying his respects to Lady Russell, and sat down close to her for ten minutes, talking with a very raised voice, but, from the clamour of the children on his knees, generally in vain. It was a fine family-piece.

Anne, judging from her own temperament, would have deemed such a domestic hurricane a bad restorative of the nerves, which Louisa's illness must have so greatly shaken; but Mrs. Musgrove, who got Anne near her on purpose to thank her most cordially, again and again, for all her attentions to them, concluded a short recapitulation of what she had suffered herself, by observing, with a happy glance round the room, that after all she had gone through, nothing was so likely to do her good as a little quiet cheerfulness at home.

Louisa was now recovering apace. Her mother could even think of her being able to join their party at home, before her brothers and sisters went to school again. The Harvilles had promised to come with her and stay at Uppercross, whenever she returned. Captain Wentworth was gone, for the present, to see his brother in Shropshire.[36]

"I hope I shall remember, in future," said Lady Russell, as soon as they were reseated in the carriage, "not to call at Uppercross in the Christmas holidays."[37]

Every body has their taste in noises as well as in other matters; and sounds are quite innoxious,[38] or most distressing, by their sort rather than their quantity. When Lady Russell, not long afterwards, was entering Bath on a wet afternoon,[39] and driving through the long course of streets from the Old Bridge to Camden-place,[40] amidst the dash of other carriages, the heavy rumble of carts and drays,[41] the bawling of newsmen, muffin-men and milkmen,[42] and the ceaseless clink of pattens,[43] she made no

33. Tressels, or trestles, are supports, either in the form of a horizontal bar with diverging legs at each end or of a tripod. They are holding up the trays.

34. Brawn is a specially prepared type of pork, usually taken from the head and foreparts of a boar. A wide variety of pies, both hot and cold, were eaten at the time, and not only for dessert. Both brawn and pies, particularly mince pies, had long been popular staples of the Christmas season.

35. The large room that would allow so many to gather together would have required a powerful fire. (For a picture of a contemporary family gathering similar to the one described here, see p. 249.)

36. This is his brother Edward, the clergyman, whose residence in Shropshire was mentioned earlier (p. 140). For the location of Shropshire, see map, p. 512.

37. This is another indication of Lady Russell's more formal and elegant tastes, compared to the Musgroves. Of course, her politeness keeps her from making such a comment until seated in the carriage with Anne.

38. *innoxious:* innocuous.

39. For the raininess of Bath, see p. 337, note 16.

40. The Old Bridge is the bridge at the southern tip of Bath. Lady Russell would use it to enter the city since she is coming from Somersetshire, which is south of Bath (see map, p. 513); since that time the bridge has been rebuilt as a footbridge, and vehicles crossing the river use the nearby Churchill Bridge. The Old Bridge lies at the opposite end of Bath from Camden Place, which is why they must travel a long course (see map, p. 516).

41. *drays:* low carts for carrying heavy loads, used especially for beer. Carts and drays would generally be used for local conveyance of goods, as opposed to wagons for longer distances. One contemporary writes, "We apply the term *cart* to a vehicle for carrying luggage, etc. that has two wheels, and the term *waggon* to one that has four."

42. Much of the commerce in English towns at this time was conducted by street peddlers who continually walked around and yelled out for people to buy their wares. Muffin men sold what are now known in the United States as English muffins; many such ready-to-eat items were sold on the street. For pictures of newsmen of the time attracting customers, and of someone selling buns in the street, see pp. 255 and 257.

43. Pattens were attachments to shoes designed to keep the feet dry. They consisted of a wooden sole, straps to hold the sole to the shoe, and a large, horizontal iron ring beneath the sole that would elevate the wearer above the ground. They would have been widely worn on a rainy day like this, and their iron rings would have clinked loudly in Bath because of its paved streets. Pat-

complaint. No, these were noises which belonged to the winter pleasures;[44] her spirits rose under their influence; and, like Mrs. Musgrove, she was feeling, though not saying, that, after being long in the country, nothing could be so good for her as a little quiet cheerfulness.

Anne did not share these feelings. She persisted in a very determined, though very silent, disinclination for Bath; caught the first dim view of the extensive buildings, smoking in rain,[45] without any wish of seeing them better; felt their progress through the streets to be, however disagreeable, yet too rapid; for who would be glad to see her when she arrived? And looked back, with fond regret, to the bustles of Uppercross and the seclusion of Kellynch.

Elizabeth's last letter had communicated a piece of news of some interest. Mr. Elliot was in Bath. He had called in Camden-place; had called a second time, a third; had been pointedly attentive: if Elizabeth and her father did not deceive themselves, had been taking as much pains to seek the acquaintance, and proclaim the value of the connection, as he had formerly taken pains to shew neglect. This was very wonderful,[46] if it were true; and Lady Russell was in a state of very agreeable curiosity and perplexity about Mr. Elliot, already recanting the sentiment she had so lately expressed to Mary, of his being "a man whom she had no wish to see." She had a great wish to see him. If he really sought to reconcile himself like a dutiful branch, he must be forgiven for having dismembered himself from the paternal tree.

Anne was not animated to an equal pitch by the circumstance; but she felt that she would rather see Mr. Elliot again than not, which was more than she could say for many other persons in Bath.[47]

She was put down in Camden-place; and Lady Russell then drove to her own lodgings, in Rivers-street.[48]

Newsmen in street, crying out or blowing to attract customers.

[From Andrew Tuer, *Old London Street Cries* (New York, 1887), p. 69]

tens were most frequently worn by servants, though there is some indication that in Bath they attained greater acceptance among wealthy people. For a picture, see next page.

44. Winter was the time when Lady Russell normally came to Bath and the time when it was liveliest.

45. Her view on arrival corresponds to Jane Austen's own experiences. In a letter after arriving on her second known visit, she writes, "It has rained almost all the way, & our first view of Bath has been just as gloomy as it was last November twelvemonth" (May 17, 1799). Two years later, when the family moved to Bath, she writes, "The first view of Bath in fine weather does not answer my expectations; I think I see more distinctly thro' Rain.—The sun was got behind everything, and the appearance of the place from the top of Kingsdown, was all vapour, shadow, smoke, & confusion" (May 5, 1801).

46. *wonderful*: astonishing.

47. Anne means her father and sister, as well as Mrs. Clay. That she looks more eagerly on the prospect of seeing Mr. Elliot again, after only a brief glimpse, speaks volumes about her feelings for her own family.

48. *Rivers-street*: a street in the fashionable northern part of the city and thus not too far from the Elliots' residence (see map, p. 516). The street contains many distinguished houses.

Bath city map from 1801.

[From Emma Austen-Leigh, *Jane Austen and Bath* (London, 1939), frontispiece]

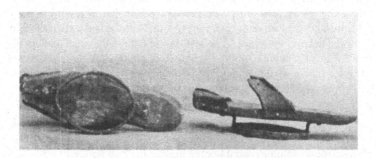

Pattens.

[From Alice Meade Earle, *Two Centuries of Costume in America* (New York, 1903), p. 362]

Woman selling buns in the street.

[From John Ashton, *The Dawn of the XIXth Century in England* (London, 1906)]

Camden Crescent, residence of Sir Walter (clothing is from a later period).

[From Mowbray Aston Green, *The Eighteenth Century Architecture of Bath* (Bath, 1904), p. 200]

Chapter Three

Sir Walter had taken a very good house in Camden-place,[1] a lofty, dignified situation, such as becomes a man of consequence; and both he and Elizabeth were settled there, much to their satisfaction.

Anne entered it with a sinking heart, anticipating an imprisonment of many months, and anxiously saying to herself, "Oh! when shall I leave you again?" A degree of unexpected cordiality, however, in the welcome she received, did her good. Her father and sister were glad to see her, for the sake of shewing her the house and furniture, and met her with kindness. Her making a fourth, when they sat down to dinner, was noticed[2] as an advantage.

Mrs. Clay was very pleasant, and very smiling; but her courtesies and smiles were more a matter of course.[3] Anne had always felt that she would pretend what was proper on her arrival; but the complaisance[4] of the others was unlooked for. They were evidently in excellent spirits, and she was soon to listen to the causes. They had no inclination to listen to her. After laying out for[5] some compliments of being deeply regretted in their old neighbourhood, which Anne could not pay, they had only a few faint enquiries to make, before the talk must be all their own. Uppercross excited no interest, Kellynch very little, it was all Bath.

They had the pleasure of assuring her that Bath more than answered their expectations in every respect. Their house was undoubtedly the best in Camden-place; their drawing-rooms had many decided advantages over all the others which they had either seen or heard of;[6] and the superiority was not less in the style of the fitting-up,[7] or the taste of the furniture. Their acquaintance was exceedingly sought after. Every body was wanting to visit them. They had drawn back from many introductions, and

1.   *Camden-place:* one of the grandest streets in Bath. Built in the 1780s, and currently known as Camden Crescent, it is in a very high location and offers spectacular views of the hills east of Bath. The houses, which form an architectural unity, are all on one side, allowing each to face the view without impediment (for a picture, see p. 257; for its location, see map, p. 516).

The site had been slated for an even grander development, but landslips forced much of the plan to be abandoned, leaving a truncated, though still impressive, crescent. Some have suggested that Jane Austen chose Camden Place as an appropriate symbol for Sir Walter's own decayed aspirations to grandeur (though in general she rarely uses symbolism).

Crescents are a prominent feature of Bath. The oldest and largest, Royal Crescent, is probably the leading landmark of the city.

2.   *noticed:* mentioned, pointed out.

3.   They are part of the obsequious, flattering behavior she always displays, especially toward Sir Walter and his family.

4.   *complaisance:* civility, politeness.

5.   *laying out for:* searching for, attempting to obtain.

6.   The drawing rooms are where they would entertain guests and show off their finest possessions, and they are the rooms they would be able to visit in other houses and compare with their own. Having more than one drawing room indicates their affluence.

7.   *fitting-up:* furnishing.

still were perpetually having cards left by people of whom they knew nothing.[8]

Here were funds of enjoyment! Could Anne wonder that her father and sister were happy? She might not wonder, but she must sigh that her father should feel no degradation in his change; should see nothing to regret in the duties and dignity of the resident land-holder;[9] should find so much to be vain of in the littlenesses of a town;[10] and she must sigh, and smile, and wonder too, as Elizabeth threw open the folding-doors,[11] and walked with exultation from one drawing-room to the other, boasting of their space, at the possibility of that woman, who had been mistress of Kellynch Hall, finding extent to be proud of between two walls, perhaps thirty feet asunder.[12]

But this was not all which they had to make them happy. They had Mr. Elliot, too. Anne had a great deal to hear of Mr. Elliot. He was not only pardoned, they were delighted with him. He had been in Bath about a fortnight; (he had passed through Bath in November, in his way to London, when the intelligence of Sir Walter's being settled there had of course reached him, though only twenty-four hours in the place, but he had not been able to avail himself of it):[13] but he had now been a fortnight in Bath, and his first object, on arriving, had been to leave his card in Camden-place,[14] following it up by such assiduous endeavours to meet, and, when they did meet, by such great openness[15] of conduct, such readiness to apologize for the past, such solicitude to be received as a relation again, that their former good understanding was completely re-established.

They had not a fault to find in him. He had explained away all the appearance of neglect on his own side. It had originated in misapprehension entirely. He had never had an idea of throwing himself off;[16] he had feared that he was thrown off, but knew not why; and delicacy had kept him silent. Upon the hint of having spoken disrespectfully or carelessly of the family, and the family honours, he was quite indignant. He, who had ever boasted of being an Elliot, and whose feelings, as to connection,[17] were only

8. Visiting cards had become a standard part of upper-class life at this time, especially in towns, where a wider variety of possible acquaintances existed and where social life was more carefully organized. People would stop at a house whose inhabitants they wished to meet, and if told they were not at home by the servants—which was a standard practice, even when people were at home—the visitors would leave a card showing their name. Those receiving the cards could then decide whether they wished to pursue the acquaintance by returning the visit.

9. The dignity of the landholder would be his leading position in the local area. The duties would include helping the poor, setting an example of good conduct, showing hospitality to the neighborhood, managing his estate (which would provide employment for many people), working with the local clergy on any important religious matters, and, in the case of many landowners, taking the lead in local government. Prevailing ideas, which Anne shares, celebrated such duties as central occupations of landowners and a critical justification for their privileged social and economic position. Someone like Sir Walter, who merely enjoyed the profits from his land without providing anything in return, would represent a violation of this ideal.

10. This probably refers to the striving for distinction and popularity among the other inhabitants, which would seem petty compared to activities in the country because no larger social purpose is being pursued.

11. Folding doors had the advantage of opening very wide, so that one could convert the two adjacent rooms into one large room if entertaining many people.

12. Town houses, which were normally, as they are in Camden Crescent, part of a row of houses, were not large in area. They could have only two or three rooms per floor, though they often had numerous floors, which was the main means of providing additional space.

13. A fuller history of Mr. Elliot's stay in Bath and his decision to reestablish contact with Sir Walter is given on p. 390.

14. This was indeed his main object in moving to Bath.

15. *openness*: frankness, lack of reserve or secrecy.

16. *throwing himself off*: casting himself off, disowning himself from the family.

17. *connection*: family ties or relationships.

too strict to suit the unfeudal tone of the present day![18] He was astonished, indeed! But his character and general conduct must refute it. He could refer Sir Walter to all who knew him; and, certainly, the pains he had been taking on this, the first opportunity of reconciliation, to be restored to the footing of a relation and heir-presumptive, was a strong proof of his opinions on the subject.

The circumstances of his marriage too were found to admit[19] of much extenuation. This was an article[20] not to be entered on by himself; but a very intimate friend of his, a Colonel Wallis, a highly respectable man, perfectly the gentleman, (and not an ill-looking man, Sir Walter added) who was living in very good style in Marlborough Buildings,[21] and had, at his own particular request, been admitted to their acquaintance through Mr. Elliot, had mentioned one or two things relative to the marriage, which made a material difference in the discredit of it.

Colonel Wallis had known Mr. Elliot long, had been well acquainted also with his wife, had perfectly understood the whole story. She was certainly not a woman of family, but well educated, accomplished, rich, and excessively in love with his friend.[22] There had been the charm. She had sought him. Without that attraction, not all her money would have tempted Elliot, and Sir Walter was, moreover, assured of her having been a very fine[23] woman. Here was a great deal to soften the business. A very fine woman, with a large fortune, in love with him! Sir Walter seemed to admit it as complete apology, and though Elizabeth could not see the circumstance in quite so favourable a light, she allowed it be a great extenuation.[24]

Mr. Elliot had called repeatedly, had dined with them once, evidently delighted by the distinction of being asked, for they gave no dinners in general;[25] delighted, in short, by every proof of cousinly notice, and placing his whole happiness in being on intimate terms in Camden-place.

Anne listened, but without quite understanding it. Allowances, large allowances, she knew, must be made for the ideas of those who spoke. She heard it all under embellishment. All that

18. He means respect for family ties, a central feature of the feudal system of the Middle Ages. In speaking of the present he is probably thinking of the growing intellectual currents, connected with increasingly powerful democratic movements and events like the French Revolution, that were challenging everything considered feudal, whether strong family ties or the respect for hierarchy associated with this. In the decades preceding this novel a number of writings had appeared in England advocating more democratic ideas, though at this time they had attained only a limited influence. In positioning himself in opposition to these unfeudal trends, Mr. Elliot is certainly saying what will appeal strongly to Sir Walter, obsessed as he is with social rank and his own family's traditions.

19. *admit:* be capable.

20. *article:* matter, subject.

21. *Marlborough Buildings:* a grand street and set of buildings next to the Royal Crescent (several streets in Bath share a name with the buildings next to them); see map, p. 516. It was a very fashionable address, which indicates the wealth of Colonel Wallis.

22. This means the woman's family, though rich, had low origins. The good education she received, which would have made her accomplished, was one of the principal ways such families made their children eligible for marriage with people of a higher social level, such as Mr. Elliot. This could then raise the status of the whole family. Given Sir Walter's strong disapproval of social climbing (p. 36), it is a testament to Mr. Elliot's powers of persuasion, as well as perhaps to how manipulable Sir Walter is, that he wins such complete approval of his earlier actions from the latter.

23. *fine:* attractive.

24. The end of this sentence should read "allowed it *to* be a great extenuation." The omission of "to" is probably a printer's error; elsewhere in Jane Austen where the same or similar wording is used, the "to" is included.

25. A later passage will mention this habit of not giving dinners and its supposed conformity to prevailing customs among the elite of Bath (p. 418).

sounded extravagant or irrational in the progress of the reconciliation might have no origin but in the language of the relators. Still, however, she had the sensation of there being something more than immediately appeared, in Mr. Elliot's wishing, after an interval of so many years, to be well received by them. In a worldly view, he had nothing to gain by being on terms with Sir Walter, nothing to risk by a state of variance.[26] In all probability he was already the richer of the two, and the Kellynch estate would as surely be his hereafter as the title. A sensible man! and he had looked like a *very* sensible man, why should it be an object to him? She could only offer one solution; it was, perhaps, for Elizabeth's sake. There might really have been a liking formerly, though convenience and accident had drawn him a different way, and now that he could afford to please himself, he might mean to pay his addresses[27] to her. Elizabeth was certainly very handsome, with well-bred, elegant manners, and her character might never have been penetrated by Mr. Elliot, knowing her but in public, and when very young himself. How her temper[28] and understanding[29] might bear the investigation of his present keener time of life was another concern, and rather a fearful one. Most earnestly did she wish that he might not be too nice,[30] or too observant, if Elizabeth were his object,[31] and that Elizabeth was disposed to believe herself so, and that her friend Mrs. Clay was encouraging the idea, seemed apparent by a glance or two between them, while Mr. Elliot's frequent visits were talked of.[32]

Anne mentioned the glimpses she had had of him at Lyme, but without being much attended to. "Oh! yes, perhaps, it had been Mr. Elliot. They did not know. It might be him, perhaps." They could not listen to her description of him. They were describing him themselves; Sir Walter especially. He did justice to his very gentlemanlike appearance, his air of elegance and fashion,[33] his good shaped face, his sensible eye, but, at the same time, "must lament his being very much under-hung,[34] a defect which time seemed to have increased; nor could he pretend to say that ten years had not altered almost every feature for the worse. Mr. Elliot appeared to think that he (Sir Walter) was looking exactly as he

26. *variance:* discord, estrangement.

27. *pay his addresses to:* court (for the purpose of marriage).

28. *temper:* emotional qualities.

29. *understanding:* intellectual qualities.

30. *nice:* fastidious, careful, delicate.

31. The object of his (marital) attentions. Anne's wish is that he not discover the truth about Elizabeth until they have married. That even someone as just and generous as Anne is in effect wishing, for the sake of a sister who has always mistreated her, that someone else make an unhappy marital choice, through an ignorance that Anne herself could correct, shows the strength of family partiality in this society, even in the absence of affection.

32. The frequency of his visits suggests he does have some purpose in mind, though whether it is Elizabeth is still uncertain.

33. Fashion could refer not just to stylishness but also to social position. A person of fashion was one from the elite ranks of society; an air of fashion could suggest membership in those ranks.

34. *under-hung:* having a lower jaw that protrudes too far, especially beyond the upper jaw.

had done when they last parted"; but Sir Walter had "not been
able to return the compliment entirely, which had embarrassed
him.[35] He did not mean to complain, however. Mr. Elliot was better to look at than most men, and he had no objection to being
seen with him any where."

Mr. Elliot, and his friends in Marlborough Buildings, were
talked of the whole evening. "Colonel Wallis had been so impatient to be introduced to them! and Mr. Elliot so anxious that he
should!"[36] And there was a Mrs. Wallis, at present only known to
them by description, as she was in daily expectation of her confinement,[37] but Mr. Elliot spoke of her as "a most charming
woman, quite worthy of being known in Camden-place," and as
soon as she recovered, they were to be acquainted. Sir Walter
thought much of Mrs. Wallis; she was said to be an excessively
pretty woman, beautiful. "He longed to see her. He hoped she
might make some amends for the many very plain faces he was
continually passing in the streets. The worst of Bath was, the number of its plain women. He did not mean to say that there were no
pretty women, but the number of the plain was out of all propor-
tion. He had frequently observed, as he walked, that one handsome face would be followed by thirty, or five and thirty frights;
and once, as he had stood in a shop in Bond-street,[38] he had
counted eighty-seven women go by, one after another, without
there being a tolerable face among them. It had been a frosty
morning, to be sure, a sharp frost, which hardly one woman in a
thousand could stand the test of. But still, there certainly were a
dreadful multitude of ugly women in Bath; and as for the men!
they were infinitely worse. Such scare-crows as the streets were
full of![39] It was evident how little the women were used to the
sight of any thing tolerable, by the effect which a man of decent
appearance produced. He had never walked any where arm in
arm with Colonel Wallis, (who was a fine military figure, though
sandy-haired)[40] without observing that every woman's eye was
upon him; every woman's eye was sure to be upon Colonel Wallis." Modest Sir Walter! He was not allowed to escape, however.
His daughter and Mrs. Clay united in hinting that Colonel Wal-

35. Sir Walter's comment reveals his obsession with looks, his foolish susceptibility to such obvious flattery as Mr. Elliot's statement about his not aging at all, and—one of his few good points—a strong enough sense of courtesy to produce discomfort when he cannot return a compliment.

36. Mr. Elliot's keen anxiety for them to meet Colonel Wallis will be explained later (p. 392).

37. This means she is expected to give birth any day. A woman's confinement, also called her lying-in, was the time from the birth of her baby through her subsequent recovery. It usually lasted a month, or a little more, for medical opinion held that such a period of strict rest was necessary to ward off the postnatal dangers threatening the mother and the baby. At the outset the mother was kept to her bed, and often shielded from strong light; subsequently, in gradual stages, she was allowed to receive more visitors and to leave, first her bed, then her room, then, at the conclusion, her home. A similar caution frequently attended the period just before birth, which is why strangers are currently unable to see Mrs. Wallis.

38. *Bond-street:* one of the principal shopping streets in Bath (see map, p. 516).

39. This is another example of the tendency then to regard excessive thinness as unattractive (see p. 231, note 28).

40. Sir Walter's abomination of freckles has already been described (p. 66), and since freckles frequently accompany sandy hair, it is likely he has a similar disdain for such a hair color.

C.W.T.
after Pri

Woman's cap.

[From Elisabeth McClellan, *Historic Dress in America, 1800–1870* (Philadelphia, 1910), p. 67]

lis's companion might have as good a figure as Colonel Wallis, and certainly was not sandy-haired.[41]

"How is Mary looking?" said Sir Walter, in the height of his good humour. "The last time I saw her, she had a red nose, but I hope that may not happen every day."

"Oh! no, that must have been quite accidental. In general she has been in very good health, and very good looks since Michaelmas."

"If I thought it would not tempt her to go out in sharp winds, and grow coarse, I would send her a new hat and pelisse."[42]

Anne was considering whether she should venture to suggest that a gown, or a cap,[43] would not be liable to any such misuse, when a knock at the door suspended every thing. "A knock at the door! and so late! It was ten o'clock. Could it be Mr. Elliot?[44] They knew he was to dine in Lansdown Crescent.[45] It was possible that he might stop in his way home, to ask them how they did. They could think of no one else. Mrs. Clay decidedly thought it Mr. Elliot's knock." Mrs. Clay was right. With all the state[46] which a butler and foot-boy could give,[47] Mr. Elliot was ushered into the room.

It was the same, the very same man, with no difference but of dress. Anne drew a little back, while the others received his compliments, and her sister his apologies for calling at so unusual an hour, but "he could not be so near without wishing to know that neither she nor her friend had taken cold the day before, &c. &c." which was all as politely done, and as politely taken as possible, but her part must follow then. Sir Walter talked of his youngest daughter; "Mr. Elliot must give him leave to present him to his youngest daughter" — (there was no occasion for remembering Mary) and Anne, smiling and blushing, very becomingly shewed to Mr. Elliot the pretty features which he had by no means forgotten, and instantly saw, with amusement at his little start of surprise, that he had not been at all aware of who she was. He looked completely astonished, but not more astonished than pleased; his eyes brightened, and with the most perfect alacrity he welcomed the relationship, alluded to the past, and entreated to be received

41. Perceiving that Sir Walter is fishing for a compliment, they respond that he was the one toward whom every woman's eye was really turned. Sir Walter has enough decorum to wish to avoid having to make the observation himself and enough foolish vanity to be delighted, as the next line indicates, when such an obvious ploy elicits praise from two people who, as inhabitants of his house, have a natural interest in flattering him.

42. *pelisse:* a garment that, like a hat, is for wearing outside (see p. 125, note 19, and picture on p. 121).

43. Caps were standard articles of clothing for women (see picture, p. 267). Generally made of soft material such as muslin or satin, they were normally worn indoors, which is why Anne thinks of them in this context. They helped keep the hair clean (means for washing hair were very limited then) and allowed women to take less trouble fixing their hair. Thus they were especially likely to be worn by married women such as Mary, or older women, neither of whom would have as strong a reason to make themselves more attractive by revealing their hair. In a letter Jane Austen writes, "I have made myself two or three caps to wear of evening since I came home, and they save me a world of trouble as to hair-dressing" (Dec. 1, 1798).

44. They suspect Mr. Elliot because it would be too late for less intimate acquaintances to visit—though wealthy people, especially in towns, tended to maintain fairly late hours. Such hours are indicated by their speculation that Mr. Elliot might be stopping on his way back from dinner.

45. *Lansdown Crescent:* another of the three prominent crescents of Bath (see map, p. 516, and picture on p. 273). It is higher than either Camden Place or Royal Crescent, and larger than Camden Place, and was singled out for praise by contemporary writers. One declared that it "appears so elevated, that it looks more like an aerie than a habitation for men" (Richard Warner, *Bath Characters*). It is possible that Mr. Elliot's acquaintance there is meant to signify that he moves, at least part of the time, in wealthier circles than Sir Walter does.

46. *state:* pomp, ceremony, grandeur.

47. A butler was a high-ranking servant whose duties could include answering the door and attending to guests. Footboys, or footmen, were lower servants who could also perform that function, especially in the absence of a butler. Usually both would not usher in a single guest. Sir Walter's procedure is presumably meant to impress guests: advertising the master's wealth was in many respects the most important function of footmen, who were frequently dressed in very gaudy liveries and whose main tasks were such public ones as

as an acquaintance already. He was quite as good-looking as he had appeared at Lyme,[48] his countenance improved by speaking, and his manners were so exactly what they ought to be, so polished, so easy,[49] so particularly agreeable, that she could compare them in excellence to only one person's manners. They were not the same, but they were, perhaps, equally good.[50]

He sat down with them, and improved their conversation very much. There could be no doubt of his being a sensible man. Ten minutes were enough to certify that. His tone, his expressions, his choice of subject, his knowing where to stop, — it was all the operation of a sensible, discerning mind. As soon as he could, he began to talk to her of Lyme, wanting to compare opinions respecting the place, but especially wanting to speak of the circumstance of their happening to be guests in the same inn at the same time, to give his own route, understand something of hers, and regret that he should have lost such an opportunity of paying his respects to her. She gave him a short account of her party, and business at Lyme. His regret increased as he listened. He had spent his whole solitary evening in the room adjoining theirs; had heard voices—mirth continually; thought they must be a most delightful set of people—longed to be with them; but certainly without the smallest suspicion of his possessing the shadow of a right to introduce himself.[51] If he had but asked who the party were! The name of Musgrove would have told him enough. "Well, it would serve to cure him of an absurd practice of never asking a question at an inn, which he had adopted, when quite a young man, on the principle of its being very ungenteel to be curious.[52]

"The notions of a young man of one or two and twenty," said he, "as to what is necessary in manners to make him quite the thing, are more absurd, I believe, than those of any other set of beings in the world. The folly of the means they often employ is only to be equalled by the folly of what they have in view."[53]

But he must not be addressing his reflections to Anne alone; he knew it; he was soon diffused again among the others, and it was only at intervals that he could return to Lyme.

accompanying their employers when they went out, delivering messages, waiting at table, and standing around and awaiting orders from the house's inhabitants. At the same time, Sir Walter's hiring of a footboy indicates he is making his show on the cheap, for the wages of a footboy were typically one-third or less of the wages of a footman.

48. This description differs a little from the statement on p. 200, when Mr. Elliot was seen at Lyme, that he, "though not handsome, had an agreeable person [i.e., pleasant appearance]." The somewhat stronger praise here could be an inconsistency on the part of the author, or it could be a suggestion that Anne's own opinion of Mr. Elliot, for whatever reason, has improved.

49. *easy*: unembarrassed; free from awkwardness or stiffness.

50. The other person is Captain Wentworth, the person consistently on Anne's mind and forming her standard of excellence. The comparison here suggests a possible rivalry between the two, at least in her head.

51. Current etiquette prescribed strict rules about introducing oneself to others.

52. Ideas of gentility scorned excessive curiosity, especially if it meant prying into others' affairs or asking them inappropriate questions. It would not mean, however, never asking a question at an inn. Mr. Elliot's having formed a conscious program when young of making himself genteel gives an important clue to his character, revealing his concern for status and at least some of the reason for his highly correct manners.

53. The statement suggests that Mr. Elliot now believes it is folly to wish to be as fashionable and genteel as possible, but his behavior and his opinions at other points show a continued concern for such values.

His enquiries, however, produced at length an account of the scene she had been engaged in there, soon after his leaving the place. Having alluded to "an accident," he must hear the whole. When he questioned, Sir Walter and Elizabeth began to question also; but the difference in their manner of doing it could not be unfelt. She could only compare Mr. Elliot to Lady Russell, in the wish of really comprehending what had passed, and in the degree of concern for what she must have suffered in witnessing it.

He staid an hour with them. The elegant little clock on the mantle-piece[54] had struck "eleven with its silver sounds,"[55] and the watchman[56] was beginning to be heard at a distance telling the same tale, before Mr. Elliot or any of them seemed to feel that he had been there long.

Anne could not have supposed it possible that her first evening in Camden-place could have passed so well![57]

Rowlandson. Delin. 1813.
"Past one o'clock, an' a fine morning!"

Watchman crying out the time.

[From Andrew Tuer, *Old London Street Cries* (New York, 1887), p. 37]

54. Clocks small enough to fit on a mantelpiece were widely available then.

55. The origin of this phrase, which seems, based on the quotation marks, to be from a particular text, has never been identified for certain. One commentator, Patricia Meyer Spacks, suggests the phrase may allude to a line in *The Rape of the Lock* by Alexander Pope, a poet Jane Austen certainly knew well: "And the pressed watch returned a silver sound."

The phrase does not represent a literal description of the operation of the clock, for the component parts of a clock were made of other metals than silver, usually brass or steel. Clocks were standard parts of a home, designed for elegant appearance as well as utility.

56. A watchman was someone who would patrol a town after dark, crying out the time and keeping watch for possible trouble. Watchmen in London then would cry the time every half hour. See illustration on facing page for a contemporary picture (the lantern and stick were standard).

57. Her unexpected felicity, a contrast to her anticipations of imprisonment at the start of the chapter, suggests that her stay in Bath may turn out to be less miserable than she feared.

Lansdown Crescent, where Mr. Elliot dines (from a contemporary drawing).

[From Mowbray Aston Green, *The Eighteenth Century Architecture of Bath* (Bath, 1904), p. 188]

Chapter Four

*T*here was one point which Anne, on returning to her family, would have been more thankful to ascertain, even than Mr. Elliot's being in love with Elizabeth, which was, her father's not being in love with Mrs. Clay; and she was very far from easy about it, when she had been at home a few hours. On going down to breakfast the next morning, she found there had just been a decent pretence on the lady's side of meaning to leave them. She could imagine Mrs. Clay to have said, that "now Miss Anne was come, she could not suppose herself at all wanted"; for Elizabeth was replying, in a sort of whisper, "That must not be any reason, indeed. I assure you I feel it none. She is nothing to me, compared with you"; and she was in full time to hear her father say, "My dear Madam,[1] this must not be. As yet, you have seen nothing of Bath. You have been here only to be useful. You must not run away from us now. You must stay to be acquainted with Mrs. Wallis, the beautiful Mrs. Wallis. To your fine[2] mind, I well know the sight of beauty is a real gratification."[3]

He spoke and looked so much in earnest, that Anne was not surprised to see Mrs. Clay stealing a glance at Elizabeth and herself.[4] Her countenance, perhaps, might express some watchfulness; but the praise of the fine mind did not appear to excite a thought in her sister. The lady could not but yield to such joint entreaties, and promise to stay.

In the course of the same morning, Anne and her father chancing to be alone together,[5] he began to compliment her on her improved looks; he thought her "less thin in her person,[6] in her cheeks; her skin, her complexion, greatly improved—clearer, fresher.[7] Had she been using any thing in particular?" "No, nothing." "Merely Gowland,"[8] he supposed. "No, nothing at all." "Ha! he was surprised at that"; and added, "Certainly you cannot do

1. *My dear Madam:* a more formal address than most people would use, especially toward someone who is relatively young and a close acquaintance. It may result from his wishing to maintain some distance between them or from his general formality.

2. *fine:* refined, delicate.

3. This last line signals Mrs. Clay's successful flattery, in convincing Sir Walter that she shares his own great interest in physical appearance. It thus forms a fitting capstone to Sir Walter's earnest invitation to Mrs. Clay and the greater affection for her that it indicates.

4. Mrs. Clay's glance around, like Anne's observance of her, results from the serious implications of Sir Walter's words, especially his praise of her mind, for prevailing rules of propriety counseled against an unmarried man paying compliments directly to an unmarried woman unless he had serious intentions toward her. Sir Walter's is a limited compliment, but it could signal more to come.

5. The wording suggests that only chance, and never intention, would bring them together.

6. *person:* physical person. For the tendency not to equate thinness with beauty, see p. 231, note 28.

7. The compliments of Sir Walter, someone always focused on appearance and inclined to criticize that of others, indicate that the improvement in Anne's looks seen at Lyme has persisted, and thus that her hope of enjoying a "second spring of youth and beauty" may be coming true (p. 230).

8. Gowland was a popular skin lotion of the time. It had been created in the mid-1700s by John Gowland, and promoted, first by Gowland and then by the succeeding owners of the formula, with pamphlets in which its curative properties were extolled, particularly with respect to "cutaneous eruptions" of the skin (in one pamphlet Gowland is hailed as the apothecary to the king). It in fact contained corrosive substances that would strip away the top layer of the skin.

better than continue as you are; you cannot be better than well; or I should recommend Gowland, the constant use of Gowland, during the spring months. Mrs. Clay has been using it at my recommendation, and you see what it has done for her. You see how it has carried away her freckles."[9]

If Elizabeth could but have heard this! Such personal praise might have struck her, especially as it did not appear to Anne that the freckles were at all lessened. But every thing must take its chance. The evil of the marriage would be much diminished, if Elizabeth were also to marry. As for herself, she might always command a home with Lady Russell.

Lady Russell's composed mind and polite manners were put to some trial on this point, in her intercourse in Camden-place. The sight of Mrs. Clay in such favour, and of Anne so overlooked, was a perpetual provocation to her there; and vexed her as much when she was away, as a person in Bath who drinks the water,[10] gets all the new publications,[11] and has a very large acquaintance, has time to be vexed.

As Mr. Elliot became known to her, she grew more charitable, or more indifferent, towards the others. His manners were an immediate recommendation; and on conversing with him she found the solid so fully supporting the superficial, that she was at first, as she told Anne, almost ready to exclaim, "Can this be Mr. Elliot?" and could not seriously picture to herself a more agreeable or estimable man. Every thing united in him; good understanding, correct opinions, knowledge of the world,[12] and a warm heart. He had strong feelings of family-attachment and family-honour, without pride or weakness; he lived with the liberality of a man of fortune, without display; he judged for himself in every thing essential, without defying public opinion in any point of worldly decorum.[13] He was steady, observant, moderate, candid,[14] never run away with by spirits[15] or by selfishness, which fancied itself strong feeling; and yet, with a sensibility to what was amiable[16] and lovely, and a value for all the felicities of domestic life, which characters of fancied enthusiasm and violent agitation sel-

9. Freckles were, along with almost every other imaginable ailment or defect of the skin, mentioned by the seller of Gowland as something his lotion could cure.

10. Drinking the warm mineral waters that flowed from beneath the ground and that supplied the baths was a favorite activity of visitors to Bath. Though the waters were not praised for their taste, they were frequently lauded as healthful, and many people made drinking them part of their daily routine (for a picture of a royal visitor drinking the waters, see p. 286).

11. Bath, in addition to other sources of amusement, was supplied with a number of booksellers and circulating libraries (the latter were often run by booksellers). It even had publishers of its own. Hence it would be an excellent place to keep abreast of new books and pamphlets.

12. *world*: society, different walks of life; possibly also the specific connotation of elite society.

13. This represents the ideal mean, with regard to the issue of independence vs. social conformity, promoted by Jane Austen. She satirizes those who blindly conform to whatever happen to be prevailing notions. At the same time, in *Sense and Sensibility* she presents a heroine, Marianne, whose strong Romantic ideas lead her to disregard social decorum and to rely only on her personal feelings in governing her behavior, which ends up creating pain for others and disaster for herself. In contrast, her sister Elinor, who follows established decorum and controls her feelings, avoids causing such harm. In an exchange with Marianne, she explains that while she has criticized the latter's lack of civility to others, she has never "advised you [Marianne] to adopt their sentiments or conform to their judgments in serious matters."

14. *candid*: fair-minded or generous in one's opinions; inclined to think well of others.

15. *spirits*: eagerness, vehemence.

16. *amiable*: kind, benevolent, worthy of love.

dom really possess.[17] She was sure that he had not been happy in marriage. Colonel Wallis said it, and Lady Russell saw it; but it had been no unhappiness to sour his mind, nor (she began pretty soon to suspect) to prevent his thinking of a second choice. Her satisfaction in Mr. Elliot outweighed all the plague of Mrs. Clay.

It was now some years since Anne had begun to learn that she and her excellent friend could sometimes think differently; and it did not surprise her, therefore, that Lady Russell should see nothing suspicious or inconsistent, nothing to require more motives than appeared, in Mr. Elliot's great desire of a reconciliation. In Lady Russell's view, it was perfectly natural that Mr. Elliot, at a mature time of life, should feel it a most desirable object, and what would very generally recommend him, among all sensible people, to be on good terms with the head of his family; the simplest process in the world of time upon a head naturally clear, and only erring in the heyday of youth. Anne presumed, however, still to smile about it; and at last to mention "Elizabeth." Lady Russell listened, and looked, and made only this cautious reply: "Elizabeth! Very well. Time will explain."[18]

It was a reference to the future, which Anne, after a little observation, felt she must submit to. She could determine nothing at present. In that house Elizabeth must be first; and she was in the habit of such general observance as "Miss Elliot," that any particularity of attention seemed almost impossible.[19] Mr. Elliot, too, it must be remembered, had not been a widower seven months. A little delay on his side might be very excusable. In fact, Anne could never see the crape round his hat,[20] without fearing that she was the inexcusable one, in attributing to him such imaginations; for though his marriage had not been very happy, still it had existed so many years that she could not comprehend a very rapid recovery from the awful[21] impression of its being dissolved.[22]

However it might end, he was without any question their pleasantest acquaintance in Bath; she saw nobody equal to him; and it was a great indulgence now and then to talk to him about Lyme, which he seemed to have as lively a wish to see again, and to see more of, as herself. They went through the particulars of their first

17. Lady Russell's evaluation reflects her own strong belief in rational self-control. It also echoes points made elsewhere in Jane Austen, who consistently presents "characters of fancied enthusiasm and violent agitation" in a critical light. This novel's treatment of Louisa Musgrove and Captain Benwick is one example.

18. This suggests that, contrary to what has just been explained, Lady Russell already suspects a further motive in Mr. Elliot, namely an interest in Anne.

19. Any attention directed particularly to Anne seemed impossible.

20. Crape, because of its dull finish, was frequently used for mourning attire, which was supposed to have nothing shiny about it. In a letter discussing how she will mourn for her brother's just-deceased wife, Jane Austen writes that her bonnet will be covered with crape (Oct. 15, 1808).

If the crape around Mr. Elliot's hat is his sole remaining mourning article, as implied by the wording of the sentence, then he is in a later stage of mourning. Custom dictated two or three stages, with each stage involving a reduction of the number of mourning articles or their darkness. When Mr. Elliot was in Lyme, approximately two months prior to this (see chronology, p. 488), he was probably in an earlier stage, for Anne notices, after two passing encounters with him and a view of his servant in the street, that they are both in mourning, and crape around a hat might not have sufficed for that; the servant is also described as having traded his livery for mourning clothes (see pp. 200 and 204).

21. *awful*: worthy of respect or awe.

22. Anne is naturally attributing to someone else her own delicacy and regard for others. The real nature of Mr. Elliot's feelings, on this matter and other ones, will eventually be revealed in great detail in Chapter IX of Volume II.

meeting a great many times. He gave her to understand that he had looked at her with some earnestness. She knew it well; and she remembered another person's look also.[23]

They did not always think alike. His value for rank and connexion she perceived to be greater than hers. It was not merely complaisance, it must be a liking to the cause, which made him enter warmly into her father and sister's solicitudes on a subject which she thought unworthy to excite them. The Bath paper[24] one morning announced the arrival of the Dowager Viscountess Dalrymple,[25] and her daughter, the Honourable Miss Carteret;[26] and all the comfort of No. —, Camden-place, was swept away for many days; for the Dalrymples (in Anne's opinion, most unfortunately) were cousins of the Elliots; and the agony was, how to introduce themselves properly.

Anne had never seen her father and sister before in contact with nobility, and she must acknowledge herself disappointed. She had hoped better things from their high ideas of their own situation in life, and was reduced to form a wish which she had never foreseen—a wish that they had more pride,[27] for "our cousins Lady Dalrymple and Miss Carteret"; "our cousins, the Dalrymples," sounded in her ears all day long.

Sir Walter had once been in company with the late Viscount, but had never seen any of the rest of the family, and the difficulties of the case arose from there having been a suspension of all intercourse by letters of ceremony, ever since the death of that said late Viscount, when, in consequence of a dangerous illness of Sir Walter's at the same time, there had been an unlucky omission at Kellynch. No letter of condolence had been sent to Ireland.[28] The neglect had been visited on the head of the sinner, for when poor Lady Elliot died herself, no letter of condolence was received at Kellynch, and, consequently, there was but too much reason to apprehend that the Dalrymples considered the relationship as closed. How to have this anxious business set to rights, and be admitted as cousins again, was the question; and it was a question which, in a more rational manner, neither Lady Russell nor Mr. Elliot thought unimportant. "Family connexions were always

23. The other person is Captain Wentworth, who was prompted by Mr. Elliot's look to glance at Anne with greater appreciation (p. 200).

24. *Bath paper:* one newspaper in Bath, the *Bath Chronicle*, listed the most prominent arrivals into Bath. In 1799 it referred to the arrival of "Mr. and Mrs. E. Austin," a probable (misspelled) reference to Jane Austen's brother Edward, the heir of a considerable estate, and his wife (cited in Maggie Lane, *A Charming Place*, p. 23). Jane Austen herself and her parents were not wealthy and prominent enough to receive such a mention upon their arrival, though in her first letter written from Bath, she notes, "There was a very long list of Arrivals here, in the Newspaper yesterday" (May 17, 1799).

25. A viscountess is the wife of a viscount, the fourth-highest rank of nobility—the others are duke, marquess, earl, and, after viscount, baron. This puts the viscountess at a higher rank than Sir Walter. Dowager is the title given to widows of those with titles. When this woman's husband died, his heir, most likely his son, became the new viscount, and his wife, if she existed, became Viscountess Dalrymple. "Dowager" allows the widow, while retaining the title of viscountess, to be distinguished from the current holder of the title.

26. "The Honourable" is a courtesy title given to the children of viscounts and barons. Carteret is the family name, which normally differs from the name of the noble title; thus the mother's full name would be "——Carteret, Dowager Viscountess Dalrymple."

Many dowagers came to Bath. They would frequently no longer be able, or wish, to remain in the family home once their sons' families moved there. In *Mansfield Park* a wealthy woman in such a position moves to Bath "with true dowager propriety" (she lacks a title, but "dowager" was sometimes used for any wealthy and prominent widow). Lady Dalrymple, as shortly explained, has only come to Bath for three months; she also came last year, so she may divide her time between it and London or other resort towns, at all of which she could enjoy the society of many other wealthy people. This would also make such places suitable for finding a husband for Miss Carteret.

27. *Pride and Prejudice*, even as it condemns pride generally, especially that based purely on birth, does indicate some sympathy for certain kinds of pride, such as the pride in one's goodness that could spur action to conform to that self-image. In this case, Anne is disappointed that her father's and sister's sense of their own dignity has not dissuaded them from undignified behavior.

28. It would not be unusual for an Irish noble family to have relations in England or to visit an English resort like Bath. Ireland at the time was part of the United Kingdom and governed from London; more significantly, Ireland was dominated by the so-called Anglo-Irish, descendants of English settlers whose great wealth and power was supported by Britain as a way of maintaining Protestant and British control over Ireland, and who thus had strong

worth preserving, good company always worth seeking; Lady Dalrymple had taken a house, for three months, in Laura-place, and
would be living in style. She had been at Bath the year before, and
Lady Russell had heard her spoken of as a charming woman. It
was very desirable that the connexion should be renewed, if it
could be done, without any compromise of propriety on the side
of the Elliots."

Sir Walter, however, would choose his own means, and at last
wrote a very fine[29] letter of ample explanation, regret and entreaty,
to his right honourable[30] cousin. Neither Lady Russell nor Mr.
Elliot could admire the letter; but it did all that was wanted, in
bringing three lines of scrawl from the Dowager Viscountess.
"She was very much honoured, and should be happy in their
acquaintance." The toils of the business were over, the sweets
began. They visited in Laura-place,[31] they had the cards of Dowager Viscountess Dalrymple, and the Hon. Miss Carteret, to be
arranged wherever they might be most visible;[32] and "Our cousins
in Laura-place,"—"Our cousins, Lady Dalrymple and Miss
Carteret," were talked of to every body.

Anne was ashamed. Had Lady Dalrymple and her daughter
even been very agreeable, she would still have been ashamed of
the agitation they created, but they were nothing. There was no
superiority of manner, accomplishment, or understanding.[33]
Lady Dalrymple had acquired the name of "a charming woman,"
because she had a smile and a civil answer for every body. Miss
Carteret, with still less to say, was so plain and so awkward, that
she would never have been tolerated in Camden-place but for her
birth.[34]

Lady Russell confessed that she had expected something better;
but yet "it was an acquaintance worth having," and when Anne
ventured to speak her opinion of them to Mr. Elliot, he agreed to
their being nothing in themselves, but still maintained that as a
family connexion, as good company, as those who would collect
good company around them, they had their value. Anne smiled
and said,

"My idea of good company, Mr. Elliot, is the company of

feelings of affinity with Britain. The Anglo-Irish formed the majority of the Irish nobility. In fact, many Irish peerages were conferred on English families who were not considered worthy of English peerages. This, along with the greater number of Irish peers relative to the population and their lesser wealth and political power compared to English peers, gave them lower prestige. It is possible Jane Austen made the Dalrymples Irish for this reason, for their lesser status, as peers go, makes Sir Walter's obsequiousness even more foolish. In a letter from Lyme she gives a sense of her own probable low opinion of Irish nobility by speaking of "the Hon^{bl} Barnwalls, who are the son & son's wife of an Irish Viscount—bold queerlooking people, just fit to be Quality at Lyme" (Sept. 14, 1804). While her strictures are most obviously directed at their personal qualities, her words about being quality, i.e., the elite class, at Lyme, a small town that did not cater to a particularly selective clientele, suggest a low opinion of their social status as well.

29. *fine:* fancy, ornate (often in an affected manner).

30. *right honourable:* a designation conferred on nobles below the rank of marquess. Sir Walter would use it when addressing Viscountess Dalrymple in his letter to her.

31. *Laura-place:* a grand, diamond-shaped square in the eastern part of Bath (see map, p. 516). This area, across the river from the rest of the city, formed, along with the north, the principal direction of Bath's expansion in the years preceding the novel. It was very fashionable. In *Northanger Abbey*, the heroine stays in Pulteney Street, which adjoins Laura Place, and during Jane Austen's time in Bath, she and her family lived for a while on Sydney Place in this area; they were not in a position to afford Laura Place itself.

Since the Elliots are the ones who zealously wish for the connection, their feelings would inspire them to visit first, but etiquette would probably also dictate a first visit from them, as the ones already resident in Bath (see also p. 75, note 57).

32. Trays for holding visiting cards were standard equipment. Visitors would place their cards on them, but they could also serve as places to display cards one had received. Since these trays were in front hallways, their contents would be visible to all who came to the house.

33. *understanding:* intellect.

34. Anne's experience replicates one of Jane Austen herself. While staying at the estate of her wealthy brother Edward she met a Lady Elizabeth Finch-Hatton, the daughter of an earl, and her daughter. She comments, "I have discovered that Ly Eliz:^{th} for a woman of her age & situation, has astonishingly little to say for herself, & that Miss Hatton has not much more" (Aug. 24, 1805).

clever, well-informed people, who have a great deal of conversation; that is what I call good company."

"You are mistaken," said he gently, "that is not good company, that is the best. Good company requires only birth, education and manners, and with regard to education is not very nice.[35] Birth and good manners are essential; but a little learning is by no means a dangerous thing in good company, on the contrary, it will do very well. My cousin, Anne, shakes her head. She is not satisfied. She is fastidious. My dear cousin,[36] (sitting down by her) you have a better right to be fastidious than almost any other woman I know; but will it answer? Will it make you happy? Will it not be wiser to accept the society of these good ladies in Laura-place, and enjoy all the advantages of the connexion as far as possible? You may depend upon it, that they will move in the first set in Bath this winter, and as rank is rank, your being known to be related to them will have its use in fixing your family (our family let me say) in that degree of consideration which we must all wish for."

"Yes," sighed Anne, "we shall, indeed, be known to be related to them!"—then recollecting herself, and not wishing to be answered, she added, "I certainly do think there has been by far too much trouble taken to procure the acquaintance. I suppose (smiling) I have more pride than any of you; but I confess it does vex me, that we should be so solicitous to have the relationship acknowledged, which we may be very sure is a matter of perfect indifference to them."

"Pardon me, my dear cousin, you are unjust to your own claims. In London, perhaps, in your present quiet style of living, it might be as you say;[37] but in Bath, Sir Walter Elliot and his family will always be worth knowing, always acceptable as acquaintance."

"Well," said Anne, "I certainly am proud, too proud to enjoy a welcome which depends so entirely upon place."[38]

"I love your indignation," said he; "it is very natural. But here you are in Bath, and the object is to be established here with all the credit and dignity which ought to belong to Sir Walter Elliot. You talk of being proud, I am called proud I know, and I shall not wish to believe myself otherwise, for our pride, if investigated,

35. *nice*: fastidious, discriminating.

36. "My dear" is often used before mother, father, sister, or brother, but it is rarely used with cousins in Jane Austen. The only other example is the foolish and excessively formal Mr. Collins in *Pride and Prejudice*. Mr. Elliot's use of the term—and he says "my dear cousin" twice more in this brief conversation—marks the great, if not excessive, courtesy of his manners, as well as the earnestness of his wish to win Anne's favor.

37. London was not only far larger than Bath, but also where the wealthiest and highest-ranking people in England congregated, so the Elliots could never hope to be in the first set there. Their chances would be further undermined by the "quiet style of living" mentioned by Mr. Elliot, for leading families in London would typically give elaborate entertainments and participate in the political and cultural life of the capital.

38. Their continued disagreement over the value of rank suggests a fundamental divide between Anne and Mr. Elliot, though it is kept from being too apparent by the politeness and goodwill of both, and by their agreement over Mrs. Clay, which Mr. Elliot, eager to downplay their differences, proceeds to cite. Anne's refusal to accede to his perspective may result in part from the misery that high regard for rank, on the part of her father and Lady Russell, caused her by leading her to reject Captain Wentworth. If so, it would form one more way that event continues to influence her.

would have the same object, I have no doubt, though the kind may seem a little different. In one point, I am sure, my dear cousin, (he continued, speaking lower, though there was no one else in the room) in one point, I am sure, we must feel alike. We must feel that every addition to your father's society, among his equals or superiors, may be of use in diverting his thoughts from those who are beneath him."

He looked, as he spoke, to the seat which Mrs. Clay had been lately occupying, a sufficient explanation of what he particularly meant;[39] and though Anne could not believe in their having the same sort of pride, she was pleased with him for not liking Mrs. Clay;[40] and her conscience admitted that his wishing to promote her father's getting great acquaintance,[41] was more than excusable in the view of defeating her.

Interior of Pump Room, visit of Princess Caroline to drink the waters. Note the Bath chair inside the building.

[From Mowbray Aston Green, *The Eighteenth Century Architecture of Bath* (Bath, 1904), p. 203]

39. This is the first indication of Mr. Elliot's own worries about Mrs. Clay. The degree and importance of this will be revealed later (pp. 390–394).

40. Anne's dislike of Mrs. Clay indicates she is not indifferent to status, because her strong objection to a possible marriage between Mrs. Clay and Sir Walter seems to be based at least partly on her belief in its social inappropriateness and on the shame it would bring to the family. Anne never speaks very harshly of Mrs. Clay's personal qualities, and she herself would not be directly harmed by the marriage since she would not be displaced as mistress of the household.

41. *great acquaintance:* friendship or acquaintance with people of high, or great, social position.

West end of Bath Street, with the Cross Bath on right. The Hot Baths are just behind the Cross Bath (from a contemporary picture).

[From Emma Austen-Leigh, *Jane Austen and Bath* (London, 1939), p. 8]

Chapter Five

While Sir Walter and Elizabeth were assiduously pushing their good fortune in Laura-place, Anne was renewing an acquaintance of a very different description.

She had called on her former governess, and had heard from her of there being an old school-fellow in Bath,[1] who had the two strong claims on her attention, of past kindness and present suffering. Miss Hamilton, now Mrs. Smith, had shewn her kindness in one of those periods of her life when it had been most valuable. Anne had gone unhappy to school,[2] grieving for the loss of a mother whom she had dearly loved, feeling her separation from home, and suffering as a girl of fourteen, of strong sensibility and not high spirits,[3] must suffer at such a time; and Miss Hamilton, three years older than herself, but still from the want[4] of near relations and a settled home, remaining another year at school,[5] had been useful and good to her in a way which had considerably lessened her misery, and could never be remembered with indifference.

Miss Hamilton had left school, had married not long afterwards, was said to have married a man of fortune, and this was all that Anne had known of her, till now that their governess's account brought her situation forward in a more decided but very different form.

She was a widow, and poor. Her husband had been extravagant; and at his death, about two years before, had left his affairs dreadfully involved.[6] She had had difficulties of every sort to contend with, and in addition to these distresses, had been afflicted with a severe rheumatic fever, which finally settling in her legs, had made her for the present a cripple.[7] She had come to Bath on that account, and was now in lodgings near the hot-baths,[8] living in a

1. Girls from wealthy families frequently had a governess if they were educated at home. Anne would have had hers in the years before she went to school. The governess may know about Anne's old schoolfellow from having connections with the school or with a teacher there, for governesses and schoolteachers were drawn from the same source, unmarried women from genteel backgrounds who needed to earn money, these being the only jobs considered suitable for genteel women. The heroine of Charlotte Brontë's *Jane Eyre* works as a teacher before becoming a governess, a course Anne's governess could have followed, and one that might have led her to recommend the school for Anne.

2. Many girls went to boarding schools for a few years (though not all—Anne might never have gone had her mother not died). Bath had a number of schools, and its proximity to Kellynch would make it a logical place for Anne to go. For what was usually taught, see p. 77, note 66.

3. This is an indication that Anne's general quietness and reserve existed even before the unhappy end of her affair with Captain Wentworth.

4. *want*: lack.

5. By seventeen a girl was usually finished with her education, but there was no standardized curriculum that forced anyone to finish at a particular time. Thus a girl could easily remain another year if her family could pay for it.

6. *involved*: entangled.

7. Rheumatic fever is an illness characterized by the sudden onset of a variety of severe symptoms, with the heart and joints being particularly affected. Now believed to result from a reaction to a streptococcus infection, it was first diagnosed in the late eighteenth century and may have been an actual new disease. Called rheumatic fever ("fever" was applied then to a variety of ailments), or acute rheumatism because of its effect on the joints, it was distinguished from normal, or chronic, rheumatism by a number of features. These included its sudden onset, its effects on the heart, its fatality in some instances, and its almost exclusive focus on the young—those in their teens were the most likely to contract it, followed by those in their twenties, as is the case with Mrs. Smith (at present, a year or two later, she is thirty—see p. 298). The inflammation and pain also tended to migrate, often rapidly, from one area to another, which is why Mrs. Smith's pain is described as "finally settling in her legs." The words "for the present" are also apt, for usually the affliction of the joints would cease after a while, though the disease could cause long-term damage to the heart.

8. *hot-baths*: the hottest of several baths in the city, all of which were within

very humble way, unable even to afford herself the comfort of a servant,[9] and of course almost excluded from society.

Their mutual friend answered for the satisfaction which a visit from Miss Elliot[10] would give Mrs. Smith, and Anne therefore lost no time in going. She mentioned nothing of what she had heard, or what she intended, at home. It would excite no proper interest there. She only consulted Lady Russell, who entered thoroughly into her sentiments, and was most happy to convey her as near to Mrs. Smith's lodgings in Westgate-buildings,[11] as Anne chose to be taken.

The visit was paid, their acquaintance re-established, their interest in each other more than re-kindled. The first ten minutes had its awkwardness and its emotion.[12] Twelve years were gone since they had parted, and each presented a somewhat different person[13] from what the other had imagined. Twelve years had changed Anne from the blooming, silent, unformed girl of fifteen, to the elegant little woman of seven and twenty, with every beauty excepting bloom, and with manners as consciously right as they were invariably gentle; and twelve years had transformed the fine-looking, well-grown Miss Hamilton, in all the glow of health and confidence of superiority, into a poor, infirm, helpless widow, receiving the visit of her former protegeé as a favour; but all that was uncomfortable in the meeting had soon passed away, and left only the interesting charm of remembering former partialities and talking over old times.

Anne found in Mrs. Smith the good sense and agreeable manners which she had almost ventured to depend on, and a disposition to converse and be cheerful beyond her expectation. Neither the dissipations of the past—and she had lived very much in the world,[14] nor the restrictions of the present; neither sickness nor sorrow seemed to have closed her heart or ruined her spirits.

In the course of a second visit she talked with great openness, and Anne's astonishment increased. She could scarcely imagine a more cheerless situation in itself than Mrs. Smith's. She had been very fond of her husband,—she had buried him. She had been used to affluence,—it was gone. She had no child to connect her

close proximity (see map, p. 515; for a picture of the adjacent Cross Bath, see p. 287). Warm bathing was sometimes recommended for rheumatic fever and other ailments striking the joints.

9. Not having a servant would be a true mark of limited means and reduced status. Servants were considered essential to living a decent life by the classes depicted in Jane Austen, and in fact it would cost little to hire the cheapest kind, an unskilled maid.

10. *Miss Elliot:* what this friend, as a nonrelation, would call Anne. She uses this rather than "Miss Anne Elliot" because she does not know Elizabeth (see also p. 137, note 58).

11. *Westgate-buildings:* a street and buildings in the lower, old part of town (it was the original site of the west gate of the city). The street was very close to the baths, and thus would be an excellent location for someone who is frequenting them for her health, as Mrs. Smith is soon revealed to be doing, but who is unable to afford to be conveyed long distances. The street's unfashionable location would also make lodgings there more affordable.

In a letter regarding her family's debate over possible new locations in Bath, Jane Austen mentions Westgate Buildings as one, and writes, "Westgate Buildings, tho' quite in the lower part of the Town are not badly situated themselves; the street is broad, & has rather a good appearance" (Jan. 3, 1801). She does say, however, that other locations are preferable. For a picture, see p. 307.

12. *emotion:* agitation; mental disturbance or excitement.

13. *person:* personal appearance; in this case, it also probably means general persona.

14. *in the world:* in fashionable society. Its inhabitants were often noted for their dissipations, a word often used then to describe a life of profligacy, hedonism, and moral laxness.

with life and happiness again, no relations to assist in the arrangement of perplexed affairs,[15] no health to make all the rest supportable. Her accommodations were limited to a noisy parlour,[16] and a dark bed-room behind, with no possibility of moving from one to the other without assistance, which there was only one servant in the house to afford,[17] and she never quitted the house but to be conveyed into the warm bath.[18]—Yet, in spite of all this, Anne had reason to believe that she had moments only of languor and depression, to hours of occupation and enjoyment. How could it be?—She watched—observed—reflected—and finally determined that this was not a case of fortitude or of resignation only.[19]—A submissive spirit might be patient, a strong understanding[20] would supply resolution, but here was something more; here was that elasticity of mind,[21] that disposition to be comforted, that power of turning readily from evil to good, and of finding employment which carried her out of herself, which was from Nature alone. It was the choicest gift of Heaven; and Anne viewed her friend as one of those instances in which, by a merciful appointment,[22] it seems designed to counterbalance almost every other want.

There had been a time, Mrs. Smith told her, when her spirits had nearly failed. She could not call herself an invalid now, compared with her state on first reaching Bath. Then, she had indeed been a pitiable object—for she had caught cold on the journey, and had hardly taken possession of her lodgings, before she was again confined to her bed, and suffering under severe and constant pain; and all this among strangers—with the absolute necessity of having a regular nurse, and finances at that moment particularly unfit to meet any extraordinary expense. She had weathered it however, and could truly say that it had done her good. It had increased her comforts by making her feel herself to be in good hands. She had seen too much of the world, to expect sudden or disinterested attachment any where, but her illness had proved to her that her landlady had a character[23] to preserve, and would not use her ill; and she had been particularly fortunate in her nurse, as a sister of her landlady, a nurse by profession,[24] and

15. *perplexed affairs:* messy or entangled or uncertain finances.

16. "Parlour" was the term generally used for a small sitting room. One that was more spacious and luxurious would be called a drawing room.

17. *afford:* supply. The house is a rooming house. Such houses were a common feature of English towns, frequently run by landladies, and Bath contained many, of varying levels of comfort and cost. Rooming houses normally employed servants, often multiple ones—that this house has only one indicates its modest level and hence the reduced circumstances of Mrs. Smith.

18. She could be conveyed into the bath by means of a Bath sedan chair (see p. 337, note 18) or a wheelchair. While certain forms of wheelchair had been around for a while, shortly before this time an improved version called a Bath chair had been developed in Bath, whose invalid population created a large demand for such a device. The chair had one small wheel in front and two large ones in back, with a handle allowing the rider to steer while an attendant pushed it from behind.

19. Anne would have a natural interest in studying and reflecting on this case, for much of her life has been spent trying to achieve fortitude and resignation in the face of distress. Mrs. Smith's resilience links her to Anne and makes her an appropriate friend (Captain Wentworth's friends are also shown to share important characteristics with him; see p. 189, note 39).

20. *understanding:* intellect, mind.

21. *elasticity of mind:* buoyancy of character or disposition; ability to overcome depression or despair.

22. *appointment:* decree or allotment. In other words, heaven has arranged it so that her special gift of mental fortitude counterbalances her other misfortunes. Anne's attributing such a gift to her suggests, perhaps with a touch of admiring envy on Anne's part, that Mrs. Smith does not need to struggle for calm and composure as Anne does.

23. *character:* reputation. "Character" could mean a work reference allowing one to gain new employment; in this case, the landlady would wish to maintain her house's reputation as a desirable residence. Thus Mrs. Smith has been able to rely on someone's own self-interest to obtain good treatment.

24. The term "profession" applied to nurses at the time only in a very loose sense, for there was no regular training or certification for nurses, much less any kind of organization. Most nursing was done at home, by family members and servants, as seen earlier in the cases of little Charles Musgrove and Louisa. Among those who earned a living as nurses, some worked in the small number of hospitals existing at the time; a much larger number worked

who had always a home in that house when unemployed, chanced to be at liberty just in time to attend her. — "And she," said Mrs. Smith, "besides nursing me most admirably, has really proved an invaluable acquaintance. — As soon as I could use my hands, she taught me to knit,[25] which has been a great amusement; and she put me in the way of making[26] these little thread-cases, pin-cushions and card-racks,[27] which you always find me so busy about, and which supply me with the means of doing a little good to one or two very poor families in this neighbourhood.[28] She has a large acquaintance, of course professionally, among those who can afford to buy, and she disposes of my merchandize. She always takes the right time for applying. Every body's heart is open, you know, when they have recently escaped from severe pain, or are recovering the blessing of health, and nurse Rooke thoroughly understands when to speak. She is a shrewd, intelligent, sensible woman. Hers is a line for seeing human nature; and she has a fund of good sense and observation which, as a companion, make her infinitely superior to thousands of those who having only received "the best education in the world," know nothing worth attending to.[29] Call it gossip if you will; but when nurse Rooke has half an hour's leisure to bestow on me, she is sure to have something to relate that is entertaining and profitable, something that makes one know one's species better.[30] One likes to hear what is going on, to be *au fait*[31] as to the newest modes of being trifling and silly. To me, who live so much alone, her conversation I assure you is a treat."[32]

Anne, far from wishing to cavil at the pleasure, replied, "I can easily believe it. Women of that class have great opportunities, and if they are intelligent may be well worth listening to. Such varieties of human nature as they are in the habit of witnessing! And it is not merely in its follies, that they are well read; for they see it occasionally under every circumstance that can be most interesting or affecting. What instances must pass before them of ardent, disinterested, self-denying attachment, of heroism, fortitude, patience, resignation — of all the conflicts and all the sacri-

as private nurses like the person mentioned here. In either case, a nurse had a status similar to that of a servant and performed cleaning as well as strictly nursing tasks. This nurse's periodic unemployment and need to live with her sister indicate the precarious nature of her position.

25. Mrs. Smith is taught to knit by her nurse because, while knitting was widely practiced by the lower classes, it was at that time rare among upper-class women, who instead devoted themselves to decorative forms of needlework. The only other women in Jane Austen's novels described as knitting are Mrs. Bates and her granddaughter Jane Fairfax in *Emma*, both of whom, like Mrs. Smith, are in difficult economic circumstances and thus more likely to prefer an activity with a strong practical benefit.

26. *in the way of making:* in a position to make.

27. Thread cases are folding cases with pockets in which pieces of thread would be kept; thread was not sold loose then and was wound around pieces of bone or wood, so it would be helpful to have pockets for arranging different threads in an orderly and accessible fashion. Pincushions hold pins, which were fairly expensive then and so worth taking the trouble to avoid losing. Both of these would be useful for women engaged in needlework. Card racks hold visiting cards, popular items in Bath (see p. 261, note 8).

28. One reason, in addition to benevolence, for Mrs. Smith to value these acts of charity is that they would affirm, amid her current economic distress, her upper-class status, for helping the poor was a basic activity of wealthy women. Thus, even as her knitting signifies her social descent, the use she makes of her knitted products signifies something more elevated.

29. In her novels Jane Austen consistently indicates respect for being thoughtful and well-informed and liking to read, but she does not necessarily associate that with formal schooling, and she sometimes speaks satirically of fashionable or expensive schools. She herself went to school only briefly.

30. This may represent Jane Austen's own sentiments. Her letters show a continual interest in news of others, while her novels display her continual fascination with the intricacies and varieties of human character. She may also object to those who denigrate such curiosity as mere craving for gossip.

31. *au fait:* thoroughly conversant or well-informed.

32. Nurse Rooke's frequent sharing of interesting gossip may be another sign of her shrewdness and intelligence. It would be a useful service for a nurse to perform for a confined patient, one that might raise the patient's spirit—at a time when physical means of curing ailments were very limited—and that would enhance the value of the nurse's services, making the patient more likely to retain her and recommend her to others.

fices that ennoble us most. A sick chamber may often furnish the worth of volumes."[33]

"Yes," said Mrs. Smith more doubtingly, "sometimes it may, though I fear its lessons are not often in the elevated style you describe. Here and there, human nature may be great in times of trial, but generally speaking it is its weakness and not its strength that appears in a sick chamber; it is selfishness and impatience rather than generosity and fortitude, that one hears of.[34] There is so little real friendship in the world! — and unfortunately" (speaking low and tremulously) "there are so many who forget to think seriously till it is almost too late."[35]

Anne saw the misery of such feelings. The husband had not been what he ought, and the wife had been led among that part of mankind which made her think worse of the world, than she hoped it deserved. It was but a passing emotion however with Mrs. Smith, she shook it off, and soon added in a different tone,

"I do not suppose the situation my friend Mrs. Rooke is in at present, will furnish much either to interest or edify me. — She is only nursing Mrs. Wallis of Marlborough-buildings[36] — a mere pretty, silly, expensive,[37] fashionable woman, I believe — and of course will have nothing to report but of lace and finery. — I mean to make my profit of Mrs. Wallis, however. She has plenty of money, and I intend she shall buy all the high-priced things I have in hand now."

Anne had called several times on her friend, before the existence of such a person was known in Camden-place. At last, it became necessary to speak of her. — Sir Walter, Elizabeth and Mrs. Clay returned one morning from Laura-place, with a sudden invitation from Lady Dalrymple for the same evening, and Anne was already engaged, to spend that evening in Westgate-buildings. She was not sorry for the excuse. They were only asked, she was sure, because Lady Dalrymple being kept at home by a bad cold, was glad to make use of the relationship which had been so pressed on her, — and she declined on her own account with great alacrity — "She was engaged to spend the evening with an old

33. The term "volumes" would have particular resonance then because most books, including Jane Austen's novels, were published in multiple, separate volumes.

Anne here espouses ideals of stoic fortitude akin to those she discussed earlier with Captain Benwick (see p. 192). Such ideas were fundamental to this culture, advocated on the basis of both religious and nonreligious principles. The ideals were frequently applied to sickness, with almost everyone arguing for the necessity and worthiness of fortitude and resignation in the face of illness, and extolling the great character of those who demonstrated such virtues. A further spur to such attitudes was the lack of many other means of coping with illness, given the inability of contemporary medicine to cure many ailments, or even to offer relief from the terrible pain that often accompanied them. At the same time, the intensity of such miseries made people frequently admit the difficulty, or impossibility, of being as stoic and resigned as they would like.

34. Mrs. Smith's skepticism clearly reflects her own recent trials and is part of a cynicism about human beings that she displays elsewhere. It also probably reflects Jane Austen's own perspective, for in both her novels and her letters she describes the querulousness of those who suffer from illness or believe themselves to be suffering. If so, it would be one of the occasional points on which she signals a difference between herself and her heroine.

This whole issue had a particular poignancy for Jane Austen, for it was while finishing this novel that she came down with the illness—possibly Addison's disease, a failure of the adrenal glands—that killed her. Based on the testimony of family members and some letters from that time she seems to have demonstrated uncomplaining fortitude, even as her pain worsened and the possibility of recovery became more remote. In a letter written two months before her death, when she was already suffering greatly, she manages to write, with evident self-mockery, "I was interested in all you wrote, though with all the Egotism of an Invalid I write only of myself" (May 22, 1817). In fact, she was calm enough about the matter of illness in those final months to begin work on a novel, Sanditon, in which she satirizes those who come to a seaside resort in quest of health, including a trio of siblings with a ludicrous obsession with their ailments.

35. "To think seriously" sometimes meant specifically to think about religious matters. Thus when Mrs. Smith speaks of "almost too late" she may mean not thinking about one's soul and its fate until one is about to die.

36. Mrs. Wallis and her husband, Colonel Wallis, have already been mentioned as friends of Mr. Elliot (see pp. 262–268); the coincidental connection with Nurse Rooke will lead to important revelations later. The latter is attending Mrs. Wallis because, as mentioned earlier, she is having a baby (see also p. 267, note 37).

37. *expensive*: extravagant, given to lavish expenditure.

schoolfellow." They were not much interested in any thing relative to Anne, but still there were questions enough asked, to make
it understood what this old schoolfellow was; and Elizabeth was
disdainful, and Sir Walter severe.

"Westgate-buildings!" said he; "and who is Miss Anne Elliot to
be visiting in Westgate-buildings?[38] — A Mrs. Smith. A widow Mrs.
Smith, — and who was her husband? One of the five thousand Mr.
Smiths whose names are to be met with every where. And what is
her attraction? That she is old and sickly. — Upon my word, Miss
Anne Elliot,[39] you have the most extraordinary taste! Every thing
that revolts other people, low company, paltry rooms, foul air,[40]
disgusting associations are inviting to you. But surely, you may put
off this old lady till to-morrow. She is not so near her end, I presume, but that she may hope to see another day. What is her age?
Forty?"

"No, Sir, she is not one and thirty;[41] but I do not think I can put
off my engagement, because it is the only evening for some time
which will at once suit her and myself. — She goes into the warm
bath[42] to-morrow, and for the rest of the week you know we are
engaged."

"But what does Lady Russell think of this acquaintance?" asked
Elizabeth.

"She sees nothing to blame in it," replied Anne; "on the contrary, she approves it; and has generally taken me, when I have
called on Mrs. Smith."

"Westgate-buildings must have been rather surprised by the
appearance of a carriage drawn up near its pavement!"[43] observed
Sir Walter. — "Sir Henry Russell's widow, indeed, has no honours
to distinguish her arms;[44] but still, it is a handsome equipage,[45]
and no doubt is well known to convey a Miss Elliot. — A widow
Mrs. Smith, lodging in Westgate-buildings! — A poor widow,
barely able to live, between thirty and forty[46] — a mere Mrs.
Smith, an every day Mrs. Smith, of all people and all names in the
world, to be the chosen friend of Miss Anne Elliot, and to be preferred by her, to her own family connections among the nobility
of England and Ireland![47] Mrs. Smith, such a name!"

38. *Westgate-buildings:* Though the houses on this street are fairly grand, its location in the poorer and lower part of town would make it an object of scorn by anyone as conscious of wealth and status as Sir Walter. In 1780 one aristocrat, Lord Herbert, declared, "I cannot bear to go into the Lower Town" (quoted in Hembry, *The English Spa,* p. 126). Westgate Buildings could be a particular object of loathing because the street was very close to Avon Street, the center of the area in which the poorest and least reputable inhabitants resided. Anne's lack of concern about such matters is another mark of her profound difference with the rest of her family.

39. *Miss Anne Elliot:* a sign of Sir Walter's formality, even to his own daughter, as well as probably a reminder to her of the difference in her status from that of a "mere Mrs. Smith."

40. Foul air would be regarded not simply as unpleasant but as dangerous, for medical opinion regarded bad air as a prime cause of illness. It would be especially common in poorer sections of town, which, in Bath and other towns and cities then, were characterized by overcrowding and poor sanitation.

41. *not one-and-thirty:* thirty; this construction appears elsewhere in Jane Austen.

42. *warm bath:* this probably means either the King's or Queen's Bath, which, according to a contemporary guidebook, had temperatures of around 100 degrees Fahrenheit (the Hot Bath had a temperature as high as 117, and the Cross Bath one of 93–94). The book says that the former baths are "chiefly used by hospital invalids, or by persons of the lower class of life" (John Feltham, *A Guide to all the Watering and Sea-Bathing Places,* p. 26).

43. *pavement:* sidewalk.

44. The family arms would be displayed on the carriage. Not everyone had the right to display arms. It required a license. But by this time more than ten thousand families possessed the right, so a knight like Sir Henry Russell, or his widow, certainly would, even if these arms were undistinguished in the eyes of a baronet like Sir Walter.

45. *equipage:* carriage plus horses and servants attending it.

46. One factor in Sir Walter's contempt is that widows were very numerous in Bath. They, like many others, found it an attractive place of retirement; their presence is indicated by the census of 1811, which shows the population of Bath as just over 60% female, as opposed to 52% for England as a whole.

47. This suggests that Lady Dalrymple is also linked to the English nobility—no other noble connection to the Elliots is ever mentioned, and

Mrs. Clay, who had been present while all this passed, now thought it advisable to leave the room, and Anne could have said much and did long to say a little, in defence of *her* friend's not very dissimilar claims to theirs, but her sense of personal respect to her father prevented her. She made no reply. She left it to himself to recollect, that Mrs. Smith was not the only widow in Bath between thirty and forty, with little to live on, and no sirname of dignity.[48]

Anne kept her appointment; the others kept theirs, and of course she heard the next morning that they had had a delightful evening. — She had been the only one of the set absent; for Sir Walter and Elizabeth had not only been quite at her ladyship's service themselves, but had actually been happy to be employed by her in collecting others, and had been at the trouble of inviting both Lady Russell and Mr. Elliot; and Mr. Elliot had made a point of leaving Colonel Wallis early, and Lady Russell had fresh arranged all her evening engagements in order to wait on[49] her.[50] Anne had the whole history of all that such an evening could supply, from Lady Russell. To her, its greatest interest must be, in having been very much talked of between her friend and Mr. Elliot, in having been wished for, regretted, and at the same time honoured for staying away in such a cause. — Her kind, compassionate visits to this old schoolfellow, sick and reduced, seemed to have quite delighted Mr. Elliot.[51] He thought her a most extraordinary young woman; in her temper, manners, mind,[52] a model of female excellence. He could meet even Lady Russell in a discussion of her merits; and Anne could not be given to understand so much by her friend, could not know herself to be so highly rated by a sensible man, without many of those agreeable sensations which her friend meant to create.

Lady Russell was now perfectly decided in her opinion of Mr. Elliot. She was as much convinced of his meaning to gain Anne in time, as of his deserving her; and was beginning to calculate the number of weeks which would free him from all the remaining restraints of widowhood, and leave him at liberty to exert his most open powers of pleasing.[53] She would not speak to Anne

Sir Walter would certainly be one to bring it up if he could. It is possible that her family does have English ties (see p. 281, note 28). It is also possible that Sir Walter is simply overstating the case from vanity.

48. Sir Walter's differing attitudes toward Mrs. Clay and Mrs. Smith indicate his inconsistency, for he is in many respects more guilty with the former of the faults he finds in his daughter relative to Mrs. Smith. Anne only visits her widowed friend, while his lives permanently with the family. Moreover, Mrs. Smith, while poorer than Mrs. Clay at present, comes from a higher social position, something Sir Walter should be able to guess from her being an old schoolfellow of Anne's. That Mrs. Clay's flattery and external deference make Sir Walter overlook all this shows how foolish he can be, even with regard to his own principles of social distinction.

49. *wait on:* call upon, visit.

50. The actions of Mr. Elliot and Lady Russell demonstrate again the difference between them and Anne on this important point, one that is just about to play a critical role in Anne's decision about him and disagreement with her.

51. It will later turn out that Mr. Elliot and Mrs. Smith know each other, but he definitely seems not to recognize her here. It is possible Anne did not mention her name, but that is unlikely, especially since Sir Walter regards its commonplace character as worthy of remark. More likely, that same commonplace character keeps Mr. Elliot from wondering if this is the same Mrs. Smith he knows.

52. *temper, manners, mind:* these three terms would together refer to all her personal qualities.

53. One year was the standard period of mourning for those who had lost a wife or husband. Those who abbreviated it could face severe censure. Not long after this Anne will say, "Mr. Elliot's wife has not been dead much above half a year" (p. 370), so there would still be a number of weeks remaining before he would be free. Lady Russell's beginning to calculate them suggests her eagerness.

with half the certainty she felt on the subject, she would venture on little more than hints of what might be hereafter, of a possible attachment on his side, of the desirableness of the alliance,[54] supposing such attachment to be real, and returned. Anne heard her, and made no violent exclamations. She only smiled, blushed, and gently shook her head.

"I am no match-maker, as you well know," said Lady Russell, "being much too well aware of the uncertainty of all human events and calculations. I only mean that if Mr. Elliot should some time hence pay his addresses to[55] you, and if you should be disposed to accept him, I think there would be every possibility of your being happy together. A most suitable connection[56] every body must consider it—but I think it might be a very happy one."

"Mr. Elliot is an exceedingly agreeable man, and in many respects I think highly of him," said Anne; "but we should not suit."

Lady Russell let this pass, and only said in rejoinder, "I own[57] that to be able to regard you as the future mistress of Kellynch, the future Lady Elliot—to look forward and see you occupying your dear mother's place, succeeding to[58] all her rights, and all her popularity, as well as to all her virtues, would be the highest possible gratification to me.—You are your mother's self in countenance[59] and disposition;[60] and if I might be allowed to fancy you such as she was, in situation, and name, and home, presiding and blessing in the same spot,[61] and only superior to her in being more highly valued! My dearest Anne,[62] it would give me more delight than is often felt at my time of life!"

Anne was obliged to turn away, to rise, to walk to a distant table, and, leaning there in pretended employment,[63] try to subdue the feelings this picture excited. For a few moments her imagination and her heart were bewitched. The idea of becoming what her mother had been; of having the precious name of "Lady Elliot" first revived in herself; of being restored to Kellynch, calling it her home again, her home for ever, was a charm which she could not immediately resist.[64] Lady Russell said not another word, willing to leave the matter to its own operation; and believing that, could

54. *alliance:* marriage.

55. *pay his addresses to:* court (for the purpose of marriage).

56. *connection:* link established by marriage.

57. *own:* admit.

58. *succeeding to:* inheriting.

59. *countenance:* appearance and (possibly) demeanor.

60. *disposition:* general mental bent or tendencies. The term had a broader connotation at this time than it does today.

61. This probably means to sit at the head of the table and bless the food. "Preside" often refers specifically to the first action, though it can also refer to directing affairs in general (both usages are found in Jane Austen). Either usage could apply to a future mistress of a household—who could preside at table and would always manage the household generally—though the reference to "the same spot" suggests the first meaning.

62. *dearest Anne:* this, like "dear someone," was frequently used by family members and friends, and usually with "my" as in this case. Jane Austen uses the designation at times in her letters.

63. This probably means needlework, which was such a prevalent activity among ladies that it was often called simply "work."

64. This is the most significant temptation Anne faces in the novel. It is particularly seductive for her because of all the disappointments and suffering she has experienced: the loss of her mother, the neglect by her father and sister, the years of regret after rejecting Wentworth, and the recent pain of witnessing his coldness to her and pursuit of other women. Her ability to resist it, as immediately revealed, constitutes a strong proof of her character. The match offers many advantages from the standpoint of wealth and position and attention by others, but she still rejects it on grounds, more than anything, of moral principle.

Mr. Elliot at that moment with propriety have spoken for him-self!—She believed, in short, what Anne did not believe. The same image of Mr. Elliot speaking for himself, brought Anne to composure again. The charm of Kellynch and of "Lady Elliot" all faded away. She never could accept him. And it was not only that her feelings were still adverse to any man save one; her judgment, on a serious consideration of the possibilities of such a case, was against Mr. Elliot.

Though they had now been acquainted a month, she could not be satisfied that she really knew his character. That he was a sensible man, an agreeable man,—that he talked well, professed good opinions, seemed to judge properly and as a man of principle,—this was all clear enough. He certainly knew what was right, nor could she fix on any one article[65] of moral duty evidently transgressed; but yet she would have been afraid to answer for his conduct. She distrusted the past, if not the present. The names which occasionally dropt of former associates, the allusions to former practices and pursuits, suggested suspicions not favourable of what he had been. She saw that there had been bad habits; that Sunday-travelling had been a common thing;[66] that there had been a period of his life (and probably not a short one) when he had been, at least, careless on all serious matters;[67] and, though he might now think very differently, who could answer for the true sentiments of a clever, cautious man, grown old enough to appreciate a fair character?[68] How could it ever be ascertained that his mind[69] was truly cleansed?

Mr. Elliot was rational, discreet, polished,—but he was not open. There was never any burst of feeling, any warmth of indignation or delight, at the evil or good of others. This, to Anne, was a decided imperfection. Her early impressions were incurable.[70] She prized the frank, the open-hearted, the eager character beyond all others. Warmth and enthusiasm did captivate her still. She felt that she could so much more depend upon the sincerity of those who sometimes looked or said a careless or a hasty thing, than of those whose presence of mind never varied, whose tongue never slipped.[71]

65. *article:* item; clause or provision. This last meaning, usually used in relation to written documents, may be suggested because it would link articles of moral duty with the "thirty-nine articles," the basic tenets of the Church of England. Such religious principles were considered to be intimately linked to morality.

66. Frequent Sunday traveling was often regarded as a sign of bad character. There was a strong belief in the sanctity of the Sabbath, which meant refraining on Sunday from many activities, including travel; travel, which usually took a long time then, would also tend to preclude going to church. There had been a movement in the decades prior to this novel to improve adherence to the rules regarding the Sabbath, especially those prohibiting drinking, working, and traveling, since these rules were frequently violated. In 1802 the Society for the Suppression of Vice came into being, and, among other things, tried to pressure government officials to enforce Sabbath laws more zealously. These efforts, which seem to have had some, though far from universal, success, were linked to the growing evangelical movement, which sought to inspire greater moral and religious devotion in various aspects of life and also promoted certain political causes, including the abolition of the slave trade. It is possible this had some influence on Jane Austen, for after expressing a dislike for evangelicals in a letter from Jan. 24, 1809, she declares sympathy for them in a letter of Nov. 18, 1814. As regards this novel, the serious thoughtfulness of its heroine would make her likely to respect strict religious principles, as she does here.

67. *serious matters:* religious matters (possibly). See p. 297, note 35.

68. *fair character:* good name or reputation.

69. *mind:* inner character. The term then referred not just to the intellect.

70. By "early impressions" she probably means falling in love with Captain Wentworth, which has so clearly left a permanent imprint on her mind. It is possible that her long experience of the unhappiness in her father's house, with its surface polish and lack of warmth, has influenced her as well.

71. In addition to her "early impressions," her recent experience with Wentworth and other members of naval society, especially at Lyme, have probably helped inspire this attitude. Thus both he and Lyme continue to play a critical role in the story and in Anne's development. At the same time, it is also significant that her decision to reject Mr. Elliot does not stem from any lingering hope of attaining Captain Wentworth instead.

Mr. Elliot was too generally agreeable. Various as were the tempers in her father's house, he pleased them all. He endured too well,—stood too well with every body. He had spoken to her with some degree of openness of Mrs. Clay; had appeared completely to see what Mrs. Clay was about, and to hold her in contempt; and yet Mrs. Clay found him as agreeable as anybody.[72]

Lady Russell saw either less or more than her young friend, for she saw nothing to excite distrust. She could not imagine a man more exactly what he ought to be than Mr. Elliot;[73] nor did she ever enjoy a sweeter feeling than the hope of seeing him receive the hand of her beloved Anne in Kellynch church, in the course of the following autumn.[74]

72. In these respects Mr. Elliot is part of a category that appears consistently in Jane Austen. In all her novels but her first, *Northanger Abbey*, there is a young man with great surface charm and attractiveness who tempts the heroine to a degree. The previous four—Willoughby, Wickham, Henry Crawford, and Frank Churchill—all prove untrustworthy in some respect, though in varying degrees. More will eventually be revealed about the true nature of Mr. Elliot's character.

73. Anne's decision reveals her clear independence from Lady Russell. She is capable of deciding completely on her own, and the good judgment and high moral standards she has shown throughout the novel suggest that her verdict is more worthy of trust than her friend's.

74. Mr. Elliot's mourning would end by the summer (see p. 301, note 53; and chronology, p. 487), and this would allow a decent interval between his proposal and the marriage, something the highly proper Lady Russell would desire.

Westgate Buildings, where Mrs. Smith lives.

[From Mowbray Aston Green, *The Eighteenth Century Architecture of Bath* (Bath, 1904), p. 196]

Chapter Six

*I*t was the beginning of February; and Anne, having been a month in Bath, was growing very eager for news from Uppercross and Lyme.[1] She wanted to hear much more than Mary communicated. It was three weeks since she had heard at all. She only knew that Henrietta was at home again; and that Louisa, though considered to be recovering fast, was still at Lyme;[2] and she was thinking of them all very intently one evening, when a thicker letter than usual from Mary was delivered to her,[3] and, to quicken the pleasure and surprise, with Admiral and Mrs. Croft's compliments.[4]

The Crofts must be in Bath! A circumstance to interest her. They were people whom her heart turned to very naturally.

"What is this?" cried Sir Walter. "The Crofts arrived in Bath?[5] The Crofts who rent Kellynch? What have they brought you?"

"A letter from Uppercross Cottage, Sir."[6]

"Oh! those letters are convenient passports. They secure an introduction.[7] I should have visited Admiral Croft, however, at any rate. I know what is due to my tenant."

Anne could listen no longer; she could not even have told how the poor Admiral's complexion escaped; her letter engrossed her. It had been begun several days back.

February 1st,——.

"MY DEAR ANNE,

"I make no apology for my silence, because I know how little people think of letters in such a place as Bath. You must be a great deal too happy to care for Uppercross, which, as you well know, affords little to write about. We have had a very dull Christmas; Mr. and Mrs. Musgrove have not had one dinner-party all the holidays.[8] I do not reckon the Hayters as any body. The holidays, however, are

1. This chapter marks the beginning of a new phase in the novel, when Anne's attention—and much of the action—returns to those she had seen at Uppercross and Lyme. It is appropriate that it comes just after she reached an important decision regarding her principal new acquaintance since then, Mr. Elliot.

2. The reason why Louisa remains at Lyme, despite her improved condition, will soon become clear.

3. For the thickness of Mary's letter, see p. 313, note 15.

4. The Crofts could have sent their compliments orally to the servant who took the letter and then delivered it to Anne with the message, or they could have included a brief note to her. In either case, their presence in Bath would be apparent to Anne.

5. Sir Walter may say this after being presented with the Crofts' visiting card. It is stated later (p. 318) that they "considered their intercourse with the Elliots as a mere matter of form," which suggests they would at least wish to preserve the proper forms of courtesy.

6. Many characters in Jane Austen use "sir" or "ma'am" when speaking to their parents, so this is not necessarily a sign of particular formality. But usually they vary that usage with "papa/mamma" or "father/mother"; the younger Musgroves use only these latter designations. In contrast, Anne is shown only using "sir," here and on p. 298.

7. Sir Walter's assumption is that the Crofts have not brought a letter from his daughter out of kindness but out of a wish to establish their connection with him and secure his goodwill, thereby inducing him to visit them.

8. Dinner parties were central to Christmas celebrations, which then involved mostly feasting and gatherings of family and friends. Christmas trees and the exchange of presents and cards would develop only later as significant parts of the holiday.

over at last: I believe no children ever had such long ones.[9] I am sure I had not. The house was cleared yesterday, except of the little Harvilles; but you will be surprised to hear that they have never gone home. Mrs. Harville must be an odd mother to part with them so long. I do not understand it. They are not at all nice children, in my opinion; but Mrs. Musgrove seems to like them quite as well, if not better, than her grand-children. What dreadful weather we have had! It may not be felt in Bath, with your nice pavements; but in the country it is of some consequence.[10] I have not had a creature call on me since the second week in January, except Charles Hayter, who has been calling much oftener than was welcome. Between ourselves, I think it a great pity Henrietta did not remain at Lyme as long as Louisa; it would have kept her a little out of his way. The carriage is gone to-day, to bring Louisa and the Harvilles to-morrow. We are not asked to dine with them, however, till the day after, Mrs. Musgrove is so afraid of her being fatigued by the journey, which is not very likely, considering the care that will be taken of her; and it would be much more convenient to me to dine there to-morrow. I am glad you find Mr. Elliot so agreeable, and wish I could be acquainted with him too; but I have my usual luck, I am always out of the way when any thing desirable is going on; always the last of my family to be noticed. What an immense time Mrs. Clay has been staying with Elizabeth! Does she never mean to go away? But perhaps if she were to leave the room vacant we might not be invited. Let me know what you think of this. I do not expect my children to be asked, you know. I can leave them at the Great House very well, for a month or six weeks.[11] I have this moment heard that the Crofts are going to Bath almost immediately; they think the admiral gouty.[12] Charles heard it quite by chance: they have not had the civility to give me any notice, or offer to take any thing. I do not think they improve at all as neighbours. We see nothing of them, and this is really an instance of gross inattention. Charles joins me in love, and every thing proper.

Yours, affectionately,
MARY M——."

9. This means the Musgroves' children have returned to school.

10. Local roads in the country varied in quality (see p. 247, note 16), and, since they were normally unpaved, bad weather could make travel on them very difficult. In contrast, streets in Bath began to be paved in the early eighteenth century, and eventually it became standard throughout the city, especially on streets in the affluent parts of town.

11. This is a remarkable statement considering that Mary has just criticized Mrs. Harville for leaving her children with Mrs. Musgrove. Moreover, Mrs. Harville has the excuse, which Mary does not, of needing the children gone so she can nurse someone else. Earlier, during her two weeks at Lyme, Mary had no apparent hesitation in leaving her children with only her servants (see p. 229, note 16).

12. Gout was a common affliction of the time, concentrated particularly among older gentlemen like the admiral (it struck men far more than women). It results from an excess of uric acid in the blood, which can cause inflammation and agonizing pain in various joints, most especially those of the big toe. What usually brings it on is excessive consumption, generally over many years, of alcohol and foods rich in purine, which include various types of meat and fish. At the time, people understood its connection with a rich diet but not its exact physiological causes; there was also little treatment for it, other than moderation in eating and drinking.

Coming to Bath, or other spas, was one of the most popular treatments, to the point that the city became associated with sufferers from gout. In a letter Jane Austen suggests her brother may travel to Bath for a possible case of gout (June 19, 1799). Its warm waters were a particular attraction for those suffering from ailments of the joints, as also seen in Mrs. Smith's use of them for her rheumatic fever. In the case of gout, the waters, both when drunk and bathed in, could produce an initial aggravation of the symptoms, but medical opinion considered this to be ultimately salutary. In *Northanger Abbey* the heroine is able to go to Bath because Mr. Allen, an older friend of the family, is seeking treatment for gout and invites her along, while Tobias Smollett's *Humphry Clinker*, one of the best-known novels of the eighteenth century, begins with a similar venture to Bath and the nearby spa of Clifton by the gouty main character, Matthew Bramble.

"I am sorry to say that I am very far from well; and Jemima has just told me that the butcher says there is a bad sore-throat very much about.[13] *I dare say I shall catch it; and my sore-throats, you know, are always worse than any body's."*[14]

So ended the first part, which had been afterwards put into an envelop, containing nearly as much more.

"I kept my letter open, that I might send you word how Louisa bore her journey, and now I am extremely glad I did, having a great deal to add. In the first place, I had a note from Mrs. Croft yesterday, offering to convey any thing to you; a very kind, friendly note indeed, addressed to me, just as it ought; I shall therefore be able to make my letter as long as I like.[15] *The admiral does not seem very ill, and I sincerely hope Bath will do him all the good he wants. I shall be truly glad to have them back again. Our neighbourhood cannot spare such a pleasant family.*[16] *But now for Louisa. I have something to communicate that will astonish you not a little. She and the Harvilles came on Tuesday very safely, and in the evening we went to ask her how she did, when we were rather surprised not to find Captain Benwick of the party, for he had been invited as well as the Harvilles; and what do you think was the reason? Neither more nor less than his being in love with Louisa, and not choosing to venture to Uppercross till he had had an answer from Mr. Musgrove;*[17] *for it was all settled between him and her before she came away, and he had written to her father by Captain Harville. True, upon my honour. Are not you astonished? I shall be surprised at least if you ever received a hint of it, for I never did. Mrs. Musgrove protests solemnly that she knew nothing of the matter. We are all very well pleased, however; for though it is not equal to her marrying Captain Wentworth,*[18] *it is infinitely better than Charles Hayter; and Mr. Musgrove has written his consent, and Captain Benwick is expected to-day. Mrs. Harville says her husband feels a good deal on his poor sister's account; but, however, Louisa is a great favourite with both. Indeed Mrs. Harville and I*

13. Jemima has already been identified as Mary's nursery maid (see p. 86). Her receiving news from the butcher and passing it on to her mistress shows the way local gossip circulates. She may have spoken to the butcher while out herself—Mrs. Musgrove criticized her for going out too much—or when the butcher came to the house on business. It is also possible she and the butcher are more than friends: servant girls would often marry workingmen (and then leave service), and butchers were especially likely candidates since their jobs gave them frequent reason to call at houses.

14. It is notable that Mary worries about a sore throat only on her own account and not on her children's account.

15. Mary's letter, described as thicker than usual, can be longer because it is going via the Crofts rather than the post office. Postal rates were very high during this period—the postal service was used to raise revenue, and the government's need for money to fight the wars with Napoleon had made it increase rates considerably—and the cost of a letter varied according to the number of sheets. In this case Mary probably had some space remaining on her existing sheet and decided to save it to add news about Louisa, but the Crofts' offer made her feel free to begin a new sheet. Mary's thinking about such matters is a sign of consideration for Anne, for the cost of letters was borne by the recipient. Jane Austen's own letters reveal a strong attention to holding down cost: she adds short messages from succeeding days onto many letters, saves space with a variety of abbreviations, and even writes across lines she has already written (making the new lines perpendicular to the old ones) or writes upside down in the space between existing lines.

16. This second part of Mary's letter demonstrates how easily she switches from querulousness to good humor: it required only a kind note from Mrs. Croft to reverse completely her view of the Crofts and to inspire her with greater cheer about everything. Mary's letters are almost the only ones in *Persuasion*; in other novels Jane Austen makes much greater use of them. Some of her early literary efforts were written entirely in the form of letters, a style of composition popular in the eighteenth century, and in her novels she shows the influence of that style by using letters to reveal character as well as to convey information.

17. The answer from Mr. Musgrove would be his consent to their marriage: saying a man was in love with a woman usually meant he wished to marry her. Asking parental consent, particularly of the father, was standard at this time. Men would usually ask the father's consent in person; Captain Benwick's use of a letter may result from his general shyness and quietness.

18. Captain Benwick is a commander (see p. 324), a lower rank than Captain Wentworth's. This, and his greater youth, also means he has made less money. Moreover, while Wentworth is brother-in-law to an admiral, Benwick's family is never mentioned, suggesting he has no relation of distinction.

quite agree that we love her the better for having nursed her.[19]
*Charles wonders what Captain Wentworth will say; but if you
remember, I never thought him attached to Louisa; I never could
see any thing of it. And this is the end, you see, of Captain Benwick's being supposed to be an admirer of yours. How Charles could
take such a thing into his head was always incomprehensible to me.
I hope he will be more agreeable now. Certainly not a great match
for Louisa Musgrove; but a million times better than marrying
among the Hayters.*"

Mary need not have feared her sister's being in any degree prepared for the news. She had never in her life been more astonished. Captain Benwick and Louisa Musgrove![20] It was almost too
wonderful[21] for belief; and it was with the greatest effort that she
could remain in the room, preserve an air of calmness, and
answer the common questions of the moment.[22] Happily for her,
they were not many. Sir Walter wanted to know whether the
Crofts travelled with four horses,[23] and whether they were likely
to be situated in such a part of Bath as it might suit Miss Elliot[24]
and himself to visit in; but had little curiosity beyond.

"How is Mary?" said Elizabeth; and without waiting for an
answer, "And pray what brings the Crofts to Bath?"

"They come on the Admiral's account. He is thought to be
gouty."

"Gout and decrepitude!" said Sir Walter. "Poor old gentleman."[25]

"Have they any acquaintance here?" asked Elizabeth.

"I do not know; but I can hardly suppose that, at Admiral
Croft's time of life, and in his profession, he should not have
many acquaintance in such a place as this."

"I suspect," said Sir Walter coolly, "that Admiral Croft will be
best known in Bath as the renter of Kellynch-hall. Elizabeth, may
we venture to present him and his wife in Laura-place?"

"Oh! no, I think not. Situated as we are with Lady Dalrymple,
cousins, we ought to be very careful not to embarrass her with
acquaintance she might not approve. If we were not related, it

19. The description of Mary's stay at Lyme speaks of her "sense of being so very useful" (p. 244). But, among her specific activities, it never lists nursing, which suggests her usefulness probably existed mostly in her own head.

20. Anne's surprise is probably shared by the reader. But, while no direct indication of such a development appeared earlier, Captain Benwick never came to Uppercross, despite his professed interest in Anne and Charles and Mary's invitation, and Louisa remained in Lyme even after getting better. The reason for both is now apparent. It is possible that Louisa is being fetched at this time because Captain Benwick's proposal prompted her to send word that she finally wished to return home.

21. *wonderful*: astonishing.

22. The sense of what this could mean for her is beginning to affect her, but at this point she keeps her mind focused on other things.

23. For four horses, and Sir Walter's concern with that, see p. 11, note 34.

24. "Miss Elliot" would be what Sir Walter would call Elizabeth when speaking.

25. Sir Walter, who has already been shown frequently lamenting the effects of aging on others, associates gout with decrepitude because it usually afflicted people later in life, often becoming worse as people aged. It also was a disease noted for afflicting the wealthy, whose rich, meat-based diet, heavy consumption of alcohol, and frequently sedentary lifestyle made them especially vulnerable to it. The Prince Regent, the effective head of state in Britain at this time and a notorious glutton, suffered acutely from it, as had many monarchs over the centuries.

All this gave gout a certain social cachet, which may account for Sir Walter's "poor old gentleman," an unusually compassionate exclamation from him. Sir Walter's relative sympathy—a notable contrast to his generally like-minded daughter's immediate transition to wondering what the admiral's arrival will mean for them socially—may also stem from worries regarding himself. He, a wealthy, middle-aged man, is in the category of people most likely to begin suffering from the disease. In fact, it was often regarded as a normal and expected stage of life for gentlemen, though Sir Walter's concern with his appearance may have made him less likely to indulge in the excessive eating and drinking that often brought it on. "Poor old gentleman" is also ironic coming from Sir Walter, for he is probably older than Admiral Croft—Sir Walter being fifty-four, and Admiral Croft's wife being thirty-eight (p. 92). Sir Walter's vanity and good looks make him perceive himself to be younger than he is.

would not signify; but as cousins, she would feel scrupulous as to any proposal of ours. We had better leave the Crofts to find their own level. There are several odd-looking men walking about here, who, I am told, are sailors. The Crofts will associate with them!"[26]

This was Sir Walter and Elizabeth's share of interest in the letter; when Mrs. Clay had paid her tribute of more decent attention, in an enquiry after Mrs. Charles Musgrove, and her fine little boys,[27] Anne was at liberty.

In her own room she tried to comprehend it. Well might Charles wonder how Captain Wentworth would feel! Perhaps he had quitted the field, had given Louisa up, had ceased to love, had found he did not love her. She could not endure the idea of treachery or levity, or any thing akin to ill-usage between him and his friend. She could not endure that such a friendship as theirs should be severed unfairly.[28]

Captain Benwick and Louisa Musgrove! The high-spirited, joyous, talking Louisa Musgrove, and the dejected, thinking, feeling, reading Captain Benwick, seemed each of them every thing that would not suit the other. Their minds[29] most dissimilar! Where could have been the attraction? The answer soon presented itself. It had been in situation. They had been thrown together several weeks; they had been living in the same small family party; since Henrietta's coming away, they must have been depending almost entirely on each other, and Louisa, just recovering from illness, had been in an interesting state,[30] and Captain Benwick was not inconsolable. That was a point which Anne had not been able to avoid suspecting before;[31] and instead of drawing the same conclusion as Mary, from the present course of events, they served only to confirm the idea of his having felt some dawning of tenderness toward herself. She did not mean, however, to derive much more from it to gratify her vanity, than Mary might have allowed. She was persuaded that any tolerably pleasing young woman who had listened and seemed to feel for him, would have received the same compliment. He had an affectionate heart. He must love somebody.

26. There are many naval officers in Bath (see p. 321, note 39), but they would not wear their uniforms off duty, so Sir Walter and Elizabeth can only suspect that these men are sailors.

27. "Fine little boys" would be Mrs. Clay's flattering language.

28. It is remarkable that, after hearing news with such tremendous implications for herself, Anne's first conscious thoughts involve concern about the possibility of wrong behavior or suffering by others. In a letter to her niece about the novel, Jane Austen writes, "You may *perhaps* like the Heroine, as she is almost too good for me" (March 23, 1817).

29. *minds:* general inner characters.

30. *interesting state:* condition that touches or arouses concern in others.

31. This confirms Anne's perceptiveness about Captain Benwick's true character. Captain Wentworth, though having known Benwick far better than Anne has, later confesses himself to be completely astounded by the event (p. 346). Her earlier observation about Louisa's feelings for Captain Wentworth being "a little fever of admiration" rather than real love is also vindicated (p. 156).

She saw no reason against their being happy. Louisa had fine naval fervour to begin with, and they would soon grow more alike. He would gain cheerfulness, and she would learn to be an enthusiast for Scott and Lord Byron;[32] nay, that was probably learnt already; of course they had fallen in love over poetry. The idea of Louisa Musgrove turned into a person of literary taste, and sentimental reflection, was amusing, but she had no doubt of its being so. The day at Lyme, the fall from the Cobb, might influence her health, her nerves, her courage, her character to the end of her life, as thoroughly as it appeared to have influenced her fate.

The conclusion of the whole was, that if the woman who had been sensible[33] of Captain Wentworth's merits could be allowed to prefer another man, there was nothing in the engagement to excite lasting wonder; and if Captain Wentworth lost no friend by it, certainly nothing to be regretted. No, it was not regret which made Anne's heart beat in spite of herself, and brought the colour into her cheeks when she thought of Captain Wentworth unshackled and free. She had some feelings which she was ashamed to investigate. They were too much like joy, senseless joy![34]

She longed to see the Crofts, but when the meeting took place, it was evident that no rumour of the news had yet reached them. The visit of ceremony was paid and returned,[35] and Louisa Musgrove was mentioned, and Captain Benwick too, without even half a smile.[36]

The Crofts had placed themselves in lodgings in Gay-street,[37] perfectly to Sir Walter's satisfaction. He was not at all ashamed of the acquaintance, and did, in fact, think and talk a great deal more about the Admiral, than the Admiral ever thought or talked about him.

The Crofts knew quite as many people in Bath as they wished for, and considered their intercourse with the Elliots as a mere matter of form, and not in the least likely to afford them any pleasure. They brought with them their country habit of being almost always together. He was ordered to walk, to keep off the gout,[38] and Mrs. Croft seemed to go shares with him in every thing, and

32. This discussion of their meeting of minds also suggests affinities between them even before their romance. Louisa was already an enthusiast of sorts, though not for poetry. She had ardently declared her willingness to suffer accidents rather than be separated from the man she loved and her determination never to abandon what she set out to do (pp. 160 and 166). Both declarations also had an element of showing off in front of Captain Wentworth, just as Benwick's ardent quoting of poetic lines of despair were arguably intended, at least in part, to make an impression on Anne. Their falling in love with each other, so soon after she had displayed such interest in Wentworth and he had proclaimed himself to be inconsolable about Fanny Harville, suggests the less than profound nature of their earlier ardor, as well as the overall limitations of their characters. It also suggests the limitations of enthusiasm in general, and in doing so it tempers the novel's tendency to celebrate warmth and spontaneity. Just as refusal to be persuaded can go too far, so can fervor and reliance on emotion. Anne's controlled passion forms the ideal mean.

33. *sensible:* cognizant.

34. After worrying about others and trying to understand what has happened, the personal implications for Anne finally emerge to the surface in her mind—though she still tries to control and subdue the emotions they provoke. Her joy would be enhanced by her recent decision to reject Mr. Elliot, for it means she has no feelings to hinder or complicate her hope for a renewal of Captain Wentworth's affection.

35. This means there were two meetings, first at the Elliots' and then at the Crofts'.

36. Anne does not divulge anything. She has not been authorized to, and, having no particular connection to the participants, she would not consider herself justified in doing so.

37. *Gay-street:* a street in a good part of town, though not as grand or as fashionably situated as Camden Place. This probably accounts for Sir Walter's satisfaction: the Crofts' situation is not so bad as to taint Sir Walter by association, but it is definitely inferior to his. He had earlier expressed similar satisfaction with the admiral's social position being an ideal one of moderate inferiority (see p. 46).

38. Regular exercise was recommended as one of the best cures for gout. The phrase "keep off the gout" stems from the disease's normal pattern, in which bouts of intense pain, often lasting a few weeks, alternated with periods of remission. The admiral is now in the latter and hoping to avoid a new bout of pain. Were he in the midst of an attack it is unlikely he would be walking at all, for the usual concentration of pain in the feet or legs tended to immobilize the sufferer.

to walk for her life, to do him good. Anne saw them wherever she
went. Lady Russell took her out in her carriage almost every
morning, and she never failed to think of them, and never failed
to see them. Knowing their feelings as she did, it was a most attractive picture of happiness to her. She always watched them as long
as she could; delighted to fancy she understood what they might
be talking of, as they walked along in happy independence, or
equally delighted to see the Admiral's hearty shake of the hand
when he encountered an old friend, and observe their eagerness
of conversation when occasionally forming into a little knot of the
navy, Mrs. Croft looking as intelligent and keen as any of the officers around her.[39]

Anne was too much engaged with Lady Russell to be often
walking herself, but it so happened that one morning, about a
week or ten days after the Crofts' arrival, it suited her best to leave
her friend, or her friend's carriage, in the lower part of the town,
and return alone to Camden-place; and in walking up Milsom-
street,[40] she had the good fortune to meet with the Admiral. He
was standing by himself, at a printshop window, with his hands
behind him, in earnest contemplation of some print,[41] and she
not only might have passed him unseen, but was obliged to touch
as well as address him before she could catch his notice. When he
did perceive and acknowledge her, however, it was done with all
his usual frankness and good humour. "Ha! is it you? Thank you,
thank you. This is treating me like a friend. Here I am, you see,
staring at a picture. I can never get by this shop without stopping.
But what a thing here is, by way of a boat. Do look at it. Did you
ever see the like? What queer fellows your fine painters must be,
to think that any body would venture their lives in such a shape-
less old cockleshell as that. And yet, here are two gentlemen stuck
up in it mightily at their ease, and looking about them at the rocks
and mountains, as if they were not to be upset the next moment,
which they certainly must be. I wonder where that boat was
built!" (laughing heartily) "I would not venture over a horsepond
in it.[42] Well," (turning away) "now, where are you bound? Can I
go any where for you, or with you? Can I be of any use?"

39. Admiral Croft would likely encounter many he knew, for Bath was a popular residence for retired military officers. Such men, having been stationed at various places, often overseas, throughout their careers, were less likely to have strong ties to a local area in Britain, and would find congenial a place where many others without current employment were gathered.

The happy, friendly society they form is also an indication that Bath does not have to be the place of cold, heartless elegance that Anne feared before her arrival.

40. *Milsom-street*: one of the leading shopping streets in Bath. It would be a natural place to encounter someone (in the next chapter it will be the setting for an even more significant encounter). It also represents the most direct route between the lower part of the town and Camden Place (see map, p. 516).

41. The print trade was a major business at this time, with a great variety of prints available to buyers. Large windows that could attract customers by displaying wares had become a standard feature of many stores by this time, and print shops were naturally leading examples of this trend, with their windows serving as free picture galleries for those walking on the street.

42. Romantic landscapes were popular for paintings and prints, and they often included lakes and mountains, as well as figures in the landscape who were enjoying their beauties, in a boat or on land. It is not known if Jane Austen had a particular picture in mind; she could easily have seen a number with a scene such as the admiral describes. It is even possible that she had heard one of her two naval brothers opine on the flimsiness of boats in pictures such as this. A naval officer would certainly know, for in addition to commanding a large sailing ship, he would have ample experience with smaller boats, which were needed to convey people between ships or between ship and shore. Landscape painters of the time, with their intense focus on the beauties of nature, would not necessarily worry about accuracy in practical matters. Thus the episode suggests a nice comic contrast between Romantic idealism and the highly unromantic practicality of someone like Admiral Croft.

"None, I thank you, unless you will give me the pleasure of your company the little way our road lies together. I am going home."

"That I will, with all my heart, and farther too. Yes, yes, we will have a snug[43] walk together; and I have something to tell you as we go along. There, take my arm; that's right; I do not feel comfortable if I have not a woman there. Lord! what a boat it is!" taking a last look at the picture, as they began to be in motion.

"Did you say that you had something to tell me, sir?"

"Yes, I have. Presently. But here comes a friend, Captain Brigden; I shall only say, 'How d'ye do,' as we pass, however. I shall not stop. 'How d'ye do.' Brigden stares to see anybody with me but my wife. She, poor soul, is tied by the leg. She has a blister on one of her heels, as large as a three shilling piece.[44] If you look across the street, you will see Admiral Brand coming down and his brother. Shabby fellows, both of them! I am glad they are not on this side of the way. Sophy cannot bear them. They played me a pitiful trick once—got away some of my best men.[45] I will tell you the whole story another time. There comes old Sir Archibald Drew and his grandson. Look, he sees us; he kisses his hand to you; he takes you for my wife.[46] Ah! the peace has come too soon for that younker.[47] Poor old Sir Archibald! How do you like Bath, Miss Elliot? It suits us very well. We are always meeting with some old friend or other; the streets full of them every morning; sure to have plenty of chat; and then we get away from them all, and shut ourselves into our lodgings, and draw in our chairs, and are as snug as if we were at Kellynch, ay, or as we used to be even at North Yarmouth and Deal.[48] We do not like our lodgings here the worse, I can tell you, for putting us in mind of those we first had at North Yarmouth. The wind blows through one of the cupboards just in the same way."

When they were got a little farther, Anne ventured to press again for what he had to communicate. She had hoped, when clear of Milsom-street, to have her curiosity gratified; but she was still obliged to wait, for the Admiral had made up his mind not to begin, till they had gained the greater space and quiet of Bel-

43. *snug:* enjoyable, comfortable. The word would naturally occur to the admiral, for it was also used as a term of praise for ships.

44. It would be a large blister if the admiral is not exaggerating, for the diameter of a three-shilling piece was just under an inch and a half (3.5 centimeters). As the product of her walks with him to keep off his gout, it would show the extent of her marital devotion. Mention of this coin dates the novel precisely, for this denomination was issued as a silver coin only from 1811, three years before the action is set, to 1816, the year the novel was finished. In general the only shilling coins issued by the British government were one-shilling pieces.

A shilling was, along with the pound and the pence, one of the three basic British monetary units. Twelve pence made a shilling, and twenty shillings made a pound.

45. Staffing ships was a perpetual problem for the navy, especially during major wars that mobilized large numbers of ships, for the supply of skilled seamen never sufficed to fill all the ships. For this reason, the navy used press gangs to force every skilled man they could find into service. Even with this, most ships had to include a number of poor or inexperienced crewmen. Thus losing those who were good sailors would be a major grievance of a captain (as Admiral Croft probably was when this occurred). This could happen through administrative order: if, as he said, both these men did it, the likelihood is that one was in a position of influence or power to have the order issued on behalf of the other; favors for relatives or friends were a frequent practice in the navy.

46. His mistaking her for Mrs. Croft is what makes him kiss his hand: such an intimate gesture could be justified to the wife of a friend.

47. *younker:* youngster, specifically a boy or junior seaman in the navy. He presumably means Sir Archibald's grandson. Sir Archibald himself might not be in the navy, though it is likely he is, and met Admiral Croft that way, while receiving his title from meritorious service there; it was common practice for sons to follow their fathers or grandfathers into the navy. The peace would have come too soon for the grandson because it makes advancement far more difficult, due to the reduced size of the navy and the fewer possibilities of distinguishing oneself by action. Some who were junior seamen could remain that always. Sympathy for this grandson would be what inspires the "Poor old Sir Archibald" that immediately follows. It also could be the grandson who kissed his hand, perhaps with the idea that in his situation he needs to curry as much favor from high-ranking naval officers as possible.

48. Yarmouth and Deal were both naval bases where the admiral had been stationed. Each was mentioned previously by him or by Mrs. Croft (pp. 134 and 174). See map, p. 512, for locations.

mont,[49] and as she was not really Mrs. Croft, she must let him have his own way. As soon as they were fairly ascending Belmont, he began,

"Well, now you shall hear something that will surprise you. But first of all, you must tell me the name of the young lady I am going to talk about. That young lady, you know, that we have all been so concerned for. The Miss Musgrove, that all this has been happening to. Her christian name—I always forget her christian name."[50]

Anne had been ashamed to appear to comprehend so soon as she really did; but now she could safely suggest the name of "Louisa."

"Ay, ay, Miss Louisa Musgrove, that is the name. I wish young ladies had not such a number of fine christian names. I should never be out, if they were all Sophys, or something of that sort. Well, this Miss Louisa, we all thought, you know, was to marry Frederick. He was courting her week after week. The only wonder was, what they could be waiting for, till the business at Lyme came; then, indeed, it was clear enough that they must wait till her brain was set to right. But even then, there was something odd in their way of going on. Instead of staying at Lyme, he went off to Plymouth, and then he went off to see Edward.[51] When we came back from Minehead,[52] he was gone down to Edward's, and there he has been ever since. We have seen nothing of him since November. Even Sophy could not understand it.[53] But now, the matter has taken the strangest turn of all; for this young lady, this same Miss Musgrove, instead of being to marry Frederick, is to marry James Benwick. You know James Benwick."

"A little. I am a little acquainted with Captain Benwick."

"Well, she is to marry him. Nay, most likely they are married already, for I do not know what they should wait for."[54]

"I thought Captain Benwick a very pleasing young man," said Anne, "and I understand that he bears an excellent character."[55]

"Oh! yes, yes, there is not a word to be said against James Benwick. He is only a commander,[56] it is true, made[57] last summer, and these are bad times for getting on,[58] but he has not another

49. *Belmont:* currently lower Lansdown Road, it was north of Milsom (see map, p. 516). To get there Admiral Croft and Anne would have used George Saint, another large and busy thoroughfare. This is why the admiral waited to speak until Belmont, which, being a residential street and also very steep, would not have attracted as much traffic.

50. Earlier Admiral Croft said he could not tell Louisa from Henrietta (p. 174).

51. His visits to Plymouth and to his brother in Shropshire were both spoken of earlier (pp. 250 and 252). By this point he would have been in Shropshire well over a month (see chronology, p. 489). Visits to family at this time often were long, due to the slowness and difficulty of traveling: Jane Austen's visits to family members often extended beyond a month. But staying away from Lyme that long would be odd behavior if he truly loved Louisa. He will later explain the reason for his actions (p. 464). They have obviously helped facilitate Louisa's engagement to Captain Benwick.

52. Minehead is a coastal town in northern Somerset (see map, p. 513). Earlier he and Mrs. Croft were said to "be going away for a few weeks, to visit their connexions in the north of the county" (p. 240).

53. He obviously thinks Mrs. Croft especially able to discern Wentworth's motives, whether because she is his sister or because she has shown shrewdness in understanding people. She is earlier pictured as helping to guide him in many things, and it is probable that Admiral Croft has come to rely heavily on her judgment, especially for nonnaval matters.

54. The admiral's expectation of immediate marriage fits with his description, and defense, of the quickness—measured in days—with which he and his wife married after meeting (p. 174). He does not seem like the type to wait or worry about the niceties of courtship etiquette.

55. *bears an excellent character:* has an excellent reputation.

56. A commander, sometimes called master and commander, was someone who could command sloops or other small ships. Though called captain, he would rank below a regular post-captain, such as Captain Wentworth, who could command larger vessels.

57. *made:* promoted.

58. As discussed above (note 47), the opportunities for naval officers to advance during peacetime were significantly less. Those lower in rank would suffer especially from this, since it might keep them from ever rising higher.

fault that I know of. An excellent, good-hearted fellow, I assure you, a very active, zealous officer too, which is more than you would think for, perhaps, for that soft sort of manner does not do him justice."

"Indeed you are mistaken there, sir. I should never augur[59] want of spirit[60] from Captain Benwick's manners. I thought them particularly pleasing, and I will answer for it they would generally please."

"Well, well, ladies are the best judges; but James Benwick is rather too piano[61] for me, and though very likely it is all our partiality, Sophy and I cannot help thinking Frederick's manners[62] better than his. There is something about Frederick more to our taste."

Anne was caught. She had only meant to oppose the too-common idea of spirit and gentleness being incompatible with each other, not at all to represent Captain Benwick's manners as the very best that could possibly be, and, after a little hesitation, she was beginning to say, "I was not entering into any comparison of the two friends," but the Admiral interrupted her with,

"And the thing is certainly true. It is not a mere bit of gossip. We have it from Frederick himself. His sister had a letter from him yesterday, in which he tells us of it, and he had just had it in a letter from Harville, written upon the spot, from Uppercross.[63] I fancy they are all at Uppercross."

This was an opportunity which Anne could not resist; she said, therefore, "I hope, Admiral, I hope there is nothing in the style of Captain Wentworth's letter to make you and Mrs. Croft particularly uneasy. It did certainly seem, last autumn, as if there were an attachment between him and Louisa Musgrove; but I hope it may be understood to have worn out on each side equally, and without violence.[64] I hope his letter does not breathe the spirit of an ill-used man."

"Not at all, not at all; there is not an oath[65] or a murmur[66] from beginning to end."

Anne looked down to hide her smile.

"No, no; Frederick is not a man to whine and complain; he has

59. *augur:* project, anticipate.

60. *want of spirit:* lack of ardor, courage.

61. *piano:* soft, mild. The term, from the Italian for "soft," was rarely used outside of musical contexts; the term for the musical instrument is a shortened version of "pianoforte" ("soft-strong" in Italian), and derives from the ability to play the same note either softly or loudly.

62. *manners:* general outward conduct and demeanor.

63. This suggests a little delay in the arrival of the news to Captain Wentworth. Anne received her letter from Mary when the Crofts arrived, said to have been a week to ten days ago. In her letter Mary wrote that Captain Benwick was expected that day. If he asked Mr. Musgrove for permission then, the engagement was announced, and Harville wrote to Wentworth, the latter should have received the news a number of days ago, for it would not have taken a letter long to reach him. Since it is hard to imagine Mr. Musgrove not announcing his consent immediately, especially since everyone there knew of the engagement, it is probable that Captain Benwick's shyness made him hesitate to ask, or, perhaps even more likely, that Captain Harville delayed writing to Captain Wentworth, either out of fear that the news would pain his friend or because of his own distressed feelings at Benwick's quick switch from mourning Harville's sister to loving Louisa. Captain Harville will later be shown as deeply afflicted on this account.

64. *violence:* fury; vehement or violent feelings. The term did not necessarily refer to physical violence, and it is doubtful Anne would be thinking of that.

65. *oath:* curse; profane word or expression.

66. *murmur:* expression of grumbling or discontent.

too much spirit for that. If the girl likes another man better, it is very fit she should have him."

"Certainly. But what I mean is, that I hope there is nothing in Captain Wentworth's manner of writing to make you suppose he thinks himself ill-used by his friend, which might appear, you know, without its being absolutely said. I should be very sorry that such a friendship as has subsisted between him and Captain Benwick should be destroyed, or even wounded, by a circumstance of this sort."

"Yes, yes, I understand you. But there is nothing at all of that nature in the letter. He does not give the least fling[67] at Benwick; does not so much as say, 'I wonder at it, I have a reason of my own for wondering at it.' No, you would not guess, from his way of writing, that he had ever thought of this Miss (what's her name?) for himself. He very handsomely hopes they will be happy together, and there is nothing very unforgiving in that, I think."

Anne did not receive the perfect conviction which the Admiral meant to convey, but it would have been useless to press the enquiry farther. She, therefore, satisfied herself with commonplace remarks, or quiet attention, and the Admiral had it all his own way.

"Poor Frederick!" said he at last. "Now he must begin all over again with somebody else. I think we must get him to Bath.[68] Sophy must write, and beg him to come to Bath. Here are pretty girls enough, I am sure. It would be of no use to go to Uppercross again, for that other Miss Musgrove, I find, is bespoke[69] by her cousin, the young parson. Do not you think, Miss Elliot, we had better try to get him to Bath?"

67. *fling*: a scoffing or sarcastic remark, thrown out in passing.

68. Bath was indeed a good place to find a mate. In addition to the presence of so many visitors of roughly similar class, it provided greater opportunities than were generally available at the time for relatively free socializing with the opposite sex. The two principal characters in *Northanger Abbey* meet in Bath and ultimately marry, and in *Emma* one character visits Bath and returns with a wife.

69. *bespoke by*: engaged to.

Milsom Street, one of the main shopping streets in Bath (from a contemporary illustration).

[From Mowbray Aston Green, *The Eighteenth Century Architecture of Bath* (Bath, 1904), p. 154]

Chapter Seven

While Admiral Croft was taking this walk with Anne, and expressing his wish of getting Captain Wentworth to Bath, Captain Wentworth was already on his way thither.[1] Before Mrs. Croft had written, he was arrived; and the very next time Anne walked out, she saw him.

Mr. Elliot was attending his two cousins and Mrs. Clay. They were in Milsom-street.[2] It began to rain, not much, but enough to make shelter desirable for women,[3] and quite enough to make it very desirable for Miss Elliot to have the advantage of being conveyed home in Lady Dalrymple's carriage, which was seen waiting at a little distance; she, Anne, and Mrs. Clay, therefore, turned into Molland's,[4] while Mr. Elliot stepped to Lady Dalrymple, to request her assistance. He soon joined them again, successful, of course; Lady Dalrymple would be most happy to take them home, and would call for them in a few minutes.

Her ladyship's carriage was a barouche,[5] and did not hold more than four with any comfort. Miss Carteret was with her mother; consequently it was not reasonable to expect accommodation for all the three Camden-place ladies.[6] There could be no doubt as to Miss Elliot. Whoever suffered inconvenience, she must suffer none, but it occupied a little time to settle the point of civility between the other two. The rain was a mere trifle, and Anne was most sincere in preferring a walk with Mr. Elliot. But the rain was also a mere trifle to Mrs. Clay; she would hardly allow it even to drop at all, and her boots were so thick![7] much thicker than Miss Anne's; and, in short, her civility rendered her quite as anxious to be left to walk with Mr. Elliot, as Anne could be, and it was discussed between them with a generosity so polite and so determined, that the others were obliged to settle it for them; Miss

1. This means he left just after learning of Louisa's engagement (see p. 326).

2. *Milsom-street*: see p. 321, note 40, and picture on p. 329.

3. Women were considered more delicate physically, and, thanks to their homebound routines, were less accustomed to exposure to inclement weather than men. Moreover, women's clothing was more lightweight and delicate and thus more easily soaked and likely to be damaged by water; the hems of their long skirts could also quickly become wet and muddy from walking in the rain.

4. *Molland's*: see p. 333, note 11.

5. A barouche was a carriage with two seats facing each other, but, unlike the similar coach, each seat was large enough only for two; it also differed from a coach in having a top that folded down, allowing it to be either a closed or open carriage (see picture below). Barouches were expensive and highly fashionable, and thus appropriate vehicles for a viscountess. In a visit to her brother in London, Jane Austen rode in a barouche at one point. She wrote to her sister, "I liked my solitary elegance, & was ready to laugh all the time, at my being where I was—I could not but feel that I had naturally small right to be parading about London in a Barouche" (May 24, 1813).

6. The walk from Milsom Street to Camden Place would be fairly lengthy and would also involve going up a steep hill (see map, p. 516).

7. Boots had recently become fashionable for women, especially for out-

A barouche. The top is folded down, making it an open carriage.

[From Ralph Straus, *Carriages and Coaches* (London, 1912), p. 232]

Elliot maintaining that Mrs. Clay had a little cold already, and Mr. Elliot deciding on appeal, that his cousin Anne's boots were rather the thickest.[8]

It was fixed accordingly that Mrs. Clay should be of the party in the carriage; and they had just reached this point when Anne, as she sat near the window, descried, most decidedly and distinctly, Captain Wentworth walking down the street.

Her start was perceptible only to herself; but she instantly felt that she was the greatest simpleton in the world, the most unaccountable and absurd! For a few minutes she saw nothing before her. It was all confusion. She was lost; and when she had scolded back her senses, she found the others still waiting for the carriage, and Mr. Elliot (always obliging) just setting off for Union-street[9] on a commission of Mrs. Clay's.

She now felt a great inclination to go to the outer door; she wanted to see if it rained. Why was she to suspect herself of another motive? Captain Wentworth must be out of sight. She left her seat, she would go, one half of her should not be always so much wiser than the other half, or always suspecting the other of being worse than it was. She would see if it rained.[10] She was sent back, however, in a moment by the entrance of Captain Wentworth himself, among a party of gentlemen and ladies, evidently his acquaintance, and whom he must have joined a little below Milsom-street.[11] He was more obviously struck and confused by the sight of her, than she had ever observed before; he looked quite red. For the first time, since their renewed acquaintance, she felt that she was betraying the least sensibility of the two. She had the advantage of him, in the preparation of the last few moments. All the overpowering, blinding, bewildering, first effects of strong surprise were over with her. Still, however, she had enough to feel! It was agitation, pain, pleasure, a something between delight and misery.

He spoke to her, and then turned away. The character of his manner was embarrassment. She could not have called it either cold or friendly, or any thing so certainly as embarrassed.[12]

door wear. They were generally made of leather, had some decoration, and came up to the ankle (for this reason they were often called half boots). Thus, though better than shoes for the rain, they were not as hardy as men's full-length boots, which was another reason for women to avoid rain.

8.   Mr. Elliot's decision in favor of Anne could result from his preference for her and avowed dislike of Mrs. Clay. Another possibility is suggested by later events (see p. 479, note 27).

9.   *Union-street*: a small street near Molland's (see map, p. 515). Toward the end of the novel it will be the site of an even more fateful encounter between Anne and Captain Wentworth than the one about to happen now.

10.   The clear suggestion is that Anne is looking for Captain Wentworth, even as she is assuring herself that she wishes only to see if it rained. The reference to halves of her indicates her awareness of a divided self. One reason why part of her would not wish to look for him (or acknowledge doing so) is that she does not want to think herself too eager for him. She also may want to shield herself from possible disappointment, since she still cannot know whether he has any interest in her. She would not wish to overthrow the calmness and steadiness of mind that she has struggled so hard to attain by carelessly indulging false hopes. Another reason is that rules of propriety dictated that a woman should not look directly at a man, but wait for him to make all the advances, even visual.

11.   Molland's was one of the leading confectioners and pastry shops in Bath, selling both sweet and nonsweet foods. Such shops could be popular places for wealthy people to gather and meet; Molland's included the inducement of space for customers to dine. A number of chance encounters in Jane Austen occur in shops. Many, especially those catering to affluent customers, encouraged casual browsing and extended visits through spacious, pleasant atmospheres and ample seating for customers.

For Captain Wentworth's probable route from below Milsom Street, see map, p. 516.

12.   This is the first time, excepting the immediate aftermath of the accident at Lyme, that he has seemed less calm and assured than she when they are together. This reversal will continue through much of the last part of the book.

At the same time, his approaching her to speak, and the exchange that now follows, represents the first time in the novel—excepting the carriage ride back from Lyme, when he spoke only from necessity—that he has initiated friendly conversation with her.

After a short interval, however, he came towards her and spoke again. Mutual enquiries on common subjects passed; neither of them, probably, much the wiser for what they heard, and Anne continuing fully sensible of his being less at ease than formerly. They had, by dint of being so very much together, got to speak to each other with a considerable portion of apparent indifference and calmness; but he could not do it now. Time had changed him, or Louisa had changed him. There was consciousness of some sort or other. He looked very well, not as if he had been suffering in health or spirits, and he talked of Uppercross, of the Musgroves, nay, even of Louisa, and had even a momentary look of his own arch significance as he named her; but yet it was Captain Wentworth not comfortable, not easy, not able to feign that he was.

It did not surprise, but it grieved Anne to observe that Elizabeth would not know him. She saw that he saw Elizabeth, that Elizabeth saw him, that there was complete internal recognition on each side;[13] she was convinced that he was ready to be acknowledged as an acquaintance, expecting it, and she had the pain of seeing her sister turn away with unalterable coldness.

Lady Dalrymple's carriage, for which Miss Elliot was growing very impatient, now drew up; the servant came in to announce it.[14] It was beginning to rain again, and altogether there was a delay, and a bustle, and a talking, which must make all the little crowd in the shop understand that Lady Dalrymple was calling to convey Miss Elliot. At last Miss Elliot and her friend, unattended but by the servant, (for there was no cousin returned)[15] were walking off; and Captain Wentworth, watching them, turned again to Anne, and by manner, rather than words, was offering his services to her.

"I am much obliged to you," was her answer, "but I am not going with them. The carriage would not accommodate so many. I walk. I prefer walking."

"But it rains."

"Oh! very little. Nothing that I regard."

13. She, unlike Mary, had been present when he courted Anne (p. 56).

14. In addition to a coachman, a woman of Lady Dalrymple's wealth would usually be accompanied by at least one footman, who would ride on the outside and perform services such as taking messages, helping people in and out of the carriage, and announcing the carriage. A footman would also indicate his employer's identity and importance through his fancy livery.

15. Mr. Elliot has not returned yet from his commission for Mrs. Clay.

A *Modern Belle going to the Rooms at Bath*.

A Bath chair (from a contemporary illustration). The woman's headdress and the umbrella covering it are satirical exaggerations.

[From *Works of James Gillray* (London, 1849)]

After a moment's pause he said, "Though I came only yester-day, I have equipped myself properly for Bath already, you see,"[16] (pointing to a new umbrella)[17] "I wish you would make use of it, if you are determined to walk; though, I think, it would be more prudent to let me get you a chair."[18]

She was very much obliged to him, but declined it all, repeat-ing her conviction, that the rain would come to nothing at pres-ent, and adding, "I am only waiting for Mr. Elliot. He will be here in a moment, I am sure."

She had hardly spoken the words, when Mr. Elliot walked in. Captain Wentworth recollected him perfectly. There was no dif-ference between him and the man who had stood on the steps at Lyme, admiring Anne as she passed, except in the air and look and manner of the privileged relation and friend. He came in with eagerness, appeared to see and think only of her, apologised for his stay, was grieved to have kept her waiting, and anxious to get her away without further loss of time, and before the rain increased; and in another moment they walked off together, her arm under his, a gentle and embarrassed glance,[19] and a "good morning to you," being all that she had time for, as she passed away.

As soon as they were out of sight, the ladies of Captain Went-worth's party began talking of them.

"Mr. Elliot does not dislike his cousin, I fancy?"

"Oh! no, that is clear enough. One can guess what will happen there. He is always with them; half lives in the family, I believe. What a very good-looking man!"

"Yes, and Miss Atkinson, who dined with him once at the Wal-lises, says he is the most agreeable man she ever was in company with."[20]

"She is pretty, I think; Anne Elliot; very pretty, when one comes to look at her. It is not the fashion to say so, but I confess I admire her more than her sister."

"Oh! so do I."

"And so do I. No comparison. But the men are all wild after Miss Elliot. Anne is too delicate for them."

16. Bath is in the west of England, which is the rainiest part of the country, thanks to the moist ocean air brought by the prevailing westerly winds. It is especially rainy in the winter, the time when this conversation occurs.

17. Umbrellas as a protection against rain had first come into significant use in the early eighteenth century (umbrellas for protection against the sun, or in ceremonial functions, had long existed in various parts of the world). In England, they caught on more slowly than in other parts of Europe and were for a while derided as odd or foreign or effeminate. But by the last decades of the century they had attained wide popularity and become a standard personal item, especially for wealthier people.

18. *chair:* a sedan chair for transportation. Sedan chairs consisted of an enclosed seat carried by two men, one in front and one behind, using two long poles attached to the bottom of the seat (for a picture, see p. 335). They were a prominent feature of Bath because of the difficulty of getting carriages through the narrow streets of the old sections of the city (though in the 1790s, not long before the novel's date, a rebuilding program had widened many streets). In a letter written just after arriving in Bath, Jane Austen writes, "My Uncle overwalked himself at first & can now only travel in a Chair" (June 2, 1799). Chairs, not necessarily covered, could also be used to carry people all the way into and out of the baths, allowing them to avoid changing vehicles or walking; some houses were specially designed so that the residents could be carried all the way to or from their beds (for an example of chairs being taken inside a room in Bath, see picture on p. 286). Their popularity is shown by the detailed regulations drawn up by the city of Bath, which included a precise schedule of rates to be charged, depending on the distance traveled. Chairs could be easily hailed and would certainly be available in a popular commercial location such as this.

19. Presumably she feels a little embarrassed about being arm in arm with another man after Captain Wentworth has just shown such friendliness toward her.

20. Their gossip suggests the smallness of the Bath social world. It also means that, immediately after arriving in Bath, Captain Wentworth is hearing others speculate that Anne will marry another man and support their speculations with observations on that man's feelings, his footing in Anne's family, and the prevailing high opinion of his social charms.

Anne would have been particularly obliged to her cousin, if he would have walked by her side all the way to Camden-place, without saying a word. She had never found it so difficult to listen to him, though nothing could exceed his solicitude and care, and though his subjects were principally such as were wont to be always interesting—praise, warm, just, and discriminating, of Lady Russell, and insinuations highly rational against Mrs. Clay. But just now she could think only of Captain Wentworth. She could not understand his present feelings, whether he were really suffering much from disappointment or not; and till that point were settled, she could not be quite herself.[21]

She hoped to be wise and reasonable in time; but alas! alas! she must confess to herself that she was not wise yet.[22]

Another circumstance very essential for her to know, was how long he meant to be in Bath; he had not mentioned it, or she could not recollect it. He might be only passing through. But it was more probable that he should be come to stay. In that case, so liable as every body was to meet every body in Bath, Lady Russell would in all likelihood see him somewhere.[23]—Would she recollect him? How would it all be?

She had already been obliged to tell Lady Russell that Louisa Musgrove was to marry Captain Benwick. It had cost her something to encounter Lady Russell's surprise; and now, if she were by any chance to be thrown into company with Captain Wentworth, her imperfect knowledge of the matter might add another shade of prejudice against him.

The following morning Anne was out with her friend, and for the first hour, in an incessant and fearful sort of watch for him in vain; but at last, in returning down Pulteney-street,[24] she distinguished him on the right hand pavement at such a distance as to have him in view the greater part of the street. There were many other men about him, many groups walking the same way, but there was no mistaking him. She looked instinctively at Lady Rus-

21. Thus Anne experiences the first direct conflict in attention between Mr. Elliot and Captain Wentworth, and she focuses all her thoughts on the latter.

22. Again Anne struggles for composure; it has taken only a brief exposure to Captain Wentworth to place her once more in that position.

23. One reason for this frequent meeting in Bath—seen both in this novel and in the other Austen novel set in the city, *Northanger Abbey*—is that Bath was not very large. The central part of the city stretched not much more than half a mile, and even the outlying residential districts did not extend much farther (see map, p. 516). There were also only a few main shopping streets, all close to one another. Finally, the city had many common social events—balls, plays, concerts—that tended to bring large numbers of people together, though, as explained below, Sir Walter and his family do not often attend these events; whether Lady Russell does is never indicated.

24. *Pulteney-street:* A main thoroughfare in eastern Bath (see map, p. 516). It is not clear where Anne and Lady Russell are returning from. One possibility is Sydney Gardens, a popular place for walking at the end of Pulteney Street; another is the hilly area east of Bath, which was a popular venue for drives.

Curtains of the time.

[From Thomas Arthur Strange, *English Furniture in the 18th Century: A Guide to Collectors*, p. 358]

sell; but not from any mad idea of her recognising him so soon as she did herself. No, it was not to be supposed that Lady Russell would perceive him till they were nearly opposite. She looked at her however, from time to time, anxiously; and when the moment approached which must point him out, though not daring to look again (for her own countenance she knew was unfit to be seen), she was yet perfectly conscious of Lady Russell's eyes being turned exactly in the direction for him, of her being in short intently observing him. She could thoroughly comprehend the sort of fascination he must possess over Lady Russell's mind, the difficulty it must be for her to withdraw her eyes, the astonishment she must be feeling that eight or nine years should have passed over him, and in foreign climes and in active service too, without robbing him of one personal grace!

At last, Lady Russell drew back her head. — "Now, how would she speak of him?"

"You will wonder," said she, "what has been fixing my eye so long; but I was looking after some window-curtains, which Lady Alicia and Mrs. Frankland were telling me of last night. They described the drawing-room window-curtains of one of the houses on this side of the way, and this part of the street, as being the handsomest and best hung of any in Bath, but could not recollect the exact number, and I have been trying to find out which it could be; but I confess I can see no curtains hereabouts that answer their description."[25]

Anne sighed and blushed and smiled, in pity and disdain, either at her friend or herself.[26] — The part which provoked her most, was that in all this waste of foresight and caution, she should have lost the right moment for seeing whether he saw them.[27]

A day or two passed without producing any thing. — The theatre[28] or the rooms,[29] where he was most likely to be, were not fashionable[30] enough for the Elliots, whose evening amusements were solely in the elegant stupidity[31] of private parties,[32] in which they were getting more and more engaged; and Anne, wearied of such a state of stagnation, sick of knowing nothing, and fancying herself stronger because her strength was not tried,[33] was quite impatient for the concert evening. It was a concert for the benefit

25. Since the early 1700s curtains had become increasingly common in English homes and were made of a variety of fabrics and colors. By 1800 the most popular type of curtains hung from a rod and opened horizontally; this meant that a portion of the curtains would be visible from the outside. For examples of contemporary curtains, see picture on previous page.

26. The ambiguity results from not knowing if Lady Russell really was looking only at curtains. If so, Anne would be the object of pity and disdain for assuming that others are as focused on Captain Wentworth as she is. If not, Lady Russell would be the object for being unable to admit her own interest in him. The exact truth is deliberately left uncertain. My guess is that while Lady Russell is too honest to lie directly—in other words, she was not staring at Wentworth—it is possible she did perceive him briefly and turned to looking at curtains to avoid looking more in his direction.

27. This, like her possible mistake about Lady Russell, suggests some irony at the expense of Anne. In other Austen novels powerful romantic feelings often lead an otherwise sensible heroine into foolish feelings or behavior.

28. The theater was a prominent feature of life in Bath (see p. 429, note 103).

29. *the rooms:* the Assembly Rooms. There were two in Bath, the Lower Rooms and the Upper Rooms, each with rooms for dancing, cards, and refreshment. They were the leading venues for social life in Bath, with an important event, usually a dance, occurring most nights at one set of rooms; there was a general Bath social schedule to keep these events from clashing.

30. *fashionable:* socially elite.

31. *stupidity:* dullness, tedium.

32. The Elliots' disdain for public amusements reflects a change in Bath at this time, one noted by various observers. Throughout the 1700s public events had dominated social life, and visitors were strongly encouraged to attend. But the city's growing popularity, along with increasing affluence and improvements in the ease and speed of transportation, swelled the ranks of middle-class visitors, and this made those in the top echelons of society recoil. The high aristocracy gradually ceased coming at all, while those a little lower, like the Elliots, turned to select gatherings among themselves, however dull such gatherings might be. In contrast, Captain Wentworth does not allow his choice of entertainment to be dictated by such considerations.

In her preface to *Northanger Abbey*, published at the same time as *Persuasion* but written thirteen years earlier, Jane Austen notes that many things, including manners, have changed in the interval. This change in Bath is probably part of what she had in mind, for in the earlier novel, unlike here, much of the action in Bath centers around public gatherings.

33. She may mean her strength for participating in more active events or,

of a person patronised by Lady Dalrymple.[34] Of course they must attend. It was really expected to be a good one, and Captain Wentworth was very fond of music. If she could only have a few minutes conversation with him again, she fancied she should be satisfied; and as to the power of addressing him she felt all over courage[35] if the opportunity occurred. Elizabeth had turned from him, Lady Russell overlooked him; her nerves were strengthened by these circumstances; she felt that she owed him attention.

She had once partly promised Mrs. Smith to spend the evening with her; but in a short hurried call she excused herself and put it off, with the more decided promise of a longer visit on the morrow. Mrs. Smith gave a most good-humoured acquiescence.

"By all means," said she; "only tell me all about it, when you do come. Who is your party?"

Anne named them all. Mrs. Smith made no reply; but when she was leaving her, said, and with an expression half serious, half arch, "Well, I heartily wish your concert may answer;[36] and do not fail me to-morrow if you can come; for I begin to have a foreboding that I may not have many more visits from you."[37]

Anne was startled and confused, but after standing in a moment's suspense, was obliged, and not sorry to be obliged, to hurry away.

perhaps even more, her strength for facing Captain Wentworth with equanimity ("knowing nothing" probably refers to her having learned nothing about him since the encounter at the shop). The line below about feeling the courage to address him suggests this concern is greatly in her mind.

34. Concerts were another popular form of evening entertainment in Bath, with the finest performers in England sometimes featured. They were usually held on Wednesdays (see chronology, p. 491, for sequence of days). Like theatrical performances, they were often advertised as being for the benefit of a specific person or persons; concerts' close connection with various charities caused them to be frequently called benefits. Aristocrats like Lady Dalrymple would often exercise patronage of this type.

35. *all over courage:* generally courageous.

36. *answer:* be satisfactory.

37. The reasons for Mrs. Smith's not replying when she hears who is of Anne's party, and then for wondering whether she will see much of Anne anymore, will be revealed soon.

Chapter Eight

Sir Walter, his two daughters, and Mrs. Clay, were the earliest of all their party, at the rooms in the evening; and as Lady Dalrymple must be waited for, they took their station by one of the fires in the octagon room.[1] But hardly were they so settled, when the door opened again, and Captain Wentworth walked in alone.[2] Anne was the nearest to him, and making yet a little advance, she instantly spoke. He was preparing only to bow and pass on, but her gentle "How do you do?" brought him out of the straight line to stand near her, and make enquiries in return, in spite of the formidable father and sister in the back ground. Their being in the back ground was a support to Anne; she knew nothing of their looks, and felt equal to every thing which she believed right to be done.

While they were speaking, a whispering between her father and Elizabeth caught her ear. She could not distinguish, but she must guess the subject; and on Captain Wentworth's making a distant bow, she comprehended that her father had judged so well as to give him that simple acknowledgment of acquaintance, and she was just in time by a side glance to see a slight curtsey from Elizabeth herself. This, though late and reluctant and ungracious, was yet better than nothing, and her spirits improved.

After talking however of the weather and Bath and the concert, their conversation began to flag, and so little was said at last, that she was expecting him to go every moment; but he did not; he seemed in no hurry to leave her; and presently with renewed spirit, with a little smile, a little glow, he said,

"I have hardly seen you since our day at Lyme. I am afraid you must have suffered from the shock, and the more from its not overpowering you at the time."

She assured him that she had not.

1. *octagon room:* One of the three principal rooms in the Upper Rooms (see p. 341, note 29). The other rooms were the Ball Room (the largest of the three) and the Tea Room (see diagram below). The Octagon Room, named for its shape, was originally built as a card room, but the interference from the constant circulation of people through the room caused a separate card room to be built off the Octagon Room. By this point it was used primarily as a place for meetings (in *Northanger Abbey* the heroine meets friends there before a ball) and for music (though not for this concert).

2. Anne had guessed Captain Wentworth would come due to his love of music. It was earlier mentioned as an important taste they had in common (p. 88), so it is appropriate it should draw them together here for what will be their most sustained and important conversation so far. In contrast, early in the novel, at the first dinner they both attend, their common interest in music led to an encounter that underlined their complete estrangement (see p. 137, note 60).

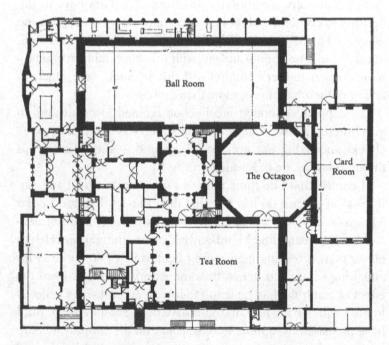

Diagram of the Assembly Rooms.

[From Mowbray Aston Green, *The Eighteenth Century Architecture of Bath* (Bath, 1904), p. 161]

"It was a frightful hour," said he, "a frightful day!" and he passed his hand across his eyes, as if the remembrance were still too painful; but in a moment half smiling again, added, "The day has produced some effects however—has had some consequences which must be considered as the very reverse of frightful.—When you had the presence of mind to suggest that Benwick would be the properest person to fetch a surgeon, you could have little idea of his being eventually one of those most concerned in her recovery."

"Certainly I could have none. But it appears—I should hope it would be a very happy match. There are on both sides good principles and good temper."[3]

"Yes," said he, looking not exactly forward—"but there I think ends the resemblance. With all my soul I wish them happy, and rejoice over every circumstance in favour of it. They have no difficulties to contend with at home, no opposition, no caprice, no delays.—The Musgroves are behaving like themselves, most honourably and kindly, only anxious with true parental hearts to promote their daughter's comfort. All this is much, very much in favour of their happiness; more than perhaps—"[4]

He stopped. A sudden recollection seemed to occur, and to give him some taste of that emotion[5] which was reddening Anne's cheeks and fixing her eyes on the ground.—After clearing his throat, however, he proceeded thus,

"I confess that I do think there is a disparity, too great a disparity, and in a point no less essential than mind.—I regard Louisa Musgrove as a very amiable, sweet-tempered girl, and not deficient in understanding;[6] but Benwick is something more. He is a clever man, a reading man—and I confess that I do consider his attaching himself to her, with some surprise.[7] Had it been the effect of gratitude, had he learnt to love her, because he believed her to be preferring him, it would have been another thing. But I have no reason to suppose it so. It seems, on the contrary, to have been a perfectly spontaneous, untaught feeling on his side, and this surprises me. A man like him, in his situation! With a heart pierced, wounded, almost broken![8] Fanny Harville was a very

3. *temper:* dispositions, emotional qualities. Anne's interrupted speech, "But it appears—I should hope . . ."—a rare fragmentary sentence from her—indicates the hesitation with which she approaches the topic of Louisa. She knows it may affect him strongly, though without knowing how, and that it is a matter with momentous implications for herself.

4. He stops because he seems about to segue to a comparison of the Musgroves' behavior with that of Anne's family and friends during his courtship of her. His concern with the subject is shown by his repetitive, "no difficulties . . . , no opposition, no caprice, no delays."

5. *emotion:* agitation. Her "fixing her eyes on the ground" here parallels his "looking not exactly forward" just above; each evidently finds it difficult to look at the other. Her looking even more away corresponds both to her generally more reserved character and to the greater modesty that women were expected to show, especially when talking to men.

6. *understanding:* intellect, intelligence.

7. For the first time Captain Wentworth gives his full verdict on Louisa Musgrove. It indicates his lack of regret at losing her and his high standards for true attachment. Since Anne certainly is clever, and a reader—her conversations with Benwick about poetry could have reminded Captain Wentworth of that, assuming he overheard them or learned from someone what they involved—she would meet his standards, and he may intend this as a signal to her.

8. This could easily describe Captain Wentworth's heart after Anne's rejection of him. His suddenly emotional tone, after calmly assessing Captain Benwick's situation, suggests that the strong parallels with his own situation are beginning to overpower him, especially since he is discussing them with the very person who pierced his heart.

superior creature; and his attachment to her was indeed attach-ment. A man does not recover from such a devotion of the heart to such a woman!—He ought not—he does not."[9]

Either from the consciousness,[10] however, that his friend had recovered, or from some other consciousness, he went no farther; and Anne, who, in spite of the agitated voice in which the latter part had been uttered, and in spite of all the various noises of the room, the almost ceaseless slam of the door, and ceaseless buzz of persons walking through, had distinguished every word, was struck, gratified, confused, and beginning to breathe very quick, and feel an hundred things in a moment.[11] It was impossible for her to enter on such a subject; and yet, after a pause, feeling the necessity of speaking, and having not the smallest wish for a total change, she only deviated so far as to say,

"You were a good while at Lyme, I think?"

"About a fortnight.[12] I could not leave it till Louisa's doing well was quite ascertained. I had been too deeply concerned in the mischief[13] to be soon at peace. It had been my doing—solely mine. She would not have been obstinate if I had not been weak.[14] The country round Lyme is very fine.[15] I walked and rode a great deal; and the more I saw, the more I found to admire."

"I should very much like to see Lyme again," said Anne.

"Indeed! I should not have supposed that you could have found any thing in Lyme to inspire such a feeling. The horror and dis-tress you were involved in—the stretch of mind, the wear of spir-its!—I should have thought your last impression of Lyme must have been strong disgust."[16]

"The last few hours were certainly very painful," replied Anne: "but when pain is over, the remembrance of it often becomes a pleasure. One does not love a place the less for having suffered in it, unless it has been all suffering, nothing but suffering—which was by no means the case at Lyme. We were only in anxiety and distress during the last two hours; and, previously, there had been a great deal of enjoyment.[17] So much novelty and beauty! I have travelled so little, that every fresh place would be interesting to me—but there is real beauty at Lyme: and in short" (with a faint

9. This statement about man's constancy in love foreshadows the lengthy debate on the matter, and the letter that follows it, at the climax of the novel (pp. 442–454).

10. The other consciousness is presumably his awareness of how much what he said applies to himself and his feelings toward Anne. In the last part of his statement he not only became more passionate, indicated by his emphatic concluding words and confirmed by the description just below of his "agitated voice," but he also switched to discussing man in general, rather than specifically Captain Benwick.

11. His words have so overwhelmed her that at this point she can hardly sort through them. On p. 352 she will consider more calmly their meaning and implications.

12. It probably was a little longer than two weeks. For the reasons and Captain Wentworth's actions in the interval, see chronology, p. 489.

13. *mischief*: harm, injury. The term had a stronger, less innocuous connotation than it does today.

14. It is characteristic that he would attribute his mistake to weakness, for, as seen in his condemnation of Anne for repudiating their engagement, weakness is something he particularly abhors (see p. 114). At the same time, by admitting this fault in himself, he undermines this earlier condemnation of her.

15. The area around Lyme is very hilly and offers many views of the sea. His appreciation of natural beauty gives him another link with Anne.

16. *disgust*: distaste. This term had a weaker connotation then.

17. Anne's ability to focus on what is pleasant in an experience that included great distress may result in part from the often forlorn circumstances of her life so far, which have forced her to savor what enjoyment she can find.

blush at some recollections) "altogether my impressions of the place are very agreeable."

As she ceased, the entrance door opened again, and the very party appeared for whom they were waiting. "Lady Dalrymple, Lady Dalrymple," was the rejoicing sound; and with all the eagerness compatible with anxious elegance,[18] Sir Walter and his two ladies stepped forward to meet her. Lady Dalrymple and Miss Carteret, escorted by Mr. Elliot and Colonel Wallis, who had happened to arrive nearly at the same instant, advanced into the room. The others joined them, and it was a group in which Anne found herself also necessarily included. She was divided from Captain Wentworth. Their interesting, almost too interesting conversation must be broken up for a time; but slight was the penance compared with the happiness which brought it on! She had learnt, in the last ten minutes, more of his feelings towards Louisa, more of all his feelings, than she dared to think of![19] and she gave herself up to the demands of the party, to the needful civilities of the moment, with exquisite, though agitated sensations. She was in good humour with all. She had received ideas which disposed her to be courteous and kind to all, and to pity every one, as being less happy than herself.

The delightful emotions were a little subdued, when, on stepping back from the group, to be joined again by Captain Wentworth, she saw that he was gone. She was just in time to see him turn into the concert room.[20] He was gone—he had disappeared: she felt a moment's regret. But "they should meet again. He would look for her—he would find her out long before the evening were over—and at present, perhaps, it was as well to be asunder. She was in need of a little interval for recollection."[21]

Upon Lady Russell's appearance soon afterwards, the whole party was collected, and all that remained, was to marshal themselves, and proceed into the concert room; and be of all the consequence in their power, draw as many eyes, excite as many whispers, and disturb as many people as they could.[22]

Very, very happy were both Elizabeth and Anne Elliot as they walked in. Elizabeth, arm in arm with Miss Carteret, and looking

18. Their eagerness is balanced by their anxiety to maintain their elegance, which would require staying calm and composed.

19. Captain Wentworth's words proved both his lack of love for Louisa and the probability of his continued love for Anne, but at this juncture she dares to think consciously only of the former point. On p. 352 she will finally acknowledge all.

20. The room being used for the concert is evidently the Ball Room, the largest room in the building (for they move into it from the Octagon Room, and later people are described as going to get tea, which would be served in the next largest room, the Tea Room—see diagram on p. 345).

21. These are Anne's words to herself. She is obviously trying to make the best of her disappointment at Captain Wentworth's disappearance.

22. Their behavior is similar to Elizabeth's in the previous chapter, when she wished to alert everyone in the shop to her being picked up by Lady Dalrymple's carriage.

on the broad back of the dowager[23] Viscountess Dalrymple before her, had nothing to wish for which did not seem within her reach; and Anne—but it would be an insult to the nature of Anne's felicity, to draw any comparison between it and her sister's; the origin of one all selfish vanity, of the other all generous attachment.[24]

Anne saw nothing, thought nothing of the brilliancy of the room.[25] Her happiness was from within. Her eyes were bright, and her cheeks glowed,—but she knew nothing about it. She was thinking only of the last half hour, and as they passed to their seats, her mind took a hasty range over it. His choice of subjects, his expressions, and still more his manner and look, had been such as she could see in only one light. His opinion of Louisa Musgrove's inferiority, an opinion which he had seemed solicitous to give, his wonder at Captain Benwick, his feelings as to a first, strong attachment,—sentences begun which he could not finish—his half averted eyes, and more than half expressive glance,—all, all declared that he had a heart returning to her at least; that anger, resentment, avoidance, were no more; and that they were succeeded, not merely by friendship and regard, but by the tenderness of the past; yes, some share of the tenderness of the past. She could not contemplate the change as implying less.— He must love her.[26]

These were thoughts, with their attendant visions, which occupied and flurried her too much to leave her any power of observation; and she passed along the room without having a glimpse of him, without even trying to discern him. When their places were determined on, and they were all properly arranged, she looked round to see if he should happen to be in the same part of the room, but he was not, her eye could not reach him; and the concert being just opening, she must consent for a time to be happy in an humbler way.

The party was divided, and disposed of on two contiguous benches: Anne was among those on the foremost, and Mr. Elliot had manœuvred so well, with the assistance of his friend Colonel Wallis, as to have a seat by her.[27] Miss Elliot, surrounded by her

23. *dowager:* see p. 281, note 25.

24. This is a rare editorial comment on the part of the author. Usually she allows her moral judgments to emerge from the story and dialogue or through the reflections of the characters.

25. The Assembly Rooms in which this scene occurs were elaborately decorated, and they would have plenty of illumination during events (this is what is principally meant by "brilliancy"). This would contrast with the dim lighting of most places at night, due to the high cost of candles or oil for lamps.

26. Anne has finally managed to compose her feelings enough to consider fully what Captain Wentworth told her and to register its ultimate implications.

27. This indicates both Mr. Elliot's continued interest in Anne and the willingness of Colonel Wallis to assist him in his designs. The full extent of Colonel Wallis's assistance will be revealed in the next chapter.

cousins, and the principal object of Colonel Wallis's gallantry,[28] was quite contented.

Anne's mind was in a most favourable state for the entertainment of the evening: it was just occupation enough: she had feelings for the tender, spirits for the gay, attention for the scientific,[29] and patience for the wearisome; and had never liked a concert better, at least during the first act. Towards the close of it, in the interval succeeding an Italian song,[30] she explained the words of the song to Mr. Elliot. — They had a concert bill[31] between them.

"This," said she, "is nearly the sense, or rather the meaning of the words, for certainly the sense of an Italian love-song must not be talked of,[32] — but it is as nearly the meaning as I can give; for I do not pretend to understand the language. I am a very poor Italian scholar."[33]

"Yes, yes, I see you are. I see you know nothing of the matter. You have only knowledge enough of the language, to translate at sight these inverted, transposed, curtailed Italian lines, into clear, comprehensible, elegant English. You need not say anything more of your ignorance. — Here is complete proof."

"I will not oppose such kind politeness; but I should be sorry to be examined by a real proficient."

"I have not had the pleasure of visiting in Camden-place so long," replied he, "without knowing something of Miss Anne Elliot; and I do regard her as one who is too modest, for the world in general to be aware of half her accomplishments, and too highly accomplished for modesty to be natural in any other woman."[34]

"For shame! for shame! — this is too much of flattery. I forget what we are to have next," turning to the bill.

"Perhaps," said Mr. Elliot, speaking low, "I have had a longer acquaintance with your character than you are aware of."

"Indeed! — How so? You can have been acquainted with it only since I came to Bath, excepting as you might hear me previously spoken of in my own family."

"I knew you by report long before you came to Bath. I had heard you described by those who knew you intimately. I have

28. *gallantry:* courteous attention of a man to a woman.

29. *scientific:* this probably means more sophisticated or complicated music, the type that would require more attention. A contemporary writer on Bath, Pierce Egan, speaks of the "scientific Linley" (referring to the composer Thomas Linley the Elder, 1733–1795). I have been unable to locate a more precise definition of the term as applied to music, but it is clearly intended to denote music that would represent a change from pieces that are predominantly tender or gay.

The program's variety would be normal. The ruling principle of concerts at the time was miscellany. They would contain a wide array of pieces, usually of different types, with both instrumental and vocal selections.

30. This would probably be a song from an Italian opera. Italian opera had long been very popular, such that even the operas of leading non-Italian composers of the previous century, such as Handel and Mozart, were usually in Italian. Excerpts from these operas were generally the main feature of concert programs.

31. The few surviving concert bills from Regency Bath include the words of the vocal music being performed (according to Piggott, *The Innocent Diversion*).

32. Many of the songs from Italian operas were love songs. The lyrics tended to consist of banal or extravagant expressions of tender affection, enhanced by several repetitions and considerable musical elaboration.

33. Languages were one of the principal subjects taught to girls at boarding schools, and Italian was, after French, the most popular language (girls would not learn Latin or Greek, which were central to boys' education at this time).

34. Mr. Elliot's smooth charm and flattery contrast with Captain Wentworth's words earlier, which were more open and heartfelt and often less polished.

been acquainted with you by character[35] many years. Your person,[36] your disposition,[37] accomplishments,[38] manner—they were all described, they were all present to me."

Mr. Elliot was not disappointed in the interest he hoped to raise. No one can withstand the charm of such a mystery. To have been described long ago to a recent acquaintance, by nameless people, is irresistible; and Anne was all curiosity. She wondered, and questioned him eagerly—but in vain. He delighted in being asked, but he would not tell.[39]

"No, no—some time or other perhaps, but not now. He would mention no names now; but such, he could assure her, had been the fact. He had many years ago received such a description of Miss Anne Elliot, as had inspired him with the highest idea of her merit, and excited the warmest curiosity to know her."

Anne could think of no one so likely to have spoken with partiality of her many years ago, as the Mr. Wentworth, of Monkford, Captain Wentworth's brother. He might have been in Mr. Elliot's company, but she had not courage to ask the question.

"The name of Anne Elliot," said he, "has long had an interesting sound to me. Very long has it possessed a charm over my fancy; and, if I dared, I would breathe my wishes that the name might never change."[40]

Such she believed were his words; but scarcely had she received their sound, than her attention was caught by other sounds immediately behind her, which rendered every thing else trivial. Her father and Lady Dalrymple were speaking.

"A well-looking man," said Sir Walter, "a very well-looking man."

"A very fine young man indeed!" said Lady Dalrymple. "More air[41] than one often sees in Bath.—Irish, I dare say."[42]

"No, I just know his name. A bowing acquaintance. Wentworth—Captain Wentworth of the navy.[43] His sister married my tenant in Somersetshire,—the Croft, who rents Kellynch."

Before Sir Walter had reached this point, Anne's eyes had caught the right direction, and distinguished Captain Wentworth, standing among a cluster of men at a little distance. As her eyes

35. *character:* reputation.

36. *person:* personal appearance.

37. *disposition:* inner character or tendencies.

38. *accomplishments:* a term frequently used for a woman's talents and knowledge. For more on what these accomplishments usually were, see p. 77, note 66.

39. Mr. Elliot's reasons for remaining silent, in addition to a wish to stimulate continued curiosity, are revealed in the next chapter.

40. In other words, he wishes she would become his wife, and thus always have the name of Elliot. He does not dare to say that explicitly, at least in part, because the etiquette of mourning dictates that he wait longer out of respect for his first wife. His increasingly fulsome compliments to Anne have already been leading in this direction, for such compliments were usually, in this society, an indication of serious feelings and intentions.

This moment is significant not just for the first open avowal of Mr. Elliot's hopes, but also for Anne's reaction. Rather than absorb the full import of his words, she is easily distracted by other sounds, and it turns out they relate to Captain Wentworth, thus ensuring that they seize all her attention.

41. *air:* stylish or impressive appearance.

42. Lady Dalrymple, living in Ireland herself, may be naturally inclined to think that an impressive-looking man is Irish.

43. Sir Walter and Elizabeth were earlier shown as being willing to grant at least a cold bow and curtsey to Captain Wentworth. Praise from Lady Dalrymple would make them even more favorably disposed toward him.

fell on him, his seemed to be withdrawn from her. It had that appearance. It seemed as if she had been one moment too late; and as long as she dared observe, he did not look again: but the performance was re-commencing, and she was forced to seem to restore her attention to the orchestra, and look straight forward.

When she could give another glance, he had moved away. He could not have come nearer to her if he would; she was so surrounded and shut in: but she would rather have caught his eye.

Mr. Elliot's speech too distressed her. She had no longer any inclination to talk to him. She wished him not so near her.

The first act was over.[44] Now she hoped for some beneficial change; and, after a period of nothing-saying amongst the party, some of them did decide on going in quest of tea.[45] Anne was one of the few who did not choose to move. She remained in her seat, and so did Lady Russell; but she had the pleasure of getting rid of Mr. Elliot; and she did not mean, whatever she might feel on Lady Russell's account, to shrink from conversation with Captain Wentworth, if he gave her the opportunity. She was persuaded by Lady Russell's countenance that she had seen him.

He did not come however. Anne sometimes fancied she discerned him at a distance, but he never came. The anxious interval wore away unproductively. The others returned, the room filled again, benches were reclaimed and re-possessed,[46] and another hour of pleasure or of penance was to be set out, another hour of music was to give delight or the gapes,[47] as real or affected taste for it prevailed.[48] To Anne, it chiefly wore the prospect of an hour of agitation. She could not quit that room in peace without seeing Captain Wentworth once more, without the interchange of one friendly look.

In re-settling themselves, there were now many changes, the result of which was favourable for her. Colonel Wallis declined sitting down again, and Mr. Elliot was invited by Elizabeth and Miss Carteret, in a manner not to be refused, to sit between them;[49] and by some other removals, and a little scheming of her own, Anne was enabled to place herself much nearer the end of

44. Thus the previous intervals, one that allowed for a lengthy conversation and for looking around and observing people, did not represent an actual intermission between acts. One characteristic of concerts then, as well as plays and operas, was a greater tolerance for speaking and moving around during the performance on the part of the spectators.

45. They went to the Tea Room (see p. 351, note 20; and the diagram on p. 345).

46. One reason for having benches at concerts was that most concerts at the time were held in venues also used for other purposes, as is the case here; thus seats that could be easily removed would be more practical.

47. *the gapes:* bouts of yawning.

48. The description suggests many spectators were not there for the sake of the music. Sir Walter and Elizabeth have already been described as coming for the sake of Lady Dalrymple; others have undoubtedly come because Bath concerts were a prominent part of the public social schedule, and, following the rules of that schedule, dances usually did not occur on concert nights. Moreover, taste for music could be a mark of social distinction, especially for women—hence the reference to "affected taste." *Emma, Pride and Prejudice,* and *Sense and Sensibility* all have snobbish female characters who profess great appreciation for music, even as their actions demonstrate the opposite.

49. Elizabeth, who has long been interested in Mr. Elliot, may be disturbed that he has been paying so much attention to Anne instead of herself.

the bench than she had been before, much more within reach of
a passer-by. She could not do so, without comparing herself with
Miss Larolles, the inimitable Miss Larolles,—but still she did it,
and not with much happier effect;[50] though by what seemed prosperity in the shape of an early abdication in her next neighbours,
she found herself at the very end of the bench before the concert
closed.

Such was her situation, with a vacant space at hand, when Captain Wentworth was again in sight. She saw him not far off. He
saw her too; yet he looked grave, and seemed irresolute, and only
by very slow degrees came at last near enough to speak to her. She
felt that something must be the matter. The change was indu-
bitable. The difference between his present air and what it had
been in the octagon room was strikingly great.—Why was it? She
thought of her father—of Lady Russell. Could there have been
any unpleasant glances? He began by speaking of the concert,
gravely; more like the Captain Wentworth of Uppercross;
owned[51] himself disappointed, had expected better singing; and,
in short, must confess that he should not be sorry when it was
over. Anne replied, and spoke in defence of the performance so
well, and yet in allowance for his feelings, so pleasantly, that his
countenance improved, and he replied again with almost a
smile.[52] They talked for a few minutes more; the improvement
held; he even looked down towards the bench, as if he saw a place
on it well worth occupying; when, at that moment, a touch on her
shoulder obliged Anne to turn round.—It came from Mr. Elliot.
He begged her pardon, but she must be applied to, to explain Italian again. Miss Carteret was very anxious to have a general idea of
what was next to be sung. Anne could not refuse; but never had
she sacrificed to politeness with a more suffering spirit.

A few minutes, though as few as possible, were inevitably con-
sumed; and when her own mistress again, when able to turn and
look as she had done before, she found herself accosted by Captain Wentworth, in a reserved yet hurried sort of farewell. "He
must wish her good night. He was going—he should get home as
fast as he could."[53]

50. Miss Larolles is a character in Frances (or Fanny) Burney's novel *Cecilia*; Burney was one of Jane Austen's favorite novelists, and she cites *Cecilia*, along with Burney's *Camilla* and Maria Edgeworth's *Belinda*, as leading examples of novels in her impassioned defense of the form in *Northanger Abbey*. Miss Larolles is a member of the fashionable London society that is satirized in *Cecilia*. She talks constantly and with great rapidity and lack of restraint, uses highly exaggerated expressions to describe everything, and contradicts herself frequently, especially in declaring how horrible she finds people or places or events that she simultaneously makes clear are precious to her.

The incident that forces the comparison upon Anne also occurs at a concert. Miss Larolles explains that she has moved to the outside of her bench to talk to passersby, with a particular hope of speaking to Mr. Meadows, the ultrafashionable young man whose attentions she continually seeks even as she just as continually complains of his extreme rudeness. She fails, however, in this object, furthering the parallel between her action and Anne's.

Anne's ready remembrance of the incident indicates how much of a reader she is, for it is only a brief, minor episode in a long novel.

51. *owned*: acknowledged.

52. Anne, as she did when Captain Wentworth first entered before the concert, is attempting to encourage him. This greater initiative, however limited, marks a significant change from the first half of the book, when she could do nothing but watch and wait and wonder what might be going through his mind. She will continue to play a more active role until the end.

53. His abrupt behavior here deepens the contrast already seen between him and the consummately polite Mr. Elliot. It is appropriate that, in the only scene in which the two men are both present for a sustained period, they should display such opposite characteristics.

"Is not this song worth staying for?" said Anne, suddenly struck by an idea which made her yet more anxious to be encouraging.

"No!" he replied impressively,[54] "there is nothing worth my staying for"; and he was gone directly.[55]

Jealousy of Mr. Elliot! It was the only intelligible motive. Captain Wentworth jealous of her affection![56] Could she have believed it a week ago[57]—three hours ago! For a moment the gratification was exquisite. But alas! there were very different thoughts to succeed. How was such jealousy to be quieted? How was the truth to reach him? How, in all the peculiar[58] disadvantages of their respective situations, would he ever learn her real sentiments? It was misery to think of Mr. Elliot's attentions.—Their evil was incalculable.[59]

54. *impressively*: in a manner that would make an impression.

55. *directly*: immediately.

56. This has completed the reversal of their situations: Captain Wentworth is now forced to suffer many of the same feelings Anne did when she saw him earlier with Louisa and Henrietta

57. Her encounter with Captain Wentworth in Molland's shop was exactly six days ago (see chronology, p. 490).

58. *peculiar*: particular.

59. One reason her fears are so great is that prevailing social rules would prevent her from establishing contact with him and thereby communicating her true feelings. An unmarried woman could not write to an unmarried man to whom she was not related, nor visit him, nor invite him to her home. Her father and sister, as the head and mistress of the household, could invite him, but, even with their lesser aversion toward him, there is no reason to assume they would do so, for the Elliots' social circles are clearly different from his. This also means Anne is unlikely to encounter him at any of the private parties she attends. Moreover, the Elliots' preference for such parties—the concert being a rare exception—means that Anne will seldom be at the public dances and entertainments where he is likely to spend his evenings.

In contrast, Mr. Elliot will have continual access to Anne, which means that reports of his attentions to her will continue reaching Captain Wentworth's ears. All this suggests a strong possibility that he might leave Bath, which is not his home after all, before he learns the truth about her affections.

Chapter Nine

Anne recollected with pleasure the next morning her promise of going to Mrs. Smith; meaning that it should engage her from home at the time when Mr. Elliot would be most likely to call; for to avoid Mr. Elliot was almost a first object.

She felt a great deal of good will towards him. In spite of the mischief[1] of his attentions, she owed him gratitude and regard, perhaps compassion. She could not help thinking much of the extraordinary circumstances attending their acquaintance; of the right which he seemed to have to interest her, by every thing in situation, by his own sentiments, by his early prepossession.[2] It was altogether very extraordinary.—Flattering, but painful. There was much to regret. How she might have felt, had there been no Captain Wentworth in the case, was not worth enquiry; for there was a Captain Wentworth: and be the conclusion of the present suspense good or bad, her affection would be his for ever. Their union, she believed, could not divide her more from other men, than their final separation.[3]

Prettier musings of high-wrought love and eternal constancy, could never have passed along the streets of Bath, than Anne was sporting with from Camden-place to Westgate-buildings.[4] It was almost enough to spread purification and perfume all the way.[5]

She was sure of a pleasant reception; and her friend seemed this morning particularly obliged to her for coming, seemed hardly to have expected her, though it had been an appointment.[6]

An account of the concert was immediately claimed; and Anne's recollections of the concert were quite happy enough to animate her features, and make her rejoice to talk of it. All that she could tell, she told most gladly; but the all was little for one who had been there, and unsatisfactory for such an enquirer as

1. *mischief:* harm.

2. *prepossession:* preconception in her favor. She is thinking of his having heard her praises before he met her.

3. This passage shows that Anne has completely rejected Mr. Elliot, even before the important revelations of the rest of this chapter. It also raises again the issue of constancy in love that will be so memorably discussed in the next-to-last chapter (pp. 442–446).

4. She would have a long time to do this, for the two streets are at opposite ends of Bath (see map, p. 516).

5. The wording of this paragraph suggests some irony toward Anne on the part of the author. It is notable that this, and a couple of exchanges with Mrs. Smith during which Anne seems to adopt a naively idealistic perspective (pp. 294 and 382), all occur in the later part of the novel, when Anne's fortunes have improved, and she does not need to be as much an object of sympathy.

6. At their last meeting, Mrs. Smith expressed doubt, just as Anne was leaving, about seeing her much in the future (p. 342).

Mrs. Smith, who had already heard, through the short cut of a laundress[7] and a waiter,[8] rather more of the general success and produce of the evening than Anne could relate; and who now asked in vain for several particulars of the company. Every body of any consequence or notoriety in Bath was well known by name to Mrs. Smith.

"The little Durands were there, I conclude," said she, "with their mouths open to catch the music; like unfledged sparrows ready to be fed. They never miss a concert."

"Yes. I did not see them myself, but I heard Mr. Elliot say they were in the room."

"The Ibbotsons—were they there? and the two new beauties, with the tall Irish officer,[9] who is talked of for one of them."

"I do not know.—I do not think they were."

"Old Lady Mary Maclean? I need not ask after her. She never misses, I know; and you must have seen her. She must have been in your own circle, for as you went with Lady Dalrymple, you were in the seats of grandeur; round the orchestra, of course."

"No, that was what I dreaded. It would have been very unpleasant to me in every respect. But happily Lady Dalrymple always chooses to be farther off; and we were exceedingly well placed— that is for hearing; I must not say for seeing, because I appear to have seen very little."

"Oh! you saw enough for your own amusement.—I can understand. There is a sort of domestic enjoyment to be known even in a crowd, and this you had. You were a large party in yourselves, and you wanted nothing beyond."

"But I ought to have looked about me more," said Anne, conscious while she spoke, that there had in fact been no want of looking about; that the object only had been deficient.

"No, no—you were better employed. You need not tell me that you had a pleasant evening. I see it in your eye. I perfectly see how the hours passed—that you had always something agreeable to listen to. In the intervals of the concert, it was conversation."

Anne half smiled and said, "Do you see that in my eye?"

7. *laundress:* this could refer to someone who worked for a particular house as a laundry maid or someone who took laundry from various families and washed it elsewhere. The latter was especially likely in towns, where people often lacked space for the elaborate laundry facilities required then to clean clothes.

8. The most likely explanation is that the waiter was at the concert and then told the laundress, who had dealings with Mrs. Smith or her landlady. Waiters and laundresses could easily know one another. Jane Austen often shows information being spread by such means, for while different social classes lived mostly separate lives, they would still have necessary business dealings with one another, and those in the poorer classes would be interested in those who employed them.

9. Irish officers were plentiful in both the navy and the army, especially the latter, where they were disproportionately represented. The principal reason was the greater poverty and more limited economic opportunities in Ireland, which made a military career more attractive.

"Yes, I do. Your countenance perfectly informs me that you were in company last night with the person, whom you think the most agreeable in the world, the person who interests you at this present time, more than all the rest of the world put together."

A blush overspread Anne's cheeks. She could say nothing.

"And such being the case," continued Mrs. Smith, after a short pause,[10] "I hope you believe that I do know how to value your kindness in coming to me this morning. It is really very good of you to come and sit with me, when you must have so many pleasanter demands upon your time."

Anne heard nothing of this. She was still in the astonishment and confusion excited by her friend's penetration, unable to imagine how any report of Captain Wentworth could have reached her. After another short silence—

"Pray," said Mrs. Smith, "is Mr. Elliot aware of your acquaintance with me? Does he know that I am in Bath?"

"Mr. Elliot!" repeated Anne, looking up surprised. A moment's reflection shewed her the mistake she had been under. She caught it instantaneously; and, recovering courage with the feeling of safety, soon added, more composedly, "are you acquainted with Mr. Elliot?"

"I have been a good deal acquainted with him," replied Mrs. Smith, gravely, "but it seems worn out now. It is a great while since we met."

"I was not at all aware of this. You never mentioned it before. Had I known it, I would have had the pleasure of talking to him about you."

"To confess the truth," said Mrs. Smith, assuming her usual air of cheerfulness, "that is exactly the pleasure I want you to have. I want you to talk about me to Mr. Elliot. I want your interest[11] with him. He can be of essential service to me; and if you would have the goodness, my dear Miss Elliot,[12] to make it an object to yourself, of course it is done."

"I should be extremely happy—I hope you cannot doubt my willingness to be of even the slightest use to you," replied Anne;

10. Mrs. Smith pauses because she thinks her guess, one she fears to be true, has just been confirmed. She will soon learn its falsity.

11. *interest:* personal influence.

12. Mrs. Smith will continue to address her as "my dear Miss Elliot" throughout the conversation. Social rules dictated that, despite their friendliness, they would not use first names, for they had no family connections (Lady Russell uses Anne's first name, but she is a longtime friend of Anne's mother who has preserved a strong intimacy with the Elliot family). Mrs. Smith, however, could indicate her affection by adding "dear," often used at the time when addressing people.

"but I suspect that you are considering me as having a higher claim on Mr. Elliot—a greater right to influence him, than is really the case. I am sure you have, somehow or other, imbibed such a notion. You must consider me only as Mr. Elliot's relation. If in that light, if there is any thing which you suppose his cousin might fairly ask of him, I beg you would not hesitate to employ me."

Mrs. Smith gave her a penetrating glance, and then smiling, said,

"I have been a little premature, I perceive. I beg your pardon. I ought to have waited for official information.[13] But now, my dear Miss Elliot, as an old friend, do give me a hint as to when I may speak. Next week? To be sure by next week I may be allowed to think it all settled, and build my own selfish schemes on Mr. Elliot's good fortune."

"No," replied Anne, "nor next week, nor next, nor next. I assure you that nothing of the sort you are thinking of will be settled any week. I am not going to marry Mr. Elliot. I should like to know why you imagine I am."

Mrs. Smith looked at her again, looked earnestly, smiled, shook her head, and exclaimed,

"Now, how I do wish I understood you! How I do wish I knew what you were at! I have a great idea that you do not design to be cruel, when the right moment comes. Till it does come, you know, we women never mean to have any body. It is a thing of course among us, that every man is refused—till he offers. But why should you be cruel?[14] Let me plead for my—present friend I cannot call him—but for my former friend. Where can you look for a more suitable match? Where could you expect a more gentlemanlike, agreeable man? Let me recommend Mr. Elliot. I am sure you hear nothing but good of him from Colonel Wallis; and who can know him better than Colonel Wallis?"[15]

"My dear Mrs. Smith,[16] Mr. Elliot's wife has not been dead much above half a year.[17] He ought not to be supposed to be paying his addresses to[18] any one."

13. Mrs. Smith means an official announcement of their engagement.

14. She means cruel to Mr. Elliot, by rebuffing him even though she welcomes his advances. Deliberate cruelty toward lovers, especially rejecting someone simply to force him to woo and plead more fervently, was a stratagem often attributed to women. One character in *Pride and Prejudice*, Mr. Collins, absurdly persists in believing that a clear rejection of his proposal by the heroine must be a deceptive ploy on her part.

15. This plea for Mr. Elliot will cause much questioning by Anne later.

16. *My dear Mrs. Smith:* Anne, here and elsewhere, uses the same formal but affectionate style of address as Mrs. Smith.

17. The appropriate mourning period for a spouse was generally a year (see p. 301, note 53).

18. *paying his addresses to:* courting (for the purpose of marriage).

"Oh! if these are your only objections," cried Mrs. Smith, archly, "Mr. Elliot is safe, and I shall give myself no more trouble about him. Do not forget me when you are married, that's all. Let him know me to be a friend of yours, and then he will think little of the trouble required, which it is very natural for him now, with so many affairs and engagements of his own, to avoid and get rid of as he can—very natural, perhaps. Ninety-nine out of a hundred would do the same.[19] Of course, he cannot be aware of the importance to me. Well, my dear Miss Elliot, I hope and trust you will be very happy. Mr. Elliot has sense to understand the value of such a woman. Your peace will not be shipwrecked as mine has been. You are safe in all worldly matters,[20] and safe in his character. He will not be led astray, he will not be misled by others to his ruin."

"No," said Anne, "I can readily believe all that of my cousin. He seems to have a calm, decided temper, not at all open to dangerous impressions. I consider him with great respect. I have no reason, from any thing that has fallen within my observation, to do otherwise. But I have not known him long; and he is not a man, I think, to be known intimately soon. Will not this manner of speaking of him, Mrs. Smith, convince you that he is nothing to me? Surely, this must be calm enough. And, upon my word, he is nothing to me. Should he ever propose to me (which I have very little reason to imagine he has any thought of doing),[21] I shall not accept him. I assure you I shall not. I assure you Mr. Elliot had not the share which you have been supposing, in whatever pleasure the concert of last night might afford:—not Mr. Elliot; it is not Mr. Elliot that—"

She stopped, regretting with a deep blush that she had implied so much; but less would hardly have been sufficient. Mrs. Smith would hardly have believed so soon in Mr. Elliot's failure, but from the perception of there being a somebody else. As it was, she instantly submitted, and with all the semblance of seeing nothing beyond; and Anne, eager to escape farther notice, was impatient to know why Mrs. Smith should have fancied she was to marry

19. Mrs. Smith's words indicate her cynical attitude. Her casual dismissal of Anne's statement about mourning may reflect the same; in contrast, Lady Russell, while wishing Anne to marry Mr. Elliot, still displays respect for the need to wait the appropriate period of time.

20. *worldly matters*: this refers particularly to finances, social standing, and other practical or material matters.

21. This is an odd statement, considering the degree of attention Mr. Elliot has shown her, and his declaration that he wished her name always to remain the same (p. 356). The text did state that she only believed those to be his words, her attention being distracted at that moment. It is possible that her wish that they had not been said, along with her focus on Captain Wentworth, made her blot them from her mind. It is also possible Anne's modesty makes her loath to avow openly that a man who has not proposed is interested in her. Moreover, already fearing the effects of Captain Wentworth's belief in her attachment to Mr. Elliot, she may be trying to avoid any statement that, through the inevitable circulation of gossip, could give support to that belief.

Mr. Elliot, where she could have received the idea, or from whom she could have heard it.

"Do tell me how it first came into your head."

"It first came into my head," replied Mrs. Smith, "upon finding how much you were together, and feeling it to be the most probable thing in the world to be wished for by every body belonging to either of you; and you may depend upon it that all your acquaintance have disposed of you in the same way.[22] But I never heard it spoken of till two days ago."

"And has it indeed been spoken of?"

"Did you observe the woman who opened the door to you, when you called yesterday?"

"No. Was not it Mrs. Speed, as usual, or the maid? I observed no one in particular."[23]

"It was my friend, Mrs. Rooke—Nurse Rooke, who, by the by, had a great curiosity to see you, and was delighted to be in the way to let you in. She came away from Marlborough-buildings[24] only on Sunday; and she it was who told me you were to marry Mr. Elliot. She had had it from Mrs. Wallis herself,[25] which did not seem bad authority. She sat an hour with me on Monday evening, and gave me the whole history."[26]

"The whole history!" repeated Anne, laughing. "She could not make a very long history, I think, of one such little article of unfounded news."

Mrs. Smith said nothing.

"But," continued Anne, presently, "though there is no truth in my having this claim on Mr. Elliot, I should be extremely happy to be of use to you, in any way that I could. Shall I mention to him your being in Bath? Shall I take any message?"

"No, I thank you: no, certainly not. In the warmth of the moment, and under a mistaken impression, I might, perhaps, have endeavoured to interest you in some circumstances. But not now: no, I thank you, I have nothing to trouble you with."

"I think you spoke of having known Mr. Elliot many years?"

"I did."

22. Friendly, intimate conversation between an unmarried man and woman could lead quickly to expectations of marriage in this society (for more, see 463, note 86). These expectations would be strengthened here by general knowledge of Anne's good character and Mr. Elliot's charm and by the extreme suitability of the match for her, for she has arrived at an age when a woman's chances of marriage were fading rapidly, and Mr. Elliot, a man already rich and in line to inherit the Kellynch property and a baronetcy, would be far superior, from a social and financial perspective, to anything Anne could normally expect in her situation.

23. Anne's thinking the woman, in fact the nurse, might be the maid indicates the low status of nurses then, for people's social level at the time was indicated by their dress and manner. That even such a generous person as Anne took little notice of her also indicates how much servants, for persons of Anne's class, existed in the background, taken for granted and only occasionally the object of serious attention, unless one was the mistress of a household, responsible for supervising their labor.

24. *Marlborough-buildings:* the residence of the Wallises. See also p. 263, note 21.

25. Mrs. Wallis has already been identified as the wife of Mr. Elliot's friend. At the time Anne arrived in Bath, she was about to give birth. That nurse Rooke "came away . . . only on Sunday" means that she stopped attending Mrs. Wallis only then. It was standard for wealthy women giving birth to hire a monthly nurse, someone who arrived just before the delivery and attended the mother through her confinement. For Mrs. Wallis and confinement, see p. 267, note 37. It is now approximately a month and a half since Anne arrived in Bath (see chronology, p. 489), so Mrs. Wallis's confinement has been around five weeks, a normal period. Its end will be marked by her appearance, in a few days, at a party of the Elliots (see p. 468).

26. This means that Mrs. Smith heard this before she expressed doubt about the continuation of her friendship with Anne (p. 342), for that occurred on the day of the concert (a Wednesday—see chronology, p. 491).

"Not before he married, I suppose?"

"Yes; he was not married when I knew him first."

"And—were you much acquainted?"

"Intimately."

"Indeed! Then do tell me what he was at that time of life. I have a great curiosity to know what Mr. Elliot was as a very young man. Was he at all such as he appears now?"

"I have not seen Mr. Elliot these three years," was Mrs. Smith's answer, given so gravely that it was impossible to pursue the subject farther; and Anne felt that she had gained nothing but an increase of curiosity. They were both silent—Mrs. Smith very thoughtful. At last,

"I beg your pardon, my dear Miss Elliot," she cried, in her natural[27] tone of cordiality, "I beg your pardon for the short answers I have been giving you, but I have been uncertain what I ought to do. I have been doubting and considering as to what I ought to tell you. There were many things to be taken into the account. One hates to be officious, to be giving bad impressions, making mischief. Even the smooth surface of family-union seems worth preserving, though there may be nothing durable beneath. However, I have determined; I think I am right; I think you ought to be made acquainted with Mr. Elliot's real character. Though I fully believe that, at present, you have not the smallest intention of accepting him, there is no saying what may happen. You might, some time or other, be differently affected towards him. Hear the truth, therefore, now, while you are unprejudiced. Mr. Elliot is a man without heart or conscience; a designing, wary, cold-blooded being, who thinks only of himself; who, for his own interest or ease, would be guilty of any cruelty, or any treachery, that could be perpetrated without risk of his general character. He has no feeling for others. Those whom he has been the chief cause of leading into ruin, he can neglect and desert without the smallest compunction. He is totally beyond the reach of any sentiment of justice or compassion. Oh! he is black at heart, hollow and black!"[28]

27. *natural*: normal.

28. Mrs. Smith's language is highly melodramatic, an appropriate beginning for what is certainly the most melodramatic part of the novel.

Anne's astonished air, and exclamation of wonder, made her pause, and in a calmer manner she added,

"My expressions startle you. You must allow[29] for an injured, angry woman. But I will try to command myself. I will not abuse him. I will only tell you what I have found him. Facts shall speak. He was the intimate friend of my dear husband,[30] who trusted and loved him, and thought him as good as himself. The intimacy had been formed before our marriage. I found them most intimate friends; and I, too, became excessively pleased with Mr. Elliot, and entertained the highest opinion of him. At nineteen, you know, one does not think very seriously, but Mr. Elliot appeared to me quite as good as others, and much more agreeable than most others, and we were almost always together. We were principally in town,[31] living in very good style. He was then the inferior in circumstances, he was then the poor one; he had chambers in the Temple,[32] and it was as much as he could do to support the appearance of a gentleman.[33] He had always a home with us whenever he chose it; he was always welcome; he was like a brother. My poor Charles, who had the finest, most generous spirit in the world, would have divided his last farthing[34] with him; and I know that his purse[35] was open to him; I know that he often assisted him."

"This must have been about that very period of Mr. Elliot's life," said Anne, "which has always excited my particular curiosity. It must have been about the same time that he became known to my father and sister. I never knew him myself, I only heard of him, but there was a something in his conduct then with regard to my father and sister, and afterwards in the circumstances of his marriage, which I never could quite reconcile with present times. It seemed to announce a different sort of man."

"I know it all, I know it all," cried Mrs. Smith. "He had been introduced to Sir Walter and your sister before I was acquainted with him, but I heard him speak of them for ever. I know he was invited and encouraged, and I know he did not choose to go. I can satisfy you, perhaps, on points which you would little expect; and

29. *allow*: make allowance.

30. While "dear" is used in many contexts in Jane Austen's novels, this is the only time it is prefixed to "husband" or "wife." Mrs. Smith's usage may be an attempt, conscious or unconscious, to reaffirm her affection for him, for she is telling a story that does not reflect well on his judgment or on the position he left her in after his death.

31. *town*: London.

32. This means he was attending either the Inner Temple or the Middle Temple; they, along with Gray's Inn and Lincoln's Inn, constituted the four Inns of Court that qualified people for the bar, i.e., to be practicing barristers. Each Inn required five years' attendance, or three years for university graduates. The only specific requirement during that time was to go to a minimum number of dinners held at the Inn: the idea was that this would give the student a chance to associate with others in the legal world, including established barristers connected with the Inn. Otherwise students were on their own to pick up what knowledge they could, either by reading or by observing and assisting practicing lawyers.

33. At this time a gentleman would be distinguished by significant external characteristics. The most obvious would be the quality of his clothing: it was expected that a gentleman, like a lady, would always dress in a manner marking his status. A gentleman was also expected to live in a luxurious home in a good part of town, to have servants to attend him, to travel in carriages rather than by foot, and to spend money freely and generously. Those who failed to do these things would quickly be identified and, if they were too derelict, be scorned socially.

This would be a problem for those studying the law, for many were in pinched circumstances. Enrollment at one of the Inns required a fee, and living in London cost even more. Mr. Elliot's circumstances suggest that, while he may have inherited or received some money from his parents, it was not a large amount. This could help account for the ambition he displays.

34. A farthing is the smallest unit of English money. It is one-fourth of a pence, which in turn is one-twelfth of a shilling, or one–two hundred and fortieth of a pound. In Jane Austen's novels it is mentioned only as part of expressions like these, in which it signifies the smallest possible sum.

35. *purse*: monetary funds or resources.

as to his marriage, I knew all about it at the time. I was privy to all the fors and againsts, I was the friend to whom he confided his hopes and plans, and though I did not know his wife previously, (her inferior situation in society, indeed, rendered that impossible)[36] yet I knew her all her life afterwards, or, at least, till within the last two years of her life, and can answer any question you wish to put."

"Nay," said Anne, "I have no particular enquiry to make about her. I have always understood they were not a happy couple. But I should like to know why, at that time of his life, he should slight my father's acquaintance as he did. My father was certainly disposed to take very kind and proper notice of him. Why did Mr. Elliot draw back?"

"Mr. Elliot," replied Mrs. Smith, "at that period of his life, had one object in view—to make his fortune, and by a rather quicker process than the law.[37] He was determined to make it by marriage. He was determined, at least, not to mar it by an imprudent marriage; and I know it was his belief, (whether justly or not, of course I cannot decide) that your father and sister, in their civilities and invitations, were designing a match between the heir and the young lady; and it was impossible that such a match should have answered his ideas of wealth and independance.[38] That was his motive for drawing back, I can assure you. He told me the whole story. He had no concealments with me. It was curious, that having just left you behind me in Bath, my first and principal acquaintance on marrying, should be your cousin; and that, through him, I should be continually hearing of your father and sister. He described one Miss Elliot, and I thought very affectionately of the other."

"Perhaps," cried Anne, struck by a sudden idea, "you sometimes spoke of me to Mr. Elliot?"

"To be sure I did, very often. I used to boast of my own Anne Elliot, and vouch for your being a very different creature from—" She checked herself just in time.[39]

"This accounts for something which Mr. Elliot said last night," cried Anne. "This explains it. I found he had been used to hear of

36. Mrs. Smith came from a genteel background. She could not otherwise have attended a boarding school that Sir Walter would let one of his children attend. This meant she would not have socialized with someone of significantly lower status, for while current mores urged courtesy and affability between people of different levels, they discouraged real intimacy.

37. Mr. Elliot's decision first to pursue and then to abandon the law would make sense given both his own character and the nature of a legal career then. The bar, meaning the upper reaches of the law, was probably the most popular of the genteel professions for those, like Mr. Elliot, interested in wealth, for some who pursued it attained great riches, along with a corresponding fame and prestige. Moreover, while connections would be helpful, success could be attained purely through talent.

Yet this success was highly uncertain. The law was often depicted as a lottery, for barristers were largely on their own to drum up business, and many failed completely. Even those who succeeded might have to endure a long period of deprivation first. Aspiring lawyers like Mr. Elliot, if they wished to have a decent chance of success, also needed to master large amounts of material that even successful lawyers admitted to be dry and tedious, and to do so without formal teaching or institutional guidance. They did this while residing in London, which meant they were constantly being tempted away from work by the extraordinary array of diversions the city offered. All this could operate as a powerful spur for a man like Mr. Elliot to opt for a different path to affluence.

38. *independance:* financial independence. A marriage with Elizabeth would have given him a dowry of ten thousand pounds (that is the amount later identified as Anne's dowry, p. 474, and daughters were almost always given the same dowry). That would be a good sum, but not enough by itself to provide a truly affluent income. It is also probable that he would have been required, before the marriage, to sign a settlement giving an annual sum to his wife for her own private expenses, called pin money, and a guarantee of money to be given to any children of his. These were standard parts of marriage agreements among the landed classes.

Mr. Elliot ultimately married a woman from a commercial family, which normally did not use strict settlements. This meant he would not be bound by such restrictions, and that the father of the bride, unlike many landowners, could endow her with as great a sum as he wished and ensure it was in readily available cash. This made such brides more attractive to many men of the time seeking fortunes (for more, see p. 383, note 45).

39. Mrs. Smith knows that Anne would be distressed to hear her sister disparaged, however much Anne herself would be aware of its just nature.

me. I could not comprehend how. What wild imaginations one forms, where dear self is concerned! How sure to be mistaken! But I beg your pardon; I have interrupted you. Mr. Elliot married, then, completely for money? The circumstance, probably, which first opened your eyes to his character."

Mrs. Smith hesitated a little here. "Oh! those things are too common. When one lives in the world,[40] a man or woman's marrying for money is too common to strike one as it ought. I was very young, and associated only with the young, and we were a thoughtless, gay set, without any strict rules of conduct. We lived for enjoyment. I think differently now; time and sickness, and sorrow, have given me other notions; but, at that period, I must own I saw nothing reprehensible in what Mr. Elliot was doing. 'To do the best for himself,' passed as a duty."

"But was not she a very low[41] woman?"

"Yes; which I objected to, but he would not regard. Money, money, was all that he wanted. Her father was a grazier,[42] her grandfather had been a butcher,[43] but that was all nothing. She was a fine[44] woman, had had a decent education, was brought forward by some cousins, thrown by chance into Mr. Elliot's company,[45] and fell in love with him; and not a difficulty or a scruple was there on his side, with respect to her birth. All his caution was spent in being secured of the real amount of her fortune, before he committed himself.[46] Depend upon it, whatever esteem Mr. Elliot may have for his own situation in life now, as a young man he had not the smallest value for it. His chance of the Kellynch estate was something, but all the honour of the family he held as cheap as dirt. I have often heard him declare, that if baronetcies were saleable, any body should have his for fifty pounds, arms and motto, name and livery included;[47] but I will not pretend to repeat half that I used to hear him say on that subject. It would not be fair. And yet you ought to have proof; for what is all this but assertion? and you shall have proof."

"Indeed, my dear Mrs. Smith, I want none," cried Anne. "You have asserted nothing contradictory to what Mr. Elliot appeared to be some years ago. This is all in confirmation, rather, of what

40. *in the world:* in fashionable society.

41. *low:* of inferior social rank; or coarse and vulgar in her behavior and culture. The usual assumption in this society was that the two meanings went together.

42. *grazier:* someone who grazes and feeds cattle for the market.

43. A butcher was a humble profession. In contrast, a grazier, who owned cattle, would have some wealth. Thus the father had already risen relative to the grandfather, though, logically, in the same general business of beef.

44. *fine:* very good-looking.

45. The history of this woman and her family exhibits a standard process of social climbing in this society. Earlier generations have advanced economically, to the point that the family could afford to send a daughter to a fine school, where she would acquire higher-class education, manners, and speech—and possibly friendships in that sphere. She could then be introduced to someone from a high-ranking family who needed money and was willing to overlook her origins for the sake of an ample dowry. This process happened most often with a wife from a lower background, for while money could come from either spouse, social standing came principally from the husband, since a wife took on his status, as would any children of theirs. The main anomaly in this case is the speed of the family's rise: usually one's poorer ancestors needed to be more generations in the past before one could truly be accepted or considered as a marriage partner. Only Mr. Elliot's desperation for money made him overlook her immediate origins, while others, like Anne and Mrs. Smith here and Sir Walter earlier, show an acute awareness of them.

46. Frequently the fortunes of potential marriage partners were widely known. Throughout Jane Austen's novels characters speak openly, and knowledgeably, of the precise fortunes of others, especially those who are unmarried. But in this case, unlike others, the bride was from a completely different social circle, so her situation was less likely to be known. Mr. Elliot may have attempted not only to find out what her father intended to settle on her, but also to persuade that father, under threat of not marrying her, to increase the amount. Marriage normally involved a detailed legal agreement about the financial contributions and benefits of each side, and hard bargaining about the exact terms could precede the agreement.

47. The Elliot arms and motto were part of their listing in the baronetage (p. 4); high-ranking families would generally have them (for more on arms, see p. 299, note 44). Liveries were also specific to families (see p. 41, note 39).

we used to hear and believe. I am more curious to know why he should be so different now?"

"But for my satisfaction; if you will have the goodness to ring for Mary[48]—stay, I am sure you will have the still greater goodness of going yourself into my bed-room, and bringing me the small inlaid box[49] which you will find on the upper shelf of the closet."[50]

Anne, seeing her friend to be earnestly bent on it, did as she was desired. The box was brought and placed before her, and Mrs. Smith, sighing over it as she unlocked it, said,

"This is full of papers belonging to him, to my husband, a small portion only of what I had to look over when I lost him. The letter I am looking for, was one written by Mr. Elliot to him before our marriage, and happened to be saved; why, one can hardly imagine. But he was careless and immethodical, like other men, about those things;[51] and when I came to examine his papers, I found it with others still more trivial from different people scattered here and there, while many letters and memorandums[52] of real importance had been destroyed. Here it is. I would not burn it, because being even then very little satisfied with Mr. Elliot, I was determined to preserve every document of former intimacy. I have now another motive for being glad that I can produce it."

This was the letter, directed to "Charles Smith, Esq.[53] Tunbridge Wells,"[54] and dated from London, as far back as July, 1803.

"Dear Smith,

"I have received yours. Your kindness almost overpowers me. I wish nature had made such hearts as yours more common, but I have lived three and twenty years in the world, and have seen none like it. At present, believe me, I have no need of your services, being in cash again.[55] Give me joy: I have got rid of Sir Walter and Miss.[56] They are gone back to Kellynch, and almost made me swear to visit them this summer, but my first visit to Kellynch will be with a surveyor,[57] to tell me how to bring it with best advantage to the hammer.[58] The baronet, nevertheless, is not unlikely to marry again; he is quite fool enough. If he does, however, they will leave

48. Mary's being called only by her first name indicates she is a servant; Mrs. Smith's residence was earlier described as having one (p. 293, note 17). As for ringing, Mrs. Smith could be referring to a pulley attached by wires to bells in the servants' quarters, as existed in better houses (see p. 71, note 44), or, in such a modest rooming house, she could simply mean a bell sitting on a table.

49. An inlaid box had ornamentation of some type embedded in its surface. Putting such ornamentation on boxes was a standard decorative activity of genteel ladies, the sort that Mrs. Smith might have been taught in the school she attended with Anne.

Portable locked boxes — and Mrs. Smith is shortly described as unlocking this one — were widely used at this time for storing valuables and personal items. They were especially common for those renting lodgings, who needed to worry not only about theft but also about the inquisitiveness of the landlady or landlord and other lodgers.

50. A closet then usually meant a small room.

51. Mrs. Smith may speak of other men also being careless as a way of deflecting blame from her husband, whom she obviously cherishes despite the distress that his folly and negligence have brought upon her.

52. *memorandums:* notes and records, especially to help remember things.

53. Esquire is an informal title often assumed by gentlemen (see p. 3, note 4).

54. Tunbridge Wells is a town south of London, named for wells supplying mineral waters considered beneficial for health. By the eighteenth century it had developed into one of the most popular spa and resort towns in England, one that was particularly favored by the nobility. Mr. Smith's being there — and at the height of its summer season, when it was noted for its high prices — gives proof of the heedless life of pleasure Mrs. Smith has already mentioned, one that led to her current poverty.

55. This sentence neatly summarizes Mr. Elliot's attitude to his friend.

56. *Miss:* Miss Elliot, i.e., Elizabeth. The abbreviated usage is probably meant to be derogatory.

57. *surveyor:* someone who examines houses, land, or other property in order to calculate their value.

58. *bring it . . . to the hammer:* sell it by auction (the phrase comes from a small hammer used by auctioneers to indicate a sale). Thus his plan is not to destroy the property but to sell it, once he learns how he can obtain the best price. Usually the heir to a landed estate was prevented from selling by the

me in peace, which may be a decent equivalent for the reversion.[59]
He is worse than last year.

*"I wish I had any name but Elliot. I am sick of it. The name of
Walter I can drop, thank God! and I desire you will never insult me
with my second W. again, meaning, for the rest of my life, to be only
yours truly,*

WM. ELLIOT."[60]

Such a letter could not be read without putting Anne in a glow;
and Mrs. Smith, observing the high colour in her face, said,

"The language, I know, is highly disrespectful. Though I have
forgot the exact terms, I have a perfect impression of the general
meaning. But it shews you the man. Mark his professions to my
poor husband. Can any thing be stronger?"[61]

Anne could not immediately get over the shock and mortification of finding such words applied to her father.[62] She was obliged
to recollect that her seeing the letter was a violation of the laws of
honour,[63] that no one ought to be judged or to be known by such
testimonies, that no private correspondence could bear the eye of
others, before she could recover calmness enough to return the
letter which she had been meditating over, and say,

"Thank you. This is full proof undoubtedly, proof of every
thing you were saying. But why be acquainted with us now?"

"I can explain this too," cried Mrs. Smith, smiling.

"Can you really?"

"Yes. I have shewn you Mr. Elliot, as he was a dozen years ago,
and I will shew him as he is now. I cannot produce written proof
again, but I can give as authentic oral testimony as you can desire,
of what he is now wanting, and what he is now doing. He is no
hypocrite now. He truly wants to marry you. His present attentions to your family are very sincere, quite from the heart. I will
give you my authority; his friend Colonel Wallis."

"Colonel Wallis! are you acquainted with him?"

"No. It does not come to me in quite so direct a line as that; it
takes a bend or two, but nothing of consequence. The stream is as

strict settlement governing the estate. But such a settlement needed to be renewed each generation, by having the current holder and the next in line, once the latter came of age, unite to break the entail dictating the succession and form a new one. This usually happened automatically when the heir was a son, bound to his father by both natural deference and current financial dependence. But a more distant heir like Mr. Elliot would not be so bound, especially if, as is certainly true here, he feels contempt for the current holder. Moreover, such an heir was less likely to feel beholden to the family traditions urging the preservation of its patrimony, and thus more willing to sell the estate for the sake of immediate gain. In Mr. Elliot's case, having procured a fortune by other means and become recently interested in the title he is to inherit, he may have abandoned by now his plan to sell Kellynch.

59. The reversion is Mr. Elliot's inheritance of the Kellynch estate, if Sir Walter dies without a male heir. If Sir Walter did marry and produce a son, he would supersede Mr. Elliot, thereby depriving the latter of the estate.

60. It is certainly very convenient that Mrs. Smith happens to possess a letter that so fully reveals Mr. Elliot's opinions of Sir Walter and Elizabeth. One might question the plausibility of this letter. It certainly reveals a different Mr. Elliot from the calm, careful, calculating man who has appeared so far, and who spoke of his concern for gentility even when young (p. 271, note 52). But it is possible to imagine that during those years Mr. Elliot was not always worried about gentility, especially in the face he showed to a close friend, and that, harboring strong feelings about Sir Walter, he was happy to express them to this friend with great frankness, perhaps inspired further by some youthful bravado in exhibiting contempt for his high-ranking relations and indifference to his possible inheritance. Moreover, his overwhelming focus on his immediate financial needs could make him somewhat heedless of any money he was likely to receive only after many years have passed.

61. The two women, despite their sympathy with each other, still have different thoughts aroused by the letter, Anne thinking of its strictures against her father and Mrs. Smith of what it reveals about the writer's insincerity toward her husband.

62. Anne's mortification demonstrates the power of family feeling in this society: despite knowing the good reasons for such a low opinion of her father, it still shocks and pains her to see them openly expressed.

63. Such laws would dictate not spying into other people's private communications without their permission. The good characters in Jane Austen are extremely scrupulous about such matters. For example, the heroine of *Pride and Prejudice* purposefully leaves the room to avoid being exposed to information that is supposed to remain a secret, even though this information would be of great importance to her.

good as at first; the little rubbish it collects in the turnings, is easily moved away. Mr. Elliot talks unreservedly to Colonel Wallis of
his views on you—which said Colonel Wallis I imagine to be in
himself a sensible, careful, discerning sort of character; but
Colonel Wallis has a very pretty silly wife, to whom he tells things
which he had better not, and he repeats it all to her. She, in the
overflowing spirits of her recovery,[64] repeats it all to her nurse;[65]
and the nurse, knowing my acquaintance with you, very naturally
brings it all to me. On Monday evening my good friend Mrs.
Rooke let me thus much into the secrets of Marlborough-
buildings. When I talked of a whole history therefore, you see, I
was not romancing[66] so much as you supposed."

"My dear Mrs. Smith, your authority is deficient. This will not
do. Mr. Elliot's having any views on me will not in the least
account for the efforts he made towards a reconciliation with my
father. That was all prior to my coming to Bath. I found them on
the most friendly terms when I arrived."

"I know you did; I know it all perfectly, but—"

"Indeed, Mrs. Smith, we must not expect to get real information in such a line. Facts or opinions which are to pass through
the hands of so many, to be misconceived by folly in one, and
ignorance in another, can hardly have much truth left."

"Only give me a hearing. You will soon be able to judge of the
general credit due, by listening to some particulars which you can
yourself immediately contradict or confirm. Nobody supposes
that you were his first inducement. He had seen you indeed,
before he came to Bath and admired you, but without knowing it
to be you. So says my historian at least. Is this true? Did he see you
last summer or autumn, 'somewhere down in the west,' to use her
own words, without knowing it to be you?"

"He certainly did. So far it is very true. At Lyme; I happened to
be at Lyme."

"Well," continued Mrs. Smith triumphantly, "grant my friend
the credit due to the establishment of the first point asserted. He
saw you then at Lyme, and liked you so well as to be exceedingly
pleased to meet with you again in Camden-place, as Miss Anne

64. Her recovery from childbirth. A woman at this time would have even stronger reasons than now for "overflowing spirits" (i.e., exuberance). First, she and her baby had survived: cases in which one or both died were a regular occurrence (Jane Austen refers to both in letters). Second, since women were valued for procreation more than anything, a successful mother gained social prestige and, in many cases, greater approval from her husband and other members of her family.

65. For the nurse, and childbirth and recovery, see p. 375, note 25.

66. *romancing*: exaggerating or inventing in the manner of romances. A "romance" at the time meant a story that was remote from ordinary life, whether in its setting, in the incidents of its plot, or in the nature of its characters; it did not necessarily mean a story centered around love, though love was frequently an important element. For centuries most works of imaginative literature had been, broadly speaking, romances of this type. The rise of the novel in the eighteenth century introduced large numbers of stories set in current society, with characters such as one might normally meet and plots that could plausibly happen in ordinary life. Commentators of the time remarked on the novelty and importance of this literary development. At the same time, romances still existed and were often popular.

Jane Austen always preferred stories that were not romances. She did, however, receive a suggestion to write one. James Stanier Clarke, librarian to the Prince Regent, who had corresponded with her about dedicating *Emma* to the prince (the latter was a great fan of her novels), mentioned in a subsequent letter that he had been appointed secretary to the Prince of Cobourg, and he suggested for her next publication that "any Historical Romance illustrative of the History of the august house of Cobourg, would just now be very interesting." Jane Austen, after thanking him politely, wrote, "I am fully sensible that an Historical Romance founded on the House of Saxe Cobourg might be much more to the purpose of Profit or Popularity, than such pictures of domestic Life in Country Villages as I deal in—but I could no more write a Romance than an Epic Poem.—I could not sit seriously down to write a serious Romance under any other motive than to save my Life, & if it were indispensable for me to keep it up & never relax into laughing at myself or other people, I am sure I should be hung before I had finished the first Chapter" (April 1, 1816). When Clarke persisted in offering suggestions for a future novel her response was to compose, for her own amusement, a "Plan for a Novel" that ridicules his suggestions by sketching a story in which the various absurdities of romances are taken to ridiculous extremes.

One irony of the use of the term "romancing" at this juncture is that Mrs. Smith's tragic story of her husband and Mr. Elliot, and the coincidence of her knowing him and being able to share such thorough information with Anne, brings this episode closer to the implausible contrivances of a romance than almost anything else in Jane Austen's novels.

Elliot, and from that moment, I have no doubt, had a double motive in his visits there. But there was another, and an earlier; which I will now explain. If there is any thing in my story which you know to be either false or improbable, stop me. My account states, that your sister's friend, the lady now staying with you, whom I have heard you mention, came to Bath with Miss Elliot and Sir Walter as long ago as September, (in short when they first came themselves) and has been staying there ever since; that she is a clever, insinuating, handsome woman, poor and plausible,[67] and altogether such in situation[68] and manner,[69] as to give a general idea among Sir Walter's acquaintance, of her meaning to be Lady Elliot, and as general a surprise that Miss Elliot should be apparently blind to the danger."[70]

Here Mrs. Smith paused a moment; but Anne had not a word to say, and she continued,

"This was the light in which it appeared to those who knew the family, long before your return to it; and Colonel Wallis had his eye upon your father enough to be sensible[71] of it, though he did not then visit in Camden-place; but his regard for Mr. Elliot gave him an interest in watching all that was going on there,[72] and when Mr. Elliot came to Bath for a day or two, as he happened to do a little before Christmas,[73] Colonel Wallis made him acquainted with the appearance of things, and the reports beginning to prevail.—Now you are to understand that time had worked a very material change in Mr. Elliot's opinions as to the value of a baronetcy. Upon all points of blood and connexion, he is a completely altered man. Having long had as much money as he could spend, nothing to wish for on the side of avarice or indulgence, he has been gradually learning to pin his happiness upon the consequence[74] he is heir to. I thought it coming on, before our acquaintance ceased, but it is now a confirmed feeling. He cannot bear the idea of not being Sir William. You may guess therefore that the news he heard from his friend, could not be very agreeable, and you may guess what it produced; the resolution of coming back to Bath as soon as possible, and of fixing[75] himself here for a time, with the view of renewing his former

67. *plausible*: ingratiating, pleasing, agreeable.

68. *situation*: this could be referring to her social position, which would make a marriage with Sir Walter such an advancement, or to her situation in his household, which gives her the opportunity to win his affections.

69. *manner*: behavior, demeanor (toward Sir Walter).

70. Elizabeth would be in particular danger because a wife of Sir Walter would displace Elizabeth as mistress of the house, the one who manages its affairs and has the power of deciding who is invited there. It also would displace her as the leading person in her father's affections.

71. *sensible*: aware, cognizant.

72. This would be plausible given the small scale of Bath society (see p. 338 especially for further indications of this).

73. Mr. Elliot was mentioned earlier as stopping briefly in Bath after the stop in Lyme where he first saw Anne (p. 260). He had explained to Sir Walter that he failed to visit only because, being in Bath a mere twenty-four hours, he had lacked the time or opportunity. This account suggests that he might have had a little more time than that, and it was really lack of interest that made him stay away.

74. *consequence*: social position, distinction.

75. *fixing*: settling.

acquaintance and recovering such a footing in the family, as
might give him the means of ascertaining the degree of his danger, and of circumventing the lady if he found it material.[76] This
was agreed upon between the two friends, as the only thing to be
done; and Colonel Wallis was to assist in every way that he could.
He was to be introduced, and Mrs. Wallis was to be introduced,
and every body was to be introduced.[77] Mr. Elliot came back
accordingly; and on application was forgiven, as you know, and re-
admitted into the family; and there it was his constant object, and
his only object (till your arrival added another motive) to watch
Sir Walter and Mrs. Clay. He omitted no opportunity of being
with them, threw himself in their way, called at all hours—but I
need not be particular on this subject. You can imagine what an
artful man would do; and with this guide, perhaps, may recollect
what you have seen him do."

"Yes," said Anne, "you tell me nothing which does not accord
with what I have known, or could imagine. There is always something offensive in the details of cunning. The manœuvres of selfishness and duplicity must ever be revolting, but I have heard
nothing which really surprises me. I know those who would be
shocked by such a representation of Mr. Elliot, who would have
difficulty in believing it; but I have never been satisfied. I have
always wanted some other motive for his conduct than
appeared.—I should like to know his present opinion, as to the
probability of the event he has been in dread of; whether he considers the danger to be lessening or not."

"Lessening, I understand," replied Mrs. Smith. "He thinks Mrs.
Clay afraid of him, aware that he sees through her, and not daring
to proceed as she might do in his absence. But since he must be
absent some time or other, I do not perceive how he can ever be
secure, while she holds her present influence. Mrs. Wallis has an
amusing idea, as nurse tells me, that it is to be put into the marriage articles[78] when you and Mr. Elliot marry, that your father is
not to marry Mrs. Clay. A scheme, worthy of Mrs. Wallis's understanding, by all accounts; but my sensible nurse Rooke sees the
absurdity of it.—"Why, to be sure, ma'am," said she, "it would not

76. *material:* essential, necessary. Thus his entire presence in Bath stems from his design to separate Sir Walter and Mrs. Clay.

77. It was Colonel Wallis's sympathetic explanation of Mr. Elliot's marriage that persuaded Sir Walter to drop his resentment regarding it (p. 262). Colonel Wallis was just shown at the concert assisting Mr. Elliot's attempts to gain a seat next to Anne (p. 352).

78. The marriage articles were the specific provisions of the legal agreement drawn up by the bride's and groom's respective families before a marriage. The agreement centered around the financial contributions and obligations of each side. Provisions like the one Mrs. Wallis imagines would not be part of the articles, which is why Mrs. Smith calls the scheme one worthy of Mrs. Wallis's (limited) understanding, or intelligence.

prevent his marrying any body else." And indeed, to own the truth, I do not think nurse in her heart is a very strenuous opposer of Sir Walter's making a second match. She must be allowed to be a favourer of matrimony you know, and (since self will intrude) who can say that she may not have some flying visions of attending the next Lady Elliot, through Mrs. Wallis's recommendation?"[79]

"I am very glad to know all this," said Anne, after a little thoughtfulness. "It will be more painful to me in some respects to be in company with him, but I shall know better what to do. My line of conduct will be more direct. Mr. Elliot is evidently a disingenuous, artificial, worldly[80] man, who has never had any better principle to guide him than selfishness."

But Mr. Elliot was not yet done with. Mrs. Smith had been carried away from her first direction,[81] and Anne had forgotten, in the interest of her own family concerns, how much had been originally implied against him; but her attention was now called to the explanation of those first hints, and she listened to a recital which, if it did not perfectly justify the unqualified bitterness of Mrs. Smith, proved him to have been very unfeeling in his conduct towards her, very deficient both in justice and compassion.

She learned that (the intimacy between them continuing unimpaired by Mr. Elliot's marriage) they had been as before always together, and Mr. Elliot had led his friend into expenses much beyond his fortune.[82] Mrs. Smith did not want to take blame to herself, and was most tender of throwing any on her husband; but Anne could collect[83] that their income had never been equal to their style of living, and that from the first, there had been a great deal of general and joint extravagance.[84] From his wife's account of him, she could discern Mr. Smith to have been a man of warm feelings, easy temper,[85] careless habits, and not strong understanding,[86] much more amiable[87] than his friend, and very unlike him—led by him, and probably despised by him.[88] Mr. Elliot, raised by his marriage to great affluence, and disposed to every gratification of pleasure and vanity which could be commanded without involving[89] himself, (for with all his self-

79. Nurse Rooke would naturally favor matrimony—which at that time almost always involved at least the attempt to have children—from a wish for more opportunities to work as a monthly nurse for women giving birth. She would be especially likely to find such employment from affluent women, as any wife of Sir Walter would be. In a letter Jane Austen shows the importance of recommendations when she writes of someone getting a nurse who, though with "no particular charm either of person or manner," is pronounced by local people "to be the best nurse that ever was" (Nov. 17, 1798).

80. *worldly:* devoted to the affairs of this world (in a pejorative sense); interested in success and money.

81. *direction:* course or line of discussion.

82. Most wealthy people then got their fortunes through inheriting them. Thus if someone like Mr. Smith spent beyond his means he could easily exhaust that fortune, with limited means of remedying his situation.

83. *collect:* gather.

84. This suggests that Mrs. Smith bears some of the responsibility for her distress, and that may be one reason she is so keen to throw all the blame on Mr. Elliot. Anne's reaction to the history indicates that, as bad as Mr. Elliot's treatment of his friend was, he was not the only one at fault.

85. *easy temper:* thoughtless disposition; one that was averse to taking trouble.

86. *understanding:* intellect, mind.

87. *amiable:* kind, good-natured.

88. The above letter from Mr. Elliot to Mr. Smith suggests a relationship in which the former regularly asked for, and received, money from the latter.

89. *involving:* entangling, creating difficulties for. In other words, Mr. Elliot was happy to engage in any gratification that did not cost him anything or land him in any trouble.

indulgence he had become a prudent man) and beginning to be rich, just as his friend ought to have found himself to be poor,[90] seemed to have had no concern at all for that friend's probable finances, but, on the contrary, had been prompting and encouraging expenses, which could end only in ruin.[91] And the Smiths accordingly had been ruined.

The husband had died just in time to be spared the full knowledge of it. They had previously known embarrassments[92] enough to try the friendship of their friends, and to prove that Mr. Elliot's had better not be tried; but it was not till his death that the wretched state of his affairs was fully known. With a confidence in Mr. Elliot's regard, more creditable to his feelings than his judgment, Mr. Smith had appointed him the executor of his will;[93] but Mr. Elliot would not act, and the difficulties and distresses which this refusal had heaped on her, in addition to the inevitable sufferings of her situation,[94] had been such as could not be related without anguish of spirit, or listened to without corresponding indignation.

Anne was shewn some letters of his on the occasion, answers to urgent applications from Mrs. Smith, which all breathed the same stern resolution of not engaging in a fruitless trouble, and, under a cold civility, the same hard-hearted indifference to any of the evils it might bring on her. It was a dreadful picture of ingratitude and inhumanity; and Anne felt at some moments, that no flagrant open crime could have been worse. She had a great deal to listen to; all the particulars of past sad scenes, all the minutiæ of distress upon distress, which in former conversations had been merely hinted at, were dwelt on now with a natural indulgence. Anne could perfectly comprehend the exquisite relief, and was only the more inclined to wonder at the composure of her friend's usual state of mind.

There was one circumstance in the history of her grievances of particular irritation. She had good reason to believe that some property of her husband in the West Indies,[95] which had been for many years under a sort of sequestration[96] for the payment of its own incumbrances,[97] might be recoverable by proper measures;

90. *ought to have found himself to be poor:* should have perceived that he was becoming poor.

91. Mr. Elliot might have particularly encouraged Mr. Smith in expenses, such as lavish entertaining and dining or travel to fashionable resorts, whose fruits Mr. Elliot could have also enjoyed.

92. *embarrassments:* financial difficulties.

93. Mr. Smith could have appointed Mrs. Smith; a woman had the right to be an executor, or, more precisely, executrix.

94. This refers to her severe illness (see p. 288).

95. Britain had many colonies in the West Indies, which tended to be very profitable from the cultivation and sale of sugar. The plantations there were worked by slave labor, so there is a good chance that Mr. Smith's property included slaves. It is not certain if Jane Austen meant this to be significant: the issue of the slave trade, whose recent abolition in Britain had been a major political issue, is mentioned in both *Mansfield Park* and *Emma*, and the former novel includes a character with substantial property in the West Indies. A letter of hers, in which she refers admiringly to a book by Thomas Clarkson, one of the leaders of the movement to ban the trade, suggests that she sympathized with the movement (Jan. 24, 1813). At the same time, her letters do not suggest a strong interest in politics, and in the above-mentioned "Plan for a Novel" (see p. 389, note 66), she ridicules the idea of making a novel a vehicle for political speechifying.

The most likely reason, from the perspective of the story, for having the property be in the West Indies is that its distance would add to the difficulties Mrs. Smith suffers in recovering it. Moreover, if this property were in Britain, it might not even be hers to recover, for most landed property there was bound by entails that caused it, on the death of its current holder, to descend to the next male relative. A man, however, could bequeath nonentailed property completely to his widow, as Mr. Smith has apparently done.

96. *sequestration:* the appropriation of income from a property.

97. An incumbrance, or encumbrance, is a claim on property. What this probably means is that Mr. Smith's debts related to this property, while not causing him to lose it, had given creditors the right to appropriate the income.

and this property, though not large, would be enough to make her comparatively rich. But there was nobody to stir in it. Mr. Elliot would do nothing, and she could do nothing herself, equally disabled from personal exertion by her state of bodily weakness,[98] and from employing others by her want of money.[99] She had no natural connexions[100] to assist her even with their counsel, and she could not afford to purchase the assistance of the law. This was a cruel aggravation of actually streightened means.[101] To feel that she ought to be in better circumstances, that a little trouble in the right place might do it, and to fear that delay might be even weakening her claims, was hard to bear!

It was on this point that she had hoped to engage Anne's good offices with Mr. Elliot. She had previously, in the anticipation of their marriage, been very apprehensive of losing her friend by it; but on being assured that he could have made no attempt of that nature, since he did not even know her to be in Bath, it immediately occurred, that something might be done in her favour by the influence of the woman he loved, and she had been hastily preparing to interest Anne's feelings, as far as the observances due to Mr. Elliot's character would allow,[102] when Anne's refutation of the supposed engagement changed the face of every thing, and while it took from her the new-formed hope of succeeding in the object of her first anxiety, left her at least the comfort of telling the whole story her own way.

After listening to this full description of Mr. Elliot, Anne could not but express some surprise at Mrs. Smith's having spoken of him so favourably in the beginning of their conversation. "She had seemed to recommend and praise him!"

"My dear," was Mrs. Smith's reply, "there was nothing else to be done. I considered your marrying him as certain, though he might not yet have made the offer, and I could no more speak the truth of him, than if he had been your husband. My heart bled for you, as I talked of happiness. And yet, he is sensible, he is agreeable, and with such a woman as you, it was not absolutely hopeless. He was very unkind to his first wife. They were wretched together. But she was too ignorant and giddy for respect, and he

98. Mrs. Smith would not have been prevented from taking legal action because she is a woman. Married women at this time suffered serious legal restrictions, for in the eyes of the law they were considered part of their husbands. But single women and widows could act independently.

99. Lawyers collected fees according to which specific services they rendered, with the fees being regulated by the government. The fees were not necessarily exorbitant—many, in addition to the wealthy, hired lawyers—but they certainly would add up in a complicated suit, as Mrs. Smith's sounds like it could be. In addition, contingent fees, allowing someone with no money to hire a lawyer on the basis of anticipated winnings, were not legal at this time.

100. *natural connexions:* connections, i.e. relations, by blood. Her relations by her marriage may not be good candidates for assisting her, since, if they exist, they might resent Mr. Smith's having left her all his property—many men left a substantial portion of their fortunes to other family members instead of leaving it all to the widow. In an unfinished novel by Jane Austen, *The Watsons,* one man condemns a relative of the family for leaving all his fortune to his widow.

101. *streightened means:* straitened, i.e., inadequate, monetary resources.

102. She was planning to reveal her history, and her predicament about Mr. Smith's property, while concealing, as much as possible, anything that might reflect badly on Mr. Elliot's character, or reputation. She presumably could not have avoided mentioning his failure to act as executor, but she might have attributed it to a misunderstanding or to his being distracted by other matters.

had never loved her. I was willing to hope that you must fare better."[103]

Anne could just acknowledge within herself such a possibility of having been induced to marry him, as made her shudder at the idea of the misery which must have followed. It was just possible that she might have been persuaded by Lady Russell![104] And under such a supposition, which would have been most miserable, when time had disclosed all, too late?

It was very desirable that Lady Russell should be no longer deceived;[105] and one of the concluding arrangements of this important conference, which carried them through the greater part of the morning,[106] was, that Anne had full liberty to communicate to her friend every thing relative to Mrs. Smith, in which his conduct was involved.

103. Mrs. Smith's excuse is a feeble one. Having hardly heard Anne mention Mr. Elliot, and never with any special affection, she had no reason to imagine her deeply in love. Nor would she have reason, from her knowledge of Anne, recently strengthened by their conversations, to believe that Anne would either crave the social advantages of a match with Mr. Elliot or simply accede to the possible wishes of her family. Her willingness to visit Mrs. Smith, despite the latter's poverty and unfashionable location, already testifies to Anne's independence of mind and lack of concern with rank. All this, and her knowledge of Anne's good sense and strict principles, would give Mrs. Smith sufficient reason to expect Anne to heed information regarding Mr. Elliot's bad character, especially when backed by the proof of Mr. Elliot's letter.

One possible explanation is that Mrs. Smith's cynicism, seen at various points, has made her assume that anyone, even someone who seems as high-minded as Anne, would automatically seize the chance at a marriage that is socially and financially advantageous. Another is that this cynicism, along with the desperation of her circumstances, has made her willing to sacrifice her friend to her own interest in having access to Mr. Elliot. A final explanation is that the episode is not plausible and exists only to provide otherwise unavailable information about Mr. Elliot. Many commentators have pointed to this subplot as the weakest element in the novel and speculated that, had Jane Austen's health permitted her to revise the novel more thoroughly, she would have substantially altered and improved this aspect of the story.

104. This shows the potentially tragic turn the story could have taken, due to Lady Russell's excessive regard for social rank. It also shows the significance of Anne's clear rejection of Mr. Elliot before Captain Wentworth's reappearance, for her decision indicated how much she had learned the lesson of not being too persuadable and had learned over the years to judge well for herself.

105. She thinks only of undeceiving Lady Russell, and not her father, even though the latter has established much greater intimacy with Mr. Elliot. Anne may fear that he would not listen, or she may believe that the truth about Mr. Elliot's feelings toward Sir Walter and reasons for recently seeking reconciliation would be so painful and embarrassing for Sir Walter that it would be better to spare him the knowledge.

106. This would be much of the day, for at this time "morning" referred to the entire day until dinner, which was usually around four or five o'clock.

Chapter Ten

A nne went home to think over all that she had heard. In one
point, her feelings were relieved by this knowledge of Mr.
Elliot.[1] There was no longer any thing of tenderness due to him.
He stood, as opposed[2] to Captain Wentworth, in all his own
unwelcome obtrusiveness; and the evil of his attentions last night,
the irremediable mischief he might have done, was considered
with sensations unqualified, unperplexed.[3]—Pity for him was all
over. But this was the only point of relief. In every other respect,
in looking around her, or penetrating forward,[4] she saw more to
distrust and to apprehend.[5] She was concerned for the disappointment and pain Lady Russell would be feeling, for the mortifications which must be hanging over her father and sister, and had
all the distress of foreseeing many evils, without knowing how to
avert any one of them.—She was most thankful for her own
knowledge of him. She had never considered herself as entitled to
reward for not slighting an old friend like Mrs. Smith, but here
was a reward indeed springing from it!—Mrs. Smith had been
able to tell her what no one else could have done. Could the
knowledge have been extended through her family!—But this was
a vain idea. She must talk to Lady Russell, tell her, consult with
her, and having done her best, wait the event[6] with as much composure as possible; and after all, her greatest want[7] of composure
would be in that quarter of the mind which could not be opened
to Lady Russell, in that flow of anxieties and fears which must be
all to herself.[8]

She found, on reaching home, that she had, as she intended,
escaped seeing Mr. Elliot; that he had called and paid them a
long morning visit; but hardly had she congratulated herself, and
felt safe till to-morrow, when she heard that he was coming again
in the evening.

1. Anne's relief signals another result of the revelations about Mr. Elliot, which is that they have confirmed the complete correctness of her preference for Captain Wentworth. He has turned out to be far superior to Mr. Elliot, and far more suitable for Anne. This unambiguous affirmation of the rightness of the romantic hero for the heroine is also a feature of Jane Austen's other novels. In each case the charming seducer who, like Mr. Elliot, tempts the heroine is ultimately proven to be completely wrong for her, whether because of fatal defects of character or because of prior involvement with another woman.

2. *opposed*: opposite, contrary.

3. *unperplexed*: not confused or uncertain.

4. *penetrating forward*: discerning what is to come.

5. *apprehend*: anticipate with fear or dread.

6. *event*: result.

7. *want*: lack.

8. Meaning her anxieties relating to Captain Wentworth.

"I had not the smallest intention of asking him," said Elizabeth, with affected carelessness, "but he gave so many hints; so Mrs. Clay says, at least."

"Indeed I do say it. I never saw any body in my life spell[9] harder for an invitation. Poor man! I was really in pain for him; for your hard-hearted sister, Miss Anne, seems bent on cruelty."[10]

"Oh!" cried Elizabeth, "I have been rather too much used to the game to be soon overcome by a gentleman's hints.[11] However, when I found how excessively he was regretting that he should miss my father this morning, I gave way immediately, for I would never really omit an opportunity of bringing him and Sir Walter together. They appear to so much advantage in company with each other! Each behaving so pleasantly! Mr. Elliot looking up with so much respect!"[12]

"Quite delightful!" cried Mrs. Clay, not daring, however, to turn her eyes towards Anne.[13] "Exactly like father and son! Dear Miss Elliot,[14] may I not say father and son?"

"Oh! I lay no embargo[15] on any body's words. If you will have such ideas! But, upon my word, I am scarcely sensible of his attentions being beyond those of other men."

"My dear Miss Elliot!" exclaimed Mrs. Clay, lifting up her hands and eyes, and sinking all the rest of her astonishment in a convenient silence.

"Well, my dear Penelope,[16] you need not be so alarmed about him. I did invite him, you know. I sent him away with smiles. When I found he was really going to his friends at Thornberry-park[17] for the whole day to-morrow, I had compassion on him."[18]

Anne admired[19] the good acting of the friend, in being able to shew such pleasure as she did, in the expectation, and in the actual arrival of the very person whose presence must really be interfering with her prime object. It was impossible but that Mrs. Clay must hate the sight of Mr. Elliot; and yet she could assume a most obliging, placid look, and appear quite satisfied with the curtailed license of devoting herself only half as much to Sir Walter as she would have done otherwise.

To Anne herself it was most distressing to see Mr. Elliot enter

9. *spell*: intimate or hint at one's desire.

10. For the idea of female cruelty in rebuffing lovers, see p. 371, note 14.

11. Elizabeth means the game of flirtation, specifically the male practice of pretending affection for a woman simply to have the fun of rousing her interest. The idea of this as common practice is, like that of female cruelty, found in various writings of the period, especially in conduct books warning women of the dangers posed by seductive men. At the same time, social rules of the time meant that such men needed to be careful, for if they were too explicit in expressing interest in a woman, they could find themselves committed to her in the eyes of others and obligated, by social pressure or even legal action, to marry her (for more, see p. 465, note 91). This is why Elizabeth suggests that someone as experienced as she is knows to ignore mere hints, which, since they would not commit a man, could be freely dropped.

12. Elizabeth's description is not only ironic in the light of what has just been revealed about Mr. Elliot and his true feelings and designs regarding Sir Walter, but it also suggests, in her insistence on inviting Mr. Elliot, that, despite her above avowal of indifference, she is eager to see him for her own sake. Supposed concern for Mr. Elliot and her father simply provides a good cover. She will continue this pretense as she denies noticing Mr. Elliot's attentions and explains that she invites him purely out of compassion.

13. This suggests that Mrs. Clay, who was just described by Mrs. Smith as suspecting that Mr. Elliot sees through her designs, also probably suspects Anne of discerning at least some of her motives. She is certainly shrewd enough to perceive how much more intelligent Anne is than Elizabeth.

14. *Dear Miss Elliot*: This indicates both her aspiration to close friendship with Elizabeth and the latter's tolerance of that (for Mrs. Clay would not dare use such an intimate designation if she did not know Elizabeth approved).

15. *embargo*: prohibition.

16. Elizabeth reciprocates the show of friendship with "my dear," while, by using only a first name, she confirms Mrs. Clay's social inferiority.

17. *Thornberry-park*: no place with that name has been clearly identified. It is likely the author simply made it up as a plausible destination for Mr. Elliot: the houses of wealthy landowners were often called "Park" (as in the place that provides the setting and the title of *Mansfield Park*).

18. See note 22, below, for this journey. It is hard to see how compassion would demand inviting him because he would be gone for a single day.

19. *admired*: marveled at.

the room; and quite painful to have him approach and speak to her. She had been used before to feel that he could not be always quite sincere, but now she saw insincerity in every thing. His attentive deference to her father, contrasted with his former language, was odious; and when she thought of his cruel conduct towards Mrs. Smith, she could hardly bear the sight of his present smiles and mildness, or the sound of his artificial good sentiments. She meant to avoid any such alteration of manners as might provoke a remonstrance on his side. It was a great object with her to escape all enquiry or eclat;[20] but it was her intention to be as decidedly cool to him as might be compatible with their relationship, and to retrace, as quietly as she could, the few steps of unnecessary intimacy she had been gradually led along. She was accordingly more guarded, and more cool, than she had been the night before.

He wanted to animate her curiosity again as to how and where he could have heard her formerly praised; wanted very much to be gratified by more solicitation; but the charm was broken: he found that the heat and animation of a public room were necessary to kindle his modest cousin's vanity; he found, at least, that it was not to be done now, by any of those attempts which he could hazard among the too-commanding claims of the others.[21] He little surmised that it was a subject acting now exactly against his interest, bringing immediately into her thoughts all those parts of his conduct which were least excusable.

She had some satisfaction in finding that he was really going out of Bath the next morning, going early, and that he would be gone the greater part of two days. He was invited again to Camden-place the very evening of his return; but from Thursday to Saturday evening his absence was certain.[22] It was bad enough that a Mrs. Clay should be always before her; but that a deeper hypocrite should be added to their party, seemed the destruction of every thing like peace and comfort. It was so humiliating to reflect on the constant deception practised on her father and Elizabeth; to consider the various sources of mortification preparing for them! Mrs. Clay's selfishness was not so complicate[23] nor so

20. *eclat*: public sensation or notice; scenes that would attract notice.

21. In a general gathering like this, he must pay frequent attention to the others and cannot devote all his efforts to conversing with Anne, as he had been able to do at the concert, where the others were often distracted by all that was happening.

22. The wording here is misleading. It is currently Thursday evening (the concert was on Wednesday evening, and Anne spent most of this day with Mrs. Smith). Thus, Mr. Elliot will really be absent on Friday and Saturday, or, as stated in the preceding sentence, "the greater part of two days." For more on the sequence of events, which can be plotted more precisely for the end of the novel than for any previous section, see chronology, p. 491.

23. *complicate*: intricate; difficult to understand or unravel.

revolting as his;[24] and Anne would have compounded for[25] the marriage at once, with all its evils, to be clear of Mr. Elliot's subtleties, in endeavouring to prevent it.

On Friday morning she meant to go very early to Lady Russell, and accomplish the necessary communication; and she would have gone directly after breakfast but that Mrs. Clay was also going out on some obliging purpose of saving her sister trouble, which determined her to wait till she might be safe from such a companion. She saw Mrs. Clay fairly off, therefore, before she began to talk of spending the morning in Rivers-street.

"Very well," said Elizabeth, "I have nothing to send but my love. Oh! you may as well take back that tiresome book she would lend me, and pretend I have read it through. I really cannot be plaguing myself for ever with all the new poems[26] and states of the nation[27] that come out. Lady Russell quite bores one with her new publications. You need not tell her so, but I thought her dress[28] hideous the other night. I used to think she had some taste in dress, but I was ashamed of her at the concert. Something so formal and *arrangé*[29] in her air! and she sits so upright![30] My best love, of course."

"And mine," added Sir Walter. "Kindest regards. And you may say, that I mean to call upon her soon. Make a civil message. But I shall only leave my card.[31] Morning visits are never fair by[32] women at her time of life, who make themselves up so little.[33] If she would only wear rouge,[34] she would not be afraid of being seen; but last time I called, I observed the blinds were let down immediately."

While her father spoke, there was a knock at the door. Who could it be? Anne, remembering the preconcerted visits, at all hours, of Mr. Elliot, would have expected him, but for his known engagement seven miles off. After the usual period of suspense, the usual sounds of approach were heard, and "Mr. and Mrs. Charles Musgrove" were ushered into the room.

Surprise was the strongest emotion raised by their appearance; but Anne was really glad to see them; and the others were not so sorry but that they could put on a decent air of welcome; and as

24. Hers is easier to unravel because she is simply trying to get Sir Walter to propose to her; his intrigue to prevent such a marriage necessarily involves more intricate and subtle maneuvers. As for why her design is less revolting, one reason is that trying to achieve a marriage, even one considered socially unsuitable by most people, is an inherently more honorable course than trying to foil others' possible marriage simply to secure one's inheritance. Another is that Mrs. Clay's modest means and need to support two children makes her scrambling for money more understandable than the efforts of the wealthy and childless Mr. Elliot to attain even greater wealth and a title. Finally, while both are practicing deception, his is more pronounced. Her professions of friendship mask only a wish to become even more intimate with the family than she acknowledges. His professions of regard mask a complete lack of interest, and perhaps complete contempt.

25. *compounded for:* accepted, agreed to.

26. Poetry was very popular at this time, with poems often outselling novels. For more, see p. 193, notes 58–62.

27. *states of the nation:* books about current affairs. That this and poetry seem to constitute the principal types of books read by Lady Russell indicates her serious and thoughtful tastes.

28. *dress:* attire. The term then referred to everything one was wearing, not to the principal garment worn by women (which was called a gown). Hence there are also references in Jane Austen to the dress of a man.

29. *arrangé:* French for "arranged." It likely has a connotation of overly studied.

30. Contemporary standards emphasized the virtue of sitting upright; lolling on a sofa or bed, unless one was sick or elderly, was frowned upon. Lady Russell's apparent propensity for sitting upright indicates her highly correct manners, a point underlined by having someone as formal and as concerned with manners and appearance as Elizabeth call her excessive in this regard.

31. Visiting cards, in addition to being used to introduce oneself and establish contact, could be used to indicate one had called on an acquaintance.

32. *fair by:* fair to. "By" is used elsewhere where we would now use "to."

33. Because "morning" then meant most of the day, he is basically saying one should not visit her when daylight allows one to see her well—existing means of artificial light provided only dim illumination.

34. Rouge was sometimes used by women at this time. In the eighteenth

soon as it became clear that these, their nearest relations, were not arrived with any views of accommodation in that house, Sir Walter and Elizabeth were able to rise in cordiality, and do the honours of it very well. They were come to Bath for a few days with Mrs. Musgrove, and were at the White Hart.[35] So much was pretty soon understood; but till Sir Walter and Elizabeth were walking Mary into the other drawing-room,[36] and regaling[37] themselves with her admiration, Anne could not draw upon Charles's brain for a regular history of their coming, or an explanation of some smiling hints of particular business, which had been ostentatiously dropped by Mary, as well as of some apparent confusion as to whom their party consisted of.[38]

She then found that it consisted of Mrs. Musgrove, Henrietta, and Captain Harville, beside their two selves. He gave her a very plain, intelligible account of the whole; a narration in which she saw a great deal of most characteristic proceeding. The scheme had received its first impulse by Captain Harville's wanting to come to Bath on business. He had begun to talk of it a week ago; and by way of doing something, as shooting was over,[39] Charles

Exterior of the Pump Room (street lamps are from a later period).

[From Mowbray Aston Green, *The Eighteenth Century Architecture of Bath* (Bath, 1904), p. 196]

century cosmetics, including rouge, had been popular, especially among very wealthy and fashionable women, as well as among some men. By the early nineteenth century cosmetics had begun to fall out of favor, though many still used them discreetly. A principal reason was the growing taste for a simpler and more natural look, in clothing and hairstyles as well as facial appearance. A popular beauty guide from 1811, *The Mirror of Graces*, advocates such a look and strenuously denounces white makeup, widely used in the previous century. The author does say, however, that rouge, because it simply replicates the natural redness of the cheeks, can be *tolerated*, though not recommended, when it comes to women who have lost that natural redness. Lady Russell might be among those who take an even stricter view, though we cannot know whether she actually uses no cosmetics—almost anyone might fall short of the mark there in Sir Walter's eyes—or whether, if she does not, it results from disapproval or from simple unwillingness to take the trouble.

35. *White Hart*: one of the leading inns in Bath at the time. It was on Stall Street, opposite the Pump Room (see p. 423, note 85) in the center of Bath (see map, p. 515). The facing picture was made near the former location of the White Hart.

36. They would normally receive guests, especially just two guests, in only one drawing room, but since they wish to show off their possessions to Charles and Mary they are now taking them to the other drawing room.

37. *regaling*: gratifying or delighting.

38. Mary presumably likes to play with revealing information about a wedding, which the news turns out to be. At the same time, her disapproval of Charles Hayter, the groom in one wedding, may make her reluctant to reveal much about it, and this could account for the confusion described.

39. The official shooting season for the two principal game birds, partridges and pheasants, extended from September 1 until January 31. There was a strong taboo among country gentlemen against killing birds out of season, a taboo reinforced by a fine of 5 pounds, a substantial sum, per bird killed.

had proposed coming with him, and Mrs. Harville had seemed to like the idea of it very much, as an advantage to her husband;[40] but Mary could not bear to be left, and had made herself so unhappy about it that, for a day or two, every thing seemed to be in suspense, or at an end. But then, it had been taken up by his father and mother. His mother had some old friends in Bath, whom she wanted to see;[41] it was thought a good opportunity for Henrietta to come and buy wedding-clothes for herself and her sister;[42] and, in short, it ended in being his mother's party, that every thing might be comfortable and easy to Captain Harville; and he and Mary were included in it, by way of general convenience. They had arrived late the night before. Mrs. Harville, her children, and Captain Benwick, remained with Mr. Musgrove and Louisa at Uppercross.

Anne's only surprise was, that affairs should be in forwardness[43] enough for Henrietta's wedding-clothes to be talked of: she had imagined such difficulties of fortune to exist there as must prevent the marriage from being near at hand; but she learned from Charles that, very recently, (since Mary's last letter to herself) Charles Hayter had been applied to by a friend to hold a living for a youth who could not possibly claim it under many years;[44] and that, on the strength of this present income, with almost a certainty of something more permanent long before the term in question,[45] the two families had consented to the young people's wishes,[46] and that their marriage was likely to take place in a few months, quite as soon as Louisa's. "And a very good living it was," Charles added, "only five-and-twenty miles from Uppercross, and in a very fine country—fine part of Dorsetshire.[47] In the centre of some of the best preserves in the kingdom, surrounded by three great proprietors, each more careful and jealous than the other; and to two of the three, at least, Charles Hayter might get a special recommendation.[48] Not that he will value it as he ought," he observed, "Charles is too cool about sporting. That's the worst of him."

"I am extremely glad, indeed," cried Anne, "particularly glad

40. Mrs. Harville may think the trip will take his mind off Captain Benwick's forgetting Fanny Harville so soon; Captain Harville will later show himself to be much grieved on his sister's account.

41. Since Bath was a popular retirement destination, especially for widows, and is close to Uppercross, she probably has a number of friends there.

42. Buying wedding clothes was a standard part of marriage preparations. It meant not only clothes for the wedding itself—in fact, at this time weddings were mostly modest affairs, and the bride's gown one that could also be worn on other occasions. It also meant outfitting the bride with items she could wear afterward and that would help her start her new life. In *Emma* being able to display fine clothes is mentioned as a privilege of the newly married woman, while in *Pride and Prejudice* the heroine's mother shows more interest in whether one daughter will be able to select good wedding clothes than in almost anything else about the marriage.

Bath would be a natural destination for those buying wedding clothes, for its many affluent visitors had caused it to abound in stores; it was perhaps second only to London as a contemporary shopping center (and London would be both more expensive and much farther away for those living in Somerset). Jane Austen herself mentions shopping for clothes in many of her letters from Bath, and in one, written shortly before the family was to move there, she writes that she will wait to buy a new gown there (Jan. 25, 1801).

43. *forwardness:* advancement toward completion.

44. This means the living, i.e., position as clergyman for a parish, is controlled by one wishing to give it eventually to someone, probably a relation now too young to hold it. Charles Hayter has been hired to perform the duties and collect the income until this designee comes of age. This would make a substantial difference in Charles Hayter's situation, for the income of a living was usually much higher than that of a curate, his current position (see p. 45, note 48, for curates).

45. This could be the curacy at Uppercross, something already discussed as a possibility for him (pp. 148 and 196), though he could be sure of that only as long as the current holder, who is old, stays alive. Charles had earlier spoken of his cousin's good chance of getting something from the bishop (p. 146); he may have meant a permanent living and be alluding to that now.

46. Thus, as easygoing and sympathetic to the young people as the Musgroves are, they consent to the engagement only when adequate means are assured. This issue will soon arise again, with particular pertinence to Anne.

47. Dorsetshire is immediately southeast of Somersetshire (see map, p. 513).

48. Preserves refer to areas of land for game. Preserves were an increasingly prominent feature of the countryside in this period—the word itself, with this meaning, had only recently developed. They had arisen due to the increased

that this should happen: and that of two sisters, who both deserve equally well, and who have always been such good friends, the pleasant prospects of one should not be dimming those of the other—that they should be so equal in their prosperity and comfort. I hope your father and mother are quite happy with regard to both."

"Oh! yes. My father would be as well pleased if the gentlemen were richer, but he has no other fault to find. Money, you know, coming down with money—two daughters at once[49]—it cannot be a very agreeable operation, and it streightens[50] him as to many things. However, I do not mean to say they have not a right to it. It is very fit they should have daughters' shares;[51] and I am sure he has always been a very kind, liberal[52] father to me.[53] Mary does not above half like Henrietta's match. She never did, you know. But she does not do him justice, nor think enough about Winthrop. I cannot make her attend to the value of the property. It is a very fair match, as times go;[54] and I have liked Charles Hayter all my life, and I shall not leave off now."

"Such excellent parents as Mr. and Mrs. Musgrove," exclaimed Anne, "should be happy in their children's marriages.[55] They do every thing to confer happiness, I am sure. What a blessing to young people to be in such hands! Your father and mother seem so totally free from all those ambitious feelings which have led to so much misconduct and misery, both in young and old![56] I hope you think Louisa perfectly recovered now?"

He answered rather hesitatingly, "Yes, I believe I do—very much recovered; but she is altered: there is no running or jumping about, no laughing or dancing; it is quite different.[57] If one happens only to shut the door a little hard, she starts and wriggles like a young dab chick in the water;[58] and Benwick sits at her elbow, reading verses, or whispering to her, all day long."

Anne could not help laughing. "That cannot be much to your taste, I know," said she; "but I do believe him to be an excellent young man."

"To be sure he is. Nobody doubts it; and I hope you do not

demand for game that was caused by improved methods of killing, including better guns. Landowners would foster the breeding of game in the preserves, while also protecting the animals being bred through the systematic killing of any creatures who preyed on them.

The proprietors' jealousy could be directed against poachers or other landowners: once people took the trouble to cultivate preserves, they also frequently took steps, such as no trespassing notices, to discourage other country gentlemen from pursuing game on their land. At the same time, they could always make exceptions for friends or for those whose goodwill they sought: in Charles Hayter's case, someone with good connections with two of the proprietors would presumably give him his special recommendation.

49. The strict settlement governing landed property usually dictated a certain amount for each daughter's dowry. But this did not necessarily mean the sum was set aside in a specific investment or account. Instead, much of the family's money would be invested in and used for the estate to maximize its profitability. Thus a landowner like Mr. Musgrove might have to take special steps, or restrict other expenditures, when he needed large sums quickly, as he would when raising the money for two different dowries.

50. *streightens*: straitens, i.e., restricts (in this case financially).

51. The standard settlement gave the estate itself to the eldest son, while allotting a specified amount, of much lesser value, to younger sons and daughters. The former would use it to begin their careers, the latter to marry.

52. *liberal*: generous financially.

53. As explained before, Charles and Mary do not own property of their own but rely primarily on grants from Mr. Musgrove (p. 85, note 19). Hence any financial constraints on his father would affect Charles. That may be why Charles bothers to mention it, even as he professes his lack of complaint.

54. The end of the European war in 1814 led to increased imports of food from overseas, and this hurt those gaining their income from land.

55. Anne's reaction to the news differs completely from Charles's. He speaks of the financial aspects of the marriage, she of the young people's happiness.

56. An odd statement, considering that Charles has just said, "My father would be as well pleased if the gentlemen were richer," suggesting he is not "totally free" of ambitious feelings. Anne, who at other points attributes her own high-mindedness to others, may engage in excessive praise here because it was ambition regarding a daughter's marriage that caused her such misery.

57. This suggests one reason for her affinity with Captain Benwick now.

58. A dabchick is a small grebe, a type of diving waterfowl.

think I am so illiberal[59] as to want every man to have the same objects and pleasures as myself. I have a great value for Benwick; and when one can but get him to talk, he has plenty to say. His reading has done him no harm, for he has fought as well as read.[60] He is a brave fellow. I got more acquainted with him last Monday than ever I did before. We had a famous set-to[61] at rat-hunting all the morning, in my father's great barns;[62] and he played his part so well, that I have liked him the better ever since."[63]

Here they were interrupted by the absolute necessity of Charles's following the others to admire mirrors and china;[64] but Anne had heard enough to understand the present state of Uppercross, and rejoice in its happiness; and though she sighed as she rejoiced, her sigh had none of the ill-will of envy in it. She would certainly have risen to their blessings if she could, but she did not want to lessen theirs.

The visit passed off altogether in high good humour. Mary was in excellent spirits, enjoying the gaiety and the change; and so well satisfied with the journey in her mother-in-law's carriage with four horses,[65] and with her own complete independence of Camden-place, that she was exactly in a temper to admire every thing as she ought, and enter most readily into all the superiorities of

Elegant party with a woman playing a harp and attracting attention.
[From William Combe, *The Dance of Life* (London, 1817; 1903 reprint), p. 232]

59. *illiberal:* narrow-minded.

60. Though this was not a predominantly warrior society, those men who served in the army or navy tended to have greater prestige than any others, with the possible exception of landed gentlemen, and it was considered important for all men to be courageous and to be able and willing to fight if needed.

61. *set-to:* fight, contest.

62. These are the largest barns on his estate, which would naturally attract rats.

63. In *Sense and Sensibility* Jane Austen declares that a sportsman "esteems only those of his sex who are sportsmen likewise." Charles has just disclaimed such an attitude, but he still manifests it strongly, first in his saying earlier that the worst of Charles Hayter is his being "too cool about sporting," and now in explaining that his good opinion of Captain Benwick was truly gained from the latter's successful performance in hunting rats.

64. Large wall mirrors were a common feature of interiors then, especially in rooms used for company. The reason was that they added considerably to the brightness of rooms by reflecting the dim light given off by candles or lamps. The picture on the facing page shows a contemporary room with numerous mirrors. These mirrors frequently had elaborate gilded frames, which would make them worth showing to others.

China, whether in the form of dishes or purely decorative pieces, was also a standard feature of affluent homes at this time, frequently displayed in glass cases or on top of tables and other surfaces.

65. Four horses, in addition to making the ride faster, were a sign of affluence and distinction.

the house, as they were detailed to her. She had no demands on her father or sister, and her consequence[66] was just enough increased by their handsome drawing-rooms.[67]

Elizabeth was, for a short time, suffering a good deal. She felt that Mrs. Musgrove and all her party ought to be asked to dine with them, but she could not bear to have the difference of style, the reduction of servants, which a dinner must betray, witnessed by those who had been always so inferior to the Elliots of Kellynch.[68] It was a struggle between propriety and vanity; but vanity got the better, and then Elizabeth was happy again. These were her internal persuasions.—"Old-fashioned notions—country hospitality[69]—we do not profess to give dinners[70]—few people in Bath do—Lady Alicia[71] never does; did not even ask her own sister's family, though they were here a month: and I dare say it would be very inconvenient to Mrs. Musgrove—put her quite out of her way. I am sure she would rather not come—she cannot feel easy with us.[72] I will ask them all for an evening; that will be much better—that will be a novelty and a treat. They have not seen two

Elegant party of the time, such as Sir Walter and Elizabeth hope to have.

[From William Combe, *The History of Johnny Quae Genus* (London, 1822; 1903 reprint), p. 201]

66. *consequence*: social importance or prestige.

67. "Just enough" implies that Mary might not wish to have her consequence increased too much by her father and sister's house. While glad to gain some prestige from their nice living arrangements, she does not want them to outshine her and her husband, or to owe too much of her own importance to them. A similar mixture of feelings will characterize Mary's reaction at the end to Anne's change of condition (see p. 476).

68. Most servants' labor was done out of the sight of guests (much was also done out of the sight of those living in the house). Hence in general others could only speculate on the number of servants employed by the family—as they might well do, for it was an important measure of status. The Elliots have already been shown trying to maximize the numbers attending on those arriving at their door (see p. 269, note 47). Such expedients would meet their limits at a formal dinner, however, for there a large number of servants would normally be visible, if they were available, due to the elaborate labor required to serve the various courses and attend to the guests.

The reduction of the Elliots' staff, a product of their own reduced resources, would have been encouraged by the conditions of urban living. A town house, being much smaller, required considerably less labor, since much of what servants did involved cleaning the house and its furnishings. Moreover, servants boarded with their employers, and while they could be, and often were, crammed into tight quarters with other servants, a smaller house inevitably imposed limits on the number that could be hired. Finally, wages for servants were generally higher in towns.

69. Hospitality was a long-standing country tradition; the Musgroves were earlier described as frequently inviting people to their house. One reason was the strong local ties of people in the country. Another was that hospitality bolstered the social prestige and influence of landowners.

70. The Elliots were mentioned as generally not giving dinners (p. 262), so Elizabeth is not simply fabricating this reason. But they also had made an exception for Mr. Elliot, who is only their cousin, while Elizabeth is making no such exception now for her own sister.

71. "Lady + first name" is used only by a woman who is the daughter of a duke, marquess, or earl, the three highest ranks of nobility. Thus Lady Alicia is of very high rank, making her a natural model for Elizabeth to follow.

72. She may be right that Mrs. Musgrove and others in her family would not feel easy, but Elizabeth also may be thinking of how uncomfortable she might feel from seeing the Musgroves' lack of polish, especially in her own dining room and in front of those the Elliots associate with in Bath.

such drawing-rooms before.[73] They will be delighted to come to-morrow evening. It shall be a regular[74] party—small, but most elegant." And this satisfied Elizabeth:[75] and when the invitation was given to the two present, and promised for the absent, Mary was as completely satisfied. She was particularly asked to meet Mr. Elliot, and be introduced to Lady Dalrymple and Miss Carteret, who were fortunately already engaged to come; and she could not have received a more gratifying attention.[76] Miss Elliot was to have the honour of calling on Mrs. Musgrove in the course of the morning, and Anne walked off with Charles and Mary, to go and see her and Henrietta directly.

Her plan of sitting with Lady Russell must give way for the present. They all three called in Rivers-street for a couple of minutes; but Anne convinced herself that a day's delay of the intended communication could be of no consequence, and hastened forward to the White Hart, to see again the friends and companions of the last autumn, with an eagerness of good-will which many associations contributed to form.[77]

They found Mrs. Musgrove and her daughter within, and by themselves, and Anne had the kindest welcome from each. Henrietta was exactly in that state of recently-improved views,[78] of fresh-formed happiness, which made her full of regard and interest for every body she had ever liked before at all; and Mrs. Musgrove's real affection had been won by her usefulness when they were in distress. It was a heartiness, and a warmth, and a sincerity which Anne delighted in the more, from the sad want of such blessings at home. She was intreated to give them as much of her time as possible, invited for every day and all day long, or rather claimed as a part of the family; and in return, she naturally fell into all her wonted ways of attention and assistance, and on Charles's leaving them together, was listening to Mrs. Musgrove's history of Louisa, and to Henrietta's of herself, giving opinions on business,[79] and recommendations to shops,[80] with intervals of every help which Mary required, from altering her ribbon[81] to settling her accounts, from finding her keys,[82] and assorting her trinkets,[83] to trying to convince her that she was not ill-used by any

73. They would use both drawing rooms for the evening party, for they would need the space for card tables. In contrast, a dinner party might require the use of only one drawing room, before and after the meal.

74. *regular*: well-ordered, correctly done.

75. This is the most sustained glimpse we get of Elizabeth's mind. It shows that while she does have a sense of propriety—in fact, it may be her most important moral principle—even it is relatively weak.

76. *attention*: act of courtesy or politeness.

77. Anne's decision to delay her message shows how much more she cares about all related to the Musgroves than about Elliot affairs. For the route from Camden Place to Rivers Street and then to the White Hart, see map, p. 516.

78. *views*: expectations, prospects.

79. *business*: what one is busy about; that is, the Musgroves' errands and tasks.

80. There was a great variety of shops in Bath, so someone who had been living there would naturally be able to point out which were best for various wares.

81. Ribbons could be used in various ways in the dress of the time; they were especially likely to be found on the head, either directly on the hair or on hats and caps. In Mary's case, sitting inside, the strongest likelihood is that the ribbon in question is attached to her cap (see also p. 269, note 43).

82. As the mistress of her house, Mary would be in charge of most household accounts, and would keep the household keys. The household keys, of which there was usually only one set, were of great importance and prestige, which is why Mary has brought hers with her to Bath rather than leaving them with a servant. They were used especially for the various places—rooms, cupboards, boxes—where valuable items were stored.

83. *trinkets*: small ornaments, especially personal jewelry. These could include necklaces, earrings, bracelets, brooches, and hair ornaments.

body; which Mary, well amused[84] as she generally was in her station at a window overlooking the entrance to the pump-room,[85] could not but have her moments of imagining.

A morning of thorough confusion was to be expected. A large party in an hotel ensured a quick-changing, unsettled scene. One five minutes brought a note, the next a parcel,[86] and Anne had not been there half an hour, when their dining-room, spacious as it was,[87] seemed more than half filled: a party of steady old friends were seated round Mrs. Musgrove, and Charles came back with Captains Harville and Wentworth. The appearance of the latter could not be more than the surprise of the moment. It was impossible for her to have forgotten to feel, that this arrival of their common friends must be soon bringing them together again. Their last meeting had been most important in opening his feelings; she had derived from it a delightful conviction; but she feared from his looks, that the same unfortunate persuasion, which had has-

Exterior of the Pump Room (from a contemporary picture).

[From Emma Austen-Leigh, *Jane Austen and Bath* (London, 1939), p. 46]

84. *amused:* entertained, occupied.

85. *pump-room:* the Pump Room was a large room where the Bath waters could be drunk; its name came from the pumps that raised the water from below. It was a prominent place for people to meet others and converse, as the heroine of *Northanger Abbey* does on several occasions. Most likely the opportunity to observe the many people entering and leaving the Pump Room is what draws Mary to her vantage point and keeps her at least mostly occupied and entertained. For contemporary pictures of the interior and the exterior, see below and facing page. Mary would look out on the street from the side of the Pump Room shown in the exterior picture; the picture on p. 410 gives an even more exact sense of the vantage point.

86. The parcel is presumably from a shop.

87. This would be part of their apartment at the inn. Better inns often had such accommodations for large, affluent parties.

Interior of the Pump Room (from a contemporary picture).

[From Emma Austen-Leigh, *Jane Austen and Bath* (London, 1939), p. 8]

tened him away from the concert room, still governed.[88] He did not seem to want to be near enough for conversation.

She tried to be calm, and leave things to take their course; and tried to dwell much on this argument of rational dependance[89]— "Surely, if there be constant attachment on each side, our hearts must understand each other ere long. We are not boy and girl, to be captiously irritable, misled by every moment's inadvertence,[90] and wantonly playing with our own happiness." And yet, a few minutes afterwards, she felt as if their being in company with each other, under their present circumstances, could only be exposing them to inadvertencies and misconstructions of the most mischievous[91] kind.

"Anne," cried Mary, still at her window, "there is Mrs. Clay, I am sure, standing under the colonnade,[92] and a gentleman with her. I saw them turn the corner from Bath-street[93] just now. They seem deep in talk. Who is it?—Come, and tell me. Good heavens! I recollect.—It is Mr. Elliot himself."[94]

East side of Bath Street, from which Mr. Elliot emerges to meet Mrs. Clay. Store signs and advertisements are from a later time.

[From Mowbray Aston Green, *The Eighteenth Century Architecture of Bath* (Bath, 1904), p. 198]

88. The concert was two days ago (see chronology, p. 491), and this is their first time together since then. The Musgroves' arrival provides a basis for their meeting that they would not have had otherwise (see p. 363, note 59, for the barriers to their seeing each other). It thus helps solve a difficulty in the plot: in Jane Austen's initial version of the novel, she had to contrive an awkward, and not completely plausible, meeting at the Crofts' residence to bring Anne and Captain Wentworth together once more. This passage also indicates that Anne has not forgotten this happy product of the Musgroves' arrival—it may be this thought that made her eager to leave Lady Russell and come here. Captain Wentworth may have thought of this too, though his behavior at the moment does not suggest it.

89. *dependance:* confidence, trust. His argument at the concert that a man does not forget a superior woman he truly loved would give her a rational basis of confidence or trust.

90. *inadvertence:* oversight.

91. *mischievous:* harmful (in a serious, not playful way).

92. *colonnade:* a series of columns supporting a roof or covering. There were several built in the vicinity of the baths, providing a sheltered passageway for those going to or from the baths. Some, such as those on each side of Bath Street (see next note; for a picture, see facing page), consist of one row of columns with a building forming the other side of the passage. What Mary would be able to see from a window at the White Hart, across Stall Street, is the colonnade extending north from the Pump Room, which has two rows of columns and is open on both sides (see illustration on p. 410; for location, see map, p. 515).

93. *Bath-street:* a short street perpendicular to Stall Street, and hence a natural place for Mr. Elliot and Mrs. Clay to have emerged from. The street was created to connect the Cross Bath to the King's and Queen's Baths, which are part of the same complex as the Pump Room (see map, p. 515).

94. It takes Mary a moment to recognize him because she has had only one brief glimpse of him at Lyme. This will not stop her from shortly expressing indignation that anyone would imagine she could not easily recognize him.

"No," cried Anne quickly, "it cannot be Mr. Elliot, I assure you. He was to leave Bath at nine this morning, and does not come back till to-morrow."[95]

As she spoke, she felt that Captain Wentworth was looking at her; the consciousness of which vexed and embarrassed her, and made her regret that she had said so much, simple as it was.

Mary, resenting that she should be supposed not to know her own cousin, began talking very warmly about the family features, and protesting still more positively that it was Mr. Elliot, calling again upon Anne to come and look herself; but Anne did not mean to stir, and tried to be cool and unconcerned. Her distress returned, however, on perceiving smiles and intelligent glances pass between two or three of the lady visitors, as if they believed themselves quite in the secret. It was evident that the report concerning her had spread; and a short pause succeeded, which seemed to ensure that it would now spread farther.[96]

"Do come, Anne," cried Mary, "come and look yourself. You will be too late, if you do not make haste. They are parting, they are shaking hands.[97] He is turning away. Not know Mr. Elliot, indeed!—You seem to have forgot all about Lyme."

To pacify Mary, and perhaps screen her own embarrassment, Anne did move quietly to the window.[98] She was just in time to ascertain that it really was Mr. Elliot (which she had never believed), before he disappeared on one side, as Mrs. Clay walked quickly off on the other; and checking the surprise which she could not but feel at such an appearance of friendly conference between two persons of totally opposite interests, she calmly said, "Yes, it is Mr. Elliot certainly. He has changed his hour of going, I suppose, that is all—or I may be mistaken; I might not attend";[99] and walked back to her chair, recomposed, and with the comfortable[100] hope of having acquitted herself well.[101]

The visitors took their leave; and Charles, having civilly seen them off, and then made a face at them, and abused them for coming,[102] began with—

"Well, mother, I have done something for you that you will like. I have been to the theatre, and secured a box for to-morrow

95. For his stated departure and return, see p. 406, and chronology, p. 491.

96. Anne's inability to speak, which makes her situation worse, obviously results from surprise, but it also may be a product of the passive role of observer that her longtime circumstances have forced upon her. She is now again, as she was at the concert, in a position where she must do something to counteract the misleading impressions in Captain Wentworth's mind.

97. Shaking hands was a sign of closeness in this society. In Jane Austen's novels it almost never occurs between an unmarried woman and an unmarried man unless they are related or one of them is engaged. A contemporary guide to etiquette and beauty, *The Mirror of Graces* (1811), warns women against shaking hands, declaring, "When any man, who is not privileged by the right of friendship or of kindred, attempts to take her hand, let her withdraw it immediately, with an air so declarative of displeasure, that he shall not presume to repeat the offence. . . . A touch, a pressure of the hands, are the only external signs a woman can give of entertaining a particular regard for certain individuals" (p. 170). Hence Mrs. Clay's willingness to shake Mr. Elliot's hand represents a significant gesture on her part.

98. Thus Anne does begin to act, albeit in a limited way. Her difficulty in trying to alert Captain Wentworth about her feelings is compounded by the prevailing rules of feminine propriety, which dictated that she should not make overt advances to him. The heroine of *Pride and Prejudice*, in the latter part of that novel, is in a similar situation of waiting and trying to give what encouragement she can to the man she loves. In both cases the woman had rejected an earlier offer of marriage from the man, which naturally makes him more hesitant about approaching her and asking again.

99. *might not attend*: may not have attended. "Might" is used here as the past tense of "may," as it was once before (see p. 169, note 44).

100. *comfortable*: pleasant, reassuring, encouraging.

101. Thus Anne ultimately turns the sighting of Mr. Elliot, which had seemed initially such an unlucky chance, to her advantage. In a sense she has passed her first test of action. At the same time, this change of fortune shows that all events are not conspiring against the heroine, as is frequently the case in novels of the time, including those by the two novelists who influenced Jane Austen the most, Samuel Richardson and Frances (or Fanny) Burney. They present such extremes of misfortune to underline certain moral messages and for the sake of dramatic tension. Jane Austen, while valuing both of these things, especially the first, values realism at least as highly, which means avoiding what clearly violates the normal experience of life.

102. Charles's behavior serves as a reminder of the Musgroves' rougher man-

night.[103] A'n't[104] I a good boy? I know you love a play; and there is room for us all. It holds nine. I have engaged Captain Wentworth. Anne will not be sorry to join us, I am sure. We all like a play. Have not I done well, mother?"

Mrs. Musgrove was good humouredly beginning to express her perfect readiness for the play, if Henrietta and all the others liked it, when Mary eagerly interrupted her by exclaiming,

"Good heavens, Charles! how can you think of such a thing? Take a box for to-morrow night! Have you forgot that we are engaged to Camden-place to-morrow night? and that we were most particularly asked on purpose to meet Lady Dalrymple and her daughter, and Mr. Elliot—all the principal family connexions—on purpose to be introduced to them? How can you be so forgetful?"

"Phoo! phoo!" replied Charles, "what's an evening party? Never worth remembering. Your father might have asked us to dinner, I think, if he had wanted to see us.[105] You may do as you like, but I shall go to the play."

"Oh! Charles, I declare it will be too abominable if you do! when you promised to go."

"No, I did not promise. I only smirked and bowed, and said the word 'happy.' There was no promise."

"But you must go, Charles. It would be unpardonable to fail. We were asked on purpose to be introduced. There was always such a great connexion between the Dalrymples and ourselves. Nothing ever happened on either side that was not announced immediately. We are quite near relations, you know: and Mr. Elliot too, whom you ought so particularly to be acquainted with! Every attention is due to Mr. Elliot. Consider, my father's heir—the future representative of the family."

"Don't talk to me about heirs and representatives," cried Charles. "I am not one of those who neglect the reigning power to bow to the rising sun.[106] If I would not go for the sake of your father, I should think it scandalous to go for the sake of his heir. What is Mr. Elliot to me?"

The careless expression was life to Anne, who saw that Captain

ners, and thus of their limitations, even with the greater friendliness and good cheer that their presence in Bath has brought to Anne.

103. The theater was one of the most popular entertainments in Bath and a major attraction of the city. Spurred by the presence of large numbers of affluent people in search of amusement, the principal Bath theater flourished enough to become in 1768 the first theatrical company to receive a royal patent. Its success continued in subsequent years, and in 1804 a guidebook said that it and its affiliated Bristol theater "have long been held next in consideration to those of London" (Feltham, *Guide to all the Watering and Sea-Bathing Places*, p. 41).

Hiring a box at the theater would be standard for those as affluent as the characters here. Boxes were very popular: theaters constructed in this period had several levels of boxes, covering both sides and often the rear as well; in some of the grander playhouses between one-third and one-half of the seats were in the boxes. Seats in boxes could be sold separately, or the whole box could be taken—Charles's wording suggests he has done the latter. A new, very grand theater had been opened in Bath in 1805: it contained three tiers of boxes, including twenty-six private boxes (boxes completely secluded by a floor-to-ceiling partition). The latter also enjoyed special suite of rooms for relaxing and a separate entrance from the rest of the audience.

104. "A'n't," or its variants "an't" and "ain't," was considered incorrect grammar then and is used in Jane Austen by less polished or less educated characters.

105. Charles's reaction suggests that, despite all Elizabeth's rationalizations about an invitation for an evening party being as good or better (pp. 418–420), others are aware of the superior hospitality, and desirability, of a dinner party.

106. This statement would have a particular resonance at this time, for one of the central themes in British politics over the preceding century had been the conflict between the king and the heir to the throne, and the followers of each. As the reigning sovereign, and thus the person who could appoint people to high office, dispense other favors, and determine policy (along with Parliament), the king would collect supporters around him. At the same time, many who disagreed with the king's policies or simply had not been fortunate enough to enjoy his patronage would congregate around the king's eldest son, who could offer the certainty that, barring premature death, he would eventually become king and be able to act as his supporters wished. Those gathered around him often constituted the main political opposition in the country. As the king seemed to be nearing his end, the number of those who gravitated to the heir apparent, i.e., "the rising sun" in Charles's words, would naturally increase.

Wentworth was all attention, looking and listening with his whole soul; and that the last words brought his enquiring eyes from Charles to herself.

Charles and Mary still talked on in the same style; he, half serious and half jesting, maintaining the scheme for the play; and she, invariably serious, most warmly opposing it, and not omitting to make it known, that however determined to go to Camden-place herself, she should not think herself very well used, if they went to the play without her. Mrs. Musgrove interposed.

"We had better put it off. Charles, you had much better go back, and change the box for Tuesday.[107] It would be a pity to be divided, and we should be losing Miss Anne too, if there is a party at her father's; and I am sure neither Henrietta nor I should care at all for the play, if Miss Anne could not be with us."[108]

Anne felt truly obliged to her for such kindness; and quite as much so, moreover, for the opportunity it gave her of decidedly saying—

"If it depended only on my inclination, ma'am, the party at home (excepting on Mary's account) would not be the smallest impediment. I have no pleasure in the sort of meeting, and should be too happy to change it for a play, and with you. But, it had better not be attempted, perhaps."

She had spoken it; but she trembled when it was done, conscious that her words were listened to, and daring not even to try to observe their effect.

It was soon generally agreed that Tuesday should be the day, Charles only reserving the advantage of still teasing his wife, by persisting that he would go to the play to-morrow, if nobody else would.

Captain Wentworth left his seat, and walked to the fire-place; probably for the sake of walking away from it soon afterwards, and taking a station, with less barefaced design, by Anne.[109]

"You have not been long enough in Bath," said he, "to enjoy the evening parties of the place."

"Oh! no. The usual character of them has nothing for me. I am no card-player."[110]

107. Playbills and other notices show Tuesday, Thursday, and Saturday to be the standard days for performances at this time, though some performances on other days (excepting Sundays) occur. The "to-morrow night" that Charles originally secured is a Saturday (see chronology, p. 491). In a letter from Bath Jane Austen writes of attending a play on Saturday (June 19, 1799).

108. This statement signals Anne's increasing integration into the Musgroves' circle, especially since, in contrast to some earlier incidents, Mrs. Musgrove is not praising Anne because of any service she is rendering the family but simply out of fondness for her and a wish for her presence. This statement has additional value for Anne now, with Captain Wentworth present. It is possible that hearing Anne so highly praised helps motivate his friendlier approach to her immediately after this.

109. Fireplaces were the only form of heat in rooms. During the winter they needed to burn strongly, which could make the immediate vicinity of the fireplace excessively warm, even as more distant areas of the room remained cool. Hence moving toward the fire from cooler areas and away from it again after being warmed would be a common procedure, one enabling Captain Wentworth to end up near Anne without alerting others that this was his real intention.

110. Cards were one of the most popular forms of indoor amusement at the time, with many different games being played; Jane Austen's characters are frequently described playing cards. They were especially popular in Bath, where the concentration of people with ample leisure encouraged frequent playing and, in many cases, heavy gambling. Anne and Captain Wentworth assume as a matter of course, and turn out to be correct, that this evening party will center around cards.

"You were not formerly, I know. You did not use to like cards; but time makes many changes."

"I am not yet so much changed," cried Anne, and stopped, fearing she hardly knew what misconstruction.[111] After waiting a few moments he said—and as if it were the result of immediate feeling—"It is a period, indeed! Eight years and a half is a period!"[112]

Whether he would have proceeded farther was left to Anne's imagination to ponder over in a calmer hour; for while still hearing the sounds he had uttered, she was startled to other subjects by Henrietta, eager to make use of the present leisure for getting out, and calling on her companions to lose no time, lest somebody else should come in.

They were obliged to move. Anne talked of being perfectly ready, and tried to look it; but she felt that could Henrietta have known the regret and reluctance of her heart in quitting that chair, in preparing to quit the room, she would have found, in all her own sensations for her cousin, in the very security of his affection, wherewith to pity her.

Their preparations, however, were stopped short. Alarming sounds were heard;[113] other visitors approached, and the door was thrown open for Sir Walter and Miss Elliot, whose entrance seemed to give a general chill. Anne felt an instant oppression, and, wherever she looked, saw symptoms of the same. The comfort, the freedom, the gaiety of the room was over, hushed into cold composure, determined silence, or insipid talk, to meet the heartless elegance of her father and sister. How mortifying to feel that it was so!

Her jealous eye was satisfied in one particular. Captain Wentworth was acknowledged again by each, by Elizabeth more graciously than before. She even addressed him once, and looked at him more than once. Elizabeth was, in fact, revolving a great measure.[114] The sequel explained it. After the waste of a few minutes in saying the proper nothings, she began to give the invitation which was to comprise all the remaining dues of the Musgroves.[115] "To-morrow evening, to meet a few friends, no formal party." It was all said very gracefully,[116] and the cards with

111. While Anne's not being changed could mean she still loves Captain Wentworth, it could also mean she is still swayed by or susceptible to those influences that earlier caused her to reject him. Her hesitation shows the difficulties created by the mixed legacy of her past experience with Captain Wentworth.

112. This is the first time he has ever directly alluded to their earlier relationship.

113. The sounds are presumably alarming not because they know who might be arriving, but because they feel any guests to be unwelcome. The face Charles made at their earlier visitors suggests the general desire for a conclave that consists only of the family and its closest friends.

114. *revolving a great measure*: considering or pondering an important step.

115. This is all she believed she still owed them as relations and perhaps as former neighbors as well.

116. The good manners of Sir Walter and Elizabeth when it comes to public behavior will be mentioned later (p. 468).

which she had provided herself, the "Miss Elliot at home," were laid on the table,[117] with a courteous, comprehensive smile to all; and one smile and one card more decidedly for Captain Wentworth. The truth was, that Elizabeth had been long enough in Bath, to understand the importance[118] of a man of such an air and appearance as his. The past was nothing. The present was that Captain Wentworth would move about well in her drawing-room. The card was pointedly given, and Sir Walter and Elizabeth arose and disappeared.

The interruption had been short, though severe; and ease and animation returned to most of those they left, as the door shut them out, but not to Anne. She could think only of the invitation she had with such astonishment witnessed; and of the manner in which it had been received, a manner of doubtful meaning, of surprise rather than gratification, of polite acknowledgment rather than acceptance. She knew him; she saw disdain in his eye, and could not venture to believe that he had determined to accept such an offering, as atonement for all the insolence of the past. Her spirits sank. He held the card in his hand after they were gone, as if deeply considering it.

"Only think of Elizabeth's including every body!" whispered Mary very audibly. "I do not wonder Captain Wentworth is delighted! You see he cannot put the card out of his hand."

Anne caught his eye, saw his cheeks glow, and his mouth form itself into a momentary expression of contempt, and turned away, that she might neither see nor hear more to vex her.

The party separated. The gentlemen had their own pursuits, the ladies proceeded on their own business, and they met no more while Anne belonged to them. She was earnestly begged to return and dine, and give them all the rest of the day; but her spirits had been so long exerted, that at present she felt unequal to more, and fit only for home, where she might be sure of being as silent as she chose.

Promising to be with them the whole of the following morning, therefore, she closed the fatigues of the present, by a toilsome walk to Camden-place,[119] there to spend the evening chiefly in

117. Elizabeth is the one to distribute cards, and hence invitations, because she is the mistress of the house.

118. *importance*: social consequence.

119. The walk to Camden Place would be toilsome not only because of Anne's anxieties regarding Captain Wentworth but also because of its long and steep ascent.

listening to the busy arrangements of Elizabeth and Mrs. Clay for the morrow's party, the frequent enumeration of the persons invited, and the continually improving detail of all the embellishments which were to make it the most completely elegant of its kind in Bath, while harassing herself in secret with the never-ending question, of whether Captain Wentworth would come or not? They were reckoning him as certain, but, with her, it was a gnawing solicitude never appeased for five minutes together. She generally thought he would come, because she generally thought he ought; but it was a case which she could not so shape into any positive act of duty or discretion, as inevitably to defy the suggestions of very opposite feelings.[120]

She only roused herself from the broodings of this restless agitation, to let Mrs. Clay know that she had been seen with Mr. Elliot three hours after his being supposed to be out of Bath; for having watched in vain for some intimation of the interview from the lady herself, she determined to mention it; and it seemed to her that there was guilt in Mrs. Clay's face as she listened. It was transient, cleared away in an instant, but Anne could imagine she read there the consciousness of having, by some complication of mutual trick, or some overbearing authority of his, been obliged to attend (perhaps for half an hour) to his lectures and restrictions on her designs on Sir Walter. She exclaimed, however, with a very tolerable imitation of nature,[121]

"Oh dear! very true. Only think, Miss Elliot, to my great surprise I met with Mr. Elliot in Bath-street![122] I was never more astonished. He turned back and walked with me to the Pump-yard.[123] He had been prevented setting off for Thornberry, but I really forget by what[124]—for I was in a hurry, and could not much attend, and I can only answer for his being determined not to be delayed in his return. He wanted to know how early he might be admitted to-morrow.[125] He was full of 'to-morrow'; and it is very evident that I have been full of it too ever since I entered the house, and learnt the extension of your plan, and all that had happened, or my seeing him could never have gone so entirely out my head."

120. Duty might dictate coming, whether as an acknowledgment of Elizabeth's courtesy in inviting him, as a sign of friendship to Anne, or as something that would please his friends, the Musgroves, and his sister and her husband (the Crofts are later described as attending the party, which would be expected since they are Sir Walter's tenants). Discretion might dictate staying away, to avoid any conflicts or uneasiness that could arise from visiting the home of those who had earlier treated him with disdain, or to avoid seeing the woman he loves with another man who is courting her and is widely expected to marry her. Yet, since all of these reasons are fairly weak, Anne remains undecided as to what might ultimately sway him.

121. *imitation of nature:* appearance of acting naturally. "Nature" and "imitation of nature" were often used in connection with art; pictures or works of literature that represented people accurately were praised for imitating nature well.

122. *Bath-street:* see p. 425, note 93.

123. *Pump-yard:* an open area just north of the Pump Room and very close to Bath Street (see map, p. 515).

124. A later development suggests this might have been a planned delay on his part, done for the very purpose of having this meeting (p. 478).

125. He would presumably like to arrive at the Elliots' before the other guests.

Chapter Eleven

One day only had passed since Anne's conversation with Mrs. Smith; but a keener interest had succeeded, and she was now so little touched by Mr. Elliot's conduct, except by its effects in one quarter, that it became a matter of course the next morning, still to defer her explanatory visit in Rivers-street.[1] She had promised to be with the Musgroves from breakfast to dinner. Her faith was plighted, and Mr. Elliot's character, like the Sultaness Scheherazade's head, must live another day.[2]

She could not keep her appointment punctually, however; the weather was unfavourable, and she had grieved over the rain on her friends' account, and felt it very much on her own,[3] before she was able to attempt the walk. When she reached the White Hart, and made her way to the proper apartment,[4] she found herself neither arriving quite in time, nor the first to arrive. The party before her were Mrs. Musgrove, talking to Mrs. Croft, and Captain Harville to Captain Wentworth, and she immediately heard that Mary and Henrietta, too impatient to wait, had gone out the moment it had cleared, but would be back again soon, and that the strictest injunctions had been left with Mrs. Musgrove, to keep her there till they returned.[5] She had only to submit, sit down, be outwardly composed, and feel herself plunged at once in all the agitations which she had merely laid her account of tasting a little before the morning closed. There was no delay, no waste of time. She was deep in the happiness of such misery, or the misery of such happiness, instantly. Two minutes after her entering the room, Captain Wentworth said,

"We will write the letter we were talking of, Harville, now, if you will give me materials."[6]

Materials were all at hand, on a separate table; he went to it, and nearly turning his back on them all, was engrossed by writing.

1. It is now Saturday; she spoke with Mrs. Smith on Thursday. Anne's delay in telling Lady Russell introduces some awkwardness into the story, for it makes the conversation with Mrs. Smith, which formed the longest chapter in the book, of even less relevance to the main plot, since it does not even lead to an alteration in Lady Russell's attitude. At the same time, the delay does underline the true nature of Anne's priorities.

2. The Sultaness Scheherazade is the ostensible narrator of *The Arabian Nights*. In the story she has married a king, or sultan, who executes each new wife the morning after the wedding in order to prevent her from ever being unfaithful. To forestall this fate Scheherazade tells the king a story that is still unfinished when morning arrives, promising to finish it come evening. The king's eagerness to hear the end makes him postpone her execution for one day, but the next night she also begins a new story and leaves it uncompleted. This continues night after night until at last the king relents from his murderous design; the tales told by her constitute the book. In the case of Mr. Elliot's character, or reputation, the reprieve it wins, at least as regards Lady Russell's opinion, promises to be only temporary.

The *Arabian Nights*, which emerged in various versions in the Middle East, first came to the attention of European readers in the early 1700s with a French translation of one version by Antoine Galland. An English translation of that soon followed, and the book became very popular, with a particular appeal for children but with many adult readers as well. This popularity grew further in the early 1800s, as its exotic origin and many fantastical elements fit in well with the Romanticism of the period.

3. It is characteristic of Anne's unselfish and sympathetic nature that she "grieved" over the sufferings of her friends and only "felt" her own.

4. An apartment could be a room or a suite of rooms, but it is the latter in this case. The previous chapter referred to the Musgroves' dining room, and it soon becomes apparent that Anne has joined others in a sitting room that is separate from the bedrooms.

5. In the previous chapter Mrs. Musgrove indicated how much she valued Anne's company, rather than just her usefulness (p. 430). Now Henrietta, and even Mary, do the same.

6. Captain Wentworth asks about writing materials. The ones on hand are on a separate table because a number of different materials were needed then. They included, in addition to paper, a quill pen, an inkwell (often a glass bottle) into which the pen was dipped, a penknife to sharpen the easily dulled quill, and a pounce-pot, or sander, to sprinkle a drying substance over the paper, since the highly liquid ink would otherwise blot (chalk was the favored substance; the term "sander" derived from the earlier use of sandarac, a resin). To this would be added materials for sealing the letter (see p. 451, note 46).

Mrs. Musgrove was giving Mrs. Croft the history of her eldest daughter's engagement, and just in that inconvenient tone of voice which was perfectly audible while it pretended to be a whisper. Anne felt that she did not belong to the conversation, and yet, as Captain Harville seemed thoughtful and not disposed to talk, she could not avoid hearing many undesirable particulars, such as "how Mr. Musgrove and my brother[7] Hayter had met again and again to talk it over; what my brother Hayter had said one day, and what Mr. Musgrove had proposed the next, and what had occurred to my sister Hayter, and what the young people had wished, and what I said at first I never could consent to, but was afterwards persuaded to think might do very well," and a great deal in the same style of open-hearted communication—Minutiæ which, even with every advantage of taste and delicacy which good Mrs. Musgrove could not give, could be properly interesting only to the principals.[8] Mrs. Croft was attending with great good humour, and whenever she spoke at all, it was very sensibly. Anne hoped the gentlemen might each be too much self-occupied to hear.[9]

"And so, ma'am, all these things considered," said Mrs. Musgrove in her powerful whisper, "though we could have wished it different,[10] yet altogether we did not think it fair to stand out any longer; for Charles Hayter was quite wild[11] about it, and Henrietta was pretty near as bad; and so we thought they had better marry at once, and make the best of it, as many others have done before them. At any rate, said I, it will be better than a long engagement."

"That is precisely what I was going to observe," cried Mrs. Croft. "I would rather have young people settle[12] on a small income at once, and have to struggle with a few difficulties together, than be involved in a long engagement. I always think that no mutual—"

"Oh! dear Mrs. Croft," cried Mrs. Musgrove, unable to let her finish her speech,[13] "there is nothing I so abominate for young people as a long engagement.[14] It is what I always protested against for my children. It is all very well, I used to say, for young people to be engaged, if there is a certainty of their being able to

7. *brother*: brother-in-law.

8. Mrs. Musgrove's lack of taste and delicacy make the account even less interesting to others, like Mrs. Croft, than it would be in any case. "Good Mrs. Musgrove" refers to her moral goodness, i.e., her kindness and benevolence. Jane Austen distinguishes this from taste or delicacy, which would make the speaker present her account well and refrain from introducing inappropriate or overly private details. In Jane Austen's scale of values, kindness and benevolence matter more than taste, but the latter is still important, and the ideal person, such as Anne, has both.

9. It is not clear if Anne does not wish them to hear because she always wishes others not to experience something uncomfortable, even if she is experiencing it, or because she feels that a conversation between two women about marriage would be especially uncongenial to a man, or because she feels that the gentlemen's lack of any family connection makes the subject even less relevant and interesting to them than to her.

10. Presumably she means they could have wished the manner and speed with which the engagement proceeded to be different, not the match itself. Except for Charles Musgrove's mentioning earlier that his father could have wished Charles Hayter to be richer—in which the former may have even been projecting his own opinions onto his father—there has been no sign of objection to the marriage on the part of the Musgroves, especially Mrs. Musgrove.

11. *wild*: passionate.

12. *settle*: marry.

13. Mrs. Musgrove's abrupt interruption is another sign of her inferior manners and the lack of delicacy mentioned above.

14. In a letter to her niece Jane Austen expresses similar sentiments. The niece is wondering whether to marry a man, and Jane Austen tentatively advises against it, focusing on his lack of independent means and the long delay that could entail: "I should dread the continuance of this sort of tacit engagement, with such an uncertainty as there is, of *when* it may be completed.—Years may pass, before he is Independent.—You like him well enough to marry, but not well enough to wait" [emphasis in original] (Nov. 30, 1814).

marry in six months, or even in twelve, but a long engagement!"

"Yes, dear ma'am," said Mrs. Croft, "or an uncertain engagement; an engagement which may be long. To begin without knowing that at such a time there will be the means of marrying, I hold to be very unsafe and unwise, and what, I think, all parents should prevent as far as they can."[15]

Anne found an unexpected interest here. She felt its application to herself, felt it in a nervous thrill all over her,[16] and at the same moment that her eyes instinctively glanced towards the distant table, Captain Wentworth's pen ceased to move, his head was raised, pausing, listening, and he turned round the next instant to give a look—one quick, conscious look at her.[17]

The two ladies continued to talk, to re-urge the same admitted truths, and enforce[18] them with such examples of the ill effect of a contrary practice, as had fallen within their observation, but Anne heard nothing distinctly; it was only a buzz of words in her ear, her mind was in confusion.

Captain Harville, who had in truth been hearing none of it, now left his seat, and moved to a window; and Anne seeming to watch him, though it was from thorough absence of mind, became gradually sensible that he was inviting her to join him where he stood. He looked at her with a smile, and a little motion of the head, which expressed, "Come to me, I have something to say"; and the unaffected, easy kindness of manner which denoted the feelings of an older acquaintance than he really was, strongly enforced the invitation. She roused herself and went to him. The window at which he stood, was at the other end of the room from where the two ladies were sitting, and though nearer to Captain Wentworth's table, not very near. As she joined him, Captain Harville's countenance reassumed the serious, thoughtful expression which seemed its natural character.

"Look here," said he, unfolding a parcel[19] in his hand, and displaying a small miniature painting,[20] "do you know who that is?"

"Certainly, Captain Benwick."

"Yes, and you may guess who it is for. But (in a deep tone) it was not done for her. Miss Elliot, do you remember our walking

15. The principle of marrying only with sufficient means is another one endorsed by Jane Austen, and by various characters in her novels; in this case the two families consented only after Charles Hayter's income improved (p. 412). Austen makes clear that while she believes it is terrible to marry only for money, when there is no affection, it is certainly foolish to marry solely on the basis of love, without any means of support. She herself seems to have followed this advice when young, for she and a young man, Tom Lefroy, separated from each other, despite apparent attraction between them, because neither had enough money to enable them to marry.

16. Her thrill would come from hearing Captain Wentworth's own sister endorse the principle on which Anne rejected him, for at the time of their engagement it was highly uncertain, since he was only starting out in the navy, whether and when they would have the means to marry.

17. It is not clear if Captain Wentworth's look is conscious in the same sense as the word is still used today, i.e., a product of his acute consciousness of how meaningful those words are for Anne and himself, or in the sense of guilty, another meaning of the word at the time. The latter could result from his thinking, as he listens to Mrs. Croft, that he has judged Anne too harshly for exercising the same prudent caution when she broke off their engagement. His pausing, perhaps to reflect on his sister's words, might suggest the latter represents at least part of the explanation.

18. *enforce:* strengthen; press home (an argument).

19. "Parcel" frequently referred to small packages wrapped in paper, as is the case here.

20. Miniature paintings had long been popular, especially for portraits, and their popularity had greatly increased during the late eighteenth century. They were particularly valued because their small size allowed them to be carried or worn about the neck, thereby keeping the image of the person portrayed always at hand; they were thus especially suitable for those in love, as in this case. (For a picture of a contemporary woman wearing one around her neck, see p. 473.)

together at Lyme, and grieving for him? I little thought then—but no matter. This was drawn at the Cape.[21] He met with a clever young German artist at the Cape,[22] and in compliance with a promise to my poor sister, sat to him, and was bringing it home for her.[23] And I have now the charge of getting it properly set for another![24] It was a commission to me! But who else was there to employ? I hope I can allow[25] for him. I am not sorry, indeed, to make it over to another. He undertakes it—(looking towards Captain Wentworth) he is writing about it now." And with a quivering lip he wound up the whole by adding, "Poor Fanny! she would not have forgotten him so soon!"

"No," replied Anne, in a low feeling voice. "That, I can easily believe."

"It was not in her nature. She doated on him."

"It would not be the nature of any woman who truly loved."[26]

Captain Harville smiled, as much as to say, "Do you claim that for your sex?" and she answered the question, smiling also, "Yes. We certainly do not forget you, so soon as you forget us. It is, perhaps, our fate rather than our merit. We cannot help ourselves. We live at home, quiet, confined, and our feelings prey upon us.[27] You are forced on exertion. You have always a profession, pursuits, business of some sort or other, to take you back into the world immediately, and continual occupation and change soon weaken impressions."[28]

"Granting your assertion that the world does all this so soon for men, (which, however, I do not think I shall grant) it does not apply to Benwick. He has not been forced upon any exertion. The peace turned him on shore at the very moment, and he has been living with us, in our little family-circle, ever since."

"True," said Anne, "very true; I did not recollect; but what shall we say now, Captain Harville? If the change be not from outward circumstances, it must be from within; it must be nature, man's nature, which has done the business for Captain Benwick."

"No, no, it is not man's nature. I will not allow it to be more man's nature than woman's to be inconstant and forget those they do love, or have loved. I believe the reverse. I believe in a true

21. The Cape of Good Hope is at the southern tip of Africa and is now part of South Africa. It had been captured by Britain because it stood at the juncture of the Atlantic and Indian oceans, making it a critical location for a country with naval interests around the world and whose ships had to pass by the Cape en route to its most important colony, India (the Suez Canal did not yet exist). Cape Town, the city at the Cape, became a British naval base, which is where Captain Benwick's ship would have stopped.

22. South Africa, whose principal European settlers were Dutch, starting in the 1600s, also received a large number of German settlers over the years. Jane Austen's naval brother Francis, who stopped at the Cape, described the colony there in a letter as a mixture of many nations.

23. Captain Harville's sister obviously wished to have a picture of Captain Benwick. This would be natural for someone engaged or married to a naval officer, whose duties would keep him away from home for many months.

24. To set a picture is to place it in a frame. Captain Benwick must have been planning to do this after he returned home, either because he lacked the opportunity to do so at the Cape, or because he thought the quality of frames or framing work would be better in England. Then, learning of Miss Harville's death, he had no reason to frame it, until his engagement to Louisa meant there was someone else who desired his picture.

25. *allow:* make allowances.

26. Anne here commences the most important conversation in the novel. Absent from the first version, it was a final inspiration of the author. It provides a superb lead-up to the resolution of the plot—much better than a meeting at the Crofts' that had earlier served that purpose—while also revealing more of the two main characters, and their feelings for each other, and drawing together a number of critical themes already developed.

27. Anne is describing, at least in part, her own situation over the last eight years. But her description would also apply to any genteel woman who lost her man in some way, though many of these women would have more distractions than Anne, whether from duties as mistress of a house, the function Elizabeth performs in the Elliot family, or from a more active family or social life. Many, lacking her habits of continual reflection, would also be less prone to being preyed on by their feelings than Anne.

28. One inspiration for this observation would be the contrast between her own situation and Captain Wentworth's. As he explained earlier (p. 124), he was able to channel his impatience for doing something, after the end of their engagement, into naval activity. Her statement suggests that she assumes he was able, thanks to this activity, to forget her and thereby to suffer less. The truth of this assumption will soon be a matter of debate.

analogy between our bodily frames and our mental; and that as our bodies are the strongest, so are our feelings;[29] capable of bearing most rough usage, and riding out the heaviest weather."[30]

"Your feelings may be the strongest," replied Anne, "but the same spirit of analogy will authorise me to assert that ours are the most tender. Man is more robust than woman, but he is not longer-lived; which exactly explains my view of the nature of their attachments. Nay, it would be too hard upon you, if it were otherwise. You have difficulties, and privations, and dangers enough to struggle with. You are always labouring and toiling, exposed to every risk and hardship. Your home, country, friends,[31] all quitted. Neither time, nor health, nor life, to be called your own. It would be too hard indeed" (with a faltering voice) "if woman's feelings were to be added to all this."[32]

"We shall never agree upon this question"—Captain Harville was beginning to say, when a slight noise called their attention to Captain Wentworth's hitherto perfectly quiet division of the room. It was nothing more than that his pen had fallen down, but Anne was startled at finding him nearer than she had supposed, and half inclined to suspect that the pen had only fallen, because he had been occupied by them, striving to catch sounds, which yet she did not think he could have caught.[33]

"Have you finished your letter?" said Captain Harville.

"Not quite, a few lines more. I shall have done in five minutes."

"There is no hurry on my side. I am only ready whenever you are.—I am in very good anchorage here," (smiling at Anne) "well supplied, and want for nothing.—No hurry for a signal at all.[34]— Well, Miss Elliot," (lowering his voice) "as I was saying, we shall never agree I suppose upon this point. No man and woman would, probably. But let me observe that all histories are against you, all stories, prose and verse. If I had such a memory as Benwick, I could bring you fifty quotations in a moment on my side the argument,[35] and I do not think I ever opened a book in my life which had not something to say upon woman's inconstancy. Songs and proverbs, all talk of woman's fickleness. But perhaps you will say, these were all written by men."[36]

29. This analogy of body and mind was used by many people at the time, whether in relation to the difference between the sexes or to other matters.

30. Captain Harville will continue to use numerous naval metaphors; Admiral Croft does the same. Captain Wentworth also uses them but less frequently, a sign of his wider reading and broader mind.

31. "Friends" at this time could include family members, and it probably does here.

32. Anne is offering an idealized vision of men's professions, for most did not call for such risks or such separation from home. She may be offering this compliment to men to encourage acceptance of her arguments and avoid any antagonistic feelings that could arise from disagreement.

Ironically, Anne's argument, though presented in defense of women, bears similarities to arguments presented then in favor of traditional roles for women. Hannah More, a leading evangelical writer, argued that a domestic role suited women because they were more emotional, and their feelings would interfere with successful performance of jobs outside the home.

33. He may be overhearing them. If so, this conversation reverses his and Anne's positions during an earlier important conversation, in which she overheard him praise Louisa Musgrove for her firmness and thereby implicitly criticize Anne for lacking that same quality (pp. 166–168). In this case, the speaker has reason to suspect the listener's awareness, which means she must anticipate his hearing whatever else she says.

34. Harville makes a series of analogies between himself and a ship. Being well supplied was critical for naval vessels because they were frequently away from any port for long periods. An elaborate system of signals existed to convey information and orders to ships, such as those to leave their anchorage or other existing position.

35. These last words should read "my side of the argument." The omission of the "of" is probably a printer's error; other passages in Jane Austen with the same or similar wording use the "of."

36. Much of the literature of preceding centuries did lament woman's supposed inconstancy. Most of it also, as he allows, was written by men. But the case was far from being as uniform as he asserts—his own limited reading leads him to an overly absolute generalization. There were plenty of stories showing male betrayal as well as ones showing female betrayal. The issue itself also became a point of dispute in many works of literature.

One of these is "Henry and Emma," the poem that occurred to Anne at an earlier point (see p. 223, note 94). Its portrait of a dedicated and faithful woman begins with a declaration that it will refute "Whatever has been writ, whatever said / Of Female Passion feign'd, or Faith decay'd." Another is

"Perhaps I shall.—Yes, yes, if you please, no reference to examples in books. Men have had every advantage of us in telling their own story. Education has been theirs in so much higher a degree; the pen has been in their hands.[37] I will not allow books to prove any thing."

"But how shall we prove any thing?"

"We never shall. We never can expect to prove any thing upon such a point. It is a difference of opinion which does not admit of proof. We each begin probably with a little bias towards our own sex, and upon that bias build every circumstance in favour of it which has occurred within our own circle,[38] many of which circumstances (perhaps those very cases which strike us the most) may be precisely such as cannot be brought forward without betraying a confidence, or in some respect saying what should not be said."[39]

"Ah!" cried Captain Harville, in a tone of strong feeling, "if I could but make you comprehend what a man suffers when he takes a last look at his wife and children, and watches the boat that he has sent them off in,[40] as long as it is in sight, and then turns away and says, "God knows whether we ever meet again!" And then, if I could convey to you the glow of his soul when he does see them again; when, coming back after a twelvemonth's absence perhaps, and obliged to put into another port,[41] he calculates how soon it be possible to get them there, pretending to deceive himself, and saying, 'They cannot be here till such a day,' but all the while hoping for them twelve hours sooner, and seeing them arrive at last, as if Heaven had given them wings, by many hours sooner still! If I could explain to you all this, and all that a man can bear and do, and glories to do for the sake of these treasures of his existence! I speak, you know, only of such men as have hearts!" pressing his own with emotion.[42]

"Oh!" cried Anne eagerly, "I hope I do justice to all that is felt by you, and by those who resemble you. God forbid that I should undervalue the warm and faithful feelings of any of my fellow-creatures. I should deserve utter contempt if I dared to suppose that true attachment and constancy were known only by woman.

Shakespeare's *Twelfth Night*, which contains an exchange in which the Duke Orsino declares first that, contrary to what is often said, "Our [men's] fancies are more giddy and unfirm," before switching, after he broods on his own rejection in love, to a denunciation of the feebleness of women's love. In reply, Viola, who is disguised as a boy, proclaims that "they [women] are as true of heart as we," and tells a story of a woman, by which she means herself, who pined away in unrequited love and "sat like Patience on a monument, / Smiling at grief." Jane Austen, who cited this last line in *Northanger Abbey*, may have been inspired by this dialogue here, for its picture of a long-suffering woman bears some resemblance to Anne.

37. At this time there had been moves to improve the quality of women's education, but it still was inferior to men's, especially at the higher levels— no universities admitted women. As for books, while women had come to constitute a substantial portion of those who wrote novels, men dominated virtually all other fields of literary endeavor.

38. This evocation of inherent bias suggests there may always be a certain division and lack of agreement between the sexes, though the example of Anne herself, through her generous admission of her own probable partiality, suggests the possibility of establishing some concord or harmony.

39. Anne alludes to a basic difficulty in their conversation, which is that they are prohibited, for various reasons of discretion, from citing some of the individual cases they know. These could include Louisa Musgrove, an example of female inconstancy if she had genuinely loved Captain Wentworth earlier; Wentworth himself, an example of male inconstancy if he had once stopped loving Anne; and Anne, a strong example of female constancy. Anne's reference to this difficulty, along with her statement, "We never can expect to prove any thing," may be an attempt to end the conversation, now that she has reason to suspect Captain Wentworth of hearing.

40. They would have rowed with him to the ship, and then returned to shore in the boat.

41. It was common for naval ships to have to change their port of arrival, and this frequently forced naval wives to have to travel for long distances, and at short notice, to meet their husbands.

42. Captain Harville's whole speech represents a switch to a more personal and emotional argument. It may be a sign of his sensing that they have reached an impasse, rationally speaking. His heartfelt fervor is also an ironic comment on Anne's earlier evocation of woman's especially acute feelings.

It is possible that Jane Austen, in this vivid description of a returning sailor's feelings, was inspired by her observations, or even the direct statements, of her naval brothers, who both had families. More generally, Captain Harville's description of the anguished feelings of officers when

No, I believe you capable of every thing great[43] and good in your married lives. I believe you equal to every important exertion, and to every domestic forbearance, so long as—if I may be allowed the expression, so long as you have an object. I mean, while the woman you love lives, and lives for you. All the privilege I claim for my own sex (it is not a very enviable one, you need not covet it) is that of loving longest, when existence or when hope is gone."[44]

She could not immediately have uttered another sentence; her heart was too full, her breath too much oppressed.

"You are a good soul," cried Captain Harville, putting his hand on her arm quite affectionately. "There is no quarrelling with you.[45]—And when I think of Benwick, my tongue is tied."

Their attention was called towards the others.—Mrs. Croft was taking leave.

"Here, Frederick, you and I part company, I believe," said she. "I am going home, and you have an engagement with your friend.—To-night we may have the pleasure of all meeting again, at your party," (turning to Anne). "We had your sister's card yesterday, and I understood Frederick had a card too, though I did not see it—and you are disengaged, Frederick, are you not, as well as ourselves?"

Captain Wentworth was folding up a letter in great haste, and either could not or would not answer fully.

"Yes," said he, "very true; here we separate, but Harville and I shall soon be after you, that is, Harville, if you are ready, I am in half a minute. I know you will not be sorry to be off. I shall be at your service in half a minute."

Mrs. Croft left them, and Captain Wentworth, having sealed his letter with great rapidity,[46] was indeed ready, and had even a hurried, agitated air, which shewed impatience to be gone. Anne knew not how to understand it. She had the kindest "Good morning, God bless you," from Captain Harville, but from him not a word, nor a look. He had passed out of the room without a look![47]

She had only time, however, to move closer to the table where he had been writing, when footsteps were heard returning; the

separated from their families has a sound basis: "surviving naval correspondence confirms that however distracted by the business of their ship, husbands were invariably anxious about their wives at home, particularly if they had children" (Margarette Lincoln, *Naval Wives & Mistresses*, p. 175).

43. *great:* distinguished, grand, notable in achievement. It is used here along with "good," i.e., morally virtuous, because at this time "great" had yet to develop the sense of "extremely good," applicable to anything.

44. The fervor of Anne's statement suggests she knows what it means to be without hope and without an object, though it could be argued that she was still able to follow Captain Wentworth's career and perhaps harbor some secret hope of seeing him again. In that respect her situation differed from Captain Benwick's.

It is possible she intended her words as a message to Captain Wentworth, for she would know that he could easily grasp them as a ringing affirmation of her persistent love for him. In his letter on pp. 452–454 he declares, referring to this speech, that she sinks her voice, which suggests she was not trying to be overhead, though it cannot be known which part of the speech he had in mind. Her natural modesty and delicacy might make her reluctant to express such feelings loudly. But, whatever her intention, the role played by her words means that, after being a passive figure for most of the novel, her actions play a vital role in bringing about the denouement.

45. Captain Harville's affectionate gesture suggests the establishment of a true rapport between him and Anne that, at least on this more elemental level, overcomes much of the gulf between the sexes suggested above. It thus in a sense foreshadows the far more important rapprochement that follows. It is also a testament to both their good characters that an argument in which they never cease to disagree, at least in part, ends with their being on friendlier terms than they were at the beginning.

46. Envelopes as we know them did not exist then (the term "envelope" referred to the outside sheet of a letter). The sheets of paper were simply folded together and sealed. Sealing was accomplished first by either melting sealing wax over the outside, often with the aid of a special instrument to allow the melting to occur without mishap, or by placing a wafer made of a paste between the sheets, after which, using either procedure, the adhesive substance would be stamped with a seal. That Captain Wentworth accomplished all this with great rapidity indicates both his long practice at sealing—naval officers wrote many letters—and his current state of agitation.

47. Anne's surprise at his abrupt and cold departure would be natural in any case, especially after their recent increased friendliness, but she would be more shocked if she believed he had heard some of her recent words.

door opened; it was himself. He begged their pardon, but he had forgotten his gloves,[48] and instantly crossing the room to the writing table,[49] and standing with his back towards Mrs. Musgrove, he drew out a letter from under the scattered paper, placed it before Anne with eyes of glowing entreaty fixed on her for a moment, and hastily collecting his gloves, was again out of the room, almost before Mrs. Musgrove was aware of his being in it—the work of an instant!

The revolution which one instant had made in Anne, was almost beyond expression. The letter, with a direction[50] hardly legible, to "Miss A. E——,[51] was evidently the one which he had been folding so hastily. While supposed to be writing only to Captain Benwick, he had been also addressing her![52] On the contents of that letter depended all which this world[53] could do for her! Any thing was possible, any thing might be defied rather than suspense. Mrs. Musgrove had little arrangements of her own at her own table; to their protection she must trust, and sinking into the chair which he had occupied, succeeding to[54] the very spot where he had leaned and written, her eyes devoured the following words:

"*I can listen no longer in silence. I must speak to you by such means as are within my reach. You pierce my soul. I am half agony, half hope.[55] Tell me not that I am too late, that such precious feelings are gone for ever. I offer myself to you again with a heart even more your own than when you almost broke it eight years and a half ago.[56] Dare not say that man forgets sooner than woman, that his love has an earlier death. I have loved none but you. Unjust I may have been, weak and resentful I have been, but never inconstant. You alone have brought me to Bath. For you alone I think and plan.—Have you not seen this? Can you fail to have understood my wishes?[57]—I had not waited even these ten days, could I have read your feelings, as I think you must have penetrated mine. I can hardly write. I am every instant hearing something which overpowers me. You sink your voice, but I can distinguish the tones of that voice, when they would be lost on others.—Too good, too excellent*

48. Gloves were a basic accessory for both men and women, worn in many circumstances. Men's gloves, at least for everyday use, were usually made of leather or suede. They would also be a natural accessory to forget when leaving a room: it quickly becomes clear that Captain Wentworth has forgotten his deliberately to give him a good excuse for returning briefly.

49. Writing tables were a special category of tables at the time (see picture on p. 457).

50. *direction:* address or dedication of a letter.

51. Abbreviations were common in letters. He ends by abbreviating his own name.

52. A critical reason for him to use this means of communication, in addition to his spontaneous reaction to what he has heard, is that regular correspondence between unmarried people who were not already engaged was considered improper. By leaving, almost as if by accident, a note on the table, which she could then happen to find, he was, in a certain sense, circumventing this prohibition.

53. *this world:* earthly life.

54. *succeeding* to: inheriting, taking his place in.

55. Wentworth's passionate language contrasts him with other Jane Austen heroes, who are often much cooler and more rational. It also fits with the more intense emotional tone of this novel compared to others of hers. The letter itself is arguably the moment of highest emotion in her works.

56. His precision on the length of time indicates how fully aware he is of what occurred before and of what this interval of separation has meant.

57. He is probably thinking particularly of the concert, when in fact she did come to understand his feelings. At the same time, he is failing to appreciate the difficulties of her situation, having to discern his exact motive while they saw so little of each other and while he, when they did meet, remained often silent and aloof.

creature! You do us justice indeed. You do believe that there is true attachment and constancy among men.[58] *Believe it to be most fervent, most undeviating in*

                                                      F. W."[59]

"*I must go, uncertain of my fate; but I shall return hither, or follow your party, as soon as possible. A word, a look will be enough to decide whether I enter your father's house this evening, or never.*"

Such a letter was not to be soon recovered from. Half an hour's solitude and reflection might have tranquillized her; but the ten minutes only, which now passed before she was interrupted, with all the restraints of her situation,[60] could do nothing towards tranquillity. Every moment rather brought fresh agitation. It was an overpowering happiness. And before she was beyond the first stage of full sensation, Charles, Mary, and Henrietta all came in.

The absolute necessity of seeming like herself produced then an immediate struggle; but after a while she could do no more.[61] She began not to understand a word they said, and was obliged to plead indisposition and excuse herself. They could then see that she looked very ill—were shocked and concerned—and would not stir without her for the world. This was dreadful! Would they only have gone away, and left her in the quiet possession of that room, it would have been her cure; but to have them all standing or waiting around her was distracting, and, in desperation, she said she would go home.

"By all means, my dear," cried Mrs. Musgrove, "go home directly and take care of yourself, that you may be fit for the evening. I wish Sarah was here to doctor you, but I am no doctor myself.[62] Charles, ring and order a chair.[63] She must not walk."

But the chair would never do. Worse than all! To lose the possibility of speaking two words to Captain Wentworth in the course of her quiet, solitary progress up the town (and she felt almost certain of meeting him) could not be borne. The chair was earnestly protested against; and Mrs. Musgrove, who thought only of one sort of illness, having assured herself, with some anxiety, that there

58. He is obviously writing this while listening to her last statement during the exchange with Captain Harville (see p. 448). He naturally focuses on her avowed belief that men can also be constant, rather than her final claim of greater female constancy in certain unenviable circumstances.

59. The letter climaxes the gradual rapprochement of the two main characters. It also provides a coda to the debate between Anne and Captain Harville over the relative constancy of men and women. Harville had seemed, without conceding completely, to admit he could not counter her, due to the strong example of Captain Benwick. Now Captain Wentworth offers himself as an example on the other side of the equation. The question is whether his behavior over the course of the novel supports his claim of always having loved Anne, or if it is more a testament to his current passionate feelings. His coldness toward her and his interest in Louisa Musgrove do not suggest continued love—unless those actions are interpreted as attempts to counteract the underlying love he still harbored and wished not to acknowledge.

Whatever the verdict, the question does put Anne in a paradoxical position. If Captain Wentworth's claim of constant love is true, she would in effect lose the argument with Captain Harville, for his love would be an example of loving long "when hope is gone." But she would gain the powerful consolation of knowing herself to have been truly beloved all those years. If his assertion is not true, or at least exaggerated, her argument would be vindicated, but she might find less emotional comfort.

60. The restraints would be her inability to concentrate on all she was feeling and thinking without the distractions and demands of others. The primacy of social ties meant that she could not simply go off on her own, with no regard for how it might affect others.

61. Anne has spent much of the novel struggling to control her emotions, maintain outward composure, and meet her social obligations—usually with success. Here she finally experiences feelings that no amount of struggle can subdue.

62. A doctor could mean anyone who practiced medicine or treated people, even informally. Sarah is probably Mrs. Musgrove's servant; it was common then for people of all classes to cultivate a knowledge of home remedies.

63. *chair*: for transport back to her home (see p. 337, note 18).

had been no fall in the case; that Anne had not, at any time lately, slipped down, and got a blow on her head; that she was perfectly convinced of having had no fall, could part with her cheerfully, and depend on finding her better at night.

Anxious to omit no possible precaution, Anne struggled, and said,

"I am afraid, ma'am, that it is not perfectly understood. Pray be so good as to mention to the other gentlemen that we hope to see your whole party this evening. I am afraid there has been some mistake; and I wish you particularly to assure Captain Harville, and Captain Wentworth, that we hope to see them both."

"Oh! my dear, it is quite understood, I give you my word. Captain Harville has no thought but of going."

"Do you think so? But I am afraid; and I should be so very sorry! Will you promise me to mention it, when you see them again? You will see them both again this morning, I dare say. Do promise me."

"To be sure I will, if you wish it. Charles, if you see Captain Harville any where, remember to give Miss Anne's message. But indeed, my dear, you need not be uneasy. Captain Harville holds himself quite engaged, I'll answer for it; and Captain Wentworth the same, I dare say."

Anne could do no more; but her heart prophesied some mischance, to damp the perfection of her felicity. It could not be very lasting, however. Even if he did not come to Camden-place himself, it would be in her power to send an intelligible sentence by Captain Harville.[64]

Another momentary vexation occurred. Charles, in his real concern and good nature, would go home with her; there was no preventing him. This was almost cruel! But she could not be long ungrateful; he was sacrificing an engagement at a gunsmith's to be of use to her;[65] and she set off with him, with no feeling but gratitude apparent.

They were in Union-street,[66] when a quicker step behind, a something of familiar sound, gave her two moments' preparation for the sight of Captain Wentworth. He joined them; but, as if

64. She could send a message by Captain Harville, because he was a married man and therefore could receive a letter from her. Her successful reassurance to herself, even as her heart is fearing otherwise, suggests she is regaining some of her composure.

65. England was known internationally at the time for having the best gunsmiths, and provincial gunsmiths were widespread enough that decent guns could easily be procured without going to London—though the ones in Bath would certainly be better than any in the country, which is why Charles would wish to visit one here. Charles's passion for shooting would naturally make his appointment at a gunsmith of great importance to him.

66. Union Street is a short street almost immediately north of the White Hart (see map, p. 515). Hence Captain Wentworth has not gone far. He has presumably been waiting for Anne: he would probably not wish to wait right outside the inn, since others in their party might see him from the window and wonder what he is doing, and has chosen nearby Union Street since it would be the beginning of her route back to her lodgings.

Writing table of the time.

[From Thomas Arthur Strange, *English Furniture in the 18th Century: A Guide to Collectors,* p. 319]

irresolute whether to join or to pass on, said nothing—only looked. Anne could command herself enough to receive that look, and not repulsively.[67] The cheeks which had been pale now glowed, and the movements which had hesitated were decided. He walked by her side. Presently, struck by a sudden thought, Charles said,

"Captain Wentworth, which way are you going? only to Gay-street,[68] or farther up the town?"

"I hardly know," replied Captain Wentworth, surprised.

"Are you going as high as Belmont?[69] Are you going near Camden-place? Because if you are, I shall have no scruple[70] in asking you to take my place, and give Anne your arm to her father's door. She is rather done for this morning, and must not go so far without help.[71] And I ought to be at that fellow's in the market-place.[72] He promised me the sight of a capital gun he is just going to send off; said he would keep it unpacked to the last possible moment, that I might see it; and if I do not turn back now, I have no chance. By his description, a good deal like the second-sized double-barrel[73] of mine, which you shot with one day, round Winthrop."[74]

There could not be an objection. There could be only a most proper alacrity, a most obliging compliance for public view; and smiles reined in and spirits dancing in private rapture. In half a minute, Charles was at the bottom of Union-street again, and the other two proceeding together; and soon words enough had passed between them to decide their direction towards the comparatively quiet and retired gravel-walk,[75] where the power of conversation would make the present hour a blessing indeed; and prepare for it all the immortality which the happiest recollections of their own future lives could bestow.[76] There they exchanged again those feelings and those promises which had once before seemed to secure every thing, but which had been followed by so many, many years of division and estrangement. There they returned again into the past, more exquisitely happy, perhaps, in their re-union, than when it had been first projected; more tender, more tried, more fixed in a knowledge of each other's char-

67. *repulsively:* coldly, repellently; in a manner tending to repulse.

68. *Gay-street:* the street where the Crofts live (see p. 319, note 37). Charles may assume that Captain Wentworth is planning to visit the admiral (Mrs. Croft is still in the room with Mrs. Musgrove). Gay Street would not be that far up the town and thus would not take Anne much closer to her residence, as Charles hopes Captain Wentworth could.

69. *Belmont:* a street on the route from where they are to Anne's residence at Camden Place (see map, p. 516).

70. *scruple:* hesitation.

71. His concern and insistence on assisting her reflect the chivalrous protection of women that was considered to be a basic duty of men, especially gentlemen.

72. *market-place:* an area with numerous commercial stalls that is directly east of Union Street (see map, p. 515). Hence it is in a different direction from the one in which Anne is going.

73. Double-barreled shotguns were the instruments of choice for shooting birds. They were a recent development, made possible by improvements in gun manufacture that allowed for shorter barrels, which meant that guns with two barrels would not be excessively heavy. Perfected in the years around 1800, they very quickly rose to preeminence, thanks to the great advantage they offered of firing off two shots in quick succession. They came in various sizes.

74. Winthrop is the residence of the Hayters, where everyone went on their long walk in the country. Charles's statement indicates they also went that far afield during their shooting, which would not be unusual in their search for birds.

75. *gravel-walk:* a walk that goes between Queen Square to the grassy area, a favorite place for promenading, just beneath the Royal Crescent. The walk, which is still in existence, though it is now paved, has grass and trees around it and hence provides a quieter atmosphere than the street. It also lies away from Anne's route home, a sign that she is hardly worrying about her destination. For the entire route they took, see map, p. 516.

76. The words would be remembered continually during their future lives and be the perpetual subject of happy recollections.

acter, truth, and attachment; more equal to act, more justified in acting.[77] And there, as they slowly paced the gradual ascent, heedless of every group around them, seeing neither sauntering politicians,[78] bustling house-keepers, flirting girls, nor nursery-maids and children, they could indulge in those retrospections and acknowledgments, and especially in those explanations of what had directly preceded the present moment, which were so poignant and so ceaseless in interest. All the little variations of the last week were gone through; and of yesterday and to-day there could scarcely be an end.

She had not mistaken him.[79] Jealousy of Mr. Elliot had been the retarding weight, the doubt, the torment. That had begun to operate in the very hour of first meeting her in Bath; that had returned, after a short suspension,[80] to ruin the concert; and that had influenced him in every thing he had said and done, or omitted to say and do, in the last four-and-twenty hours. It had been gradually yielding to the better hopes which her looks, or words, or actions occasionally encouraged; it had been vanquished at last by those sentiments and those tones which had reached him while she talked with Captain Harville; and under the irresistible governance of which he had seized a sheet of paper, and poured out his feelings.

Of what he had then written, nothing was to be retracted or qualified. He persisted in having loved none but her. She had never been supplanted. He never even believed himself to see her equal. Thus much indeed he was obliged to acknowledge—that he had been constant unconsciously, nay unintentionally; that he had meant to forget her, and believed it to be done. He had imagined himself indifferent, when he had only been angry; and he had been unjust to her merits, because he had been a sufferer from them.[81] Her character was now fixed on his mind as perfection itself, maintaining the loveliest medium of fortitude and gentleness; but he was obliged to acknowledge that only at Uppercross had he learnt to do her justice,[82] and only at Lyme had he begun to understand himself.

At Lyme, he had received lessons of more than one sort. The

77. This suggests some advantages to both of them from having waited, even as they have suffered many disadvantages over the last eight years.

78. The term "politicians" was not applied just to those in politics, but sometimes to those who showed characteristics, such as being crafty, thought typical of politicians. In *Emma* one character says of a man he has not met that he would hate to find him "the practised politician, who is to read every body's character, and . . . to be dispensing flatteries all around." Hence in this case, "politicians" could refer to a variety of people.

79. At this point the novel can finally provide a complete history of Captain Wentworth and what he has been thinking and feeling. Until now, with one brief exception (p. 116), all the reader's knowledge of him has come from what Anne has observed or guessed based on her own understanding of him. This, even with her astuteness and past experience with him, has meant that much of his mental evolution has remained shrouded. This is a necessary consequence of Jane Austen's telling the novel almost completely from the perspective of the heroine. This procedure leads consistently to final passages of retrospective explanation on the part of the hero, like the one that is commencing here.

80. The short suspension, or pause, in his jealousy would have occurred in the moments when Anne was able to speak in a friendly and encouraging tone to him.

81. This implies that he now perceives Anne's original refusal of him to be a sign of her merit, or at least to have come from the meritorious qualities of her character. He presumably means her strong sense of duty.

82. The question is what he is referring to at Uppercross. He never gave any indication there of altering his opinion of Anne, even though he did perform services for her such as lifting the child off her and getting her to ride home with the Crofts. He may mean that his frequent exposure to her and inevitable observation of her behavior (such as the nursing of her nephews) reminded him of her virtues, which in turn could have made him reflect more charitably on the possible reasons for her earlier refusal.

passing admiration of Mr. Elliot had at least roused him, and the scenes on the Cobb, and at Captain Harville's, had fixed[83] her superiority.

In his preceding attempts to attach himself to Louisa Musgrove (the attempts of angry pride), he protested that he had for ever felt it to be impossible; that he had not cared, could not care for Louisa; though, till that day, till the leisure for reflection which followed it, he had not understood the perfect excellence of the mind[84] with which Louisa's could so ill bear a comparison; or the perfect, unrivalled hold it possessed over his own. There, he had learnt to distinguish between the steadiness of principle and the obstinacy of self-will, between the darings of heedlessness and the resolution of a collected mind. There, he had seen every thing to exalt in his estimation the woman he had lost, and there begun to deplore the pride, the folly, the madness of resentment, which had kept him from trying to regain her when thrown in his way.

From that period his penance had become severe.[85] He had no sooner been free from the horror and remorse attending the first few days of Louisa's accident, no sooner begun to feel himself alive again, than he had begun to feel himself, though alive, not at liberty.

"I found," said he, "that I was considered by Harville an engaged man! That neither Harville nor his wife entertained a doubt of our mutual attachment.[86] I was startled and shocked. To a degree, I could contradict this instantly; but, when I began to reflect that others might have felt the same—her own family, nay, perhaps herself, I was no longer at my own disposal. I was hers in honour if she wished it. I had been unguarded. I had not thought seriously on this subject before.[87] I had not considered that my excessive intimacy must have its danger of ill consequence in many ways; and that I had no right to be trying whether I could attach myself to either of the girls, at the risk of raising even an unpleasant report,[88] were there no other ill effects. I had been grossly wrong, and must abide the consequences."

He found too late, in short, that he had entangled himself;[89] and that precisely as he became fully satisfied of his not caring for

83. *fixed:* established, settled (in his mind).

84. *mind:* inner character.

85. In Jane Austen main characters who have made serious errors are consistently forced to undergo some kind of penance for their errors. This helps them learn from their mistakes and correct their faults, and ultimately it makes them more deserving of happiness.

86. In this society people were quick to assume an engagement existed if a young man and woman who were both unmarried spent time together and exhibited a mutual liking. One reason was the prevailing strong belief in marriage and the assumption that almost everyone wished to marry (in fact around 90% of the population did marry). Another was that unmarried men and women had limited ability to socialize together; often the most that people interested in each other could do was to exhibit extra friendliness in the midst of general social events, to dance or engage in other activities more frequently with each other, and, perhaps, to separate on occasion from the larger group for brief tête-à-têtes. Thus, when a couple did those things, it was generally assumed that they had serious intentions toward one another.

87. One reason for his mistake is that, as someone who had spent most of the previous eight years serving at sea, he would have had limited exposure to the rituals and rules of courtship.

88. His involvement with them, if not followed by a proposal of marriage, could lead to an unpleasant report about one of them, such as that she had tried to lure him into marriage or had jilted him after encouraging him. Any such report would damage her reputation.

89. *entangled himself:* ensnared or bound himself to another person. "Entanglement" was often used for cases in which someone had fallen in love with or become pledged to another.

Louisa at all, he must regard himself as bound to her, if her sentiments for him were what the Harvilles supposed. It determined
him to leave Lyme, and await her complete recovery elsewhere.[90]
He would gladly weaken, by any fair means, whatever feelings or
speculations concerning him might exist;[91] and he went, therefore, to his brother's, meaning after a while to return to Kellynch,
and act as circumstances might require.

"I was six weeks with Edward," said he, "and saw him happy.[92]
I could have no other pleasure. I deserved none. He enquired
after you very particularly; asked even if you were personally
altered, little suspecting that to my eye you could never alter."

Anne smiled, and let it pass. It was too pleasing a blunder for a
reproach. It is something for a woman to be assured, in her eight-
and-twentieth year, that she has not lost one charm of earlier
youth: but the value of such homage was inexpressibly increased
to Anne, by comparing it with former words,[93] and feeling it to be
the result, not the cause of a revival of his warm attachment.

He had remained in Shropshire, lamenting the blindness of his
own pride,[94] and the blunders of his own calculations, till at once
released from Louisa by the astonishing and felicitous intelligence of her engagement with Benwick.

"Here," said he, "ended the worst of my state; for now I could at
least put myself in the way of happiness, I could exert myself, I
could do something. But to be waiting so long in inaction, and
waiting only for evil, had been dreadful.[95] Within the first five
minutes I said, "I will be at Bath on Wednesday," and I was. Was
it unpardonable to think it worth my while to come? and to arrive
with some degree of hope? You were single. It was possible that
you might retain the feelings of the past, as I did; and one encouragement happened to be mine. I could never doubt that you
would be loved and sought by others, but I knew to a certainty
that you had refused one man at least, of better pretensions than
myself: and I could not help often saying, Was this for me?"[96]

Their first meeting in Milsom-street afforded much to be said,
but the concert still more. That evening seemed to be made up of
exquisite moments. The moment of her stepping forward in the

90. This would also be why he did not see Louisa while still in Lyme (pp. 248–250).

91. This is a fair means because he himself is not breaking with Louisa. A basic principle of this society was that a man should not break an engagement with a woman. One who did so would be censured and could even be sued in court by the woman for damages. Since Captain Wentworth never actually proposed to Louisa, he ran no such risk, nor would he have suffered as much general censure, but his own strict scruples made him feel honor-bound to behave as if he had proposed. *Sense and Sensibility* hinges partly around a man who entered into an engagement with a woman and later does not feel free to end it, even though he has come to regret it.

Women were, in contrast, considered free to break an engagement, though it was still a serious step and, depending on the circumstances and whether the woman had done this before, it might cause her to be labeled a jilt. An important reason for the difference was that the man, being the one who made the initial offer, was considered to have enjoyed adequate time to be certain of his choice. Jane Austen herself, after accepting an offer of marriage from a man whose family she was visiting, decided the next day to break it off; this did not create any serious problems for her, but she still felt sufficiently uncomfortable, and fearful of ill will from the other family, to insist that she and her sister leave for home at once.

92. It is possible his stay with his brother was longer than six weeks. For the potential problem with this part of the chronology, see p. 489.

93. The former words were those, which Mary repeated to Anne, that she was "so altered he should not have known [her] again" (p. 114). He spoke them the first time he had seen her since their separation; that now he does not even recall them indicates the revolution in his attitude over the course of the novel.

94. Shropshire is the home of his brother. The blindness of his pride refers to the pride that made him angry at Anne, unwilling to allow for her possible good reasons for having refused him, and determined not to attempt a reconciliation.

95. "Waiting in inaction" is a naval term, and it is something that Captain Wentworth would particularly dislike, both because of his personality and because his own naval career so far has involved stations requiring frequent activity (see p. 126). Some naval officers had to spend years on duties, such as maintaining a continual blockade outside enemy ports, that involved long periods of waiting; such officers would have at least grown more accustomed to the condition than Captain Wentworth.

96. He refers to learning that Anne had refused Charles Musgrove (p. 168).

octagon room to speak to him, the moment of Mr. Elliot's appearing and tearing her away, and one or two subsequent moments, marked by returning hope or increasing despondence, were dwelt on with energy.

"To see you," cried he, "in the midst of those who could not be my well-wishers, to see your cousin close by you, conversing and smiling, and feel all the horrible eligibilities[97] and proprieties of the match! To consider it as the certain wish of every being who could hope to influence you! Even, if your own feelings were reluctant or indifferent, to consider what powerful supports would be his! Was it not enough to make the fool of me which I appeared? How could I look on without agony?[98] Was not the very sight of the friend who sat behind you, was not the recollection of what had been, the knowledge of her influence, the indelible, immoveable impression of what persuasion had once done—was it not all against me?"

"You should have distinguished," replied Anne. "You should not have suspected me now; the case so different, and my age so different. If I was wrong in yielding to persuasion once, remember that it was to persuasion exerted on the side of safety, not of risk. When I yielded, I thought it was to duty; but no duty could be called in aid here. In marrying a man indifferent to me,[99] all risk would have been incurred, and all duty violated."[100]

"Perhaps I ought to have reasoned thus," he replied, "but I could not. I could not derive benefit from the late knowledge I had acquired of your character. I could not bring it into play:[101] it was overwhelmed, buried, lost in those earlier feelings which I had been smarting under year after year. I could think of you only as one who had yielded, who had given me up, who had been influenced by any one rather than by me.[102] I saw you with the very person who had guided you in that year of misery. I had no reason to believe her of less authority now.—The force of habit was to be added."

"I should have thought," said Anne, "that my manner to yourself might have spared you much or all of this."

"No, no! your manner might be only the ease[103] which your

He was described at the time as pausing, presumably in thought, when he heard it. Charles had better pretensions than Captain Wentworth because he had much more secure financial prospects, being destined to inherit a substantial landed estate. A match with him would also have offered Anne a home in her own neighborhood, among a family she already knew, and a way of life, as the mistress of an estate, similar to her mother's. The earlier description of Anne's refusal, and her satisfaction with the decision afterward, did not suggest that it was made for Captain Wentworth's sake (p. 52 and p. 82). But it is not surprising he might imagine that to be her reason.

97. *eligibilities*: things that make it fit or suitable.

98. Thus Captain Wentworth experienced very similar feelings to what Anne experienced when she saw him with Louisa and Henrietta Musgrove.

99. *indifferent to me*: that I was indifferent to.

100. Anne is correct from a logical point of view, but it is probably unrealistic, as he suggests in reply, for her to expect him, from his more limited vantage point, to have perceived the differences as clearly as she did. Her mistake is similar to Captain Wentworth's in imagining that she must have discerned fully his feelings after he came to Bath (p. 452). It shows how even the most kindred souls can still fail to achieve complete comprehension of each other.

101. *bring it into play*: make use of it, activate it.

102. Captain Wentworth was angry that she had allowed anyone else, even a close friend and substitute mother like Lady Russell, to influence Anne rather than himself. The statement shows his unreasonableness, as does, even more, his continuing for years afterward to allow such anger to distort his judgment. This, along with the highly charged description of his own feelings in these passages, indicates that he is still learning to control his feelings as well as Anne has learned to control hers. One reason for his greater difficulty is that he has not been forced to spend years practicing and developing her strong self-control.

103. *ease*: absence of awkwardness or embarrassment; tranquillity.

engagement to another man would give. I left you in this belief; and yet—I was determined to see you again. My spirits rallied with the morning, and I felt that I had still a motive for remaining here."

At last Anne was at home again, and happier than any one in that house could have conceived. All the surprise and suspense, and every other painful part of the morning dissipated by this conversation, she re-entered the house so happy as to be obliged to find an alloy in some momentary apprehensions of its being impossible to last. An interval of meditation, serious and grateful, was the best corrective of every thing dangerous in such high-wrought felicity; and she went to her room, and grew steadfast and fearless in the thankfulness of her enjoyment.[104]

The evening came, the drawing-rooms were lighted up,[105] the company assembled. It was but a card-party, it was but a mixture of those who had never met before, and those who met too often—a common-place business, too numerous for intimacy, too small for variety; but Anne had never found an evening shorter. Glowing and lovely in sensibility[106] and happiness, and more generally admired than she thought about or cared for, she had cheerful or forbearing feelings for every creature around her. Mr. Elliot was there; she avoided, but she could pity him. The Wallises; she had amusement in understanding them.[107] Lady Dalrymple and Miss Carteret; they would soon be innoxious[108] cousins to her. She cared not for Mrs. Clay, and had nothing to blush for in the public manners of her father and sister. With the Musgroves, there was the happy chat of perfect ease; with Captain Harville, the kind-hearted intercourse of brother and sister; with Lady Russell, attempts at conversation, which a delicious consciousness cut short;[109] with Admiral and Mrs. Croft, every thing of peculiar[110] cordiality and fervent interest, which the same consciousness sought to conceal;[111]—and with Captain Wentworth, some moments of communication continually occurring, and always the hope of more, and always the knowledge of his being there![112]

It was in one of these short meetings, each apparently occupied in admiring a fine display of green-house plants,[113] that she said—

104.This shows the ideal of balance that is often found in Jane Austen: an excess of anything, even happiness, can be dangerous. In this case Anne is finally content when she can be steadfast rather than highly wrought. In the original draft of the novel this passage presents the idea of excess in happiness even more sharply: "It was necessary to sit up half the Night, & lie awake the remainder to comprehend with composure her present state, & pay for the overplus of Bliss, by Headake [*sio*] and Fatigue."

105. The lighting up of the rooms is mentioned particularly because one notable feature of evening parties and entertainments was that they were the only time large amounts of artificial illumination were used. Otherwise the high cost of lighting caused people, even the wealthy, to be sparing in its use. On a special occasion the most likely form of illumination was wax or spermaceti (whale oil) candles—both much better but also much more expensive than the standard tallow candles. Many would be hung in a chandelier, which had become a standard fixture in affluent homes. Oil lamps, potentially even more powerful but very costly to fill, were also used.

106. *sensibility*: acute or aroused feelings. The positive connotation given to the term here shows a possible relaxation of the critical attitude toward sensibility seen in *Sense and Sensibility*. For more on this issue, see p. 279, note 17.

107. Mrs. Wallis has recently finished her confinement—see p. 267, note 37, and p. 375, note 25—and thus can attend the party. Anne can have amusement, or occupation, in understanding them because she has already heard much about them without having seen them yet.

108. *innoxious*: innocuous.

109. The delicious consciousness would be her awareness of her engagement, which she knows will confound Lady Russell. It may be delicious to Anne because it will force Lady Russell to confront the error of her earlier persuasion of Anne and her mistaken opinion of Captain Wentworth.

110. *peculiar*: particular.

111. She knows that her engagement will give them a more particular and fervent interest in one another, but she cannot reveal that yet.

112. It would be impolite to separate very long from the main party for private conversation, especially if there were many friends and relatives there.

113. Greenhouses had become very popular in England, allowing the production and display of plants that could not be grown there or could not be grown throughout the year. Hence the Elliots can display plants even though it is now February. It is possible that, rather than being purchased, the plants came from their own greenhouse, since some nicer town houses included one.

"I have been thinking over the past, and trying impartially to judge of the right and wrong, I mean with regard to myself; and I must believe that I was right, much as I suffered from it, that I was perfectly right in being guided by the friend whom you will love better than you do now. To me, she was in the place of a parent. Do not mistake me, however. I am not saying that she did not err in her advice. It was, perhaps, one of those cases in which advice is good or bad only as the event[114] decides;[115] and for myself, I certainly never should, in any circumstance of tolerable similarity, give such advice. But I mean, that I was right in submitting to her, and that if I had done otherwise, I should have suffered more in continuing the engagement than I did even in giving it up, because I should have suffered in my conscience.[116] I have now, as far as such a sentiment is allowable in human nature, nothing to reproach myself with,[117] and if I mistake not, a strong sense of duty is no bad part of a woman's portion."[118]

He looked at her, looked at Lady Russell, and looking again at her, replied, as if in cool deliberation,

"Not yet. But there are hopes of her being forgiven in time. I trust to being in charity with her soon. But I too have been thinking over the past, and a question has suggested itself, whether there may not have been one person more my enemy even than that lady? My own self. Tell me if, when I returned to England in the year eight, with a few thousand pounds, and was posted into the Laconia,[119] if I had then written to you, would you have answered my letter? would you, in short, have renewed the engagement then?"

"Would I!" was all her answer; but the accent was decisive enough.[120]

"Good God!" he cried, "you would! It is not that I did not think of it, or desire it, as what could alone crown all my other success. But I was proud, too proud to ask again. I did not understand you. I shut my eyes, and would not understand you, or do you justice. This is a recollection which ought to make me forgive every one sooner than myself. Six years of separation and suffering might have been spared. It is a sort of pain, too, which is new to me. I

114. *event:* result, outcome.

115. Her meaning is presumably that, because Lady Russell's advice was founded principally on her pessimism about Captain Wentworth's chances, its rightness would inevitably be determined by how well his career went. Anne stated earlier that she would have preferred the engagement even if his lack of success had forced her to wait for years (p. 54), but perhaps she considers that, from a more objective point of view, Lady Russell's caution would have been vindicated by such a turn of events.

116. She would have suffered because of her violation of the principle of duty toward parents or parental figures, a basic tenet of this society. This point also seems to contradict her earlier statement: "She was persuaded that . . . she should yet have been a happier woman in maintaining the engagement, than she had been in the sacrifice of it" (p. 54). There, however, she was focusing on the general wisdom of renouncing the engagement, encapsulated in the question of whether she would give similar advice to another young person. It did not address specifically whether Anne would have been happier in continuing the engagement *after* Lady Russell had issued her advice to the contrary, and thereby imposed an obligation on Anne. Thus Anne's position may be consistent, though it is also possible that now that she no longer suffers from her earlier decision, she is less inclined to condemn the reasoning behind it.

117. She alludes to the Christian idea of universal human sinfulness and the great danger of proudly believing oneself to be free of sin or weakness.

118. *portion:* dowry; or, what one has been allotted, whether by specific events or by fate in general. Anne probably has both meanings in mind (and both are found elsewhere in Austen). The latter would fit because her own course of life until now has inculcated that sense of duty in her, and because the many social obligations of women would make such a sense valuable, both for fulfilling these obligations and for being contented while doing so. The former meaning could be appropriate since, dutifulness would be important in a wife: discussions of marriage then emphasized its many duties, with a particular emphasis on those of a wife. Anne, in alluding to such a dowry, could have in mind her current lack of a regular monetary one, due to her father's indebtedness (see p. 475, note 7).

119. This would have been two years after his first proposal. Of greater importance than his few thousand pounds was his promotion to captain, necessary to command a frigate like the *Laconia*. This promotion was a crucial one, for it meant that he was certain, if he lived, to become an admiral and rise through its ranks, since advancement at that level was based purely on seniority. Below the level of captain there was no assurance of rising higher.

120. In addition to the better position of Captain Wentworth just described,

have been used to the gratification of believing myself to earn every blessing that I enjoyed. I have valued myself on honourable toils and just rewards.[121] Like other great men under reverses," he added with a smile, "I must endeavour to subdue my mind to my fortune. I must learn to brook being happier than I deserve."

Anne's willingness at this point to override her earlier caution would have probably resulted from her not having had other acceptable offers in the interval, which meant she would be getting closer to being past the age of marital eligibility. It could have stemmed as well from an increased sense, as she matured, of independence and ability to form her own judgments.

121. The navy, due to the opportunities it provided to rise through merit, as Captain Wentworth seems to have done, could encourage this sense of desert.

Woman of the time wearing and holding a portrait miniature.

[From *Stuart; American School* (Boston, 1906), plate VII]

Chapter Twelve

Who can be in doubt of what followed? When any two young people take it into their heads to marry, they are pretty sure by perseverance to carry their point, be they ever so poor, or ever so imprudent, or ever so little likely to be necessary to each other's ultimate comfort. This may be bad morality to conclude with,[1] but I believe it to be truth; and if such parties succeed, how should a Captain Wentworth and an Anne Elliot, with the advantage of maturity of mind, consciousness of right, and one independent[2] fortune between them, fail of bearing down every opposition? They might in fact have borne down a great deal more than they met with, for there was little to distress them beyond the want[3] of graciousness and warmth. — Sir Walter made no objection, and Elizabeth did nothing worse than look cold and unconcerned. Captain Wentworth, with five-and-twenty thousand pounds, and as high in his profession as merit and activity could place him,[4] was no longer nobody. He was now esteemed quite worthy to address[5] the daughter of a foolish, spendthrift baronet, who had not had principle or sense enough to maintain himself in the situation in which Providence had placed him,[6] and who could give his daughter at present but a small part of the share of ten thousand pounds which must be hers hereafter.[7]

Sir Walter indeed, though he had no affection for Anne, and no vanity flattered, to make him really happy on the occasion, was very far from thinking it a bad match for her. On the contrary, when he saw more of Captain Wentworth, saw him repeatedly by daylight and eyed him well,[8] he was very much struck by his personal claims,[9] and felt that his superiority of appearance might be not unfairly balanced against her superiority of rank;[10] and all this, assisted by his well-sounding name,[11] enabled Sir Walter at

1. It would be bad morality to conclude with because it violates the principle of obedience to parents and the need to seek parental consent in marriage. The strength of this belief is shown in the contemporary reaction to the novel. Of three reviews of the novel just after it appeared, two complained of its moral tendency. One of them, in the *British Critic*, declared that the novel "contains parts of very great merit; among them, however, we certainly should not number its *moral*, which seems to be, that young people should always marry according to their own inclinations and upon their own judgment" (emphasis in original).

2. *independent:* sufficient.

3. *want:* lack.

4. His current rank of captain has been attained by the merit of his actions. The higher rank of admiral, and its various gradations, would all be attained by seniority.

5. *address:* apply to (with the intention of marrying).

6. The idea that providence placed people in their station of life was common then. It was generally accompanied by the idea that people should fulfill the duties of their station well, which Sir Walter has not by spending beyond his means and being forced to cease presiding over the estate.

7. This would be her dowry, guaranteed as part of the strict settlement binding the estate; it had probably been established on the marriage of Sir Walter and his wife. Normally a daughter would receive her dowry upon her marriage, thereby contributing to the fortune of the new couple. Sir Walter's debts prevent him from fulfilling most of that obligation. But she will eventually get it; even if Sir Walter never gives her the remainder, upon his death the estate will be required to pay it.

8. The weak artificial illumination of the time meant that one could see people well only by daylight. Sir Walter already showed a consciousness of this when discussing Lady Russell's appearance (see p. 409, note 33).

9. *personal claims:* claims of personal appearance.

10. These are, of course, Sir Walter's supreme values.

11. As mentioned earlier by Sir Walter, Wentworth was the family name of the Earls of Strafford (p. 45, note 49).

last to prepare his pen with a very good grace for the insertion of the marriage in the volume of honour.[12]

The only one among them, whose opposition of feeling could excite any serious anxiety, was Lady Russell. Anne knew that Lady Russell must be suffering some pain in understanding and relinquishing Mr. Elliot, and be making some struggles to become truly acquainted with, and do justice to Captain Wentworth. This however was what Lady Russell had now to do. She must learn to feel that she had been mistaken with regard to both; that she had been unfairly influenced by appearances in each; that because Captain Wentworth's manners[13] had not suited her own ideas, she had been too quick in suspecting them to indicate a character of dangerous impetuosity; and that because Mr. Elliot's manners had precisely pleased her in their propriety and correctness, their general politeness and suavity, she had been too quick in receiving them as the certain result of the most correct opinions and well regulated mind.[14] There was nothing less for Lady Russell to do, than to admit that she had been pretty completely wrong, and to take up a new set of opinions and of hopes.[15]

There is a quickness of perception in some, a nicety[16] in the discernment of character, a natural penetration, in short, which no experience in others can equal, and Lady Russell had been less gifted in this part of understanding[17] than her young friend. But she was a very good woman, and if her second object was to be sensible and well-judging, her first was to see Anne happy. She loved Anne better than she loved her own abilities;[18] and when the awkwardness of the beginning was over, found little hardship in attaching herself as a mother to the man who was securing the happiness of her other child.[19]

Of all the family, Mary was probably the one most immediately gratified by the circumstance. It was creditable to have a sister married, and she might flatter herself with having been greatly instrumental to the connexion,[20] by keeping Anne with her in the autumn; and as her own sister must be better than her husband's sisters, it was very agreeable that Captain Wentworth should be a

12. This is the Baronetage, which came in multiple volumes. Sir Walter was earlier shown updating his family entry by writing in new information of importance.

13. *manners:* outer qualities or behavior.

14. *mind:* inner character.

15. This change in Lady Russell is plausible, but it could be argued that its being only summarized at the end is a weakness in the novel. The limited development of Lady Russell as a character, relative to her importance, has already been discussed (p. 247, note 18). In the last part of the book she never appears at all, despite being in Bath the whole time and despite her frequent recurrence in Anne's thoughts (the last time she is more than mentioned is in Volume II, Chapter Seven).

16. *nicety:* subtlety, minute accuracy.

17. *part of understanding:* portion of her intellect.

18. *abilities:* mental powers, cleverness.

19. The other child is Anne—once she is done "attaching herself as a mother" to Captain Wentworth, she has two children in effect.

20. *connexion:* connection—that is, one formed by marriage.

richer man than either Captain Benwick or Charles Hayter.—
She had something to suffer perhaps when they came into contact again, in seeing Anne restored to the rights of seniority,[21] and
the mistress of a very pretty landaulette,[22] but she had a future to
look forward to, of powerful consolation. Anne had no Upper-
cross-hall before her, no landed estate, no headship of a family;[23]
and if they could but keep Captain Wentworth from being made
a baronet, she would not change situations with Anne.

It would be well for the eldest sister if she were equally satisfied
with her situation, for a change is not very probable there. She
had soon the mortification of seeing Mr. Elliot withdraw; and no
one of proper condition[24] has since presented himself to raise
even the unfounded hopes which sunk with him.

The news of his cousin Anne's engagement burst on Mr. Elliot
most unexpectedly. It deranged his best plan of domestic happiness, his best hope of keeping Sir Walter single by the watchfulness which a son-in-law's rights would have given. But, though
discomfited and disappointed, he could still do something for his
own interest and his own enjoyment. He soon quitted Bath; and
on Mrs. Clay's quitting it likewise soon afterwards, and being next
heard of as established under his protection in London,[25] it was
evident how double a game he had been playing, and how determined he was to save himself from being cut out by one artful[26]
woman, at least.

Mrs. Clay's affections had overpowered her interest, and she
had sacrificed, for the young man's sake, the possibility of scheming longer for Sir Walter. She has abilities, however, as well as
affections; and it is now a doubtful point whether his cunning, or
hers, may finally carry the day; whether, after preventing her from
being the wife of Sir Walter, he may not be wheedled and
caressed at last into making her the wife of Sir William.[27]

It cannot be doubted that Sir Walter and Elizabeth were
shocked and mortified by the loss of their companion, and the discovery of their deception in her. They had their great cousins, to
be sure, to resort to for comfort; but they must long feel that to flat-

21. A woman's status was raised by being married. Thus Mary enjoyed precedence over Anne, her older sister, when she was married and Anne was not. Anne's marriage returns the precedence to her.

22. *landaulette:* a small carriage with a folding top, which allowed it to be either open or closed (see picture, p. 483). Unlike completely open carriages, such as a gig or a curricle, it was not driven from the passenger seat but by a coachman from a special seat in front. This would be standard for a carriage used by a woman, for women rarely drove. The landaulette, like its larger cousin the landau, was a fashionable vehicle (a barouche-landau is a major source of boasting by a snobbish character in *Emma*). This would undoubtedly be a large part of Mary's suffering on seeing Anne in possession of one, a suffering that would be made worse if Mary herself continued to lack a carriage, a condition she laments early in the novel.

23. This all represents Charles Musgrove's inheritance, and thus what Mary will share in, at least provided Charles outlives his father.

24. *condition:* social position.

25. Mrs. Clay is under his protection because a woman who went to live with a man out of wedlock became a social outcast and would have a hard time finding a place to live, including with her own family. In *Mansfield Park* a woman who abandons her husband for another man ends up exiled to a distant retreat, supported by her family but not allowed to associate with them further. Thus Mrs. Clay's only hope is to remain with Mr. Elliot: he, as a man, would be subject to far less censure or ostracism, and as long as he consents, she could enjoy a comfortable enough existence in London, with its many amusements and the presence of some others living a similar life.

26. *artful:* crafty, wily.

27. This surprising plot development has been given a little preparation, most especially by the meeting between Mr. Elliot and Mrs. Clay spied by Mary. Anne also reflected earlier on how he made himself as agreeable to Mrs. Clay as to anyone else (p. 306), and the incident when Mrs. Clay disputed with Anne over who should walk with Mr. Elliot instead of riding in the carriage might have resulted from Mrs. Clay's allowing her eagerness to be with Mr. Elliot overpower her discretion (p. 330). This development also serves some useful functions. It wraps up this subplot and resolves the question of what will happen between Sir Walter and Mrs. Clay. It confirms Mrs. Smith's revelations about Mr. Elliot's duplicitous character. Finally, it metes out just deserts all around, with Mr. Elliot and Mrs. Clay left to punish each other, Sir Walter and Elizabeth forced to endure some humiliation, and Anne spared having to worry further about Mrs. Clay's intrigues in her father's house.

ter and follow others, without being flattered and followed in turn, is but a state of half enjoyment.

Anne, satisfied at a very early period of Lady Russell's meaning to love Captain Wentworth as she ought, had no other alloy to the happiness of her prospects than what arose from the conscious-ness of having no relations to bestow on him which a man of sense could value. There she felt her own inferiority keenly. The dis-proportion in their fortune was nothing; it did not give her a moment's regret;[28] but to have no family to receive and estimate him properly; nothing of respectability, of harmony, of good-will to offer in return for all the worth and all the prompt welcome which met her in his brothers and sisters,[29] was a source of as lively pain as her mind could well be sensible[30] of, under circum-stances of otherwise strong felicity.[31] She had but two friends in the world to add to his list, Lady Russell and Mrs. Smith. To those, however, he was very well disposed to attach himself. Lady Rus-sell, in spite of all her former transgressions, he could now value from his heart. While he was not obliged to say that he believed her to have been right in originally dividing them, he was ready to say almost every thing else in her favour;[32] and as for Mrs. Smith, she had claims of various kinds to recommend her quickly and permanently.

Her recent good offices[33] by Anne had been enough in them-selves; and their marriage, instead of depriving her of one friend, secured her two. She was their earliest visitor in their settled life; and Captain Wentworth, by putting her in the way of recovering[34] her husband's property in the West Indies; by writing for her, act-ing for her, and seeing her through all the petty difficulties of the case, with the activity and exertion of a fearless man and a deter-mined friend, fully requited the services which she had rendered, or ever meant to render, to his wife.

Mrs. Smith's enjoyments were not spoiled by this improvement of income, with some improvement of health, and the acquisition of such friends to be often with, for her cheerfulness and mental alacrity did not fail her; and while these prime supplies of good remained, she might have bid defiance even to greater accessions

Yet it has serious problems of plausibility. Both Mr. Elliot and Mrs. Clay have been shown as careful, unemotional characters, governed primarily by calculations of self-interest, and their running away together risks their interests. In his case, it does serve to remove the danger of her marrying Sir Walter, while also providing him sexual companionship, something hard for an unmarried man to procure in this society without resorting to prostitutes — this is what is meant by the words "his own enjoyment." But by angering Sir Walter, Mr. Elliot will no longer be able to intervene in case another woman tries to snare him. Moreover, if Mr. Elliot felt the need to establish an even more intimate footing in the family, he always had the option of marrying Elizabeth. That would bind him even more closely to Sir Walter than marrying Anne would have. Elizabeth is a far less appealing person, but she is attractive and has good external manners, something Mr. Elliot values, while she, unlike Anne, shares completely his high regard for rank; Mr. Elliot's first marriage also indicates that he does not mind having a wife he does not respect if the marriage serves his interests.

As for Mrs. Clay, her affection for Mr. Elliot would need to be so strong as to override all other considerations. Unless she can wheedle him into marriage — and she has no means of pressuring him, while he seems like a difficult person to wheedle or manipulate — she has made herself a social outcast. She can no longer associate with most people, and if he abandons her, she could be left with no one and scarcely any means of even supporting herself. She has also alienated her family, which would be her one remaining refuge in the event of his abandonment. Her action would bring social disgrace upon them, while forever tarnishing the lives of her children, and probably harming, perhaps fatally, her father's business as an attorney, especially by causing him to lose the vital custom of Sir Walter.

28. Her lack of concern could result from her own nonmaterialistic character or from the greater wealth that men usually brought to a marriage.

29. The plural for both brother and sister is used because in-laws are included. Hence it means the Crofts and Edward Wentworth and his wife (the existence of the latter is mentioned on p. 140).

30. *sensible:* cognizant, conscious.

31. A fundamental principle seen in Jane Austen is that marriage is never simply the union of two individuals. It always involves a larger circle of people, and the best couples are those whose love for each other goes along with goodwill toward, and good relations with, others.

32. Thus both Captain Wentworth and Lady Russell end up adjusting their ideas about each other.

33. *offices by:* services to.

34. *putting her in the way of recovering:* helping her to be able to recover.

of worldly prosperity.[35] She might have been absolutely rich and perfectly healthy, and yet be happy. Her spring of felicity was in the glow of her spirits, as her friend Anne's was in the warmth of her heart. Anne was tenderness itself, and she had the full worth of it in Captain Wentworth's affection. His profession was all that could ever make her friends wish that tenderness less;[36] the dread of a future war all that could dim her sunshine.[37] She gloried in being a sailor's wife, but she must pay the tax[38] of quick alarm for belonging to that profession which is, if possible, more distinguished in its domestic virtues than in its national importance.

THE END.

35. This is playful irony at the expense of the romantic idea, which some literature of the time promoted, that wealth was inimical to happiness. In *Sense and Sensibility* the highly romantic Marianne argues that the two have nothing to do with each other, before admitting that she still considers a very substantial sum to be necessary for a decent existence. Jane Austen, while never celebrating wealth as the key to happiness or advocating the sacrifice of other values for its sake, always indicated that wealth could be a good thing and certainly did not mar life.

36. Her friends wish her tenderness to be less because it makes her worry more about the dangers that a naval captain inevitably runs whenever he goes to sea.

37. During the time when the novel is supposed to finish, early 1815, Napoleon escaped from his exile in Elba, reassumed the throne of France, and caused a renewal of warfare. But this lasted only a few months, at the end of which Napoleon was defeated for good, and it led to little action on the part of the navy. Jane Austen, writing in 1816, would have known that, but she could not have known that the British navy would not experience another major war until a hundred years later.

38. *pay the tax:* suffer the burden.

A landaulette. The front seat is for a driver.

[From Ralph Straus, *Carriages and Coaches* (London, 1912), p. 232]

Chronology

Persuasion is the one Jane Austen novel whose year can be precisely identified, for the text indicates at an early point that it is "the summer of 1814." Austen also provides exact birth dates for several important characters and states the year during which background events occurred. At the same time, she did not consult a calendar when writing the novel, for at one point February 2 is described as a Tuesday (see below) but in fact February 2, 1815, was a Thursday.

VOLUME I		**PAGE**
March 1, 1760	Birth of Sir Walter Elliot	2
1780	Birth of Mr. Elliot	384
	Says in letter of 1803 that he has lived 23 years.	
July 15, 1784	Marriage of Sir Walter and Lady Elliot	2
June 1, 1785	Birth of Elizabeth Elliot	2
August 9, 1787	Birth of Anne Elliot	2
November 20, 1791	Birth of Mary Elliot	2
1801	Death of Lady Elliot	2
	Text says 1800, but it is almost certainly 1801 (this was possibly a printer error). Just below it says the marriage lasted 17 years, Elizabeth and Anne were 16 and 14 (p. 6), and 13 years had passed (p. 6). This same information is repeated at later points.	
1801–1804	Anne attends school in Bath	26
	She went for three years after her mother's death.	
1802	Mrs. Smith (then Miss Hamilton) leaves school	288
	She is described as "remaining another year at school" after Anne's arrival.	
1802–1803	Sir Walter and Elizabeth seek out Mr. Elliot	12

They saw him two springs in London, and in a letter of July 1803, Mr. Elliot writes he has seen them this year and last year (p. 384).

Late 1803 or   Marriage of Mr. and Mrs. Smith   288
Early 1804   *She married shortly after leaving school, but she says a letter of July 1803 was prior to the marriage (p. 384). Also it was approximately 11 years before January 1815, for she is 30 then (p. 298), and she was 19 when she met Mr. Elliot, presumably just after her marriage to Mr. Smith (p. 378).*

1804   Marriage of Mr. Elliot   12
After not seeing Mr. Elliot in 1803, Sir Walter's "next tidings were that he was married." It occurred after the Smith marriage, for Mr. Elliot confided in Mrs. Smith about his plans (pp. 380–382).

February 1806   Battle of St. Domingo, as a result of which   48
Frederick Wentworth was made commander

Summer 1806   Visit of Captain Wentworth in Somerset;   48
romance and engagement with Anne

Late 1806   Engagement broken; Captain Wentworth departs   52
Their acquaintance lasted "a few months."

Late 1806 or   Captain Wentworth given command of the *Asp*   124
Early 1807   *He strongly wished to be at sea and doing something then (due to his rejection by Anne).*

Autumn 1808   Return of Captain Wentworth to England;
promotion to captain; assignment to the *Laconia*   126
He later says it was in 1808 (p. 470).

1809 or 1810   Anne refuses Charles Musgrove's offer of marriage   52
She was "about two-and-twenty."

December 16, 1810   Marriage of Charles and Mary   2

1812   Death of Dick Musgrove   96

Severe wound suffered by Captain Harville   180
Both events occurred "two years before."

1812–1813   Engagement of Captain Benwick and
Fanny Harville   184
"They had been a year or two waiting" to marry before her death in the summer of 1814.

Death of Mr. Smith   288
It was "about two years before" January 1814.

This is later described as a Tuesday (p. 312), which
conflicts with the 1815 calendar (see above).

February 3	Mary finishes her letter	314
	She probably finished the day after the above events,	
	for she mentions learning of them "in the evening."	
Early February	Crofts arrive in Bath and deliver letter to Anne	308
	This is probably a day or two after Mary finished	
	her letter. She writes on February 1 that "the Crofts	
	are going to Bath almost immediately" (p. 310).	
Early to Mid-	Captain Wentworth learns of Louisa's engagement	464
February	*He quickly resolves to be in "Bath on Wednesday."*	
	Captain Wentworth writes to his sister about	
	the news	326
	Admiral Croft says Captain Wentworth had just	
	learned the news from Captain Harville (p. 326).	
1–2 Days Later	Mrs. Croft receives letter from Captain Wentworth	326
Mid-February	Anne walks with Admiral Croft	320
	This was "about a week or ten days after the Crofts'	
	arrival [in Bath]," in early February. It is the day after	
	they received Captain Wentworth's letter (p. 326).	

From this point on, for the only sustained period in the novel, the events can be
precisely chronicled. The overall sequence would occur in mid- to late February.

Wednesday	Captain Wentworth arrives in Bath	464
	He was on his way to Bath on the day of Anne's walk	
	with Admiral Croft (p. 320). It would probably take	
	a little more than a day to go from Shropshire to	
	Bath, which would mean his arrival happened the	
	next day and Anne's walk with the admiral	
	happened on Tuesday.	
Thursday	Anne encounters Captain Wentworth at	
	Molland's shop	332
	He says he arrived in Bath "yesterday" (p. 336). It	
	is also "the very next time Anne walked out" after	
	her walk with the admiral (p. 330).	
Friday	Anne and Lady Russell see Captain Wentworth	338
	It was "the following morning."	
Saturday–Sunday	Anne does not see him again and anticipates the	
	concert	340

"A day or two passed [after above sighting] without producing any thing."

Sunday	Nurse Rooke leaves Mrs. Wallis	374
	She was attending her after childbirth.	
Monday	Mrs. Smith sees Nurse Rooke	374
	Mrs. Smith hears of the rumors of Anne and Mr. Elliot.	
Wednesday	Anne sees Mrs. Smith briefly during the day	342
	She calls on her the day of the concert.	
	Evening concert; Anne talks to Captain Wentworth	344
	Bath concerts normally occurred on Wednesday evenings (see p. 343, note 34).	
Thursday	Anne visits Mrs. Smith and learns Mr. Elliot's history	364
	Mr. Elliot joins Sir Walter's family in the evening	404
Friday	Mr. Elliot leaves for Thornberry Park	406
	He said on previous day he would be away "tomorrow."	
	Arrival of Musgroves in Bath	408
	Anne joins Musgroves and sees Captain Wentworth	420–434
	Mr. Elliot seen meeting Mrs. Clay	424
Saturday	Anne goes to the Musgroves' rather than to Lady Russell's	438
	Wentworth proposes to Anne	452
	Party at Elliots' in the evening	468
	Invitations given by the Elliots on the previous day were for "to-morrow evening" (p. 432).	
Soon After	Announcement of Anne and Captain Wentworth's engagement	474
	Mr. Elliot and Mrs. Clay depart Bath together	478

Bibliography

EDITIONS OF *PERSUASION*

Chapman, R. W., ed., *The Novels of Jane Austen, Vol. V: Northanger Abbey and Persuasion* (Oxford, 1933)

Spacks, Patricia Meyer, ed., *Persuasion: A Norton Critical Edition* (New York, 1995)

Todd, Janet, and Antje Blank, eds., *The Cambridge Edition of the Works of Jane Austen: Persuasion* (Cambridge, 2006)

WORKS BY JANE AUSTEN

Jane Austen's Letters, ed. by Deirdre Le Faye (Oxford, 1995)

Jane Austen's "Sir Charles Grandison," ed. by Brian Southam (Oxford, 1980)

The Oxford Illustrated Jane Austen, 6 vols., ed. by R. W. Chapman (Oxford, 1988)

WORKS RELATING TO JANE AUSTEN

Biographical

Austen, Caroline, *Reminiscences of Caroline Austen* (Guildford, 1986)

Austen-Leigh, J. E., *A Memoir of Jane Austen and Other Family Recollections* (Oxford, 2002; originally published 1871)

Austen-Leigh, William, and Richard Arthur Austen-Leigh, *Jane Austen: A Family Record,* revised and enlarged by Deirdre Le Faye (Boston, 1989)

Harman, Claire, *Jane's Fame: How Jane Austen Conquered the World* (Edinburgh, 2009)

Honan, Park, *Jane Austen: Her Life* (New York, 1989)

Le Faye, Deirdre, *Jane Austen: The World of Her Novels* (New York, 2002)

Mitten, G. E., *Jane Austen and Her Times* (Philadelphia, 2003; originally 1905)

Myer, Valerie Grosvener, *Jane Austen: Obstinate Heart* (New York, 1997)

Ross, Josephine, *Jane Austen: A Companion* (New Brunswick, NJ, 2003)

Critical

Auerbach, Emily, *Searching for Jane Austen* (Madison, 2004)

Axelrad, Arthur M., *Jane Austen Caught in the Act of Greatness* (U.S.: 1st Books, 2003)

Babb, Howard S., *Jane Austen's Novels: The Fabric of Dialogue* (Columbus, OH, 1962)

Bush, Douglas, *Jane Austen* (New York, 1975)

Cecil, Lord David, *A Portrait of Jane Austen* (New York, 1979)

Craik, W. A., *Jane Austen: The Six Novels* (London, 1965)

Dadlez, E. M., *Mirrors to One Another: Emotion and Value in Jane Austen and Hume* (Chichester, 2009)

Duckworth, Alistair M., *The Improvement of the Estate: A Study of Jane Austen's Novels* (Baltimore, 1971)

Dwyer, June, *Jane Austen* (New York, 1989)

Emsley, Sarah, *Jane Austen's Philosophy of the Virtues* (New York, 2005)

Gard, Roger, *Jane Austen's Novels: The Art of Clarity* (New Haven, 1992)

Gomme, Andor, "On Not Being Persuaded," *Essays in Criticism* 16, 1966: 170–184

Gooneratne, Yasmine, *Jane Austen* (Cambridge, 1970)

Graham, Peter, *Jane Austen and Charles Darwin* (Aldershot, 2008)

Grey, J. David, ed., *The Jane Austen Companion* (New York, 1986)

Hardy, John, *Jane Austen's Heroines: Intimacy in Human Relationships* (London, 1984)

Harris, Jocelyn, *A Revolution Almost Beyond Expression: Jane Austen's Persuasion* (Newark, DE, 2007)

Jones, Vivien, *How to Study a Jane Austen Novel* (Basingstoke, Hampshire, 1987)

Kennedy, Margaret, *Jane Austen* (London, 1950)

Konigsberg, Ira, *Narrative Technique in the English Novel: Defoe to Austen* (Hamden, CT, 1985)

Kroeber, Karl, *Styles in Fictional Structure: The Art of Jane Austen, Charlotte Brontë, George Eliot* (Princeton, 1971)

Lascelles, Mary, *Jane Austen and Her Art* (Oxford, 1939)

Lauber, John, *Jane Austen* (New York, 1993)

Liddell, Robert, *The Novels of Jane Austen* (London, 1963)

Litz, J. Walton, *Jane Austen* (New York, 1965)

MacDonagh, Oliver, *Jane Austen: Real and Imagined Worlds* (New Haven, 1991)

Mansell, Darrel, *The Novels of Jane Austen: An Interpretation* (London, 1973)

McMaster, Juliet, *Jane Austen the Novelist* (Basingstoke, 1996)

Moler, Kenneth L., *Jane Austen's Art of Illusion* (Lincoln, NE, 1968)

Mooneyham, Laura, *Romance, Language and Education in Jane Austen's Novels* (New York, 1988)

Morris, Ivor, *Jane Austen and the Interplay of Character* (London, 1999)

Mudrick, Marvin, *Jane Austen: Irony as Defense and Discovery* (Princeton, 1952)

Nardin, Jane, *Those Elegant Decorums: The Concept of Propriety in Jane Austen's Novels* (Albany, NY, 1973)

Paris, J. Bernard, *Character and Conflict in Jane Austen's Novels* (Detroit, 1978)

Roberts, Warren, *Jane Austen and the French Revolution* (New York, 1979)

Scott, P. J. M., *Jane Austen* (London, 1982)

Southam, B. C., ed., *Jane Austen: The Critical Heritage*, 2 vols. (London, 1968–1987)

———, *Jane Austen: Northanger Abbey and Persuasion: A Casebook* (London, 1976)

Spacks, Patricia Meyer, ed., *Persuasion: A Norton Critical Edition* (New York, 1995)

Stovel, Bruce and Lynn Weinlos Gregg, *The Talk in Jane Austen* (Alberta, 2002)

Ten Harmsel, Henrietta, *Jane Austen: A Study in Fictional Conventions* (The Hague, 1964)

Thomson, Clara Linklater, *Jane Austen: A Survey* (London, 1929)

Weisenfarth, Joseph, *The Errand of Form: An Assay of Jane Austen's Art* (New York, 1967)

Winborn, Colin, *The Literary Economy of George Crabbe and Jane Austen* (Aldershot, 2004)

WORKS OF HISTORICAL BACKGROUND

General Histories and Reference

Craik, W. A., *Jane Austen in Her Time* (London, 1969)

Encyclopaedia Britannica; or, A Dictionary of Arts, Sciences, and Miscellaneous Literature, 3rd ed. (Edinburgh, 1797), and 4th ed. (Edinburgh, 1810)

Halevy, Elie, *A History of the English People in the Nineteenth Century*, vol. I: *England in 1815*, translated by E. I. Watkin and D. A. Barker, 2nd ed. (London, 1949)

McKendrick, Neil, John Brewer, and J. H. Plumb, *The Birth of a Consumer Society: the Commercialization of Eighteenth-Century England* (Bloomington, IN, 1982)

Olsen, Kirstin, *All Things Austen: An Encyclopedia of Austen's World*, 2 vols. (Westport, CT, 2005)

Porter, Roy, *English Society in the Eighteenth Century*, rev. ed. (London, 1990)

Rule, John, *Albion's People: English Society, 1714–1815* (London, 1992)

Todd, Janet, ed., *Jane Austen in Context* (New York, 2005)

Turberville, A. S., ed., *Johnson's England: An Account of the Life and Manners of His Age*, vols. I and II (Oxford, 1933)

Language of the Period

The Compact Edition of the Oxford English Dictionary (Oxford, 1971)

Johnson, Samuel, *Dictionary of the English Language*, ed. by Alexander Chalmers (London, 1994; reprint of 1843 ed.)

Page, Norman, *The Language of Jane Austen* (Oxford, 1972)

Phillipps, K. C., *Jane Austen's English* (London, 1970)

Pinion, F. B., *A Jane Austen Companion* (London, 1973)

Room, Adrian, *Dictionary of Changes in Meaning* (New York, 1986)

Schapera, I., *Kinship Terminology in Jane Austen's Novels* (London, 1977)

Stokes, Myra, *The Language of Jane Austen: A Study of Some Aspects of Her Vocabulary* (New York, 1991)

Tucker, Susie, *Protean Shape: A Study in Eighteenth-Century Vocabulary and Usage* (London, 1967)

Cultural and Literary Background

Ali, Muhsin Jassim, *Scheherazade in England* (Washington, DC, 1981)

Bradbrook, Frank W., *Jane Austen and Her Predecessors* (Cambridge, 1966)

Brewer, John, *The Pleasures of the Imagination: English Culture in the Eighteenth Century* (New York, 1997)

Caracciolo, Peter L., ed., *The Arabian Nights in English Literature* (New York, 1988)

Clark, Kenneth, *The Gothic Revival* (London, 1962)

Fara, Patricia, *An Entertainment for Angels: Electricity in the Enlightenment* (New York, 2002)

Murdoch, John, et al., *The English Miniature* (New Haven, 1981)

Reynolds, Graham, *English Portrait Miniatures* (Cambridge, 1988)

Marriage and the Family

Gillis, John R., *For Better, For Worse: British Marriages, 1600 to the Present* (New York, 1985)

Jones, Hazel, *Jane Austen and Marriage* (London, 2009)

Stone, Lawrence, *The Family, Sex and Marriage in England, 1500–1800* (London, 1977)

Tadmor, Naomi, *Family and Friends in Eighteenth-Century England: Household, Kinship, and Patronage* (Cambridge, 2001)

Trumbach, Randolph, *The Rise of the Egalitarian Family: Aristocratic Kin-*

ship and Domestic Relations in Eighteenth-Century England (New York, 1978)

Wolfram, Sybil, *In-Laws and Outlaws: Kinship and Marriage in England* (Beckenham, Kent, 1987)

The Position of Women

Barker, Hannah, and Elaine Chalus, eds., *Women's History: Britain, 1700–1850: An Introduction* (London, 2005)

Brophy, Elizabeth Bergen, *Women's Lives and the 18th-Century English Novel* (Tampa, 1991)

Hill, Bridget, *Women Alone: Spinsters in England, 1660–1850* (New Haven, 2001)

Horn, Pamela, *Victorian Countrywomen* (Oxford, 1991)

Perkin, Joan, *Women and Marriage in Nineteenth-Century England* (London, 1989)

Shoemaker, Robert B., *Gender in English Society, 1650–1850: The Emergence of Separate Spheres?* (London, 1998)

Tague, Ingrid H., *Women of Quality: Accepting and Contesting Ideals of Femininity in England, 1690–1760* (Woodbridge, UK, 2002)

Vickery, Amanda, *The Gentleman's Daughter: Women's Lives in Georgian England* (London, 1998)

Children and Childbearing

Bayne-Powell, Rosamond, *The English Child in the Eighteenth Century* (New York, 1939)

Fletcher, Anthony, *Growing Up in England: The Experience of Childhood, 1600–1914* (New Haven, 2008)

Lewis, Judith Schneid, *In the Family Way: Childbearing in the British Aristocracy, 1760–1860* (New Brunswick, NJ, 1986)

Steward, James Christen, *The New Child: British Art and the Origins of Modern Childhood* (Berkeley, 1995)

Housekeeping and Servants

Adams, Samuel and Sarah, *The Complete Servant* (Lewes, 1989; originally published 1825)

Bayne-Powell, Rosamond, *Housekeeping in the Eighteenth Century* (London, 1956)

Davidson, Caroline, *A Woman's Work Is Never Done: A History of Housework in the British Isles, 1650–1950* (London, 1982)

Dillon, Maureen, *Artificial Sunshine: A Social History of Domestic Lighting* (London, 2002)

Gerard, Jessica, *Country House Life: Family and Servants, 1815–1914* (Oxford, 1994)

Hardyment, Christina, *Home Comfort: A History of Domestic Arrangements* (Chicago, 1992)

Hecht, J. Jean, *The Domestic Servant Class in Eighteenth-Century England* (London, 1956)

Hill, Bridget, *Servants: English Domestics in the Eighteenth Century* (Oxford, 1996)

Horn, Pamela, *Flunkeys and Scullions: Life Below Stairs in Georgian England* (Stroud, 2004)

——, *The Rise and Fall of the Victorian Servant* (Stroud, 2004)

Laing, Alastair, *Lighting* (London, 1982)

Sambrook, Pamela, *The Country House Servant* (Stroud, 1999)

Stuart, Dorothy Margaret, *The English Abigail* (London, 1946)

Turner, E. S., *What the Butler Saw: 250 Years of the Servant Problem* (New York, 1962)

Entails and Settlements

English, Barbara, and John Saville, *Strict Settlement: A Guide for Historians* (Hull, 1983)

Erickson, Amy Louise, *Women and Property in Early Modern England* (London, 1993)

Habakkuk, John, *Marriage, Debt and the Estates System: English Landownership, 1650–1950* (Oxford, 1994)

Holcombe, Lee, *Wives and Property: Reform of the Married Women's Property Law in Nineteenth-Century England* (Oxford, 1983)

Spring, Eileen, *Law, Land, and Family: Aristocratic Inheritance in England, 1300 to 1800* (Chapel Hill, 1993)

Money and Finance

Bird, James Barry, *The Laws Respecting Landlords, Tenants, and Lodgers* (London, 1801)

Dowell, Stephen, *A History of Taxes and Taxation in England* (London, 1884)

Friedberg, Robert, *Coins of the British World: Complete from 500 A.C. to the Present* (New York, 1962)

Landed Society

Baronetage of England (London, 1806)

Beckett, J. V., *The Aristocracy in England, 1660–1914* (Oxford, 1986)

Bence-Jones, Mark, and Hugh Montgomery-Massingberd, *The British Aristocracy* (London, 1979)

Book of the Ranks and Dignities of British Society, attributed to Charles Lamb (London, 1805; reprinted 1924)

Cannon, John, *Aristocratic Century: The Peerage of Eighteenth-Century England* (Cambridge, 1984)

Debrett's Illustrated Baronetage (London, 1808)

Dugdale, William, *The Antient Usage in Bearing of Such Ensigns of Honour as are commonly call'd Arms* (Oxford, 1682)

Greene, D. J., "Jane Austen and the Peerage," *PMLA* 68 (1953): 1017–1031.

Mingay, G. E., *English Landed Society in the Eighteenth Century* (London, 1963)

——, *The Gentry: The Rise and Fall of a Ruling Class* (New York, 1976)

The New Baronetage of England (London, 1804)

Stone, Lawrence, and Jeanne C. Fawtier Stone, *An Open Elite? England 1540–1880* (Oxford, 1984)

Thompson, F. M. L., *English Landed Society in the Nineteenth Century* (London, 1963)

The Rural World

Bovill, E. W., *English Country Life, 1780–1830* (London, 1962)

Eastwood, David, *Governing Rural England: Tradition and Transformation in Local Government, 1780–1840* (Oxford, 1994)

——, *Government and Community in the English Provinces, 1700–1870* (New York, 1997)

Horn, Pamela, *The Rural World, 1780–1850: Social Change in the English Countryside* (New York, 1980)

Keith-Lucas, Brian, *The Unreformed Local Government System* (London, 1980)

Rackham, Oliver, *The History of the Countryside* (London, 1986)

Wade Martins, Susanna, *Farmers, Landlords, and Landscapes* (Macclesfield, Cheshire, 2004)

Williamson, Tom, *The Transformation of Rural England* (Exeter, UK, 2002)

Williamson, Tom, and Liz Bellamy, *Property and Landscape* (London, 1987)

Urban Life

Adburgham, Alison, *Shopping in Style: London from the Restoration to Edwardian Elegance* (London, 1979)

Corfield, P. J., *The Impact of English Towns, 1700–1800* (Oxford, 1982)

Cox, Nancy, *The Complete Tradesman: A Study of Retailing, 1550–1820* (Aldershot, 2000)

Cruickshank, Daniel, and Neil Burton, *Life in the Georgian City* (London, 1990)

Ellis, Joyce M., *The Georgian Town, 1680–1840* (Basingstoke, 2001)

Girouard, Mark, *The English Town: A History of Urban Life* (New Haven, 1990)

Mui, Hoh-Cheung, and Lorna H. Mui, *Shops and Shopkeeping in Eighteenth-Century England* (Kingston, Ontario, 1989)

Orchard, Vincent, *Tattersalls* (New York, 1954)

The Professions

Corfield, Penelope J., *Power and the Professions in Britain, 1700–1850* (New York, 1995)

Reader, W. J., *Professional Men: The Rise of the Professional Classes in Nineteenth-Century England* (London, 1966)

The Church and the Clergy

Collins, Irene, *Jane Austen and the Clergy* (London, 1994)

Francis Brown, C. K., *A History of the English Clergy, 1800–1900* (London, 1953)

Hart, A. Tindal, *The Curate's Lot* (Newton Abbot, 1971)

Jacob, W. M., *The Clerical Profession in the Long Eighteenth Century, 1680–1840* (Oxford, 2007)

Virgin, Peter, *The Church in an Age of Negligence* (Cambridge, 1989)

Whitaker, Wilfred Barnett, *The Eighteenth-Century English Sunday* (London, 1940)

The Navy and Army

Blake, Nicholas, *Steering to Glory: A Day in the Life of a Ship of the Line* (London, 2005)

Great Britain, Admiralty, *Navy List* (London, 1815)

Holmes, Richard, *Redcoat: The British Soldier in the Age of Horse and Musket* (London, 2001)

Hubback, John H., *Jane Austen's Sailor Brothers* (London, 1906)

King, Dean, *A Sea of Words: A Lexicon and Companion for Patrick O'Brian's Seafaring Tales* (New York, 1995)

Lavery, Brian, *Nelson's Navy: The Ships, Men and Organisation, 1793–1815* (London, 1989)

Lewis, Michael, *England's Sea-Officers: The Story of the Naval Profession* (London, 1939)

———, *A Social History of the Navy, 1793–1815* (London, 1960)

Lincoln, Margarette, *Naval Wives & Mistresses* (London, 2007)

Representing the Royal Navy: British Sea Power, 1750–1815 (Aldershot, 2002)

MacDonald, Janet, *Feeding Nelson's Navy* (London, 2004)

Marcus, G. J., *Heart of Oak: A Survey of British Sea Power in the Georgian Era* (London, 1975)

Rodger, N. A. M., *The Command of the Ocean* (New York, 2006)
The Wooden World: An Anatomy of the Georgian Navy (New York, 1986)
Southam, Brian, *Jane Austen and the Navy* (London, 2005)
Steel, David, *Steel's Original and Correct List of the Royal Navy* (London, 1813)

Medicine

Buchan, William, *Domestic Medicine* (New York, 1815; based on London ed.)
Cooper, Samuel, *First Lines of the Practice of Surgery* (Hanover, NH, 1815; based on London ed.)
Copeman, W. S. C., *A Short History of the Gout and Rheumatic Diseases* (Berkeley, 1964)
Digby, Anne, *Making a Medical Living: Doctors and Patients in the English Market for Medicine, 1720–1911* (Cambridge, UK, 1994)
Dingwall, Robert, Anne Marie Rafferty, and Charles Webster, eds., *An Introduction to the Social History of Nursing* (London, 1988)
English, Peter, *Rheumatic Fever in America and Britain* (New Brunswick, NJ, 1999)
French, Roger, and Andrew Wear, eds., *British Medicine in an Age of Reform* (London, 1991)
Kamenetz, Herman, *The Wheelchair Book* (Springfield, IL, 1969)
King, Lester, *The Medical World of the Eighteenth Century* (Chicago, 1958)
Lane, Joan, *A Social History of Medicine: Health, Healing and Disease in England, 1750–1950* (London, 2001)
Loudon, Irvine, *Medical Care and the General Practitioner, 1750–1850* (Oxford, 1986)
Porter, Roy, and Dorothy Porter, *In Sickness and in Health: The British Experience, 1650–1850* (New York, 1989)
———, *Patient's Progress: Doctors and Doctoring in Eighteenth-Century England* (Stanford, 1989)
Porter, Roy, and G. S. Rousseau, *Gout: The Patrician Malady* (New Haven, 1998)
Scudamore, Charles, *A Treatise on the Nature and Cure of Gout and Rheumatism* (London, 1817)

Law and Lawyers

Abel-Smith, Brian, and Robert Stevens, *Lawyers and the Courts: A Sociological Study of the English Legal System, 1750–1965* (London, 1967)
Baker, J. H., *An Introduction to English Legal History*, 2nd ed. (London, 1979)
Birks, Michael, *Gentlemen of the Law* (London, 1960)

Brooks, Christopher, *Lawyers, Litigation, and English Society since 1450* (London, 1998)

Duman, Daniel, *The Judicial Bench in England, 1727–1875: The Reshaping of a Professional Elite* (London, 1982)

——, *The Laws Respecting Women* (London, 1777; reprinted 1974)

Lemmings, David, *Professors of the Law: Barristers and English Legal Culture in the Eighteenth Century* (Oxford, 2000)

Robson, Robert, *The Attorney in Eighteenth-Century England* (Cambridge, 1959)

Education

Chandos, John, *Boys Together: English Public Schools, 1800–1864* (New Haven, 1984)

Gardiner, Dorothy, *English Girlhood at School: A Study of Women's Education Through Twelve Centuries* (London, 1929)

Books and Newspapers

Black, Jeremy, *The English Press, 1621–1861* (Stroud, 2001)

Bronson, Bertrand H., *Printing as an Index of Taste in Eighteenth-Century England* (New York, 1958)

Clarke, Bob, *From Grub Street to Fleet Street: An Illustrated History of English Newspapers to 1899* (Aldershot, 2004)

St. Clair, William, *The Reading Nation in the Romantic Period* (Cambridge, UK, 2004)

Libraries

Hamlyn, H. M., "Eighteenth-Century Circulating Libraries in England," *Library*, Fifth Series I (1947), pp. 197–218.

Manley, K. A., "Booksellers, Peruke-Makers, and Rabbit-Merchants: the Growth of Circulating Libraries in the Eighteenth Century," in Myers, Robin, Michael Harris, and Giles Mandelbrote, eds., *Libraries and the Book Trade* (New Castle, 2001)

Writing

Finlay, Michael, *Western Writing Implements in the Age of the Quill Pen* (Carlisle, Cumbria, 1990)

Whalley, Joyce Irene, *Writing Implements and Accessories: From the Roman Stylus to the Typewriter* (Newton Abbot, Devon, 1975)

The Postal Service

Hemmeon, J. C., *The History of the British Post Office* (Cambridge, MA, 1912)

Joyce, Herbert, *The History of the Post Office* (London, 1893)

Kay, F. George, *Royal Mail: The Story of the Posts in England from the Time of Edward IVth to the Present Day* (London, 1951)

Transportation

Copeland, John, *Roads and Their Traffic* (Newton Abbot, Devon, 1968)
Dyos, H. J., and D. H. Aldcroft, *British Transport: An Economic Survey from the Seventeenth Century to the Twentieth* (Leicester, 1969)
Felton, William, *A Treatise on Carriages* (London, 1796)
Jackman, W. T., *The Development of Transportation in Modern England* (London, 1962)
Luton Museum and Art Gallery, *The Turnpike Age* (Luton, 1970—reprint of contemporary work by G. Gray)
McCausland, Hugh, *The English Carriage* (London, 1948)
Pawson, Eric, *Transport and Economy: The Turnpike Roads of Eighteenth-Century Britain* (New York, 1977)
Reid, James, *Evolution of Horse-Drawn Vehicles* (London, 1933)
Sparkes, Ivan, *Stagecoaches and Carriages* (Bourne End, 1975)
Stratton, Ezra, *World on Wheels* (New York, 1878)
Whatney, Marylilan, *The Elegant Carriage* (London, 1961)
Wilkinson, T. W., *From Track to By-Pass: A History of the English Road* (London, 1934)

Theater

Leacroft, Richard, *The Development of the English Playhouse* (Ithaca, 1973)
Lowndes, William, *The Theatre Royal at Bath* (Bristol, 1982)
Southern, Richard, *The Georgian Playhouse* (London, 1948)
Theatre Royal, Bath Playbills, 1800–1817: portfolio (Stead Collection, 1933)

Music and Dance

Hart, Miriam, *Hardly an Innocent Diversion: Music in the Life and Writings of Jane Austen* (Ohio U., 1999)
Loesser, Arthur, *Men, Women and Pianos: A Social History* (New York, 1954)
Piggott, Patrick, *The Innocent Diversion: A Study of Music in the Life and Writings of Jane Austen* (London, 1979)
Rensch, Roslyn, *Harps and Harpists* (Bloomington, 1989)
Richardson, Philip J. S., *The Social Dances of the Nineteenth Century in England* (London, 1960)
Sharp, Cecil, *The Country Dance Book* (Wakefield, 1972–76)
Weber, William, *The Great Transformation of Musical Taste: Concert Programming from Haydn to Brahms* (Cambridge, UK, 2008)
Wollenberg, Susan, and Simon McVeigh, eds., *Concert Life in Eighteenth-Century Britain* (Aldershot, 2004)

Wood, Melusine, *Historical Dances: Twelfth to Nineteenth Century* (London, 1982)

Outdoor Sports

Arkwright, William, *The Pointer and His Predecessors* (London, 1906)
Griffin, Emma, *Blood Sport: Hunting in Britain since 1066* (New Haven, 2007)
Held, Robert, *The Age of Firearms: A Pictorial History* (New York, 1957)
Lascelles, Robert, *Letters on Sporting* (London, 1815)
Longrigg, Roger, *The English Squire and His Sport* (New York, 1977)
[Magne de Marolles], adapted and translated by John Acton, *An Essay on Shooting* (London, 1791)
Munsche, P. B., *Gentlemen and Poachers: The English Game Laws, 1671–1831* (Cambridge, UK, 1981)
Needham, T. H. [pseud.], *The Complete Sportsman* (London, 1817)
Pollard, Hugh B. C., *Pollard's History of Firearms* (New York, 1985)
Selwyn, David, *Jane Austen and Leisure* (London, 1999)
The Sportsman's Dictionary (London, 1807)

Weather and Umbrellas

Crawford, T. S., *History of the Umbrella* (New York, 1970)
Farrell, Jeremy, *Umbrellas and Parasols* (London, 1985)
Wheler, Dennis, and Julian Mayes, eds., *Regional Climates of the British Isles* (New York, 1997)

Lyme Regis and the Seaside

Austen-Leigh, Emma, *Jane Austen and Lyme Regis* (Folcroft, PA, 1976)
Feltham, John, *A Guide to All the Watering and Sea-Bathing Places* (London, 1804)
Fowles, John, *A Short History of Lyme Regis* (Boston, 1982)
Gosling, Ted, and Lyn Marshall, *Lyme Regis* (Dover, NH, 1993)
Lane, Maggie, *Jane Austen and Lyme Regis* (Chawton, 2003)
Lencek, Lena, and Gideon Bosker, *The Beach: The History of Paradise on Earth* (New York, 1998)
Roberts, George, *The History of Lyme-Regis, Dorset* (Sherborne, 1823–2007 reprint)
Walton, John K., *The English Seaside Resort: A Social History, 1750–1914* (New York, 1983)

Bath

Barbeau, Alfred, *Une Ville d'Eaux Anglaise au XVIIIe Siecle* (Paris, 1904)
Borsay, Peter, *The Image of Georgian Bath, 1700–2000* (Oxford, 2000)

Davis, Graham, and Penny Bonsall, *A History of Bath: Image and Reality* (Lancaster, 2006)

Egan, Pierce, *Walks through Bath* (Bath, 1819)

Fawcett, Trevor, *Bath Administered* (Bath, 2001)

——, *Bath Commercialised* (Bath, 2002)

——, *Bath Entertained* (Bath, 1998)

Feltham, John, *A Guide to All the Watering and Sea-Bathing Places* (London, 1804)

Hembry, Phyllis, *The English Spa* (London, 1990)

Ibbetson, Julius, *A Picturesque Guide to Bath, Bristol Hot Wells, the River Avon, and the Surrounding Country* (London, 1793)

Ison, Walter, *The Georgian Buildings of Bath* (London, 1948)

Lane, Maggie, *A Charming Place: Bath in the Life and Novels of Jane Austen* (Bath, 1988)

McIntyre, Sylvia, "Bath: The Rise of a Resort Town, 1660–1800," in Peter Clark ed., *Country Towns in Pre-Industrial England* (Leicester, 1981)

Neale, R. S., *Bath, 1680–1850: A Social History* (London, 1981)

Ragg, Laura Maria Roberts, *Jane Austen in Bath* (London, 1938)

Robertson, Charles, *Bath: An Architectural Guide* (London, 1975)

Warner, Richard, *Bath Characters, or, Sketches from Life* (London, 1807)

Gardens and Landscaping

Batey, Mavis, *Jane Austen and the English Landscape* (Chicago, 1996)

Jacques, David, *Georgian Gardens: The Reign of Nature* (Portland, OR, 1984)

Laird, Mark, *The Flowering of the Landscape Garden: English Pleasure Grounds, 1720–1800* (Philadelphia, 1999)

Quest-Ritson, Charles, *The English Garden: A Social History* (London, 2001)

Stuart, David, *Georgian Gardens* (London, 1979)

Houses and Cottages

Arnold, Dana, ed., *The Georgian Country House: Architecture, Landscape and Society* (Stroud, Gloucestershire, 1998)

Aslet, Clive, *The National Trust Book of the English House* (Harmondsworth, Middlesex, 1985)

Cook, Olive, *The English House through Seven Centuries* (New York, 1983)

Girouard, Mark, *Life in the English Country House: A Social and Architectural History* (New Haven, 1978)

Tinniswood, Adrian, *Life in the English Country Cottage* (London, 1995)

Interior Decoration

Blacker, Mary Rose, *Flora Domestica: A History of British Flower Arranging, 1500–1930* (London, 2000)

Edwards, Ralph, and L. G. G. Ramsey, *The Connoisseur's Period Guides to the Houses, Decoration, Furnishing and Chattels of the Classic Periods*, vol. 4: *The Late Georgian Period, 1760–1810*, Vol. 5: *The Regency Period, 1810–1830* (London, 1958)

Gloag, John, *Georgian Grace: A Social History of Design from 1660 to 1830* (London, 1956)

Harrison, Molly, *People and Furniture: A Social Background to the English Home* (London, 1971)

Jagger, Cedric, *The World's Great Clocks and Watches* (London, 1977)

Morley, John, *Regency Design, 1790–1840* (London, 1993)

Musgrave, Clifford, *Regency Furniture, 1800–1830* (London, 1970)

Parissien, Steven, *The Georgian House in America and Britain* (New York, 1995)

——, *Regency Style* (Washington, D.C. 1992)

Pilcher, Donald, *The Regency Style, 1800 to 1830* (New York, 1948)

Vickery, Amanda, *Behind Closed Doors: At Home in Georgian England* (New Haven, 2009)

Watkins, Susan, *Jane Austen in Style* (New York, 1996)

Female Decorative Activities

Forest, Jennifer, *Jane Austen's Sewing Box* (Millers Point, New South Wales, 2009)

Rutt, Richard, *A History of Hand Knitting* (London, 1987)

Beauty and Fashion

Ashelford, Jane, *The Art of Dress: Clothes and Society, 1500–1914* (New York, 1996)

Buck, Anne, *Dress in Eighteenth-Century England* (London, 1979)

Byrde, Penelope, *A Frivolous Distinction: Fashion and Needlework in the Works of Jane Austen* (Bristol, 1979)

Corson, Richard, *Fashions in Hair: The First Five Thousand Years* (New York, 1965)

Fashions in Makeup: From Ancient to Modern Times (New York, 1972)

Cunnington, C. Willett, *English Women's Clothing in the Nineteenth Century* (Mineola, NY, 1990; originally published 1937)

——, and Phyllis Cunnington, *A Handbook of English Costume in the Eighteenth Century* (Boston, 1972)

Dickinson, Robert, *An Essay on Cutaneous Diseases, Impurities of the Skin, and Eruptions of the Face* (London, 1800)

Ewing, Elizabeth, *Everyday Dress, 1650–1900* (London, 1984)

Gowland, John, *An Essay on Cutaneous Diseases, and All Impurities of the Skin* (London, 1792)

Lady of Distinction, *The Mirror of Graces; or, The English Lady's Costume* (London, 1811)

McKendrick, Neil, John Brewer, and J. H. Plumb, *The Birth of a Consumer Society* (London, 1982)

Pratt, Lucy, and Linda Woolley, *Shoes* (London, 1999)

Styles, John, *Dress of the People: Everyday Fashion in Eighteenth-Century England* (New Haven, 2007)

Williams, Neville, *Powder and Paint* (London, 1957)

Food and Dining

Lane, Maggie, *Jane Austen and Food* (London, 1995)

Palmer, Arnold, *Movable Feasts* (New York, 1952)

Pimlott, J. A. R., *The Englishman's Christmas: A Social History* (Atlantic Highlands, NJ, 1998)

Trusler, John, *The Honours of the Table, or Rules for Behaviour during Meals* (London, 1791)

Wilson, C. Anne, *Food and Drink in Britain: From the Stone Age to Recent Times* (London, 1973)

Etiquette

Banfield, Edwin, *Visiting Cards and Cases* (Trowbridge, 1989)

Cunnington, Phillis, and Catherine Lucas, *Costume for Births, Marriages, and Deaths* (New York, 1972)

Curtin, Michael, "A Question of Manners," *Journal of Modern History* 57:3 (Sept. 1985), pp. 396–423

Fritzer, Penelope Joan, *Jane Austen and Eighteenth-Century Courtesy Books* (Westport, CT, 1997)

Morgan, Marjorie, *Manners, Morals and Class in England, 1774–1858* (New York, 1994)

Ross, Josephine, *Jane Austen's Guide to Good Manners* (New York, 2006)

Taylor, Lou, *Mourning Dress: A Costume and Social History* (London, 1983)

Wildeblood, Joan, *The Polite World: A Guide to the Deportment of the English in Former Times* (London, 1973)

Female Conduct Books

Advice of a Mother to Her Daughter, by the Marchioness of Lambert; *A Father's Legacy to His Daughters,* by Dr. Gregory; *The Lady's New Year's Gift, or, Advice to a Daughter,* by Lord Halifax, in *Angelica's Ladies Library* (London, 1794)

Burton, John, *Lectures on Female Education and Manners* (London, 1793; reprint ed., New York, 1970)

Chapone, Hester, *Letters on the Improvement of the Mind* (Walpole, NH, 1802; first published London, 1773)

Gisborne, Thomas, *An Enquiry into the Duties of the Female Sex* (London, 1796)

Murry, Ann, *Mentoria, or, the Young Ladies Instructor* (London, 1785)

Pennington, Sarah, *An Unfortunate Mother's Advice to Her Absent Daughters* (London, 1770)

Trusler, Rev. Dr. John, *Principles of Politeness, and of Knowing the World, in Two Parts* (London, 1800)

Ideas of the Gentleman

Carter, Philip, *Men and the Emergence of Polite Society, Britain 1660–1800* (Harlow, Essex, 2001)

Castronovo, David, *The English Gentleman: Images and Ideals in Literature and Society* (New York, 1987)

Maps

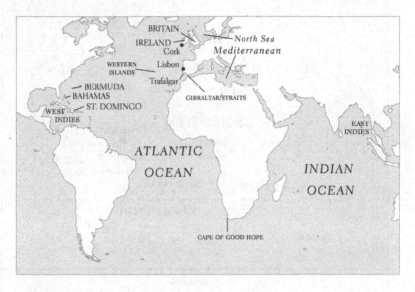

West Indies: Where Captain Wentworth sailed; and Mrs. Smith has property.

Bahamas; Bermuda: Where the Crofts have sailed.

St. Domingo: Site of British naval victory, in which Captain Wentworth won promotion.

Western Islands (Azores): Where Captain Wentworth had a cruise in which he gained great prize money.

Gibraltar/Straits: British naval base where Dick Musgrove was left ill; straits controlling access to the Mediterranean.

Trafalgar: Cape and site of major British naval victory, in which Admiral Croft fought.

Lisbon: Where Captain Wentworth and Admiral Croft each stopped.

Cork: British naval base, where Admiral Croft was.

North Sea: Where Admiral Croft probably sailed (see p. 135, note 53).

Mediterranean: Where Captain Wentworth had a profitable cruise.

Cape of Good Hope: Where Captain Benwick had his portrait done.

East Indies: Where the Crofts have been stationed.

ENGLAND

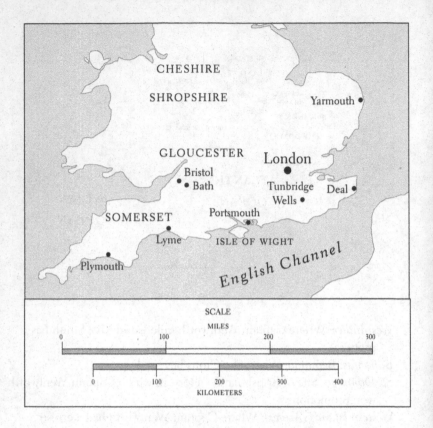

Plymouth: Important British naval base, where Captain Wentworth's
   ship was almost wrecked, and where he later traveled
   (from Portsmouth) to console Captain Benwick.
Somerset, Lyme, Bristol, Bath: See next page.
Cheshire: County where the Elliot family originated.
Shropshire: County where Captain Wentworth's brother lives.
Gloucester: County where Lady Elliot was from.
Portsmouth: Britain's largest and most important naval base.
Isle of Wight: Island noted for its natural beauties.
Tunbridge Wells: Fashionable spa where Mr. Smith was.
Deal: Naval base where the Crofts lived.
Yarmouth: Naval base where the Crofts lived.

SOMERSET AREA

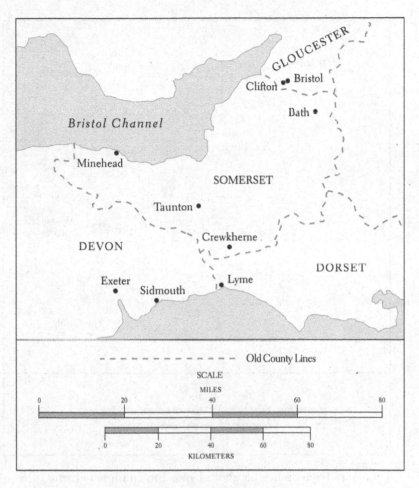

Exeter: Where the Miss Musgroves attended school.

Minehead: Where the Crofts visited relatives.

Sidmouth: Seaside resort visited by Mr. Elliot before he came to Lyme.

Somerset: County in which most of the main characters live.

Taunton: County seat, where Mr. Shepherd met Admiral Croft.

Lyme: Seaside resort town where many characters go.

Crewkherne: First important stop on the road from Lyme.

Dorset(shire): County in which Charles Hayter gets a church position.

Clifton: resort town (next to Bristol) where the Musgroves vacationed.

Bath: Leading spa and resort town in England.

LYME

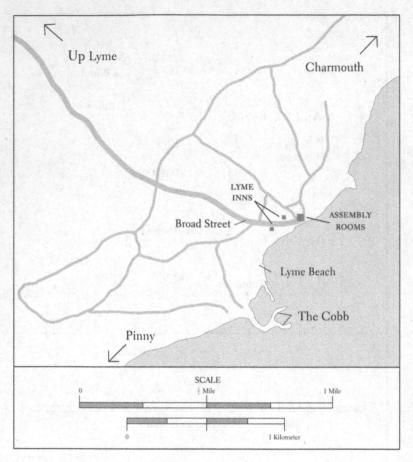

Up Lyme

Charmouth

LYME
INNS

Broad Street

ASSEMBLY
ROOMS

Lyme Beach

The Cobb

Pinny

SCALE

0   ½ Mile   1 Mile

0   1 Kilometer

Up Lyme: Town on heights above Lyme and en route to Lyme.

Pinny: Scenic spot praised by Jane Austen.

Broad Street: Main street in Lyme; it is steep and ends abruptly at the coastline.

Lyme Inns: At one of which the visitors to Lyme stayed.

The Cobb: Curved structure that is Lyme's most distinctive feature; this is where the visitors to Lyme walked, and Louisa Musgrove had her accident.

Charmouth: Nearby resort town, where Mary bathed in the sea while staying in Lyme.

CENTRAL BATH

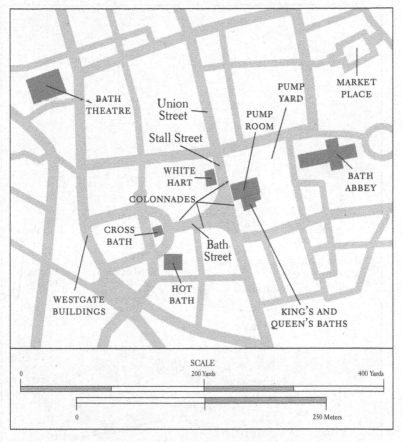

SCALE

0   200 Yards   400 Yards

0   250 Meters

Union Street: Where Captain Wentworth catches up with Anne after she reads his letter.

Market Place: Where Charles has an appointment with a gunsmith.

Westgate Buildings: Where Mrs. Smith lives.

Bath Street: Street from which Mr. Elliot and Mrs. Clay emerge together.

Colonnades: Where Mr. Elliot and Mrs. Clay stop to talk (at colonnade near the Pump Room).

White Hart: Inn where the Musgroves are staying.

Pump Room: Where Bath waters are drunk, and whose entrance Mary overlooks from her window at the White Hart Inn.

Pump Yard: Where Mrs. Clay says Mr. Elliot accompanied her to.

BATH

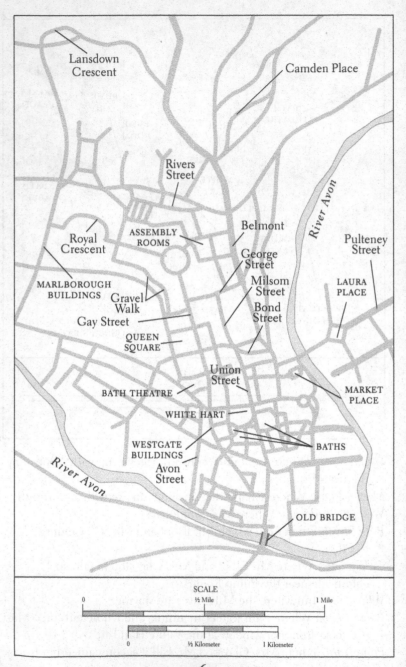

Lansdown Crescent

Camden Place

Rivers Street

River Avon

Belmont

Royal Crescent

ASSEMBLY ROOMS

George Street

Pulteney Street

MARLBOROUGH BUILDINGS

Milsom Street

LAURA PLACE

Gravel Walk

Bond Street

Gay Street

QUEEN SQUARE

Union Street

BATH THEATRE

MARKET PLACE

WHITE HART

WESTGATE BUILDINGS

BATHS

Avon Street

River Avon

OLD BRIDGE

SCALE

0   ½ Mile   1 Mile

0   ½ Kilometer   1 Kilometer

Lansdown Crescent: Where Mr. Elliot dines.

Camden Place: Where Sir Walter and his family live.

Rivers Street: Where Lady Russell lives.

Marlborough Buildings: Where the Wallises live.

Assembly Rooms: Where the concert occurs at which Anne and Captain Wentworth meet.

Belmont: Quiet street where Anne and Admiral Croft converse.

Gravel Walk: Secluded walk where Anne and Captain Wentworth go after they meet in Union Street.

Gay Street: Residence of the Crofts.

Queen Square: Where the Miss Musgroves do not want their parents to rent a place if they go to Bath.

Milsom Street: Main shopping street, where, at Molland's shop, Anne and Captain Wentworth first meet in Bath.

Bond Street: Another main shopping street, where Sir Walter observes numerous unattractive people.

Laura Place: Where Lady Dalrymple lives.

Pulteney Street: Where Anne and Lady Russell see Captain Wentworth when in a carriage.

Bath Theatre: Where Charles buys tickets and the Musgroves plan to go.

Union Street: Where Captain Wentworth catches up with Anne after she reads his letter.

Market Place: Where Charles has an appointment with a gunsmith.

Westgate Buildings: Where Mrs. Smith lives.

White Hart: Inn where the Musgroves are staying.

Old Bridge: Where Lady Russell and Anne enter Bath.